Adele Parks w [illegible] ead English Language and [illegible] duating she has lived in Italy and Africa but has spent most of her adult life in London. She lives in Chiswick, with her husband and son. Her novels, *Playing Away*, *Game Over*, *Larger than Life*, *The Other Woman's Shoes*, *Still Thinking of You* and *Husbands*, are all bestsellers and are published in over twenty different countries.

www.adeleparks.com

ADELE PARKS

Perfect Partners

GAME OVER

LARGER THAN LIFE

PENGUIN BOOKS

PENGUIN BOOKS

Published by the Penguin Group
Penguin Books Ltd, 80 Strand, London WC2R 0RL, England
Penguin Group (USA) Inc., 375 Hudson Street, New York, New York 10014, USA
Penguin Group (Canada), 90 Eglinton Avenue East, Suite 700, Toronto, Ontario, Canada M4P 2Y3
(a division of Pearson Penguin Canada Inc.)
Penguin Ireland, 25 St Stephen's Green, Dublin 2, Ireland (a division of Penguin Books Ltd)
Penguin Group (Australia), 250 Camberwell Road,
Camberwell, Victoria 3124, Australia (a division of Pearson Australia Group Pty Ltd)
Penguin Books India Pvt Ltd, 11 Community Centre,
Panchsheel Park, New Delhi – 110 017, India
Penguin Group (NZ), cnr Airborne and Rosedale Roads, Albany,
Auckland 1310, New Zealand (a division of Pearson New Zealand Ltd)
Penguin Books (South Africa) (Pty) Ltd, 24 Sturdee Avenue,
Rosebank, Johannesburg 2196, South Africa

Penguin Books Ltd, Registered Offices: 80 Strand, London WC2R 0RL, England

www.penguin.com

Game Over first published by Penguin Books 2001
Larger Than Life first published by Penguin Books 2002
This combined edition published 2005
1

Printed in England by Clays Ltd, St Ives plc

ISBN-13: 978-0-141-02736-4
ISBN-10: 0-141-02736-3

GAME OVER

For my Significant Exes

1

'What an inauspicious start to married life,' Josh comments.

'Is there such a thing as an auspicious start?' I ask. He grins at me and Issie scowls. *She* likes weddings. The rain is falling so hard it's bouncing off the pavements and up my skirt. I'm bloody cold and wish the bride would stop hugging her mother and simply get in the car. I look closer. Maybe she isn't so much hugging as clinging. Maybe the seriousness of what she's done has hit her and she's having second thoughts. Issie shakes the remnants of confetti from the blue box but misses the bride and groom. The confetti settles on the grubby road. The filthy street is a stark contrast to the finery of their clothes, the car, the flowers, the smiles that radiate.

'Josh, what's the proper name for a squashed cube?' I ask, pointing to the little blue box of confetti. 'They should redesign this packaging,' I add.

'No!' Issie looks horrified, as if I'd suggested exposing my bikini line to the vicar. 'Weddings are about tradition.'

'Even if tradition means tacky and predictable?' Two big sins in my book.

'By definition,' she defends. Then she leaps forward to jostle for a front position to catch the bouquet. She nervously hops from one foot to the other, her sleek, blonde, shoulder-length hair brushing her right shoulder, then her left, then her right again. Issie is a fidget. I am a still person. She continually rubs her hands together, taps her feet, jerks her knee. She once read that this constant nervous activity uses thirty calories an hour, more than a Mars bar a day, pounds in a year, a whole dress size in a lifetime. Her constant unfocused activity strikes me as a fairly accurate metaphor for how she lives her life.

I don't try to catch the flowers. I don't try for two reasons. One, Issie will lynch me if I catch them. She's spent the entire reception spiking the drinks of single women, in the hope that this will diminish their co-ordination. And two, it's bollocks.

No really, the whole marriage thing is bollocks. I mean I'm as happy as the next one to have an excuse to wear a hat and drink champagne. Generally, wedding receptions are a laugh, a big, fun party. But that's as far as it goes for me. Beyond that, it's bollocks. I'm not a man. And I'm not a lesbian. I'm not even a man hater – Josh is one of my best friends and he's a man. I'm a single, successful, attractive, 33-year-old, heterosexual. I just don't want to get married. Ever.

Clear?

Issie doesn't catch the flowers and she looks as though the disappointment will break her.

'A drink, Cas? Issie?' asks Josh, in an effort tc cheer her up. He doesn't wait for a response but turns back to the hotel and heads directly for the bar. He knows that we'll willingly join him for a drink Martini-style: any time, any place, anywhere. We elbow through the elegant crowds. This morning they sat demurely in church pews but they have now abandoned any semblance of civilization. The exit of the bride, the groom and the oldies leaves the rest of the guests free to indulge in what brought us to the wedding in the first place. The opportunity for some hedonistic, no strings attached, unashamed sex.

I selected my target in the church, before the 'I dos'. I relocate him. He's tall, dark and handsome. Admittedly, he doesn't look that bright. Rather too in love with himself to allow room for anyone else. Perfect. Deep and meaningful is an over-rated phenomenon. Shallow and meaningless but well endowed gets such a hard press.

It's important to pick out a target early on in the proceedings and it's important to let him know he's it. I smile. Directly at him. If at this point he looks around and tries to locate the recipient of my smile, I'll instantly go off him. I like my men to be arrogant enough to know that I'm flirting with them.

He passes the test by grinning back at me. Only turning to catch his reflection in the mirror that hangs behind the bar. He grins again. This time at himself. The difference in appreciation is fractional. I don't mind. Vanity is a safety net. I flick my hair and turn away. Job done.

Issie and Josh are still fighting their way to the bar. I call them back.

'What? I was nearly at the front,' Issie complains.

'Don't worry, drinks are on their way,' I assure.

'Oh.' She relaxes into the chintz chair. Josh lights a fag, trusting me. We are all familiar with my routine. Josh and Issie know all about me.

Josh is like a brother to me. We met aged seven over our suburban fences. It is this meeting that makes me believe in fate. We met when our families' stars were crossing. His in the ascendant. Mine spiralling downwards.

That summer we shared Rubik's cubes, cream soda and an uneasy sense of impending change. Our childish sixth sense told us that we were both powerless in the face of adult whim. The five-bedroom detached, in Esher, Surrey, that my mother and I had thought was a dream home turned out to be a temporary residence. That summer my father announced that he was in love with another woman and couldn't live without her. My mother showed rare wit and emotional honesty by asking whether he'd prefer cremation or burial. My father moved out immediately following his announcement. I was to see him three more times in my life. A week later when he came to collect his records and he brought me a Lundby doll's house (presumably to replace the real home he was destroying). A month later when he took me to the zoo (I cried the entire afternoon, saying that the animals behind the bars upset me. In fact, they didn't, but I was determined that both my father and I would have a terrible afternoon – after all, my mother and I were having plenty of them). And the following Christmas (when I refused to open his present or sit on his knee). After that, he just sent Christmas and birthday cards, which petered out before I was ten. Josh's seventh summer wasn't great either: he was told that he was to be wrenched from his comfortable local primary school and prepped at the hallowed ground of Stowe. Thinking about it, perhaps it wasn't so much a sixth sense. The prep-school prospectuses and the endless rows were a giveaway. Although very nearly entirely submerged in our own terror, we settled into an uneasy mutual sympathy that passed as companionship. Sulkily learning to rollerskate and eating raw gooseberries has an enormous bonding effect. I still think he got the best deal. At that time we had lived in identical homes, distinguishable only by the colour of the Formica on the kitchen units. I was never to live in anything so spacious again. He, in anything so compact. As a child I identified the difference. His father kept quiet about his affairs.

I suspect that our childish friendship, although intense in a sharing gobsmacker type of way, would have petered out except that we met again, aged twelve, at a county tennis tournament. Josh recognized that knowing a girl, any girl, would improve his standing at Stowe. I was attracted by his rounded vowels, and even at that early age had recognized that competition was healthy, a challenge that the boys at

Westford Comprehensive rose to. It turned out that we still liked each other. We liked each other so much that Josh insisted on disappointing his teachers and parents by joining me at Manchester University. They'd had their sights set on an establishment that was a little older and altogether less red-brick. I was determined to go to Manchester; for the trendy bands, the radical students union, the men in turned-up Levis and DMs, but mostly for the outstanding media studies course.

Josh is tall, six foot two, blond. If I look at it objectively, I have to admit he is the most attractive man I know that I haven't slept with. Whenever I introduce him to my girl friends and colleagues, they unilaterally swoon, they go on and on about how fanciable he is. He is what's described as 'handsome' or 'dashing'. Invariably, because they lack imagination, they assume we are an item. I explain that I like him far too much to complicate things by having sex with him.

In fact, I love him. He is one of the three people I love in the world. I love my mother in a no-nonsense, non-demonstrative kind of way. And I love Issie.

Issie and I met at Uni. In her first term she read biology, then chemistry and finally chemical engineering. It wasn't so much that she'd finally found her vocation, it's just that her tutor wouldn't hear of another change of direction. Issie is frighteningly intelligent and alarmingly optimistic. It's an unusual combination, which largely leaves her dissatisfied. She's a little taller than most women are (five foot nine) and a little thinner (UK size ten), achieved through the constant fidgeting rather than gym visits. Therefore she's slim but untoned. She bewails her wobbly upper arms and potbelly but hasn't, in the fifteen years I've known her, ever seriously considered stomach crunches or lifting weights (unless you count carrying heavy shopping bags). She's a natural blonde: eyelashes and brows prove it. Therefore she doesn't tan but has a sprinkling of freckles on her (wide) nose and (slim) shoulders. She has the sexiest mouth in the Western world. It's broad and red. Women describe her as stunning. Men are diametrically opposed; they either fail to notice her at all, her paleness rendering her invisible, or they want to be her knight in shining armour and put her on a pedestal. I don't think either of these responses suits her. Issie's fierce intellect and brutal honesty ought to be dignified with something more than indifference or insulation. But then there's a lot of things that ought to happen and won't. I don't hold much hope for Issie finding a man that is worthy of her. Especially since her optimism has overpowered her intelligence and she has spent her adult life in a stalwart but senseless crusade to discover hidden depths in the men she dates. I've explained on countless occasions that there isn't a pot of gold at the end of the rainbow.

It's really Josh who is responsible for Issie's and my friendship. He spotted her at Freshers' Week and developed an intense crush on her. He begged me to befriend her. I did. By the time I discovered how much I liked her and how ethereal and fragile she was, Josh had slept with half of the students in Withington and Fallowfields. I decided that she was far too special to allow him to have his wicked and transient way with her. I discouraged both parties, in what I admit to be a Machiavellian manner. I pointed out his shortcomings to her and other women's attractions to him. It was a successful ploy.

I still think I made the right decision.

If they'd wanted each other so much, they'd have found a way to make it happen.

We settled into a healthy flirty relationship where we often confused who fancied whom. Instead of any of us sharing each other's beds, in the second and third years, we shared a student house. Just the three of us, loath to let anyone else into our inner sanctum. This was sensible, as arguments over who bought the last loo roll and put an empty milk carton back in the fridge put a full stop to any romantic notion any one of us harboured.

We were typical students. We avoided lectures, joined clubs and societies – rugby (Josh), Literary Soc. (Issie), wine appreciation (me); we drank copious amounts in the Uni. bar, relied on last-minute cramming for exams and shagged relentlessly. We were atypical in that none of us fell victim to the statistic that says one third of all graduates meet their long-term partner at university. We were all hopeless at anything long-term. Issie fell in love with every man she shagged. It was a warped attempt at respectability. She shagged until the men she was shagging got fed up with her reading metaphysical poetry as foreplay. Josh fell in love with every woman he screwed, at least until he'd eaten breakfast and sometimes for days on end. He was forever breaking hearts. I never fell in love and often got bored before the first post-coital cigarette.

This youthful pattern set us on the path we would follow throughout our twenties and, likely as not, until we draw our pensions. This thought doesn't bother Josh or me. The law chambers which he so successfully wafts around offer enough intelligent and willing women for him to fall in and out of love *ad infinitum*. The same can be said of my job in the media. The abundance of loose-moralled young men is a necessary criterion for any job offer I accept. I have no illusions about commitment, which makes me a deeply attractive proposition to men who have no intention to commit – 99.99 per cent of them. So I use and abuse. It's easier all round. Actually, I don't do too much abuse. To abuse someone they have to be emotionally involved and in my experience men are happy to forgo this nicety if good head is on offer. So when I leave their beds failing to leave my telephone number on the empty fag packet or when I shoo them out of my flat with the empty promise that I'll call, no one really minds that much.

Issie is a lab technician at a huge pharmaceutical company. Her white coat is quite fetching but I know Issie is still looking for something more than a quick game of doctors and nurses. I'm always telling her it will be a fruitless search and she wants to count herself lucky that we have each other to love.

'Can I offer you a drink?' I never say yes to this question without first checking out the origin, however busy the bar is. I look up and see Mr Tall, Dark and Handsome. On cue. He is presumptuously holding a bottle of Bollie and a fistful of glasses. I like presumption, extravagance and the recognition that my friends will want a drink too. He has sparkling green eyes and the floppy-haired look that was all the rage when I was nineteen. I resist telling him that since *Brideshead Revisited*, no man (other than Hugh Grant) has ever successfully pulled off this look. I resist because besides the height, eyes and cheekbones, I like his suit.

'Fine.' I grin.

He does the usual stuff: he asks me my name, and I tell him it's Cas and he says, 'Oh, what's Cas short for?' And I explain it's short for Jocasta and I grin and add, 'I was named after my father's mother, very Oedipal.' And sometimes they get this reference and sometimes they don't but it doesn't matter because either way they grin maniacally. Because usually by this time the men I talk to are well and truly in lust with me. They may not be interested in references to Greek plays but they are extremely interested in the possibility of steamy foreplay. They are checking out my full, pert tits or my long, brown, muscular legs, depending on whether they are breast or leg men. And, if their tastes are more sophisticated and long, black, glossy hair, or clear skin, or slim hips, or blue eyes, or straight white teeth turn them on, I can offer all these things too.

Believe me, I know I'm blessed.

I wear my hair long, because it drives men wild. They look at me and see a sexy bitch or a nineteenth-century heroine, whichever is their bag. Strictly speaking, I think my personality would suit a razor-sharp, chin-length bob, but I work in television and 'give them what they want' is my war cry.

I ask his name and try to commit it to memory. I ask what he does, and he does something or other. It doesn't matter. His prospects only matter to women who want a future. I notice he has very large feet and this is exciting. In my experience (wide and varied) the old adage is true. I constantly touch him. Little light touches on his arm and shoulder. I even pick off an imaginary piece of lint from his breast pocket. It always amazes me that men fall for this clichéd crap but they always do. I run my tongue around my lips, my teeth and the olive in his Martini. He is not vulnerable. He knows this routine. He's played it himself on countless occasions. He's a little bit taken aback that it's being played to him but my audacity excites. He tries to regain control of at least the conversation and asks what I do for a living. I tell him that I'm a TV producer for the new terrestrial channel, TV6, and this, if we were in any doubt, clinches it.

My glamorous job has huge pulling power. My job *is* glamorous, especially in comparison to most people's jobs. It is an affectation of those who work in TV to continually deny that the job is fun or alluring. It's a way of neutralizing our guilt at the hideously high salaries we earn. It is undoubtedly more glamorous to sell TV airtime than baked beans at a leading supermarket. It is unquestionably more exciting to spot Des O'Connor in the lifts than Dave Jones from accounts. However, TV is also bloody hard work. I've been in the business for twelve years now. I started as a gofer on *Wake Up Britain* straight after Uni. The pay was a pittance but I was thrilled. I had a job in *television*. I spent most of my time in a state of perpetual fear. I had no responsibility so the level of misdemeanour that I could aspire to was putting sugar in someone's coffee when they'd distinctly asked for saccharin. My most constant dread was that my clothes, hair, figure, accent, jokes were unacceptable. I spent all my money on the right clothes (black) and the right hairstyles (long, short, very short, long again, black, blonde, red, black again), happily reinventing myself until I could be myself. It was vital to me to do well. Not just well but best. No job was too small for me to accept it cheerfully. No ambition was too large for me to hold it greedily. I worked obscene hours, even working once on Christmas Day, which wasn't really a hardship. Holidays bore me. It was worth it. I leapt ahead of my peers and by the time I was twenty-three I was chief researcher. I rushed through the ranks of associate producer and producer, and I reached the dizzy heights of executive producer the week before my thirtieth birthday. It's who I am. It's what I am.

'That must be fascinating,' Mr Tall, Dark, Handsome with Green Eyes comments.

'It is. As we are now living in the digital age and there are hundreds of extra channels all fighting for the consumer mind share, it's extremely tough.' I don't bother to tell him that besides the terrestrial channels, BBC 1 and 2, ITV, Channels 4 and 5 and TV6, there are 200 digital satellite channels, 500 digital cable channels and 70 digital terrestrial channels on offer, not to mention interactive television, the Internet and home shopping. Yet viewing time per capita has declined. The more we have to watch, the less often we tune in. So the challenge hasn't let up; I'm constantly being asked to introduce more demanding or aggressive promotions, programmes or plans. I don't bother to mention it because even Josh, my most devoted listener, glazes over when I give too much detail. I know I can be boring about my work but it means so much to me. I try to think of an entertaining star story. In the corridors of power I often bump into someone famous, especially those who are famous for being famous – they make themselves very available. I like them the least and admire them the most. It's much harder than being famous for being talented. I know a story about has-been soap stars won't interest.

'I eat my sandwiches in the same canteen as Davina McCall.' That gets him.

I wake up to birds screeching and a swarm of bees hovering threateningly above me. I fully expect to open my eyes and see a fan whirling from the ceiling. It takes me some seconds to understand that my pounding head is not because I'm on set in *Apocalypse Now and Again* but that the audibility of feathered friends is due to the fact that the windows of the country-house hotel bedroom are wide open. The night before it had been a good idea. I'd insisted on it. Naturally, as I am paying £170 a night (not on expenses), I wanted my money's worth. Shortbread biscuits, mini bottles of shampoo, shower cap and fresh air.

The swarm of bees turns out to be a Lone Ranger. This is a relief. I survey the room. The debris suggests I had a really good time last night. I move my head a fraction; the hangover confirms it.

I concentrate on focusing: empty champagne bottle, empty

mini bar, horizontal wardrobe and handsome stranger in my bed.

A result.

His name eludes me. This is not a disaster but it is an irritation. It seems rude, even by my standards, to ask a man to leave without addressing him on a first-name basis. Big boy, although an adequate term of endearment last night, seems faintly ridiculous in the harsh light of day. I'm saved from immediately confronting this dilemma as the phone rings.

Tring, trinnnnnng, tring, trinnnnnng. The tone is definitely getting more insistent. I feel around for the handset.

'Cas?'

'Issie.' I pull myself on to my elbow. 'You OK?'

'No.'

I try to concentrate on her story. It starts well – scored with one of the ushers. But it gets muddled through her tears. Seemingly she had a passion session last night. Peppered with orgasms, blowjobs and him murmuring, 'You are amazing.' This morning she'd woken up to him trying to sneak out of her room. She'd asked for his number. He gave her one but it was made up. It was one digit too many.

'He called me Zoë,' she wails. It's true Zoë isn't generally the accepted shortening of Isabelle, however familiar the parties involved. 'How could he forget my name?'

'I don't know, honey. I really don't. What's your room number?' I want to stroke her hair, hunt a tissue from my handbag, blow her nose and pour a substantial G&T. I want to make her better. I hurriedly climb out of bed. Momentarily noting the slight strain in my groin. I turn and have a last wistful look at big boy. I wouldn't have minded a bit of early morning naughtiness. But it is out of the question. Issie needs me. I don't even have time to wash off the sperm and smell of rubber.

'Hey big—' I stop myself. 'Hey.' I shake him gently. He opens his eyes and tries to pull me back into bed.

'What's the rush?' he asks with a lazy grin. I manœuvre away from all his hands, pull a jumper on and throw his shirt at him.

'My friend called. I'm going round to her room.'

'I'll wait for you,' he offers.

'No, that would be' – I play with the idea of saying tedious and opt for the more polite approach – 'too kind but unnecessary. She's very upset; I might be gone all morning. All day.'

'Should I leave you my card?'

'Yes, great. Do that.' I kiss him on his forehead and feel a bit like his mother. How young this guy looks in the daylight. Of course I have no intention of calling him, but I'd like to have his name. I keep immaculate mental records in these matters.

Issie opens the door; she's wrapped in a sheet.

'Oh Issie.' I hug her. Fighting down the swell of irritation that washes over me when I see her tear-stained face. I'm annoyed at him for doing it to her. I'm annoyed at her for doing this to herself. 'Have you called Josh?'

'He's incognito.'

'Oh, makes sense. I saw him slope off with that woman in the huge navy hat.'

'Which one?' asks Issie. 'There were a dozen navy hats.'

'The Emu one.'

'Oh.' She grins, despite herself, and I think, not for the first time, that Issie is too nice to be treated like this.

I put on the mini kettle and throw the biscuits to her. She needs the sugar. She catches them with one hand and this simple gesture makes my heart swell with pride. It is so unfair. There is no way Issie would ever have managed to do something so cool in front of a guy she fancied. Women are always so much nicer, more composed and funnier when blokes aren't around. Why can't we be our best selves in front of them?

'Did you have full sex?' I ask, trying to establish the level of disappointment.

'Yes.' She sounds guilty.

'Don't sweat it, forget it. I'm not your mum.' But I know she's wracked with shame and an overwhelming sense of self-loathing. She's explained it often enough. I try to cheer her up. 'I also had full sex and I'm not expecting to see him again either.'

'But you don't care. You have no feelings.' Fair point. I shrug. I'm as hard as nails on the outside. Scratch the surface and I'm as hard as nails on the inside. Impenetrable. Well, emotionally impenetrable, not the other. Not frigid. Technically, I guess, for want of a more user-friendly term, I'm a slapper. I start to run her a bath. I'm overly generous with the bubble bath. Bubbles are so frivolous. They never fail to cheer me up.

'Was it good sex?' I shout above the running tap.

'Not particularly – we hardly know each other.'

So why is she so upset? I walk back into the bedroom and start to drag her towards the bathroom.

'What did I do wrong?' she wails. I've heard this question so often that I have a stockpile of answers. '*You* did nothing wrong.' 'Men are simply incapable of more.' Etc., etc. None of it helps. She still regularly has her heart stomped upon.

Whilst she's in the bath I order room service. We require serious comfort food so I order a big, greasy fried breakfast (powerful medicine for hangovers and broken hopes), a pile of pastries and huge steaming mugs of hot chocolate. I quickly shower whilst Issie flicks through the Sunday papers. We eat breakfast lying on the massive bed, wrapped in luxurious, white towelling dressing gowns. I couldn't be happier. To me this is a perfect Sunday morning. I know Issie would be happier if I were a man.

'But why does it matter?' I ask, genuinely confused. 'You had your servicing and you don't have to put up with the inane conversation this morning. Best of both worlds.'

Issie sighs. 'What if the conversation wasn't inane but stimulating?'

'It's a bit unlikely, isn't it?'

She sighs again, very deeply this time. I know I am trying her patience.

'No, it's not unlikely. Men are people, Cas, and they are capable of relationships.'

It's not that I think men are any more awful or dishonest than women where such matters are concerned. That's such an archaic view. But as soon as sex comes into the equation, integrity, candour and decency invariably make a swift exit. Someone is bound to get hurt. I simply prefer it if it's not me. Or Issie. Or Josh.

I catch sight of my reflection in the dressing-table mirror. I can see what other people see, a five-foot-seven, size eight woman, with huge blue eyes and long dark hair. Sexy, cool, flawless. But it *still* surprises me that they can't see what I can. The seven-year-old chubby tyke, left behind by her father. Not only was I not pretty enough to make my father stay, I actually suspected it was my fault he'd left. Had I been naughty? Was it something to do with digging up his vegetable plot with Josh? By the time I realized this wasn't the case at all, and it was actually more to do with Miss Hudley – his buxom, blonde and willing secretary – it was too late. I'd spent a decade blaming myself. Rationale and reason were too tardy. The psychology isn't difficult to figure out. Intense feelings of betrayal, blah, blah, blah. I have a complex about men not loving me enough to stay and about their general ability to be faithful. My defence is a life awash with cynicism, constraint and calculation. And it's an extremely effective preclusion to pain. I hurt before I can be harmed. I dump before I'm damaged. I never get involved.

'The mistake everyone makes is thinking sex and love are at all compatible. Why? No one imagines they are in love because they feel hungry or tired or cold. Why imagine you are if you feel randy?'

'Oh, you are too clever for me.' Issie evades my argument. She doesn't think I'm clever, she thinks I'm cruel, but she's too polite to say so.

I had planned to spend Sunday afternoon with my mother, and Issie decides to join me, as she can't face a Sunday afternoon on her own. I'm pleased she's joining me but frustrated that she thinks there is such a thing as 'on your own' when you live in a city with seven million inhabitants, dozens of museums, scores of galleries, hundreds of shops, and millions of bars and restaurants.

When we arrive at my mother's, she is sitting in the garden reading a romantic novel. I pointedly put down the bag of improving books that I have brought for her. She thanks me, but I doubt she'll swap the stolen glances and passionate embraces to learn more about the trials of the Irish during the potato famine. My mother is delighted to have both Issie and me to fuss over and immediately scuttles to the kitchen to put on the kettle.

Mum lives in a small, immaculate house in Cockfosters. The house is crammed full of furniture that she rescued from her marriage. My mother brought everything from our five-bedroom detached home and put it into her two-bedroom terraced house. The result is overpowering. It is impossible to walk through a room without banging your hip on a sideboard or stubbing your toe on a chair. In some rooms furniture is literally piled up on top of other bits of furniture. Chair on table, poof on chair. There are two beds in each bedroom, although no one ever stays. I wish she'd throw it all out. I wish she'd start again at Heal's. The house is stuck in a time warp and so is Mum. When she married my father everyone commented that there was an amazing resemblance between her and Mary Quant. It was a very successful look at the time. She's never been able to leave it behind. Over thirty-five years later she still wears her hair in a thick dark bob. She applies a home dye kit every three weeks. She wears her skirts too short and a ton of eyeliner. I find her look mildly embarrassing. Not simply because she's unfashionable and being a trend leader is important to me, but because of what her look signifies. It is a very public statement that she has not been able to move on since my father left her. She's never said so, but I know that she's preserving herself in this way. She hopes that one day father will come home and the last twenty-six years will be magically erased. A modern-day Miss Haversham.

My mother is a tall, strong-looking woman. The height comes from her thighs, which are slightly longer than average. She's kept her figure. The only concession to her age is that her tummy is gently rounding, comfortably protruding but certainly not huge. Her back is broad and her shoulders wide. Her body tells of capability. Her face is thin and she has high cheekbones. Her nose is narrow and straight, giving the impression that life's discomforts slip from her without disturbing her. But her chin is pointy and juts out to catch all pain and atrocity. She has watery blue eyes that punctuate the solidness of her face. And because her eyes are the window to all her delight and disgust she often hides them behind dark glasses, even in the winter. I've inherited this from my mother. Whilst I don't actually wear dark glasses I do see the world as a slightly shady place.

'Did you get my message on Tuesday?' Mum asks. I don't say yes and that it made my day. I say yes but I've been too busy to call back. She nods.

'How was the wedding?' She knows all about my social life and what I do with myself on a daily basis. It's a tactic to avoid living a life of her own.

'Fluffy,' I reply.

'Beautiful.' Issie smiles.

'What a shame about the rain, especially as today is so beautiful. Isn't that always the way?'

'They must have expected rain or at least thought there was a fair probability. It is August, it is England.' I don't know why I do this. Behave badly. But I always do. My mother always brings out the worst in me. The moment I am in her presence I am incapable of being polite, let alone charming. I become petulant, sulky, churlish and unreasonable. My mother authorizes this appallingly childish behaviour by silently indulging me. The harder she tries to please, the meaner I become. I always leave her house ashamed of myself.

'Ignore her,' says Issie.

'Oh, I do,' giggles my mum.

'You know how she hates weddings.'

I pretend to have an overwhelming interest in the yellow patches of grass on the lawn. My mother cuts me a piece of chocolate fudge cake. It was my favourite as a child. I consider telling her I'm dieting but it's a lie. I'd only be doing it to be pathetic.

'Did Josh enjoy the wedding?'

'Seemed to,' I mutter. I know where this conversation is leading. It's leading where every conversation my mother ever has about Josh leads. She mistakenly labours under the belief that Josh and I would make a 'lovely couple'. She insists on deliberately misconstruing his innocent acts of friendship as overtures. Her inference would irritate me, but I comfort myself with the thought that my mother knows absolutely nothing about the male psyche.

'Didn't he want to come for tea too?'

'He was otherwise engaged.' I haven't the heart to elaborate – she looks crushed as it is. Rallying herself, my mother turns to Issie.

'Issie, are you courting at the moment?' asks Mum as she passes Issie a slice of cake. Issie and I avoid catching each other's eye because although we are thirty-three years old we still think the word 'courting' is hysterical. Hearing it said out loud is enough to send us into peals of helpless giggles.

'No.' Issie manages the single syllable by cramming a load of fudge cake into her mouth.

'Oh. What a shame. Are you working too hard? You're not neglecting your social life are you? Don't forget there's more to life than work.' My mum and I agree on one thing. If Issie wants a man it should be possible.

'It's not work. It's just that all the men I meet are bastards.' Mum blushes at Issie's expletive. I'm amused and watch the exchange with interest. My mum and I run through this routine every week. It amazes me that whilst her marriage made her so unhappy, she still thinks it's the answer to everyone else's dreams.

'I met someone last night.' I catch Issie's eye – we both know she is giving my mother false hope. 'But I took his number down incorrectly, one digit too many.' She's just bending the truth to protect the feelings of an older lady. Anyone would do it. My mother and Issie then spend an hour looking at the telephone number working out which is likely to be the wrong digit. This is one of the most pointless exercises I've ever witnessed. I spray the roses, which have a spot of greenfly.

2

He is appallingly ugly. And whilst most people are embarrassed by their physical drawbacks, Nigel Bale, my boss, is blissfully unaware that he looks like Hissing Sid. His mannerisms are, by some way, less attractive. He is very tall and should be skinny, but he has wide, middle-aged woman's hips and a pot belly. The pot belly is a testament to the numerous occasions he's cornered some poor, defenceless junior in the pub and drunk them under the table or, more accurately, into bed. He has large feet and fat fingers. He's balding. The hair he does have is greasy, serving to glue his dandruff to his exposed scalp. And yet he is inconceivably arrogant, confident and vain. So much so that he will not recognize himself from this description. He considers himself to be the most intelligent of the male species and although he doesn't come across as crushing competition on a day-to-day basis at TV6, he is mistaken. He firmly believes he is irresistible to the opposite sex. Sadly, to many he is.

It's his bank balance. It is huge. Massive.

And he is powerful. Extremely so.

Two compelling aphrodisiacs. I am ashamed to be female when I see Hissing Sid surrounded by an entourage of young vixens, willing to lie back and think of the Bank of England. It disgusts me that these women, always attractive and often intelligent, are too lazy to think of anything more creative than sleeping with the boss to ensure a promotion.

I can sense his presence, and this isn't entirely to do with his body odour and bad breath. A deathly hush has fallen.

Hissing Sid is oozing his way across the open-plan office towards me. I brace myself for his visit by starting to breathe through my mouth.

I force myself to look up. Nigel is leaning over my desk. He has no perception of personal body space and does not seem to understand that I don't want to be close to him. Could his mother? I think of dead fish in a fishmonger's window.

'A word, if you please,' he sprays. He mistakenly believes that the fake Dickensian language is distinguished. Flapping my arms, encouraging the air between us to circulate as quickly as possible, I follow him back to his office. As Controller of Entertainment and Comedy (a position he secured by uniquely blending bullying, bullshitting and – much as it pains me to admit it – a genuine business acumen) Bale has three offices. The executive office on the sixth floor, which is bigger than my flat, heaves with mahogany and teak, deep shag-pile carpets (literally), and numerous pictures of Bale with celebs. It doesn't work for me – I still don't think he is interesting, I still think he is offensive. This office is straight out of a set from *Dynasty*. This man is blissfully unaware that New Romantics are passé and even their retro revival has been and gone. His second office is a *pied à terre* in Chelsea. I shudder to think what kinds of contracts are negotiated there. I've never visited. The third office is the one on our floor, which he is currently leading me to. Again, huge – this time very modern and open. Not so that we are encouraged to drop in on him (no one wants to) but so that he can terrify us through constant surveillance.

Although visiting Bale's office is unpleasant, at least I am one of the few heterosexual women in TV6 who is safe from his advances. He obviously asked me to sleep with him when we first met, but I refused. He quickly became distracted by a far prettier but less fastidious PA. By the time she received her

P45 (following her justified but failed attempt to bring a sexual harassment case to court) I'd proved that I was actually quite good at my job. Lascivious Bale is, but stupid he is not. He realized that actively pursuing me as a lay was unlikely to be successful and would certainly limit my productivity. More concerned with the bottom line than any bottom, he's since left me more or less alone. He occasionally takes the odd pot shot, when he's had one or two dozen too many. He leers at me or sprays his spittle in my direction, but a friendly hint that Mandy in Comedy finds him really attractive is usually enough to distract him.

Bale nods towards the leather chair that is strategically positioned to be four inches lower than his. It's a ham-fisted attempt at intimidation. I sigh; this man is a parody. I sit down and wait.

He waits too.

Silently.

Then he grins. It's the cruellest smile I've ever seen and it totally fails to ignite his eyes. I wonder if he is going to sack me. I feel a bead of sweat run down my back. It's cold. If he calls me Jocasta this is serious.

'Jocasta, I want an idea.' He bangs his fist on the desk. I force myself not to jump. I know we are at war. But then, I always am. His gesture is unnecessary but I understand his motivation. He knows, as well as I do, that every eye on the floor is turned towards us. He likes to appear passionate; it's very new millennium.

'We're in trouble, Cas.' Because he calls me Cas, I realize that *we* may be in trouble but *I* am not. He needs me. I allow myself to relax enough to take in what he is saying. He flings the channel's weekend viewing figures over the desk. I don't pick them up to examine them. I don't have to. I checked them this morning at 7.30 a.m. They are terrible.

Not content with being one of the youngest executive producers at ITV and managing some of the strongest shows for a main commercial channel, two years ago I decided I needed new challenges. I took a leap of faith and joined a consortium led by a group of guys with enough venture capital and balls to bid for the franchise of a new channel. Our team won the bid for TV6 by insisting that instead of being yet another publisher broadcaster, filling airtime with programmes shipped in from the US, we would produce new programmes. I had visions of producing challenging, dynamic, informative and startling programmes. I threw away my six-figure salary, company Porsche, obscene expense account, private healthcare, pension and gym membership, and moved to TV6. To be clear, this was not an act of altruism. My end goal was not to educate and entertain the great British public. I just thought that this novel approach would generate huge viewing figures, that the channel would be an unprecedented success and that I'd get more material rewards than I've ever had before. The added benefit, the incalculable advantage, would be that I would have control. A smaller pond to swim in perhaps, but I'd certainly be a much bigger fish. A shark.

I'd honestly believed that the public wanted new programming. New thoughts, new ideas. It pains me to admit that this was a misjudgement on my part. It's unusual that I miscalculate human nature and it's unprecedented that my miscalculation is rosy. It appears that the general public is very happy with repeats of *Different Strokes* and *Fame*. Channels that, three years ago, looked as though they'd never sail are beginning to race in the white waters. It could be that I am on the *Titanic*.

'The competition are whipping our ass. Have you seen their Internet policy? They're not fucking around.' He throws a competitive annual report in my direction. I've read it. 'And they are capturing the youth market.' He throws another annual report my way. Again, I've seen it. 'Youth is the name of the game. We should go after that.'

'What and be a "me too"?' I comment scathingly. I notice that the slats in the blinds in Bale's office are damaged. I briefly wonder who he's fucked up against them. Bale ignores my put-down.

'Let's employ some designers with trendy jeans. We could get the girl on reception to serve our clients vodka and Red Bull.' He looks at me hopefully. My eye falls on his desk. He has a mug with a dozen identical, yellow, sharp pencils. All this in the digital age. Oblivious, he carries on. 'They could listen to trance music and send their friends text messages. They could wear blades to work.'

'And that would help with the schedule, would it?'

'It would bring fresh ideas.'

'Bale, we are too old. Even the lads and ladettes we know are aspiring to "me-time" and their own pads. We can't do anything for the teen market.'

'Well what then?' he asks petulantly. I bet he'd already chosen the bunny outfit for the receptionist.

'I don't know. Late twenties and early thirties are always rich pickings.' I know I'm clasping at straws. 'We should think of a schedule that targets them.'

'Yeah, they all have more money than sense, no direction and lots of time. How about sport?'

'I've never believed in encouraging sports fanaticism, the next thing you know they are actually playing, which involves turning off their TV sets. We don't want them out playing sport. We want them slouched in front of the box. Besides, ASkyA are there.'

'Yes, whilst I think about it, write a complaint letter. ASkyA are running sports updates throughout their ad breaks on sports programmes. They'll be charging advertisers a premium for that. Where there's advertising there is money for programme development,' he warns.

'You could argue that it distracts the viewer from the advert. Maybe it's worth less money.'

'Yeah, send a spoiler letter to the advertisers,' he instructs.

'Get your secretary to do it,' I counter.

We glare at one another. Both livid and arrogant.

And scared.

'I want an idea,' he yells again. 'A single idea, but a big one. A humongous one. A bloody big-dick-swinging one. An astonishing, unique, bang-those-bastards-and-their-new-shows-into-the-ground-idea.' He changes tack. He leans towards me and starts to whisper menacingly, 'The tabloids and the men's mags have a host of new wannabe babes who present meaningless shows and are prepared to pose topless for publicity.' I'm about to condemn this, when he adds, 'You're going to have to come up with something really good to top that.' He wipes his mouth with the back of his hand. The idea of topless wannabes has made him salivate. 'Got it?'

'Something arresting.' I'm trying to sound cool but I keep my hands by my sides so he doesn't see them quiver. I hope my mastery of understatement irritates him.

'A ginormous, fucking, ratings-rocketting idea. Now go away and have it.' He dismisses me.

I get back to my desk and give in to the shaking. I light a cigarette and swallow back a cold double espresso. Artificial stimulants are a way of life. For all Bale is as ugly as a slapped arse, he is good at his job. I do, grudgingly, admire him. He has a point. I've been trying to ignore our flagging ratings, positively denying the competition's success. But the weekend runs are indisputable: TV6 is in big trouble.

Our office is in north London. A peculiar idiosyncrasy in the microclimates means that it rains more than average here. Or so it seems to me. It's late August. It has certainly been summer in every other part of London. I have seen pavement cafés exploding throughout Soho; crowds of office workers have exploited every coffee and lunch break by pouring into the streets in the West End. Girls in skimpy sundresses and strappy sandals have been spotted as far as Hammersmith. But in Islington it's bleak. To be specific, in TV6 it's bleak.

'Everything OK?' asks Fi. Fi is my assistant and has been for eighteen months. I employed her because she reminds me of myself. She is committed, ambitious and dedicated. She's cold comfort in times of a crisis.

'Fine.' I turn to my PC and hope she'll get the hint. I like to work things out for myself.

'Is there anything I can help with?'

'No,' I reply automatically. Although I employed Fi, I don't trust her 100 per cent. It isn't that Fi has done anything to lose my trust. In fact, when she first joined TV6, she worked very hard to be a 'chum', but eventually she realized I don't do 'chum'. And I don't trust. These are policies.

'If it's Bale, maybe I can have a word,' she offers. I sigh, depressed by the implication. Am I supposed to think she's being helpful? I look up at her and she is twirling her fine blonde hair around her finger, tapping her foot and smiling to herself. The implication is that she has a special relationship with Bale. Has she? Has she slept with him? Oh, awful thought. I look closer and she defiantly returns my gaze. Her ice-blue eyes, sparkling out above her high, chiselled cheekbones, lock on mine for a fraction of a second. Then she starts to walk away. She is striking. Her mother is Norwegian and she has inherited her Scan. confidence and good looks. She's one of those women who can make a beady bag and a friendship bangle look cool rather than childish. She is five foot ten; she has no hips, no thighs, no stomach. She is the ideal woman, as far as women are concerned. Generally Bale likes his women a little curvy, but then that is a generalization. It's possible they've had sex. However, I don't want to ask her. What's the point? She wouldn't have to tell me the truth. If she has slept with him she will have no influence over him, whatever she thinks to the contrary. But it is possible that he's still trying to seduce her, and if this is the case I can't afford to alienate her. She could be useful.

'Hey, Fi. Yeah, you can help. Organize a meeting between our team after lunch. We need a brainstorm.' I smile. We both know the smile is business. She grins back and I'm relieved. She probably hasn't slept with him yet. I normally know about such things long before the participants do. I consider warning her but decide not to. She'll either think I am jealous or too old to know better. Advice, by its very nature, is there to be ignored.

Our office is a huge glass building that seems to rise endlessly upwards. It's turned inside out like the Pompidou Centre. There is an odd mix of ritz and tat. Diet Coke and watery hot drinks from vending machines are consumed around Conran aluminium tables. There are plants oxygenating the room but I suspect the nod towards green and leafy is a losing battle. Since television studios are some of the few places left in London where people can still smoke, most feel it is obligatory. A dense smoky haze fills our days. People don't move around much, they stay at their desks. This suggests that there is a substantial amount of genuine industry but not much communication. Calling a meeting indicates the seriousness of my issue. Through the glass partition I see my team congregate. It's like watching a bunch of anxious relatives waiting by a sick bed. The analogy is frighteningly close to the reality. I'm pleasantly surprised to see that they possibly realize as much; everyone appears slightly nervous and sweaty. They are trying hard to look as though they are not trying at all. Their names are Thomas and Mark (the creative team), Jacquelyn (production secretary), Diana (marketing manager), Graham (sponsorship and advertising manager), Deborah (PR officer), Richard (broadcast strategy and scheduling manager) and Fi. Because we work in TV they are known as Tom, Jaki, Di, Gray, Debs, Ricky and Fi. There was nothing we could do with Mark.

The team look at one another to discover a suitable expression to draw their faces into. They are trying to decide whether to look racked with professional concern, coolly indifferent or bright and optimistic. The problem with my industry is that a very large part of it is populated by those who refuse to leave their student years behind them. They dress like students. Everyone is ill-looking thin. Dressing down is an art form. The merest hint of trying, an iota of personal pride, will be condemned. Everyone looks as though they do too many drugs, and smoke and drink too much. It's fair. Besides looking like students, the attitudes are similar, too. It is only students who could have arrived at the concepts of 'essay crisis' or 'no milk in the fridge crisis'. These are not crises. Crises are earthquakes, famines and tidal waves. My team understands that the cancellation of the Christmas karaoke act is a crisis but have no concept that twelve weeks of plummeting ratings is a crisis. If they do get the concept and panic about it for fifteen minutes or so, they can't hold the concept. It's usual that mid-brainstorm or meeting, someone suggests that we need to go to the pub for a 'break from the intensity'. On our return the original subject of the meeting is forgotten and the debate has moved on to whether salt and Linneker are a better flavour crisp than cheese and onion.

I don't feel like this. There is nothing more important than my job.

I never enter a meeting room without first thinking through exactly what I want to say, how I want to say it and what effect I want to have. Fi being keen and ambitious, whilst slightly threatening and nauseous, is useful. She'll really want to crack this. I've slept with both Mark and Tom, although neither of them knows about the other. (FYI, Mark is better-looking, Tom is better in bed. He tries harder.) It should be easy to keep their attention. Especially as by happy chance I am wearing an unnecessarily tight T-shirt and bootleg jeans that cling in all the right places. I haven't slept with Gray so the outfit will be doubly effective. Debs and Di like to keep in with me as I occasionally give them tips on hair conditioners or the latest 'must have' fashion statement. Ricky's gay so he does the same for me.

'Afternoon,' I breeze.

'Afternoon,' they mumble sulkily. For a nanosecond I think they are going to add 'miss', but they don't.

'What's this?' I ask, pointing sceptically towards a cardboard box in the centre of the table. It's overflowing with balloons, Christmas decorations, crayons, sticky-backed plastic, old magazines, a toy trumpet, several Comic Relief noses and a cappuccino.

'Oh, that's my coffee,' says Di, reaching into the box and rescuing her drink. She takes a huge slurp, oblivious to my disdain.

'Yes, that's clear. What is the rest of it?' I fear Debs has been let down by her childminder again and had to bring her five-year-old son into work. I hope not – Bale just isn't in the mood.

'It's the creativity box,' pipes up Fi, enthusiasm oozing from every pore. I look at her, waiting for a more meaningful explanation. She tries, 'It's to help stimulate more creative thoughts.' Even if I hadn't read Fi's CV I would know by this comment that she had an idyllic childhood, went to the best public schools for young ladies and had a father who adored her. How else could she be this happy with life? I think I'll piss on her parade.

'Remind me, Fi, which industry do we work in?'

'TV.' She looks cautiously around the room, unsure where this questioning is going.

'And wouldn't you agree that TV is generally considered a creative industry?'

'Well, yes, but—'

'We're not bloody management consultants, we don't need sticky-backed plastic to prove we are capable of ideas.' I don't raise my voice. I don't have to. She sheepishly drags the box off the table and tries to hide it behind the more conventional ideas aid, the flip chart. The others disloyally look away, distancing themselves from her. That doesn't impress me either.

'OK. You have read the brief. We have to come up with a hero show, something that will draw in the viewers and the advertisers; interest of the press would be a bonus. Mr Bale has articulated the problem here, rather succinctly, I'm sure you'll agree.' I read, '"We need a 'bang-those-bastards-and-their-new-shows-in-to-the-ground-idea".' The team treat themselves to a nervous giggle. I'm tough, but Bale is a tosser and our common loathing of him unites us again. I roll up my sleeves and sit on the side of the table, smiling and allowing the good humour to penetrate. 'So what's the competition doing?'

'ITV are concentrating on their main stable of shows,

successful soaps, quiz games that make people rich and buying in blockbuster films that earned a fortune in the box office. Here's their schedule for the next four months. The docusoap features heavily too,' says Ricky. He's done his homework efficiently. Unfortunately the news is depressing. The room falls silent again; the good mood has evaporated.

'What about Channel 4's scheduling this year?' asks Fi hopefully.

'Just as strong,' adds Ricky, embarrassed to be twisting the knife. 'They have everything. Arts, music, drama, comedy, entertainment, lifestyle, leisure, documentaries, film premières and something called "4 later".'

'What's that – porn?' asks Mark.

'I don't expect they even need porn,' answers Tom.

I read the descriptor. 'It's porn,' I assure. No one knows whether we should be glad that C4 have resorted to this or depressed because it will be a crowd pleaser. I clap my hands. 'OK, to business. No idea is a daft idea, any thoughts, please?' I pick up the marker and stand with my pen poised in front of the flip chart.

Silence.

'Come on,' I encourage. 'Don't let those schedules intimidate you. I really think you can overestimate a period drama with high production values, big stars and great plots. I think they are too highbrow. Let's catch another niche market.'

Fi gets it. 'Drama is too expensive for TV6. Entertainment is cheap.'

'Exactly,' I bolster. 'With entertainment the main outgoing is people's pride and common sense.'

'What about a game show?' offers Tom. The look on his face suggests that he thinks he's just invented electricity.

'Good,' I assure. He'll be the first to go, when the P45s are being dished up. 'Now try and think of what *type* of game show.' I consider whether, if the worst comes to the worst, I could retrain as a primary school teacher. I have all the core skills.

We bandy a few game show ideas around but they've all been done before. Often on bigger budgets than we have available. We talk it round and round.

'We could diversify. We could buy a publishing house or a football team,' suggests Gray. He's thinking of the free tickets that he could blag for his friends.

'That's a stupid idea,' comments Di.

'Gary, the commercial director, likes it.'

'I think it is a great idea,' says Di.

'Can we keep to the point, please,' I instruct. It's getting hot and late. I call out for more coffee and Coke. The rest of London's workforces teem out of their offices and escape into pubs for a long cool lager. This isn't an option for my team.

'How about a "fly-on-the-wall" programme?' asks Jaki. 'They are cheap and popular.'

'Absolutely. On which subject?'

'The police force?' offers Mark. 'We could expose their ruthless tactics and racist tendencies.'

'They do a pretty good job of that themselves, without TV,' points out Jaki.

'The fire brigade?' offers Ricky. I know he's simply getting hot and sweaty over the idea of them swinging down their pole. He's a sucker for uniforms.

'Been done.'

His disappointment is criminal.

'Banker-wankers?'

'Same as the police force, really.'

'The gas board?'

'Done.'

'Electricity?'

'And water. Nothing left to be said on the utilities scams.'

'Or builders or mechanics.'

'It's all been done before,' sighs Mark. 'It's all too undemanding and formulaic.'

'We are talking about an escapist medium,' I remind him. 'No one wants demanding. Demanding is how we describe our kids, red bills and the lover we no longer want to have sex with.'

We fall silent again. I look at the trash that's lying on the table. Numerous empty cans of diet Coke, overflowing ashtrays, curling sandwiches. This mountain of debris and my Patek Philippe watch tell me it's time to call it a day.

'OK, go home. Go and see your partners and kids.' I flop back into my chair and put my head on the desk. The cool surface is a relief. 'But don't stop thinking about this. The idea may come to you on the tube or in the bath or whilst you're making love.'

'You're sick,' grins Jaki. She seems to think that part of her job description as production secretary is to tell me how it is.

'Look, Jaki, football is not a matter of life and death, it's more important than that. And TV? TV is more important than football.'

She laughs and closes the door behind her.

But I'm not joking.

3

I live on my own, in a spacious pseudo-loft apartment in a trendy part of East London. I say pseudo because it's not in the loft, it's on the second floor. But I do have exposed brickwork and genuine iron girders that keep the roof from falling in. My space is the antithesis of both the abandoned family home in Esher and my mother's two-up-two-down in Cockfosters. It's modern and light and empty. I only allow things into my flat if they are both useful and beautiful. Except for the men who visit, which would be asking too much. My two favourite possessions are my charcoal-grey B&B Italia couch that seats umpteen and my B&O TV, which is the size of a screen at a small local cinema. I love my flat and Issie hates it, for the same reason: it's clinical and impersonal. Issie keeps trying to introduce chintz by buying me floral bathmats and tea cosies for Christmas. I return the favour by buying her aluminium, slim-line pasta jars, which she can't open.

Josh and Issie both have keys to my flat, as I do to their homes. We are Londoners so we don't literally drop in on one another. But sometimes we make arrangements to go round to each other's pads for supper, as it's nice to occasionally come home to the smell of cooking and the clink of someone pouring you a G&T. Tonight I'm delighted we've made this plan. I need their company. I push open my door and am hit by delicious cooking smells.

'You're late,' shouts Josh from the kitchen. He's responsible for the delicious smells. I drop my bags and PC and head straight for the kitchen.

'What's cooking?' I enquire, lifting lids and spooning small amounts of heaven into my mouth.

'Out,' he snaps, playfully swiping at my hands and trying to replace the lids. 'You have to wait.' But he can't resist showing off. 'It's *peperoni con acciughe e capperi.*'

'Chargrilled peppers with anchovy and capers,' translates Issie, as she hands me a glass of Australian Chardonnay. 'Mountadam, Eden Valley 1996,' she assures, knowing it's important to me.

'And *maiale arrosto con aceto balsamico,*' interrupts Josh.

I turn helplessly to Issie. She fills in, 'Roast pork with balsamic vinegar.'

'Fantastic.' Funny, I'm never irritated by Josh's pretension of insisting on calling every dish he cooks by its Italian name. 'Have I got time to shower off my shit day?'

'Yes, if you are quick.'

Sometimes we chatter non-stop throughout supper and sometimes we watch TV, entertaining ourselves by hurling abuse or a book at the commentary, but tonight we eat in comfortable silence. Or at least I think it is comfortable until Issie asks, 'What's up, Cas? You're really quiet tonight.' She's given me authority over the remote control. Normally I love this but tonight, as a diversionary tactic, the remote control is a failure.

I realize I'm grateful to be asked and I slip into child mode, hoping that surrogate Mum and Dad can sort things out for me. There's only Issie and Josh, in the entire world, who I let see me when I feel vulnerable or down.

'It's work,' I whine.

'Naturally. We never expect you to say it's man trouble,'

comments Josh. I don't have man trouble – that's the advantage of seeing them as sex objects rather than soul mates.

'The channel's viewing figures are down for the twelfth week in a row. It's serious. Bale's talking redundancies. Problem is we haven't got a hero show. We haven't even got a strong soap.'

'What about *Teddington Crescent*?' Issie is as intimate with my programming schedule as I am.

'The lives and loves of the inhabitants of Milton Keynes don't have what it takes to knock *Corrie* or *Brookie* off their spots. We haven't got a principal game show, or a lead chat show host. Poor ratings – that's viewership,' I translate, but it's unnecessary as they are both educated in my media speak, 'affect the advertisers we can draw. Without advertising money we can't invest in cool shows. It's a vicious circle.' I pause. They don't interrupt but allow me to find the words. 'The worst of it is that Bale has made it into my problem.' I check to see if they are as pissed off as I am. They both make an admirable job of looking horrified. Satisfied, I continue. 'Despite his obscene pay cheque he has renounced all responsibility and said I have to come up with a winning idea. He's—'

'So rotten. He's repellent, revolting, ridiculous,' jokes Josh.

'A plethora of R words.' Issie grins and tries to get me to cheer up.

I scowl. 'He's a shit.' I'm not going to allow them to brighten me out of my despair. 'I'm scared.'

Everyone is silent. They know my job is my world. Josh sits down next to me and puts his arm round me.

'I'm fucking scared,' I say with unusual honesty.

'I don't see the problem. You'll come up with the idea,' he comforts. Normally I love his confidence in me but I shrug, because right now, I don't think his confidence is founded. My head is aching. Everything's fuzzy.

'Maybe.' I know that it is my problem and neither of them can really offer a solution, so I change the subject. 'Did I get any post?'

'Its on the mantelpiece.'

Two bills, council tax and water – marvellous. Three pieces of junk mail, all for pizza delivery services. I spy another heavy white envelope.

'Hell, another wedding,' I sigh. 'It's nearly September, for Christ's sake. Haven't these people any decency? Plaguing me throughout my autumn months as well as the summer.' I'm only half kidding, but it's great to see Issie look het up.

'Who is it this time?' she asks.

'Jane Fischer is marrying Marcus Phillips,' I read. 'Have we met him?'

'Yup,' confirms Josh. 'He was at Lesley and James's wedding last week. He was an usher. The blonde one, with the red waistcoat. Jane wasn't there – some prior commitment, probably another wedding.'

Issie and I freeze.

'Bastard,' we assert in unison.

I pass Issie the invite so she can see the betrayal for herself. Issie fingers the white card, caressing the embossing, and sighs. It's not turning out to be a good day for either of us.

'That explains the reluctance to give a real telephone number.'

'Will either of you marry me?' asks Josh, realizing that Issie's had a disappointment but not knowing the exact nature.

'No,' I say.

'Yes,' says Issie, 'but only for the dress.'

We all laugh. We've run through this routine zillions of times. When we graduated Josh promised to marry whichever one of us wasn't married by the time we were twenty-five. Twenty-five came and went. None of us had managed to find a life partner but we were forced to admit that, at that precise moment in time, we didn't fancy each other. We decided not to go ahead but put the deal back to when we hit thirty, assuming that we'd be so desperate by then we'd all be less fastidious. Thirtieth parties came and went, but Josh said he couldn't choose between us and as bigamy is an offence, punishable in the highest courts in the land, we all agreed to think about it again in the year 2005. However, Josh does regularly ask us to marry him, just so we feel good about ourselves. He often tries to coincide it with our menstrual cycles, which with the passing of time he has reluctantly become intimate with.

'Can you believe that Marcus guy slept with me just days before he sent out invites to his wedding?'

'Yes,' I reply.

She scowls and mutters, 'Well, of course you only expect the worst from people,' she grumbles. 'Can *you* believe it?' Issie turns to Josh. It's an annoying habit of hers to think that there is a male and a female point of view on these things. She often dismisses my point of view and turns to Josh 'because he's a man and he knows how men think'. Invariably Josh agrees with me.

'It's commonplace. The last fling and all that,' says Josh, and although I know that what he is saying upsets Issie I feel vindicated. 'I make a conscious effort to look up ex-girlfriends just before they get married, on the grounds that I might exploit the last fling thing,' he adds.

'Do you?' cries Issie, horrified.

'Do you?' I say, and once again my respect for him is renewed. Josh tries to settle his face in an expression that will please both of us, a subtle mix between contrition and pride. He gives up and ends up just grinning at me.

'Tell me,' I beg. Josh is a wonderful friend and I love him

for very many reasons and one of them is that he's unscrupulous and we can share tactics.

'It never fails. It's the combination of the near-legalized indiscretion. Women figure that once they've slept with you, they might as well sleep with you again.' I raise my eyebrows. Personally I'm not too fond of repeat performances – they give the wrong message. Josh catches my glance and understands my scepticism.

'I'm generalizing,' he explains. 'Normal women. Everyone wants a final fling but a safe final fling. The ex is that. It's worked for me on several occasions. One last night of unbridled passion but without the complications that Marcus risked by starting up a new liaison.' Issie scowls. Josh shrugs apologetically. But what can he do? He's spent years apologizing to Issie for his half of the human race, but really it's not his fault. Now he simply shrugs off her disappointments.

'That's it! That's it! Genius,' I congratulate. 'You are a genius.' I cry and hug Josh. Josh happily accepts my hugs but he hasn't got a clue why I'm so excited. 'That's the idea for the fucking amazing ratings-rocketing programme. A *Blind Date* meets *The Truman Show*.'

'What?' asks Josh. Issie simply stares; she rarely expects to follow my devious mind.

'A fly-on-the-wall plus. We get couples, the week before their wedding, to come on to the show and tell us all about why they are getting married.' I rush to explain but my tongue can't keep up with my grey matter and I doubt I'm making sense. 'Loads of sucker stuff about how they knew from the moment they saw each other and how there could never be anyone else for them. Then we find out which one of them is gagging for a bit of extra-curricular—'

'But—' Issie tries to interrupt me.

'There will be one,' I assure forcefully. 'Then we manœuvre

a meeting between that party and an ex. Then we let nature take its course.'

'Will it work?'

'Of course it will work. There is nothing more seductive than an ex.'

Issie eyes me sceptically.

'Except perhaps Gucci,' I concede. I'm thrilled. 'It has everything! Voyeurism, trivialization of sex, manipulation.'

'It's a terrible idea,' shouts Issie.

I'm genuinely bewildered. 'It's brilliant.'

'It's the principle I object to,' she adds.

'I don't deal in principles – they are no longer legal tender.'

'More is the pity.'

I start to imagine the marketing and PR. 'He's put on a pound or two, maybe lost a bit of hair, but otherwise he's unchanged. He was the love of your life when you were twenty-one and ten years have gone by. Yet he has that same boyish grin, he still calls you by your nickname and he remembers that you bought your hair gel in goldfish bowls at Superdrug. How can you resist?' I'm warming to my theme.

'Flirting with nostalgia is perilous,' warns Issie.

'That's its selling point,' I confirm.

'You could wreck lives. Be responsible for cancelled weddings,' she squeals.

'We'd pay for the wedding if it fell through.'

Josh looks at me as though I've just crawled out from under the rim of the loo. This surprises me.

'What?' I demand, hotly. 'I'm saving taxes. Your hard-earned taxes.' I think this will get him. Josh is in the 40 per cent bracket. He has private healthcare and went to public school, so my very reasonable argument that taxes aren't just for the building and deconstruction of our roads but for the building and reconstruction of our healthcare and future has never washed with him. Now I'm grateful.

'If these people married, they would sooner or later divorce, dragging their five children through the courts. The children would be emotionally scarred and, no doubt, perpetrate the scenario by re-enacting their parents' failed marriages. The total legal aid costs could run into hundreds of thousands.'

'Christ, Cas, you deserve a medal,' bites Josh sarcastically.

I choose to ignore the sarcasm. 'I knew you'd see it my way.'

I can hardly sleep with excitement. I fine-tune the details. I consider that perhaps it is too much to expect every couple, weeks away from marriage, to have cracks in their relationships, but I could advertise. I reason that no one is going to come forward and volunteer that they are feeling restless or randy. People lack such emotional honesty or self-awareness. I know – I've operated in the so-called adult world for sixteen sexually active years and I've yet to find anyone who is prepared to call a spade a shovel. But perhaps there is another way. Perhaps I could attack it from the other side. I've seen countless examples of paranoia, jealousy, insecurity and mistrust. Now *that* is an angle! Maybe I could advertise for people who doubt their partners and want to test them before they make that final commitment. Then all TV6 will have to do is manœuvre a situation where the mistrusted party comes into contact with the threatening ex and then . . . And then! I hug myself. Obviously it depends on the mistrusted partner never having a clue that they are being tested. Total secrecy. But that shouldn't be too hard to achieve. In my experience secrecy between couples is pretty commonplace. I know this is big. I can see it now. The reaction of the duped, the hypocrisy of the rogue partners. All on live TV. It is pure brilliance! It's so cruel. It's so honest. I can smell my success and it makes me feel sexy.

I switch on my bedside light and feel under my bed in an attempt to unearth my electronic diary. I hesitate. Problem with repeat performances is that they invariably lead to unnecessary complications. The guy involved thinking I really care, him thinking he does, or his wife finding out and thinking both of us do. Yet, needs must. I really can't be bothered to get dressed and drag myself to my club to pick up something fresh. The diary beeps at me. Steven Arnold? No, I think he just got married. That would be awful timing. Keith Bevon? No, psycho, stalker tendencies. Phil Bryant? Didn't he emigrate? George Crompton, or perhaps his brother Jack? Oh no, too late in the day for the complex sibling thing – 'Why did you ring me rather than my brother?' 'Is mine bigger than his?' Lord, it's enough to bring on a headache. Miles Dodd? Good idea, not too clingy, not too involved – with me or anyone else. Prepared to hold back until I come. Yes, Miles will do nicely. Disappointingly his line is engaged. Well, at least it's just his line. Joe Dorward. It takes me a moment to place him. Oh yes, the researcher on that pop quiz show on Channel 4. I met him at a workshop several months ago. I hadn't found him sexy at first – good-looking, yes, but not clever enough to really turn me on. I figured I could run verbal rings around him, which is rarely attractive. However, after three or four glasses of champagne I was less fastidious. It had panned out quite well. As Josh says, it's not *verbal* stimulation you want in bed. I call his number. He picks up.

'Hey, Joe,' I murmur.

I wake up and Joe is already up. I can hear him in the kitchen, whistling and fixing breakfast. He brings up a coffee and tells me that he's been to the 7–11 to buy croissants, that they'll be ready soon. I tell him I don't eat breakfast and struggle to sit up.

'Water?'

He rushes to the bathroom and returns with a glass of water. I'm so dehydrated that I ignore the fact that this glass of water has undoubtedly passed through five other bodies before me. Joe climbs back into bed and starts nibbling my shoulder. In the cold light of day I realize that first impressions are always right. He is dumb. Admittedly, he is extremely handsome and, I suppose, sexy, in an obvious sort of way. But how come I hadn't noticed those puppy-dog eyes shining with devotion? That overloud laugh that erupts every time I say anything, even unfunny things like my name and that nodding bloody head that agrees with *everything* I say. It's nauseating. He still smells good and, thinking about it objectively, he is a shag. But he's so certainly besotted. I try to think of the things that could put him off me. Perhaps if I showed him my cellulite or my untrimmed bikini line he'd leave the flat (unlikely). Maybe if I insist on watching Oprah, or pick the pubes from between my teeth with my toenails. I can't think of any antisocial behaviour that is antisocial enough to discourage him. I realize that the only way to get him to lose interest is to pretend to be in love with him. I doubt I have the energy. His large legs, erotic last night, look overwhelming today. I push him away, get out of bed, locate his trousers and throw them at him.

'Get dressed. I've a big day today.'

'Bale, I have the answer.' I charge into his office, shooing his secretary away with a single, withering glance. I decline the seat and the cigar he offers. He really is a twat. However, he is my twat boss and I want to impress him.

'I have the Idea.'

'I'm all ears,' he sneers. Actually, he does have jug ears but he's all teeth, not all ears. I resist the jibe and start to tell him about my idea. Although I've stormed into his office at 10.50 a.m. to give the impression of an employee who knows her worth and won't be bullied, I have actually been in the office since 8.15 a.m. rehearsing this meeting. I have perfected a pitch that guarantees punch but appears spontaneous, that is irresistible and, most of all, assured. Besides the presentation of the pitch, I have paid immaculate attention to the detail of the presentation of the person. I'm wearing a Dries Van Noten white cotton slip dress with heavy boots on bare legs. The look I've achieved is naïve charm, but the boots hint at something a whole lot tougher. I'm showing enough cleavage to secure his attention.

'OK.' I take a deep breath. 'The brief was to have a high-profile programme that will attract viewers, advertising budgets and the press.' Bale nods cautiously. 'You want notoriety on a shoestring,' I add for clarity.

'I never said notoriety.'

'But you agree we need to be noticed.' He nods. The nod is fractional. I know this is because if there is ever a debate with the executive committee regarding this programme, Bale will deny he gave consent. Sod him. I tell him my idea.

'It's a bit unlikely, isn't it?' says Bale cautiously.

'Why do you say that?'

'Well, the premiss you're working from is that we need couples who are just about to skip towards the altar but are paranoid enough to think that their dearest is not 100 per cent kosher and he fancies a bit of pork with his ex-totty.'

The analogy is repulsive. Offensive to a number of religions, vegetarians and women, but yes, basically Nigel has it. I try to encourage him.

'Look, I've done my research. There are 6.6 marriages per 1,000 population in the UK. Which is roughly 11,000 per week. It's one of the highest marriage rates in the world, twenty-ninth highest, actually. But we also have one of the highest divorce rates too—'

'Well, you can't divorce unless you marry,' says fucking Einstein. I smile icily.

'The divorce rate is 3.2 per 1,000 population. Ninth highest in the world.'

'And your point is?'

'Do you know in how many cases the ex is cited in court? Thirty-seven per cent. There are countless rekindlings of old flames and remarriages to ex-partners each year. The ex is so compelling. I give you Liz Taylor and Richard Burton, Fergie and Prince Andrew, Melanie Griffith and Don Johnson.' Bale's beginning to be interested. He knows a good idea when he sees one.

'Isn't that Melanie one with that Banderas one now?'

I sweep his objections away by ignoring them. 'Bale, we can't fail.'

'Would there really be people who would do this?'

I can't believe Bale is questioning whether there are enough exhibitionist/paranoid/jealous types in the world.

'We are looking at a pilot series of six episodes. Two couples per episode. We only need twelve couples. We have the entire British population to choose from.'

Bale nods. 'People are so hideous.'

He should know. I fake cordiality. 'It makes good television. Think back to 1974, Paul Rogers' documentary *The Family*. You know what I'm talking about?' The show has superstar status in the history of TV. Everyone knows of it. It was the first fly-on-the-wall.

'Oh, the one where Rogers sat, for months, with a camera

in the front room of some family from the commuter belt? The marriage broke down as a consequence.'

'Yes. I don't think it was simply to do with Mr Wilkins's dislike of audio equipment. It was because Mrs Wilkins admitted on national TV that her husband was not the father of her last child.'

'That's right.' Bale is leering and chuckling at the same time. 'Dirty bitch.'

'But ask yourself why, Bale. Why would she divulge such a thing to the entire world? Maybe it *was* simply stress, but she invited that stress into her home. Why would she do that? Maybe she wanted to make the confession? Maybe she wanted to blow apart her sanitized semi? Or was it to guarantee that she didn't pass from this world to the next without her Andy Warhol requisite fifteen minutes of fame?'

'Or maybe she wanted to teach him a lesson?' adds Bale. 'Hurt him? Or beg his forgiveness in a forum too public to allow him to reject her?'

'Exactly. We don't know. There are myriad reasons that motivate people. Think of the radio wedding a few years back. People are prepared to trot down the aisle, with absolute strangers, to get their Warhol fifteen minutes. Although in the Birmingham couple's case, it wasn't so much fifteen minutes as seven and a half months, 185 minutes of TV air time, 207 minutes of radio airtime and 58 column inches in the press.'

Bale taps his pen on the desk. He's getting excited. I go for closure.

'There are countless fly-on-the-wall programmes about marriage: the run-up to the proposal, the wedding, the first year. I've heard that Channel 4 are developing a documentary on consummation.' I'm making this up, but I want Bale's budget. I am immoral most of the time and amoral where business is concerned. 'I'm proposing a twist to a proven formula. The contributors are to be in the studio when the actions of all parties are exposed. The live audience is key. It's overpowering. The thing about exes is that they never go away. Even those to whom you haven't given a second thought in over a decade, whom you've never seen since you parted, are important. There is always a nagging curiosity about what happened to the one that got away, or the one you threw away.'

Bale, a true businessman, sees the potential. 'You think it will work.' He states this as a fact rather than as a question.

'Yes,' I enthuse. 'I admit that it is dependent upon the credulity, stupidity and vanity of the British population.' I take a deep breath. 'It can't fail.'

'But if it gets as big, as you say it will, how will we keep attracting people on to the show?'

'We'll film enough shows for a series before we go live. We'll have watertight release forms so that the guests can't retract their permission. Bale, I'll work out the detail. Don't you worry.' I'm desperate, so I gently pat his arm.

Bale nods. 'OK, Cas. Go to finance and work out a budget.'

I want to punch the air. He senses it. 'Hey, don't get carried away. I'm not a millionaire.'

That's another one of Bale's relentless lies. But I don't care. I've got a programme and it's a winner!

4

'Josh, hi, it's me. Guess what? Bale went for it! The infidelity with an ex show.'

'And I'm supposed to think that's a good thing.'

'Oh, come on, Josh.' It's not like him to be down on me. 'I'm back on top.'

'Which is where you most like to be.' Josh laughs, despite himself.

'Both literally and metaphorically,' I add cheekily.

'Are you flirting with me, Cas?' Josh asks, but not seriously.

'I'd be flirting if it was anyone but you,' I assure him.

'Cold comfort.'

'We're going to call it *Sex with an Ex*. What do you think?'

'I'm trying not to think about it.'

I sigh, disappointed by his lack of enthusiasm. 'Look, I've got to ring off – there's so much to do. I just wanted to tell you my good news. After all, you more or less gave me the idea.'

'Oh, horrible thought. Bye now.'

I put the phone down and do my best to push Josh's reserved response to the back of my mind. Instead I focus on the fact that Bale is as grateful as I could hope. He has offered to pay me a bonus related to the ratings we secure. I'm likely to make a killing. My success has duly subdued Fi and I have decided to be magnanimous. I don't trust her, but practically speaking she is my assistant and I need her to be closely involved in this project – there is so much to do.

We start with the advert.

Are you about to get married? Do you trust your affianced 100 per cent? Is there an ex in his or her past who could still affect your future? Please write in complete confidentiality to P.O. Box . . .

Such a simple call to action.

'Will it work?' asks Fi.

'If I know anything about human nature, this will work.'

'Where should we place the ad?'

'Initially in the sad, loser magazines, *Gas* and *Gos*.' I throw a couple of mags over to her. I respect Fi enough not to expect her to be familiar with them. She picks up the mags and begins to flick through them.

'My God, these are obscene. Don't these people have any self-respect?'

I don't look up from my budget sheets. 'No.'

She starts to read the contents page. '"I Had Sex with 100 Men in Three Years", "I had a Threesome with my Mate and his Girlfriend", "The Crotchless Knickers are by the Booby Drops – Working in a Sex Shop", "We're Sex-perts – Women Who Really Rate Themselves in Bed"!'

'It's ideal,' I interrupt. 'The readers are willing to bare their souls and their bodies for a measly fiver and a couple of column inches on the letters page. These people are looking for platforms. They're a gift. However, Fi, I don't want to be another Jerry Springer. I don't simply want the oddballs of this world. We are going to have to think of an extremely clever incentive to attract normal people.'

Fi groans. 'But it will be easier to get horrid people on the show. They have no self-awareness and also they've had fewer opportunities.'

I glare at her. Easy (unless relating to my sexual morals) is not a word I like in my vocabulary. I know that the success of the show will lie in whether I can make the average viewer feel uncomfortable. There are zillions of fly-on-the-wall and chat show programmes where the guests are modern-day ghouls. Normally the viewer sits back, cushy on their chintz. They comment that the characters on talk shows are priceless, pure escapism. Chat shows do a public service: people watch and thank God that their own lives are better than these are. I want *Sex with an Ex* to be a different sort of show. I want cosy couples to stiffen in each other's company. I want them to struggle for conversation in the ad break. I want them to move apart a fraction and doubt each other. This show is their lives, whatever class, age, race or religion they are.

'So who do you want to attract?'

'Joe and Joanne public. The people we trust. Policemen, nurses, librarians, teachers, the guys at Carphone Warehouse.' Fi eyes me sceptically.

Eventually we agree to place the advert on the TV6 web page and the internal electronic noticeboard, to send a researcher to gyms and clubs to do some on-the-spot recruiting, and to place a telephone line after our *Don't Try This Alone* programme. It does quite well on the early evening slot.

Any reservations Fi had regarding the number of volunteers we'd find are soon swept away. Within days of placing the adverts we are inundated with responses; they arrive by the sackful. The world, it appears, is full of those who are about to pledge love until death do them part but actually fear a much more secular separation. It was as I'd expected. They are the most depressing reads ever.

My girlfriend, Chrissie, is the sweetest, kindest, most loving woman I have ever known. I'm honoured that she accepted my proposal and agreed to be my wife. We are due to marry in four weeks' time. We are having a big do, no expense spared. After all, you only do it once. We plan to have a large family and one day live by the sea. I love her and she loves me. She says so all the time.

Do you think she'd ever be unfaithful?

I only ask because my best mate reckons he saw her in a pub with an ex-boyfriend of hers. I'm sure it was innocent but when I asked her about it, she said he must have made a mistake . ...

I get married in seven weeks' time. I love my fiancé so much and I'm sure that he loves me, pretty sure. But not absolutely certain. There was a girl he went to college with. She ditched him for an American rower. My best friend got very drunk at a dinner party last night and said some really mean things. She said that I caught him on the rebound, that he's out of my league. I wonder – if he had the choice, would he choose me?

. . . I found letters, you see. Why would she keep his letters?

. . . When you marry you give up your past. You have to. I'm ready for it. But is he? He's always been a bit of a one for the ladies. Nothing serious. He's just a flirt. He can't help himself. He doesn't mean any harm by it. It doesn't bother me. Too much. It's just that my mum says that men like him never change. It's not that there is an individual ex that I'm threatened by. To be frank there are dozens . . .

There are a number of psychotics. People who said they'd rather see their partner dead than unfaithful. I believe them and pass their letters on to the police.

We employ a team to trawl through the responses, but Fi and I can't resist an occasional morbid dip into them.

Although the letters are in many ways individual there is a commonality. There is a mustard ripeness of those desperate to confirm their own supremacy in their partner's affections.

'Do you think they'll all look hideous?'

'Why do you suppose that, Fi?'

'Well, to be so desperate, so insecure?'

I throw over to her a picture of one of the letter writers. The woman in question is thirty-two, slim, blonde, elegant. She has enclosed a CV detailing that she has a first from Cambridge and a Ph.D. from Harvard. Fi looks amazed. To shake her further, I pass a photo of the fiancé. He is smart and mediocre. Fi looks bewildered.

'He is so ordinary.'

'Yup, to you. But to her he is a god.'

'I don't get it.' She shakes her head wearily.

'Nor do I, babe. Maybe it's a London thing.' I don't believe this, but I think it might be a comfort. 'Anyway, get her on the show.'

The team is gathering around the mountain of letters, which appear to have a magnetic force. I take advantage of their presence, 'OK, status. Have you seen the lawyers, Jaki?'

'Yes. We have to be extremely careful, but the terms aren't impossible. For those who know they are being filmed and are part of the set-up we can use any footage we like, as long as the punter is informed that the tape is running. "Informing" them can be as simple as posting a notice saying cameras are in operation, and to be super-safe, we must get the guests to sign this.' She waves a weighty document, about the thickness of the *Yellow Pages*. 'The fine print will bore the proverbials off most guests and they'll sign. You can use CCTV footage as long as the local council agrees. I'm working on clearance. Those cameras are everywhere – shops, garages, on street lamps in dark alleys' – I like the fact that she's been thinking laterally – 'libraries, public car parks, hotel foyers.'

'I can't imagine these public and commercial bodies will agree, though, will they?' asks Fi.

'As I say, I'm working on clearance but as long as all the correct legal documents are in place no one seems too squeamish about blowing the whistle. Restaurants and hotels see it as free publicity. However, taping the dupe is much more difficult. If someone doesn't know they are being taped it's illegal to show footage of them, unless they are committing a criminal act and it's to help the course of justice.'

'Oh,' I sigh. This isn't good news. The whole premiss of the show depends on catching these guys and gals red-handed, so to speak.

Jaki continues. 'The only way round it is to conceal their identity. Do it all through implication. So, for example, show stills of the dupe and current fiancé/fiancée, which the fiancé/fiancée will have released. Then show stills of the "tempting party" and then when filming the actual seduction scene we'll have to be creative with those black banners that obscure identity or body parts. It will be clear whether the dupe has fallen or not, without having to actually say so.'

I think about it. As the film will be shown for the first time in front of a live audience and all the parties, it will be impossible for the dupe to deny if he/she is the person committing infidelity. And even if they do, the guaranteed ensuing row will still make great TV. I can't lose. 'Sounds manageable. Anything else?'

'In addition, you can't show any actual lewd acts, even after the watershed. We must bleep out the C word, at a minimum, and other expletives if you want to avoid controversy.'

'Which I don't.'

Jaki shrugs. 'It's your call. In summary Mr and Ms J. Bloggs have very few legal rights over their privacy.'

'Fantastic. Document everything. Remember the golden rule.'

Jaki nods. 'Yes, I have it tattooed on my cranium, "Thou shalt cover thy arse."'

'Precisely. OK, Ricky, what did the scheduler say?'

'Oh, you know, the usual bollocks that their responsibility is to heighten the built-in tension between random luck and rules in a game structure – between the predictable and inconceivable, the controllable and the frenzy, which creates enjoyment, blah blah. Need I go on?'

'No. What slot do we have?'

'They offered us seven thirty on Saturday night, going out against Cilla.'

'That's stupid. *Blind Date* has been running for sixteen years. It still pulls in over seven million viewers. I'd never think of running a head-to-head.' I pause. 'Well, at least not until towards the end of the series. What else did they offer? It's hardly as though we are flush with brilliant programmes.'

'Monday at ten.'

'Take it. Gray, how are the sponsorship and advertising deals coming along?'

'Good. The advertising is all in place. The TV trailers are set up and we've optioned press and poster adverts – the exact placement will be confirmed a few weeks before the first show. As for sponsorship, we have a lead. A teenage retail store is interested in sponsoring the show. It would be a cash-and-barter deal. You know the type of thing: the guest would be obliged to wear their gear, etc. The creatives have come up with some suggested break-bumper ideas.'

Gray cautiously puts the ideas on the table. It's an unsubtle play on the words 'top shaft'. The creative team annoy me on a number of counts. They are incapable of accepting a creative brief without whining that they are overworked, which is unlikely to be the case in a channel struggling to come up with programmes; they take long lunches; they switch off their mobiles; they never accept advice, use dictionaries or attend meetings. They proudly admit to reading the *Sport* and comment on the size of the tits of their female colleagues. And finally, worst of all, their ideas are puerile. Gray reads my face.

'You think they're puerile, don't you?'

'Yes,' I confirm. 'It won't work. The Independent Television Commission won't touch it. And even if we could get it through, it says the wrong things about the show. Get Mark and Tom to come up with some more up-market directions.'

I push open the pub door and am hit by the familiar and comforting smell of beer-soaked carpets, cigarette smoke, and salt and vinegar crisps. It's mid-September and although the sun is weakly trying to battle with the autumnal winds I'm glad Josh has decided to sit inside rather than in the beer garden. I spot him immediately. He is sitting in the corner reading *Private Eye*, oblivious to the adoring looks he is attracting from the small gaggles of women office workers. I weave my way towards him and kiss him on the cheek. He puts down his reading matter and, grinning, points to the vodka and orange which is waiting for me.

'Cheers.' We clink glasses. 'How did you know it was a vodka day?' I normally drink gin and tonic except when I'm under extreme pressure at work, when I drink vodka and orange. I like to think the orange cordial will somehow compensate for the fact that I haven't eaten a proper meal for days.

'Well, since you started this *Sex with an Ex* project, neither

Issie nor I have heard from you. I figured if you hadn't had time to call us in ten days you wouldn't have had time to eat either.'

'Sorry,' I mumble. Josh shrugs. I don't have to say much more. I'm still reeling from the ticking off he gave me this morning when he finally got through to me at work. He'd made it quite clear that he was sick of talking to my answering machine. I'd insisted that given a choice, of course, I'd prefer to be drinking with him and Issie, but developing a new show monopolizes my time, whether I like it or not. Josh swept aside my objections and bullied me into coming out for a drink with him. To be honest I was grateful to concede. 'Where's Issie tonight?'

'Yoga. She said she might join us later. So in the meantime you'll just have to put up with me boring you with stories about court.'

'Bore away.' I grin, because Josh is anything but boring. He is a good storyteller. He practises criminal law and is always full of amusing anecdotes about his day-to-day dealings with the dregs of society. We chat about his work and his flat (he wants my advice on bathroom tiles and I agree to go shopping with him next Saturday); he tells me about his latest flirtation, which he doesn't appear to be that enthusiastic about – although he assures me that she has stunning legs. The chat is comfortable and relaxed. I listen intently and whilst I'm bursting to talk about *Sex with an Ex* I resist. Josh knows me well enough to know I am practising extreme self-restraint and so finally allows me centre stage.

'And what about you? How's *Sex with an Ex* panning out?'

This is what I've been waiting for. I know that I can discuss all aspects of the show with Josh without the reserve I have to employ when talking to anyone else. In the office it is of paramount importance that I appear confident and assured at all times. I can't express any doubts or misgivings even about small things, like the colour of the set design. With Josh, on the other hand, I can bounce from extreme confidence to misgivings and back again in one easy move, without him thinking any the less of me. I sigh.

'I don't want this show to be tacky, but I am working against the odds. When we don't have good ideas we have to employ amazingly expensive actors and construct lavish set designs – it's an attempt to distract the viewer.' I explain. '*Sex with an Ex* is a good idea so we are investing sweet FA in the production. I've seen the set – it shivers dangerously whenever anyone sneezes or shouts loudly. If only Bale would dig a little deeper into those pockets of his. I know they are not limitless, but they are fathoms deep.'

'Is Bale being tight?'

'He did, at least, agree to a warm-up act – you know, someone to keep the audience amused during the commercial break.'

'Well, that's something.'

'Yes, the epitome of generosity. He suggested we pick up some act from Covent Garden and pay them thirty quid,' I bite sarcastically.

'Who are you getting as the presenter?'

'Well, I wanted Zoë Ball, Yasmin Le Bon or Nigella Lawson, but Bale instructed me to go and get "some new totty" straight out of drama school. That way he won't have to pay her more than a few grand for the series.'

Josh laughs. 'Typical Bale.'

'Absolutely. Even so, I'm optimistic. After interviewing for ever we found the perfect presenter. She is busty, with short spiky hair and personality. She wears cropped tops and baggy trousers. She's young.' I don't add that I see this as an advantage because she's too young to feel particular about the tragedy bus she is if not driving certainly stamping tickets on.

'Have you worked out the detail of the show's structure?'

'Yup. We advertised and were inundated with responses from the paranoid and jealous. We interview these individuals on tape. We draft in the threatening ex and interview them too. The motivation of the ex is usually revenge or desperation (if they were dumped), curiosity or vanity (if they were the dumpee). We then follow all parties (including the unsuspecting dupe) for a week, intercutting the preparations for the wedding and the possible betrayal. The key to the show is that we bring all the guests back and play the footage live. The unsuspecting dupe thinks they are going to be on *Who Wants to be a Billionaire* or something similar, right up until the moment they are on stage. It will be on stage that the letterwriter gets to either faint with relief or discover if their worst fears have been founded.' I stop and check Josh's reaction. He's very pale and sweaty-looking. Perhaps he's been drinking too much. 'You do think it will work?'

'Yes, sadly I think you're on to a winner.'

Pleased, I stand up to get the drinks. Issie calls Josh's mobile to say that she's not going to join us because she doesn't fancy being in a pub after meditating. We stay until last orders and I have a great time.

As I climb into a cab, Josh wishes me luck with the show and makes me renew my promise to help him shop for bathroom tiles. I nod, blow him a kiss and fall back on to the leather seat. My slightly inebriated state brings with it a sense of well-being and all is right with the world. I really should make more of an effort to see more of my friends.

I find the interviews with the selected couples obscene and

fascinating at once, and have insisted on conducting as many of them as possible myself.

'So, Jenny, you wrote to us in response to the article you saw in *Gas*. Let's run through the details of the letter, so you can confirm them for me and I can get them straight in my head.' I laugh in a jolly oh-silly-me-I-find-it-so-hard-to-retain-information way. I find it gets them onside. 'Do you mind?'

Jenny shakes her head. The movement is exaggerated. She is trying to appear confident and assured. However, she is chainsmoking full strength Benson and Hedges, lighting another before the first stops smouldering – not the actions of a confident woman. Jenny is skinny but not the fashionably anorexic skinny that is prevalent in the studio. She's skinny because she can't afford to smoke and eat. We all have choices. According to my notes Jenny is twenty-three. She looks forty-five but then I suspect she was born looking forty-five. I suppose the advantage is she'll still look forty-five when she's sixty-five. Her face is pinched and reminds me of a balloon the day after the party, all shrivelled and twisted into a knot. She's had a lifetime of poor school results, no chances and no splendour, which is why she's here.

'Jenny, you must be very excited by the chance to be on TV?'

'Too right, yeah.'

'And it's been explained to you exactly how the show works?' This is code speak for 'You know the humiliation you are about to undergo?'

'Yeah.'

'You wrote to me because you think there is a possibility that your fiancé, Brian Parkinson, is being unfaithful. Or at least he would be, given the chance.' I tilt my head and quietly cluck.

'Yeah.'

'And you mention in your letter that you have your suspicions as to who the object of affection is.'

'Too right, yeah. My best friend, Karen.'

'Karen Thompson,' I read from my notes. She nods again and swaps stub for fresh fag. 'Can you give me a brief history?'

'Brian was going with Karen when I met him.'

'And that was when?'

'I was seventeen.'

The story is bleak. Brian has yo-yoed between Karen and Jenny for the past six years. It's hard to understand what drives the change of allegiance. I think it is something to do with which of the two women is employed at the time and can supply money for his fags and booze. The only cheering thought for humanity is that the women have not allowed Brian's indecision to come between them. More often than not, all three of them go to their local together. I'm not delicate but I wonder how any of them live, not knowing whom Brian will want to go home with on any given night.

'She'd be better getting it on with Roy, Brian's brother. After all, she's my bridesmaid and Roy's the best man. It's traditional, ain't it?' She slaps my thigh and laughs. But the laugh is tinny and nervous. She stops suddenly and leans close into me. I know from Issie and a number of my other friends that she is about to indulge in a confession. In a more religious age she would be offering up prayers to Mary the virgin mother, saint of desperate cases.

'I really wouldn't like to lose him, darlin'. I love him. But if I'm going to lose him, it'd better be before the wedding.'

I back away, disentangling myself from the woman's cigarette fumes and her earnest stare.

My interview with Karen is almost identical, except Karen is as fat as Jenny is skinny. Her arms wobble when she raises a glass of beer to her mouth. Her life has been one of steaming hot chips wrapped in newspaper and pastry cakes with custard. She's wearing a flowered tent. I pull Fi to one side.

'Fi, has she had her clothing allowance?' I ask horrified. There are some shows that encourage their guests to wear bright outfits, so that they look like fat sugared almonds. This isn't supposed to be one of those.

'Ya, but we couldn't find anything in Harvey Nics to fit her,' Fi whispers back.

'Well, what about a high-street store?'

'We couldn't find a researcher who was prepared to go and find out.'

I sigh and resign myself to the tent. I wonder how the colours will work against the backdrop of the set.

Karen, the 'other woman', explains that she thinks she has as much right to Brian as Jenny has.

'After all, I was with him first.' But people aren't like pieces of furniture or clothes; 'I saw him first' isn't exactly a reason to lay claim to someone. I remind Karen that Brian must love Jenny, or else he wouldn't have proposed. Karen corrects me and points out that it was Jenny who proposed and in fact she bought her own ring too. She admits that she is still sleeping with Brian. She shakes her tits at the camera: 'He likes something to get hold of.' I leave the room.

'That is so depressing,' comments Fi.

'What is?' I ask.

'The way both of those women want the same man and by this time next week one of them will have been rejected. Don't you think that's awful?'

'I think that's the point of the show. Now, here's the rest of the schedule. I want you to take a cameraman and stay with Jenny. Get lots of shots of her trying her wedding dress on, interviews with her mum, something to depict their financial struggle to put on the best wedding reception they can afford and a shot of her on her own, preferably in a church.'

'So you are expecting Brian to choose Karen, then?' asks Fi.

'Not so much actively choose, more like his dick will jump out of his trousers through habit. Now, I need the logistics crew to work out where the camera should be for the grand seduction. Karen is planning to seduce him over a pint and some pork scratchings in their local.'

'Very glamorous,' says Fi wryly.

'She's not a glamorous girl. And he's not a glamorous boy. It should be on their usual turf – we don't want to arouse suspicions. Besides which, our budget is a pittance. Now go to it.'

Next I interview Tim Barrett. I think that Tim has a good career ahead of him as a criminal. Not because he appears particularly vicious, immoral or crooked but because he would be impossible to identify in a line-up. He is neither extraordinarily skinny nor obscenely fat. He is, in fact, of average build, average height, average looks and average intelligence. His hair is mid-brown; his eyes are a brown/grey/green colour. I forget which. After close investigation I discover that the only thing that distinguishes him at all is his fanatical, obsessive jealousy in relation to his fiancée, Linda. He runs through his suspicions regarding three of her exes. I don't think his suspicions are founded. But that's irrelevant. As he tells the stories he fidgets on his chair, moving from one buttock to the other. His hands appear to have developed an independent personality. *They* are animated. He picks up his coffee cup, puts it down again, he picks up a pen, pencil, ashtray, clipboard, biscuit. Everything, other than the biscuit, is put into his mouth. After he has spent fifteen minutes boring me with his paranoia and insecurity I think that this girl deserves a fling. If we do manage to cause a rift between them we will be providing a public service. I instruct a private detective to track down some of her exes immediately.

My next interview is with a petite brunette, Chloe. Chloe is an advertising executive in a small advertising agency in Bristol. She is more like the type of guest that I crave for the show. She is certainly attractive, with shoulder-length, curly hair, a winning smile and a neat, sharp body, which she is obviously and justifiably proud of. She's aged twenty-five. She's bright, funny.

And insecure.

I imagine that generally she hides it quite well. I imagine that her acquaintances and colleagues describe her as confident. But behind her back her friends discuss her ugly neediness. After chatting to her for four and a half minutes it is obvious to anyone who has ever read any popular psychology books (and I've read them all) that she is a woman who loves too much. She believes she is half a person unless she has a boyfriend. The men she meets believe she is an entire person, until they become her boyfriends. On sensing her dependency, their cocks go limp and they leave her. However, as I listen to her chat, it seems to me that her fiancé, Rod, breaks the mould. He actually likes her dependency; it makes him feel valued. But her historical, consistent failure has eroded her trust and faith in the concept of fidelity. Instead of being grateful to have found Rod and keeping her head down, Chloe is hitting the self-destruct button by testing him.

On national TV.

As the interview comes to a close and I have all the details I need regarding Rod's exes, I ask Chloe why she feels compelled to verify his fidelity on TV. She must know that she is risking personal humiliation and universal disdain.

She shrugs and with a bravado which we both know to be fake replies, 'I think if you are going to be a failure, you should try to be as conspicuous as you can about it. Who wants to be a run-of-the-mill failure?'

I love this wisdom. You've got to hand it to the British public. There's an Aristotle in every one of them.

'The queue for the live audience is massive – it stretches the entire length of the car park,' laughs Fi excitedly. This is a good sign. The PR vehicle must have done its job.

'What do they look like?' I ask. The correct live audience is essential. There are lots of things that the majority of us will do in our homes that we wouldn't do in public. Things like: cheer at other people's insecurities, rejection and fear, encourage savagery and disloyalty, positively celebrate humiliation and distress. I need people who are either honest or stupid enough to have these reactions on live TV.

'Generally poor and unhealthy-looking. But they appear oblivious to their aesthetic drawbacks – they're oozing excitement,' says Fi.

This is exactly what I want to hear. An anonymous voice cries, 'Spot checking, ladies and gents.' Nobody has a clue what that means, if anything at all, but it has the desired effect and the audience squirm with nervous expectancy. I don't blame them. It is exhilarating. We put on a bit of a show to get them in the mood. The runner's bleep pings incessantly; she ignores the increasingly desperate calls. The director (long-haired and self-important by necessity), production manager (a grumpy git – it's a professional qualification) and the stage manager (careworn and exhausted) huddle in a corner debating furiously about some technical point or other. The production executive is running around the set as though her life depends upon it. A plethora of cameramen – dressed entirely in black, baggy combat trousers and Ted Baker shirts, Cats or DKNY trainers – are standing around, trying to look casually indifferent, as though their lives *and* souls depend upon it. The set, although flimsy, is attractive. The backdrop is a close-up picture of dozens of fat red hearts. At first glance the impression is romantic; a dip in the lights and the effect is satanic, open-heart surgery on stage. There are the compulsory comfy couches in the middle of the stage, ensuring everyone gets the best view of the gallows.

'Where did he come from?' I am referring to the warm-up act. He is a fat, northern comedian who has blatantly been on the circuit longer than Schumacher. He looks like a pantomime dame and his requests for the audience to 'Go wild, go crazy' illicit nothing more than a few embarrassed titters. Fi shrugs, 'He does well with the *Kin's Kismet* audience.'

I listen to him telling a few mucky jokes. He is the only one laughing.

'What were you thinking of? I've told you I want an up-market show. Which bit of the word up-market is it that you don't understand?' I snap. Somewhere I can hear someone say, 'Thirty seconds to live.'

'You told me to deal with the detail,' she defends.

I'm not in the mood for debating. 'I want him off the show by next week, Fi.' The voice in my earpiece says, 'Twenty seconds.' I tune back in to the fat man.

'It's a live show tonight, so if you are sitting next to somebody you shouldn't be, move.' The audience finally begins to smirk. 'Ten seconds.'

'Did you see anyone move, Fi?' I ask. I'm always thinking about potentially adulterous relationships. 'Eight, seven, six.' There is a swell of expectancy.

'Now a big hand for Katie Hunt, this evening's presenter.' The audience starts to clap their hands raw for the remote chance that there may be a nanosecond mug shot on TV. The fat man tries to get Katie to twirl like a modern-day Anthea.

This is proof, if we needed it, that he has had his day. Katie wouldn't twirl if Robbie Williams asked her to. Katie casts him a withering look. I'm relieved – at least she understands what type of show I'm making here.

'Three, two, one – we are on air.' The roving camera sweeps magnificently across the audience and set. The camera reminds me of an internal. It must do the same for Fi, as I notice she writes 'smear' on her hand with a felt tip. The emergence of the cameras acts as an aphrodisiac on the audience. Everyone visibly brightens; they grow a couple of inches, smile a bit wider.

'Hello, and welcome to the very first *Sex with an Ex*.' The stage manager initiates more applause; the audience catches on quickly and begins to cheer. Katie smiles back at the camera, appreciating their appreciation.

'You smell the same.'

'Smell? What do I smell of?' He is mildly irritated. Scrupulously clean at all times, he has made a particular effort tonight.

'My youth.' She smiles.

She leans closer to inhale him again. She notices he is quivering. She notices she is. He turns a fraction and he is staring into her eyes, straight past the pupils, and directly hitting her mind and soul. She is sixteen again. Which makes him eighteen. She has been propelled back to the doorstep of her parental home. The season is irrelevant; she feels warm and safe. It's late at night, very late, because although they abide by the curfew and get her home by 10.45 p.m., they are literal: she is home but not in her home. It's past midnight and they are still sitting on the step. They can't go in because her mother is waiting up in her nylon dressing gown. Her mum will want to know what the film was like, and she'll make a cup of coffee and stay up and drink it with them. They don't want to talk to anyone else. They never do.

Did. 'Did' is the correct verb because she's not sixteen, she's twenty-six and she's not on the step of her mum and dad's house in Croydon. She's actually just bumped into Declan outside Pronuptia bridal shop.

'Big box,' he comments, grinning, and he's just the same. The grin is just the same; it lights up her stomach and a bit lower.

'Er, yes.' She hesitates. The natural thing to say next is, 'It's my wedding dress,' but Abbie doesn't say the natural thing. She says, 'Wow, it's been a long time.'

'Yes. Ten years.' He pauses for a moment and then adds, 'Four months, two weeks and about eight days.'

Delighted and shocked, Abbie blushes and glances both ways up the street. She's not sure what or who she's looking for. But she's relieved not to see anyone she knows. 'I don't believe you've been counting.'

'Fair cop. I haven't. I just made up the stuff about months and weeks.' They both laugh because it always was easy for him to make her laugh.

'Fancy a drink?' he adds casually. And why shouldn't she? It's just a drink. She hasn't anything else planned except a night in with a face pack. Lawrence is out tonight – rugby practice.

They make their way to a nearby wine bar that he knows. She is impressed with the way he takes charge and really he couldn't have chosen better. As she pushes open the door, she is overwhelmed by the smell of fags and booze, by the litter of noise and dark suits. Money and irresponsibility, the most potent aphrodisiacs. The wine bar is packed. Smart bods forcing their way to the bar, into each other's psyches and beds. The suits are Armani and the bed linen will be Egyptian cotton. It's Abbie's kind of bar, full of deeply attractive and arrogant media types, all of whom have disposable incomes matched only by their disposable lifestyles. She hasn't been to a bar like this for ages. It was in a bar like this that she met Lawrence. But once they'd been together for a few months such dens of sin were superfluous. It was easier to sin on the settee in his flat.

The music pumps through Abbie and Declan's brains and rushes to her knickers and his cock. Music just does that. No one is dancing, it's a bar not a club, and although Abbie is tempted to sculpt out a space on the designer scuffed wooden floor, she's far too shy to do so. Besides which she's still carrying her huge box with her bridal dress and six-foot veil. Where would she put it? What is she thinking of? Bringing her dress into a smoky bar? She notes that she's tapping her foot. In fact, her leg is jerking almost uncontrollably. She wants to dance. She needs to whoosh and swirl. Suddenly she understands stripping. Music does equate to sex. It thumps and jars and consumes and fills and ultimately relieves. Abbie prefers to make love to music, rather than in silence. It helps to create the mood. Whichever mood she wants. Fast and frantic or slow and seductive. Abbie shakes her head. What is she thinking of? Sex, that's what. Why is she thinking of sex? She's not out with her fiancé; she's with Declan. She should not be thinking of sex.

'Drink?' she yells. She orders him a Becks and herself two gin and tonics. She downs one at the bar and then returns to her seat with the other. She doesn't normally try to calm her nerves with drink. Then again she's not normally nervous with men. She's been with Lawrence for three years so she can't remember the last time she felt flirtatious or sexy. But she is nervous with Declan.

And flirty.

And sexy.

'So you don't drink Bacardi and Coke any more?' He smiles.

'No.' She smiles back. 'And I assumed you'd moved on from Woodpecker cider. Cheers.'

They clink glasses. They fall silent, as they have so much to say. She wants to ask him why he never wrote once he went to university. Why didn't he reply to any of her letters? She remembers the endless *waiting for the postman, the fruitless, pointless hoping. The answer is he met a girl from Nottingham in Freshers' Week. For the first two terms it seemed like love. He reads her mind and says, 'I never was much of a letterwriter.'*

He wants to ask her who she lost her virginity to and was it good. The answer is that, furious and bored with waiting for his letters and calls, she eventually climbed into bed with his cousin within hours of blowing out the candles on her seventeenth birthday cake. Yes, it was good, very good.

She reads his mind and assures him, 'Pretty average, really. Like everyone's first time.'

They both start to laugh at the cosmic connection that seems undamaged by the years of neglect. They had always found talk easy. Indulging in endless outpouring of thoughts, views, dreams and emotions. Now they exchange suppositions, opinions, histories and sentiments. They don't notice the difference. It is still there, the familiar but indefinable sense of possibility. He'd always filled her with such a pure sense of adventure. She loves Lawrence dearly, but he doesn't create that sense of future possibilities; he brings with him a sense of future stability. She thought it was impossible to feel sixteen unless you were *sixteen, but now she is within inches of Declan, it's back, that overwhelming sense of YESness. Her mood is buoyant as she drinks those first few G&Ts. Quickly they pass a respectable G&T hour, so they swap to red wine.*

'Aren't you hot?' he yells over the crowd.

'Hot?' she asks with feigned nonchalance.

'You are still wearing your gloves.'

Slowly she peels them off, revealing her engagement ring.

'When?' he asks.

'Two weeks,' she answers. The answer does not create the same rush she experienced this morning when she checked her countdown calendar.

'He's a lucky man,' says Declan, but he won't look at Abbie. 'We should be celebrating. I'll buy us some champagne.'

Occasionally when she wanders around Heal's furniture department or sits at a dinner party with Lawrence, Abbie finds herself idly wondering whether, if she'd met Declan later in life, he would have been 'the One'. Occasionally Abbie has wondered what sleeping with Declan would be like. The front step of her parents' house didn't offer the correct opportunity. As she watches him at the bar she believes that it can't hurt to find out.

As Abbie pushes back the hotel sheets and climbs on top of Declan she is sixteen again. As she leaves the hotel room, three hours later, under the cover of darkness she feels her twenty-six years and to be frank she rather likes it. Declan was a lovely part of her past and that's where he should be. She's walking with a swagger. It's the swagger of a confident young woman who knows she's marrying the right man.

When Lawrence watches the tape he misinterprets the John Wayne stance and is disgusted.

For a moment the studio is silent. Awash with betrayal, regret and fear. Lawrence is staring at Abbie. His jaw is hanging open, which is unbecoming. He looks like the dumb animal Abbie has reduced him to. It's complex. I admit that. I signal frantically for camera two to move in tightly. Close up, close up. I want to see every muscle twitch, every emotion exposed. Abbie is shaking so violently that I think she may spontaneously combust. I suspect she wishes she could. She resolutely stares at the floor. Too humiliated and ashamed to think beyond how she can get out of the studio, she doesn't even attempt to catch Lawrence's eye. She's forgotten that Declan ever existed. Declan is trying to look unconcerned. He is sitting back in his chair, with his long legs casually crossed, and he's tapping his toe. His brave performance is exposed as the act it is when camera three picks up the fact that he is tearing at his own skin, digging his nails so deeply that his quicks are brilliant white. Boy, are they regretting it now. They are a mass of sweaty palms, quivering lips and knotted intestines. Their faces ask what they've done.

I wish I'd never written the letter.

I'm sorry. I'm sorry.

Fuck.

Lawrence breaks the silence. 'Why did you do it?' he upbraids.

'Why didn't you trust me?' accuses Abbie.

'Fuck,' says Declan.

That's the cue for the audience. They become animals. They boo and hiss and spit and claw. They are collectively relieved that, in this instance, it is someone else who has been fucked over. Unscathed, they fly into an uncontrollable frenzy. The savages hurl abuse and insults. I think that if they'd had rotting fruit to hand they'd have used it. They despise Lawrence for being cuckolded. They loathe Abbie for being a slut. And they forgive Declan because he has got a cute grin and he's a bit of a lad. The synthesized music pipes cheerfully through the studio. Oblivious to the fact that Abbie is sobbing hysterically and has to be carried off the stage. Her legs buckle. It's a sad pathetic sight. I hope camera two got a close-up.

'Good job, Cas.'

'Thank you.'

'Way to go, Cas.'

'Thanks.'

'High five, Cas.'

'Yes, very high.' I efficiently accept the congratulations and charge through the corridors with the air of someone who has a mission. Thing is, I have. My heart is pounding; the blood is rushing through my being. The show only finished minutes ago but already I know it is a huge success. Massive. The audience won't leave and we have had to call in security. Lawrence punched Declan. Live on stage! I'm delighted. It couldn't have gone better if I'd scripted it. Then Jenny, Brian and Karen – what a horror show! Brian wasn't sure if it was the worst or best day of his life. The audience loved his unashamed cockiness.

I walk into my office, which is awash with flowers and champagne. Good news sure does travel quickly. I had expected to be doused in congratulations and good wishes. After all, nearly everyone at TV6 is scared of me and therefore they try hard to ingratiate themselves. But I never calculated a result as big as this. I'm delirious, but I know that it is essential that I appear unmoved.

'Where should I put these flowers?' asks Fi.

'Anywhere.' I casually read the cards. There's one from Josh and Issie. It reads, 'You are an unscrupulous, overly ambitious, single-minded exploiter. Well done. Love, your best friends.'

I grin. There is another from Bale. It reads, 'Big things get bigger very quickly.'

'You are *so* profound,' I mutter.

'I'll crack open this bubbly, shall I?' asks Fi. She's holding a bottle of vintage Veuve Clicquot.

'If you like. As long as you understand that this isn't a celebration.'

Her smile vanishes. 'Isn't it?' She is genuinely dumbfounded.

'No, it isn't. We need to see the overnight runs and also the log call book before we can really celebrate. In fact, I think I'll go and sit in the log room now to talk to the duty manager.'

'But I've booked Bibendum. The team's looking forward to it. They've worked so hard over the last eight weeks.'

It's true we've all worked regular fourteen-hour days.

'On whose budget?'

She's crushed. She's silent. I relent. 'OK, you guys go along and I'll catch you up. If the news is good, I'll pay. If it's not, I'll pay.'

Sometimes I'm nice like this but it's just to confuse them.

I make my way through the rabbit warren of corridors, leaving the sound of popping champagne corks behind me. I stumble past piles of A4 paper and mountains of clip files (the paperless office is a figment of management consultants' imaginations). I note dozens of plastic crates that haven't been unpacked in the twenty-four months that we've been here. I wonder if someone knows something that I don't. As I approach the normally silent log room, where all complaints and compliments are handled, I am struck by a general buzz of activity.

I wake up with an aching back and neck, a furry mouth and a fuzzy brain. Not enough sleep. It's a huge effort, but I force concentration. I establish the following facts: I'm not in a bed, my own or a stranger's; I'm not hung over, but there is a glob of saliva on my desk where my head has been. I consider that this is one of the reasons I'm careful about intimacy. Imagine if I had woken up with the man of my dreams, if such a thing existed, and there had been a string of saliva on the pillow. It would certainly put him off. Far too human. However, such speculation is irrelevant, as my pillow last night was a box file, my bed companion a portable computer. I try to think it through. I'm here because—

The phone rings. I reach for it and automatically chant, 'Cas Perry, TV6. Good . . .' – I hesitate and check my watch. It's 7.15 a.m. – 'morning,' I confirm, confident that it is morning, but I'm less sure why anyone would be calling me at this hour.

'Thank God,' says Josh.

'Oh, hi,' I mutter, reaching for my fag packet. I light up and inhale. The nicotine hits me behind the eyeballs. That's better.

'We were so worried. Where the hell have you been?'

'Hey, don't come on all marital with me,' I laugh. 'I've been here all night. Did you see the programme?'

'Yeah.'

'Wasn't it brilliant?' The tar and bad stuff have helped. I now know why I slept at my desk. 'We were taking calls all night. I took the last one at 4.45 a.m. The lines were jammed. TV6 has never seen anything like it!'

'Lots of complaints, then?' asks Josh sympathetically.

'Complaints, sure,' I say dismissively, 'but compliments too and applications to go on the show.' I check the latest figures in the log book. 'Two hundred and forty-seven calls!' I do some quick mental arithmetic. 'One hundred and thirty complaints! Can you believe it? I only have to get fifteen before I am obliged to take the programme to the ITC for reappraisal.'

'So that's good news?' Josh asks hesitantly. He simply doesn't get it. 'All those complaints are good news?'

'It's caused a national outcry. It's huge. It's fantastic. It's – look I can't chat. I need to call PR – we'll have to put out a press release. I wonder if any of the papers have picked anything up yet.'

'It's a shame you didn't make it to Issie's last night. We had ricotta and basil risotto, as planned.' Josh slices through my euphoria. I suddenly remember that I had promised to go straight to Issie's after the show. In fact, I'd begged them to meet up. I'd insisted that Issie miss her pottery class and that Josh skip his rugby practice. I'd worried that the show would be a disaster. We'd all known that if that was the case Issie and Josh would be the only people I'd be able to face.

'Oh, shit. Josh, I'm sorry. Fuck, I'm really sorry. I'll make it up to you. Both of you. I just got caught up here on the telephone lines. Shit. I'm sorry.' This is genuine. I feel awful. There have been occasions when Issie and Josh have let me down, always due to circumstances they couldn't control. I've sat endlessly staring at the clock wondering where they were. Why they didn't call? My irritation that their supper is ruined has turned to fear as I imagine they've been abducted or murdered or involved in a road accident. Worse, that they are dating someone unsuitable. I know that standing each other up is a bishop sin.

'I should have called,' I add meekly.

'Yes, you should have. We were worried.' Josh can't stay angry with me for long. 'The risotto was ruined. I've had to soak the dish but the stubborn bits of cheese won't come off.'

I know I'm off the hook. 'Try Fairy Liquid extra concentrated king-strength,' I laugh. 'Look, I've got to go. I'll call you tonight.'

'You'd better.'

I can see my reflection in my computer screen. By rights I should be looking rough. Last night I secured just a few hours' sleep. Over the past eight weeks I've been averaging six hours a night at best, even at weekends. I haven't had a night out in all that time. I've existed largely on sandwiches from the staff canteen and double espressos from the Italian deli round the corner. I can't remember when I last saw natural daylight or a vitamin. Either boxed or first-generation.

And yet I look *fantastic*.

Well, there is no point in my being falsely modest. I look keen and lithe and sharp and I'm glowing. I know I look like a woman who's just fallen in love. And the reason for this, the little beauty secret, tip for the top, is that the show is a *success*. I rattle around in my desk drawer looking for a toothbrush and all the other necessary toiletries. I open my stationery cupboard. I keep a full wardrobe at work for all events. A few basics: trousers from Jigsaw, T-shirts from Gap, white cotton knickers from M&S. Plus a couple of Nicole Farhi trouser suits and shirts from Pink, in case I'm unexpectedly called into a big meeting. Some Agent Provocateur underwear and a number of garments that vary in their size and transparency but are reassuringly, constantly black. These are for when I get lucky. None of this is appropriate for today. I see what's lurking behind the plastic file dividers. Eventually I select Miu Miu trousers, a slash-neck Cristina Ortiz wool jumper and Bally boots. I find a pair of clean knickers and a tiny lacy bra in my filing cabinet. I know today is my day and it's important to look the part. I go for a brisk workout and then shower in the office gym. By 8.45 a.m. I'm back at my desk.

Fi is in too. It looks like my budget was thrashed at Bibendum.

'You look crap,' I tell her, as I generously offer a can of Red Bull.

'Thank you. You look as fresh as a daisy.'

I graciously accept the compliment. After all, I do. 'Was it worth it?' I ask.

She grins. 'Yeah, I had a fantastic time. Or at least I think I did.' She holds her head steady for a moment trying, no doubt, to chase a faint memory. She gives up.

'Well, that's the main thing,' I assure.

'We went on to the Leopard Lounge. I didn't go home – I've come straight in.'

I'm impressed by her dedication. I try to ignore the brewery smells she's exhaling and fill her in on the excitement of the night in the log room.

'Sounds a gas.' She stifles a yawn. 'I'm glad it went so well.' She starts to tell me some funny tale about Di getting off with Gray, and Ricky trying to pull a transvestite. I'm glad they've had a good time. But I'm not interested. I know I'll lose most of today. The team's productivity will be severely depleted because of the necessary administration of Alka Seltzer and intravenously dripped black coffee. They'll spend hours discussing the pros and cons of the various hair of the dog cures. Choices being Bloody Mary, a pint of Guinness, fried eggs with gin. Most importantly they will all be extremely ashamed of themselves and so tomorrow I'll get commitment overdrive.

My phone rings again.

'Cas Perry, TV6. Good morning.'

'Jocasta?'

'Mum.'

'How are you, dear?'

'Brilliant. Mum, did you ring about the show?' I'm thrilled.

'Show?'

'My show. You did watch it, didn't you?' I'm devastated. I can't believe that my mother has forgotten about the show. Even when things were really hairy and busy around here, in the penultimate couple of weeks before the show went live, I'd religiously visited my mum on Sundays. I had been there in body, although, I admit, not always in spirit. I'd had to spend a lot of time on my mobile. But when I wasn't on my mobile I had taken time to tell her all about the show. Now my mother is acting as though she's never heard of it.

'Oh yes. Erm, *Best with an Ex*.' She demurely avoids the S word. Actually, I'm quite impressed with her title. I should have consulted her before the show went out. *Best with an Ex* is so much more subtle than *Sex with an Ex*. I wonder if there is any chance of a name change at this stage. My train of thought is interrupted as Mum mithers on.

'I did watch the first ten minutes but then Bob, from across the road, popped over to fix that drawer that's been sticking. You know, the third one down in the kitchen.'

Bob, one of a small number of names that my mother floats past me on a regular basis. 'Mrs Cooper said that there's a buy two and get one free offer on shampoo at Boots at the moment'; 'It's Albert and Dorothy's fortieth wedding anniversary on Saturday – they are having a supper'; 'Dr Dean was asking after you'. It's tedious keeping up with the comings and goings of these tiresome people.

'I couldn't have the television running whilst he was in the house,' comments my mother.

I'm disappointed, so move quickly to get her off the line. A non-offensive exit demands a certain amount of self-sacrifice. I agree to go shopping with her on Saturday. I regret the offer almost the moment the words are out of my mouth. It will be a disaster: it always is. For a start she will want to find a bargain in the Army and Navy store, whilst I will want to spend obscene amounts in Bond Street. If we do go to Bond Street, her face will settle into one of the expressions I can only assume she most favours, shocked or cross. Shocked at the prices and cross at life. I can't bear her sudden outbursts in small boutiques. 'That's how much? There's nothing to it! Look at the hemming. I could run you one up on the sewing machine.' Which is odd, as she has never sewn in her life. Worse than her audible disgust will be her silent condemnations of my frivolity, the incessant tutting at the cashpoint as I hand over one of my magic pieces of plastic. Therefore we usually shop at the Army and Navy store, where I destroy her pleasure by continually pointing out 'nice' things and adding for clarity, 'Nice for you, Mum.' Revenge is always hers as she buys whichever monstrosity I've picked out and gives it to me for Christmas or my birthday. All this accepted, we regularly put ourselves through this purgatory on earth. What else can I do? She's my mum. I wonder if I can get Issie or Josh to meet us for lunch.

By the time I put the phone down most of the team have arrived. Except for Tom and Mark. Their status as creatives excludes them from having to appear at work at all if they are hung over. The scene is as I'd predicted: I am in an office with the walking dead. They are pale and unshaven, and they smell of booze, sweat and sex. There is a certain amount of squabbling, the excuse being that the vending machine is all out of non-dairy creamer, the real reason being the bad heads. However, the atmosphere is immediately dissolved when Ricky bursts into the office.

'Have you seen the ratings?' he screams.

Shit, the ratings. I must have been affected by the booze fumes to allow the ratings figures to slip my mind. The number of calls we have received that have been duly logged suggests we have a stonking success on our hands. However, I can't count my poultry just yet. Ratings are the accurate measure of exactly how many people watched the show. This is the acid test.

Ricky is breathless. I know it is good news.

'Well?'

He grins. Enjoying his moment.

I humour him and extend my grin a fraction wider. 'Well?' He hesitates again. This time I consider firing him. A girl can only be so patient.

'1.4 million viewers tuned in at 10.00 p.m.' There is a whoop. The team throw off their hangovers to cheer and shout and clap and generally behave like delinquents on E, which is not so far from the fact. I stay calm.

'Well done to marketing.' I smile across to Di and Debs. I know that the number of viewers we draw in as the initial credits roll is 95 per cent down to the marketing. Keeping the viewers for longer than five minutes is down to the quality of the programme. I am at the mercy of the remote control. It's so undignified.

'And what were the numbers after the centre break?' I ask.

'1.6 million!'

Now I scream.

Really loudly.

5

'Can you believe it?' I ask Fi for the fourteenth time. 'The ratings went up. That means people actually called their friends and told them to tune in!'

'Or something good finished on the other side,' adds Fi.

I scowl. 'I've thought of that and checked the schedules. It wasn't the case. Not unless you count a documentary on the hibernation habits of bugs on hedgehogs as good TV.'

'Fair point.'

'*Can you believe it?* A follow-up interview with Declan in the *Sun*. I've got to hand it to him: he's a natural the way he worked the tabloids. And now they are begging us for the names of the people in the next shows. We'll have to work really hard to keep the can on the interviews we've already got. The trick is going to be in continually surprising the mark.' The 'mark' is the official name for the person we are tempting. We also call them Grouchos, stooges and victims. 'Can you believe it's such a success?' I complete my circular diatribe.

'Not really.' Fi grins. I glare and she corrects herself. 'Well, obviously it is a brilliant idea. We all knew that it would be a fantastic show. But the public isn't always as perceptive as we'd like to imagine. There's always a risk.'

I'm mollified by her obvious flattery. 'Very true. Exactly my point. Want another drink?' I survey the debris in front of us. It's roughly half past seven. I'm not certain. The hands on my watch have shrunk and they are randomly bending. We've been in this pub since four thirty. Celebrating. We have drunk my week's calorie allowance and smoked an entire tobacco field. I'm beginning to see Fi's more sympathetic side. In fact, I'll definitely be buying her a Christmas pressie.

'I shouldn't, but OK then. A gin and tonic. Go easy on the tonic. Best make it slim-line,' says Fi as she reaches for the bowl of cashew nuts. She offers them to me but I decline.

'I'm allergic.'

This isn't true. I'm very thin and very fit. Whenever anyone asks me how I manage this I smile and say it's genetic and effortless. This is, of course, bollocks, but I know that if there is anything more annoying than a thin woman, it's a thin woman who professes that she never diets. There's no such thing as effortlessly thin. It comes as a direct result of one or more of the following: dedication to a relentless fitness regime, being a slave to the calorie counter, drugs or an unreliable bastard of a boyfriend. I work out at the gym five times a week – minimum. I'm also an expert kick boxer, although I don't enter competitions; it's just for fun. I own a Z3 series BMW but cycle to work, six miles there and back every day. I club once a week and I never touch any saturated fat. In addition I indulge in every detox programme known to womankind. I can regularly be found swathed in seaweed or mud at Champney's or the Sanctuary.

I place the double G& (slim-line) Ts on the wooden table. Fi is chewing an ice cube thoughtfully.

'Is there anything you haven't tried?'

I think she has telepathically understood that I'm concentrating on detox programmes. But before I tell her that I've never done colonic irrigation – I just can't stand the idea of a hosepipe up my bum – she puts me on the right track.

'I mean with men?'

This is easier to answer.

'I never do three in a bed.'

'Oh?'

'Yes, I think everyone's entitled to some exclusive devotion, even if it's between twenty minutes and a few hours.' Not much of a moral, I admit, but one I'm faithful to.

'Is there an ex in your past, then, Cas?'

'No,' I say without hesitating.

'Then again you're not on the cusp of marriage.'

'Nor am I ever likely to be.'

'Then how did you know the show was going to be such a success? How did you know both Brian Parkinson and Abbie would fall? And, for that matter, all the other couples that we've already recorded?'

'I didn't *know*, absolutely *know*, but I thought the odds were with me.'

'You are so cynical.'

We have fast become confidantes. This is entirely due to the copious amounts of alcohol we've consumed; still, I am quite unable to resist the illusion of companionable intimacy. Whilst I talk about work Fi is more keen to discuss her dearth of men in relation to my plethora. On one hand it is odd; after all, she is an extreme beauty. She's also got that exotic twist of a Scandinavian parentage. If I were male I wouldn't be able to stop myself. The matter is cleared up when she admits to me that secretly all she desires is a large family and a log cabin. Men can smell women who want commitment further away than they can smell those who wear Poison perfume. The odour is just as overpowering and off-putting.

Fi is looking through *Tatler*'s 'Little Black Book'. She throws it aside and picks up *London Guide to Restaurants*. She isn't looking for somewhere to eat but she's looking at the photos of the chefs. She fancies the idea of bagging a creative, temperamental kitchen diva. I'm sceptical.

'I'd stick to the methods which are proven,' I advise.

'Like what?' asks Fi grumpily.

'Supermarkets or the company telephone directory. I don't know. I never have any trouble meeting men.'

'Yeah, you'd get lucky in a convent.' She throws the guide to one side. 'But it's such a waste. You are never even grateful.'

I stare at her. Surely that is the point.

'Why are you so eternally unimpressed?' she asks. It is the drink that has given her the confidence to ask this. 'Your first!' She's fallen on some inspiration. 'Tell me about that.'

She's looking for insight. I don't normally indulge. But a bottle of Merlot has magically appeared from nowhere and we'll have to talk about something as we drink it. Fi's stories have dried up pretty quickly. I feel obliged to entertain.

'My first.' I cast my mind back through the numerous tangled sheets and emotions I've shagged my way through. 'Maybe if he'd been faithful I could have believed in fidelity, even after my father's rather poor attempt as a role model.'

'He wasn't, then?'

'What do you think?'

'The odds are definitely against it,' admits Fi. She pours some wine into my glass. 'What was he like?'

'Beautiful,' I admit. 'I mean, I was just like the next seventeen-year-old. OK, my parents had gone pear-shaped, but you know I was *seventeen*. I was hopeful. I hadn't been sitting at the dining-room table sticking a fork into my hand to see how much pain I could sustain, like some psycho.' I sigh. 'He was twenty-six. He was beautiful and shallow. And married, as it happened.'

'No.' Fi is shocked. I grin wryly. I remember being shocked. Now disreputable behaviour never shocks me, it doesn't even disappoint me – I see it as an inevitability.

'Yeah. Slipped his mind to tell me. Until his wife turned up on my mother's doorstep. To quote the great Holly Golightly, '*Quel Rat.*'

Fi sits silently, trying to take it in. It's true it's not the conventional first lover story. That's meant to take place in the back of your parents' Volvo or at someone else's house whilst you are babysitting. It's meant to take place with some acne-ridden youth who is equally inexperienced and as smitten as you are.

'Which made me a paramour at seventeen years old,' I joke. But really it was no laughing matter at the time.

'Inadvertently,' says Fi, loyally.

'Still.' I inhale deeply.

'Still,' she admits, taking a large swig.

I'd cried for months and when I stopped crying I started hating. It took several more months for the hate to cool and when it did I was left in a pool of icy resentment. 'So I figured I should try and turn it to my advantage. No more shocks. No more surprises. I decided to have a very low expectancy threshold on what should be gained from a relationship. I don't think unconditional love is a possibility, never mind a probability, which guarantees no disappointment.'

Fi is concentrating on what I've just said as she taps out the tune playing on the jukebox with her fag pack.

'Sounds a bit extreme. Couldn't you have just dated someone your own age and sort of' – she pauses – 'I don't know, muddled along like the rest of us?'

I raise an eyebrow and she shrugs, perhaps realizing how unappealing the alternative is.

'I did date someone my own age next. He was a fop. Lovable, I guess.' I think about it, perhaps for the first time. 'Yes, certainly. But his willingness to please, at first a novelty, quickly became tiresome. Why don't we value those who most deserve to be valued?' I turn to Fi, but she's concentrating on drawing a loveheart on the table with drips of wine. 'Answers on a postcard please. Before I knew it I'd sort of fallen into a series of one-night stands, mostly with married men or commitment phobes and, on one occasion, a homosexual.'

This gets her attention. 'How did you know? Did he make you dress up and do funny things with strap-ons?'

'No, Fi, he had an opinion on my wallpaper.' I run through my sexual misadventures in my head and it could be the alcohol but this reminiscing is making me decidedly morose. I rouse myself into my more acceptable, tough, public persona. 'Just take it from me it's easier to enjoy the moment and not expect anything more because really there isn't anything more. I heartily recommend the married man.' I swallow and then refill both our glasses.

'Doesn't it bother you that someone else is getting the best bit?'

'The best bit?' I'm genuinely challenged to understand what Fi means.

'The companionship, the stability, the history, the future.'

'The dirty washing, the belching, the rows, the incessant football results.'

'But it doesn't make sense. You suffered first-hand because your father had a mistress. Why would you want to inflict the same pain on someone else?'

To be fair this is a pretty good question. Especially considering the units we've consumed on empty stomachs. It is a question I'd asked myself, once upon a time. The first time I fell for a married man it was purely accidental. I didn't really expect it to happen again. I did hate the very idea of 'the other woman'. Women who are compliant in this perpetuation of misery repelled me. After all, if there hadn't been a Miss Hudley, there wouldn't have been a deserting father and a deserted mother.

A deserted daughter.

The problem is, of course, you can take out Miss Hudley but a Miss Budley or a Miss Woodly would replace her. The choice is clear to me: become a Miss Hudley because the alternative role is worse – become the deserted wife. My mother's face, worn and weary with clinging to her pride whilst losing her husband, her home, her name and her identity, burns into my consciousness. Fear flung me into relationships with men committed to someone else. It was safer. I should have been struck by lightning when I broke the taboo the first time. I sometimes wish I had been. With alarming ease I've broken every rule and never been punished – in fact, I've often been rewarded. It seemed that what I was doing was sanctioned. Whilst I collected compliments and Cartier, tenaciously avoiding commitment or Kleenex, my friends who hoped for the Happily Ever After were discovering that the road to fairyland was long and winding. And often heartbreaking.

Somehow I've developed secret signals that repel available men or men with a penchant for commitment yet simultaneously attract married men or any of the others who don't want anything more than sex. Or maybe it's just that the numbers are in my favour. I don't say any of this to Fi. I turn back to her question and simplify.

'I'm not threatening. I don't want to be someone's girlfriend, or, horror of horrors, wife. Therefore I'm not a risk. I never demand. I never call at inconvenient times; I never criticize his wife-slash-girlfriend. And in return he has no right to ask me where I'm going or when I'll be back. He has no ability to make me fall in love with him.'

Fi stares at me. It may be that she is impressed. It may be that she is horrified. It may be that she is pissed.

'Christ, how depressing,' she moans.

‘Tell me I’m wrong,’ I challenge.

We are both silent for a long time. Eventually Fi suggests, ‘Another bottle?’

I return from the bar with a bottle and, because we both need cheering up, a couple of bankers.

‘Fi, let me introduce Ivor Jones and Mike Clark. They’re bankers.’ Fi starts to giggle. ‘That’s with a “b”,’ I hiss through clenched teeth. I’ve seen Ivor and Mike in this pub before. Over the last couple of months we have nodded to each other and occasionally I’ve accepted a drink from Ivor. They’ve been watching us all evening. Then I started to watch them watching us. When it got to the point of them watching us watching them watching us I knew it was time to say hi. They are well and identically dressed. Dark Boss suits, striped shirts, probably off-the-peg rather than Savile Row, saffron Hermes ties. They probably don’t even know they are saffron – they probably describe them as yellow. Ivor distinguishes himself by having a killer Welsh accent that largely renders him incomprehensible but is very sexy. I don’t mind incomprehensible. Most importantly Ivor is wearing a wedding ring and so I leave Mike to Fi.

Ivor’s attractions are not what one would describe as classical. His face reminds me of a soundly slapped bottom. He is pale with a sprinkling of freckles and a small snub nose. On the other hand he is tall (six-foot-two-ish), ridiculously intelligent and appallingly arrogant. Besides which he is begging for it. It would be rude not to sleep with him. His hungry, alert eyes bore into me as he showers us with awful sexist jokes. As he hands round bottles of Becks he asks, ‘How many men does it take to open a beer?’ Without waiting for a reply he tells us, ‘None. It should be opened by the time she brings it.’ Mike and Ivor laugh heartily. I do too, even though I’ve heard the joke before. Fi scowls.

Ivor is doing an emotional borderpoint check patrol. Just checking the amount of commitment I'll require. If I take his blatantly offensive jokes seriously he knows he's on dangerous territory. If I don't nettle but counter with a few sheep-shagging jokes, he knows he's in the clear. Ivor catches Fi's scowl.

'Oh, no offence. There's nothing worse than a male chauvinist pig, is there? Well, except a woman who won't do what she's told.' Again he laughs. Fi is obviously unimpressed. I'm refreshed to find a man who is honest enough to tell it as he sees it. However, for Mike's sake I hope he tries a more conventional chatting-up approach with Fi. If I could, I'd advise chocolates and compliments.

Ivor is bored with trying to control the group dynamics and his interest now lies in drawing me into a more intimate conversation. He takes advantage of Fi going to the loo and Mike going to the fag machine to invade my body space. He's sitting on my right and he edges closer. I have nowhere to move, even if I wanted to. He puts his left arm along the back of the scruffy tartan settee. It reminds me of being in the pictures, aged thirteen.

'So how old are you, Cas?'

'Thirty-three.' I never hesitate here. I'm proud to be thirty-three. I think it has much more kudos than, say, twenty-six or eighteen. I certainly feel better than I did then. It's only women who have a biological Timex who have a problem with saying their post-thirty ages out loud. Pointless really – it's not as though denial will turn the hands back. Anyway, I know I don't look thirty-three. As if to prove a point and somewhat predictably, Ivor raises his eyebrows. He doesn't bother with the cheap compliment that I don't look my age. He knows I'll have been told this often enough. Instead he keeps the conversation on track.

'So when are you going to settle down and make an honest man of your boyfriend?'

'Honesty is not my thing. I don't have a boyfriend and I don't want to be a wife.' I smile efficiently. So Ivor's scored a hat trick, discovering the three most important facts in one conversational turn. He taps my leg with his right hand.

'You're a wicked woman, Cas.'

This isn't strictly true. But for immediate purposes it will do as a character ensemble.

'So what do you want?'

I could tell him that I want world peace. I want Issie to find the man of her dreams. I want Josh to stop having wet dreams. I want my mother to redecorate and I want massive ratings on the next episode of *Sex with an Ex*.

'That's for me to know and you to find out,' I whisper as I move closer, allowing my breast to rub against his arm. I realize I'm not conforming to the traditional role of coy female. But playing hard to get is only useful if you want to keep the man in question, which I never do. I approve of the invention of paper knickers, cups, napkins, knives and forks. I adore the disposable. I smile broadly. He gulps his designer beer. Amnesia has hit. The words 'for better, for worse' etc. are temporarily erased from Ivor's mind.

'You know, just before you joined us Fi and I were discussing the fact that I make an adorable mistress.' My voice is devoid of emotion and I could have just commented on the autumnal weather. The contrast between the piping hot statement and the Arctic delivery causes Ivor's cock to stiffen. It's just too much fun to resist. I look from his cock to his eyes, back to his cock. His gaze follows mine. He blushes and crosses his legs. But to be honest, he hasn't a chance. 'You see, I enjoy it. All of it. Dressing up, having food eaten off me. I never worry that the chocolate ice cream will stain the sheets.'

'Meet me outside in ten minutes,' he says, leaving before he's finished his beer. I wonder how he's going to hold his erection for ten minutes, as he looks fit to explode. 'I need to call my wife. It's just—' I stop him saying any more. I don't need his excuses.

'Save it for her.'

He shows willing, in fact much too willing. His enthusiasm briefly battles with his ludicrously macho self-image. The enthusiasm wins. Ivor manages to restrain himself in the short cab ride that takes us to a hotel, and whilst he checks in. If 'restraint' can be used to describe a man who is intermittently swilling out my ear with his tongue. However, somewhat disappointingly for us both, he shoots his load in the hotel lift. I have very little to do with the act. Besides being there. It's a depressing thought, but I have to face it. He could have downloaded some images from the Pamela Anderson website. His premature ejaculation has sobered both of us. I'm left frustrated. Hardly the culmination to the evening celebrating my ratings that I was expecting. I stare at Ivor, who can barely face me. The lift stops.

'I haven't spoken to my wife for eighteen months.' Inwardly I sigh. If I'd realized this I wouldn't have touched Ivor with a barge pole. I look at him. He's grinning. 'I don't like to interrupt her.'

Another one of his jokes. We are both relieved and indulge in juvenile sniggers. His humour, for what it is, has saved the day. It's not that I think this man is particularly irresistible but I do admire an ability to laugh in the face of adversity. Although I no longer want carnal knowledge of him I am aware that he has just shed out £185 for a hotel room. The least I can do is help him attack the mini bar. By the time he unlocks the hotel bedroom door it's pretty clear that neither of us wants sex. We do both, however, need a bit of a confidence boost. I've never had the Pamela Anderson thought before but now I can't shake it.

'I've never done this before,' he offers as an explanation, justification and apology all at once.

'You don't—' I plan to say, 'You don't say,' but I catch a glimpse of Ivor sitting on the edge of the bed. His head is in his hands. It could be the alcohol, but I think he is genuinely upset. I change tack. 'You don't have to apologize. There's a first time for everyone.'

'It's just that recently my wife and I haven't been getting along too well.'

'Married long?' I ask as I light a cigarette.

'Four years.'

Ah, the seven-year itch. Everything is fast-track in London. I inhale deeply.

'We're moving house and trying for a baby. Things are tense.'

'Oh.' I'm engrossed in the mini bar. The hasty offload I can forgive, but if it's marriage guidance he's after I'd prefer it if he got a counsellor. I pour myself a brandy and try to change the subject. 'Know any more jokes?' It appears that the sexist and irreverent jokes have dried up. He's insisting on showing me that he's a decent bloke. He's wasting his time; it's an oxymoron and it's late. He fishes in his wallet and pulls out a picture of his wife.

'This is Julie.' I hate this name and face business. I light another cigarette and realize that I haven't smoked my first one yet. Irritated I stub it out.

'Very nice,' I comment, after taking a cursory glance at the picture. Julie looks like a pleasant enough woman, curvaceous, jolly, uncomplicated. She looks like a wife.

'I do love her,' pleads Ivor.

I take pity. Which is unusual. Am I due? It could be that. When I'm hormonal I'm moved by *Heartbeat*.

'Look, it's OK.' I sit next to him on the bed and stroke his head as if he is a Labrador. I am practised at letting them off the hook. Admittedly it's usually post coital rather than pre. Normally I use the gentle let-down as an efficient way to get them to vacate my bedroom. 'Nothing happened,' I insist. I consider sharing my Pammie theory but I'm not feeling *that* charitable. I wonder if he'd have resisted me if I was an ex of his. I doubt it. It's the uncharted waters that are scaring him. 'It was the combination – availability and alcohol. My availability and your alcohol. It gets them every time.' I try to grin. 'Now go home to your wife.'

He readily accepts my suggestion and scrambles to his feet. He pushes his arm into the sleeve of his jacket, which, I note, he hadn't let go of. His readiness to leave me momentarily stings, so just before the bedroom door slams closed I yell, 'And don't get mixed up in capers you can't handle.'

It's useful advice.

6

I couldn't have wished for a better outcome. Declan enjoyed his fifteen minutes of fame so much that he ached for more. He has a talent for the kiss-and-tell. Which arguably isn't a nice characteristic, but it is commonplace. And commercially admirable. Within a week of the first show he has appeared in most tabloids, giving sordid details of various aspects of his and Abbie's relationship, immediate and distant past. Some of it is undoubtedly true. He has been interviewed on local radio and TV stations, he has an agent and rumour has it that he is reading a couple of screenplays. There's no truth to this rumour. I know. My PR team initiated it.

Lawrence has asked his boss for an overseas posting but this has not shaken off the rat pack. It simply means he has become the Pied Piper for the European paparazzi as they maniacally search for him.

Abbie has gone underground. However, her actual presence isn't such a loss, as a number of her friends, family and associates are available to make comment. The woman who sold her the wedding dress offered extraordinary insight, as did the vicar who should have married them, three or four of Abbie's other ex-boyfriends and perhaps, most questionably, her hairdresser.

'Fi, can you believe her hairdresser betrayed her?' I ask, aghast.

Jenny, Brian and Karen have gone one step further. They've happily handed over letters they've written each other, posed for photographs with their families and finally invited *OK* to cover their wedding, although we are still unsure whose wedding it will be.

We have created a real live soap opera. By week two we have secured ratings of 1.8 million. By week three there've been two articles in the serious press discussing the nature and motivation of betrayal. The ratings tip 2 million.

'What's making you grin so much?' I ask Jaki, looking up from the letters commenting on the show. 'Have you been promoted and they've failed to tell me?'

Jaki laughs. 'No, but they should.' I admire her; she never misses a trick. 'No, it's something else. I was at a dinner party on Saturday night.'

'Oh yeah, what did you eat?'

She perches on my desk and Fi stops working on her laptop. There is nothing we like better than a good conversation about food. Conversations about food have an advantage over actually eating. You can take an avid interest without jeopardizing your waistline. Conversations about food are better than conversations about sex, which are often mildly pervy or frustrating. I'm not sure how to rank conversations about food and actually having sex. It's close.

Jaki details her menu comprehensively, taking an inordinate amount of time to describe the chocolate soufflé. We hungrily hang on her descriptions of double cream and blackberry sauce. When she's told us that the mints were Benedict, I drag her back to her original point.

'So what's nearly as exciting as a promotion?'

'Well, after dinner we usually play games. So that the boys can get competitive legitimately.'

'And the girls whip their arses openly,' adds Fi enthusiastically.

'Exactly. Sometimes we play Outburst or Trivial Pursuit but more often than not we prefer the more revealing Truth or

Dare. This week someone, not me, suggested playing *Sex with an Ex*.'

'Nooooo,' Fi and I chorus. We both immediately understand the importance of being absorbed into real-life popular culture. And so damn quickly!

'It was brilliant. Everyone had to name *the* ex in their past. You were right, Cas: there is always one who can send a thrill through the groin or heart. Then they had to say whether they would risk an uncomplicated, no-strings-attached, one-for-old-times'-sake bonk.'

'But wasn't it all couples at that dinner party?' I protest. We are a small team; the stuff we don't know about each other's private lives isn't worth knowing. Believe me.

'Yup. Ellie and James, Daisy and Simon, Nige and Ali and Toby and me. That was the attraction. A public outing.'

'So what happened?' asks Fi, excitedly playing with a staple gun. I take it from her before she causes serious bodily harm.

'Well, to start with everyone lied through their teeth. Those who I reckoned would do it became extremely demure. Those who wouldn't tried to pretend they had an experimental streak – which they blatantly don't have. But as the alcohol flowed the truth began to emerge.'

'And?' Fi and I chorus. We both know the result we want.

'Huge rows. Ali walked out, Ellie burst into tears, Daisy and Simon's party was ruined.'

'Wheeeey heeeeey,' squeals Fi. 'Our first row.'

'But think,' adds Jaki, 'if we were having this row in Clapham, how many similar rows must be taking place both north and south of the river, up and down the country! It's become a matter of national debate.'

'Jaki, go to marketing and tell them to slap a copyright on the board game, if they haven't already. They should be talking to game manufacturers before anyone else does. I wonder if we could get it out before Christmas?'

'That's only four weeks away,' Jaki protests. I silence her with a glance. She rushes off. Her dark Afro hair and pert bum sway jauntily.

'Did you notice, Fi, Jaki never said how her evening panned out with Toby?'

By the end of November, on week four, the ratings rip through the 4.5 million viewers' mark, and Bale insists I start interviewing again for a second series. The initial pilot series was scheduled to run six episodes. I have enough material to go to ten.

'Ten,' yells Bale. 'You are far too conservative. Interview enough couples for twenty shows.' I try to object and explain that the show will only work whilst we can surprise the stooges – that's why we filmed so many shows in advance.

Bale glowers away my objections. 'Cas, have you seen last night's ratings?' I shrug. I hope my shrug implies that I am far too busy having a fabulous social life, juggling several other projects at work and actively contributing to society by doing charity work to have checked the ratings. The reality is I checked the ratings this morning, before I went to the gym. I have worked out my related bonus and mentally spent it half a dozen times.

'Have you any idea how big this is? It's more ratings than this channel has ever had on a single show. It's the same number as ITV gets for—' – he names one or two really big shows that ITV has as staples on their schedule. 'It's more ratings than—' – he names one of our competitors – 'has ever had.' He's not telling me anything new. I know this. 'I've had offers from other channels to buy us out.'

I startle. I didn't know this.

He reassures me, 'Of course I'm not going to take them. Our lawyers are selling the idea to networks in the States, Australia and Asia. Murdoch wants to meet me!'

'I'm very pleased for you,' I reply coolly as I help myself to tissues from his desk and wipe his heinous spittle off my face.

'Yeah, it's good. I think we were helped by Melvin Bragg and Sue Lawley both condemning the show.'

'It's good. You're good.' Bale smiles. He's genuinely pleased with me. And why not? I've just saved his channel. More, I've probably made his career. I smile back and hand Bale the latest draft of my terms and conditions. It's not at all eighties in its scale. I'm not looking for a Boxster convertible or a six-figure salary. Although I'm confident that the bonuses will take me there. Bale picks up the paper and holds it at a distance. He eyes me suspiciously. He doesn't need to be afraid. The most demanding perk I've requested is that my mum gets to meet Tom Jones when we do *The Audience with Tom Jones* show on Christmas Eve. I've also suggested that Issie's younger brother gets a temporary placement as a cameraman during his university vacation and that Josh can have half a dozen tickets for the Cup Final. Bale doesn't know this and naturally assumes the worst. He feels compelled to be nasty.

'Yes, you are good. It is relatively easy to reach the dizzy heights of your chosen profession if you're not hampered by morals and squeamish sentimentality.'

'You'd know best, Bale,' I reply and leave his office. I'll give him some privacy to review the T&Cs.

Kirsty had thought long and hard about this after the private detective contacted her. At first it'd seemed ridiculous. She thought some of her mates were winding her up. But then she began to understand. A new show. Something to do with confidence in fidelity. To be specific, Eva Brooks had contacted the TV station to say that she had some doubts about her fiancé Martin McMahon. Did any of those names mean anything to Kirsty? They did. They meant the taste of metal and bile in her mouth.

The private detective was not wearing a long raincoat and a beret. In fact, she looked rather more like one of those women who stop you in shopping centres and ask if you'll spare a few minutes for market research. The private detective, Sue, liked her tea strong with two sugars.

Kirsty considered the proposition for two days solid. She was unable to keep her mind on her job and kept irritating the doctors by giving them the wrong patient notes. They nagged and grumbled at her. Ironically it was their irritation that coerced her into accepting the role, rather than a wish to wreak revenge on Martin. Well, why shouldn't she be on TV? It had to be more glamorous than her job here as a receptionist, in the dowdy little practice, in her small town. The same small town she'd been born and bred in, and if she wasn't careful would be buried in too. Sue promised that Kirsty would get a complimentary haircut and makeover, an allowance for her outfit for the show and some publicity photos afterwards. Sue thought Kirsty had a great chance as a model but she warned time was of the essence.

Kirsty didn't care for Martin at all any more. She was surprised to hear that Eva thought of her as a threat. He'd chosen Eva over her before, hadn't he? Oh shit he had. What made Kirsty think he'd choose her over Eva this time? Her knees nearly buckle under her. The humiliation was painful last time – the stinging, scorching disappointment as he explained that Kirsty was a really fun girl but absolutely not marrying material. Whereas Eva, with her posh university qualifications and green Wellingtons, was. Kirsty had tried to comfort herself with the thought that their kids would look like horses. But the thought didn't really keep her warm at night.

Still, it was a long time ago and she was far too sensible not to move on. In the last ten months she'd only thought of Martin occasionally, like when her sister had a baby, her birthday or when one of the patients did something hilarious at work. But that was natural – that wasn't hankering. Christ, what if he rejected her again? Still, the channel didn't want her to get him to propose, just to have some fun. To compromise himself. She figures it will be easy.

Kirsty waits for Martin outside the high-street bank where he is assistant manager. She doesn't often come into London. It's busy and cold and she remembers why.

'Martin.' She steps through the throng. He is with a couple of colleagues. They are all dressed identically, even the women.

'Kirsty, my goodness. What are you doing here? God, it's nice to see you.'

And Kirsty knows him well enough to know that he is being genuine. She sighs, relieved, not just because the channel will get what they want but because something, somewhere very deep inside her, melts. He cares. Not enough. Not consistently. But he does care. Martin nods his colleagues away, assuring them he'll catch them up in the pub.

'Erm, I came up to meet a friend for lunch. I heard you got engaged so I thought I'd pop by and drop off a congratulations card.' She holds out the card and beams, 'Congratulations.'

'Thanks.' He reaches for the card and their fingers bump.

'I'm really pleased for you.' Kirsty stretches her amazing smile a fraction wider.

'Yeah, thanks.' Martin seems quite embarrassed and quickly thrusts the card into his suit pocket without reading it. 'Do you fancy a drink?'

He's not wasting any time.

'Should we catch up with your friends?' offers Kirsty.

'No. I know the bar they are going to; it's really loud. We won't

be able to hear ourselves think, let alone talk. Let's go somewhere quieter.'

'I know just the place,' says Kirsty.

It surprises Martin that Kirsty knows a local pub, which turns out to be absolutely perfect, because she doesn't come up to town that much. Then Martin sighs to himself. Maybe she does come into town now. He doesn't know much about her life. He always felt it pointless to keep in touch with old flames, especially ones who obviously have such different ambitions and expectations in life. Besides which, Eva wouldn't hear of it.

He only expected to have a quick one, but this is their third round. It is good to be out with a bird who drinks pints again. Instead of the obligatory gin and tonic. Nice that she gets a round in, too, and isn't above going to the bar herself. Christ, Kirsty has fantastic tits. He'd forgotten how magnificent they are. She's still very chatty, too. She still makes little sense. She keeps wittering on about cameras. There again he's not being that rational either. Psychologists rate getting married as equally stressful as bereavement; people do odd things under stress. For example, right now all he wants to do is snog the lips off Kirsty.

With every day a new triumph emerges. The *Evening Standard* runs a story on the weddings that have been cancelled by couples who have appeared on the show and the financial implications for the industries involved. The *Express* picks up the lead and runs a story on how many weddings, up and down the country, have been cancelled since the show began.

'A 120 per cent increase on the exact same period last year!' cries Debbie. We are ecstatic. The *Express* hasn't said that *Sex with an Ex* is responsible, but the implication is there. If the show is responsible we are creating a national reaction. It's big. It's bigger than the 'Free Deirdre Campaign' that ITV ran in reaction to a *Coronation Street* storyline.

The *Mail* spots the same potential story as we do. They track down a couple who have called off their wedding recently to ask them why. People quite unconnected with the show, people who've never appeared, had no desire to appear and would probably be horrified at the idea of appearing, admit that frank discussions on the sex appeal of an ex-lover have led to a discovery of 'fundamental disagreements, which can't be ignored'.

Debs is reading from the morning paper. 'This is it. This is the quote we need to use for our latest press release.' She is literally jumping up and down.

'What does it say?' I ask.

'"I am regretful," says the would-be-groom. "I believe our parting of the ways was a direct result of staying in to watch TV on Monday."' Debs stops reading and asks, 'Why do people use such ridiculous and pompous vocabulary when talking to the press? I'm sure he doesn't normally say such stupid things as "parting of the ways".'

'Very astute, Debs. What else did he say?' I ask, trying to keep her on track.

'"I wish we'd gone to the pub as we'd originally planned. But you see we were saving up. I wish I'd never heard of the show *Sex with an Ex*."' Debs puts the paper down with a satisfied flourish.

'Ah well, he sounds like a prick. By the way, Kirsty is doing well. I saw her in *B Magazine* the other day and I understand she has a contract with some modelling agency.'

All this points to the fact that the show only has a shelf life of one or two episodes. It is becoming almost impossible to lure people on to the show, as the entire nation appears to be on infidelity alert. The plan is to use the kudos from this show to launch other programmes. My phone rings, interrupting Debs's newspaper review.

'Hi, stranger.'

'Hi, Issie.' I wait for her justified complaints. I never ring her, or Josh. I'm totally absorbed in my work. Have I visited my mum recently? It's a relief that she skips it.

'Fancy a night out?'

'Well, yes, but it's just that I'm still interviewing. Bale's keen to commission another series.'

'Then what? Another and another?'

'He seems to think so. I'm sceptical. I mean how gullible does he think the general public is?'

'Well, you may as well have a night out. You can't continue working at this rate *ad infinitum*.'

'What have you got in mind?' I ask.

'A drink? Grab some pasta? Somewhere where we can talk and catch up. I feel I haven't seen you for weeks.'

I wonder if this is code for 'I've been ditched.'

'OK, let's try Papa Bianchi's,' I suggest. 'The food's fine, not exactly Michelin star, but it's cheap and cheerful and most importantly the waiters understand the importance of having a laugh and getting lashed.' I don't mention that it is also in spitting distance of the studio and I'll be able to return to work after we've dined, but when I give her the address she'll guess.

'OK, hold the line until I get a pen.'

I can hear the music from Issie's radio drift through the telephone line. I hear her scrabble around for a pen. I know where she's looking. She'll be starting in the telephone table drawer – futile. She'll progress to the kitchen drawers, the jamjar on the windowsill and then behind the cushions on the settee. She'll find a number of pens but none of them will work, the pencils will be blunt. For a scientist Issie is extremely disorganized. She's back on the line.

'Couldn't find a pen. An odd earring that I've been looking for, a telephone number and a recipe but no pen.'

'Try your handbag.'

'Good idea.' She leaves the line again and this time the hunt is successful.

Issie takes down the details of where and when we are going to meet and I put down the phone. I'm pleased to have averted the inevitable disaster of her arriving late because she's lost or going to the wrong place and not arriving at all. My life is made up of a series of these small services which make other people's lives more comfortable. If only people realized.

I turn back to Fi and the problem of an increasingly moral nation. I know this squeamishness is hypocrisy and I don't expect it to be sustained, but it is an irritation.

'You know what, Fi?'

'What?'

'This new morality that the British public have so inexplicably developed' – I'm scornful – 'may work to our advantage.'

'How come?'

'Well, as I predicted, they've fallen. One after another. We really are living in a faithless society. Fidelity, or the lack of it, knows no boundaries. Indiscriminately it rages and rocks the lives of anyone who dares to trust.'

'But it is brilliant television,' adds Fi, not getting my drift.

'But somewhat depressing,' I assert.

'Well, yes, it is,' she confirms. 'In fact, we had a letter from a silkworm farm in Ireland today.'

'Really?' This trivia momentarily distracts me.

'Yes. Apparently last year, this farm – I forget its name – won the Queen's Award for Industry and some other shield thing for their exports. Apparently this year demand has dipped perceptibly.'

'Honestly.' I'm delighted. Fi doesn't catch my drift.

'I know, it is a huge responsibility, isn't it?'

'Responsibility bollocks, it's a huge story.' Sometimes Fi lets me down. 'Anyway, what was I talking about? Oh yeah. Whilst interviewing next week I want you to actively look for those you think have a chance of resisting.'

'I thought you said people like that didn't exist,' protests Fi.

'Prove me wrong.' She looks nervous. I try to be helpful. 'Pick the under-confident who don't believe they are attractive to one individual, let alone two. Or pick those who are too driven by public recognition to risk public humiliation.'

'What, like budding politicians?'

'Yes, or Freemasons.'

'You are a sensation! You are a fucking marvel.'

'Thank you, Nigel.'

'Where did you find them?'

'Believe me, it took some doing.'

'Your timing is immaculate. We've had six shows and just when there was a danger of infidelity becoming a foregone conclusion, you find a couple who resist.'

I smile at him. I'm trying not to look excited but to be honest I'm delighted too. We found a couple who although probably tempted were not stirred, so to speak. These people amazed me. They resisted not simply because the ex turned out to be a Clash bore or knew all the lyrics to every Duran Duran song, not just because they were worried about the chiffon and lace industry, not just because they feared being caught. But because they believed in it. Fidelity.

Loving.

Cherishing. They wanted to be exclusive lovers. For ever.

'Suckers,' I comment.

'Still, it's brilliant television,' adds Fi.

This it is. It brings the house down. This is what people want to believe in. It tantalizes. I've made it a possibility again, the Happily Ever After. We plan to do a massive follow-up show. By paying for the most OTT wedding. We are investigating the possibility of getting Westminster Abbey. It's short notice but providing there are no obscure foreign royalty or minor member of the aristocracy booked in I think we'll pull it off. I'm going to give the public what they want.

'Next week we can go back to the cheats.'

It's late and it's 24 December. I look up from my desk and note that there is no one else left in the office except the cleaner. I note that he is wearing a Santa hat and a red nose. The red nose is real. I close down my PC and decide to lock it away rather than take it home for Christmas. My phone rings.

'Cas Perry, evening.'

'Cas, you silly tart. What are you doing in the office on Christmas Eve?'

'Hi, Josh,' I sigh, too tired to tell him how pleased I am he's called. 'Just finishing off, actually.'

'Good. We're in the Goose and Crown. Come and join us.'

'Who's there?'

Josh names a number of our friends. I look at my watch. It's 8.40 p.m. – not too late to join them. I can't remember the last time I got pissed with genuine mates.

'I'd love to. I'll be there in twenty minutes.'

Suddenly I am awash with Christmas cheer and so give the cleaner a bottle of malt whisky that some advertiser sent me. He's disproportionately pleased. I received about a dozen similar gifts this Christmas and can't relate to his excitement. I call the lift and experience the unusual sensation of being relieved to leave the building. It is a glass elevator not unlike the one that appears in *Willy Wonka's Chocolate Factory*; it glides up and down in a graceful, effortless movement. As the lift takes me to the ground floor I mentally checklist the next show. This is the hundredth time I've done this – I know everything is fine but I do it anyway. It's habit. The building is dark, only illuminated by fairy lights. I pass the meeting areas. One has a photocopier in it and is always empty. The other has a Mars bar dispenser and a coffee machine. The latter room is always heaving. It's a good place to catch up on conversations about the male menopause. No one is there now. They've all gone home to start basting turkey or stuffing their wives. I pass a few words with the receptionist, which I do every Christmas. We comment on how quickly it's come around again. This time, however, I mean it. I've been so busy that I've completely missed autumn. Which is a shame because, if I was pushed to comment, I'd say that autumn is my favourite season. I nod to the security guard and then head towards the huge glass rotating doors. I'm already imagining downing my first vodka and orange.

'Jocasta Perry.' A voice slices across the tranquillity.

I don't have a chance to reply or to establish where it's coming from.

'Do you know what it is like to feel humiliation? Betrayal? Do you understand the pain? I don't suppose you do with breasts like those.'

The woman who is shouting at me is in her early thirties. She has presumably been sitting in reception waiting for me but I hadn't noticed her until she'd called out. She has fine, highlighted, shoulder-length hair. It isn't particularly styled. She's a comfortable size twelve or fourteen. I don't think I actively know her and yet she has a vaguely familiar face. She looks a lot like a lot of women. She walks across the foyer and is within a foot of me. She is pointing a plump finger at me: she's so agitated she is actually shaking and as a result the strap of her handbag keeps slipping down her shoulder. Each time it does this she stops for a second and hitches the strap back on to her shoulder. Smart mac. Gucci bag. Where do I know this woman from?

'The people who write the letters – do you know what motivates them? Have you the slightest idea?' I look at the security guard and make it clear that I want him on standby. Whoever this woman is, she is obviously buoyed up by Christmas spirit(s). 'I don't suppose you do. You obviously love yourself so much you can't love anyone else enough to be made vulnerable.'

As I can't believe I know her, I consider it a near impossibility that she knows me. Even my best friends would be reticent to claim they *know* me. So what right does she have to draw such conclusions? Cast such aspersions?

Still, she's right.

She isn't shouting or threatening, but her powerful anger is obvious. She's controlling the menace, but only to show me she can. I mentally run through my Filofax and index cards. Finally I place her.

'I know you. It's Libby, isn't it?' I hold out a hand for her to shake. Libby was on one of our early shows. She'd suspected her fiancé still had a thing for his ex. She'd been right. I remember Libby because she had had such lovely taste. I remember her showing me her wedding dress and the bridesmaids' dresses; they'd been exquisite. Yes, lovely taste, except in men, that is.

She nods curtly. 'I was scared but I was with him. Now I'm scared and alone.'

I touch her arm. She smells of teenage perfume which reminds me of Fairy Liquid. I doubt this is Libby's because of her impeccable taste. I suspect that she went for a quick one after work and with the combination of gin and Christmas songs on the jukebox she has become maudlin. I imagine her mates geeing her on to come and track me down to tackle me. One or two of her really good friends will have tried to stop her. On noting her determination they've done the next best thing – doused her in their perfume.

'He'd have left anyhow,' I comfort.

She starts to sob. 'Would he? Would he?'

The receptionist gives her a cup of tea and the security guard leads her to the settee. She's telling them how lonely she is. I think she should be evicted from the building, but as it is Christmas I won't report the lax approach of the receptionist or the guard. I head towards the door.

'Merry Christmas, Libby,' I shout. I pause, waiting for her to wish me a Happy New Year.

She doesn't. Instead she grips my arm and asks, 'Have you ever looked in the mirror and been disappointed with your reflection?' I turn to face her and she meets my gaze. 'Well, I loathe mine.'

7

It's New Year's Eve. I have two things to celebrate this evening. One, Christmas is over. I've watched *The Sound of Music* with my mum and I'm now Julie-Andrews-free for another year. And two, it's not the millennium. That was hell. The horrible expectancy of it all. I started planning my millennium New Year's Eve in February 1997, as I was terrified that I'd choose the wrong option for this once-in-a-lifetime opportunity. I couldn't decide. Cottage in the Cotswolds? Black tie in Vegas? Beach in Mauritius? There was just too much choice and every one of them with its advantages. It wasn't simply a question of enjoying myself. I presumed that I'd manage to pull that off just about anywhere, but I soon came to realize that wherever I chose said something about me. Did I want to say Vegas or Cotswolds? Did I want glitz or serenity? In the end Josh, Issie and I had a posh dinner at Issie's house. Josh cooked, I provided the champagne. Issie's contribution, besides the venue, was that she managed not to have her heart broken. A first for a New Year's Eve, at least in my memory. We then drunkenly walked up and down the River Thames, getting crushed by the crowds and watching the fireworks and the backs of several million revellers. It was great. Now, in a blink of an eye, it's New Year's Eve again. With all its hellish accessories. Not only does the thought of the little black dress ruin Christmas indulgence, but this year I'm not spending it with Issie and Josh. Issie is going to her parents' party in Marlow and Josh is in Scotland with the family of his latest girlfriend.

On the up side, I am going to a glitzy industry party and if I'm not going to be with Issie and Josh, this is my second choice. Everyone who is anyone in TV will be at the Gloucester Hotel in Mayfair tonight. I *have* to be there. Especially this year, as I'm riding high. Perhaps the highest I've ever been. My show is the talk of the industry. I also consider that it is actually impossible not to score at these events. And I'm ready for it. Thinking about it, I've been going through a bit of a dry patch of late. There was Joe, in late August. And then the botched attempt with Ivor, which doesn't count. I thrust these disconcerting thoughts aside, comforting myself with the fact that the combination of my current success, the fact that it is New Year's Eve and the loose morals of those who work in the media industry mean I'm guaranteed great sex tonight. You can smell the testosterone as soon as you walk into the hotel foyer. I bristle. We have tried to disguise it with Calvin Klein perfume and aftershave, bow ties and posh frocks, but lust is tangible. A thick tension is staining the air. And although this may sound lairy, it's not. It's exciting. It's fun. It's fan-fucking-tastic.

Literally.

My targets fall into two categories: victim or sparring partner. I prefer the latter but hey, a time and a place. I see him by the time we sit down to dinner. He's on the next table. He's glittering in the candlelight. He's not wearing a wedding ring. After a few discreet enquiries I discover that he has a long-term girlfriend but she's not here tonight. The very best combination – challenging but not insurmountable. I want this to be a one-night thing and really I can't be arsed to put in weeks of prep. Chances are he'll be going through a rough patch. They always are. He'll tell me that this is because his girlfriend doesn't understand him. Of course the opposite is true.

The dinner passes in a blur of laughter and champagne. Bale is as pompous as hell, but at least I don't get caught under the mistletoe with him, as Di does. Fi, Ricky and I have a huge giggle, spreading gossip, spiking drinks and strutting our stuff on the dance floor. I'm having so much fun that I almost forget that I plan to score. But as the clocks strike midnight and Fi and Ricky both disappear to snog their chosen boys, I look around for my target. Of course it's not a coincidence that he is standing just a few feet away from me. He wasn't oblivious to the smouldering glances I threw across the melon balls; nor was he averse to returning them.

I don't kiss him on the dance floor because he does have a girlfriend. I can do without the gossip and uproar which would ensue after such an obvious display of our intentions. Instead I lean very closely in to him so that my lips are a fraction from his lobe. His hairs stand up and brush my lips. I move an almost indiscernible bit closer, letting my tit scrape against his arm. He trembles. My groin flinches.

'Have you got a room?' He nods. The atmosphere is damp with lust. 'What number?' He tells me immediately. I feel so powerful. 'Walk to your room. Don't walk too fast because I need to leave a respectable interval between you leaving and me following, but I don't want to lose you.' I give his arm a squeeze. We both understand. He nods a drunken nod, happy to follow my instructions to the letter.

I keep a safe distance and then I catch him up in his corridor. I'm quite tired so I don't bother with anything too athletic against the wall, which I could have done to politely fill the embarrassing gap as he fumbles with the key, desperate to get it in the lock. I'm not sure if this is drink, nerves or excitement, but it doesn't bode well. Eventually he opens the door. Unaccountably my mood changes. I think I'm bored by his inability. I'm no longer looking forward to this. Still, I'm here.

He's on a promise and I think it is dishonest to pull out at this stage. It wouldn't be polite. I'm many things but a prick teaser isn't one of them. I make the decision to get it over with as quickly as possible. I really am tired and it would have been wiser to have had an early night.

I shrug away his attempt to offer me something from the mini bar.

'You go ahead.'

He pours himself a whisky. He then tries to light a cigarette but fails and spills the matches on the floor. He's very nervous and I feel almost maternal. Is he too young for this? Am I too old? I take pity and decide to encourage him. Delicate thing, the male ego. I've often thought of those soapy bubbles that you make by blowing a lot of hot air through a little plastic device. Easy to inflate, easy to pop and easy to grow again.

'Hey, tiger.' I prize the whisky tumbler out of his hand and kiss him. Fine. Quite good really. But then, it is just kissing. He lunges for my zip and tugs at it. The dress is Versace and cost me nearly a thousand quid. I play a tactful manœuvre where I shimmy out of it doing a little mini striptease. He loves it. And I save my dress. To be fair, he is trying – he just lacks subtlety. He's kneading my breasts as though he's trying to massage a muscle out of spasm. We are lying on the bed and suddenly his fingers are deep inside me. Better. OK one, two is fine. Jesus, I hope he knows fisting is just an expression.

'Would you like me to go down on you?' he asks. That's novel – I've never been called upon to have an opinion before.

'Would you like to?' I ask, grinning.

'Well, I don't mind, if it's really what you want. It's not actually my favourite. But I'm happy to oblige if it will make you come.' I guess this is sweet, in a way. But sweet is not sexy. I now seriously wonder if anything he can think of will make me come. Being called a prick teaser seems like an attractive option.

I disengage and go to the bathroom. When I emerge I'm wearing a towelling robe and I've cleaned my teeth. The vibes I'm giving off are Mary Ellen *à la* Walton family rather than Sue Ellen, Ewing family temptress.

'Goodnight.' I smile, pecking him on the cheek. I pull the dressing gown tightly around me, turn the light out and deliberately roll away from him. I don't even care that he doesn't seem too disappointed.

I scramble for my mobile, which slices through my dreamless sleep. It's Issie.

'*Happy New Year!* Where are you?' Her voice is a unique blend of excitement, frustration, anger and concern.

'In a hotel in' – I scrabble around for the note pad next to the telephone – 'Mayfair.'

'Who with?'

I look at the empty bed. I feel the sheets next to me. They are still warm. They smell of male sweat. I can hear the shower running.

'His name's Ben.' I hear her tut. I know the conclusion she has naturally drawn and I haven't the energy to correct her diagnosis of events. Instead I confirm it. 'It was New Year's Eve. It was just physical.'

'It's always just physical. That's the problem,' she sighs. She doesn't seem impressed. 'You are heading for trouble. You're on overdrive. You've been working too hard. When did you last go home?'

'Not sure. What day is it?'

It turns out to be Sunday. I haven't slept or bathed in my flat since Christmas morning and before that a week last

Tuesday. I did stay at my mum's on Boxing Day, but besides that I've been using the facilities at the gym and work.

'You need a rest,' says Issie. But she's wrong – I thrive on activity. I'm at my creative best when I'm hyper. Ordinary people may need to rest after such intensive work periods but I'm strong. I'm fine.

I think I'm going to cry.

'I'm so tired,' I wail. 'It was awful. In fact, I can't remember when I last had good sex. I'm so tense. I'm going straight from here to my masseur. My neck is so tight I can barely move.'

'You can't go to your masseur, it's New Year's Day. They'll be closed. Look, Josh's called. He's missing us. He's on a flight back down here. I'm going to the airport to pick him up. I'll swing by your flat first. Then we can all go for a walk, clear the hangovers.'

Thanks, Issie. What a darling.

It is so bloody cold that the stag that are, allegedly, in Richmond Park are nowhere to be seen.

'They're hibernating,' suggests Issie.

Josh wraps an arm around each of us.

'If you think this is cold, you should have been in Scotland. Now *that* was cold.'

'How was Scotland?' As I say this I can see my breath on the air. I pull my jacket tighter round me.

'Fine. Alcoholic. Tartan,' he comments non-committally.

'Gone off her, then?' The 'her' in question is Katherine, Josh's latest girlfriend. Issie and I quite like her. She's been hanging around with Josh for a couple of months now. We had high hopes but I can already tell from the tone of his voice, and the fact that he's back here with us instead of in St

Andrews with her and her parents, that I ought to start talking about her in the past tense.

'I finished it,' Josh confirms. Issie and I slyly exchange glances.

'Nice timing,' we chorus.

Josh shrugs apologetically.

'How was your night, Issie?' I ask.

'Really good, actually. Family all well and I met someone really nice at my parents' party.'

'Someone really nice and male?' I try to clarify. It sounds unlikely.

Issie grins and nods. The cold wind has whipped up spots of colour on her cheeks. I understand why Elizabethan poets used to mither on about their heroines having cheeks like roses. Issie is glowing.

'You look fantastic, Issie. Did you score?'

She grins sheepishly. 'I was at my parents'.' Good point, no opportunity. 'But I did give him my telephone number.'

'Home or work?' asks Josh.

'Both, and my mobile. And my e-mail and my fax,' says Issie. This time Josh and I exchange the glances.

'He hasn't called yet, though.' Issie suddenly scrambles for her mobile. She checks her message facility and the text messages. Nothing.

'It's far too early for him to call,' Josh comforts her. Although neither he nor I think that Issie's chap will call. He'll have detected the fact that whilst one hand was handing over all her telephone numbers, the other hand was flicking through a copy of *Brides and Setting Up Home.*

'Should I call him?' asks Issie.

'Do you have his number?'

'Yes, his mother gave it to my mother.'

I stamp my boots hard on the freezing snow, enjoying the crunchy sound it makes and avoiding confronting the inevitable disaster Issie is driving towards. It sounds to me as though this guy is a social misfit, if his mother has to try to get him dates. I don't share my theory with Issie. Instead I listen to hers on sexual equality.

'I mean, it doesn't matter who rings who, really, does it? I mean we are both adults. We don't have to play games.' Neither Josh nor I comment.

We stop and buy hot chocolates from a caravan, marvelling that the guy is open on New Year's Day. The vendor assures us that he'd rather be freezing in his caravan in Richmond Park than 'stuck in the house wiv me muvver-in-law and the kids'. We all do our best to ignore this condemnation of family life and sip the creamy drinks.

Issie continues. 'I'm sure he'd respect me for calling.'

She believes the seventies' hype that a man still respects you if you call him, that he'll like you and want a relationship with you. I try to explain that the advice is thirty years out of date. In the seventies, single women would not have accepted the advice of the Land Girls. So why does Issie think that the burn-the-bra brigade have any relevance to how women of the twenty-first century should conduct their romantic and sexual liaisons?

'Call him if you like, Issie. But he'll know that you don't just happen to have two tickets for the opera – no one ever does.'

'Should I suggest the Turkish restaurant that's just opened on Romilly Street?'

'If you want to, but he knows it's code for "I like you". "I like you" leaves you exposed and will send him running.'

'You call men all the time.'

'I call because I don't want commitment. They respond

because they know that.' Issie scowls at me. But doesn't waste her breath arguing. 'If you want my advice, wait until he calls you.'

Issie gives Josh her phone and makes him promise not to let her ring until 3 January, earliest.

'What about your evening?' asks Josh, turning to me.

'Fine,' I say, without committing. 'Good food. Good company. My Versace dress stole the show. Crap sex.'

Josh's charming, confident laugh rings around the park. 'Your problem is that you are from Mars and you keep meeting men from Venus.'

I grin. 'I just wanted some good sex to round the evening off but for all my fascination with other people's sex lives right now, mine is going through a rough patch. I simply can't conjure up the energy. Of course I'm still sleeping with men but it's becoming tedious. For example, this morning I just wanted to slip away. I didn't need a post mortem, but Ben wanted to be all twenty-first century about our encounter. He wanted to discuss what it meant. I told him it meant nothing.'

Issie gasps. 'Why did you say that?'

'Because it's true,' I state simply.

'It is impossible to sleep with a stranger and not risk suffering or inflicting serious emotional carnage. Casual sex is what we enter into, not what we come out of,' Issie chides.

I blame Josh for this outburst. He gave Issie the book *Responsibility for Yourself, Reconciliation with Others* for Christmas. Apparently it was intended for me, and the book *Women Who Love Too Much* was meant for Issie. He got the tags mixed up. I thought it was hilarious.

'But I do come out unscathed, without a fractured heart and absolutely free of bitter recriminations,' I point out to Issie.

'Do the men you sleep with?' she asks.

'Yes,' I say without faltering.

Issie and Josh both draw to a dramatic halt and glare at me.

'Yes,' I insist and I try not to think of Ben's hurt look this morning or the pathetic messages Joe keeps leaving on my answering machine or the numerous Christmas cards that I received from men suggesting that we could 'do it again some time'. Problem is I can rarely remember doing it the first time. My conquests are a homogenous blur.

'Well, in your case there are two options. Either you are internalizing the damage or you are an animal. I know you are not an animal.' Issie is suddenly serious and she lets go of Josh's arm and runs to hug me.

Poor Issie. This constant search for something deep and meaningful in me is exhausting. Why can't she just accept me for what I am? Someone led by hedonism, eroticism and base animal instincts. I say nothing until at last her face settles into sad acceptance. Weary of fighting with me, she grudgingly laughs, 'Oh, OK, you *are* horrid.'

We all go back to my flat. Josh immediately goes into the kitchen to see what he can rustle up. My fridge is surprisingly well stocked. This is because my mum has a key and must have popped round today. There are fresh vegetables, leftover turkey and a load of mince pies. She's also left a small Christmas cake on the coffee table. Josh starts to chop vegetables and Issie opens some wine whilst I call my mum to thank her and wish her a Happy New Year. By the time I get off the phone, Josh has made a huge pan of thick vegetable soup. We sit with bowls on our laps in front of the TV.

'Didn't your mum want to come round?' asks Josh.

'No. I invited her but she said that she and some neighbour or other are going to put their feet up in front of the TV.'

'Bob?' offers Issie.

'Could be.' I shrug. Sometimes it seems as though Issie knows more about my mother's life than I do.

It's a big night for me. The wedding episode of *Sex with an Ex* is playing out as an hour special. Half an hour on the wedding, then half an hour on the usual programme. The fact that I secured an hour spot on primetime TV on New Year's Day is hugely exciting. For all Issie and Josh have made it quite clear that they don't approve of the programme (which I think is hypocritical of Josh, considering his behaviour was inspirational to the original concept), they both have to admit that it is compelling. Neither of them has missed a show.

'Why is she wearing a leopard-skin tracksuit?' Issie asks.

'It goes with her hair,' notes Josh. 'Why do they do it at all?' he adds incredulously.

'Fame,' I assert happily. 'It's compelling.'

'She's awful,' says Issie, 'she keeps clapping herself. Why does she do that?'

'Too much orange squash as a kid,' I offer.

The scene cuts to some moody music, something that builds to a crescendo. The audience, in its entirety, is with Tom. They want him to resist. He doesn't. The cries of protest and defence of the infidel, Tom, bleat from the TV. 'It meant nothing – it confirmed the reasons we split up.' His girlfriend ignores his wails and punches him. 'WhoooooWhoooo.' The audience erupts. Turning at once. Deciding within seconds who they'll support. Who they'll hate. They know they should be supporting people because they seem nice – they ought to prefer the sweetest personality. But invariably they cheer for the bird with the biggest tits or the guy with the cheekiest grin. They whoop and cheer and sing and goad and cry and console and condemn in the space between one commercial break and the next. The overwhelming emotion is fear.

'It's fascinating,' comments Issie. 'The men justify straying on the grounds that it's not about love and the women that it is.'

'I don't find that fascinating. I find it predictable. I'd like a woman to come on the show and say she fancied a shag,' I argue.

'It's unlikely though, isn't it? You're the only woman I know who underwent an emotional lobotomy at the age of seven.'

'Shush.' I'm not embarrassed by what she's saying, but the adverts have finished and we'll miss some of the show with her chatter.

His face is grey and his lips tight. He's sweating from every pore. His eyes are darting left to right. He doesn't know. He can't be sure. Has she slept with her ex or not?

'You know how we could improve the show?' I ask rhetorically.

'Pull it,' Josh suggests.

I fling him a filthy look. 'No. We should have two signature tunes, depending on the outcome. One for jubilation, the other for . . .'

'Humiliation?' Issie interrupts.

'Mortification?' Josh offers.

'Simply desolation,' I say.

I don't shy away from it. I cast my mind back to Christmas Eve and Libby's swollen, weeping face. She thought she was telling me something I didn't know. She wasn't. She looked just as my mother had the day my father left. I know all about desolation. I know the emotion I'm exposing on stage and I'm not frightened of it. *I'm* not the one creating it and I have no reason to feel ill at ease. I know that the couples with unfaithful partners are desolate, horrified, mystified, disappointed. But it won't last. I firmly believe I'm doing them a favour. Better now than after they've signed the form at the registrar's.

We finish the soup and I heat the mince pies and slice the Christmas cake. Issie groans, insists she can't eat another bite and then asks if there's any brandy sauce for the pud. Josh has now put himself in charge of alcohol and is as liberal with the measures as he is with his sperm. We're filthily pissed by 9.15 p.m.

It's brilliant.

'Thanks for the socks,' he says, kissing me on the cheek and sitting next to me on the sofa. I grin and put my arms around him.

'You're welcome.' I also bought him a number of more desirable pressies: big boy's toys such as a palm pad, a Swiss Army knife and a mobile phone that you can send pictures on. The gift he liked best was the computer headset that gives you access to your favourite website by talking to your computer. He wasn't even perturbed when my mother asked, 'But isn't there a button you could push instead?' Buying these presents reaffirmed my belief that even the nicest men are truly incapable of growing up. The socks are a joke. We always buy each other an old-married-couple-gift. We figure that this is as close as each of us will ever get. Josh bought me a perfunctory rolling pin. Not even one of those nice marble ones. He knows I've never had a use for a rolling pin and unless someone comes up with a creative way of utilizing one in the bedroom I'm unlikely ever to. We've offered Issie the chance to join in our game. After all, if Josh bought two women wifey gifts it would be even more realistic. She's steadfastly refused, complaining that it's too depressing a notion. I think she fears she's tempting fate. The irony is she hopes that one day she'll exchange such gifts for real.

'Have you made a New Year's resolution?' asks Issie, squeezing her slim bum between Josh and me and wiggling a bit so that we have to move to accommodate her. I slosh some more brandy into everyone's glass.

'Oh, you know, the usual – lose five pounds in weight, limit my alcohol units to just twice the recommended allowance and cut back to twenty a day. You?'

'I'm going to play it cooler with men.'

Josh and I are too drunk to bother to hide our amusement. We both spit out our brandy. Mine is aimed back into my glass; Josh isn't as houseproud and he splatters his all over my cashmere cushions. I'm laughing too much to get cross.

'What?' asks Issie, indignantly. But she knows what.

'Well, at least you are consistent. That's the same resolution you made last year and the five previous to that,' I comment.

Josh is kinder. 'To be fair, that is the very nature of our resolutions. I mean you always want to eat, smoke and drink less, Issie always wants to love less and I—'

'Always want to screw more,' Issie and I chorus.

We all laugh. It's too true for any of us to take offence.

'How about we do it for real this year?' I suggest.

'I do hope to screw more,' says Josh seriously. His average is pretty high as it stands – I doubt if he has time for that many more conquests. His behaviour is already quintessentially male. I use him as a role model.

'No, I mean this year why don't we resolve to do something different, and really do it?'

'What, like run a marathon?' suggests Issie.

'Yes, if that's what you want to do,' I encourage.

'Is it a good place to meet men?' she asks. I sigh.

We drink a whole lot more. In fact, we finish the brandy

and start on whisky. This is on top of the wine that we drank with the soup. I've certainly blown apart my resolutions, but that's all I'm certain of. Everything else is a fog. I hold my hand out in front of me, but it's blurry around the edges. Issie and Josh are both being wildly funny, coming up with more and more ludicrous resolutions that we could pledge, but I can't keep up with their thoughts. My head is smudgy and, try as I might, I can't seem to control the direction of my thoughts. I keep getting vivid flashes of Ben's serious and earnest face as he droned on about his girlfriend and whether she'd forgive him for his infidelity. I advised him to keep his trap shut. He stared out of the window as though he hadn't heard me and asked how could he forgive himself. I must be really drunk because Ben's face keeps dissolving into Ivor's and Ivor's pleading eyes melt into Joe's. I shake my head. Whisky, the devil's own urine – it always makes me weird.

'Learn a new word every day.'

'That's easy.'

'And use it.'

'Do the three peaks' challenge.'

'No way.'

Issie's ash misses the ashtray she is aiming for. She doesn't seem to notice but I watch it sprinkle to the floor in slow motion. My eyes see this. My mind sees Ben's matches scatter as he nervously tries to light a fag. I notice I'm surrounded by drooping tinsel and dropping pine needles.

'Tell the truth for a week, the whole truth and nothing but,' suggests Josh. Little white lies are a way of life for him and all philanderers. More natural than breathing.

'No, that's stupid, you'd have no friends.'

'More whisky?' I offer.

'Go on then,' they slur and hold out unsteady glasses.

'OK, how about I resolve to get married?'

'What?' Both Issie and I stare at Josh. We're dumbfounded.

'You can't marry, dummy, you've just ditched your girl, remember? And she was great, the best you've introduced us to for a while. You are a commitment phobe, remember?'

'That's not true,' argues Josh.

I defend him. 'Be fair, Issie, he is committed – very much so – in the beginning. It's sustaining the commitment that he has a problem with.'

Josh scowls good-naturedly. It's a fair cop. 'I'm very committed to you, Cas. And you too, Issie,' he adds. 'I've just never been with the right girl.'

I'm not sure what he's looking for.

Josh and I are similar in many ways. We've both had numerous sexual encounters. The big difference is Josh does believe in relationships and does expect to settle down one day. He's always telling me so. I don't know why he still expects this with his track record. For eighteen years Josh has followed a pattern. He is always desperately in love or desperately in loathe. The difference is only a matter of weeks. He bores easily. But instead of thinking that it's because there is something flawed in the concept of Happily Ever After (which seems obvious to me) Josh insists it's because he hasn't had the opportunity with the right woman yet. He repeatedly and forcefully insists that he *knows* she exists.

'OK, maybe promising to get married this year is a bit over the top. The best reception venues will be all booked up anyway. I'll take it in easy stages. I'll find the One and propose.'

'Can I be bridesmaid?' asks Issie.

'Yes.'

'Can I be best woman?' I'm humouring him.

'Maybe.' He swallows back his whisky and pours yet another. He swills the amber devil's pee around in the glass and we silently watch him silently watching it.

'You're serious, aren't you?' I ask.

'It's time,' he confirms. A cold finger traces its way along my spine. I shiver; it feels a lot like fear. Josh marry? I'd lose him. Or rather I'd lose my position as *numero uno* in his life. I share Josh with Issie but that's different. Issie isn't competition, she's complementary. I'd miss him.

'You're pissed. You don't mean this. I tell you what, you can retract it in the morning.' I smile. I wait for him to smile back and he doesn't, so I move on to Issie. 'OK, what's your resolution?'

'I like that one about running a marathon. And you?'

'I'm beginning to feel cheap and bored.' She cocks her head to one side, waiting for me to elaborate. I can't. I'm amazed I've said this much. I don't mean it. Or do I? I do.

'I'm giving it up.'

'What?'

'Casual sex, shags without thought, impulsive sex, shags with limited thought, acting on drunken whims, sleeping with someone to celebrate a promotion, or the ratings, or a pretty frock in Armani.' I pause to be certain that covers all scenarios. It does.

'What will you do?' asks Issie, with the scary honesty that only best friends can employ.

'I don't know,' I reply with the same tone. 'Celibacy?'

8

'What happened? Why did you do it, Susie? What made you do this?' Jed is being unusually dignified, under the circumstances. After all, a quarter of the British adult population have just seen his fiancée kiss her ex-lover almost in the vestry of the church, fifteen minutes before their wedding rehearsal, a week before their wedding. The film clearly shows her adjust her skirt as she emerged from behind the tombstone. Bale's terrified of lawsuits so we are not explicit but it doesn't take a Mensa IQ to work out that kissing wasn't where the action stopped.

Susie is whiter than the wedding dress that she'd proudly shown the audience just before the advert break. But then that was another lifetime. That was a pre-public outing lifetime. Susie was still playing happy families, Jed was still living in cloud cuckoo land and Andrew was still standing in the wings waiting to expose Susie's infidelity.

'I am so sorry,' whispers Susie. Which I think is a good move. Her only chance of winning the audience over is to be immediately and totally contrite. After all, Jed's a good-looking guy and natural instincts are to root for him.

It's an interesting moment, this one: when all three stooges are on the floor and they have to deal publicly with the consequences of a very private affair. Jed had thought he was in control. He hadn't actually believed Andrew was any real competition. He'd imagined that it would be exciting to be on TV, something to tell the grandkids. He'd expected Susie to choose him, despite the fact that all their friends still whispered about Andrew and Susie being a great couple, so much more passionate. I bet he's now wishing he'd simply stuck to the wedding video.

Andrew thought it was his game. He had little to lose as his and Susie's romance ended in a veil of tears and reprimands some years ago (FYI, and it's worth noting, the reason why they finished was because Susie found Andrew in bed with another woman). Andrew had happily agreed to tempt her. If he hadn't, it would look as though he was chicken shit, and that foxy detective who'd approached him would think he was only half a man.

'Why did you do it, Susie?' pleads Jed.

'I wish they'd ask more probing questions,' comments Fi. We are both standing in the wings watching the action, live.

'No, this is the crux,' I whisper back. 'The reasons why the partners fall are massively interesting. The list is endless. Closure, revenge, consolation, opportunism.'

Susie has finally found her voice.

'I am sorry, Jed. But I couldn't not. For the last three years since Andrew and I split up I saw him in every square jaw and broad shoulders. Sometimes I'd see him in front of me on the tube escalator and I'd run to catch him up, my feet pounding on the wooden slats, my heart vibrating against my tonsils. And for that heady thumping moment I wouldn't worry how I'd explain it to you. Or why I was forgiving him. I just wanted to heal myself by resting my eyes upon him. I thought then that the throbbing might go away. But it never was him. It was always someone less. Because everyone is less. Even you.'

How curious.

The audience knows that Andrew doesn't deserve such devotion, but they are thrilled. Other than Susie's very deep ugly sobs, you can hear a pin drop.

Tears are streaming down Fi's face. 'Aren't you moved, Cas?'

'Yes, I'm delighted there isn't a dry eye in the house. It's great television. What's next?'

She hands me a clipboard. 'Interviews for next week's show.'

I walk towards the interview room, ushering away a few giggling research girls who are cluttering the doorway. 'What's up with them?' I ask Fi.

'Haven't you heard? Your thinking man, he's a Greek god.'

'Not very tall, then, and with several heads?' I quip. But my sarcasm is whipped out of me as I open the door and see Darren. I can understand why Marcus is insecure. I met Marcus this morning. He is fine. He is bright enough, more interesting than most, average-looking and extremely wealthy. He obviously adores Claire. Claire realizes this is not a bad deal and I figure she adores him back. However, besides my personal belief that everyone will have an affair given the opportunity, Darren is breathtaking.

He's tall, about six foot two, with long, gypsy hair touching his chin. I don't normally go for long hair. Because, more often than not, it is accessorized with an entirely denim wardrobe and a Meatloaf album collection. But, right now, all I want to do is lose my fingers in his locks. More, I want to lose him in my Conran bâteau wooden bed. He has wide shoulders that taper to slim hips and the cutest bum. He is wearing a pale grey sweater and some old Levis. Just the right amount of effort, without suggesting he is conceited. His eyes are huge, deep brown and framed with the most stunning Bambi lashes. And best of all is his smile. He has the cheekiest smile that provokes his entire face. His eyes, his cheeks, his laugh lines.

He's a babe.

For a moment I am at a complete loss. I don't know what to say, what to do or how to stand. I am absolutely dispossessed of common sense, thirty-three years of precedent, or even a simple grasp at etiquette. I can no more think of the correct words than I could bungy jump from . . . God I can't even think where people bungy jump. My mind is blank. He smiles and I think I can hear music, which is such a cliché that I'm ready to shoot myself. My nipples are getting hard, which I think is a filthy betrayal. Can he tell? I'm literally salivating. Get a fucking grip, I instruct myself.

'Jocasta Perry,' I say in a confident, don't-think-I'm-going-to-be-impressed-by-your-stunning-good-looks-I'm-impenetrable voice. It's entirely fictional.

'Jocasta, how Oedipal.' He smiles, taking my hand and shaking it very firmly. I'm amazed not at the firmness of the handshake but at the reference. 'Jocasta or Ca—'

'Cas,' I confirm. Is this man psychic?

'Darren Smith.'

'Yes, I know.' I indicate the clipboard, which has all his personal details. Telephone number, address, date of birth. I wonder if we should start including some more intimate questions in the briefing session. Like favourite sexual position, which side of the bed he sleeps on. Mentally I pinch myself. He's just a man. I quickly draw attention to his shortcomings. We both need to be aware of them.

'Daz or Dazza?' I smile icily.

'Darren,' he confirms without the slightest hint that he's taken offence. I wonder if he realizes that I am trying to be rude. He doesn't seem stupid. He grins at me. Exposing a row of teeth which the Osmonds would be proud of. How can anyone be this gorgeous?

'Well, Darren, to business.' I sit next to him and accidentally bang my knee against his. His touch blisters through my

Joseph trousers. I actually flinch. Shaking, I reach for a glass of water.

'You OK?' He moves quickly, reaching the water before I do. Genuinely concerned, he hands me the glass. I'm incapable of telling him I'm OK. The glass slips an inch. He thinks I'm going to drop it and so guides it to my lips, watching me the whole time. His eyes bore right into me. Is he reading my mind? Does he know my knickers are in flames? I take a gulp of the water. And place the glass back on the coffee table. 'It is hot in here,' he comments and springs up to play with the air conditioning switch. He is so confident. So in control. And I'm . . .? I'm so lost. Maybe I'm sick. I glance at Fi. She's grinning. This brings me back to my senses with a jolt.

'Something funny, Fi?' I glare at her. She shakes her head and retreats to a corner of the room. I force myself back to my guest notes and back to Darren. Only one of those actions presents a problem. 'As you know, Marcus Ailsebury is about to marry your ex-girlfriend, Claire Thomson, on Valentine's Day. Just over two weeks' time. Marcus wrote to us to tell us that he feels' – I correct myself – 'fears that Claire may still hold a torch for you.' I blush. This script, normally adequate, suddenly appears to be exactly what it is. Bloody awful. I hope Darren doesn't think I'd normally use an expression like 'hold a torch'. Regardless, I carry on. 'Marcus needs to know whether his fears are founded. Now are you familiar with the format of *Sex with an Ex*?' I look up at him.

'*Sex with an Ex*? Sadly, yes.' He nods seriously. His hair falls over his left eye. I can't think of anything more attractive. He blows out of the side of his mouth. Except that. The hair almost magically falls back into place.

'Good, well, what we need you to do is—'

'Look, I'm sorry to interrupt, but I don't want to waste any more of your time than I already have.' I smile, quite happy to engage in a conversation with him. Answer questions and queries. He can have all evening. I want to hear everything he has to say.

'I'm not going to do this.'

Except that.

'I don't want to be on your show.'

I stare at him, amazed. Arsehole.

'I feel terrible that I'm letting you down and that I've probably inconvenienced a lot of people, but I had no idea, when your studio invited me here, it was for *Sex with an Ex*.' He spits out the title with undisguised contempt.

'Didn't the private detective explain it all to you?' I ask bitterly.

'No. She just said that Marcus needed some help with the wedding preparations. I thought I was being invited on to a show similar to *Surprise Surprise*.'

I consider this. It is possible that our researchers and detective deliberately misled Darren. Or at the very least kept him in the dark. They too must have recognized that Darren would be great for ratings.

'Nothing on this earth would induce me to be on *Sex with an Ex*.'

'Why not?' Frankly, I'm stunned. He's saying no. No to the opportunity of being on TV. No to the opportunity of seducing an ex. No to *me*.

'Because you are undermining everything I hold dear. Love, marriage, fidelity, constancy. I can't do it.'

I'm amazed. A man who owns up to feeling these things must be gay. But I know he's not. I mentally shake myself. Fuck. Twat. I haven't got time for this. I'm busy. I don't need some half-average-looking bloke, who has too high an opinion of himself, screwing things up for me now. I glare at him. I breathe deeply.

'But Darren, why not? Marcus wants this,' I say reasonably.

'Then Marcus is wrong.'

'He wants to test her.'

'He'd do better to trust her.'

'You're joking, right?'

'Deadly serious.'

I check my watch. I have to speed this along. I still have the other guests to meet. First interview of the New Year and I run into a hitch immediately. If I were the superstitious kind, I'd think it was an omen. But I'm not.

'Look, Darren, is this a question of money? You see we can't offer our guests hard cash, our lawyers won't let us. But we can make this worth your while in expenses. Clothes, travel, entertainment, etc.' I mentally calculate what I can up the budget to. We normally expect an outlay of up to £600 per guest.

'It's nothing to do with money.' Darren rests his head in his hands and leans back against the sofa.

'We can go up to eight hundred pounds.'

'I just think it's ignoble.'

'Fifteen hundred.'

He shakes his head fractionally. And casually crosses his legs. They are extremely long. I take a deep breath.

'Two thousand.'

He doesn't acknowledge my offer. I make a quick calculation. This man is extremely intelligent, sensitive, stunningly good-looking. Even I, *fleetingly,* had found him attractive. Until he started arsing around like this. Now I realize he's a wanker. But, generally, people aren't as perceptive as I am. Audiences will like him. Bale will love him. How much?

'Four thousand pounds.' I hear Fi gasp. Darren smiles pleasantly, too astute to be insulted. He looks extremely confident. He shakes his head. I lean close to him. My mouth is only inches away from his ear.

'It's my final offer,' I whisper. He smiles. I look closer. He's resolute. Damn.

'Big prick,' I comment to Fi, as I charge out of the room. I don't even check if the door has banged shut behind me.

'Almost certainly has,' she comments.

I glare at her. 'I wasn't commenting on his equipment,' I snarl. 'More his manner.'

'I thought he was utterly charming,' she confesses, blushing.

I sigh, irritated. 'What exactly is charming about fucking up our shooting schedule?' I rage. 'Do you think Bale will be charmed?'

'Guess not.'

I begin to charge down the corridor towards the other interview rooms. We are on an extremely tight schedule. We've moved *Sex with an Ex* from the Monday slot to Saturday, which has cranked up the pressure by one more near infeasible notch. We have to complete the interviews tonight. For both liaisons, pre and post advertisements break. We have to choose the location for the temptation scene. Tomorrow we have to arrange all the logistics for all the parties in each liaison. Film on Wednesday and Thursday and then edit on Friday. The entire team regularly work at the weekends. I don't need spanners in works. I don't have time for mistakes, misgivings or misjudgements.

'So who do we have on reserve? Give me the briefing notes.' I hold out my hand waiting for the relevant file.

'Err.' Fi looks a bit shamefaced. 'We haven't one.'

I stop abruptly. 'What?'

'We did have. But we don't now. Mr P. Kent marrying a Ms L. Gripton were in reserve but he called the wedding off. I actually think he was using the show as a way to get rid of her. But he found the courage to do it without us.' Fi smiles brightly and I consider murdering her. I don't have time. When did she become stupid?

'How fabulous for him. What a shame for Ms Gripton and what a bloody disaster for us.' I'm not shouting. I'm too angry to shout. 'We always have two reserve options. Who are the others?'

'Well, there's a bit of a problem there too,' mumbles Fi. 'The bride-to-be broke her leg. She's unlikely to try to conduct an illicit liaison when she's in a toe-to-hip cast.'

'Such bad luck,' I snarl.

'Isn't it? The wedding photos will be ruined.'

'I mean ours. Fi, go back to your office and paw over every letter we've received. See if there is anyone who we can reach tonight. Who's on next week's show? Is there a case we can bring forward? Leave no stone unturned. If you can't find anyone in the letters pile, go on the Internet and set up an emergency telephone line; run it tonight.' Fi starts to dash down the corridor. I call after her, 'Fi, do you know anyone who's engaged? Check your Filofax. I'll check mine.' Fi starts to object. I sweep away her squeamishness. 'This is important.'

I check my watch. It's 6.30 p.m. I bleep for the *Sex with an Ex* runner. I know it will take some time to locate Trixxie because our policy for employing runners is another one of Bale's economy-driven strategies. Instead of recognizing that the runner on a show is a lynchpin and needs to be astute, willing, energetic and proactive, TV6 employs the defective offspring of our big advertisers. More proof that Bale is a sycophantic stinge. He gets to suck the cock of his most important clients and at the same time is able to pay below the minimum wage, in the knowledge that Daddy will supplement with an allowance. I wait nine and a half minutes for

Trixxie to respond to my page. She is undoubtedly doing something really pressing, like smoking hash or fixing her make-up or choosing the correct piece of metal to put in her eyebrow. When she eventually does show, I realize that 'respond' is probably too kind a description.

'Like can I do something?' she asks with a tone that is somewhere between careless and gormless. She is in reality about twenty-two but looks about six, as she is anorexic-thin, wears her hair in bunchies and has a number of bruises on her legs. The bruises are not, however, the result of playground bullying but UBIs – unidentified beer injuries. Unrestrained partying is part of the job. In fact, she thinks it is the job. She's paid a pittance but she's worth less. I tell her to go directly to Darren and delay him.

'Delay him?' she drawls. Redefining the adjective non-comprehending.

'Yes. He wants to leave.'

'But he can't, he's filming this week and whatever.'

'He doesn't want to film,' I explain with what absolutely must be my last ounce of patience.

'That's bad.'

I sigh, far too aware that incompetents surround me. Trixxie stumbles on an obstacle. 'I can't force him to stay against his will or whatever.'

'I know that. You have to persuade him to stay by making it worth his while.'

'Sleeping with him?' she asks.

I look at the specimen in front of me. Darren wouldn't. I think on my feet. I need Darren on the show. He'd make a great show and more urgently, because of Fi's incompetence in securing a reserve, he's our only chance at any show. I have to keep this lead, as tenuous as it is, warm until we've explored all other angles.

'No, don't offer to sleep with him. Appeal to his better side. Say that I'm cool with his decision and would like to take him to dinner later, to show there's no hard feelings etc.' I'm sure he'll agree to dinner. He's too polite not to.

'That's big of you,' says Trixxie, beaming at me. 'Really cool. Like you could be pissed off and whatever.'

I don't bother explaining that in reality I'd like to dissect Darren into small pieces and feed him to the lions at London Zoo for inconveniencing me so. I don't think Trixxie is up to the deception. In fact, I'm not sure she is up to delivering the message. And there's something else that I don't mention. As irritating as I obviously find Darren, I'm also absolutely fascinated. He said *no* to me. He said no to *me*. Not the type of no which really means 'yes' or 'maybe'. A flat, final no. Try as I might, I can't think of him as the moralistic tosspot loser that he so obviously is.

I interview the two women involved in the other liaison for next week's show. It calms me somewhat. I predict that the guy being tested will fall. I always think that there is a better chance of unfaithfulness if the men are being tested. It's not that women are fundamentally more faithful, it's just that women are more involved in the wedding preparations and are less likely to jeopardize their big day. I check my watch. It's 8.15 p.m. I call Fi and as I feared she's not hopeful about finding a reserve at such short notice. I threaten, cajole and bribe her into working through the night. I tell her to use the overtime quota and call in any reserves from the research department that she thinks are necessary.

'And what are you going to do?' she asks.

'I'm going to take Darren for dinner.'

There's a silence. Eventually she comments, 'Tough work, but someone's got to do it.'

'It really is work,' I insist. 'I expect he's going to be fabulously dull.' I'd like to mean this but my groin obviously disagrees, as my knickers think it's 5 November. 'I don't want to spend any more time with him than I have to, but we *do* need a show,' I insist. 'I'm going to persuade him to see our point of view.'

'Well, I could go instead of you,' volunteers Fi, with an enthusiasm that has been notably lacking in the past.

'You are not manipulative enough. You'd want to sleep with him.'

'So do you.'

'But you'd fall for him emotionally. I never do that.' She can't argue with this. I continue, 'We need to understand where he's coming from. He doesn't want to do the show because he realizes that his actions will have consequences, people will be hurt and humiliated. Irritating as hell. I think all we can do is try to appeal to his disproportionate and displaced sense of decency. I'm going to explain how a programme affects more than the people on the show; advertisers will be inconvenienced, audiences will be disappointed and you and I will lose our jobs.' I hope it won't come to this but Bale is unpredictable. My head aches. I squeeze my temples.

I'm desperate to see Darren again.

But only because I need a show. I think his moralistic approach is misplaced.

Quite attractive.

Bloody irritating.

'Fi?'

'Yes.'

'What should I wear?'

We arrange to meet at the Oxo tower. Trixxie has booked the restaurant rather than the brasserie. Good work. He can't fail to be impressed by the spongy leather tub chairs, the complicated wine list, the blue-white linen tablecloths, the huge, elegant wine goblets which are designed so that even Ten-ton Tessie would feel delicately petite – or maybe that's an exclusively girl thing.

I arrive before him. I survey the restaurant. It is 9.00 p.m. and the restaurant is full of people cheerfully initiating voyages of the heart. By 2.00 a.m. the streets will be littered with the grieving casualties. This is true of every restaurant in London. I am wearing a black roll-neck jumper and an on-the-knee black wool skirt. Heavy biker boots that are so chunky my legs look matchstick-thin. I have a hunch that this is more Darren's cup of Typhoo than low necklines and high hem-lines. This is currently my sexiest outfit, albeit understated sexy. I keep it in the office, if not for this exact occasion, then certainly for something similar. Issue is I'm not sure what the exact nature of this occasion is. I'm clear that I want him in line, on board, part of the family. I do need a show.

But.

Or rather and. And, whilst I'm not sure *why*, I am sure *that* I want to see him again.

I see him arrive and I'm gratified to notice he's changed clothes too. He's wearing a light grey suit and a wide-collar, open, white shirt. It shows off his olive skin brilliantly. He looks gorgeous. He walks confidently to my table and leans in to kiss me.

Kiss me.

On the cheek.

I nearly knock over the bottle of mineral water that I've ordered, which by anyone's standards would be uncool. His kiss scorches my face. I'm sure I'm branded like an animal. It takes every ounce of courage, sense and control I have to stop myself snogging him on the spot. I feel an overwhelming pull internally. It starts in my thighs and moves upward, enveloping my lungs, intestines and throat. What is wrong with me? I have experienced sexual attraction before. Keen sexual attraction, but this . . . This is something new.

I'm not threatened.

I know I'm cool as long as he's either tediously dull or arrogant.

I already know he's neither.

He sits down and smiles at the waitress. I notice that she nearly keels over on the spot. He orders the wine, giving me a cursory opportunity to offer up a preference, but he has taken control.

'I'm really pleased that you suggested this dinner, Cas. And somewhat surprised. I didn't expect you to take my views so well. Anyway your "runner"' – he manages to say the term using inverted commas, which is exactly how I describe Trixxie – 'your runner informed me that you'd like to take me for dinner. Well, that's daft. I'm very aware that I must have inconvenienced you and I insist this is my treat.'

'But I can get this on expenses,' I offer weakly. My being weak surprises me. I rarely am. In fact, the last recorded example of my being weak was pre-toilet training. But Darren is breaking all the rules. He's not overwhelmed or intimidated by me, nor is he excessively combative. Every other man I've ever met has fallen into one of these categories.

'I know that but, really, I'd hate to profit from your show in any way and' – he pauses and raises one of his eyebrows – 'I'd really like to buy you dinner.' He has a soft, velvet voice, so I have to lean close to him to hear him. As I lean close I note that he smells amazing. If I hadn't met him in these circumstances I'd think of fucking him.

No. I wouldn't have to think.

But the thought is irrelevant, as the business I have to

concentrate on is not funny business. It's not funny at all. I have four days to get the next show in the can.

I think he's wearing Issey Miyake.

I am extremely aware that the balance of power is definitely not in my favour. I remind myself again: the primary reason for my being here is that I must persuade him to be on the show. And even if he is drop-dead gorgeous, so what?

He's drop-dead gorgeous, that's what.

I stare at the menu, pretending to be interested; a toss-up between wood-roasted squid stuffed with chilli, or red mullet in white wine, parsley and garlic sauce. No, not garlic. Really I need to broach the subject of the show.

'Why would you want to buy me dinner?'

He blushes and then drags his eyes to meet mine. 'Any man would want to take you for dinner. You're stunning.'

Bang.

I am delighted, thrilled to my core. Yes, I've heard it before. Yes, I'll hear it again but really it's never been quite so thrilling. Or terrifying. His up-front approach propels me into a unique position. I'm honest in return.

'Look, Darren. Cards on the table, I'm not here to be social. I'm here to try to persuade you to be on the show. I need you. I'm embarrassed to admit it but I need a show and you're it.' I stop and take a deep breath. The bread arrives. He doesn't comment for a while. Instead he chooses his bread. He selects the walnut one. In an effort to ingratiate myself I do the same.

'I'm sorry you didn't want to have dinner with me.'

'I didn't say—'

'I'm not going to be on your show.'

'Why not?'

'Because I couldn't face myself in the mirror every morning if I did so. Myself or my parents or siblings, friends, nieces, nephew.'

No girlfriend. He didn't mention a girlfriend.

'Why not?'

'Because you are peddling the destabilization of family values.'

I sigh. I've heard it all before. Somehow the general public has convinced itself that TV is responsible for the disintegration of the family unit. It's a way of avoiding responsibility. It's not fair.

'The family unit is under pressure for myriad reasons. Television is only one,' I argue. 'There have been countless surveys that have tried to assess the effect television has on modern society but net net, bottom line, psychologists, educationalists and moralists have failed to agree that there has been *any* effect at all. How can you expect little old me to have all the answers?' I'm trying to appear girlish and agreeable.

'You are endorsing the gradual deconstruction of decency. You are encouraging the trivialization of love and sex.' He butters his bread ferociously. He has magnificent hands. Very strong-looking. I reach for my wine.

'Darren, no one needed me to do that. There were Blackpool postcards long before TV.'

'So you accept your show is in poor taste, indecent and a contributor to the erosion of public standards?'

The waitress interrupts to take our order.

'Taste is arbitrary, it changes according to fashion. Good taste is revised with every issue of *Vogue*. Decency I understand – a regard for cultural and religious issues, i.e. sending sympathy cards when some old dear pops her Patrick Cox.' I fall back on familiar territory, sarcasm. 'But standards, are they somewhere between the two? Like giving up your seat to a pregnant woman when travelling by tube, or more emphatically not travelling on public transport at all. And who is the standard setter? The law? The Independent Television

Commission? The public? You? Are you the judge and jury in this, Darren?' I'm raising my voice. He's got me riled. The seating is tight; there's no room for hysteria. I lower my voice in an effort to regain control. 'I've always avoided racism. I don't patronize people with disabilities. There's no violence, we beep out the bad language and we don't show actual penetration.'

'How magnanimous of you.'

I'm not sure he means this. I take a deep breath. This conversation is not going in the direction I expected. It's wrong by about 180 degrees, and Issie isn't even navigating. I had planned to be beguiling, flirtatious and coquettish. This is usually a successful ruse. Instead I'm behaving like Attila the Hun's more ferocious big sister. More peculiar still, I actually do want this man to see my point of view. Not simply to get him on the show: suddenly I want him to respect me. Wanting his respect makes it impossible to flirt. How much have I drunk? We both take a break as we sip our wine. It's a '96 Puligny-Montrachet. It's very fine.

'Nice wine, good choice,' I comment.

'Thank you.' Darren is not going to be side-tracked. He pursues his line of reasoning. 'TV has exercised an unanticipated and unprecedented influence. Not since the invention of the wheel has anything been so transforming.'

Someone's dropped an Alka Seltzer in my knickers. Although I don't like his argument I am delighted that he sees the importance of TV. So few people do and as I'm passionate about it, I'm thrilled to find someone else who has an opinion, even if it is so condemning. I'm also ecstatic to be debating with him. The sparks, intellectual, emotional and sexual, are all but visible. Darren stares right at me; his divine eyes lock on mine so tightly that I can't, however hard I try, break his gaze.

'You must see how influential TV is, and therefore what a responsibility you hold. Your programmes articulate the world we live in. You're saying that deception is OK, infidelity par for the course.'

We sit, sulky and silent. Listening to the clink of bottles and cutlery, and the hum of indistinguishable voices. Indistinguishable, that is, except for the table next to ours, where I can definitely hear the nervous pleas of a guy who is being ditched. The waitress brings our food. I sip my soup, carrot and coriander. It's not particularly a favourite of mine but it was top of the menu and I didn't have time to think about my selection. He is chasing skinny bits of courgette around his plate. He doesn't seem much interested in his food either. The silence is thunderous.

'So what else do you do, Cas?'

The sudden change of conversation throws me. Else? Else? Er. I'm too exhausted to think of anything creative, flirty or interesting so I plummet for the truth.

'My friends Issie and Josh, the gym and men. Oh, and my mum – on a Sunday.'

Darren laughs. 'So nothing conventional like stamp collecting or mud wrestling then?'

I smile. 'I've tried mud wrestling.'

He laughs again. 'Tell me about the men, Cas.'

There is another tiny pulse in my groin. Is he flirting with me?

Please.

'Men fall into three categories for me. Those I'd sleep with. Those I wouldn't and Josh.'

'So who wouldn't you sleep with?'

He is flirting!

Or maybe he's just trying to get a handle.

Why don't I know? I always know men.

'My friends' boyfriends and husbands, ugly or stupid men, and men I've already slept with.' He moves his fork fractionally, indicating that he is interested and that I should carry on. 'My friends' boyfriends are safe because, despite the world being awash with infidelity and deceit, I don't do that to my friends.' This is true and the nearest I have to a moral code. 'Besides which they just aren't appealing.'

He raises an eyebrow again. Which is such a cliché and, regrettably, soooooo sexy.

'I'm not saying anyone who would go out with my mates must be unattractive, far from it. It's just that my friends and I tell each other *everything*. By the time I know about their boyfriends picking their toenails, the filthy tricks they get up to with loo brushes, the farting in bed then going under the sheets to smell it, they just aren't sexy.' He's grinning. I'm being serious. 'Intimacy breeds revulsion. The reason for not sleeping with ugly or stupid men is transparent. Men I've slept with have no allure for me. I rarely do repeat performances.' I pause.

I wonder if he's noticed that, by definition, he is a man I'd sleep with?

'You seem to have it all worked out.' I nod. Which causes his grin to broaden into a smile. Is he being ironic? 'Can I ask you something?'

'Ask away and then I'll decide if I'll answer.' In my experience, the questions people ask are just as telling as the answers they give.

'Have you been unlucky in love, as they say?' He blushes. 'I mean, I only ask because I was wondering why you have such a mercenary attitude towards love.'

I choose not to take offence.

'Of course I've been unlucky in love. If you meet a woman who hasn't been unlucky in love, look for the little electronic chip behind her ear.' I always use this line. I grin and fork a mound of food into my mouth. I wonder if he's the type of man who finds a voracious appetite on a woman a turn-on?

'So who was he?' Same old question that all men ask. I have an answer rehearsed.

'Er, my first lover,' I bluff. I pause with my fork halfway between my mouth and plate.

The implication is that the memory is so painful that momentarily I can't eat. Men like to think women are too sensitive to ever fully recover from a broken heart. It fits in with their view of us as delicate flowers.

'Was it a long-term relationship?'

These incessant questions. I hesitate. 'A couple of weeks.'

'A couple of weeks.' His tone is somewhere between incredibility and hilarity. That's not the script. He's supposed to be touched by the intensity of the affair. 'But you said your first lover.' He seems confused. 'That must have been—'

'A long time ago. Yes. I don't get over things easily. I'm very sensitive.'

He stares at me. We've only just met but we both know how untrue this is. Darren's too polite to openly refute my statement.

'But you can't still be getting over an affair that took place over a decade ago and only lasted a few weeks.'

Good point. First time it's ever been made, which goes to show that the scores of other men who I've said the same to weren't paying attention.

'What *really* hurt you?'

This is unique and I haven't got a practised answer to hand. I look at Darren and his face surprises me even more than his original line of questioning. He seems genuinely concerned. I'm genuinely perplexed. I mean, what can I say? 'My first lover irritated me but frankly my heart hasn't ever been broken. I'm just a bitch.' It seems an unlikely solution. After all, it is the truth. He tilts his head a fraction in my direction. He's astonishingly close. His long hair is falling in front of his eyes and, although not quite touching my skin, it is touching the hairs on my forehead. There is acid in my knickers. My throat is dry and my breasts are straining upwards, obviously hoping he'll swoop down and kiss them. Hello, sexual tension. I shake my head.

'Hmmm?' he prompts.

'What?' My mind has undergone a spring clean and I can't remember what he asked me. His eyes are fabulous. Brown. A cluster of really rich browns, like autumn leaves piled up under a tree. Suddenly Darren appears embarrassed.

'Sorry, I shouldn't have asked that. Erm—' He scrambles around for a recovery conversation. 'Tell me about Josh.'

I'm grateful that he's let me off the hook and garble, 'Josh is my only male, platonic friend. I've known him since we were kids. He has too much dirt on me to risk me falling out with him. He could sell to the press when I'm rich and famous.'

'Is that your ambition, to be famous?'

'Isn't it everyone's? Frankly I'm confident that Josh wouldn't do that. Despite all odds, tantrums, time and the tenuous nature of platonic love, Josh and I adore each other. We trust each other and would never hurt one another.' I pause and consider what I've just said. 'Perhaps this is *because* of all the tantrums, time and the tenuous nature of platonic love.' I grin at Darren. Suddenly I'm overwhelmed with embarrassment. Why am I saying this? I'm telling him about myself. I'm being truthful and straightforward. What has possessed me? I hate people knowing more about me than I know about them. I *never* do this. I try to hide the sudden intimacy in humour. 'Besides which, I have an incriminating photo of him dressed in suspenders and a basque. He claims this was for a *Rocky Horror Show* party but I'm not convinced.'

Darren laughs.

The conversation is snappy, intense and truthful. I'm overwhelmed. Darren and I have finished a bottle of wine. We are, in fact, halfway through our second bottle. We drift from topic to topic. My clipboard detailed that he's a tree surgeon, which apparently means that he is based at London University, where he has an office and a lab but he travels to, well, wherever there is a sick tree by the sound of it. This is at once strange – as it is so individual – and at the same time expected. It's extremely fitting; I sort of imagine him working outdoors and with his hands. This connection throws me into confusion, as I have images of rolling around a park with him. I see myself picking leaves out of my hair and twigs from my ruffled clothes. Of course he has no idea what I'm thinking but the way he stares at me suggests that he is privy to my X-rated daydream. I struggle to think of anything suitable to say.

'I've never known a tree surgeon.'

He laughs again. I guess that isn't my best line ever. I try another. 'Fantastic view of the river from here, isn't there?'

'This is one of my favourite buildings in London, actually,' agrees Darren.

'Really.' Bullseye.

'Yeah, the view is amazing, as you said, and I like the brickwork.'

'You said *one* of your favourite buildings. Which others do you like?' As if I care.

'My favourite, by some way, is the Natural History Museum, I like everything about it. How and why it was conceived. The structure, the brickwork, the lighting, the contents, the concept.' How can anyone be this animated by a building full of stuff? Not even stuff you can buy.

'What's your favourite building?' he asks.

'I haven't thought about it before. I don't think anyone's ever asked me.' I consider it for a moment. 'Bibendum. You know, the restaurant in South Kensington.'

'Why?'

I could tell him that I adore the stained-glass windows and the unusual tiling that François Espinasse designed in 1911, but I don't want him to get the impression that I'm anything other than shallow.

'It's kind of a Golden Gate. It heralds the entrance to shop heaven – Joseph, Paul Smith and Conran. Besides which they sell fabulous oysters.' I smile coolly and he laughs again.

The evening flies by and I am keenly aware that I haven't really talked about getting him to appear on the show. Which is careless of me – I rarely diversify from my agenda. I drag myself back to the point.

'So why did you and Claire split up?'

Frankly I'm confused. He's clever, handsome and filthily sexy. I only have Marcus's statement, which is an unreliable source. Marcus will have received a sanitized version of events from Claire, which he'll have distorted in his head with neurotic paranoia. If I can get Darren to reveal the reason why he and Claire split up, I'll be able to manipulate the facts to justify why he should go on the show.

Besides which I'm interested.

'We were a casualty of cohabitation.'

'What do you mean?'

'What's your phrase? Intimacy breeds revulsion. Well, in our case it certainly bred irritation. We liked one another, even loved one another well enough before we moved in together, and then it started. The rot set in.'

'What, you started to take each other for granted? Became complacent?'

'Nothing as dramatic. She didn't like the way I kept film in the fridge. I hated the way her beauty product things seemed to be procreating all over the dressing table. She hated Sky Sport.'

I gasp, shocked.

'I loathe soaps.'

I'm horrified. What that girl must have put up with.

'I like to read in bed. She likes the light out immediately. And then it escalated. She began to hate my friends. I hated her hairs in the bath. She, my laugh. Me, her mother. I'd forgotten all this until I talked to Marcus earlier today. He said she was shopping. I knew that she'd be buying Easter eggs although it's only January. Her organization was always horribly efficient. I hated it. There was no spontaneity. The truth is, we split up because we weren't suited. We're not together because it didn't work and we shouldn't be together. Why else do people ever split up? It's so easy to look back on a past relationship and idealize it.'

Thank God. This is the whole premiss of my programme.

'I've never met anyone as right as Claire was for me but it still doesn't alter the fact that she wasn't 100 per cent right.'

'90 per cent is pretty good.'

'She wasn't even that.'

'85 per cent,' I suggest.

'Nearer 65 per cent.' There is an unaccountable warm glow of delight in my stomach. He's right, 65 per cent doesn't sound like the One.

If you believe in the One.

Which I don't.

'So you are really over her?' I'm disproportionately anxious to hear his reply. Which I hate myself for.

'Yes.'

'Then what harm can there be in appearing on the show? Can't you just tempt her and leave it at that?'

Darren forces his mouth into a wry grin. Does he think I'm joking?

'You just don't get it, do you, Cas? Your show's a travesty. Besides which, I loved her once. Why would I want to hurt her? I doubt she'd be tempted by me—'

'I think she would,' I interrupt enthusiastically.

'Thank you.' Darren's face relaxes into the widest smile I've seen all evening. Ever, in fact.

Arrogant bugger!

'I didn't mean it as a compliment,' I mutter sulkily into my plate. Unperturbed, his smile widens an unfeasible fraction further.

'I'll take it as one anyway.'

I scowl but try to appear unflustered by playing with the stem of my wine glass, caressing it as though it were a brand new pashmino. 'Well, if you are convinced that Claire wouldn't fall, the programme might be good for her and Marcus. We did have one couple, before Christmas, who managed to resist.'

'Yes, I read about that. TV6 turned their wedding into a media frenzy,' says Darren with obvious disgust. 'That must have been marvellous for the ratings. Cas, haven't you been listening to me? It's not about whether she would want me or not. Any association with *Sex with an Ex* is contemptible. A need to "test" someone you should love exposes the fact that there is a problem with the relationship. I don't want to embarrass Claire or anyone else for that matter. I don't want her to know that her fiancé has this insecurity. I don't want to drag up our past, not even to entertain your – what did you say? – 8.9 million viewers.' I nod. 'I loved her and that fact is still important and private.'

He believes all this. I look at him, this six-foot-two specimen of pure sex, sitting in front of me. I don't understand him. He seems to be from another era. One that is perhaps a little more genteel. And trusting.

And pointless.

I try to think about my initial strategy.

'Look, Darren, this show isn't just about entertaining the general public. There are a lot of other serious issues hanging in the balance here.'

'Such as?'

'My job, the jobs of about thirty-five other people, advertising revenues.'

'I'm sorry.' Darren calls the waitress and asks for the bill. It's time to go. I'm disappointed. The restaurant may be empty but I don't want to leave. I try to think of something else that will be damaged if the show doesn't go ahead. There's my ratings-related bonus. I don't think it's wise to mention this. I sigh, resigned. The quiet determined way he explains his views convinces me that he won't change his mind tonight. I suppose it does sort of make sense in a horribly moral way. Never again will I attempt getting a thinking man on the show. I'll stick to Neanderthals.

We leave the restaurant and start to wander back to the tube, past the National Theatre, the Royal Festival Hall, the Hayward Gallery, the Queen Elizabeth Hall. Although it is January my shirt is sticking to my back with sweat. I hope I'm not coming down with flu. Couples are edging up to one another, the foolish myth of intimacy protecting them against the late-night chill that is settling. And it must be chilly because the people who are on their own pull their coats about them. My bag weighs a ton. It's full of my life: notebooks, Dictaphones, research manuals, schedules. The weight of it drags my shoulder down to the right, causing me to lean. I occasionally bump into Darren. Each time I do so I tut so that he, at least, is clear that it's an accidental collision and I don't like it.

My senses are on red alert. I can feel the cold night air not brushing my skin but laying icy hands on my forehead and shoulders. I hear a train rattle across Charing Cross bridge, splitting the night. Sparkly lights outline the bridges and pavements. An adult dot to dot. There is metal on my tongue. I can smell sweat, fresh and stuff that's months old. The fresh twang is mingled with Darren's aftershave. It rinses my nostrils. I tut at the dreamers hanging around the National Film Theatre, lost in nostalgia or stupefied with pointless hope.

'Look at them,' I spit. 'Incapable of getting off their arses and doing something real.'

Darren surprises me by laughing. 'Is that all you see?'

'Yes.' I look at the jugglers and pseudo-intellectuals. People happier to watch plays about other people's lives than actually live their own. 'What else is there?'

'Look again,' he insists. He puts both hands on my shoulders and turns me to look at the crowds. 'You have to look at everything from as many different angles as possible. In as many ways as possible. Look at it and try to see it differently.'

I look again and see scores of people hanging out. Some are drinking coffee sold from the cafés at the theatres. Others are standing around the buskers. Others are debating with one another or chatting animatedly about the performance they have just seen. Others are snogging the face off each other. I shrug.

'Don't you see dozens of people having a good time, improving and enjoying themselves? A mass of humanity buzzing with just being here.'

'No.'

'Again. Look closer,' he insists.

There is one old guy playing a violin. He's ancient; he has a long, white beard. He is playing Vivaldi's 'Spring'. He skips lightly through the air, barely landing before rising again, his skinny limbs tapering in effortless rhythm. Grudgingly I throw some coins into his battered Panama. He is talented. He moves his head in a slight dip, more dignified than a bow. Darren smiles at me. I smile back.

We cross over the river and reach Embankment tube station. It's heaving. A burly mass of drunks in suits and drunks in rags. Distinguishable simply by their disposable incomes. Darren fights, through the morons and marauders, to the ticket machine. He buys our tickets. Mine for east London, his for south. We're on separate lines and going in separate directions.

'Will you be OK getting home?'

'Fine. I'm a tube veteran.' This is a lie. I usually catch a cab but if I say so I'll have to explain why I've just walked half a mile to the tube station. Which I can't explain, not even to myself.

'Well, it's been great to meet you, Cas. A very entertaining evening.' Darren stops and turns to face me.

'I bet you've hated every second.'

'Not at all.' He hesitates, then adds, 'The reverse.'

I smile broadly, relieved. 'Well, goodnight.'

'Goodnight.' Neither of us moves. Suddenly this feels very date-like. Will he kiss me? Is he going to shake my hand? He leans in and I think he's going to kiss my cheek so I move my head suddenly. In fact, it appears his original target was my lips but my sudden manœuvre means that his smacker ends up somewhere between my chin and earring. We jump apart and Darren heads towards the ticket barrier. It's certain. He's going to walk out of my life and back to his trees.

And right now I can't think of anything more soul-destroying.

My reluctance over letting him go *must* be attributable to the amount of wine I've drunk. Isn't it? God, I really fear it's more than that.

'Darren!' My yell slices through the crowds and almost as though he'd been waiting, Darren responds immediately by turning and walking straight back to me. I usher him away from the tube-station crowds, back towards the river. I'm buying time as I formulate a plan.

'At the very least I have to be *seen* to have done everything in my power to persuade you to come on the show.'

'You have,' he assures.

'Not everything.'

Darren looks a bit shocked. 'Are you going to—'

I read his mind. 'No. Not that,' I interrupt, understanding at once that he thinks I am going to offer to have sex with him. I'm unaccountably insulted. Darren blushes.

'That's a relief.' Then he blushes again. 'Not that I wouldn't want to, but the circumstances are—'

I help us both out by interrupting him. Before I've even thought about what I'm going to say, or why I'm saying it, or the consequences of opening my mouth at all, habitual bullshitting kicks in.

'No, my proposition is of a different nature. I'd like to be given the chance to present my side of the story. To do that I'd need to spend some time with you. I'd need to shadow you for a day or so.' It's a gamble but I'm a player. He looks at me doubtfully.

'You won't change my mind.'

'Maybe not, but at least give me the opportunity to appear to have done my best. It will save my bacon with the guys at TV6.'

This isn't true. In fact, what I should do now is return to the studio and help Fi recruit a replacement scenario.

But after spending the evening with him I know that if he were to appear on *Sex with an Ex*, it would be the best show ever. He's delicious-looking, articulate, sexy and moral. If I could publicize his objections and how we overcame them, the entire country would support *Sex with an Ex*. There have been some objections to the show. Few and far between, and in my opinion mostly hypocritical. But those who are squeamish about weddings collapsing like stacked cards would surely throw their lot in with TV6 if someone like Darren has. Who could resist Darren? And although I can't be sure that he will be persuaded I've got to give it my best shot.

I begin to mentally rearrange my schedule and calculate how much Fi will be able to handle on her own if I'm not in the studio. At the same time that I'm making these hurried calculations, trying to predict scenarios, outcomes and consequences, Darren is leisurely weighing up the proposition, which he has taken at face value.

'I was taking the week off work, expecting to be on the show. Now I'm planning on going to see my parents and family.' With something near reluctance, he sighs, 'You won't change my mind but if it helps you out with your bosses, you can join me for a couple of days.'

'Great.' I smile. Agreeing before I know whether I mean it. 'So where do your parents live?'

'Whitby.'

'Where?'

He laughs, 'Whitby, you know, in North Yorkshire.' No, I don't know. It sounds a long way off. It sounds a different and uncivilized world. But the show must go on. How bad can it be? I nod and try to appear informed without committing myself.

'OK, Cas, I'm happy for you to shadow me, if that's the official term, but I think we'd both have a better time if you started to trust me and enjoy yourself.'

I'm not here to enjoy myself and I don't do trust. I bite my tongue and resist pointing out either of these pertinent facts.

'Trust simply leads to disappointment,' I state frankly.

'Listen to yourself, Cas. You are not convincing anyone with this super-hard bitch act.'

He is very wrong. I've convinced eight primary school teachers, twelve senior school teachers, dozens of fellow students, scores of colleges, numerous girlfriends, exactly fifty-three lovers and my mother. Even Issie, painful as it is for her, admits from time to time, 'You can be so callous.' What is this obsession with being soft? Isn't it obviously asking for trouble? Asking to end up hurt, abused, alone? I like being impenetrable. I don't want to be discovered.

Darren pauses and stares out at the river. It's twinkling, which surprises me. I always think of the Thames as a rest point for crap and sanitary towels.

'You know what I think?'

'No, bowl me over,' I sigh.

'You just want to be discovered. You want someone to make the effort and scratch the surface. You want to be loved. You just want to make it difficult. A modern-day Agamemnon challenge. You are the same as every woman I've ever met.'

I didn't realize Darren could be so insulting.

I look at him and he is gorgeous. The streetlights are reflected in the river. The reflection bounces up to illuminate Darren. He looks like an angel. He smiles and he's mucky sexy. He looks like a devil. I've never come across anything so complex and compelling in my entire life. I realize that it's going to be more important than ever, and quite possibly harder than ever, to keep up my super-hard bitch act. And whilst my mind is resolving that I won't let my guard slip for a second, I hear my disloyal tongue say, 'Oh bugger it. Go on then, show me a good time. I don't suppose you'll be able to.' I grin my challenge. But even I don't believe me.

9

We meet at King's Cross station. I spot Darren as soon as the cab sets me down. He stands out like a beacon. But then that's not so extraordinary as he's sharing the platform with prostitutes, beggars and commuters. As I approach him he takes my bag from me and briefly kisses me on the cheek. It's comfortable. It's unnerving.

'You look good,' he murmurs, smiling appreciatively.

'What, this old thing?' I shrug.

'This old thing' was actually a look achieved after nine hours' searching through Issie's wardrobes and mine. I like the final effect. It's a sort of rock-chic-meets-country-girl ensemble. I think it works, although Issie had doubts. She had questioned whether a six-hundred-quid pony-skin skirt was appropriate for a dash around North Yorkshire. I ignored her advice; after all, she doesn't read the style pages. She also kept going on about how I'd be cold in a short-sleeved jumper. I explained that my upper arms were really toned at the moment and needed full exposure. She sighed and stuffed another cardigan in my bag. I'm grateful now because it is freezing on the platform.

Issie had been a bit irritating all round, whilst I packed for this tour of duty. She commented, 'North Yorkshire sounds very romantic. Isn't that where the Brontës are from?'

'Is it? I thought it was Lancashire. Didn't all the Brontës die spinsters?' I feigned ignorance. 'Besides which, we're going to visit his family. Have you ever known families to be romantic?'

Issie reminded me of the guy she met through her mother, on New Year's Eve. I reminded her that he never called. 'So why are you going to Whitby, if you think it's going to be so dour?'

'I explained, Issie, I have to get him to agree to be on the show. It's a matter of professional and personal pride.'

'Nothing more than pride?' I've been asking myself exactly the same thing all night.

'I've explained, he'd make a great show. He'd silence our few lingering critics.'

'Nothing more than a great show?' asked Issie. She didn't sound as though she believed me. I admit Darren is interesting and funny and ridiculously fanciable. I admit that if Issie were choosing to travel halfway across the globe to visit some guy's family I'd think it was because she'd fallen for him. But the same can't be said of me, can it? I'm only doing this for the good of TV6.

'What else is there?' I asked, slipping my Manolo Blahnik lilac open-toe shoes into my bag. I would have been extremely grateful if Issie could have answered me; however, she just scowled.

'It doesn't sound like you have the faintest chance of getting him to change his mind.'

'I don't know, I might have. After all, he agreed to let me shadow him.'

'Yes, I wonder why he did that. Does he fancy you? I expect he does.'

'More likely wants the opportunity to save my soul.'

'Oh lord. His chances are poorer than yours,' laughed Issie as she walked me to my waiting cab.

Yes, Issie was extremely irritating all round.

*

'I've bought your ticket. Come on, the train is in. Platform Three – we have to run,' urges Darren.

Despite the fact that we are travelling zillions of miles to (practically) Scotland, the timetable tells me that we will arrive in Darlington in two and a half hours' time. I'm incredulous, but Darren explains it's the electric line. I'm still incredulous. What about the obligatory leaves on the track and the right and wrong types of snow? My heart plummets. Even if by some miracle the train does arrive on time, two and a half hours is going to seem like ten and a half. What will I say to Darren? It was OK chatting in the restaurant last night, but I'd had a shedload to drink. But now, in the cold light of day, I'm beginning to regret volunteering to shadow him. I know my chances of persuading Darren to appear on *Sex with an Ex* are slim. I could be on a wild goose chase! What will I do with myself outside London? How will the studio manage without me? Will Bale buy my reasoning for shadowing Darren? Besides all this, sitting on a train with a moralistic do-gooder is not my idea of fun. Even a devilishly attractive one.

The train journey is awesome.

Besides buying the ticket, Darren also had the foresight to buy up half the magazines and sweets in WH Smith's. I can't remember the last time anyone bought me sweets. Big fancy boxes of chocolates, yes, I get those by the dozen. I just pass them on to my mum. She eats some and gives the other boxes to local geriatrics (cellulite not being a major concern of theirs). But Darren hasn't bought me chocolates in a box. Instead he's bought the sweets of our childhoods: Jelly Babies, Liquorice Allsorts, Flying Saucers and Sherbet Dib-dabs. Undoubtedly I'll feel sick by the time the journey is over. Even so, it's a good call. Instead of the slow and stilted conversation I feared, we have an unlimited avenue in discussing childhood. What were your favourite sweets as a kid? (He remembers Spangles, Space Dust and Cream Soda, he agrees that Snickers definitely used to be bigger and anyway they were Marathons.) What was the first book you read? (Neither of us is sure but, satisfyingly, he's clearer on his TV viewing habits; he recalls every episode of *Mr Ben* and swears his sister looked the image of the girl who sat with the clown when there was nothing on TV.) So what was your favourite TV programme? (We agree Mark from *EastEnders* will always be Tucker from *Grange Hill*.) When did you learn to swim? (He learned after seeing the advert with the fairy godmother. I learned after seeing *Jaws*.) And whilst I remember all this I completely forget to uphold my icy reserve. Trivia, but this and reading magazines together mean that the journey to Darlington flies past.

Reluctantly I acquiesce: he does a great line in small talk.

Grudgingly I have to admit that perhaps we do have some things in common.

But nothing fundamental.

I watch the landscapes change. The parks of the south melt into the woodlands of the Midlands, and in no time at all into the rugged, Gothic hills of the north. Although it's only mid-morning, the sky in North Yorkshire is mauve with damson clouds. Not the cottonwool clouds of textbooks but strong, imposing smudges, more like a painting a child would make with a thick brush. It's breathtakingly beautiful.

But then, once you've seen a scene, it's over with. It's not as though you can wear it.

I call Bale on my mobile to explain what I'm doing. It's a difficult call, as I have to make it from the minuscule British Rail loo, awash with urine and with a dodgy door lock designed to make occupants nervous.

'If we get him on the show I'd put money on the fact that

he'll be a pin-up within weeks and he'll have his own chat show within months,' I enthuse to Bale.

'That good, hey?'

'That good,' I assert.

'And do you think Fi will manage?'

I enthusiastically sing her praises to reassure him (it doesn't – he's understandably suspicious). He wavers, trying to decide whether any guest can be worth my absence. I sense his indecision, so dramatically turn up the charm. I promise I'll give it two days and travel back overnight on Tuesday in time for Wednesday's filming. In the meantime, I reassure, he can reach me on my mobile.

When we arrive at Darlington station Darren's brother, Richard, is waiting for us. Richard is younger than Darren by three years, but he's beefier (that will be the fish and chips and Yorkshire pudding) and so looks a bit older. Darren's filled me in with details of his family. There is Sarah, who is thirty-seven, married with three kids. Darren who is thirty-three, like me. Richard, thirty, he's engaged to Shelly and finally Linda, who was a bit of a surprise to Mr and Mrs Smith. She's seventeen now. Darren is the only one who has moved away from home. I must ask why. Richard and Shelly are buying a house a few streets away from her parents. Sarah and her family live in a nearby village. I commit all these details to memory in an effort to flatter him and ingratiate myself with his family.

The two men slap each other on the back and this action instantly makes them appear boyish, but in the very best sense. Whilst not obviously showing affection by embracing, it's clear that they are delighted to see each other.

'Richard, this is Cas.' Darren hesitates and then adds, 'A friend.' I'm strangely gratified to be described as such and therefore treat Richard to my most winning smile. Naturally he's enchanted and falls over himself to help me with my luggage. I catch Darren's eye; I want to know if he's noticed that I've impressed Richard. I can't be sure; he's laughing to himself.

I am keen to leave Darlington station behind. Not that there is anything particularly wrong with the station – it has everything one expects; small WH Smith, cookie-cut café and smelly loos – but it is a station and I try to avoid public transport whenever possible. However, I'm not thrilled when Richard indicates which is his car.

'The Escort?' I ask, hoping there's been a mistake.

'Yes. The one with the red door,' says Richard.

'And the blue body,' adds Darren in case the situation demanded any more clarity. I try not to show how disgruntled I am, but quietly climb into the back seat, which I share with furry dice (honestly) and an entire forestworth of sweet wrappers.

I don't say much in the car journey from Darlington to Whitby. Instead I let Darren and Richard catch up with each other's news. As an only child I'm always fascinated to see siblings' reactions to one another. Richard is obviously delighted that Darren has paid this surprise visit. I can't imagine that my arrival anywhere would be awash with such excitement. Except perhaps for Harvey Nics – my personal shopper is always blissed out when she sees me. When Richard asks Darren how he came to have unplanned holiday, I'm unaccountably relieved that Darren fudges the answer. I'm also mollified when Darren comments vaguely that we 'met at an interview'. Richard obviously feels bad that I'm not part of the conversation and tries to include me by sharing details of the route.

'We're on the A66, heading east. We could've come across the new road. They both join at A171 to Whitby.'

I'm not sure what response is required of me. This fascination with routes, alternative routes and 'the road we could have taken' is definitely a boy thing. I nod, not committing, and turn to gaze out of the window.

I'm in a foreign land. Not least because of Richard's accent but also because of the strangeness of the landscape. It's an eclectic mix of the very modern (brand-new and impressive football stadiums, architecturally complex bridges), quaint, old-fashioned poverty (bingo halls and boarded-up shops) and stunning countryside (sheep). I notice that the women standing at the bus stops, in each village, look alike. They are fat and tired – don't they ever work out? Richard's Escort pauses at a red light for a couple of minutes and I look more closely. A woman is waiting at the bus stop; another shouts to her from a fifty-yard distance. The first one makes the bus wait whilst the other heaves her excessive weight and carrier bags to the stop. The driver of the bus becomes animated and jovial and doesn't seem to be too irritated by the delay. As the woman hoists herself on to the bus all the other travellers shout and wave to her. Am I missing something? Is she famous? I don't recognize her. But she must be because why else would they be so nice to her? The warmth they so obviously feel for one another momentarily sends a freak glow through me.

Which is a bloody miracle, considering that the temperatures I'm enduring are arctic.

As in a wartime era, the men on the streets are either very young or very old. They are malnourished. On the young men, this looks chippy and sexy; on the old men, it looks pathetic. I try to remember some facts from my geography A-level and the news in the eighties. North Yorkshire wasn't a community annihilated by the closing of the mines, was it? No, definitely not. It was a community ravaged by the collapse of the ship-building industry. I wonder where the men of working age are. Have they got on their bikes? Or are they at the Cargo Fleet Social Club doing their best to support the Bass dynasty?

I sigh, bored, losing interest in my own line of thought. A new level of tedium. It must be this place. I light a cigarette. Richard stares at me through the driving mirror. So as not to be rude I wind the window down an inch, which I think is very considerate of me in these sub-zero climes.

'Would you mind not smoking?' asks Richard.

I shift uncomfortably and for a second I'm tempted to say that yes, I would mind very much. I have a thirty-a-day habit to feed. I have a metabolism to send into frenzy. Instead I smile, falsely, and throw the cigarette out of the window. Richard doesn't congratulate me or thank me but simply nods curtly. I'm surprised. I thought he fancied me. The lust men normally experience when meeting me is, if not a licence to print money, at least a certificate which exonerates me from obeying the no-smoking signs. What is it with these Smith blokes? Don't they have hormones?

The towns disappear and soon even the villages are spasmodic. The bleak warehouses and graffitied bus stops detailing that, despite the odds, 'JEZ LUVS BREND 4EVER', vanish and are replaced by wide open fields of mud, splashed with snow, ice and the odd farmhouse. The sky is still lavender but is now streaked with silver layers of light.

'I can see the sea,' shout Richard and Darren at once. Then they both laugh. 'It's sort of a family tradition,' explains Darren. 'Not a very unique one at that. I'm sure you know the thing.' I don't, but I follow their gaze anyway.

'It's beautiful,' I sigh, despite myself. And I immediately regret saying so. My city platitude hardly captures the breathtaking splendour of the scene and I do try to make it a rule not to say anything unless it is original or cutting, yet I'm at a loss for words that are grandiose enough. I catch sight of Darren's face in the wing mirror. He smiles at me as though he finds my lacklustre comment adequate.

'You don't think you'll be too bored, then?' he asks. Does he have a tent at a funfair to practise this mind-reading thing?

'No, I think I'll find enough to amuse me,' I answer honestly, with only a smidgen of flirtation.

Richard wiggles uncomfortably.

Whitby is higgledy-piggledy. Built on an undulating coastline, the houses and teashops (closed) look precariously stacked. We steer through narrow streets and climb steep slopes. I'm suddenly in a period drama. Eventually we draw up in front of a row of terraced street houses. I am sure they are going to fall into the sea if anyone coughs too loudly. Darren assures me that the houses are tougher than they look. As they've been in place for over a hundred years. I concede he's probably right; even so I make a mental note not to move too suddenly once inside. From the outside the house looks minute and I wonder how the Smiths managed to bring up four kids in something so small. Isn't property cheaper in the north? I consider passing this comment as a way of making conversation but decide against it. We don't go in the front door but slip up an alley-cum-path, which leads to the back door.

'Alleyways are called ghauts around here,' explains Darren, doing his psychic party trick again. I wish he'd stop that, it's freaky.

I realize that the house is in fact deceptively large as it stretches back in a seemingly endless row of rooms. Mrs Smith and Linda are waiting on the back step to greet us. Mrs Smith keeps yelling to 'Father' that Darren and his friend are here. Father turns out to be Mr Smith, her husband. He doesn't get up from his chair in the sitting room but waves cheerfully from where he's sitting. This is understandable; he's watching a repeat of *The Waltons* – pretty compelling viewing. Mrs Smith eyes me mistrustfully. I know from experience that women generally, and mothers specifically, are always wary of me. I also know from experience that if I want to ingratiate myself with Darren I have to make his mother like me. It's amusing that almost always the reverse is true of a man trying to impress a woman. My mother's approval is a grade A turn-off. Mrs Smith can't drag her eyes from my skirt and mutters something about her 'being sure it's all the rage' in London. Linda, by contrast, greets me in a manner with which I am much more accustomed – unadulterated praise and flattery. She loves my hair, likes my bag, adores my skirt and would die for my shoes. Her mother tuts impatiently but I answer all her questions about where I got everything and I let her touch the fabrics. Poor kid, she probably hasn't ever seen anyone dressed in anything other than a shellsuit before. I offer to take a B&B so as not to inconvenience Mrs Smith but she won't hear of it and in fact appears offended that I've suggested it. She says that Darren can share Richard's room and I can have Darren's old room. Linda enthusiastically offers to take me to it straight away and I agree. I haven't touched up my lipstick since I arrived at Darlington.

Linda is a delight to be with. Adoring me is obviously a point in her favour and she has all the advantages that youth can offer – buoyancy, an uncynical view of the world, hardly any wrinkles and an ability to be oblivious to the humiliation of slavishly following fashion. Besides, she – like Darren – has won the gene lottery jackpot. I much prefer to be surrounded by beautiful people. Linda has thick black curly hair that she wears shoulder-length. She has Darren's to-die-for eyes and

Bambi lashes and she's slim. Perhaps her most attractive feature is that she seems to have no idea how beautiful she really is. It's a shame she lives in the armpit of nowhere and won't ever be seen. In London she'd be a hit. She could get a job in media, modelling or working in the city, all of which require more than a pretty brain. Instead she'll be consigned to marrying young, raising a football team of children and counting her stretch marks. Blissfully unaware of her fate, she chatters vivaciously and non-stop as she guides me to Darren's room.

The house, like the county, is a diverse mix of ancient and modern. I spot a warehouseworth of electrical goods: three TVs, two videos, a computer, a number of computer games, radios, hi-fi systems and all white-good mod. cons. Yet the wallpaper and carpets must have been hung and laid before the war (and I'm talking Crimean). I take in endless brass wall hangings and crocheted doilies and make a mental note that next time we are producing a period piece the props department would do well to consider Mrs Smith as a source. Whilst the fixtures and fittings are old-fashioned and, frankly, ugly, they are immaculate. My mother could run her finger along any skirting board or wardrobe top and fail to find cause for concern.

At first I'd been embarrassed by Mrs Smith's insistence that I stay in their family home. I don't do family homes. I occasionally stay over at Josh's but his parents' houses (note the plural) are so big that there is never any danger of bumping into a parent on the stairwell. Anyway, you can't justifiably call Josh's places 'family homes'. His parents are only together in a nominal sense, negating the term family. And the term home. They both take advantage of the size and number of their abodes to avoid each other. If his mother is in the country, you can put money on his father being 'up in town';

if his father is in the country, his mother is ensconced in their Spanish villa. Married bliss. Yet despite my reservations about accepting Mrs Smith's invite I do have an inexplicable, but overwhelming, curiosity with regard to Darren and so I am delighted at the prospect of sleeping in his childhood bed. I casually try to establish if the room I am about to be shown has always been Darren's and Darren's alone. Linda assures me that it has: 'This room has seen everything from bed-wetting to' – she hesitates – 'well, bedwetting, I suppose.' Too much information.

She pushes open the heavy wooden door and we both struggle to get my (extremely large) case into the (extremely small) room. Like a lot of parents, Mrs Smith has lovingly preserved the shrine of her eldest son's childhood. I feel I've just been handed Darren's diary. The room is a thumbprint. There is a skinny, hard-looking bed pushed up to the wall under the window. It gives the impression that sleeping was a low priority for the youthful Darren. I can't help but wonder if the same still holds true. There's an ancient wardrobe and a small hi-fi/dressing-table unit. It's from MFI and I expect the twelve-year-old Darren demanded it as an act of rebellion against the fifties' bedroom suites. There are posters on the wall that I would expect in the room of any male who had grown up in the seventies and stagnated in the eighties. Original Star Trek, the A Team and Starsky and Hutch, then Debbie Harry and Pam Ewing. These are the only nods towards a conventional bedroom. The rest is an Aladdin's cave meets Treasure Island meets Batman's cave. There are zillions of books. They line the windowsill and countless shelves, and the overflows are piled in precarious, wavering, waist-high stacks around the walls of the room. There's everything from *Beano Annuals* to a Reader's Digest collection of Charles Dickens's work. His taste is wide but the thing that all the books have in common is that they are well thumbed. Lying on top of the books are a number of models that have obviously been made by a young Darren. I think his mother has arranged them in date order as the ones nearest to the door are childish (although charming in their naïvety) – rockets and submarines, made from loo rolls and cornflakes boxes. Then Darren must have introduced elastic bands and Dairylea tubs to make helicopters and combine harvesters. The models grow in complexity and size until finally, in the corner opposite the door, there is a massive Meccano model about three foot high and two wide.

'It's a replica of NASA,' explains Linda. She must realize that I'm none the wiser because she starts dropping small marbles into buckets, which turn a wheel, which activates a pump, which motivates an engine, which launches a rocket etc. It's fascinating and it's more complicated than *Mouse-Trap*.

'It must have taken him hours to build.'

'It did.'

'Didn't he have any friends?'

'Hundreds,' she grins cheerfully, oblivious to my implied insult. 'But he's always been fascinated by ecology and wider than that, the universe, and—'

'The reason we are here.' I can hardly keep the smirk out of my voice.

'Absolutely,' enthuses Linda. She reminds me of the Americans – they don't get sarcasm either.

She smiles at me expectantly and, unusually, I'm shamed. I'm forced to mutter, 'It's very good.' Which is honest enough.

The *pièce de resistance* is the ceiling. Darren has painted a night sky. I look closer at the pattern of the stars and realize it's an inaccurate rendition of the Milky Way. Scientific accuracy aside, it's gorgeous. Linda smiles.

'Mam won't paint over it. Darren did it when he was thirteen and Mam loves it.'

I can't decide if this interior decorating proves that Darren is the saddest man I've ever met or . . .

The most amazing.

No, definitely a loser.

I look out of the window, which is encased with sparkling net curtains, hanging straighter than Issie.

'Is that his tree house?'

'Yes, it's mine. I built it myself,' says Darren. I jump and turn to face him. Linda looks infuriated that he's crashed our girl time. I, on the other hand, can't help but be pleased to see him.

'It's very fine,' I say. 'Most people settle for one storey and forgo the plumbing.' But I beam, making it clear that I'm impressed. Darren smiles back, and I, for once, am devoid of a sparkling putdown.

We return to the kitchen, which appears to be the epicentre of the Smith household. Mrs Smith hands me a huge mug of strong, sweet tea. I mean to tell her that I prefer black coffee or Earl Grey but I can't quite find the opportunity. The kitchen is a hive. The radio is tuned into some local station. The DJ has the strangest accent. The washing machine, dryer and dishwasher are all whirling at once. Yet despite this industry there are also great mounds of dirty plates in the sink and clean ones draining on the draining board. There are piles of ironing on at least two chairs. No one is sitting on any of the other chairs, as they are inhabited by fat, lazy, sleeping cats. Intermittently the dog, an aged Labrador, jumps up from its basket and barks at some sound outside. It amazes me that he can hear a sound outside. I can barely hear myself think. There isn't a pause in the conversation. In fact, conversation is a generous description. It seems to me that everyone is talking at once, about different things and without regard for anyone else. Yet despite this no one, except me, seems to be struggling to keep abreast and answer the correct people at the appropriate time. Linda and Mrs Smith regularly try to force food on me, which I try but fail to decline. I quickly realize that it's easier to accept the cakes, biscuits and sandwiches and leave them untouched, on the side of my plate. I do quietly sip my tea, which is surprisingly pleasant. Sarah and her husband and kids explode on to the scene. Sarah unceremoniously drops the baby she is carrying on to Mrs Smith's knee and flings her arms around her brother. The two older children, girls who are probably between three and nine years old (it's hard to guess, unless you're into kids), follow suit and climb all over Darren. Sarah's husband quietly melts away and goes to join Mr Smith watching TV in the front room.

The kitchen, bubbling before, is positively effervescent now. I desperately need a glass of champagne, or at the very least, some soluble aspirin – ASAP. My head is simply throbbing with all this noise. Darren's nieces are demanding 'twizzies', and Darren is obliging them. Sarah is demanding a cup of tea and wants to know if her mother's baked this morning. Mrs Smith assures her she has, which accounts for the delicious smell that's wafting through the house. Mrs Smith is balancing the baby on one hip and feeding it with one hand, whilst setting up the ironing board with the other hand to iron dry a skirt for Linda. Shelly and Richard arrive. There is more noise and more kissing. Shelly has brought a chocolate cake, which is cut into immediately – with no regard to whether it is a mealtime or not. Richard wants to know if Darren is 'up for a kick about' in the back garden. Shelly shows her nieces-to-be samples of material for their bridesmaid dresses. Delighted, they squeal their approval. Sarah is unpacking groceries, recalling some incident to do with her eldest daughter's (turns out to be Charlotte) school teacher, and throughout all this everyone is interrogating me about who I am and why I'm here.

Mrs Smith, Sarah and Shelly have jumped to the understandable conclusion that I am Darren's girlfriend. Understandable that is, if you don't know me. I've never been a girlfriend and I have no desire to be one. And if ever I did have the desire to be one, it wouldn't be with someone like Darren. He may be good-looking, sexy, funny and intelligent but he's definitely not my type.

I'm sure he'll make someone a lovely boyfriend.

The kind of someone who wants a lovely boyfriend.

However, it's easier to allow the Smiths to think that I'm a girlfriend than explain that actually I want Darren to seduce his ex for the edification and delight of the now astounding 8.9 million viewers. The Smith women take advantage of Darren and Richard's exit to quell their curiosity.

'So you and our Darren are friends, then?' Sarah hovers over the word 'friends' for about ten seconds. I concentrate on choosing a biscuit from the heaving plate proffered by Linda. I barely nod my head.

'Known each other long, have you? It's just that I don't recall him mentioning you,' adds Mrs Smith. I'm glad I'm not into this man – his interfering family would be a nightmare. It's obvious that they don't think anyone is good enough for 'their' Darren. I imagine that a number of years hence Mrs Smith and Sarah will be checking Darren's bride's ability to wash whites whiter than blue white. Awful thought. She'd probably have to sit an exam in pastrymaking before they'd hand him over. Poor Shelly, I imagine that she was subjected to the same hostilities when Richard first brought her home. I look at Shelly, expecting to see the browbeaten shrew of my imaginings. She grins at me cheerfully and confidently kicks a cat off a chair, plonking her own bum in its place.

'Move it, Tabby.'

Hmmm.

Charlotte's interrogation lacks subtlety, but then this is forgivable because she's still wearing Winnie the Pooh matching vest and pant sets. She cuts the preamble. 'Are you Darren's girlfriend?'

'Er, no, I'm not.' I knew the question was brewing, so why am I blushing?

'Oh.' Charlotte is unimpressed. The others are simply perplexed. 'Have you got a boyfriend?' she continues.

'No.' I would never, ever have come here if I'd realized that I was going to be humiliated in this way.

'Poor you,' says Charlotte, 'I have. His name is Alan Barker and he sings to me.' I smile at her encouragingly. She persists, 'I'm six and a half. Lucy is four. Ben isn't really a baby. He's nearly two. How old are you?'

'Don't be rude, Charlotte. You should never ask a lady her age,' says Sarah. Yet she pauses expectantly, waiting for me to answer.

'Thirty-three,' I oblige.

I notice that Shelly, Sarah and Mrs Smith exchange furtive glances. They think there is something suspect about a single thirty-three-year-old woman. I wish Darren would stop farting around with that football and come and rescue me.

'Do you have a sister?' pursues Charlotte. We haven't lost eye contact since the interrogation began. I wiggle on my seat trying to get a better view of the back of her scalp; I'm looking for a tattoo of 666.

'No.'

'A brother, then?' asks Lucy.

'I'm afraid not.' Lucy climbs on to my knee, as if to console me. I'm a bit nervous – I don't think I've ever had anything so young on my knee before, not even a kitten or a puppy. How will she balance? It appears that Lucy has got experience in this sort of thing. She expertly cuddles into me and begins to suck her thumb. I can feel her breath on my neck. I look around for approval. No one else seems to think it is at all unusual that I have a child on my lap. But it is. People don't touch me. Not unless they are paid to or it's sexual. An important distinction. I'm touched by my hairdresser, masseur, acupuncturist and personal trainer for hard cash and by men for a more amorphous fee. But this child is sitting on my lap and holding my hand, and doesn't appear to want anything from me at all. How odd.

'So what do you do for a living?' asks Sarah. I am about to offer to fill in a questionnaire but I notice that Darren and Richard have just come back inside. I bite my tongue.

'She works in TV,' jumps in Linda. Linda is the only one who is impressed by my career choice.

'What exactly do you do in television, then, dear?' asks Mrs Smith. I give my dummied-down job description, which I assume will be adequate. No one ever really understands what someone else does for a living.

'I think up ideas for programmes.'

'Ooohhhh,' the kitchen choruses.

'Did you think up *Friends*?' asks Shelly.

'No, it's American.'

'Did you think up *Blue Peter*?' asks Charlotte.

'No, before my time.'

'Did you think up that game show with the nice Mr Tyrant? The one that makes people very rich?' asks Mrs Smith.

'Or *Cold Feet*?' asks Linda hopefully.

'No, not my channel,' I add apologetically. Clearly I've failed to impress anyone.

'Oh. Well, what did you think of?' asks Sarah.

Mercifully the doorbell rings and this causes such concern that everyone, other than Darren and Lucy, leaves the kitchen.

'No one ever rings the door bell,' he explains. 'They all come round the back. It must be a delivery.'

I nod as though this outlandish behaviour was second nature to me, rather than the extraordinary adventure it is.

'Why didn't you tell them the name of your show?' he asks.

I stare at him sulkily. 'I guess I didn't think it was their cup of tea,' I mutter.

'Oh, you took a guess that they weren't part of your 8.9 million. Very astute.'

I glare at him.

He is so smug. He is so cocksure. He is so sexy.

I think it's the mouth.

10

I am unsure how I got myself into this predicament. I can't remember the point when I actually agreed to accompany Darren, Charlotte, Lucy and baby Ben to the swimming baths. The noise and confusion that reign in the Smith household are so extreme that it is possible I didn't agree at all but simply was unable to resist their collective force.

I don't do public baths. I do health spas and private gyms. I can feel the foot diseases waiting in the cracks of the tiles and despite the gallons of chlorine that the local council has tipped into the pool, I am sure that I am about to swim in neat child's wee. To add insult, I catch a glimpse of myself in the steamy mirror. It's bad. I didn't bring a costume with me and therefore I've been forced into borrowing Sarah's. Although there is evidence that Sarah has been a very attractive woman in her time, she has had three babies and has let her figure go somewhat. I get the feeling sartorial elegance is not the top of her list of priorities. The bathing suit is high street rather than high fashion. I did explain to Sarah and Shelly that I only ever wear black. They smiled and handed me this monstrosity. I think that initially it was a mass of fluorescent flowers, which thankfully have faded. The cut is all wrong. Damn, why didn't I bring my Calvin Klein costume? It's cut to maximize the length of the leg and minimize the waist. It's padded at the breast, creating a look that is undisputedly flattering. The floral number is baggy at the crotch and hips, plus the straps keep sliding off my shoulders. As if the possibility that I might fall out of the suit altogether isn't terrifying enough, suddenly I find that I'm alone in the changing rooms with two small people.

The panic rises. Not just because I haven't shaved my legs in over a week, but because Charlotte and Lucy are both looking up at me with expectancy in their eyes. It appears that everyone – Darren, his mum, Sarah, Shelly and these kids – all seem to think I am in charge.

And that I'm capable of it.

Which, I am, of course. I mean, I run a show that pulls in millions of viewers per week, for God's sake. I control budgets of hundreds of thousands of pounds, create revenues of millions. I can undress two small children and dress them again in suitable attire.

Surely.

They don't stand still. They slither and slide all over the place. They don't want to wear costumes anyway, much less their armbands, which I abandon altogether. It seems that no sooner have I got the appropriate limb in the appropriate hole than they take it out again. I do manage to get the costumes on but one is inside-out and the other is back-to-front. I realize that above all else, I must remain calm. Like any confrontation it is important not to let the adversary know that you feel menaced or panicked. I can outstare four- and six-year-olds – definitely. If only they would stay still.

'Charlotte, don't run. The floor's slippery. You might hurt yourself.' I try to make this sound like advice or a warning. It comes out sounding like I'm threatened or threatening. 'Lucy, we didn't bring your pink costume. You have to put this blue one on. Now please, stop crying. Just one more arm. Please.' Both the girls are crying (although I suspect Charlotte's are crocodile tears) and I am closer to tears than I've been in twenty-five years, when another mother offers to help.

'They're not yours, are they, pet?'

'No.' I'm irritated and relieved all at once. They aren't hers either, are they? But, in a blink of an eye, she has managed to get them both into their costumes, the right way out, and facing the right direction. Why couldn't I? Can it be that there is a mother gene that makes this stuff easier once you are a mum? Not that I ever want to be a mother, not in my wildest dreams. In fact, it's close to my worst nightmare. But I do like to be able to do things properly. I don't like to fail.

I bribe the girls into not telling Uncle Darren that the nice lady had to help with dressing them. I offer them each a pound but Charlotte informs me that the going rate is a new outfit for her Barbie doll and a trip to McDonald's. I would be annoyed but actually I admire her business acumen and I'm sure that she'll go far.

Darren doesn't comment that we've been in the dressing-room for forty-five minutes but waves cheerfully from the baby pool, where he is confidently handling a happy, gurgling Ben.

I lower myself into the pool and try not to think of the wee. I hand him the armbands for the girls. Making it clear that it's his turn.

'Will you hold Ben?' I nod, as I don't want to open my mouth for fear of what will go in it. Darren grins and hands him over. I'm relieved that he doesn't start to cry. I smile winningly at him and hope that my legendary way with men works on someone so young. Darren hoists himself out of the pool.

He is divine.

He must work out. His muscles are taut and developed. He's lean and tanned. I watch the pool water glisten as it clings to his shoulders and legs. I'd glisten too if I was clinging to that Adonis. I'm thrilled to note that his strong chest and legs are hairy but his back is clean. My nipples harden and chafe against the costume. Bloody cheap thing, no lining.

Darren puts the armbands on the girls and lowers them into the pool with me. He sits on the side, dangling his legs in the water. He drags his feet unselfconsciously through the water, bending and straightening his knees. My knees have turned to Play-Doh. My entire body is on fire. I cannot drag my gaze from him. He is utterly, utterly stunning. From his tanned feet, with neat square nails – rather than the yellow, curled nails that most men choose to sport – to his long, tight, muscular legs, to his neat, flat stomach. Six pack, forget it – this is an entire shelf at the off-licence. I want to entangle my fingers in his chest hair. Lose them there and never ever find them again. His shoulders are as rigid as they are broad. They look almost polished. He's staring out at the children and not aware that I'm studying every little droplet of chlorine that's clinging to him. His glossy hair curls rebelliously at the nape of his neck and I'm envious. I want to be that lock of hair; I want to be the drops of chlorine, pool water and pee.

Since he's occupied watching the children splash and bob, I risk taking a look at his swimwear.

WHHHOOOAAA-HHHOOO.

Hello, Big Boy.

'Should I take Ben now?'

'Erm?'

I nearly drop the baby with the embarrassment. Why did he have to choose that moment to start up a conversation? I avoid his eye as I pass the baby to him. I feel like a kid caught with her hand in the biscuit jar. I force myself to look at Darren and he's grinning again. Well, I'm pleased to be so amusing! Irritated and flustered, I sulkily pull myself on to the side of the pool as he climbs in. He tries to make conversation but I won't be mollified. It isn't until I catch him furtively checking out my tits that I start to brighten up. In fact, I feel considerably happier.

When we leave the pool we go to McDonald's. Darren is blatantly a bit surprised by my choice of dining venue. I smile and don't offer an explanation. It isn't until Lucy is on to her second chocolate shake and I've taken Charlotte to the loo twice (unaided) that it crosses my mind to check my mobile messages. I can't believe I've forgotten to call Fi or Bale. It's not as though I'm having a good time. I mean, I'm not shopping or clubbing. Normally I check my messages every twenty-five minutes when I'm out of the studio.

I've had six calls.

Hi, Cas. It's Fi. I reviewed the files through the night and have a shortlist of three possible scenarios for next week's show. Should I interview them? If so, you'll need to release more budget. Call me.

Hi, Cas, it's Josh. Issie told me that you are chasing some bloke halfway up the country. What's the angle? Is he a transvestite? Now that would make a good show. Well, call me when you get a mo.

Cas. It's Fi again. Er, I haven't heard back from you so I had to make the decision to go ahead with the interviews. I think I've found a substitute. Hope this is OK. But I didn't really have a choice. What with the timetable being so tight. Can you call me? Er, say hi to Darren for me. Tell him I was the one in baby-blue cashmere. No, scrub that.

Cas, it's Issie. Weeeellllllll? How goes it with Mr Northern Hunk?

Jocasta, it's your mother. I do hate these things. Can you hear me?

Cas. Bale. Call in.

So nothing urgent. I switch the phone back to the message facility.

By the time we drop the kids back with Sarah, I am exhausted and barely have the energy to turn down the offer of staying for supper. Which under normal circumstances I'd turn down with extreme force.

'Stay – we're having lasagne and Mam and Dad are down the pub, Richard's at Shelly's, Linda's here. There will be no one at home. You'll be rattling around an empty house.'

Hearing this, I get another surge of dynamism and almost wrench Darren's arm out of its socket as I pull him from their kitchen and bundle him into the car. Laughing, he turns the ignition.

'Had enough of kids for one day?'

I feel a twinge of guilt. Perhaps he wanted to stay and was too polite to contradict me; after all, he probably doesn't get to see his family much, being based in London. But my arms are aching with playing 'one, two, three, swwiiinnnng'. I smell of baby puke, my mind is fried with coming up with answers to the perpetual 'why' question (nearly all of which had come from Darren). Most importantly, I haven't reapplied my make-up since leaving the swimming pool.

'To be honest, yes. I'm not used to kids. No nieces or nephews.'

'Some of your friends must have children, though,' he comments.

I think about it. No, not really. Women in TV rarely nod

towards their reproductive capacity and my friends in other lines of work seem to disappear once they have babies. I suppose it's because we keep very different hours.

'No.' I smile at Darren and decide to confess, 'In fact, until today I don't think I've ever held a child, or dressed one, brushed its hair, taken it to the loo, changed a nappy or fed it.'

'Really?'

'Really,' I confirm.

I'm slightly shamefaced and don't know how Darren will take this. He obviously values these motherly skills in his women. Indeed all men like to see a woman behave perfectly with kids. Most women like to think they have a natural ability to be patient, entertaining and loving. Not me. I'm not bothered. Well, I was keen to put the shoes on the right feet but that was because I hate to be inadequate at anything. As a kid myself, I didn't like anyone else winning musical chairs. Second place is nowhere. If something is worth doing, it's worth doing well. That's always been my motto. It has nothing to do with impressing Darren. I don't care what he thinks of me. I sneak a look at him to check his reaction to my confession. Richard's car is so tiny that Darren is almost folded double. He's concentrating on the curling roads. He puts on the long beam lights and the windscreen wipers are valiantly trying to clear the pouring rain. I fear it's a losing battle. Without taking his eyes off the road, he mumbles, 'You're amazing.'

I'm amazing! I'm floating on air. My bum is absolutely refusing to stay in the car seat.

I'm amazing? Oh yeah, and how many times have I heard that before?

I'm amazing! I'm floating on air. My bum is absolutely refusing to stay in the car seat.

I'm amazing. I bet he says that to everyone.

I pretend I haven't heard and close my eyes, keen to get some sleep on the short journey back to the Smiths' house.

I wake up and a young Kevin Keegan is smiling down at me. Where am I? I'm in a single bed with itchy nylon sheets and itchy nylon bedspread. They are brown. Different shades of brown. My worst fear – I've screwed someone with bad taste. I hear children laughing in the garden and I look out of the window.

Darren.

And Charlotte and Lucy. It's a grey, bleak day. Grey grass, grey sky. But Darren and the girls are a remarkable contrast, their clothes and laughter, a colourful relief to the horizon. Impetuously I bang on the window and wave furiously. They all look up and wave back. Then I remember I haven't got any make-up on, so I dive back into bed before they can see me properly. There's a knock on the door and, before I answer, Mrs Smith bustles in. She smiles broadly and I bathe in it. Perhaps she's heard how good I was with the children yesterday and is beginning to approve of me. Not that it matters. I neither want nor need Mrs Smith's approval.

Much.

She hands me a cup of tea that's so strong the spoon can stand up in it. I take it from her and thank her.

'By, you were tired, weren't you?'

A strange feeling of unease creeps into bed with me; it gets under the sheets and disperses the cosy feeling. Oh bugger, yes, now I remember. Last night I'd been very tired. Too tired to argue my case about the show properly but tired enough to argue petulantly. We were having a laugh. In the absence of wine or gin we decided to raid his parents' cocktail cabinet. A walnut veneer monstrosity, straight from the Ark, justifiably hidden in the 'front room'. We agreed that tequila was the perfect accompaniment to cheese on toast (desperate measures for desperate times. The other choices were all fluorescent in colour and likely to have been radioactive). I had the idea of broaching the subject of the show whilst the family were out and we had the house to ourselves. I thought that as he was beginning to warm to me he might be open to discussion. He wasn't. The conversation had been brief, powerful and cold.

He turned his back to me and concentrated on grating the cheese. The hairs on the back of his neck were standing to attention. I had an overwhelming desire to blow on them.

'I'm not saying that you should have sex with Claire.' God forbid. 'Just find out what would happen. Just let fate take its course,' I argued to his very wide shoulders.

'But your programme isn't about fate or what would happen naturally if everyone was left to their own devices. Your show is designed to distort. To bring out the worst in people.' He was watching my reflection in the window against the black night sky.

'The worst in people is the norm.'

He tutted dismissively. But he did, at least, turn back to me. Or was he just turning because he needed to put the bread under the grill?

'No, it's not. You just think that the peculiar is normal because it's prevalent in *your* life.'

Fucking cheek. What does he know about my life? Well, besides the stuff we'd talked about at the Oxo tower restaurant, on the train and today. But that hardly amounts to revealing insight. He knows little more about me than what my favourite milkshake was when I was a kid. Oh, and admittedly, we had a fairly flirty but extremely coded (due to the presence of minors) conversation about condom flavours this afternoon. But then half the men at TV6 know that I prefer banana-flavour condoms.

None of them know it's chocolate milkshake.

I glared at him and said, 'Infidelity is a fact. Disloyalty is a fact.'

'OK. Maybe. But it's a horrifying fact and should remain horrifying. By continually showing betrayal as an acceptable form of entertainment you are neutralizing the horror. Are you so damaged that you can't see that?'

I was tired and sick of his sanctimonious attitude. I found I was shouting. I ignored his question and asked my own instead. 'You want to shelter who, exactly, from these cultural and moral norms of the West? I'm not suggesting anything that they aren't already endorsing, committing.'

We both fell silent as Darren concentrated on retrieving the cheese on toast from under the grill. He set it down in front of me and offered Worcester sauce. I refused it. I poured him tequila; he'd left it untouched. We ate in silence and then I went to bed, alone, defeated.

Now, I try to find my wristwatch.

'It's three thirty, pet,' says Mrs Smith, cheerfully.

'In the afternoon?' I jump up suddenly. Mrs Smith clocks my lacy negligée.

'Yes, in the afternoon. By, love, you must have been tired not to notice the cold in that flimsy thing. If you'd said you only had your underwear to sleep in I'd have lent you one of my nighties.'

Duly mortified, I crawl back into bed and cover myself from her disapproving gaze. Underwear indeed! I'd especially selected the most conventional and practical nightdress I own to bring on this trip. I normally sleep naked. If she thinks this is skimpy enough to be underwear, what would she think of my knickers?

'Darren wanted to get you up but I said, "Let her sleep." You obviously needed it. He's just taking the kids into town for a ride on the merry-go-round on the seafront. I thought that you might want to get bathed and then we can think about a bite to eat.'

I nod politely, although I'm sure my stomach will actively revolt if I try to eat anything more. Yesterday's binge of sweets, chocolate cake, scones, hamburgers and finally cheese on toast was more than I normally eat in a week. It must be the fresh air that's given me such an appetite.

'What time did you say it was?'

'It's nearly twenty to four now.'

'What day is it?' I'm not normally so vague, but then I don't normally sleep for seventeen hours. And I don't *ever* sleep in nylon sheets.

'Tuesday.'

'Oh shit.'

'Excuse me.' Mrs Smith looks horrified but I have no time to placate her.

'Shit. Shit.' I scramble in my bag looking for my mobile phone. 'Shit. Fourteen messages.' Mrs Smith tuts and leaves me to my own devices. I think it's safe to assume that any tentative strands of approval she'd been weaving my way are now well and truly snapped. So what? I turn to my messages.

The first is from Issie, reminding me that my New Year's resolution was not to have casual sex. Ha, fat chance. Darren doesn't even seem to want to swap pleasantries, never mind bodily fluids. And anyway, what is she talking about? That's not why I'm here. I'm here to endear myself to Darren so that he agrees to be on the show. Nothing more. I thought I'd explained that. All the other messages are work-related.

Cas. Please give me a call. It's Tuesday morning. What time will you be back? Have you persuaded Darren to be on the show?

Fi sounds nervous and a twinge of guilt bites as I acknowledge that I have left her in the lurch. She's a strong assistant but she hasn't had to make the decisions before. Well, maybe I micromanage too much and it's time that Fi had a bit more responsibility. She's probably doing a good job. I skip a few more messages to listen out for her voice. There are three more from Fi. The first and second are increasingly irate. The third confidently asserts that she's found a replacement for Darren, Claire and Marcus and has made the decision to reschedule the filming. She details how she's going to use the two producers back to back. One in the studio, editing, whilst the other is at the shoot and then vice versa. This is a good idea as it will help catch up on time. She says she's expecting me back by Wednesday morning and significantly repeats, 'As you promised.'

Bale is less subtle.

Cas, where the fuck are you? Getting serviced? Well, fuck that. Call me.

His three messages are all the same. I also have calls from Di, Debs and Ricky. Apparently some bishop or other has written an open letter to *The Times* condemning the show. Which is great news. Di and Debs want to know how to handle the PR. Idiots. Can't they do anything without me? Ricky is lobbying for a schedule change to coincide with Valentine's Day. He's come up against a brick wall. Or, more accurately, a homophobe executive who can block or facilitate such things. Ricky's particular breed of charm will only serve to irritate in this instance. Whereas I could undoubtedly help by just offering to take the guy to lunch. I call Ricky and tell him to set it up for Friday. I call Fi, and it's not until I tell her that I'm not travelling back tonight as originally promised but early tomorrow morning or tomorrow night at latest that I realize I've made this decision.

'But you don't need to stay, Cas. I have a replacement.'

'Yeah, but I think Darren is just about to capitulate and I still think he'd make such a good show.' This lie is vibrant scarlet but I have no conscience about it.

'He is gorgeous,' Fi agrees enthusiastically.

'If you like that kind of thing.'

'Are you having a good time?'

'Not really. He's unstable. A delight one minute and a rabid dog the next. I have to schlep round with his tedious family. It's freezing and I'm in the middle of nowhere.' It's always been an adage of mine that I don't owe every pertinent enquirer the truth, the whole truth and nothing but.

'The things you do for your job.'

'Exactly. Listen, Fi. It's probably best if you don't mention to Bale that we have a replacement. He hasn't met Darren and won't understand why I'm so actively pursuing him.' Fi titters, so for clarity I add, 'For the show.'

'Of course.' I can hear the smirk in her voice. Cow. 'Be careful you don't fall for him.'

'Impossible. I could never fancy anyone called Darren. I'm not called Kylie or Sharon.'

Fi laughs. 'I won't say a word to Bale, but you'll have to get back by first thing Thursday at the absolute latest. We can push the filming back to then but no later. I can't do the filming on my own. We need you.'

Of course they do.

After bathing I feel in need of fresh air. Avocado green has never been my colour for bathroom suites. I decide to catch up with Darren and the children. Because what else can I do? Play bowls? I walk along the pier and spot them walking down the beach, which is more or less deserted as it's January, it's the north and it's freezing. Anyone with any sense is sitting by their fireside or, less romantically but more realistically, their TV set and radiators. I wave and shout, and surprisingly Lucy and Charlotte start to pelt towards me, their little legs not keeping up with their will to be further ahead than they are. I succumb to the Calvin Klein advert factor and rush to meet them. I stoop down to hug them. I only do this because I'll look good.

'Hi,' smiles Darren.

Is last night's spat forgotten? I'm not sure, so I concentrate on the girls. I know he's watching me examine their toffee apples and take due interest in the horrid plastic novelties that they've procured on the seafront.

'You're getting the hang of this kids thing. And wellingtons too,' he comments.

I glare at him. The wellingtons are Mr Smith's. I have just endured the most embarrassing thirty minutes of my life, well beyond anything I have ever encountered to date. Mrs Smith insisted that my Mulberry wide-leg trousers were 'too good to be clarting on the beach in' and gave me a pair of her 'slacks'. She laughed out loud at my Gina Couture mules and set about finding me a pair of wellington boots. I am a size seven shoe. Which caused much astonishment as the fact was repeated throughout Whitby by Mrs Smith, who rang all her friends and asked if they had a boot that large. None of them did. It's obvious that they are still binding women's feet in North Yorkshire. I was subjected to the humiliating experience of being the most ugly of Cinderella's sisters as I tried to squeeze my feet into Shelly's size six boots. They didn't go anywhere near. I commented that cheap brands do come up small. Mrs Smith laughed and gave me Mr Smith's wellingtons. They are big and slip up and down as I walk but at least I can get into them. I didn't manage to leave the house without accepting sheepskin mitts, a kagoul, a scarf and a duffel coat. The type most people wore at school. I didn't. I refused then. However, no amount of objections could deter Mrs Smith. She kept insisting that it is bitter in January, and that I wouldn't have known anything like it. The implication is that I'm a softy southerner. I explained that I had been to the north before – in fact, I went to university in Manchester. She let out a sound somewhere between derision and pity. 'That's hardly north, is it, love?'

I look like the Michelin man. Except not as colour co-ordinated. Darren sweeps an eye over my outfit. How come he's warm *and* manages to look sophisticated and rugged?

'I see that Mam kitted you out appropriately.'

I don't dignify his sarcasm with a response. I'm not sure if he thinks he's being funny or if he's trying to be irritating.

But then I'm not sure if I *am* irritated.

Odd.

I can't remember when last I was so unsure about so many things. I want to tell Darren that I feel better for my marathon sleep. Better than I've felt for as long as I can remember. I want to tell him that I seem to have woken up with a new and startling sense of clarity and whilst I don't agree with his point of view, I do accept it. Grudgingly, I respect it. He's argued his case well. But I can't say this because if I do, how will I explain that I want to stay an extra night? How will

I explain that, despite my expectations, I like it here? It's peaceful.

And terrifying. I am trying to be honest with myself, at least. I thought my battle was with Darren. But now I see that, if it was, I've lost.

I do like him.

He's sexy, witty and intelligent, which I've come across before. But more than that, he's also gentle, decent and straightforward, which is an entirely new experience for me. I do like him, very much, and by admitting as much I realize that I have a whole new war to wage. I fear my opponent is much tougher, more devious and ruthless than Darren could ever be. I'm at war with myself. I like him, but hate myself for doing so. Because isn't this what I've been studiously avoiding all my life? I know I should pack my bag immediately and get on the train back to London. I should take myself well away from this danger zone.

But I can't.

I know if I leave now, Darren will always be with me. I'd wonder if he were for real. I'd fantasize, despite myself, that his outlook on life – open, honest, optimistic – is a possibility. I'd be ruined.

If I stay, there is a reasonable chance that Darren will expose his true self, which surely can't be as amazing as I currently believe. All I can do is maintain the cool exterior, which I've nurtured for twenty-six years, and hope that by spending more time with Darren I begin to bore of him. Not my strongest strategy ever, but my preferred option by virtue of the fact that it's my only option.

We begin to walk along the shoreline. I expect and dread that we'll settle into an uncomfortable silence. Instead Darren chats happily. He's nauseatingly well informed about the local sites and history.

'Lewis Carroll is reputed to have written much of *Alice in Wonderland* whilst sitting on these sands looking out to sea.'

'Really?' I don't turn to see where he's pointing.

'In Roman times a signal station was likely to have been erected on this spot.'

'Fascinating.' I'm rather pleased with the tone I hit. It's an enthusiastic enough word choice but the manner I deliver it in hints that I've had more fun scouring ovens.

'Let's head to Flowergate. We can pop into the Sutcliffe Gallery.'

He drags the girls and me around a billion sepia pictures. After staring at four million, seven hundred and forty-five of them I begin to admire his tenacity. The shots are absorbing, but I'm doing my level best not to betray that I think so. Darren matches my feigned disinterest by feigning oblivion to it. This game-playing is exhausting, even for a pro like me. We move on, crossing the river. Darren points to a church in the distance.

'The original dates from 110 AD. Can you see the graveyard? That's where Dracula is allegedly buried.' I smile to humour him.

'And that's St Hilda's Abbey, isn't it?' I ask.

Darren nearly keels over with shock. 'Absolutely.'

I'm gratified that he doesn't ask how I know this but instead assumes that I'm one of those terribly impressive people who know all sorts of facts about a diverse range of places and topics. A person like Darren. He's so obviously delighted with me that I can't resist elaborating.

'Did you know that the original abbey housed both men and women, but was destroyed by the Danes?'

'In 867,' he adds, nodding his head enthusiastically. It's so cold I can almost see ice in his hair but his smile shoots spears of warmth through the town. There's a direct hit in my knickers. I reflect on this and consider jumping into the river and swimming away, a long way away. Less dramatically, I resume my commentary. 'Hilda was a relative of King Oswt's, wasn't she?'

'Correct.' Darren is orgasmic. Knowledge *is* power. Luckily he doesn't ask where I gained such a detailed grasp of the history of his home town, Smallsville. He's so ridiculously pleased. A little part of me would hate to disappoint him. Truth is, Fi sent me a text message through my mobile with this and a number of other facts about Whitby. We always research our subjects thoroughly.

'Would you like a closer look at the abbey?' he asks. The abbey is on a cliff top. I could do with the workout. I nod and we set off. 'What do you think of Whitby?'

I think it's cold and I think it's unfashionable. I never thought I'd be pleased to see a Woolworths' and greet it as though it was Harrods' food hall. But just as I'm about to say this I turn to Darren. He's looking out to the sea. It's shimmering turquoise and lustrous waves are breaking on the sand, which looks pink and peach by turn. I can't see any of the greyness that had been so prevalent earlier.

'It's overwhelming,' I mutter, which is at once truthful and vague enough to satisfy.

Darren grins widely. 'Isn't it? I knew you'd love it. It's such a riot of colour and smell and sound. My senses feel electric.'

His skin looks cold and transparent, which is perfect for hanging on such strong, jilting cheekbones. My senses feel electric, too, but I'm not sure that it has much to do with the smell of fishing nets and creosote. We begin to walk through the cobbled streets. The children surprise me by not whining about having to climb up a couple of hundred steps; in fact, they are keen to do so – they want to look at old gravestones. Darren doesn't seem to think this is at all odd, so I can only assume it's a northern thing. The walk takes quite some time, as I go to extreme lengths to avoid being anywhere near a seagull. I swear Whitby seagulls are baby elephants in fancy dress. I'm almost deafened by their constant, hungry squawking. They look fierce, and whilst it may be lucky to be used as a bird's public toilet, it's a pleasure I can do without. I buy ice creams for the children and me. Darren's determined to act his age and points out that it's freezing. Charlotte looks at him pityingly, as though he is a lost soul. I can smell fish and chips or, more specifically, I can smell vinegar seeping into newspaper and, as we climb higher, I can smell smoke from the chimneys. It's different.

We finally reach the church and whilst the girls run off to find Dracula's tomb I puff furiously on a cigarette, not caring if it's taking me one step nearer to joining Drac.

'Have you heard from the studio?' asks Darren.

'Oh yes. Dozens of calls. They can't seem to muddle through without me.'

'Really?'

'Really.' I don't tell him that Fi has found a replacement for him. Because if I do tell him, he's bound to ask me why I'm still here.

'I'm sure they can't do without you, Cas. I mean such an intellectually challenging programme needs your unique input.'

I'm stung. I thought we were having a nice time, even amongst the tat and bric-à-brac. I'm trying – why can't he?

'Why do you hate me, Darren?' I ask directly.

He looks genuinely surprised. He must be taken aback by my straightforward approach.

'I don't hate you. I like you. I just don't like the programme.'

Hmmm. He likes me.

Hmmm. Obviously not enough. Part of me wants to change

the subject. Talk to him about the jet or herring industries. Indeed both those subjects suddenly appear riveting. But I can't. Darren has thrown down the gauntlet; in fact, he's spat at the family crest. I have to respond.

'But it's my programme. I thought of the concept.'

'And you are proud of that, are you?'

'I am. Very. TV6 was in deep trouble until I came up with this. People could have lost their jobs.'

'Why couldn't you think of something instructive?'

'I think this is,' I nod wryly. 'It's a warning, if anyone is sensible enough to listen. Infidelity is out there. I think I'm helping civilization come to terms with itself.'

Didn't we do this last night? Why bring it up again? I'm never going to agree with him. I know why I wanted him to see my point of view: it was to get him on the show. But why is he so urgent about my seeing *his* point of view? What can it possibly matter to him? What does he want from me?

'Your show doesn't help anyone. It *cheats* civilization.' He's raising his voice. Which encourages me to remain irritatingly calm. I adore the upper hand.

'It captivates 8.9 million viewers. Actually 9.1 million last show. Di called to tell me.'

'Oh, I admit that it holds attention, and consumes energy whilst ignoring the fundamentals of life.' He's stamping on the pavement and I don't know if it's because he's cold or furious. He's waving his arms around and a woman, walking her dog, is looking at us.

'So?'

'Your programme incessantly touches the audience but on a superficial level.' I stare at him, uncomprehending. 'Television doesn't require any acceptance of responsibility. Every one of your viewers who has hoped for an infidelity has committed a small betrayal of standards. But no one, except the poor sucker on the show, has to answer for his or her actions.'

I touch my temples. I can see his argument but he's wrong.

'No, Darren. Television merely reflects and observes society. It should not be blamed for the degeneration. It might not be pretty, but I'm just telling it how it is. Why does it make you so angry?' I sigh.

'Why don't you admit it makes you furious?' he asks.

I shrug and lick my ice cream. 'Do you want some?'

'Go on, then.' We stop and he licks my ice cream. He has to hold my hand steady to do so, because it's shaking. It must be the cold. He's right – I shouldn't be eating ice cream in January. His tongue is pink and slim.

'I don't buy your thing about collective responsibility, society, the greater good, blah blah. Bugger it. The more people I meet, the more disappointments I see.'

'So who are you responsible for?'

'Myself. And I look out for my mother, Issie and Josh when I can.'

We both fall silent. I stare at him. Looking directly into his eyes, which I rarely do, at least not when he's looking back at me. My stomach hiccups. It's stress.

'I won't be on your show.' And he manages to sound genuinely upset by this. 'That's not how I could help you.' I shrug. To be frank, I'm not even sure I want Darren on the show any more – I'm almost certain I don't.

'Don't worry about it. I'm used to helping myself.' I walk on briskly, not waiting to see if my rebuff hits as deeply as I hope it will. He doesn't need to know that I don't need him any more. It's much worse than that.

I just want him.

I call Bale and am relieved that he's in a meeting. The best I can do is leave him a message. I lie. I tell him that Darren is very near to agreeing to being on the show, that it's imperative that I get him to agree and that he can't call me because the battery on my mobile has run out. I am aware that the opposite is true – in all three cases. But I don't believe in hell.

When Darren and the girls arrive back home, about ten minutes after me, I am sweetness and light incarnate. I often pull this stunt with men. One minute moody, the next a delight. It makes them grateful. It's getting late, we've missed tea and more criminally we've made the girls miss tea. Mrs Smith offers to make sandwiches but I can't eat. I'm churned up. Sarah takes the kids home for their baths. Mr and Mrs Smith, Shelly and Richard decide to go to the pub. They ask if I want to join them. I'm absolutely desperate for a drink. As soon as I agree to go, Darren grabs his coat and says he's coming too. He obviously hasn't done enough baiting for one day.

The pub is heaving. It's full of raw and rough-looking fishermen. Who, surprisingly, look quite sexy despite their wellies. They wear black skullcaps and oilskins, which are for real, rather than a fashion statement. I seduce the Smiths, offering to buy the drinks, and I even go so far as to join them in drinking the thick, treacly stout that's obviously their favourite tipple. The pub is filthy, tasteless, well worn and patently loved. Remarkably, I soon forget the sticky, ripped lino that curls to expose a far stickier wooden floor, I ignore the tattered cushions, ragged flock wallpaper and frayed rugs as I melt into alcoholic oblivion. By my second pint, try as I might, I can't find anything shabby. Instead I'm surrounded by laughter, warmth and goodwill. It swirls like cigarette smoke, sticking to my hair, clinging to my clothes and penetrating my essence. By my third pint Mr Smith (senior) seems the wisest man I've ever known. His stories about Whitby are fascinating and his silences are profound. I forget my fears that the locals probably still indulge in cockfighting and even say so to Mr Smith. I try to dilute my prejudice by admitting it's entirely unfounded.

'Prejudice is rarely anything else,' he comments.

Shelly and Mrs Smith seem actively jolly. We play several riotous games of dominoes and I win, which satiates my competitive streak for the evening. Richard is gregarious and well informed. He's heard from Darren that I have 'extensive local knowledge'. Much to my amusement he tumbles my source. 'Someone from your studio told you about the abbey, did they?' I nod, nervous that he's blown my cover with Darren. He winks conspiratorially, taps his nose and adds, 'Mam's the word.' I'm so grateful I want to kiss him. And Darren?

Darren is unprecedented.

Darren is all the above. He is sexier than the fishermen. His anecdotes are more wise, fascinating and profound than his father's. He's more fun than the Smith women, even at their most jolly. He's charmingly competitive. He is more discreet than Richard – I don't think anyone else notices him rest his hand on my knee. Like the happy atmosphere, he immerses me. He clings harder and longer than anything I've ever known.

Which horrifies me.

I'm drunk. But not too drunk, as I already hope the hangover comes with a sense of proportion.

At a quarter to nine I announce that I have to go back to pack. Darren says he'll walk with me and I'm grateful when Mrs Smith says that she wants to go home too. In my slightly woozy state I know that if Darren wanted to touch more than my knee I'd definitely let him. When we arrive home Darren goes straight to the front room. Mrs Smith stays in the kitchen to fold some clean washing into piles for ironing and I drink a reservoir of water.

'Had a nice day, pet?' she asks. I nod enthusiastically. 'You can tell. You're a proper beauty when you smile. Really gorgeous.' She leaves me alone in the kitchen, with the compliment for company. I feel brilliant. The word 'gorgeous' rolls around my head.

Gooorgeous.

Gorggessss.

Gorgeous.

I receive a lot of compliments – some from men who want to screw me, others from the girls at TV6 who are too terrified of me not to compliment, and compliments from Mum, Issie and Josh. Mum's my mum and whilst Issie and Josh are probably genuine enough, those two say nice things about everyone. In my book, indiscriminate affability cancels out the worth. But Mrs Smith's compliment is something really special. I get the feeling that she doesn't dish them out that often.

The back door swings open and Linda tumbles in after a fun-packed evening hanging around the bus shelter. She interrupts my thoughts.

'You look like the cat that's got the cream.'

'I think I am.' I smile back. 'Cup of tea?' I've put the kettle on before she answers. Now she's grinning.

'You seem much more at home here after just forty-eight hours.'

'I am. Maybe it is the sleep, or the sea air—'

'Or being around our Darren.'

What's she implying? She's bloody cheeky for a teenager. No, thinking about it, she's absolutely normal for a teenager. I don't comment, but instead concentrate on displaying the chocolate digestives on a plate. She says, 'He always has this effect on women.'

Naturally.

'Always?' I venture.

Linda rolls her eyes. 'Well, look at him.' Fair point. 'Women watch him in the street. Everyone fancies him, from Charlotte's friends, to mine, to Sarah's. Even Mum's friends, come to think of it.' Someone has thumped me very hard. Suddenly I'm sober. 'It's just the same with the women in London. I noticed when I visited him last summer hols. There was this constant stream of women dropping in on him. "Do you fancy a drink, Darren?" "Can you loosen this lid, Darren? – oh, you are so strong!" "Oh, a man who can cook – Darren you are very special."'

I don't really like what Linda is telling me but her impressions are hilarious and I can't help but giggle. Besides, she wouldn't be telling me all this unless she was saying that I'm somehow different. Would she? Well, maybe she would. After all, she's only seventeen. Perhaps this is her unsubtle way of telling me that she (and he) have seen it all before.

'He *is* a good cook,' I comment. 'He made me cheese on toast last night and it was really special.'

'Special!' Linda is derisive and she's within her rights, considering what I've just said. I catch her eye, which is clever of me, considering the speed at which she is rolling them.

'Not you as well! I thought you'd be impervious!'

'Me what?' As soon as the words are out I regret them. She's youthful; she's likely to tell me.

'You've fallen for him.'

'I haven't.'

'Really, you haven't fallen for him?' asks Linda.

'Really.'

'What a shame, because I think he's fallen for you.'

Hallelujah, hallelujah.

Linda picks up an apple and takes a hungry bite, shrugs and leaves me to my thoughts.

Where is the cheese box? The fresh herbs? The avocado? The fridge is heaving but there is nothing I can eat. I'm faced with a dazzling selection from Rowntree and Cadbury. But fish fingers, Alphabite potato wedges and Heinz sauce were not what I had in mind for a romantic dinner for two. Where is the adult food?

What am I saying? Romantic? I've never had romantic dinners before.

Strategic, yes, but not romantic.

Still, the end result is the same: sex. So it's simply a case of semantics.

I have to have sex with Darren. It's obvious – why didn't I think of it earlier? A surefire way to dispel any fanciful notions that I may be inadvertently harbouring. Having sex with Darren would bring him down to the same level as everyone else I've ever had sex with. He's definitely not going on the show now, so there would be no concerns about a lack of professionalism if I slept with him. Nor would there be any possibility of seeing him again, which erases the possibility of tiresome consequential scenes. And as he is as sexy as hell, well, why shouldn't I have a crack? I brush away my New Year's resolution in the same way that every other year I sneak an extra fag or drink.

Unaccountably, I'm nervous. I have expertly seduced the most dazzling and dull array of individuals. Darren must be like one of them. He *must* fit into one of my types and as soon as I identify the type, I can select the most appropriate strategy. I rule out anything obvious that I would try with my bimbo boys. I rule out anything dishonest that I would try with the less scrupulous dates I've bagged. I rule out anything that requires a fake identity – he knows me too well already. I look at my clothes. An ensemble of things I've borrowed from Shelly and Sarah, plus the one or two practical pieces that Issie insisted on stealing into my case. I look dreadful, so I rule out anything that is entirely dependent on my couture. I only have tonight, so I rule out anything that requires a long lead time. I had thought of cooking for him – such an act of selflessness, the candles and, if all else fails, the wine would have the desired effect. But having seen the contents of the fridge and also considering how notoriously difficult it is to cook in someone else's kitchen, I rule that out too. Yet I'm leaving tomorrow. I really do have to catch an early train. Bale will go ballistic if I delay any longer, unnecessarily so in my opinion. Fi can handle the film crews until I get there.

I look at my watch. It's 9.15 p.m.

It's now or never.

Never is not an option. I'll have to wing it.

I track Darren down in the front room; he's listening to Radio 4. 'Let's go out. I assume there is a restaurant in Whitby that's still open after nine?' I challenge.

'Plenty. Get your coat.'

11

Darren uses the term 'restaurant' much more generously than I would. You can, after all, buy food at a hot dog stand, but I doubt that A. A. Gill would repeat purchase. The 'restaurant' has about half a dozen assorted tables, which have between two and six variegated chairs scattered casually at each. There are tablecloths but they are plastic, red and white checked. There are flowers on each table but they too are plastic. There is music but it's from a jukebox. However, the candles are real and the food is good, although the choice is limited – spag. bol. or nothing – so we have the spag. bol. Darren also orders a bottle of house red. Neither of us bothers to ask if there is a wine list. There are three other couples in the restaurant and one woman has brought her dog. Loose tits and tummies surround me. This is not the sort of place where I usually hang out. The only mercy is that I'm so far from home that no one will recognize me. I am amazed that Darren seems as comfortable here as he did in the Oxo tower. I couldn't be uneasier. I'm terrified that the provincial drabness will rub off on me. That I'll start to think wearing blue and green together is acceptable or that a good night out is getting trollied in a threadbare pub. Oh no, it's happening already. I have to make my move quickly and get back to civilization before something irrevocable happens to me.

The food and drink arrive. Darren is very quiet and my confounding lack of wit irritates me. I'm never stuck for words. Why now, when I want to be dazzling? I know the end result I'm looking for. Surely getting him to sleep with me can't be that difficult? Right now it seems impossible. I sigh and gaze around the restaurant. I notice a couple of empty nesters asking the waiter to take their photo. I watch, amazed, as he doesn't show the disdain or pity that must be filling his head. They grin and raise their glasses artificially. I'm just about to say something scathing when I notice that Darren is also looking at them and he's smiling.

Fondly.

'Isn't that marvellous?' He nods at the ugly couple. He doesn't seem to be aware of how dreadful they are, but instead starts going on about how great it is to see couples of that age happily married, still in love. I interrupt and point out that the couple are probably on a dirty weekend, and as Blackpool and Brighton were full, they've opted for Whitby. He smiles, ignores me and continues on about how he really believes in fidelity, friendship, familiarity.

'And fucking,' I add. Let's cut to the chase.

'Lovemaking is part of it. Of course, that's important.'

He means this junk and the strange thing is that, as he waxes lyrical, I *almost* begin to believe it, too. His optimism is infectious. It must be the wine. In the nick of time I recover.

'Christ, you're wet,' I spit nastily. I'm not sure why I'm being nasty. Perhaps it's habit.

Darren refuses to take offence but smiles. 'Maybe, but I prefer it to being a cynic.'

'I'm not a cynic,' I bite back. 'I'm a—'

'Realist,' he finishes for me. 'I take it that you don't believe in everlasting love?'

'Everlasting love!' I snort my contempt. 'There is no such thing. People use each other, wear each other out and then move on. You see it all the time. I bet you believe in the Loch Ness monster and Father Christmas, too,' I snap. I look at

Darren and his jaw is clenched. I'm not sure if he's angry or upset. Turns out he's both.

'Why can't you be civil? I'm doing you the favour here, remember. You invited yourself to my home. Has it been so awful for you, being here with my family and me?'

For a moment I'm floored. I sigh, sip my wine and answer honestly.

'No, actually it hasn't been awful at all. I've . . .' I hesitate and then take a deep breath, 'Really had a great time. You have a lovely family.'

Darren relaxes immediately and beams at me. 'I hoped you had but I couldn't be sure. One minute you're laughing and the next you're—'

'What?'

'Well, snarling, for want of a better word.'

I sigh again but accept his observation. 'I do believe people fall in love, or at least lust, or something. We are a very weak species, generally. But they don't stay in love, again because we're too weak. Someone always gets hurt. And in my view it's better to avoid any messiness altogether.'

'Aren't you being a little bit extreme?'

'I can't see a middle lane. Just a tiny bit in love doesn't seem to be an option.'

'Now I do agree with you there.' He pauses and then asks gently, 'Do you remember the other night at the Oxo restaurant?'

Was that just three nights ago? It seems a lifetime.

'I asked you what *really* hurt you.' I nod. 'And then I realized it was none of my business and changed the subject.' I nod again. 'I wondered if you considered it my business yet? Because I'd really like to know what hurt you so badly that you shut down?' He drops his eyes, not looking at me as he asks this question. He's playing with the condiments.

I'm amazed he cares and I want to explain it to him. I wonder if I can.

'It's just that I'm not prepared to accept the flotsam and jetsam of humanity.' He looks up quizzically. 'The debris that passes for a relationship,' I moan, weary with it all. 'Look, it doesn't exist. This exciting love thing that you are obviously searching for, it doesn't exist. I know I've had sex with over fifty men and I've never made love.'

I fall silent and wait for his reaction. He doesn't look shocked or horrified by my confession. Which – irrationally – irritates me. I really want him to be disgusted with me. It would certainly be easier if he walked away now. Or I did. But I'm not sure I can. He's waiting for a more thorough explanation.

'In my experience, and as I've mentioned it's wide and varied, people use each other and when they've finished using they leave.' I pick up my knife and scrape the edge on the plastic tablecloth. I note the irony that a rather bad cover version of 'Don't Leave Me This Way' is playing in the background.

'Who left?'

The way his voice breaks between the words 'who' and 'left' means it is absolutely impossible for me to resist.

'My father.' Stupid angry tears well up from nowhere. I'm stunned. I've kept them at bay for twenty-six years. Why now? Darren sweeps the tear away with his thumb and for a nanosecond the palm of his hand is in contact with my chin. It blisters my skin and oddly soothes it in the same instance. I look at him and despite my years of experience, despite the fact that I've only known him for a few days and despite the fact that he is devastatingly gorgeous-looking – which should always be a warning sign – I want to trust this man. I think I do trust him. Which is dangerous. I have to get a grip.

'Look, I'm sorry. Can we forget that?' I push away my tears and his thumb. 'It's been a long week and what with you pulling out of the show, I'm under a lot of pressure.' He looks hurt. Which is exactly what I want. I want him to feel guilty. I look around the restaurant, desperate for a change of subject. Unless Darren has very strong views on flock wallpaper or plastic flower arrangements, I'm pretty stuck. The evening's gone AWOL. I had thought that by pudding (it's packet trifle, so the term 'pudding' is perhaps philanthropic) we would be flirting and talking exclusively in *doubles entendres*. Instead I'm drenched in big stuff, emotions, feelings of betrayal and, more extraordinarily, feelings of trust and possibility. The stuff I arduously avoid.

'You are lucky to have so many brothers and sisters,' I comment. I admit this isn't exactly a change of subject – we are still on the personal; but it's his personal rather than mine. Which is a far safer zone. 'All this hugging and kissing stuff you do to each other, I think I'm on an American chat show.'

Darren smiles. 'Aren't all families the same?' When I don't answer he stops smiling and simply adds, 'Well, it makes for interesting Christmases.'

'Our house was always quiet. When he left he took – besides the regular income and the mock crocodile suitcases – the fire from the belly of our home. The rows stopped, for which I was grateful. My mother never cried or shouted again. But for that matter she never laughed or giggled either. She settled into an eerie calmness.'

How had that happened? I'm on about me again. I look at my empty glass. Darren sees it as a hint and refills it. I don't argue.

'She cooked for me, washed and ironed my clothes, attended my parents' evenings at school, ensured ends met.

She was perfectly adequate in every way. But I've often thought that the day my father left, I lost my mother too. It seemed she decided that loving was too risky and settled into the sanitized safety of simply caring for me. Even looking back, it seems unfair. I'd never leave her.' I wish I'd shut up. I'm boring myself, never mind Darren. I mean it's hardly the most entertaining anecdote that I could have come up with, is it? Yet I can't stop myself.

'I'm not blaming her. I mean I understand where she's coming from. But occasionally it would have been nice if she could have read a fairy tale and closed the book without sniping that the prince would have a new woman by the end of the year.'

Darren smiles sadly and I force a wry grin back. 'Side by side, we worked our way through Christmases and birthdays, holidays in Devon, O-levels, A-levels and finally university. Mum ironing and singing her anthems, 'Does Anybody Miss Me?' and 'If You Go Away'. My formative years. She is a fine mum and I know she always did her best for me. But sometimes I wish that my father had left behind brothers and sisters to fill the rooms and disguise the sound of the hissing iron and the clanking radiators.'

We both wait silently as the waiter lowers two cups of coffee on to our table. I'm sure it's instant; it's served in the type of teaset that you collect from garages and with a plastic carton of UHT milk. Still, the waiter presents it as though he'd grown the beans himself and he was serving it in a seventeenth-century silver service. I would be annoyed that he's interrupted our conversation but I like people to be involved in their work.

Darren asks, 'Do you look like your mum or dad?'

'I have two pictures of my father and, to my eternal disappointment, I am the image of that callous, deserting bastard.

The pictures were taken in 1967 and 1975. The first is a wedding picture. I rescued the half my mother cut away.'

Darren looks bemused. Of course, he comes from a family wrapped in bliss – how could he understand about wedding pictures being cut in half? I try to explain it for him. 'Oh, don't worry, it wasn't a violent, passionate act. She was very calm about it. She wanted to keep the pictures of herself because she did look wonderful, so she carefully cut around her dress. I remember her using my round-ended scissors from a play weaving kit. She sat at the kitchen table for two days. She erased him from the wedding photos, the ones of my birth, all holiday snaps. Everything. It was a thorough, systematic extermination of all evidence that he ever existed. I stole the 1975 picture before she got to it.' Darren doesn't interrupt. I check he's listening. He is. He's put down his coffee cup. Deliberately I pick mine up. 'That was the year he left us. It's a picture of him helping to blow out the seven candles on my birthday cake.'

How could he have left us, me – the very spit of him?

'Do you miss him?'

'Miss him? I don't even remember him.'

We both fall silent again. I determinedly chew the mints. Just to show that I'm not bothered. It's difficult to swallow.

'For years after he left I tried to imagine what his life was like. When I was in a traffic jam I wondered if he was in it too, or another similar one. When I listened to the radio I wondered if he listened to the same channel. But I didn't know and I'll never know because I know so little about him.'

'You could trace him,' suggests Darren gently.

'I don't want to. He's made it clear where I fit into his life – i.e. I don't. He never paid a penny in alimony or even sent a birthday card. He's given me one thing in my life and I'm grateful for it. He's taught me about loss. He's saved me from ever having a broken heart.' I try to grin. 'I've turned my heart to steel. In fact, even my closest friends question if I have one at all.' I've always believed this.

'You have a heart to break, Cas, just like everyone else.'

I'm indignant. There's no call to be insulting. 'I do not,' I assert defiantly.

'So what makes you think you are different? Your extraordinarily high consumption of sun-blush tomatoes? Because, besides that, you are pretty similar to everyone else.'

'Am I?' I ask, outraged.

'A bit sexier maybe, a bit cleverer.' He ambushes me with compliments. My outrage is melting and being replaced by pure delight. 'You are just the same, Cas. You can fall in love just as easily.'

Angry again, I retort, 'No, I can't. I'm not good on intimacy. I don't like people. They are stupid and disappointing.'

'Not everyone. You like me.'

'You are so vain.' And so right.

'You want to cop out of the human race, then? You can't just hide away, secure because you are not involved, not risking.'

'I have. I am.'

'Just because your father let your mother down it doesn't mean *you* can't find love.'

'If not him, who?' I laugh but my voice is unnaturally high.

'What?'

'If my father couldn't love me, which man can?' I'm going for closure.

'I'd like to have a go.'

Bingo.

Fuck no.

It's unnecessary. I want to sleep with him. But he doesn't need to lie to me. He doesn't need to give me a cheesy line about love. I'm surprised. I thought he was above that. And it is obviously a cheesy line because he can't mean that he wants to have a relationship with me. I've spent the last three days telling him how little I believe in, or care for, such things. Not that this is the first time that I've been faced with this kind of declaration. Men are always telling me they love me. Always have done. But I know they don't mean it and sometimes they know they don't mean it, too. It's just a rather rudimentary ritual. It's more polite than just asking for a fuck. I rarely sleep with men who go for the love angle, unless I'm certain they don't mean it. If I suspect they do mean it, I forgo the sex and turn them into good friends – using their devotion for practical purposes whenever my lawn needs mowing or my garage needs clearing.

But Darren's different.

I don't think he would talk of love unless he was serious. But then, how can he be serious after all I've said? I do want to sleep with him because I fancy him like mad. But I can't possibly sleep with him if I think it means more than just sex to him. It will only get complicated. I don't want to hurt him. He's a nice guy. I must be absolutely transparent about how I feel about him.

If only I knew.

'I don't think you are the right man to try and love me, Darren,' I grin brightly. It's a fake grin and fake brightness.

'Why is that?'

'Well, you're not my type.'

'Why not?'

Why not! Why not? God, this guy is arrogant. 'Well, you're a bit too serious and, erm, homely, for me.' Darren looks at his empty cup. I feel like the bitch everyone says I am. I try to make amends. 'I'm not saying I don't fancy you. I do fancy you. I'd be happy to fuck.'

'Sex is not supposed to be separate from love.' Darren stares at me horrified and yes, I think it is disgust I can see there. Well, that should make things simpler.

'Aghh, but I've had *great* uncomplicated sex.' I try to cheer him.

'Yes, but have you ever made love? All that variety. The flings, the shags, the affairs, the nameless wonders—' He waves his hand, dismissing the men in my past, just the way I do. 'You've never had love. It's just too easy to avoid.'

'I don't need it,' I say matter-of-factly.

'You think you are so brave, don't you, Cas?' I never indulge in these conversations. They lead nowhere. They lead to— 'Well, you're not. Being brave is trusting. Being aloof is easy.' I stifle the yawn. Go, Einstein. I reassure myself that it is only his pride that is hurt. 'You use your parents and your career to avoid intimacy because you are scared.'

'Did you go to college to come up with that?'

We glare at each other over the single bud vase with the plastic flower and the empty wine bottle that is doubling as a candleholder. I know enough about men to realize that pursuing this scenario is going to waste my time. Darren's too intense. Someone would get hurt. Yes, he's a shag, undeniably fanciable, but it's not worth it. He has bunny boiler written all over him. He obviously cares for me and I simply can't allow myself to feel the same way. I admit it would be tempting to allow myself to believe that the intensity and the caring could last. But it simply doesn't. And what if I do feel the same? What if I do . . . care for him? Where would it lead? Nowhere, that's where. I've got to be brutal to be benevolent.

'You are obsessed with love. It's not your fault. It's popular culture. You're right, TV does have a lot to answer for. This ridiculous ideal, which doesn't exist, is touted in every song, poster and book. I'm sure if the Beatles had sung songs about world peace we'd be war free by now.'

'They did.'

'Oh, well not just the Beatles, then, but everyone.' I try to joke but he remains deadly serious. He's not going to let either of us off the hook.

'Do you know what I think? Searching for love, the One, it's such a lot of wasted energy. It's embarrassing. I'm embarrassed for the human race. I think we should move on. I blame Shakespeare! Love, it's insane. Get the bill.'

It's excruciating. Darren and I travelled home from the restaurant in silence. I went to bed immediately. This morning I had my breakfast with Linda; Darren was out walking the dog. It's pouring. I packed and he came home to drive me to the station. We've travelled the entire distance without using a double-syllabled word. It's a disaster. Being here is a disaster. Opening up is a disaster. Teasing Darren is a disaster. I take solace in the fact that soon I'll be on the train to King's Cross. I can go directly to the studio and make my peace with the increasingly irate Bale. I can finish the filming and manage the editing for this week's show and by Saturday night I won't even remember Darren's name. I am determined that he'll be consigned to history.

We arrive at Darlington station. The only sound is the swish of the overworked windscreen wipers. Darren gets out of the car with me. He goes to see when the train is expected and I wait on the platform. He comes back, looking yet more miserable and pitiful than before.

'We've got nearly an hour to wait. I'm sorry, I should have checked the timetable before we set off.'

'It's OK. I should have done that.' We fall silent again. 'You don't have to stay. I can wait in the café.' The plan is that

Darren is spending the rest of the week with his family. He isn't due back in London until Sunday night. I'm relieved – I couldn't stand having to do the entire journey with him in silence.

'I'd rather wait. To see you safely on the train.'

'Make sure I do leave, hey?' I try to joke but I suddenly feel horribly lonely. Inexplicably, I realize I don't want to leave things like this. I don't want to get back on the train and go home to my flat. I don't want never to see Darren again. I've been kidding myself. This wasn't ever about whether Darren appeared on the show or not. His appearance would have made a strong show. His devastating good looks would force me into tuning into *The Generation Game*, so I can only imagine the meltdown effect he'd have on the rest of the British population, yet he's not, nor was he ever, essential to the show. We have replacements. I came to Whitby because I wanted to be with him. I don't understand why I did, but I did.

I still do.

Is he going to leave me alone here on the platform? If he does, I'll scream. He's staring at the ground. I follow his gaze and try to concentrate on what he's saying.

'As a child I used to think petrol puddles were rainbows that were a casualty of a nasty road accident.' He smiles shyly, seeing how I'll relate to such an intimate confession. He's expecting something cutting that would prevent an outpouring of memories. After all, memories only lead to knowledge and intimacy. The danger of liking the person. But suddenly I face it. I want to know more about this man. I want to know everything. What was the name of the teacher he had his first crush on? There must have been one. Who are his friends? Why does he have that little scar above his eye? Does he like pesto? Does he hate mushy peas? What does he think about amusement arcades? What does he fear most? What's he like in bed? Who is he going to fall in love with next?

Is there still a chance it could be me?

What?

'Should we go for a coffee?'

I agree immediately.

Darren doesn't want to go to the station café but opts for a small 'Italian' café run by Iranian refugees. Their Italian accents are worse than mine but their cappuccinos are convincing. We sit on the sticky wooden benches and face each other over the tiny Formica table. So tiny that our heads are almost touching. But then this is OK, as the cappuccino machine is making so much noise that I'd have to lean close to hear him anyway.

'About last night – I want to apologize,' I offer. I'm not sure what I want to apologize for but I know that I feel awful. I want to tell him that I'm sorry for my toing and froing. I'm sorry for my ice-maiden act. And most of all that I'm sorry that I haven't been able to trust him.

'No, I should apologize. I rushed things.' And whilst the words are kind the tone is curt.

'It's just that we hardly know each other.' This comes out sounding like another criticism and I want it to be an explanation for my caution.

'I wasn't proposing, Cas. I was just suggesting that we could try to get to know each other. I admit I was a bit hamfisted. But look, it doesn't matter. You made your feelings perfectly clear.'

But I didn't, did I? I couldn't have because I can't. Make things clear. It's mud. I want him. I fancy him. I respect him. I like him. He intrigues me. I'm in trouble. It strikes me, as I sit in yet another one of our silences, that our relationship to date, such as it is, has been a series of rows and silences. Which proves my point that intimacy always leads to cruelty and aggro. I look at Darren and he looks dejected and delicious. I am unaware of anything other than my pulsing sex, aching breasts and throbbing lips, all of which could be relieved if he'd just kiss me. He's not going to and I can't be tortured like this any longer. I stand up and I swear the room is partying. I put my hand on the table to steady myself. It's hot in this tiny café.

'Look . . . goodbye . . . and . . . thanks for the coffee.'

It's frantic and hurried and amazing. He touches my hand. He's not trying to restrain me. But he has. I'm rooted. His finger is resting gently on my wrist. I'm shackled. I'm ignited. I kiss him. He kisses back. Strong and dark. Engulfing. I've never kissed before. Or if I have, they were poor dress rehearsals. This is it. All the words that have fallen between us suddenly disappear, they are superfluous. We're left with naked silence. Stripped to desire. He tosses a few quid on the table and, not waiting for the change, we dash out of the café, into the rain. He points to an alleyway behind the station. I'm already heading that way; I have an in-built mechanism that helps me to locate dark streets and other possible places for fornication. The rain is still pelting down, hitting the pavement and vaulting up again. It falls through the afternoon darkness in nasty, spiky, drops, but I don't care. In fact, I'm grateful: the vicious elements mean that the streets are empty. I'm boiling over with anticipation. He takes a tight hold on my arm. We cross the road, not checking for traffic. Darren flings me up against the wall, barely pausing to check for privacy, I wrap my coat around him. His lips mesh into mine and we're kissing so hard I can't tell them apart. He scrabbles with his flies and then sinks into me. I stare into his eyes and he stares back, never losing me. Not for a second. It feels amazing. It feels important. It feels right.

He's climbing, he's filling, he's plugging. He completes me.

It's over in minutes.

I'm already scared that this will never be over.

12

Someone is holding his or her finger on my door buzzer. One of the inconveniences of my loft apartment is that it has nothing as old-fashioned as a spyhole. It is impossible to know who is at the door without talking to them, by which time it is impossible to pretend not to be in, if that is the desired course of action.

I long for the visitor to be Issie. Possibly Josh, but ideally Issie. And yet I am terrified it is. What will I tell her? What can I say? How can I possibly begin to explain my behaviour over the past two weeks?

Buuuuzzzzzzz.

This persistence demands my attention. If I ignore whoever, I'll spend the rest of the afternoon wondering who it was. I drag myself towards the intercom praying it's not Bale or Fi.

'It's me,' says Issie. 'Where the hell have you been? Open up instantly.'

I'm relieved and press the release button. Within moments she is pushing open my door. She's really pissed off with me, so much so that she doesn't bother to kiss me. I'm aware that offence is the best form of defence so I demand, 'Why didn't you use your key?'

'Lost it,' she shrugs, immediately apologetic. I tut and start making noises about the security risk and the inconvenience of getting a replacement cut. Once she's appropriately subdued I ask, 'Have you looked in your dressing-table drawer?'

'No.'

'Well, I think it's in there. With the socks.'

'Why would I keep keys with my socks?'

'Beats me, Issie, but you do.'

This exchange takes place whilst we move towards the kitchen. It's four thirty on a Sunday afternoon. Which seems the perfect time to pour not just healthy but bionic G&Ts. I certainly need mine. My interlude with the key doesn't throw Issie completely.

'What's been going on, Cas? It's not so surprising that you disappear but normally it's work-related. I called the studio and they said you had laryngitis. I called here but there was no reply. You weren't hospitalized, were you?'

I take a proper look at Issie for the first time since she arrived, and I feel pretty dreadful. She is extremely drawn and nervous-looking. I realize I'm a worry to her. Then again so are lost puppies, the axeing of trees, and the absence of clean, running water in India. Considering the issues Issie involves herself with on an on-going basis, my going AWOL for over a week is small fry. We look at one another and she pauses, immediately suspicious.

'You don't look ill. You look really well.'

It's true, to be direct – I'm a goddess. My hair, black and shiny as a matter of course, is positively glistening. My smile, previously used only for effect, is now a permanent fixture. My skin has always had a pale and interesting hue, but now I'm sporting rose-red cheeks.

'Why didn't you call me, or Josh, or your mum? We were demented. What the hell is going on?'

She's going on and on and on. Question after question after question. Few of which I'm inclined to answer and those I am more willing to respond to are far too complicated. I'm relieved when she abruptly stops mid-conversation flow, but only momentarily, as I soon realize she is staring at the dirty crockery left over from this morning's breakfast. Normally anally tidy, I have not cleared up. This and the fact that the assorted debris discloses that the breakfast was saturated fat endorsed (as opposed to freshly squeezed orange juice and an ounce of Bran Flakes – my usual) astounds Issie.

'It's not just the eggshells that have been broken, is it?' Her tone is both suspicious and delighted. I shake my head and look at the slate tiles. I wonder if I can distract her by pointing to the grime under the fridge. I doubt it. 'You've broken precedent, too, haven't you? You *never* feed men breakfast. Who's been privileged like this?'

'Darren.' Simply. Unusually I haven't the energy or inclination to fudge. In fact, I want to talk about him.

'Darren?!' Uncomprehending. 'The last time I spoke to you, you'd had a huge row. He was about to take you to the station. You were coming back to London *alone*. What happened?'

I thought I'd explained: Darren happened.

I tell Issie about the train ride to Darlington, the swimming baths, and the walks on the beach and in the graveyard. I know I'm giggling, blushing and gushing (even in this state of near-hysteria I'm gratified to note she also thinks a walk through gravestones is odd). I tell her about the pub, the restaurant and finally the hissing cappuccino machine. I tell her that suddenly (whilst sitting over an itchy, orange Formica table) it occurred to me. Suddenly I knew, more clearly than I've ever known anything in my life, that I wanted him. I wanted him beyond reason or rationale.

'Whoa there.' Issie holds her skinny hands in front of her, trying to block the overload of incomprehensible information. She used to do this when we studied Russian language at night classes. Although I am trying to be clear, it's understandable that Issie feels she's neck high in the sludgy waters of an unknown territory. She naturally assumes that when I say I wanted him, I mean sexually. Exclusively sexually. A fair assumption in light of my history.

Inaccurate.

She lights one of my cigarettes, without asking.

'I thanked him for the coffee and *tried* to walk away but—'

'But?'

'He put his hand on mine and said, "You're welcome. The pleasure really was mine, Cas."' I repeat this conversation in a stupid drawling voice, which is actually nothing like Darren's voice. It's just that I am aware that what I'm saying is serious stuff. I hope the ridiculous voice will serve to make the story funnier, less intense.

'Noooo.' Issie latches on to the idiotic voice, hoping it's a lifeboat. She assumes I'd find this action inane. Any man, trying to get inside my knickers, should know never, ever to appear sentimental once, never mind twice. I can't stand it.

Usually.

'And did he say your name like, Kez.' She says my name as though she is a drunk David Niven impersonating Jimmy Tarbuck. Unaccountably, her mocking makes me ashamed. It's always felt fine to be harsh and heinous; now it seems puerile. Darren deserves better.

'Er, to be frank, no.'

'But his hand was clammy.' Issie, understandably disconcerted, is still holding out for the reassurance of one of my 'scathing dismissal' stories, as supplied on countless occasions. Scathing dismissal stories make Issie feel better about the fact that she is horribly needy and couldn't be stinging to save her life. My cruelty to the opposite sex evens things up for her. It's no use. I'd like to help but I can't lie.

'Actually, it was cool and smooth.'

Issie nearly spills her G&T on the floor as the shock makes her overestimate the size of my coffee table.

'Careful,' I grumble, thinking about the Purves and Purves carpet.

'When you say you wanted him . . .?'

I take a deep breath. I force forward. 'I just couldn't leave him.'

As best as I can, I explain it to Issie. I tell her that the pots are still dirty because I can't bear to wash him away. I even tell her that the sheets are rank for the same reason.

'Sheets? When did we get to sheets?' she squeals.

I could tell her about the first time. No sheets, just a filthy brick wall. Hurried and frenzied. My coat left damp and grubby, in need of a clean. My scarf sticky with dried love, because I used it to wipe his dick.

And I know that if I tell Issie this she'd think this is in character, it's what she expects of me. It's what I expect of me. But if I elucidate and add that whilst the act was undoubtedly basic and animalistic, it was also bashing against the surreal. We were wrapped in a pure light that made us *us*. Distinct and apart from anyone else, we floated in an individual time dimension that no one else knew about, or could ever visit. There was a secret, silent acceptance that hearts and flowers and all that they have come to symbolize were an option, even for me. I was *there*. *I* was involved.

He completed me.

Against an alley wall.

What would she make of that? Only one way to find out.

I tell her the stuff I'd vowed not to tell her. I can't do otherwise; it bursts out. I'm overpouring with Darren. Thoughts of Darren. Memories of Darren. Imaginings about Darren. I'm not nervous exactly; it's something different to nervous. I'm excited, I'm exhilarated.

I'm terrified.

Issie listens to my garbled account of events to date; she says nothing but is wearing a ridiculous smirk on her face. The smirk broadens to a grin and then it widens an unfeasible fraction more. She's beaming as I tell her that I didn't get on a train back to London that Thursday morning, or Friday, or Saturday for that matter. Instead we booked into a tiny country house. As I repeat these facts the image of Darren licking me out, which has been more or less permanently burned on my mind, becomes 3D again.

We are in bed; limbs, sheets and senses entangled and confused. Yet as he asks, 'Here, do you like it here?' I experience an unparalleled sense of clarity and certainty. I like it there, very much. I recall my fingers (which had never looked so slim and tapering) being swallowed into his thick, black hair. I'm lying on my back and looking down at my body and his head. It's nodding slightly as he moves his tongue a fraction to send me beyond consciousness. That bit was slow. But then that was our fourth time. Or was it our fifth?

Issie is quite traditionally dumbfounded.

'We stayed in bed for three days. In the end we were more or less evicted.'

I smile to myself as I think of the exasperated chambermaid begging us to leave our room so that she could clean it.

'After that, after listening to each other's breathing, dreams, thoughts, we became . . . necessary to each other.' I struggle, then come clean. 'I couldn't let him go home alone.'

I'd have lost part of myself.

'Instead I asked him back to my apartment.'

Because if not, I'd have missed his singing in the bathroom. I'd have missed him tracing kisses from the end of my hair, to my scalp, past my ears, to my jaw line, then up – finally

– to my mouth. I'd have missed the sound of his pee hitting the loo.

'He left this morning. He had to go to the Cotswolds – a tree with measles.'

Issie is quickly piecing together my story. She's counting days on her fingers. She looks confused. She must have put two and two together and, quite unusually for Issie, she's come up with four.

'He stayed here for a week?'

'Yes.'

'But you never let men stay at your flat for more than twelve hours. That's your rule. What did you do for a week?'

'Well, besides the obvious, which took up a substantial amount of time, we went to the pub, I met his flatmate, Jock. We went for a curry, we watched vids.'

'You dated.'

'No.' I think about it. 'OK, well, yes, I suppose.'

'What about work?'

'Work?' What an odd question.

'What did you tell Bale?'

'You know, I told him I had laryngitis.' I'm irritated that she wants to talk about work.

'But Cas, when you had an emergency appendicitis you discharged yourself early because the hospital staff wouldn't let you use a mobile phone. Illness doesn't stop you working. Bale won't have believed your story about laryngitis. Why did you say laryngitis? You've never had it. Do you have any idea what it's like? How long it lasts? How contagious it is?'

Issie's panicking.

She moves towards my bookshelves and starts rooting around for a medical journal. She's obviously going to look up laryngitis. Which is sweet of her, but why is she so concerned? I can hardly bring myself to be bothered.

'You could lose your job. You are in deep do-do.'

I try not to giggle at the expression and instead I think about Darren. I smile, widely, remembering how he hesitated by the door. We'd both been trying, for a week, to get back to work. We'd both been trying, for a week, to stay glued together. Issie notes my serenity and yells, 'Aren't you worried?'

What can I say? If she doesn't get it, it proves to me what I have long suspected: Issie has never been in . . . Issie's never felt like this. It would be pointless to explain that he let me warm my (eternally) cold feet on his (eternally) hot shins, or bum, or bollocks. It would be futile to elaborate. The thing is, from that first kiss my head spun but my life stopped wobbling. I hadn't even known it was wobbling before. I know what his hair smells like. I know where he is ticklish. I've licked the inside of his nostril. I had sex until I was raw, but for the first time ever, it was entirely to do with love. My body does not feel like a gambling chit, a bargaining tool or a funfair ride. The world is Technicolor.

All of this from me! The confirmed steel heart. Poor Issie, how could she possibly understand? I consider myself the more perceptive, intuitive, sagacious of the two of us and I have no clue how this happened.

I make a move towards the kitchen to pour us both two more gigantic G&Ts. I carelessly slosh gin into the glasses and splash some tonic on top. Issie stares. She's incredulous.

'No ice?'

'It's in the freezer,' I reply, heading back to the settee.

'And lemon?' I ignore her altogether. Normally I insist on measuring the drink carefully. Pouring the gin over three ice cubes and adding a slice of lemon and lime (my own speciality). I prepare G&Ts with the same care and attention that most people reserve for cooking a three-course gourmet dinner. Today I can't be fussed. To be honest, the preparation of G&T is not interesting. It's not Darren.

I pat the settee and Issie joins me. We both curl up in front of the open fire. It isn't real. It's a very good natural gas impersonation, which is cleaner and easier. Admittedly they don't give off quite the same aroma but the difference is minuscule and I'm prepared to sacrifice that small piece of authenticity for an easier life.

'Since he left this morning I've tried to distract myself by watching videos but every one I selected was about love and stuff.' I throw my arms in the air, exasperated. 'Four different videos, I tried. I put on a selection of various CDs and read the first page of a bunch of novels; but every way I turned I bashed up against poignancy.'

Issie's smirking again. 'It surprises me that you have romantic books and vids.'

'That's the point, Issie. Before I met Darren they were just novels and films; now they are *romantic* novels and films. It's weird. The very fact that I find them romantic shows that—'

'That you're in love.'

'Don't be so bloody stupid,' I snap hastily. Issie doesn't meet my eye but concentrates on sipping her gin. 'I'm not in love.' She doesn't say anything. 'I'm not,' I insist. 'Popular culture is so manipulative.'

We are silent, watching the flames flicker. I'm thinking of Darren and me rolling around in front of it, behaving like a couple of proverbial soap stars. I don't care what Issie is thinking of.

'What are you afraid of, Cas?' Oh, she's thinking of me.

'I am in love.' The words resonate around the room. Booming and thundering into our lives. Saying the words aloud is at once a relief, and also the most horrifyingly, scary moment of my life. 'I am in love with him.'

'Really! Reallyreallyreallyreally?!' Issie jumps up and this time the G&T does go flying. I scowl as I stand up to get a cloth from the kitchen. I quietly sop up the G&T.

'Yes,' I sigh, overwhelmed for the umpteenth time today by my own emotion. We are both stunned and enjoy the confession. Issie is delirious. It's as though I've just told her I've won the lottery or that *she*'d won the lottery.

'How do you know? When did you know? Oh God, Cas, how amazing.'

I smile, making the most of my moment.

'It was when we booked into the country hotel. Terrible place, floral carpets and cluttered reception, covered in flyers advertising darts matches and provincial craft shows. He had a bag with him.'

Issie looks uncertain. I clarify.

'He'd packed condoms, toothbrush and clean boxers. So besides being mouthwateringly desirable, interesting, intelligent, moral and funny (all admirable qualities but not the ones that normally fly my kite) I realized he was presumptuous and cunning too.'

'Jackpot,' she smiles.

'Exactly,' I confirm, and I can't help it – I actually clap my hands.

I luxuriate in the memories and Issie is bathing in possibility.

'Did you know we'd end up here?' I'd asked. He dribbled champagne (house, but who cares) into my mouth from his, silencing me momentarily.

'I didn't absolutely know.' Mischievous.

'But you expected it?' Disgruntled.

He moved his lips from mine and attached them to my nipple, whilst he poured more champagne into my tummy button. He inched towards the alcohol lake, kissing and caressing my shoulder, my collarbone, my waist. He lapped up the champagne whilst I silently thanked my personal trainer – the two hundred sit-ups a day were worth it.

'I didn't expect it. I hoped for it. I told you, I'm an optimist,' Darren grinned. His lips were wet with champagne and my cum.

Artful audacity is the icing on the cake. Suddenly Darren seemed dangerous. When had he got ahead of me in our sexual chess game? Had he won? Had I? Could we both?

It seems unlikely.

Cold, steely fear puts a hand around my throat, the grip tightens, squeezing the happiness out of me. My heart, which has been residing in the roof of my mouth, plummets. What have I done? What *have* I done? This is the disaster I've spent twenty-six years trying to avoid. I am not prepared to throw caution to the wind after just two weeks.

It would be nonsense.

I won't do it.

I can't do it.

This is the worst thing that could have happened. Because now I believe in all the stuff on TV, radio, novels and cinema. It's true. You do know when you meet the One.

Your muse, your purpose, your explanation of life.

And suddenly life is shiny and glossy and worthwhile. But if the films and songs are right about falling in love, the chances are they can offer some insight into the outcome of entertaining such emotions.

Pain.

Lots of it.

Isn't my mother living proof?

Every second I was with Darren was exhilarating. Reliving it now, every second is heartbreaking as I'm plagued with thoughts of what could go wrong. When he said he loved me I was blissed out, ecstatic but now I'm petrified. When Darren was with me I believed it. I believed it all, the happily ever after, the possibility that everlasting love is an option. But my confidence is ebbing away. It's unrealistic to expect Darren to stay with me every minute of every day but when he's not with me I'm too small to fight my own demons. It was OK in Whitby when we were constantly with each other – of course he couldn't be unfaithful or leave me. But now . . . where is he now? Maybe he's not in the Cotswolds. Maybe he's with another woman. The reality is that love never lasts; falling in love is asking to be hurt, deceived and betrayed. I feel naked. I look at Issie but she's oblivious to the sudden cold chill in the air. I know she's thinking that if this happened to me, absolutely anything is possible.

But it's not.

'Of course, it can't go on,' I state, making my mind up only in the seconds that the words form in my mouth.

'What?'

Turns out Issie's lottery ticket got thrown out with the garbage. Shame.

'It's impossible.' My tone is more certain than my mind.

'But you've just said you love him,' Issie is spluttering.

'I do,' I snap. 'At this moment I love him completely, utterly, desperately, clichédly. But if I carry on like this the next thing you'll know is that I'll be giving him a pet name and wanting his babies.' I sound more harsh and resolute than I feel. I hope my voice convinces my heart.

'And what's so terrible about that?'

If I'm not mistaken she actually has tears in her eyes or perhaps her contacts are playing up. Poor Issie.

'Well, let's take it through to its logical conclusion, shall we? What if he doesn't feel the same? What if I care for him more than he cares for me?'

'But from what you said he sounds besotted.'

'Well, men always are at first, aren't they?' Even Issie should know this. Especially Issie. 'Then when the girl's hooked they stop calling. The power in every relationship sits with the person who cares least.'

'That's where you go wrong, thinking that relationships are about power.'

'*I* don't go wrong, Issie.' I lay a heavy emphasis on the 'I'. 'This would never have happened if I'd stayed in town. It's just that Whitby was, I don't know, beautiful, romantic.' I continue to search for the correct word, 'different'.

'Cas, are you sure it's the scenery and not him that you are talking about?' I glare at her. 'He sounds genuine,' she pleads.

'OK, well, scenario number two. Assuming he feels the same way that I do—'

'He does, doesn't he? I know you think he does,' squeals Issie.

I hardly dare suggest it. I think of him nibbling my fingers, brushing my hair, and looking at baby photos of me.

'Well, for the sake of this argument, let's say he does. Then what?'

'You could marry and live Happily Ever After.'

As though it really were that simple. How naive! Issie obviously hasn't learnt anything from her years of being my friend. I explain it slowly and clearly, as I'm beginning to suspect she's hard of hearing.

'There. Is. No. Such. Thing. Yes, we could marry but sooner or later (and it probably would be sooner, as these intense affairs are always the first to burn out) he'd let me down. Or I'd let him down. And that would be hell. If he can make me feel this good' – as though I was born the moment his dick delved into me – 'imagine how foul he could make me feel if he left.'

Issie hides her face in her hands. 'Who are you trying to convince?'

'No one.' Me. Me. I'm trying to convince myself, but at the same time I'd be more grateful than Issie could possibly know if she proved my argument is guff. But she can't because I'm right. I'm certain I'm right. I have to stop this going any further.

'Cas, you're thirty-three now, not seven. And just because your parents' relationship didn't work it doesn't mean there can't be successful relationships.'

I glare at her. Although Issie knows everything about my mother and father's divorce, we have an unwritten rule that we never discuss it. I am not the type to bleat on Oprah.

'Issie, one in three households are single-people households. Three in four couples who co-habit split up. Nearly one in two marriages end in divorce. Look at the facts.' Now that 'the facts' have burst (uninvited) into my consciousness they won't go away.

'But think about Nicole Kidman and Tom Cruise. They've been married for ever and they are blissful.'

'That's one example, Issie.'

'There's the Queen and Prince Philip.' I snort. She's desperate.

'There's Mr and Mrs Brown in the baker's on *Teddington Crescent*.'

'They're fictional.'

'There's my mum and dad.'

'But your mum hates your dad.'

'Not at all. She only pretends to. What about that couple on your show who didn't fall into temptation?'

'It's only a matter of time.'

Issie raises her eyes skyward.

'Oh, Cas, you poor thing.'

What can she mean? My mistake was allowing myself to become besotted by Darren. A mistake but not irrevocable. Not if I act swiftly and certainly now.

'Issie, can I come and stay with you for tonight?'

'Of course, if you want to. Why?'

'Because I know if I see him I'll weaken and I'm expecting him to pop by late tonight, when he gets back from the Cotswolds.'

'Oh, see him, pleeeease.'

'I can't, Issie. I'm not playing games here. This isn't a way to make him more interested. I have to sever all contact immediately. I can't allow this to continue. I can't make myself vulnerable.'

I simply can't. Not won't. Can't.

I whizz around my bedroom and start throwing some clothes and cosmetics into a bag. I hardly pause to consider what I'm selecting, but I do stop to smell the sheets and to take him in one last time. He is why I was born a woman, but he can never, ever know because whilst I can only just bear walking away from him, I know I would be inconsolable if he ever left me.

This vulgar state of being 'in love' – it's bound to be only temporary. The sooner I get back to my ordinary routine the better I'll feel.

It will only be a matter of time.

Very little time at that, probably.

Probably.

I pull the sheets off the bed and push them into the washing basket.

Issie realizes that she's not going to change my mind so instead settles for changing the subject. As I stuff a hairbrush and knickers in a bag she tells me that the sad loser guy from New Year has called. They've seen each other a few times.

Issie's excited because they play Connect 4 together. I can't forgive him for letting his mother fix him up. Issie chatters on but I can't keep track. I'm sure it's delightful but I'm not sure I care. How has this terrible thing happened to me? How has this wonderful thing happened to me? How can it be both at once? I've seen enough to know that it is a messy, complex, filthy state of affairs at the best of times – i.e. when you want to be in love. This is by no means the best of times. I thought I was immune. I thought I was somehow better or different – certainly cleverer. Now I understand no one is immune.

As we put on our coats, Issie sighs, 'You haven't been listening to a word I've been saying, have you?'

'I'm sorry, Issie. I've spent my entire evening forgetting about Darren,' I smile sadly.

'Why are you doing this? Don't you think there's a possibility that you are snuffing out a genuine chance of happiness?' she coaxes.

'No. It's an exercise in damage limitation.'

'I don't understand you, Cas.'

'Really? How odd. I thought I'd made myself crystal clear.' Except of course I'm lying. I don't understand me either. The bit I do understand, the fact that I *am* in love, only serves to confuse me further.

I lock the door behind me and Blu-tack an envelope to the door. It's addressed to Darren and the letter inside simply says:

Don't call.

13

Work is as foul as I thought it would be. Bale didn't swallow the laryngitis story because Fi, the bitch, showed him a photo of Darren.

'Laryngitis, my arse.'

'No, actually it's a throat infection,' I snipe back. It is a weak retort but I'm out of practice. I've been being nice to people for two weeks, for God's sake.

'I saw his picture, Jocasta. You were shagging. Getting your end away whilst the rest of us carried the can. It's shoddy. It's unacceptable. What do you have to say for yourself?'

Bale has selected his glass office for this public flaying. I know that however angry he is, he has to appear more so for the benefit of the rest of the team.

'Nigel, you are getting this out of proportion.' I only ever call him Nigel when things are desperate. I consider leaning over his desk and creating an illusion of intimacy by touching his arm, but I can't bring myself to do it. 'OK, so I trailed a candidate for the show and OK, it turned out to be a duff call because I couldn't persuade him to be on the show, but it was worth the gamble. If he'd appeared, it would have been the biggest show ever.'

'Why?'

I knew that would get him.

'This guy objects to the show on moral grounds: social and individual. He's startlingly handsome and very articulate. If he'd agreed to be on the show there isn't a person in the country who would have wanted to oppose his decision. Not the lace industry, the manager of the John Lewis wedding gift service or that bishop.' I toss the latest list of complaint letters to Bale. 'The viewers would have united. He'd have taken away the last shadow of doubt about the show. People would have clambered to appear.'

'But you couldn't persuade him?'

'No, I couldn't,' I reply to my hands.

'You tried everything?' He holds on the word 'everything' and we both know what he is asking. Did I sleep with Darren to get him to appear on the show? Yes and no. This answer is far too subtle for Bale to comprehend.

'Everything.' My face is aflame.

Bale leans very close to me and I can see the blackheads nestling in the crease between his nose and cheek.

'Maybe you're losing your touch.'

'What an arse!' I complain to Fi, as there is no one else around. Most of my team have decided that it's wiser to keep out of my way for a while. Fi is either braver or more stupid than the rest.

'I thought you'd need some company.' She hands me a double espresso. I wince as I swallow it back. It's some time since I've drunk such strong coffee. It tastes like creosote.

'It's not as though anything went wrong whilst you were away,' comments Fi.

She really is a bitch. I think it's time to remind her who the guru is.

'Yes. Well done, Fi. I saw that the ratings had stabilized at 9.1. Don't worry that you didn't get an increase with your shows. I thought they were very competently filmed, no matter what the punters thought.' I smile at her and she hesitates, not knowing whether she should smile back or not.

'You're pleased, then?'

'You held the fort. Well done.' The words say one thing, the tone another.

'Have I upset you?'

I sigh. I know I'm being a cow. Fi has produced two good shows. Without her there would have been no possibility of my taking off to Whitby, never mind staying for a week and then pulling the laryngitis stunt for another week. She's made a few minor cock-ups with the paperwork, she hasn't responded to any of the log-room calls and she hasn't helped Ricky or Di with any of the decisions they needed to make on scheduling or marketing. But, all in all, she's done a fine job. It's not her fault that I feel like crying, laughing, shouting, dancing and howling, whilst smashing and kissing everything in my eye's view. I'm turbulent. And misunderstood. Most notably, by myself.

'No, really, you have done a great job,' I assure and this time I do it with a bit more enthusiasm. Her face breaks into a massive grin.

'I hoped you'd be pleased. Now tell me what really went on. I want details.'

Fi pulls up a chair and we huddle around my PC. It is not my usual style to indulge in girly confidences but I haven't said Darren's name aloud for hours. If I don't say it soon I'll erupt. I tell her some of the things that I told Issie. I tell her about the train journey, his family, the swimming baths, the walks and the 'restaurants'. I've been talking for about twenty minutes solid and I've only just caught Fi's expression. She looks bewildered.

'What?'

'Cut the foreplay, get to the shagging.'

I stare through her and think of the lovemaking. I can't tell her. For one thing, some of the language is potentially shocking, even for a Scand. And two, it's private. It's Darren's and mine. I can't turn him into a character in a short story. The phone rings and Fi reaches for it.

'Jocasta Perry's line, Fi Spencer speaking.' I turn to my e-mail and let Fi deal with the call. I note that she's blushing. Then she giggles. Finally she says, 'I'll just check.' She covers the hand set and behaves like a pantomime dame.

'It's himmmmm,' she mouths.

'Whoooo?' I mouth back; it appears it's contagious.

Fi flaps her arms up and down and rolls her eyes. In less enlightened eras she'd have been consigned to the ducking chair for less.

'Darren.'

'I'm not here.'

Fi looks perplexed. She makes excuses to Darren and then carefully copies down all his contact numbers. As she hangs up she passes me the note with the numbers on.

'So you did sleep with him.' Her tone has changed considerably from before the call. I don't deny it; I just shrug. 'And now you've lost all interest,' she concludes. I wonder if this is what Darren has surmised. 'Christ, Cas, you are such a love-them-and-leave-them merchant that I'm beginning to think that you were born a man and had a sex change. How can you resist him?'

I take the numbers from her and put them in the bin. 'If he calls again, tell him I've left the company.'

Because of the bishop's letter, Bale and I spend the entire day working side by side. The directors are metaphorically urinating all over the leather chairs in the executive suite. It's not that any of them are particularly godly – far from it. But one or two of them are hoping to be mentioned in the Queen's next honours list. Offending the Church is only one stop away from offending the government. Bale and I talk to the duty officers who work in the log room and fully analyse the complaints and compliments that the show has received since its conception. The duty officers are loyal and pragmatic and go some way to reassuring Bale that everything is cool. I suspect the loyalty is inspired by George, the duty office manager, who talks to my breasts.

'People are always more likely to complain than praise. The Great British Public complains about everything.' George shrugs; my breasts don't comment but let him continue. 'This bishop thing, don't sweat it. It's always the mad ones who complain. I've had letters saying that we are biased against smokers, that they don't like the colour of the dress that the newscaster is wearing.' I don't interrupt to say I have some sympathy – our newscasters are sartorially challenged. 'During the Rugby World Cup we received complaints about the TV angles, that the Union Jack was upside down.'

'Was it?'

'I don't know. They said Shirley Bassey was miming, which was definitely a lie. That the action was too much for epileptics and migraine sufferers. We are no longer a nation of shop-keepers but a nation of whiners.'

I'm pleased – these examples discredit the people who complain, they seem petty and small-minded. I thank George for his time, with my special smile. It's wasted because as wide as it stretches it doesn't stretch to my breasts.

Bale and I also meet the scheduling and marketing departments. By midday we have a convincing response for the executive committee and, although we have the entire afternoon scheduled for debate, I know it won't be longer than an hour before the meeting breaks down and someone walks out. It's inevitable, with so many egos in the room. I'm delighted when my prediction comes true. The only director who really does object to my show is bullied and humiliated sufficiently for him to leave in disgust within an hour. We agree to take our response to *The Times*. I am packing away my electronic Filofax when Gary, the commercial director, taps my arm.

'Well done, girl.' I smile. He nods enthusiastically and his mop of blond curly hair bounces up and down, putting me in mind of a cherub. It strikes me that I wouldn't have drawn this comparison before my foray into sentimentality. I'm disgusted with myself. I try to concentrate on what he's saying.

'Buoyant term one. Going gangbusters. Twelve up. First stab, six up. The star performer in the quadrangle. Product categories are all up. Deal credit no deal debt. All thanks to ambitious penises. Well done, girl.'

I haven't a clue what any of this means. The language is deliberately ambiguous. But Gary smiles at me and as I have only ever seen him smile when he talks about football, I figure that the commercial director is happy.

Next I plough through my mountain of e-mail. It's hard to concentrate, because although I've instructed Jaki to divert all my calls through to her, I still jump every time my line rings. Which it does about every four minutes. At the end of the day Jaki relays the messages she's taken. Despite my instructions Darren has rung twice.

I spend the early evening running through interview tapes in the editing suites. I need the best available material for next week's show. I'm not leaving it to the editor. I'm being conscientious plus to make up for going AWOL.

And to avoid thinking about Darren. It should be easier not to think of his gut-churning smile if I'm busy.

'You've quite a way with these stooges,' comments Ed the editor.

'You think so, do you?' I don't take my eyes off the monitors.

'Yeah, you resist being patronizing, talking in short sentences and in single syllables. Quite a gift – the common touch.'

'No one's ever accused me of that before,' I comment drily.

'No one would guess how terrifying you are.' Ed looks at me. Nervous, never sure how I'll take his jokes. I smile mildly and we both concentrate on the interview.

The monitor is showing the film I made the day before I met Darren. The case is one where some bloke left his wife for some girl. The girl is now unsure if she can keep him, even though they plan to marry in a month. She thinks he wants to go back to his wife. This, I suppose, disproves the theory that one wife is as good as the next. I'm interviewing the wife. She's a rare breed, a shy Scottish woman. Her abrasive vowels rasp, 'If I were famous it wouldn't bother me so much – the stained carpet and chipped skirting board. I'd accept that he chose her.'

'I might be able to give you both.'

That's my voice on the monitor, offering her false hope. At the time I had thought that a bit of fame and glamour would make her happier. And there was a chance that he'd choose her. But rewatching the tape, just two weeks on, leaves me with an uncomfortable feeling in my stomach. Is it right to—? I stop the thought as it's forming, and for the zillionth time today, I curse Darren.

'They hate my accent,' she's wailing.

'No, they hate your long legs and massive tits. That's their motivation. Objecting to your accent is a diversionary tactic,' I assure.

'You are a true pro,' says Ed. 'Dishing out that sort of

compliment is certain to get them on side. She'll get your man for you now.'

'Actually, Ed, I just meant it,' I say as I close the door behind me.

Unusually I decide to take a bus home. I don't want to be alone in a cab. I don't want to be alone with me. I don't want to be me. I've never felt so confused and miserable in my life. And yet I wouldn't have swapped it for the world. That's the worst of it.

I look at my watch and allow myself two minutes thinking about Darren. Twenty minutes later the bus arrives. There is a huge advert for aftershave painted on the side of the bus. The model has a look of Darren. Similar eyes but not as beautiful.

The bus is a mistake because the driver won't accept my £50 note and laughs when I explain that I don't carry loose change as it ruins the shape of your pockets. In the end some skinny guy behind me offers up the £1. It's embarrassing. I am about to glare at him for his impertinence but as I catch his eye I notice that he also looks tired. Maybe he isn't paying my ride in hope of one in return. Perhaps he just wants the queue to move along.

'Thanks,' I mutter. He briefly nods, self-conscious about his own act of goodness. He's probably aware how very un-London he's being.

I go upstairs and sit at the front. I wish Darren were here with me – we could pretend to be driving the bus. As soon as I have this thought I hate myself. There. See. That's where this kind of shenanigans leads. Pathetic sentimentality! How do I know that Darren would pretend to be driving the bus? I'm acting like an arse.

Usually public transport is anonymous. That's why we are happy to pay inflated prices for an unfeasible short ride – it's part of the deal. No one will talk to you and if they can possibly help it, they will avoid looking at you too. Except for drunks who use public transport for the exact opposite reason. I rarely notice whom I'm travelling with, but today it's as if I am looking with new eyes. Nothing is anonymous; everyone seems to be acting significantly. The guy next to me, besides suffering from terrible BO, offends me on another front. He's wearing a headset, which he's singing along to. Naturally he's singing a song about everlasting love, which frankly is a load of crap. Not just his voice. I move seat and find myself sitting behind two teenage girls. They are reading *Cosmo*. They do the quiz to find their perfect men. If only it was so easy. As they read the questions aloud to one another I mentally answer them. I'm mostly Bs. By the end of the quiz the girls discover that their boyfriends are mummy's boys and misogynists respectively. I discover Darren cannot be improved upon.

When I get home I see that the answering machine light is flashing. I listen to the messages as I run a bath.

'Cas, it's me,' chimes Issie. 'Just ringing to see how things went with Bale today. Give me a call later if you want to. I'll be home from the gym at about ten.'

I smile, knowing that she's slipped in the words 'the gym' to impress me. Much to Josh's and my surprise Issie is following through on her New Year's resolution. She has a place in the London Marathon and is training hard for it. The second message is from Josh.

'Hey, Babe, how are you? How was the north? I'm going to the cinema tonight. Some sub-titled bollocks that Jane wants to see. I'm sure it will be very worthy and depressing. It's on at one of those arty cinemas that don't even sell Häagen-Dazs. I'll call you tomorrow.'

Poor Jane sounds as though she's history. I am beginning

to relax. The third message is from my mother, complaining that I didn't visit on Sunday. A spasm of guilt shoots through me. So all's well on the Western front – these are the messages that I often come into on a Monday evening. I am back on familiar territory. Darren has been a bizarre distraction but now I'm fine. I'm safe.

'Cas, it's me.' His voice saws into my sanctuary and I'm delirious. I'm disgusted. 'I guess you are still at work. If you are there, please pick up.' The voice pauses. 'I guess you're not there. I got your note.' He makes a sad little sound which sounds strangled somewhere between a laugh and a sigh. 'I knew you would do something like this. I knew you'd panic. But if you'll let me talk to you—' His voice breaks and he coughs. 'Look, I had a great time the last two weeks. So did you.' He sounds urgent now, a mix between anger and frustration – which I'm used to inciting, and tenderness – which I'm not. 'If it's any consolation, I'm scared too.' Then the tape runs out. I stand perfectly still and try to understand what I'm feeling. My God, there we have it, I'm feeling already. Not thinking, like I was a couple of weeks ago. Suddenly I'm feeling!

He did sound genuine. What does he mean, he's 'scared too'? As well as who?

I listen to the message again. And again. And again. In fact, I listen to it twelve times. By the twelfth time one thing is clear. I've lost it. I press the erase button and go to bed. Darren who?

Smith.

14

Being in love is just as painful as I always expected it to be. I wake up every morning and my first thought is of Darren. In fact, as my dreams are also littered with him, I'm beginning to find it difficult to distinguish between the two states. They smudge together. I'll be driving into work and I'll see him in every car and on every street. The excitement of spotting him is tremendous. The disappointment that it never is him is side-splitting. I walk into the TV6 building and always look around to see if he's in reception, which is a ridiculous thought, considering how much he loathes the studio and all it stands for. I listen to weather forecasts for Whitby, even though I know he's in London. How could I ever have thought that Whitby was Smallsville? Now it's everywhere I turn. TV6 is setting a new drama there; on the news yesterday there was a small piece about the myth of Dracula and there was a shot of the cemetery we visited. Issie's parents have just bought a caravan and Whitby was one of the first places they visited. Whitby is suddenly the centre of the universe. Every time the phone rings I leap and whilst I always listen to his messages, several times, I haven't returned any calls.

Initially he called often and left complicated messages. Jaki begged me to return them.

'Call him, Cas. He doesn't believe you've left the firm.'

'I've nothing to say to him.'

'Well, at least tell him that! If not for your sake, for mine. My workload has practically doubled since I started taking his calls.'

'Then you weren't working hard enough in the first place,' I replied, without looking up from my screen. 'Contact reception and get me a new extension number and next time he calls tell him I'll inform the police if he keeps pestering me.'

Darren has called round to my flat twice. Both times he conscientiously left a note detailing when he'd return, so I moved to Issie's for a while. He took the hint. The visits stopped. The calls stopped. Except for the occasional one, late at night, when he's obviously drunk – just a dulcet 'It's me.' He still sends me e-mails. He no longer sends long notes asking me to get in touch; now he simply sends links to websites that he thinks might interest me. Articles on Audrey Hepburn, surveys on TV viewing habits and yesterday an update on the latest divorce statistics released by the government. I wonder what he meant by that? It's hard to read significance into any of the articles he sends, as he doesn't introduce them or sign off with anything personal. Which I suppose is a blessing. Imagine if he wrote 'best wishes' or 'love' or 'all my love' – I'd turn into Issie, analysing the significance of each word, when there isn't any.

Facts about him erupt into my consciousness when I'm least expecting them. One moment I'm checking interview scripts, the next I'm thinking about his arguments on the collective responsibility of programming.

Which is bollocks.

But he did argue his case stylishly.

If only my thoughts of him stopped with recalling his arguments. I send myself to sleep each night remembering the way his lips felt hanging on my nipple and I wake up smiling. But only for the nanosecond it takes for my brain to explain to my heart that there will be no repeat performance.

Ever.

It seems that I know a million things about him because

I'm always considering, remembering, recollecting. Yet there is so much that I don't know. I examine trees and wonder exactly what tree surgeons do. We did talk about his work but I'd like a clearer picture. I'd like to be able to imagine every part of his day. I wonder what his flat is like and what car he drives. Then I remind myself that it is safer I don't know these things because the less I have to forget the better. And really it is only a matter of time before he's annihilated from my mind. I comfort myself with the thought that, in the beginning, everything is fascinating. The way they part their hair, the way they blow their nose, their views on government policies towards third world debt, how they like their tuna steak. Every manifestation seems enticing, but if I were still with him these things would have already become tedious. It would be impossible to keep noticing these things if they were constantly before me. The commonplace is not rare and beautiful. Interesting. Precious. Like all my memories. It's better that I have the luscious intensity intact rather than sullied through everyday wear.

I'm aware that I sound like Issie. But it's under control.

I prescribe my usual antidote and work is hot. Full of despair, betrayal, rage, depression, sweaty palms and tight throats, but other people's, not mine. Weddings bring out the worst in people, which is ideal for my purposes. The British public don't disappoint me in their levels of paranoia or jealousy; contestants fall through the doors realizing what a perfect opportunity for revenge a wedding is. Who could ask for more? A huge stage packed with an audience of the stooges' nearest and dearest (plus 10.6 million viewers and rising) available to witness the humiliation. It's a fact that during preparations for a wedding small problems escalate. A decision about a buttonhole – carnation or lily – can be make or break; therefore the turmoil that the choice between Carol and Lily can wreak should not be underestimated.

My response to the bishop's letter ran in all the quality press. Which created just the correct amount of indignation. Calls were made for the government to intervene by issuing TV programmes with certificates of classification, similar to the cinema. A sensible suggestion with which no one with any common sense could argue. Luckily the tabloids misrepresented the issue and re-opened the old debate on freedom of the media and 'big brother' censorship. The uproar is tremendous. Although the tabloids fail to articulate a sensible counter-argument to the idea of classification, there is enough contagious anger to keep the issue (and most importantly the show) in the headlines for weeks. I am delighted with the controversy. There are a number of distinct advantages, besides the incessant snowballing of the number of potential guests. I have been given the go-ahead to shoot *Sex with an Ex* episodes from now until July. Advertisers are more confident and are pledging big advertising budgets, which has allowed me the opportunity to extend the channel's programme schedule. We've bought four massive films, which are set to secure huge audiences. We've put more money into the *Teddington Crescent* soap, commissioning better writers and sets that are not made of tissue paper. We've also introduced a number of entirely new programmes – quiz shows, sit-coms and docusoaps. I am Midas.

The only disadvantages of *Sex with an Ex* being a runaway success is that Bale has become more 'hands-on' in the management of the show. Like all good bosses, his main strength is identifying a winner, created by someone else, and stealing it. Bale has never had an opportunity to pull a fast one like this on me before – I'm normally too sharp, too many steps ahead of him. But this time I unintentionally handed him the opportunity on a plate. Bale describes my trip to Whitby as my 'wild-goose-chase period'. He frequently cites it as an act of misjudgement and irresponsibility. The implication is, of course, that if I've been so heinously stupid and irrational once, there is always the danger of my doing the same thing again; perhaps when even more than a tight schedule is at stake. My twelve-year exemplary CV counts for nothing. I would resent this treatment but I know the rules we play by in this industry – I made most of them up; so I simply have to take it on the chin.

At least publicly.

Privately I'm plotting ways to circulate pictures of Bale in women's underwear, which I procured from his latest wounded jilt. She happily offered them up to me, as she has been giving Bale head for three weeks, on the back of his promise that 'he'd see her right in the firm'. In fact, he saw her right *out* of the firm with nothing more than a P45 for her effort. She'd taken the pictures during one of their more bizarre sessions. She gave them to me and I gave her a letter of recommendation based on some of her talents, other than those Bale sampled. I also suggested she concentrated on her shorthand, rather than hand jobs. But I expect the advice will have fallen on deaf ears. Once you find yourself on your back, on the back of a promise, you never get up. I'm not sure when, or if, I'll ever run the pictures on the Internet but I like knowing I have them.

Bale's insidious presence affects the entire show, largely because he doesn't understand it. The success of *Sex with an Ex* is its spontaneity. Now, speculation has been annihilated.

We have telephone lines set up for those wishing to be on the show, which are manned by counsellors. I rarely handle the interviews these days, but have a team of psychologists to do so. The channel gets involved with the stooges' wedding preparations from a very early stage in the engagement, often selecting the ring. We attend most dress fittings and censor the guest list. We bear the entire cost of any weddings that actually manage to limp to the altar but, worse than twenty parents, we exercise our right to advise on all aspects, from cake to consummation. We have teams that are specially selected for their sympathetic qualities or at least their ability to feign sympathy convincingly, and they become the friends of the stooges. We become indispensable to the ordinary people who wish to compete. Because it is about competition. Who will he choose? Does she love me alone? Nothing is left to chance. It's now very rare that when the lights go down the contestants' confidence drains and they find themselves asking, 'What am I doing here?' It's unlikely because they've been rehearsed, tutored, scripted, groomed to an inch of their lives. They know how to act if they are humiliated in front of millions (ideally a woman should cry and a man should be violent, but we sometimes turn this expectation on its head to create an extraordinary effect). They know how to act if their partner remains faithful (sweet relief mixed with assured confidence). They practise how to sit, walk, hold their hands, cry, punch and kick. I personally feel the show has lost its bite but Bale is so paranoid about the big bucks which are rolling on *Sex with an Ex* that he won't hear of returning to a more impromptu approach. I could argue my case but, unaccountably, I'm not as fired about the show as I have been in the past. I'm more concerned with getting some new shows off the ground.

I call a meeting to discuss some new ideas. Through the glass partition I watch the team cluster. They no longer look like the anxious relatives of the sick, as they did last August. It's amazing what six months and over 10 million viewers can do. They look happy and confident, proud and exhilarated. Stick that in your pipe and smoke it, Darren Smith.

'Hey, guys, how are you?'

'Hanging,' replies Tom. I stare my rebuke. It's a lie. I've seen Tom's tackle and even the most generous description would not stretch to 'hanging'.

'Cool.'

'Top.'

'Smart,' reply Mark, Jaki and Gray respectively. I hope they understand that I am responsible for their feeling of euphoria.

'Pleased to hear it. Now to business.' I glare Ricky out of his chair at the top of the table and sit there taking command of the room. Each team member gives a brief update on their department. Gray reports the massive revenue increases in sponsorship and advertising. I was expecting this; the others gasp, happy and astonished. Di gives us more good news, announcing that the exec. committee has increased our team's marketing budget by 250 per cent. Tom and Mark immediately start debating where we should go for lunch.

'Quo Vadis?'

'No, the Ivy.'

'Grow up,' instructs Fi. 'There are more important things to discuss.' She's learning.

'Like what?' spits Mark.

'Like what next?' I reply. 'We have to stay hot.' We bandy some ideas around.

'A follow-up to *Sex with an Ex*. You know, how are the couple doing? Did they make the right choice?' suggests Jaki.

'That's really obvious,' snarls Fi.

'But cheap,' Jaki defends, knowing it's me not Fi she has to impress.

'You're right, go for it,' I instruct. 'Write it up as a proposal. Make it sexy. Get some visuals.'

'How about a series on serial killers?' suggests Tom. 'Compare and contrast the Yorkshire Ripper, the Moors Murderers, that Dr Death guy.' I concentrate on concealing my disgust.

'Or something more broad, like tyrants and despots. Stalin, Hitler, Pinochet – we could have an audience participation deciding who was the most vicious,' adds Mark.

'Too gruesome,' comments Gray, and I'm relieved that someone has articulated my killjoy thoughts. 'Let's stick to what we do well, humiliating and exposing the normal blokes.'

'Yeah,' says Ricky. 'We could follow guys on their stag weekends. You know, get shots of them licking Guinness off prostitutes' breasts or being tied naked to a lamppost.'

'Good idea,' enthused Fi. 'We could film the hens puking into their handbags singing "Let Me Entertain You" whilst taking their bras off.'

'No, no. I think we should go more up-market,' comments Di.

I want to kiss her.

'Let's do some undercover work on politicians and fat cats. Let's film them standing on bar tops or licking Guinness off prostitutes' breasts.'

I want to kick her.

'Or we could do a series of celeb profiles?' I suggest.

'Absolutely,' enthuses Jaki. 'Dig up all their dirty past, lots of photos they'd rather not see published.'

'No,' I shout, marginally more forcefully than I intended. 'Something more' – I hesitate, nervous of how my suggestion will be received – 'profitable.'

'Well, skeletons in the cupboard are profitable. The advertisers are bound to see the appeal and put loads of money behind it,' comments Fi.

'I mean emotionally profitable. Perhaps we could do a show about how celebs are getting along with their millennium promise or, if they didn't make one, perhaps we can get them to pledge something improving now.'

'Maybe,' mumbles Ricky. But he doesn't sound that enthusiastic. I look at the others but they are all steadfastly concentrating on the cobweb in the right-hand ceiling corner of the room. I'm embarrassed, but push on.

'OK, maybe that's not too keen, but I'm just trying to think of something more educational than the current mix.'

'Absolutely.'

'Quite right.'

'Definitely agree,' chorus the cobweb-gazing brigade.

'Do you?' I smile enthusiastically.

'Yeah, like a programme on cross-dressing. Now that's educational.'

'Or something on plastic surgery. Perhaps some horror stories of women desperate to keep their husbands and prepared to go to amazing surgical lengths to do so – all the better if the operations have gone wrong.'

'Don't be so stereotypical,' shouts Fi. 'What about male plastic surgery stories? Penis extensions – now there's a tale to tell.' The room erupts into sniggers. I don't join in. I'm relieved when someone suggests that we need to go to the pub for a 'break from the intensity'. I'm praying that the salt and Linneker versus cheese and onion debate will overwhelm, and that the original subject of the meeting is forgotten.

15

I have never worked so hard in my life as I have these past few months. Or, more honestly, work has never been so hard. I fail to notice spring; the bit of me that appreciates green buds and blue skies was only ever a small constituent of my make-up, and has now been snuffed out completely as I surround myself with schedules, deadlines, target revenues, TVRs and ARPs. I'm not busy enough. I decide that my social life needs new impetus, so I attend every party, reception, première, dinner and event that I'm invited to. Recently I've broadened my life experiences to include visiting Le Cirque du Soleil, participating in a pony-trekking weekend in north Wales and an all-day aerobathon for charity, attending two hen nights (both with essential stripping policeman) and joining Issie's pottery class. For all this frivolity, I have no fun.

This indiscriminate acceptance of invitations has filled my hours, but there have been two annulling consequences. The first is that I've discovered that my previous opinion on mankind (considered by many to be harsh) was in fact generous. People are generally much more tedious than even I estimated. The women I meet are unilaterally obsessed with their waistlines and, as often as not, individually obsessed with some waster. The men I meet are as per my original evaluation. They are insincere commitment phobes or spineless and married. And whilst I personally am still resolutely avoiding commitment, I dislike this characteristic in others. In the past I was able to endure the trite lines and clammy hands at least until the morning after the night before. Now it's impossible for me to fake interest for as long as it takes most of them to fight their way to the front of the bar queue. Issie is thrilled that I am sticking to my New Year's resolution.

'Other than Darren you haven't had any casual sex this year.' She blushes. 'Well, including Darren you haven't had any *casual* sex.'

I don't comment.

The second consequence of my indiscriminate acceptance of invites is that by making myself more available I have made myself less desirable. I worry that I am gaining the reputation of being one of those people who attends the opening of a marmalade jar. For this reason I have resolutely turned down all invitations for this weekend. I refused an offer to fly to New York to 'shop till I drop'. The guy who made the offer was being euphemistic. He actually wanted me to shop until my knickers dropped. I said no to a reception at the Tate Modern tonight and no to drinks with the team. I refused a dinner and fancy-dress party tomorrow, and a lunch on Sunday with friends. Issie is spending the weekend doing some intensive training with a group of people who are also running the London Marathon and Josh is taking Jane to the country. Not for a romantic weekend, but to bin her. He mistakenly thinks this is the gentleman-like thing to do. Issie and I tried to explain that, almost certainly, Jane would prefer to have her heart broken on her own territory, but Josh pointed out that he'd lose his deposit on the hotel room if he no-showed. As they are both out of town I'll spend the weekend without human contact.

I am hopeful, expectant. I'm looking forward to being alone with my face pack, fridge and remote control. I sit down with a highlighter pen, the television section of the *Observer* and a bottle of gin. I circle my TV viewing for the night. *Coronation*

Street, a documentary on Brooklyn Beckham (that's our show), *Brookside*, *Friends*, and then I'll switch to cable for a movie. I catch sight of the date and automatically calculate that it's one month, three weeks, five days and eight hours since I last saw Darren.

Only quarter of an hour before *Corrie* starts.

Thirteen minutes.

Another nine minutes to go.

Still quite some time yet. I think I'll ring Mum.

'Hi, Mum.'

'Oh, hello Jocasta, dear, how are you? I was just talking about you to Bob.'

'Who?'

'Bob, you know—'

'Your neighbour.'

'Exactly!'

'What were you saying?'

'Sorry?'

'What were you saying to Bob?' I'm beginning to regret the call.

'I was just saying I wonder how Jocasta is.'

'Well, I'm fine.'

'Pleased to hear it.'

'And how are you?'

'Oh, I'm fine, except for the old problem.' I have no idea what the 'old problem' is, although doubtless she's told me on countless occasions; nor do I have any desire to find out. I move the conversation on.

'I called to ask if you fancy going shopping tomorrow. Unaccountably it's a Saturday and I haven't got a wedding to go to.' I hadn't realized that I'd called to ask this; the fifteen minutes alone before my viewing started have obviously weighed in heavily. I wait for her gushing thanks that I've decided to offer up an entire Saturday, even though it's not her birthday or anywhere near Christmas. Instead she surprises me.

'I expect people are a little nervous about inviting you to their weddings, what with your show and everything. Well, dear, I'd love to go shopping with you, but Bob and I are going to a craft fair and it's been in the diary for some time. I can't let him down – I know he'd be most disappointed and I'm looking forward to it too.'

I don't ask what kind of man enjoys a craft fair; nor do I commit myself when she adds hopefully, 'How about next week?'

I put the phone down and turn the volume up.

Whilst it's been a constructive weekend (I've filed my nails, both fingers and toes, I've tidied my cutlery drawer and I've descaled the kettle and the showerhead), by Sunday afternoon I'm beginning to wish I'd accepted the invite to lunch. I've read the Sunday papers, including the small ads for the removal of unwanted lines, fat and hair, as well as those for the addition to breasts and penises. I've watched a backlog of recorded programmes and all the soap omnibuses. In fact, most of my entertainment and all my food have been generated from radioactive boxes. Although I have ample time on my hands, I can't be arsed to drag myself to Tesco's or even Cullen's. There really is no point in buying fresh herbs and vegetables, chopping and sautéing for one. Instead I search my cupboards for inspiration. I don't find it. I can't think of a recipe that happily combines peanut butter, Carr's water biscuits and All Bran. The contents of my fridge are neither useful nor ornamental. There's a mouldering jar of capers and another of anchovies (bought for a dinner party), Tabasco, Yakult and Red Bull. Of course, there's the foundation bottle of champagne, but even I don't like drinking Veuve Clicquot alone. Instead I defrost things unsavoury. Cardboard food from cardboard boxes – singleton's food.

I can hear some kids playing in the nearby park. As far as I can tell the objective of the game is to see who can produce the most piercing scream. Very entertaining, if you're eight. I wonder what Charlotte and Lucy are up to? An aeroplane passes overhead. In the mid-distance I can hear the intermittent hum of an articulated truck whizz from factory to storage warehouse. I'm depressed. I must be. The truck seems poignant. I look around for a vessel to use as an ashtray. All the ashtrays, saucers, teacups, plant pots that are in spitting distance of my sofa are full to overflowing with ash already.

Whilst me-time is all very educative, the most overwhelming lesson appears to be that I'm pretty miserable company. Even the fact that Saturday's show was a corker, and the scheduling department have already rung to tell me we've reached 10.4 million viewers, fails to cheer me. The worst of it is, I'm not entirely alone.

As I move around my home I see Darren sprawled out on his stomach reading the Sunday papers, or I find him squeezing oranges in my kitchen, or I bump into him coming out of the shower. Naked and powerful with a white towel round his hips and water drops dripping from his hair to the carpet. But the carpet is never wet because he's only in my head and he's never in my bed.

I remember Darren first coming into my flat.

'Nice pad. Did you buy it lock, stock and barrel from a style magazine?' He'd grinned and turned to kiss me. I flung my coat on the back of my settee, not bothering to hang it in the cupboard. I kissed him back and didn't take offence.

'Funny. Issie thinks this place is impersonal, too. I think

it's anything but. I bought an empty shell and built my apartment from scratch. What could be more personal?'

Darren wrapped his arms around me and held me tightly. I breathed him in. I was shaking with the newness of it all. It was new that I was talking this way. It was new that a man was in my home and I was sharing my life, even for a week.

I stare at the windowpane, concentrating on the raindrop race, which Darren taught me. The idea is you choose a raindrop and the other person chooses another raindrop, both roughly at the same height and ideally at the top of the window. The winner is the one whose drop reaches the bottom of the window first. I win. Naturally – I'm the only one playing. I can't think of anything to amuse, charm or hearten me. Not even the fact that Josh's girlfriend will be having an even more shit time than I am. This just proves my theory about the insanity of getting involved. I pray Josh will call me soon with a debrief – I need a distraction.

I decide to replace the catchy tune of my clunking radiators and purring fridge. I force myself out of my cosy window seat and examine my cassette and CD collection. Uninvited, the memory of Darren discovering my CD collection barges into my head.

'You put some music on whilst I pour some drinks,' I'd instructed, moving towards the wine rack.

'Interesting music collection,' he commented.

'Normally described as eclectic. It's a testimony to ex-shags.'

'Ah, I see.' And he probably did, because I believe that he understood me entirely, past and present. Which is my problem.

'The Smiths and the Cure represent your adolescent angst years.'

'Correct. Actually I was an extremely buoyant adolescent but my lover was an anger ball so I faked an avid interest. Red or white?' I held up both bottles, trying to ignore my own last sentence. I realized that by faking an avid interest I'd set a pattern for a lifetime.

'Red. Something full-bodied, if you have it.'

It impressed me that Darren managed to politely knock back the plonk in Whitby without showing any snobbery or distaste when he obviously knows what he likes when it comes to wine. Maybe it was a mistake to make such a fuss about drinking Blue Nun, especially when Mrs Smith had bought it just for me. Not that it matters. None of it matters.

It still gnaws.

'And I take it that Lloyd Cole, Tom Waits, Lou Reed, Pet Shop Boys and Scott Walker are attributable to your student years?'

'Spot on. Phil, Paul, Iain, Greg and, er, Mark respectively.'

I poured the wine and handed it to him. As I re-enact this scene I use a coffee mug, which is pretty inadequate.

'Your music tastes are certainly wide and varied. REM, Blur, Red Hot Chilli Peppers, Ruben Gonzalez.' Darren sipped the wine and smiled at me. The smile then, as now, hit directly in my chest, exploded and hurled shrapnel to my throat, back of knees and knickers. I'd never felt so fine. I hurt all over.

'Not my taste in music but in men. Those CDs are credited to Nathan, Andy, Tom, Dave.

'The Judds!?' Raised eyebrow.

'I know – awful, isn't it? Peter. Take heart, his appalling musical taste was compensated by his expertise in the sack. At the time I'd even have forgiven white socks.'

'I can't take heart. I'm jealous of every last one of them.' He turned and kissed me ferociously, nearly causing me to spill my wine. He began to unbutton my shirt. His fingers teased my skin. First my collarbone, then trailing past my breast, threading down to my stomach.

I absolutely force myself back to the present.

It's bleak. I thought I knew all there was to know about loss, but not having Darren in my life is so vile and final that I wonder how I get up in the mornings. I feel like Dorothy on rewind. Instead of hitting the yellow brick road and finding myself in Technicolor Oz, I've been shoved into a monotone existence. I don't enjoy parties, or bars, or clubs. I don't like being with people, I loathe being alone. I don't zing, I don't sparkle. I don't slice with my tongue. Even work seems lacklustre. I wonder how I ever thought this life was fulfilling, let alone exhilarating. Life now sags around me. I'm nauseous with loneliness. It engulfs me.

I wish I'd never met him.

I don't mean that. I hate myself for being so disloyal. I know that I would do it all again. I'd still get on that train. It was already too late the moment I collided into his eyes in the interview room. I'd thought I was so damn smart. So élite. So untouchable. Yet whilst it hurts that only his ghost – and not his irresistible self – is in my sitting-room, him in my towelling dressing gown, me in his jumper, both of us soaked in love and cum – I know I am still in control.

Oh, only just, I admit that.

I left *him*. He didn't leave me. He doesn't know how I feel. He doesn't know how vulnerable I am.

Only I know that.

The phone rings, breaking the sound of being alone. I pounce on it. It's Josh. I know this before I pick it up.

'How'd it go?' I'm ridiculously interested, as I'm desperate to break myself out of my own indulgent apathy.

'Awful,' he groans.

'Mmm.' I sound sympathetic because I am. 'Did she take it very badly?'

'She cried.' Most of Josh is upset but a tiny bit of him is triumphant.

'Mmm.'

'It's worse doing the dumping than being the dumpee.' I doubt he means this.

'I wouldn't know,' I remind him.

'No, of course not. You've never been dumped.'

'What is the point of sticking around long enough to get your heart broken?' I challenge, more cheerfully than honestly. I want this conversation to have away from me. Strangely I haven't been honest with Josh about my feelings for Darren. Josh assumes Darren was another brief and unimportant encounter. I can't tell him how I feel because saying it aloud makes it more real. I must bury my feelings for Darren. I must.

'What did you tell her?'

'Oh, you know, the usual stuff.'

'It's just not right?'

'Yes,' he agrees enthusiastically. Although I love Josh, I'm irritated by him. I sigh, thinking of all the women who've ever cried because of the words, 'It's just not right.' Why do men only discover this when they roll off the sticky Durex?

'I know what you're thinking, but I really didn't want to hurt her.'

I relent. After all, I've known him since he played with Action Men and I played with Sindy dolls. Now it's the other way round, I can't simply abandon him. He starts to tell me about the ditching. It doesn't take long; he's a boy. If Issie were telling me about her dumping some bloke or other, we'd spend hours. We'd start with describing what both parties were wearing. We'd talk about the location selected for the scenario. It's very important to choose the correct ground. His place is good because then you get to choose when to leave and he doesn't have to stumble home in a veil of tears. Or somewhere neutral, like a bar or a party. Not his mum's. She simply won't see it from your point of view. And not – under any circumstances – your own place. He might decide not to leave, insisting that it's possible to make a go of it. It never is. Calling the police in is ugly. I know – I've done it. Now if this were Issie it would be a different story. Issie would tell me everything. She'd punctuate it with 'and then he said', 'and then I said', 'and he looked as though . . .' However close we are, Josh has too many Y-chromosomes to do this. Instead he has to act all disinterested and hard. He blows it when he asks me if I'll go round.

'I'll be there in ten.' Of course I'll go to him. I'd walk hot coals for him.

Josh likes to think he lives in Islington but in fact he lives in King's Cross. He lives in a ground-floor flat, which can most adequately and efficiently be described as 'masculine'. Until his thirtieth birthday, Josh steadfastly refused to pay as much as a cursory glance towards interior design, cleanliness or comfort. He lived in squalor – not that he seemed to notice. In fact, he often joked that filth and disorder were his best friends. I was never sure if he was referring to his domestic arrangements or me and Issie respectively. Josh only ever washed up if the corner shop had run out of paper plates and he changed his sheets less frequently than his women. His bathroom never benefited from Ajax, Jif or Domestos, all of which could be Greek islands as far as Josh was concerned. His items of furniture were my mother's cast-offs, the things she absolutely could not force into her home. This foulness was not poverty-induced, simply a male blind spot, as inexplicable as the fact that when men do become interested in their home (thirtieth birthday or marriage, whichever they meet first) they cover the squalidness in blue.

Blue walls and tiles, blue fabric, blue crockery, blue cutlery, blue loo roll, blue napkins and napkin rings (which have only ever been used once – the thirtieth birthday dinner party), blue settee, blue bed and bedding, blue dustpan and mop and finally a blue toothbrush. When Issie or I ever visited Josh whilst he was decorating we were always overly animated, fearing if we stood still for too long he'd paint us blue too.

As I walk into his flat, I'm thinking that if Josh introduced buttercup yellow in his hall or a deep red in his sitting-room it would be a vast improvement.

'Josh, why are the lights dimmed?' I ask and immediately turn them up. I start to laugh. 'Oh, I see, to show off the candles. Are you indulging in a Druid-type self-loathing session?' I kiss him on the forehead and wave the bottle I've brought.

'It's a '94 Château La Croix de Mouchet. I was saving it for a special occasion but I'm not sure when that'll be so I thought I'd bring it round.' I march directly to the kitchen to forage out some glasses.

I bump into the biggest floral arrangement ever.

'Who are the flowers for, or should I say from? God, Josh, this place looks more like a seduction scene than a dumping ground.' I suddenly guess what's going on. 'No, she didn't buy you these just before you ditched her, did she?' I'm shocked at the stupidity of some women. 'And you accepted them.' I'm less surprised by the callous nature of most men. 'Bastard.' I smile. He'll know I'm joking. Josh doesn't answer but takes the wine I'm offering and clinks my glass. I continue chattering, glad of the company, for what it is. Josh is not at his sparkly best.

'God, I've had the loneliest weekend,' I confess.

'Really?'

'Don't look so pleased about it, Josh. You know you and Issie are indispensable to me. You don't need to prove your point by both going away at once. I started having the most maudlin thoughts. I even wished there was a wedding to go to. Now isn't that a hoot?'

Josh brightens. 'Do you really?'

'What?'

'Wish there was a wedding to go to?'

'Well, since my choice this weekend was that or eat Coco Pops, by the hand directly from the box, yes, I'd prefer the wedding.' I pat the settee next to me. 'Come on, then, sit here. Tell me all about chucking Jane.' I stare at Josh. 'Hey, you look quite shaken. Are you regretting it?'

'No.' He shakes his head definitively.

'So?' He pauses for the longest time. Something is definitely upsetting him. 'Good God, Josh. You're not ill, are you?' I'm suddenly terrified.

'No. Not ill.'

'So what's up?' I link my arm through his. He shuffles awkwardly, pulling his arm away.

'I don't know how to put this.'

'Just say it, whatever it is,' I encourage. Why the sudden hesitancy? Josh and I have always spoken freely to one another. What can he have to say that's so dreadful? Suddenly he lurches for my hand.

'OK, I'll just say it. Will you marry me, Cas?'

'Ha ha.' I sip my wine.

'I'm serious,' he insists.

I look at him. His eyes are shining earnestly.

He is.

Shit.

'Well, it's a bit of a surprise. I don't know what to say.'

Probably anything but that. It's a bit lame. It's awful. Luckily Josh is too nervous to notice my inadequacies. He reaches behind a cushion and pulls out a Tiffany ring box. He magics a thick cream rose from somewhere or other.

'Bloody hell, Paul Daniels is proposing to me.' I laugh but my laugh is hollow and echoey. It doesn't fill the silence. Josh notices the silence too.

'Bugger, forgot the music.'

He jumps up and puts on his CD player. 'Ground Control to Major Tom' blares out, which makes me laugh and Josh swear. I know he's spent the afternoon walking around the house with the strainer on his head, singing along.

'Fuck, not very appropriate.' He swaps to Frank Sinatra singing 'I've Got you under my Skin.' I'm grateful for this small diversion.

'You're serious, aren't you, Josh?' I ask his back.

'I am.' He tells the wall. After fiddling with the bass and the volume for a while Josh comes back and sits next to me. He doesn't sit quite as close as he usually does. He's not actually touching me, but he is close enough for me to notice that he's shaking and there's sweat on his upper lip.

'Did you buy the ring for me or Jane?' I ask.

'You, of course!' He sounds insulted.

'Just checking.' I grin nervously. 'I wondered if this was impulse or if you'd given it a lot of thought.' His face implodes. I rush on. 'Well, it's obvious that you've given it a lot of thought, but I wasn't sure if it was me you were thinking of.' He looks even more appalled. I realize I'm an arse. 'God, I'm sorry, Josh, that's a terrible thing to say. I'm nervous.' I start to giggle. 'I've never been nervous with you before, Josh.'

'Well, I've never proposed to you before, Cas.' Josh pauses. 'Or anyone.'

'So why?'

'We're good for each other. We are alike. We've known each other for ever. No other woman ever makes me laugh the way you do. Other women bore me.'

I'm still buying time. 'So you are ready for monogamy? I assume we'd play it conventionally?'

'Yes, I'm ready. I'm bored with attaching myself to the next thing that comes along and attracts attention. Other women seem sameish. You're different.' He pauses and I know he's struggling. 'I think it's always been you. I think that's why everyone else seemed inadequate. I think you are the reason I've bounced from one conquest to the next.'

'Are you sure it's you who thinks that? It sounds suspiciously like my mother's theory. This proposal isn't the result of her finally grinding you down, is it?'

Josh smirks. He doesn't answer my question but continues, 'And I figured that you don't have any other plans.' His smirk relaxes into a wide grin. 'I mean you don't let men hang around long enough for you to even learn their surnames.'

Smith.

'It is true our getting married will delight your mum. Look, marriage is the logical next step – think government tax breaks.'

'Very romantic.' I laugh.

He turns suddenly serious. 'I'll make you happy, Cas. We love each other, don't we?'

'It's just that this is so unexpected.'

Josh laughs. 'Actually, not at all. I've been waiting for years to tell you how I feel. I suppose, conventionally, I could have started by kissing you or asking you out for a drink.'

'We're always going out for drinks together,' I point out matter-of-factly.

'Exactly. I've been at a loss as to how I should let you know how I feel. I don't know if I'd ever have got the courage but recently you've changed. You seem more serious. I knew the time was right. What do you say, Cas? Can you imagine being my wife?'

Josh is my best friend. He's mymateJosh. And here he is, mymateJosh down on one knee, a rose in one hand and a diamond cluster in the other. He's right: marriage is a ceremony that is sanctified by logic, government tax breaks, law and thousands of years of repeat performance. Josh is kind, strong, wealthy, intellectually stellar, he worships me, he does not mind my tantrums or my unmade-up face and, if that wasn't enough, he's good-looking.

None of this would convince me to marry him. I look at Josh and suddenly Darren's face looms.

Josh is safe. I'd be safe. I'd never end up torn and bitter in the divorce courts. Because much as I care for Josh, I'm not overwhelmed by him. He'll never make my heart gallop, so he'll never be able to splinter it. A network of middle-class lifelines would constantly buoy us up. Dinners out with our mutual friends, who are interested and interesting. Evenings in, playing Trivial Pursuit, and charades at Christmas. Then later there'd be prep school for the kids and exotic holidays. I like all these things. These beacons of sanitized security seem like a possibility.

I've tried to fill my Darren-bereft days in an assortment of ways. None of which has been successful. But if I were with Josh, if I marry Josh – I let the concept roll round my head – I'd be safe. Marrying Josh will stop me doing anything really terrible, like getting drunk, and calling Darren, and telling him how I feel. Marrying Josh is the ultimate protection. It's complex. It's risky but it's my only chance.

'Yes.'

'Yes what? Yes we love each other . . . or yes you'll marry me?'

'Yes and yes.'

'Aghhhhhh. God, I'm the happiest man in the world. Oh my God. Should we ring Issie?' Josh does a funny little star jump and as he lands he wiggles his hips, claps his hands and punches the air. 'No, no, best ring your mum first, or my parents – what do you think?' Josh is dashing round his flat, fitfully searching for his mobile, although there is a perfectly good landline.

'Champagne? Do you want champagne?' He keeps turning to me and blowing kisses and punching the air again. I've never seen him so happy. I had no idea. I had no idea I could make him this happy. And I'm . . . I'm happy too. Calm happy.

'Well, isn't it traditional for you to kiss me? Kind of to seal the deal,' I offer.

'Christ, yes. Sorry, Cas. I've been meaning to do this for twenty-six years.'

I pretend I haven't noticed that he is now sweating profusely. I ignore the fact that he clumsily bangs my teeth and, for a moment, I'm behind the bike shed with Barry Carter. Soon we inch into it and soon I like his kissing. We're both too practised for it to be anything other than technically brilliant.

I arrive early and seat myself facing the wall so that Issie can have the view of the restaurant. I take off my ring and put it under my napkin so that I can surprise her. Then I put it back on again – better to do the Taaaaddddddaaaa and hold my hand out as soon as she arrives. Maybe not. Back under the napkin. I'm nervous. I just wonder how Issie will take this. After all, Josh's her one and only real chance of marrying. I'm joking. I know this isn't the case, but it will irrevocably alter the dynamics. Well, does it have to?

No, it doesn't.

Yes, it does.

Issie will be delighted for us both.

Surely?

Certainly.

She's here. She kisses me, orders a Bloody Mary and cuts to the chase.

'What's your news?'

Deep breath, 'I'm marrying Josh.'

The restaurant stops. There isn't a clinking glass or thudding plate. At least I can't hear one. I watch Issie's face, waiting for her reaction.

'You're marrying Josh?' she whispers. She pauses and takes a sip of my water. Issie is obviously a little taken back.

But she's pleased.

Isn't she?

Well, she's not actively unhappy.

Is she?

'Yes, I've just said so, haven't I?' I smile broadly because engaged women smile all the time and Issie knows that. I order some wine. She fiddles with her napkin. I look at the menu. She doesn't. I wonder which one of us will change the subject first. Issie and I have only ever been 100 per cent truthful with one another. Except for the occasion when I failed to tell her Josh fancied her. But that was years ago and it worked out for the best. It would be so embarrassing now if they had slept together. Anyway the point is Issie has only ever been 100 per cent truthful with me. I don't want her to skirt this if she has an issue.

But I'm not keen to confront her brutal integrity just yet.

But I hope to God she doesn't talk about the weather.

Stay with me, Issie.

'I've got to be honest with you, Cas. I'm shocked.'

'Why?' I bluff. But I know why. Why is because I've never

shown any romantic interest in Josh and I've always been actively opposed to marriage.

'Because you've never shown any romantic interest in Josh and you've always been actively opposed to marriage.'

I glare at her. The waitress brings Issie her Bloody Mary (which is downed in one) and tells us what the specials are. I get her to repeat it twice. Issie says she'll have 'That.' I ask for 'the same'. Neither of us has any idea what we've ordered.

'Haven't you always said Josh would make a great husband?' I encourage.

'Yes,' she admits.

'Haven't you always said I should marry? Allow closeness, trust, stop hiding from intimacy?'

'Yes,' she admits.

'So what's the problem?'

'I didn't say I had a problem.'

'But you so obviously do.'

'I think you are being defensive. Do *you* think there's a problem?'

'No. I don't have a problem.'

'Good.'

'Yes, it's good.'

The waitress comes back with the wine, water and bread. I'm delighted and greet her as though she is my long-lost sister. It becomes clear that she's not going to draw up a chair and join us. I watch her scuttle back to the kitchen, leaving me alone with Issie and her interrogation.

'What about Darren?'

'Darren?' The bread in my mouth won't be swallowed. I chew and chew but it simply won't go down. I drink some more water. 'Darren who?' won't wash.

'Darren taught me a lot.' I take a deep breath. 'I owe him a great deal. He opened my eyes to the possibility of intimacy being an option for me.'

'Don't speak to me as though I am one of your TV executives,' she snaps. It's unlike Issie to be down on me. I think about what I've just said. It does sound like pretentious wank. But then I'm new to this game of speaking your heart. I'd always been content with speaking my mind, which is easy in comparison.

'Darren was important,' I admit.

'You fell in love with him.'

I can't tell Issie the truth. I can't tell her that marrying Josh is the ultimate armour. She loves Josh as much as she loves me and she wouldn't forgive me. I have no choice but to rewrite history.

'No, Issie, Darren was an infatuation.' Firm. Denying Darren hurts.

'You *said* you were in love.' Rigid.

'I was wrong.' Reasonable.

'You said you're never wrong.' Irritating.

'I was wrong about that too.' I'm almost shouting. I take a deep breath and have a stab at regaining some self-control. 'Darren told me things that no one else could tell me and he taught me to look at things differently but I didn't fall in love.'

She stares at me with naked disbelief. 'Oh, so you can't quote every single word he ever uttered to you? You didn't laugh with him? You don't talk about him constantly?'

Fair point.

'Darren was . . .' I'm struggling. '. . . exhilarating and amazing but he was a stranger. Women don't fall in love with men they've just met.'

'Of course they do!'

'Why are we talking about Darren? It's Josh I feel secure with. Josh I've known for ever.'

'That doesn't sound like love to me, it sounds like the safe choice.'

The waitress arrives with our food and we call an uneasy truce over the table. We sulkily eat our goat's cheese salad and glumly glug our wine. This isn't what I wanted. I wanted her to be happy for me.

'I admit Josh doesn't send my stomach into a somersault.'

'The way Darren did.'

I ignore her interruption. 'But that's to be expected, I've known Josh for ever.'

What am I supposed to say?

Obviously Issie's disappointed that things are changing, but things can't stay the same. I wish they could have. Meeting Darren changed everything. I'm lonely in crowds now. But I'm a survivor and marrying Josh is my best survival tactic. Whilst I'm sorry that it makes Issie uncomfortable, I am completely without option. I push on.

'Darren was about sexual attraction. I got carried away. I know I said some pretty crazy things at the time.' I glance at Issie and try to work out if I'm convincing her. I can see by her face that she wants to believe me. Almost as much as I want to believe me. I press on. 'Josh wants to marry me. I love Josh. He's like a brother to me.' Issie tries to interrupt but I hold my hand up to stop her. 'Maybe, at the moment, Josh loves me in a different way. But two people rarely love each other equally, in the same way, at the same time. We've years together, we'll even up.' I pause for maximum impact and then I plead, 'I'll be a good wife to him.' I mean this. I plan to be perfect. I'll try to make it up to Josh for not being in love with him. I'll take fastidious care in putting his needs before mine. He can choose which side of the bed to sleep on. And I'll attend all his work functions. I'll even learn the rules of rugby. Josh will get a good deal.

Issie pauses and thinks about what I've said. We sit for an eternity.

Finally she mutters, 'I can't believe you'd play games with Josh, so I have to believe that you are genuine about this, Cas.' She stares at me for about two hundred years.

'I am.' Her face relaxes into a broad, delighted and assured smile. I force a tight, relieved smile. I've often condemned her for being too trusting, saying she invites people to wipe their Manolo Blahniks on her soul. Now I'm grateful that she's so ingenuous.

We are through it. Everything is going to be brilliant from now on.

I show her my ring. She ooohs and ahhs, appropriately. She says that she definitely will not wear pink, lilac or frills. I reach into my bag and pull out the Amanda Wakeley Wedding Collection brochure. We both giggle shrilly and generally allow ourselves to get completely over-excited.

This is what girlfriends are born for.

16

A whole new world opens up in front of me. An entirely novel conversational track. An individual way to relate to my mother, Josh's mother, aunts, neighbours, women I meet at dinner parties, restaurants, art galleries, the gym – my Ph.D. in *Brides and Setting up Home*. What had I talked about before I had the cluster on my finger? It surprises and delights me that wedding preparation is an admirable substitute for sex. Which is a good thing because Josh and I have decided not to rush having sex.

'Why?' Issie doesn't understand.

'Well, we're both finding it a bit harder than we imagined crossing over from friends to lovers.'

'Isn't that a fairly major detail, since you are planning on getting married? Aren't married people supposed to be lovers?'

'Yes, and friends.' I sound defensive. 'We thought of getting through the initial embarrassment by just getting pissed and shagging each other. After all, we've both done it to other people often enough in the past. But now that seems so tacky and cheap. I realized that the reason I can't rush this is because I want it to be really special. A few more months without sex will be good for me.'

'It might grow over, you know,' teases Issie. I throw a cushion at her but we both shut up as Josh comes into the room with a tray of wine and Pringles.

'Why do I get the feeling you were talking about me?' He sits in-between us. Issie and I exchange glances.

'Just singing your praises,' Issie says.

Little white lies are a way of life. Issie could hardly say, 'Oh, actually we were just talking about yours and Cas's vow of celibacy.'

Although in the past we did discuss every aspect of our lives. The nitty gritty, not just loose morals but, when travelling in India, loose faeces too.

Tonight after Issie leaves I'll tell Josh what we were really talking about. It's a small shift in the dynamics, almost imperceptible and certainly not important.

Issie's brother is designing our wedding invites so Issie has come round tonight to help us decide on the wording. Which is the other tiny change – Issie rarely pops round just to hang out any more. She only ever visits when she has a reason. Still, there are plenty of reasons – choosing dresses and flowers, repainting Josh's flat, returning a casserole dish. Her visits are just as frequent, so it's not really a problem.

'So, Issie? Have you decided – are you going to be the bridesmaid or the best man?' asks Josh.

'I'm going to be the bridesmaid. I like the outfit better.'

'You like me better,' I screech playfully.

I notice she doesn't answer me but instead asks, 'So where are you getting married?'

We answer simultaneously and differently.

'In London,' I say.

'At home,' says Josh.

'At home,' I offer quickly.

'In London,' he presses.

'We haven't worked out the details,' I smile apologetically to Issie. Wisely, she doesn't comment.

'We do have a date,' says Josh. I snuggle closer to him.

'Well, that's good,' smiles Issie. 'When?'

'June,' I say.

'July,' says Josh at the same time. We both laugh. 'Look, I don't mind. Do what you want. I'm just thrilled. It's going to be the best party ever.' He leans in and kisses me. I wiggle away because I don't want to embarrass Issie.

Josh leaves for rugby practice and Issie and I set to on Project Wedding. I approach it exactly as I approach projects at work.

'OK, we need a list.'

Issie jumps up and finds paper and pen. I grab a bunch of bridal magazines and I open the bottle of Chardonnay.

'So you are still working on when and where?' says Issie quietly as she carefully writes 'Cas and Josh's wedding' at the top of the page. Her handwriting is round and childish and familiar.

'July and Esher, Josh's family home.'

'Good progress,' grins Issie. 'Which church?'

'A church? I hadn't thought of a church.'

'They usually feature.'

'I was thinking of a civil ceremony. Maybe in a garden or a smart hotel?' I cross my legs underneath me.

Issie gently probes, 'Have you discussed this with Josh? I mean he's quite godly.'

'Considering he plays rugby,' I add.

We both laugh. It's true Josh is a long way from being a bible basher but he does believe in God and goes to church at Easter, Christmas and at least two or three other times a year. I do recall him taking his godfather duties very seriously when he became godfather to the children of his head of chambers. I'd sort of put it down to brown nosing. But maybe not. I consider it.

'Of course he's godly, Issie. He went to a posh school which had obligatory Mass. Look, I'll discuss it with him.'

'Well, if you are hoping for a July wedding you'd better discuss it pretty damn quickly. It's April now. I take it you mean this July?' She's doodling hearts and bells on the corner of the list.

'Yes, I mean this July.'

We move on and begin to draw up a list of costs. I'm somewhat perturbed to discover that tradition has it that the bride's parents are supposed to pay for just about everything; the groom's parents get off with the odd bunch of flowers and the rings. I doubt very much that my mother has had a secret trust fund that magically matures as I meet Prince Charming. I think her budgeting for my wedding would truly have been a leap of faith; I'd hardly indicated that I was marrying material. Unless I want to give my guests sausages on sticks and cheese and pineapple chunks, Josh and I will have to pay for the wedding. I hope that won't offend anyone. People have been acting rather strangely recently. Indeed, if I'd had a pound for every time anyone had said the words 'traditional', 'the done thing' and 'expected', I'd be a millionaire. I'm surprised that these words have been showered on me with such frequency because I'd never heard them previously in my entire life.

'OK, so what else needs to be included in this project plan?' I ask.

'No one could ever accuse you of being overly romantic, could they, Cas?' grins Issie wryly.

'I just want to be well organized.'

She shrugs and then reverts to the bridal magazine; I revert to the wine bottle.

'Well, for the service, civil or church, you need wedding rings and a form of service. You need to select music and readings. You'll have to consider cars, photographers and guest accommodation. There is a lot to think about. You'll need a guest list, and an acceptance list, lists of menus, lists of drink, gift lists. There are caterers to consider. You need to book a photographer and videographer. If I were you I'd decline my dad's kind offer to bring his cinecamera along. It's older than I am. What type of reception do you want?'

'There's only one type, isn't there? The after-ceremony type.'

Issie rolls her eyes. 'Sit-down meal, buffet, melon balls and chicken or something a little less traditional, Asian, sushi, Italian, Mexican? What about your silverware, napkins, menu design, flowers? Are you going to invite children? And if so, you should consider their menu and an entertainer. What about the favours, the balloons, the seating plan? Round tables or square? Who's going to sit in the seat that is traditionally saved for the father of the bride? Will you have speeches? Will you make one?' She finally draws to a halt.

'Oh, I see. Well, what do you think?' This is the question Issie has been waiting to be asked all her life.

'Well, if it were me, I'd want it to be sit-down and with a seating plan. I wouldn't try to mix oldies and youngies – because that only works in books. I'd allow the people with things in common to sit together. I'd want tuna carpaccio, followed by tempura fish with chilli salad and Parmesan polenta and then summer berries, which I'd have stacked in huge mounds as table centrepieces. I wouldn't have a traditional cake but I'd have a bitter chocolate profiterole mound instead.'

I'm left stranded somewhere between horrified and admiring. When has Issie had time to think of all this? Then I remember she does this imaginary wedding thing instead of t'ai chi.

'Er, sounds good. Let's have that.'

'You can't have that! That's what I'm having!'

I don't point out that Issie isn't even seeing anyone on a regular basis. It doesn't seem like a nice thing to do.

'Well, erm . . .' I'm unsure what to say next. 'I don't really mind and I'm pretty sure Josh is relaxed about it too. Let's ask my mum. She'll love getting involved. Planning my wedding will cheer up her drab little life.'

'I'm not sure she thinks it's drab.'

'Oh, come on, Issie, she must! Before she married she lived an exemplary life of purity and chastity – which can hardly be a barrel of laughs. Then she fell uncontrollably in love with her husband, he exited stage left and ever since she's put her life on hold by refusing to get over him.'

'Is that how you see it?'

'Is there any other way?' I'm already dialling my mother's number, so I can't be sure, but I think I hear Issie say something about three sins I'm clear of. I watch as she moves her finger down the magazine page as she reads, which I find quaint and touching. The finger stops and hesitates.

'What about insurance?' asks Issie.

'Insurance? What will I need insurance for?'

'Theft of pressies, damage to the dress, damage to the marquee.'

'It's a wedding, not a rave.'

'The loss of deposits due to the cancellation of the wedding.'

We both pause.

'Well, let's get an estimate.'

My mother picks up the mantle. She works steadily throughout the summer and does a marvellous job of knocking the day into shape. Full of zeal, she organizes everything from the church to the caterers, tactfully asking Josh's mum's opinion every step of the way. The wedding has a profound effect on everyone. Josh's mum has become more animated than I've ever seen her before, drinking less and smiling more. As I don't have a father to do the traditional patriarchal stuff, Josh's father happily adopts the role. He invites everyone he's ever met to the wedding, talks about the 'forthcoming happy event' and, I swear, he's even taken to swaggering. This would be infuriating behaviour except, a more happy consequence, he has decided that keeping a mistress is incongruous with his current self-image. For the time being at least, he has given up his philandering. Josh is delirious. Issie hasn't actually voiced any objections. Everyone is as happy as pigs in mud. I'm relieved to be freed up from the hassle, as I can now turn back to concentrating on my work. With vengeance.

I have returned to my routine of five trips to the gym a week, cycling into the office by 8.30 a.m. and working through lunch. However, I don't often stay late now because Mum organizes imperative meetings with the dressmaker/vicar/caterers/videographer/photographer/florist, etc., on a more or less continuous basis. But then I like to be busy. I exist in a huge waft of tissue paper and ribbons with a sprinkling of rose petals.

'Someone has parked their bike in my space. Deal with it,' I bark at Jaki. 'Ricky, do you have the runs for last night's shows? Di, Debs, have either of you seen the papers today? We are mentioned in the *Guardian* for our storyline in *Teddington Crescent* and in the *Sun* for the documentary on stars' babies and in the *Star* for *Sex with an Ex*. Pretty good crop for one day, I'm sure you'll agree. Get a response out to all three editors by 10 a.m.'

Jaki puts a double espresso on my desk.

'What did you watch on TV last night?' she asks.

'No time, I was at a tiara fitting.' We take a moment to smirk at each other.

'Morning, darling,' shouts Tom generally to no one in particular.

'Afternoon,' we chorus as it's 8.45 a.m. Tom looks wounded – he's probably never been in the office so early before.

The status meeting runs exactly to plan. Gray tells me that we have received two complaints from the ITC about offensive language, but, or indeed therefore, the ratings achieved for most of our shows are as expected. The entire team negotiates with him over the predicted ratings for next season's schedule. As the advertising and sponsorship director, it is in his interest to put in 'stretch predictions'. The rest of the team see this as setting unfeasible targets. I settle the matter by diplomatically choosing a number mid-distance between the two extremes. Ricky updates me on scheduling. I'm only half listening because I notice Debs isn't listening at all but instead staring at her screensaver of George Clooney. I'm irritated by her lack of commitment. I tune back in to Ricky.

' . . . So net net what they are suggesting is to push back *Sex with an Ex*. I'll say OK, shall I?' If he hadn't closed his file quite so swiftly and tried to walk away faster than Road Runner, I mightn't have noticed.

'What did you say?'

Ricky sighs when he realizes he's stuck with my undivided attention. He has no choice other than to tell me the full tale.

Ironically, because of the success of *Sex with an Ex* TV6 is a bit flush with cash, which we've invested in big box hit movies, a move that I'd sanctioned. Now the Strategy and Scheduling Department are suggesting we take on the other commercial channels by showing the blockbuster films at a time which will necessitate *Sex with an Ex* being pushed out of peak hour. Why didn't I see that coming?

'There's not much we can do,' shrugs Ricky apologetically. 'Their case is watertight. The *Sex with an Ex* viewership has stabilized; we can pull more viewers in with an Arnie Schwarnie film. There's more violence.'

He's right. I sigh and nod.

'OK. Say we agree.'

'What, just like that?' asks Fi, amazed. 'Aren't you even going to try to think of a way to make *Sex with an Ex* bigger?'

'Look, Fi, you've got to learn which battles to fight. See the bigger picture. We are responsible for the channel, not individual shows.'

'But the show was your idea.'

'Fi, I have loads of ideas. Ten million viewers is an excellent achievement for a show of this nature. Far beyond anything we expected when we set out. Let's not get greedy. We'll pull in 12 million with the right films. And besides which, it's not as if they are suggesting we ditch *Sex with an Ex* – we're just moving it out of peak.'

'Well, if it were my show I'd be fighting tooth and nail to keep it in peak,' spits Fi, with far more passion than I'd ever seen her display before.

'It's not your show.'

As part of my self-protection campaign against Bale sidelining me, I have started to increase my own public profile. In interviews with the national press I make it clear that my personal contribution to the channel is colossal. I also make the most of my less cerebral attributes. I figure that Bale will be keener to keep me sweet if I am a public sweetheart. I'm mid-interview with a journalist from one of the big women's glossies, when Jaki announces that my mother is in reception.

'I'm sorry, we're going to have to leave it there. I'm taking my mother out for lunch,' I smile apologetically. The interview has been more demanding than I expected. The journalist and I are playing a very sophisticated game. I know he likes me but he's pretending not to; it's a matter of professional pride. I'm pretending that I'm still trying to win him over, although I know he's eating out of my hand.

He grimaces stiffly, trying to decide if I planned this interruption in the hope that he'll mention my lunch date with Mum in his article. If I have planned it, he won't mention it. If I haven't, he will. It would, after all, provide a human angle, which is notably lacking. In truth, it's a complete coincidence. Their paths wouldn't have crossed if Mum wasn't tyrannically anal about promptness and this journalist wasn't stereotypical in his tardiness.

'Just one or two more questions.' I agree and smile a candy-coated smile. 'You receive an enormous number of complaint letters about the nature of your lead show *Sex with an Ex*, from parents, teachers, local governments. Even the Church of England has condemned you—'

'I'm agnostic,' I smile my interruption.

He ignores it. 'How do you feel about the charge that you are advocating adultery?'

'Quite simply, I'm not. The ratings are just as high if the couple stay together. I see TV as a nationally authorized culture. I don't force anyone to watch or to participate in the show.' I parrot my answer, barely suppressing my yawn. It doesn't sound as convincing, to me, as it used to. I hope it convinces him. I think of a new bit to add. 'The British public is far too intelligent to be dictated to. Will you write that up as a direct quote?' He nods shyly. I know he's annoyed with himself for being acquiescent.

'Finally, how do you feel about the label that you're "the voice of your generation"?'

'I haven't heard that one before.' I titter and twitter in a vain attempt to convince him that I'm harmless. 'Truly? Off record?' I don't think I can maintain this syrupy exterior for another minute. It's such a strain. He nods.

'I'm not the voice of my generation because I'm far cleverer, far more compassionate and far crueller.'

He mulls over what I've just said. I suspect he regrets agreeing to keep that off record. It's the best quote of the interview.

If only he knew what it meant.

I stand up, indicating that it's time for him to go. Jaki ushers the journalist out of the office and brings my mum in.

'I'm sorry, I'm running late.' I blow her a kiss and my apology as I grab my jacket and handbag off the back of the chair.

'Jaki, I'm taking Mum to lunch and then we are going to choose her outfit for the wedding. I'll be out most of the afternoon.'

This isn't a problem because I do such long hours I feel entitled to take an hour or two off. Other than my team, most TV6 employees don't arrive until 11.00 a.m.; for many the real work doesn't begin until after sobering up from lunch. 'Keep checking my e-mail as I'm expecting an important decision from the executive committee, regarding the budgets for next year. I'll keep my mobile on but don't call me unless it's an emergency. Don't put anyone through except for Darren.'

'Darren?' repeats Jaki astounded. About two thousand watts charge through me.

'Did I say Darren? Oh, I meant Josh.' I'm scarlet, so I delve into my handbag pretending to be looking for a tissue to blot my lipstick and I'm not even wearing lipstick.

'Why did you say Darren?' asks Jaki.

'Oh, it must have been that journalist. He was asking the same kind of questions that that Darren bloke asked about the show. You know, did I feel responsible for the nation's adultery? Do I feel guilty for being the catalyst of so much aggro?'

My hands have suddenly got a life of their own. They are scratching my nose, moving my hair behind my ear, itching my leg. They won't stay steadily on my hips or by my sides. Jaki and Mum are both staring at me very closely. 'They were a lot alike, the journalist and er, thingy, Darren. They were both unrealistic, misguided, moralistic pricks. Sorry, Mum.' I'm apologizing for using the word 'prick' before she demands that I do.

Sorry, Darren. Somewhere deep inside I feel treacherous.

'Who's Darren?' asks Mum.

'Nobody. Some guy who didn't appear on my show.'

'Sex on legs,' says Jaki matter-of-factly.

'Sorry dear?' My mum's pretending she doesn't understand.

'Very Jude Law, but kind of more dangerous, muckier,' adds Jaki. My mother still looks bemused. 'Very Rhett Butler,' clarifies Jaki.

'Oh, I see.'

My mother and I collapse gratefully into the chairs in the Selfridges restaurant. We are carrying heavy bags and light purses and therefore truly euphoric. It's quite an achievement. We've managed to buy Mum an outfit for the wedding, which we both like. *And* the said purchase has been completed without either of us resorting to sulking, glowering, blackmail or tears. We are on a roll, so despite having already had lunch, we now order a traditional tea with scones and sandwiches. I won't touch the cakes or cream, of course. Fanatical about my food before, now I'm going to be a bride, I am rabid. Still, Mum's delighted and only worries about the extravagance for the briefest time. She does what she always does nowadays, whenever we are together: she delves into her bag and produces the *How to Plan for Your Wedding* book.

'Have you spoken to your hairdresser?'

'Yes. I've made two bookings. One so she can practise putting my hair up and then one for the wedding day. But I'm playing with the idea of getting my hair cut.'

'Oh, not your lovely hair.' Mum looks as though I've just suggested sacrificing vestal virgins to pagan gods.

'I'm too old for such long hair. What do you think of a sharp bob or a Zoë Ball crop?'

Evidently not much because my mother simply ticks the box entitled 'hairdresser' and moves the conversation on.

'Have you informed your bank and building society of your name change and ordered new business cards?'

'I don't think I'll change my name.'

'Oh.'

'Well, it's one less job,' I defend, concentrating on sipping my Earl Grey. My mother speaks a million words with her silences. Finally she moves down the list.

'You have to choose the flowers.'

I instantly know this isn't going to be as simple as picking out something fragrant and pretty.

'I was thinking hydrangeas and—'

'You can't have hydrangeas.'

'Why?'

'They're unlucky. They represent boastfulness and exposure.'

'Well, which are the lucky ones?'

'Roses are always good. They stand for love, innocence and thankfulness, depending on the colour. Or something delicate like heliotropes, which represent devotion and faithfulness, with a bit of lemon blossom. They stand for fidelity in love.'

'It's bollocks. What did you have?'

'Lemon blossom.'

'There's my point.'

My mum looks away. And I know I've hurt her. I can't quite say sorry.

'Oh, OK, heliotrope and lemon blossom it is.'

She smiles, relieved, and I'm embarrassed at how easy it is to please her.

'Have you thought about your honeymoon?'

'I'm leaving it to Josh. Which probably isn't all that wise, but it is traditional. Will you have a discreet word with him, Mum? So that he doesn't book anything too active. Don't let him book a trekking holiday to the North Pole or a canoeing safari. Beach and bars will suit me fine.' My mother makes a note.

'Has he chosen his ushers and best man?'

I stare at her with incredulity.

'It's not me who's asking, it's what the book says. Here, look: "Check your fiancé has chosen his ushers."' She points to the page.

'God, they assume we all marry simpletons, don't they? The implication is that he couldn't wipe his own nose unassisted.' My mother and I treat the surrounding tables to looks of disdain and disbelief.

'So has he chosen his ushers?' she asks.

'No,' I reply and we both giggle helplessly. I like this relaxed Mum. When the giggles subside, I say, 'I am grateful, Mum. Thank you. I know it's a lot of work.'

Mum glows and simpers. She carefully cuts her scone into halves and then quarters. There has been a mass of work and I don't know how I'd have coped without her. I hadn't expected to care about the fairy-tale day but as it approaches I really do want it to be perfect. I want a perfect bride with perfect hair, dress and make-up. Perfect Mum with all her friends attending and a hat that suits her. Perfect guests who are happy with the food and seating plan. And a perfect husband, which Josh is.

'We've had a lovely day, haven't we?' asks Mum.

'Yes,' I agree.

She doesn't pause. 'Issie mentioned a Darren to me. Pass the jam, dear.' She's desperately trying to be disingenuous but she's had no practice. I, on the other hand, am a veteran. I reach into my bag and pull out, from acres of tissue paper, the shoes I've just bought for the wedding. They are covered in tiny beads, zillions of them. They are certainly the prettiest pair of shoes I've ever seen.

'What do you think, Mum?'

'They are beautiful. Wasn't Darren the one from the north? Didn't you go on holiday with him?'

Issie really is rent-a-mouth.

'It wasn't a holiday. It was work.'

Mum falls back on the etiquette we have used for a thousand years. She refills my teacup and cuts me a slice of cake. She does this with the precision of a geisha girl. I try to be patient until the little ceremony comes to an end. It is only now that I realize she always uses this ritual to buy time. She has something important to say and she is carefully considering how best to phrase it.

'Josh is a lovely boy.'

I smile, this is fine. We both know this.

'He's been like a son to me in some ways, over the years, and certainly like a brother to you. I'm sure he loves you very much.'

'Er, Mum, this is hardly headline news. We are engaged to be married next month. Isn't this the usual state of affairs?'

Mum reaches across the table and puts her hand on top of mine. 'Do you love Josh?'

'Mum!' I'm shocked. When my father informed my mother about his affair, she could not believe it. Quite literally. I watched, from the doorway of the kitchen, as she ran to him and hung her arms around his neck. She smiled sweetly, hopefully, up at him and asked if he could possibly love the other woman as much, no more, than his wife and daughter. She had expected him to see sense and tell her, 'No, of course not.' That way we could all sweep the whole silly business under the carpet. Unfortunately, my father was unaware of the script. He'd replied that, yes, regrettably, that was the case. My mother reeled from the shock. It was at that moment that she began to construct the elaborate safety net that would protect her from any such horrors and indignities again. The most notable components of the net are that she doesn't readily show affection (I can count on one hand the number of times she's deliberately touched me). She never talks about love. And she never asks questions to which she doesn't know the answers. It bothers me that in a single afternoon, sitting in the Selfridges restaurant, my mother has broken all three of her own rules.

I figure it's a bit late in the day for my mum to take up the role of adviser. Just because I've let her choose the flowers and menu doesn't mean I want her opinion on every part of my life. She's my mother and therefore understands nothing and knows less. She's always let me pretty much make my own mistakes and learn my own lessons. Why start interfering now? Anyway, I am suddenly *piqued* with myself. Marrying Josh isn't a mistake. It is the right thing to do. He's kind and decent and easy-going and everyone likes him and he's got great career prospects and he's a good cook.

And he's not Darren.

I glare at Mum but she won't be intimidated into shutting up. Instead she says, 'I'd hate to think that all I'd taught you was sacrifice.'

I put Mum in a taxi, which very nearly spoils the day because she thinks a taxi is frivolous and sees it as yet another example of my decadence and 'odd ways'. I simply think it will save her hat box from being crushed on the tube. We all but have a stand-up fight, but we are reunited when the cab driver is rude to us and tells us to get 'bloody in, or bloody out, the bleedin', bloody cab'. I take another cab and rush back to the studio in time to sit in on the interviews of a couple of possible candidates for next week's show. The interviews finish at 7.45 p.m. and when I return to my desk I find the department empty, except for Fi.

'You're here late,' I comment.

She doesn't reply directly but grunts and glowers. I remember my mild, but public, rebuke earlier this morning and calculate that she's probably still sulking with me. I try to restore departmental harmony by telling her about the interviews.

'There was this archetypal Essex girl . . .'

It may be that she wasn't from Essex at all, but from Edinburgh or Exeter or anywhere in-between. But it's shorthand that Fi will appreciate. The girl had been describing her ex-lover. His CV read like the admission book to the Priory. A compulsive womanizer and gambler, whose idea of a day's work was a sticky-fingered sweep round the local shopping centre; a louse in every way but redeemed in her eyes because he was 'a real salt'.

I stared at the girl, non-comprehending. 'An Essex term, I presume?'

'Salt. Salt of the earth. The real thing. A fucker,' she elaborated.

'Quite,' I smiled. Knowing she'd make great TV and the warm-up act would be able to wallow in innumerable Essex jokes.

'Hey, Fi, what does an Essex girl say after her eleventh orgasm?' Fi shrugs. 'Just how many are there in a football team?'

It's an old gag, but Fi appreciates my effort and finally allows herself to smirk. I know I've won her round when she says, 'I'm just packing up. Fancy a drink? We could go to the Brave Lion.'

I'm about to decline, as is my habit, and explain that I have thirty plus e-mails to clear, when I suddenly think of my mother's fretful face in Selfridges.

If only I could leave it there.

I know that if I stay in the office on my own she'll haunt me, so I shut down my PC and grab my bag.

'Are you all right?'

'I'm fine.'

I'm not. But what can I say? How am I going to explain it to Fi, of all people? We clink glasses and sip our G&Ts.

I wonder what she meant? Sacrifice?

Fi is using her fag to orchestrate the tune playing on the jukebox. It's playing 'Always Something There to Remind Me', which seems poignant. Fuck, I'll be reading horoscopes next. I wish pubs would stick to ambient music. Sentimental lyrics and alcohol are a lethal combination. I charge towards thoughts of work, and away from ones of my mum, or Josh or the wedding.

'So tell me, Fi, if *Sex with an Ex* were your show, what would you be doing to "make it bigger"?'

Fi looks shamefaced. 'Er, sorry about this morning. I got

wound up. I was being ridiculous. As you said, I should choose my battles.'

'Apology unnecessary,' I grin. 'It's good you are so passionate about your work.' Or at least I think it is. 'Tell me, what do you think of the show at the moment?' I ask this to give the impression that I value her opinion. It's a motivational thing I learnt on a course. Fi sucks the lemon slice from her drink.

'Honestly?'

Suddenly I *do* value her opinion.

'Yeah, honestly.'

I'm indignant that she's implying that I like to hear anything other than honesty. Then I remember that I often accept half-truths, exaggeration, insincere compliments and uncalled-for criticism, knowing that they are blatant lies. It's the oil that eases the wheels I call my life. Exaggeration – of anything from quoting the sales figures to qualifications on a CV – is routine. Insincere compliments and uncalled-for criticisms are always the result of someone else having an agenda. Usually the three Ps: promotion (securing theirs, ruining the chances of mine), pay rises (earning theirs, negotiating mine), promiscuity (all of the above).

Half-truths.

This is more uncomfortable.

This is horrendous.

I drain my G&T. Issie and I are dealing exclusively in half-truths at the moment. I find it totally impossible to be frank with her or, for that matter, with my mother or Josh. To be frank with them I'd have to be honest with myself and, although I have briefly considered this, I've rejected it as the lunacy it so obviously is.

'Want another drink?' Fi is up and halfway to the bar before I nod my response.

The full truth is I have not forgotten Darren. I had expected that by now his name, if mentioned, would call a blank. That momentarily I'd struggle to place him and on placing him I'd be indifferent, cool, unconcerned.

I think of him more or less continuously and a fleeting thought sends me into a flurry of, of, of . . . happiness.

Pure unadulterated happiness. I'm happy he's on this planet somewhere. Even if that where isn't anywhere near me. All this and I'm marrying someone else in four weeks. I force myself to return to Fi. What were we talking about? Oh yeah, honesty.

She puts the drinks on the table.

'Yes. Honestly, what do you think of the show at the moment?'

'Well, it's fine.' I raise an eyebrow. 'Very good,' Fi corrects. I raise the other eyebrow. This doesn't create such a fetching effect but at least my expression corresponds with my thoughts. Fi sighs. 'It's lost its bite. There are no surprises.' She's right.

'Any ideas?'

'A few.' I wonder if she's going to share them. She must have invited me for a drink just for this opportunity. The opportunity to say, 'Actually I've sketched out a couple of ideas and a business case,' and then to reach for her satchel. I pause. She doesn't do this. I'm surprisingly relieved. Frankly a ten-hour day is enough for anyone.

'Another thing.' Fi hesitates and examines her nails. I notice that, somewhat out of character, her nails are bitten, stubby runts of nails. I wonder what's making her nervous. Or has she always bitten her nails? I can't remember.

'Go on, what other thing? Actually don't, I'll get the drinks in then you can tell me.' Odd that our glasses are already empty. I engage in that necessary hand-to-hand combat with other pushy, over-aggressive and well-dressed Londoners. Luckily I'm served immediately. It takes a rare barman to ignore me (and a rare barwoman to serve me). I squeeze my way back to Fi. I feel as though I've just spent six weeks in army training. Sensibly I've bought us both two G&Ts; two doubles, actually. Well, it saves having to tackle the assault course for at least another fifteen minutes.

'Go on. The other thing?'

'You.'

'Me?'

'You. You've changed.'

'I'm wearing eye shadow – maybe that's it. I read that eye shadow was in again,' I defend.

Fi stares. She can't decide if I'm being deliberately obtuse or uncharacteristically thick. The truth is, I'm nervous. I neck both my drinks as though they are water. Fi pushes her spare one in my direction.

'Maybe it's the engagement but—' she's steeling herself. Deciding whether to be brutally straight or not. She ploughs on. All I can do is admire her stupidity. 'You just don't seem as interested.'

'I'm very busy,' I snap with indignation.

'Of course.' Assuring.

'I can't be expected to do everything.' Defensive.

'Certainly not.' Insincere.

'You're managing.' Petulant.

'Absolutely.' Condescending.

'I'm not as interested.' Truthful.

Truthful. Fuck. That's unprecedented. I swill back another huge glug of gin.

'Oh shit, Fi, what can I say?'

Fi tilts her head, silently nods and I want to say something. I want to confide in her. I mean, I really like her. OK, it's quite a sudden intimacy, I have been resisting becoming matey. It could be something to do with the several gins that I've necked in as many minutes, but I want to talk to someone. Anyone. And Fi is the one in front of me. Two actually. There are suddenly two Fis in front of me. And a whole pile of glasses. I shake my head gently from side to side.

'Maybe because now you are getting married you are slightly less cynical and the programme is no longer as appealing?' offers Fi.

Maybe.

She could be right. I want this to be the answer.

'Or maybe it's simply that you are really busy with other things. I mean before you got engaged absolutely everything came *after* work – your friends, your family. Maybe you are simply reprioritizing because you are busier now.'

Yes, the endless lists. I'm suddenly chilled as a flash of panic hits me. Have I given the list of hymn choices to the organist?

What does she mean – 'everything came after' my work?

Fi's saying something else. I try to listen. The room is carousing. I touch my head but it still thinks it's a spinning top.

'When did you get engaged? March, wasn't it?' She doesn't wait for my confirmation. She drags heavily on her cigarette. 'Yet I'd say that your disinterest stems back further than that.' I freeze. 'Back to January. Did you make a New Year resolution not to work as hard?'

I glare at her. Both Fi and I know that she's pieced it together. She isn't absolutely spelling it out and this could be for one of a number of reasons. Either she's not drunk enough, or she still has vague enough recollections that I whip hide rather efficiently and I'm her boss, or she hasn't a lot of cash with her and she can't afford to offend me as she needs me to buy her drinks. I pause and consider what her reticence can be attributed to. Fi takes advantage of the pause by going to the bar and buying some more drinks. So she has plenty of cash.

As she sits down I blurt, 'It's Darren.'

'Darren who?'

'Darren Smith.' I resist adding 'of course'. How can she not know who Darren is? How come his name isn't embroidered on her consciousness? I feel gelded.

'Smith? I always think that's such a pointless surname. It doesn't throw any light on the matter of identification.'

I scowl at Fi. Smith is a strong name. Where would England have been without black smiths and gold smiths and plain smiths? A slightly embarrassing recollection tickles my conscience. I vaguely remember thinking Smith (and Darren) were stupid names. Over the last few months this has changed somewhat; I've been associating Smith (and Darren) and, more specifically, Darren Smith with strength, goodness and downright horniness, rather than pseudo names for adulterous couples embarking on a dirty weekend. I hunt out the more familiar part of my nature, my ability to be Machiavellian.

'Darren. You know, that stubborn git that I tried, and failed, to get on the show,' I prompt Fi. I'm trying to give the impression that he was a no mark in my grand scheme. This is stupid. Talking about Darren is stupid. Why am I doing this? It's dangerous. Fi hadn't associated my peculiar and sudden squeamishness with Darren and I should be relieved. I shouldn't be pursuing the topic. Because *no matter what* I am marrying Josh next month. Josh who isn't a risk and isn't a bad option. It's stupid to bring up another man's name in conversation.

I can't stop myself.

Saying his name aloud is a relief.

And anyway I'm only talking about him. Perhaps talking about him will help me clarify the situation. It does need clarifying because – I'm certain this is just the drink – but suddenly I can't remember why I didn't return his calls.

'The beauty? The horn?' asks Fi.

'Hmmm. Was he? Yes, I suppose, in a very obvious way he could be described as attractive. I'm referring more to his arguments on collective responsibility, taste, decency and erosion of public standards.'

I force myself to look at Fi. She's staring right back at me. It's obvious that she doesn't believe me. That's because she wasn't born yesterday. I suddenly sober up and know I have to change the subject. My mind is whitewashed. Blank. Vacant. Clean.

'I slept with him.'

'I know that.' Fi waves my confession away with a beer mat. It strikes me that when other women confess this type of thing the reaction is usually a little more stunning. Fi goes on to explain why she's not that astounded. 'But you sleep with everyone.'

'Actually I don't. Not any more. I haven't slept with anyone since Darren.'

'Not even—'

'Not even Josh.'

Fi looks as though she's just received news that there is intelligent life on Mars. More, that they are male. I take a deep breath.

'We tried but – well, it was awkward, and so we thought it's probably just the pressure.' She doesn't seem to be following me. 'Josh says it doesn't matter.'

But patently it does. Josh must be wondering how, since I've slept with half the male race in London, I can't have sex with him – my fiancé. It is a good question. He's lovely. I've slept with men I barely knew, never mind liked. Why the sudden capricious nature? Sex has never been in my head, firmly staying where it should be, in bed. Except for the mind fuck games which I played, but that was entertainment. I don't do sentimentality or lamenting lost love.

At least I didn't.

I got on. So there was never any issue about, 'I like him but I just don't fancy him'. Now I have problems with every aspect. His smell. Not that he smells terrible – the reverse is true. Josh always smells beautifully coiffured and doused in aftershave. But I want to smell *him*. His fingers, his armpits, his feet, his sperm.

But then I don't.

'Well, you know, it was bound to be difficult because we've known each other so long, in such a different context.' I look at Fi again. From her face it's clear that my explanation is mud. 'And so we thought we'd wait until after the . . . you know—'

'Wedding?' prompts Fi. I'm grateful.

'Yeah, the wedding.'

'But the real reason is because you've still got the hots for Darren.'

'I'm not saying that.'

'Oh, I thought you were.'

Another cab. This time to Josh's. I find him in front of his PlayStation. Without taking his eyes off the TV, he tells me that there's beer in the fridge.

'This is an unexpected pleasure,' he yells through to the kitchen. 'What's on your mind? If it's the ushers, don't worry, your mother's already called me. And she mentioned the honeymoon, too. I've cancelled the bungy jumping from Sydney harbour.'

I bring my beer back into the living room and don't waste any time trying to work out if he's kidding or not.

'No, nothing to do with wedding arrangements, I just – look put away the PlayStation. I've a couple of other dials for you to play with.'

I sort of dive on to him, quickly fastening my mouth on to his before he can comment on my terrible seduction line. I hastily unbutton his shirt and push it back off his shoulders. I frantically kiss his chest and neck whilst tearing at his buckle.

'What's the rush?' he asks as he tries to turn my hasty pecks into lingering kisses.

'It's time now,' I insist. 'We've waited too long.'

It's encouragement enough. After all, he is male. He jumps up and walks to the bedroom. I follow him. We undress ourselves quickly. He folds and hangs up his clothes. We get into bed and have sex.

He wants to please me, that's obvious. He strokes my head and thighs and caresses my breasts. I bury my head into his neck and squeeze my eyes shut. It's pointless. Darren is tattooed on to the inside of my lids.

It's fine, absolutely fine. I even have brief waves of orgasm, although I don't quite achieve a full climax, but then, I rarely do.

I lie on my back and stare at the ceiling. Josh props himself up on one arm and lies facing me. I pull the duvet up to my armpits. He strokes my hair.

'I'm sorry that was all a bit quick.'

'No, no, it was – fine. Great.' I'm desperate for a cigarette.

'Really, you, er, enjoyed yourself?' He wants to believe it. 'I mean, did you, er—'

'Yes, really, I came. Well, just about.'

Relieved, he reaches for his cigarettes. 'Well, that's good, then.'

'Yes.'

He hands me a lit fag and I edge up the headboard so that I can smoke it. I'm gripping on to the duvet like a Victorian virgin. We smoke in silence and then we stub out in silence.

'Do you think we are doing the right thing, Josh?'

'What a big wedding, rather than something small and intimate? Absolutely. It's going to be a great party and we've both got loads of people we have to invite – my family, your colleagues – and a few we actually want to invite. A big wedding is definitely right for us.'

I hold my breath. As I let it go, unscheduled words tumble out. 'No, I mean by getting married at all.' Double jeopardy. Gin-induced soul-searching, the worst kind.

'Well, even if we simply lived together you'd still have to have sex with me,' jokes Josh. I turn to him and see he's terrified. He coughs. 'Was it that bad?'

'No,' I smile, messing his hair and planting a big kiss on his cheek. 'You are every bit as good as you've always said.'

We laugh, me and mymateJosh. I feel more relaxed with Josh than I have done since the engagement. Obviously it was the sex thing that was stressing me out. It's better to have got that over with. I feel I can talk to him again. I push on.

'I just worry that neither of us knows how to do this. Neither of us has ever sustained a relationship for any length of time—'

'That's because we were with the wrong people. We are meant for each other.'

Of course.

'But my parents are divorced and yours just stay together to spite one another. Hardly ideal role models.' Why am I trying to reach for the self-destruct button? Marrying Josh is what I want to do. Why am I putting doubts in his mind?

'Loads of people manage.'

'Loads of people mess it up too,' I counterargue grimly. But then I remind myself: those who don't make it through are the ones who marry for the wrong reasons, for lust, for passion, because they are irrationally in love. Josh and I are quite different. We are marrying because we are alike. We are compatible. We are comfortable.

Fine.

Josh puts his hand under the duvet. He rests it on my thigh. He moves his thumb in circles. It feels like he is dragging my skin in the wrong direction.

'Again?' he asks.

Again? I hadn't thought about again. But of course there's an again. And again and again.

'I'm a bit tired actually.'

'No worries. We've got all the time in the world.' Josh turns away from me and is asleep in seconds. His breathing is deep and relaxed.

A lifetime of doing it again.

My feet are ice blocks.

17

Bale has come up with his most ridiculous, irritating and inconvenient idea yet.

'A party?' I'm incredulous.

'Yes, Jocasta, you know the sort of thing – music, drink, merriment.'

'But what for?'

'For the troops, of course. To thank them for all their hard work during the difficult times, to celebrate these delightful ones.'

Bale, nearer the bile of human meanness than the milk of human kindness, has never been within miles of being altruistic. I can't credit it now. I wonder which young PA he has his eye on. I assume that there must be someone he wants the opportunity to befuddle. Even so, it's a lot of expense to run to just to get someone drunk.

'Come off it, Bale. What's really going on?'

He comes clean. 'It's a tax break. I have to spend a certain amount on staff training and recreation.'

'I see.' I consider it. A party isn't a bad idea. If it takes place after I get back from my honeymoon I'll be tanned. I begin to mentally run through my wardrobe, considering what I should wear to cause the biggest sensation.

'All right, I'll look at organizing something in August.'

'Too late. All the invoices need to be through by the end of July. The party must take place this month.'

'In that case, no can do.' I can use this phrase with Bale – he still thinks 'ciao' is an acceptable greeting. 'Someone else will have to organize it. I'm getting married on the twenty-first.' I point out the obvious to him. 'Less than three weeks' time.'

'We'll do it before the wedding.' Bale reaches for his *Playboy* desk calendar. He concentrates on the numbers in amongst the cleavages and tight butts. 'Today is the second. Let's have the party a week on Friday – that's the thirteenth. You're not superstitious, are you? No, you're not the type. That gives you another week before your wedding to clear the invoices.' Bale stares at me. 'You always throw such good parties.'

I want to tell him that this isn't in my job description. I want to tell him that I have a number of other projects that need completing before I go on holiday. I want to tell him to go and screw himself. But there's something in his eyes that tells me this isn't up for debate. I know I'm being tested. Am I efficient and committed enough to pull off a huge corporate event the week before I get married? Or am I demob happy?

The bastard.

'No problem,' I smile and skip out of his office.

'Bugger!' I yell, once I'm safely behind my screensaver.

'What's up?' asks Fi as she passes my desk.

'The usual. Bale,' I groan. 'He's piling up my workload just to see if I fuck up. I could really do without it.'

'What's he asked you to do?'

'Arrange a party.'

'A party? Great,' enthuses Fi, miscalculating the reaction I want by about as much as is humanly possible. She sees my thunderous face and adjusts her jubilant one accordingly. 'Not great.'

'No, not great,' I snap. 'Besides all the final touches for my wedding, I have to close the books on this quarter's budgets, write a presentation to the executive committee, oversee the production of *The Murder Trilogy* drama, secure the contract on the coverage of the Tour de France, get the final episode of this series of *Sex with an Ex* in the bag and approve the casting of the Scott family in *Teddington Crescent*!'

By the time I finish my list there's more than a passing resemblance between my face and Barbara Cartland's wardrobe.

'OK. OK, I get the picture. Calm down, pink's not your colour,' says Fi. She puts her hand on my shoulder. 'I have some capacity at the moment. I'll help.'

'You will?'

'Sure.' She sounds nonchalant and not at all like the life-saver she undoubtedly is. I want to kiss her. I settle for something more conventional.

'Thank you.'

'No problem.'

Fi and I make a great team. She takes charge of arranging the party: decides the theme, arranges caterers and alcohol. She finalizes the guest list, which extends beyond staff, to include the press, minor celebs and competition winners; she sends all the invites. Fi works around the clock for two weeks. I am really impressed by her commitment and friendship. Whenever I see her, she's awash with project plans, inventories, rosters and registers. She is nearly continuously on the phone trying to drum up guests, PR interest, entertainers and glassware or she is sending e-mails, faxes and couriers to cajole, influence or sweet-talk whoever into doing whatever.

This leaves me free to tackle all my other tasks. It's imperative I leave work in shipshape condition. I really don't want to have to be making long-distance calls throughout my honeymoon. I work like a madwoman. Long hours and high levels of concentration cause my head to ache, eyes sting and temples bulge. By the time it gets round to the thirteenth

I have emptied my in-tray and signed off all the projects that are imperative. The only thing left to do, in the week between the party and the wedding, is close the books on this quarter's budgets. Then after the honeymoon I can come back to—

Well, to whatever is in my in-tray.

'All done!' I send my last e-mail of the day with a flourish of satisfaction.

'Oh good. I was worried that Cinders wasn't coming to the ball,' says Fi. She's scrabbling under her desk trying to retrieve a kitten-heel shoe. We are both high on the spirit of having achieved what was demanded of us. Despite the unreasonable nature of the demands.

'What, and miss your party? Not for the world.'

She's dressed in a white sequined Moschino number. Very ice maiden meets LA débutante. I couldn't have chosen better myself. She's obviously taken great care and spent her dowry.

'Are you getting changed?' she nags.

'I haven't thought about it.' Fi pulls a face. 'OK, OK, I'll look through my filing cabinet. There's bound to be something to wear in there.' I know she's worked hard and wants everyone to appreciate her effort by making an effort.

Fi has plumped for a theme of black and white. She said this was largely to do with the invitations being sent out so late in the day; the guests are mostly media luvvies, and a dress code stipulating one or other of these colours won't cause any problems. Despite the brief, I emerge from the loos, fifteen minutes later, with freshly applied lipstick and a scarlet Johanna Hehir dress. It's clingy, flowery and feminine. I believe in the importance of an entrance.

I follow the noise of laughter and clinking glasses and the heady perfume of fat waxy lilies up to the roof terrace where we are holding the jamboree. The lift parts and my first impression is top. Waiters, dressed in Paul Smith, carry trays of champagne. There are dozens of lanterns and fairy lights everywhere and whilst it's still too light and warm for them to be anything more than decorative, they are certainly that. There are sculptures of huge chess pieces scattered about. I'm not sure what their original purpose was intended to be but they are being used as giant ashtrays and bar stools. There are luxurious, white, faux-fur rugs hanging on the walls. The food looks exquisite; it also follows the theme of black and white – piles of scrumptious-looking caviar followed by attractive miniature summer puddings, made entirely with blackberries and served with heavy dollops of double cream. Fi has done the correct thing by serving small amounts of delicious-looking food. It barely matters what it tastes like, as most of the guests would rather polish the shoes of the entire British army than consume unanticipated calories. Still, the media luvvies look the part; as my mother would prosaically say, 'They scrub up well.' The room is awash with every label in the alphabet, from Armani to Versace.

The effect is magical.

I help myself to a glass of champagne and look for someone useful to talk to. Fi prevents this by hurtling towards me.

'OhmygodOhmygod,' she screams.

'What? Have I lipstick on my teeth?' I ask, rubbing my teeth with my finger. As I do so I notice there's soap stuck in my engagement ring; I take it off and start to gouge it out with my fingernail. Something is certainly upsetting Fi. She looks as though she is hyperventilating.

'I am so sorry. I can't think how it happened. We used mail merge. His name must have been on the wrong list,' she gabbles.

'Whose name?' I ask. But Fi can't answer because she's staring at something behind me. She looks like a rabbit terrified and trapped in the headlights of an oncoming truck. I turn.

I'm the rabbit.

'Darren? Darren?' I can hardly believe it is him. For months I've been trying to convince myself that seeing Darren again would be the worst thing that could possibly happen to me, but now I'm actually facing him, I have to admit it feels like the best. The crowds around us dwindle and there's just the two of us. Which is a nightmare because my tongue is cleaving to the roof of my mouth and I can't think of anything at all suitable to say. I slip my ring in my pocket.

He's breathtaking. He's everything I've been imagining and remembering for the last six months, but more.

I'm expecting an onslaught of anger and recriminations and try to head them off by putting us on a polite and formal note immediately.

'Are you here for the party?' Then I shoot myself. Or at least that would be a suitable penalty for such a banal conversation starter but I don't have a gun handy.

'I suppose I am,' he says, half grinning and wincing at the same time. My La Perla hiccups.

'Good, good. I'm so pleased.' I like this sentence more. It is at once honest and straightforward. Honesty and the ability to be straightforward are things I know Darren admires. 'I didn't expect to see you here,' I rush to clarify. 'Not that I invited you.' That sounds awful. 'I mean. I didn't send out the invites.' He looks confused. 'Well, it's not your sort of thing, is it?' My voice finally falters and then draws to a halt. I suspect we are both relieved.

We stand awkwardly watching other people enjoy themselves, until eventually Darren asks, 'Will Trixxie be coming along?'

I'm crushed. He's here for Trixxie. Not me.

Not that he could be here for me. Not after I've ignored him for six months.

Nor should I want him to be. I'm engaged to Josh and I don't do casual sex any more. I try to tell myself that my jealousy is a lazy hangover from my other life.

'I don't know. I don't think even Fi knows who she's invited, judging by the look of confusion on her face when she saw you. If Trixxie is coming she'll be late,' I add sulkily. He's grinning. No sign of disappointment that Trixxie may not appear. Maybe he just thought of her because I was behaving like an incompetent. I add, 'It's quite a select gathering.'

'I'm touched.'

In case he thinks I am, I clarify, 'And your name got on the list by mistake. A fault with mail-merging the wrong list.'

'Ha,' he guffaws. He actually throws his head back and laughs out loud. As ever, I'm not sure if he's laughing at me or with me. But I don't care. I just like hearing his laughter. It cheers me. It is definitely the most exhilarating sound I've ever heard.

'You don't change, do you?' he asks.

In fact, I do. I have. And if I tell him I'm engaged that would prove it.

My mouth is welded together.

I wait for him to walk away but he doesn't. Instead he asks, 'What did you think about that article on Ian Schrager's latest hotel?'

'Sorry?'

'Or the one on the Balinese spas?' He is referring to the web pages he's e-mailed to me. The one on the spas was the last one he sent, nine weeks ago. 'It's just you never said.' Darren stares at me and his stare could shatter granite. Every one of his e-mails had been selected with peculiar care. They always referred back to some conversation we'd had in the halcyon period. The two weeks when we behaved as a couple. The two weeks when we were a couple.

I cough up my voice. 'I – I often visit the Starsky and Hutch site.' The side of his mouth twitches a fraction. 'And the one about historical Oscars. In fact all the articles were interesting.'

Darren nods. It's a tight, tense nod. Hardly perceptible. I need a drink. I daren't move towards a champagne tray, in case Darren takes the opportunity to leave, so instead I flag down a waiter and insist he fetches us a couple of glasses.

Darren accepts the glass but he doesn't look comfortable.

'What should we toast to?' he asks.

I consider suggesting that we could toast to my engagement. But I don't.

'To, er, you. You look well. Let's toast to you,' I suggest.

'No. That would be far too unchivalrous. How about to *you*? You're always well, aren't you?' I don't quite know how to answer that. He doesn't sound 100 per cent genuine. I shake my head warily.

'Proposing we toast to us seems a bit off key,' he snipes.

'Suppose so,' I mutter reluctantly.

'I've got it. Here's to *Sex with an Ex*.'

I catch his eye. 'Er, *Sex with an Ex*,' I mutter, because really, here's to it. But can Darren mean that? He can't be toasting the programme. He loathes the programme. So does he mean a genuine ex? Me? Is he flirting? I clink my glass. I hope he's flirting.

I can't believe my luck. I keep expecting him to make his excuses and go and talk to someone else but he doesn't leave my side. Instead he attentively fills my glass, fetches me caviar, walks the room with me, allows me to introduce him to innumerable colleagues. He stands outside with me when I feel overwhelmed by the heaving throng and then he dances with me when I feel so happy that all I want to do is fling my body in random, jerky movements to the thumping bass. He stays right by me, carefully watching my every action, listening to my conversations with other people, and he seems to be happy to do this. We both behave as though we've seen each other every day for the last six months. Darren doesn't publicly rebuke me for my terse note and sudden disappearance; he doesn't refer to a single aspect of my despicable and undoubtedly confusing behaviour. I don't know what to make of this. Am I so insignificant to him that he can't even summon up the curiosity to ask me why I behaved so strangely? But if that is the case, why spend the evening with me? If I were more trusting, the only conclusion I could draw is that he wants answers but he won't embarrass me in front of my colleagues by demanding them. He's too polite. He cares too much.

Believing that he cares at all sends me into a state of near hysteria.

Throughout the evening he is a delight. He charms and amuses everyone. He chats to Debs, Di and Jaki, who are enraptured with his good looks and general affability. Trixxie stands speechless, with her jaw hanging open as she listens to his theories on why women find Robson Green irresistible.

'She's literally mesmerized by you,' I tease him.

'No, it's drugs,' he grins modestly.

I watch as Darren works his sorcery on the celebs who normally make it a rule not to be impressed by or even civil to anyone other than their next pay cheque. He grips the 'gentlemen' of the press by quoting their own articles back to them and having an informed opinion on the broadest range of subjects – anything from the ins and outs of India's election systems to the GDP per capita in Japan. He even impresses Bale, who, desperate to meet Darren, follows him around the room and contrives to collide in the urinals. In our two weeks together I'd painted a bleak, but accurate, picture of Bale which must now be colouring Darren's judgement. Whilst happy to talk to everyone from the bar staff to the chairman, Darren steadfastly avoids Bale and won't treat him to more than a casual wave across the room. And whilst everyone is captivated by Darren, I am bewitched. He is just as funny and interesting and polite and sincere as I remembered.

He is more sexy.

I feel as though I am swimming in champagne. Bubbles of euphoria zip through my body where blood and lungs and my nerve system used to be. I feel giddy and light-headed and light-hearted too.

Fuck – what if someone tells him about the engagement before I can?

I saw my way through the crowd of women who are congregating around him. It's slow progress and so I eventually whisper to one of them that Robbie Williams has just arrived. Fickle, they rapidly disperse, leaving Darren to me again. He looks relieved.

'Enjoying yourself?'

'Yeah, it's great meeting your friends.' There's a 'but' in his voice and I'm glad.

'Fancy going somewhere less frantic?'

He agrees immediately.

We leave the party and start to stroll aimlessly along the river. We take a similar route to the one we took in January, past the National Theatre, the Royal Festival Hall, the Hayward Gallery, the Queen Elizabeth Hall. We walk on to Westminster Bridge and stop to look at the London Eye.

'Impressive, isn't it?' comments Darren.

'Very,' I agree.

'This is what I love about London. The space, the crowds, the progress, the history. The morphing culture.'

So he starts to tell me about what he does with his time in London and how he ended up here in the first place, why he left Whitby and also how much he misses and loves it. I ask him about his family and he gives me their news. Sarah's expecting another baby and Richard and Shelly had a lovely wedding day. He shows me a photo of Charlotte receiving her certificate for swimming twenty-five metres. The image of her tiny, wet and shivering body, erect with pride, makes me smile. I ask dozens of questions but he can't give me enough information. I hadn't known I could miss anyone so much.

'They often ask about you,' he says.

'Do they really?' I'm aglow.

'Yeah, they have a pet name for you.'

'What?' I ask tentatively, not sure that I want to know.

'Naomi Campbell,' he grins.

I start to laugh. 'I'm going to pretend that is because of my fetish for shoes and modelesque looks rather than my stunning ability to throw a hissy fit.'

Darren laughs nervously, too frank to confirm or deny my suppositions. His nervousness makes me laugh louder. I'm laughing at myself and it's OK because I'm part of the Smith family jokes. He tells me how his sick trees are and makes me laugh again with descriptions of his new flatmate. We talk and walk for hours. We leave the river at Charing Cross and start to head to St James's Park; we pass Buckingham Palace and march on to Hyde Park.

I can't remember exactly when he took hold of my hand. I think it was when we crossed the Mall. I have never held any man's hand in public. It's so territorial, so tacky. Their hands are always clammy and it's difficult to walk in a straight line with someone hanging on to you.

Don't let go.

I'm firing on all cylinders. It's been a particularly warm evening, so there are still hundreds of people on the streets. Including the terrorists of the speed walker – tourists, roller bladers and pensioners. But tonight their stop-start-stop styles, dangerous speeds or dithering steps don't annoy me. They seem like part of the tapestry. As do the *Big Issue* sellers, the gangs of Euro-trash teenagers, the groups of friends finishing their picnics, the traffic wardens, the dog walkers, the mounted police riding up Birdcage Walk and the other happy couples.

Other happy couples.

Other happy *couples*.

'My feet are aching.' I finally submit. 'Let's go and get a drink somewhere.'

'OK. Where?'

'Dunno. It's late and this is not my end of town.'

And I want to take a hotel room.

It's just like that. Because besides all the hand holding, and the conversation, and the laughing, and the fact that I was desperately proud of him at the party, there's something else. There's my breasts, which have taken on a life of their own: nipples upturned and out-turned, aching, desperate for him to clutch and ply and grasp and tongue. And there are my exploding knickers. Creamy with desire. Dizzy with craving.

We hail a cab within seconds, which is fluky and seems to me to be a sign that this is meant to be. Unashamed, I instruct the cabby to take us to a hotel.

'Which one?'

'Any,' I reply, irritated by the interruption, for by now he is interrupting. He's interrupting Darren's long, filthy looks of undisguised want.

The cab pulls up outside some hotel. We pay in a daze, wildly overtipping. We muddle through the inconvenience of having to check in and decide which paper we want in the morning. And just as I think we are about to stumble into bed in a stupor, Darren stops in the foyer.

'We have to talk.'

'We've done nothing but talk all night,' I say whilst tugging at his jacket sleeve, impatiently trying to drag him towards the lifts.

'Talk about us.' The only topic we've avoided.

'But you're a boy,' I joke.

Darren won't be deterred and leads me to the hotel bar. I reason that a drink is a good idea. I haven't had one since I left the party, which will have been near nine o'clock. It's nearly twelve now; I'm in serious danger of sobering up. In the past I've often found myself in London hotel bars. I know the form. There will be a waiter who shuffles in a manner that is ostensibly discreet. Eyes averted, addressing us as 'sir' and 'madam' rather than anything that hints at our real identity. The waiter will ensure that we've located the loos, knowing that the purchase of condoms will be necessary and as likely as not somewhere to throw up the night's excesses. He will take away the dirty ashtray and leave a clean one; he'll leave a small bowl of cashew nuts and a cocktail menu. He'll expect us to get heinously drunk in an attempt to shed responsibility and any visions of consequences and he'll expect us to leave a massive tip before we stumble to our bedroom. Darren breaks precedent by ordering a lemonade. His boyish choice makes me giggle until he says, 'And you, Cas? I suggest we keep clear heads.'

I want a double vodka and a fuzzy head but I order a mineral water. We don't say anything in the time it takes the waiter to go to the bar, fix our drinks and return with them. When the drinks do arrive neither of us suggests a toast. The silence clings to my brain and congregates in my nose and throat, suffocating me.

'Why?' The question, disgustingly direct, shocks me. Darren is naïvely expecting an equally open response. He wants truth to shape all his dealings. Whilst when I stumble across it (which is rare) I view it as an obstacle. The late hour and the raw expectancy in his voice defeat me.

'Is that an all-encompassing "why"? Why didn't I call? Why didn't I return any of your messages? Why did I dodge you when you came to see me?'

'No, Cas, I know the answers to those questions.' He does? How? 'I know why you ran. I know you are terrified of commitment and I reasoned that I couldn't do anything about that except wait. I hoped time would show you that I'm serious about you. If I hadn't known at least that much about you, how do you think I could have brought myself to speak to you this evening? Don't you think I was blistering with anger and' – he pauses – 'pain? But I reasoned that whilst you hurt me you didn't do it to be cruel, although you were; you did it because you didn't know how else to behave. You hurt because you are always hurting. That's why I didn't rail at you this evening. Believe me, I wanted to.'

He pauses and I look at him. His eyes are a mass of confusion and wisdom, certainty and terror. I feel so ashamed. If he had ranted at me I could have walked away. I could have sidled back to the sanctuary of aloofness, feeling justified that he didn't understand me and never would. But he does understand me.

'I never stopped thinking about you, Cas. I never stopped

wanting you. What I'm asking you now is why won't you *allow* yourself to trust *me*?'

So he's worked it out. I'm impressed – it shows dedication. But then I know he's the dedicated type. I wonder how to answer his question. After all, he's never let me down, hurt me or disappointed me. In fact, he consistently exceeds my expectations. He has attributes and characteristics that I thought had died out with Merlin and Arthur's round table. And even they were myths.

I can't think of a logical reason why I wouldn't trust him.

I can't think of a convincing lie. So I do the next best thing. I tell the truth, a part of the truth, something like the truth.

'I do trust you.'

Darren's face, previously tight and anxious, melts into the broadest grin. He takes my chin in his hand, tilts my head and kisses me. The kiss is strong, absorbing and complete. Darren is satisfied with my answer; he thinks that his six months' wait on the sidelines has brought me to my senses. And so we move towards the lifts, to the bedrooms. I trust him but he shouldn't trust me. I am engaged to Josh. And whilst I know now, for certain, that I made that promise for the wrong reasons, I did promise. Poor Josh. Poor Darren. And if I could bring myself to like myself more, I'd feel sorry for me too. I know I should pull away from Darren, stop him kissing me, stop kissing him back and tell him about Josh instead. But I can't. I'm a coward. Whilst Darren has been the epitome of reasonableness thus far he won't understand that my fear of loving him drove me into an engagement with another man. I hardly understand it. And I want him so ferociously that I don't know how I'd continue to live if he stopped kissing me now. So whilst Darren's kissing me, and illuminating my skin with his strokes, and warming my consciousness with the words he's uttering, I am making another promise. This time to myself.

This will be the last time.

One last fling before I return to Josh. I may trust Darren but I don't trust love. And whilst Darren has arrived in my life with a certificate of authenticity, he's not carrying a lifetime warranty. Josh does. I plan to enjoy every moment of tonight and I'll make memories that will fortify and edify me for the rest of my life.

That's what I plan.

We fall on to the bed and he forcefully and repeatedly kisses me. My legs entwine around his, our hands race to rediscover every curve, crevice, ravine and fissure of each other's bodies. We shed our sticky clothes in a matter of seconds as our skin burns and bleeds into one another's. He kisses, strokes, licks every inch of my body. Exploring the obvious parts – my shoulders, my tits, my thighs, discovering the discreet parts, my toes, the crook of my elbow, the space between my fingers. I consume him. Tasting his sweat and smelling his sex. I concentrate on the feel of him, which bits of his body are rough, which are smooth. I become familiar with the texture of his hair, all his different hair. His thick, glossy locks, the downy fuzz growing in-between his buttocks, the hairs on his chest that thicken and become more coarse around his groin, the bristles that grow on his chin, right now whilst I'm with him. I listen to his heart and his breathing. Both becoming quicker and less controlled. I smell him. I taste him.

I see him.

The second before he enters me, he grabs my head in both his hands and he looks at me. He stares.

He knows me. Me with his pubes stuck to my cheek, him with my sex on his lips. I tighten my muscles in my thighs and groin in an effort to cling on to him. To keep him exactly where he is now. In me. With me. I wonder how I walked away from this. I wonder how I'll walk away a second time.

It's faster and faster and tighter and harder. I can feel my body responding and the response is rising. It's coming from my toes, circling up through my legs. But it's started in my fingers too, which seem to be lost in his hair and then running up and down his back. My arms ache with the exquisite brilliance of it. My head spins with the same shocking ecstasy. The intense feelings of luxury creep up my back and through my heart, meeting in my stomach. The meeting fulfilled in acute spasms of rapture. I jerk with sex. I jolt with sex. And when he screams out that he loves me I brim over with a feeling of gladness.

Suddenly everything is crystal. This is the last piece of the jigsaw, the glass of freezing water on a blisteringly, stifling day, the hot, creamy chocolate after an afternoon on the piste, the sunshine on a wet pavement after a summer storm, the thing the songs go on and on and on about. He's it.

Exhausted and sweating, we fall on to each other.

I watch him execute the logistics of falling asleep: peeing, putting a glass of water on the bedside table, adjusting the air conditioning, discarding the duvet and selecting a sheet instead, and I'm fascinated. I watch him turn on to his side and see that, as his breathing calms, his shoulders rise and fall steadily. I tuck tightly into him. My breasts on his back. His bum nestling in my pubes. My legs folded into his, finishing with my toes in the arch of his ankle. And it starts to fade. The throbbing anger, cynicism and mistrust that I've carried around for twenty-six years start to fade. As does the terrible feeling of loss and grief that I've been soused in since January. I am simply full of love and hope and possibility. The revelation that we are imbued with something more interesting than physical gratification is velvety. The recognition that I, too, have a need for and ability to give respect, friendship, love and passion sings around my head. This man is my destiny. This man is my life. Fuck it, I'll risk it. So he doesn't come with a warranty – so what? I'll risk it. And I'm so lucky to be able to.

'Cas, you awake?' Darren's whisper interrupts my thoughts.

'Yes,' I whisper back, although I'm unsure who we're being careful not to disturb.

'I was just wondering.'

'What?'

'Will you marry me?'

'Yes.'

I know. It's slightly unconventional that I am technically engaged to two men.

18

Here I am in the middle of realizing a dream, a dream I didn't even realize I had, and it's good. Really good. Wow. That shit about better to travel hopefully than arrive. Losers. Better to arrive spectacularly and I have.

I have! I'm drunk on euphoria (and only a little bit of fear). I want to bottle the experience and keep it on my dressing table. I know he is *it*. The One. The only one. I'm not sure how I'll maintain this constant high. But I believe it will all take care of itself.

We stay in the hotel all morning, excitedly talking about when and where we'll get married. Darren is thrilled when I admit that there's nothing I'd like more than to marry in St Hilda's Abbey, Whitby.

'You mean the church near the abbey. The actual abbey is decayed. It doesn't have a roof.'

'No. I mean the abbey. I want to be outside in the open.'

'We can look into it. I'm not sure of the rules. I suppose once ground is consecrated, it's always consecrated, long after the roof has fallen in.' He pauses and kisses a mole on my back. 'I didn't think you believed in God. What are you doing? Keeping a foot in each camp?'

'No, it's not that. It just feels right. The abbey is so beautiful. I felt calm there.'

We both confess to a hankering for a winter wedding.

'Although it will be freezing, so I have to consider erect nipples if we are getting married outdoors. They can ruin a photograph,' I comment.

'Can they?' From his tone it's obvious that he doesn't think so.

I can see me in a long fur dress and him in navy velvet. I can see it all so clearly. We talk about children, how many and their names! Then we agree that we had better get up and start telling people. I freeze. Telling people that I'm marrying Darren necessarily means telling them I'm not marrying Josh. I'm terrified and horrified. I can only imagine the pain and disappointment I'm going to cause. I turn to Darren and consider confessing everything to him. I'm sure he'll guide me, and advise me on how best to handle this awful situation. But the words don't fall out of my mouth. Instead we agree to negotiate a late checkout. I try to thrust Josh to the back of my mind. We order champagne and drink it in our room. Later we order lunch, 'our meal' (because we already have 'our' things) – cheese on toast which I can't eat. So instead we celebrate with more loving. At four o'clock the chambermaid and the manager hover, then hammer outside our door, insisting that the room has to be cleaned, as it is booked by someone else for tonight. Reluctantly we drag ourselves out of bed and into our clothes.

We say goodbye to one another in the hotel lobby, but then can't quite separate, so Darren walks me to the tube even though he is catching a bus. We say goodbye again at the ticket barrier but then decide to buy a ticket for him, just so that we can say a final goodbye on the platform. We wouldn't have parted at all but I have arrangements to meet my mum and Issie at my flat to do a final fitting of the wedding dress. The wedding to Josh, that is.

'I expect his reluctance to let you out of his sight was because he isn't sure when, or indeed if, he's ever going to see you again,' snaps Issie.

'Of course he knows he'll see me again. He trusts me. *I* trust me. We're going to see each other every day for the rest of our lives.' I giggle and do a small on-the-spot jig. I'm just so full of energy! My mother and Issie stare at me from their seats on the settee. Their faces sort of spoil the moment.

'Aren't you pleased for me?'

They exchange looks.

'Aren't you going to congratulate me on my engagement?'

Issie tuts, 'Which one, Little Miss Changie-Mindy?' I notice my mother put her hand on top of Issie's in a futile attempt to calm her.

'It does seems a little sudden,' comments my mum. Trying to walk the tightrope between tact and instruction.

'It's not sudden, I've felt like this for a long time, I've just found the courage to admit it. I haven't changed my mind, just my heart. I am still sure that infidelity, shallowness and cruelty are out there. I just no longer believe they are my only option.'

'You know, you're right. Infidelity, shallowness and cruelty are out there,' shouts Issie. 'And do you know something else? They are right here too. *You* epitomize them. What about Josh?'

Of course I haven't forgotten him. I admit that I've worked hard in the last twenty-four hours not to think of him, but he's been with me all the time. He's the shadow on my intense euphoria. Which is heartbreaking, because I do believe that all he ever wanted to do was make me happy.

'I can't marry Josh,' I state sadly.

'Well, I realized that you weren't planning on becoming a bigamist,' screams Issie. Her mouth is wide open and her face is the same colour as her tonsils.

I kneel in front of them, hoping, rather than expecting, they'll understand. Issie flings herself back against the settee;

my mother moves a fraction closer to me. Although it's hardly a herald of angels, I take this as a sign of encouragement.

I try to explain. 'I didn't believe in love – I couldn't understand why anyone would. When people talked about love it was like reading reports about war in a faraway country – it just didn't seem real. And then I . . . well . . . I guess . . . I . . .' Issie and my mother are staring at me, which is a bit offputting. 'Well . . . fell in love.'

'Visited the war zone, so to speak?' says my mother. She sounds unsure.

I plough on regardless. 'But it was really scary, so I . . . well . . . I . . .' Bugger – when did I start stuttering? 'Ran away.' Issie tuts like a budgie. 'But once I knew the war zone was real, really real, I found it impossible to ignore. Marrying Josh would be a halfway measure, like sending food parcels.'

'You want to be a foot soldier rather than part of the Red Cross,' says my mum. She still doesn't sound confident. Hearing her repeat it back to me like that, I realize how bizarre my analogy is. So I try something more conventional.

'I am so sorry that I'm going to hurt Josh. But don't you see? It would be much worse marrying him when I don't feel about him the way he does about me.'

'Yes, I see that,' says Issie. 'That was my point all the way along.'

'Darren makes jokes funnier if he laughs at them and he makes the room more homely when he enters it. He makes water cleaner, nights blacker and stars brighter if he notices them. I hadn't wanted to admit that love existed, that I'd made such a monumental, disastrous misjudgement. But I have to, because I love him. Even when I'm asleep.' At this point it seems a genuine possibility that foreign tongues have possessed me.

'I, I, fucking I. That's all we ever hear from you, Cas. What about thinking about someone else for a change?'

I stumble backwards, nearly overwhelmed by the power of Issie's words. She rarely swears and never says fuck.

'First you hurt Darren by just walking away from him, then you pick him back up when you feel like it—'

'It isn't like that, it's—'

She waves her hands in front of her, cutting through my objections. Imagine Issie's little, skinny hands being so powerful and effective.

'You are *so* selfish.' She's on her feet now and pacing around the room. 'OK, so you believe in love now – let's have a party!' She stamps her foot and with anyone else I'd have been tempted to laugh, but since this fury is coming from Issie and directed towards me, all I can do is listen.

'No, on second thoughts, let's not. Let's examine your ridiculous behaviour instead.' I think I prefer the first option, but then I don't think this is a genuine choice situation. I listen to Issie as she begins to list my crimes against humanity. The way she explains it, it appears that I have more in common with Imelda Marcos than a love of shoes. '. . . The horrible way you've treated your countless lovers. The stupid destructiveness of *Sex with an Ex* and finally your selfish, fucking, engagement to Josh.' With each accusation Issie raises her voice a decibel. I fully expect the people in the flat above to bang on the floor and ask us to keep the noise down.

My insides are raw. I want to tell her that I wasn't awful to all my lovers and anyway most of them didn't really expect anything too laudable. I want to tell her that the show saved jobs. I want to tell her that I love her *and* Josh and never meant to hurt either of them. But all these arguments seem hollow and pointless. She's heard them before. She was never that impressed. Anyway she's gone.

The door bangs behind her.

I turn to my mother. 'Do you think she was disappointed because she's not going to be bridesmaid next week?'

'Don't joke about it, Jocasta,' replies my mother sternly. 'You always rush to hide pain in jokes and it comes across badly.' Subdued, I follow her through to the kitchen. She opens the fridge and pulls out a bottle of Veuve Clicquot.

'We can always depend on you to have champagne in the fridge,' she comments. 'I've always thought that is so stylish of you.'

'Have you?' I'm so stunned I'm momentarily diverted from pondering Issie's outburst. I'd always assumed that Mum thought champagne was decadent. The only bottles my mum keeps in the fridge are brown sauce and tomato ketchup. My initial surprise is superseded by the fact that my mother expertly opens the champers and pours it into the glasses without spilling a drop. I don't think I've ever seen my mum open champagne in my life.

'Do you think Issie's right?' I want to know where I stand, but I'm not sure how much more straight talking I can take.

'Yes,' replies my mum, without taking her eyes off the drink she's pouring.

'Oh.' We both silently watch the bubbles fizz and then settle, and I wonder if I'm going to have any friends left, if I get through this at all.

'What are we celebrating?' I ask apprehensively.

'It's not quite as simple as that, is it? I mean we could raise a glass to your new engagement but that would seem rather insensitive towards Josh. Poor boy.'

I stare at my shoes. 'If only I could turn the clock back.'

'You can't. Ever,' states Mum. And as if to prove her point I notice that the only sound in the kitchen is the clock ticking.

Then in a kinder voice she adds, 'But do you know something? I'm proud of you.'

'Proud of me?' I can't believe it.

'Yes. You've recovered. You aren't letting your father ruin your life.'

'Like he did yours, you mean,' I mutter glumly. I really don't want to be reminded of my father right now. All too clearly, I remember the innumerable occasions when my mother moaned and grumbled about him. I received the subliminal message loud and clear: men are bastards.

Not all of them. I remind myself.

Expecting an onslaught of bitter regret and fury from my mother, I cling to the thought as though it were a shield. Not all of them.

'He didn't ruin mine, darling. I have a lovely life. Bob and I are very comfortable with one another.'

'Bob?' I'm amazed. Surely her life is dished. Why else would it be so quiet? Except of course if she likes it that way.

'Yes, Bob.' She smiles and doesn't elaborate. Thank God. I've had enough monumental shocks and surprises in the past twenty-four hours to last me a lifetime. I've discovered I'm capable of loving. I've learnt Darren loves me and revealed that I love him too. I've got engaged. Again. I've heard Issie say fuck. I've seen my mother open a bottle of champagne. I could not stand knowing that she has a sex life.

'I'm proud of you for falling irrationally and uncontrollably in love. I didn't know if you'd ever have the grit to do it. I thought your father and I had denied you that on top of everything else.' She pauses and then adds, 'Well done, Cas!' I think she's going to slap me on the back but she hugs me. It's a small, tight hug – not exactly the huge grasping to the huge bosom that you see in movies, but then my mother hasn't got a huge bosom.

It's the best hug I've ever received.

We pull apart and grin at one another. I think I've just come first in the egg and spoon race. I must have because my mother is every bit the proud parent.

'Issie,' I groan.

'Don't worry too much about Issie, she'll come round eventually. She's too kind not to want to see it from your point of view,' smiles Mum. Then she adds, in a tone I'm much more used to hearing from her, 'Not that you should dismiss what she said – it was spot on. You have a lot of bridges to mend and maybe some of them will never be repaired.'

I can't bear to think about that.

'Now come and tell me some more about Darren. When will I get to meet him? Don't forget to bring that bottle of champers.' She takes my hand and leads me to the sitting room.

Mum sits on the settee and I sit next to her. We while away the early evening with chatter about Darren and, more shockingly, Bob. I tell her the big things that make Darren wonderful and some of the small things too.

'He raises his eyebrow and it is sooo sexy. And he kind of ruffles his hair in a boyish way.'

'Bob does that too. Not that he has much hair. Which does, I suppose, encumber the effect.' We laugh. 'Maybe you and Darren would like to have tea with Bob and me on Sunday.'

I think of a compromise. 'Or we could all go to a restaurant.'

She sees it as that and meets me. 'Yes, that's a good idea. We can get dressed up. Make it a bit special.'

At some point I ease down the settee and find myself half slumped, half draped across Mum. My head is on her lap and she's playing with my hair. She runs her fingers over my scalp. I have Darren. I have Mum. I am as safe and as loved as a child.

Buuuuzzzzzzzz.

'Wonder who that can be,' I mutter, annoyed that my bonding time with my mother is being so rudely unglued.

Buuuuzzzzzzzz.

'Are you expecting anyone?' asks Mum.

'No.' I drag myself towards the intercom but before I open the door it opens from the outside and Issie falls through it. She's fumbling with her keys and mobile and handbag, which she drops, scattering tissues, money and make-up everywhere. I'm thrilled to see her.

'Put the TV on,' screams Issie. She's tense and still angry, which incites her to forcefully yell, '*Now*. TV6.' Yesterday this sudden boldness would have been unusual; now the unexpected is all that seems available. I do as she says.

I hear a familiar theme tune.

'*Sex with an Ex*? But the series is over.'

Issie shushes me.

'Hello. Thank you very much and welcome,' says Katie Hunt as she bounds on to the stage. Her tits are trembling and, to make the job of the close-up camera easier, her shirt is unbuttoned one more button than necessary. 'Well, ladies and gentlemen, have I got a treat for you!' She winks cheekily, the way I taught her to.

Issie hands me a gin and tonic, which I take unquestioningly. I see that she's poured Mum a sherry.

'Tonight we are featuring our very own "voice of our generation", only days before her wedding. We are going to see if she's ready to say "from this day forward", or is it a case of "from this lay forward". The audience erupts into loud oohs and phwas. 'Our celeb was given the opportunity to appear on the show but has declined, so instead we'll meet her fiancé, Joshua Dixon. A big hand, ladies and gentlemen.'

'Josh!'

The gin and tonic slips out of my hand on to the floor. The glass smashes and the liquid spills in all directions. None of us moves to mop it up.

'Josh – you don't mind if I call you Josh, do you?' Katie purrs. Josh shakes his head, always one to be taken in by a pretty face. 'Can you tell us a little bit about yourself and your relationship with your fiancée, Jocasta Perry. Tell us why you are here tonight.'

'Cas and I have known each other since we were children.'

Ahhhhh, chorus the audience, no doubt incited by the stage manager holding up a big sign reading 'HOW SWEET'. We have other ones reading 'SHAME' and 'CONDEMN'. The signs were Bale's idea.

'I love Cas. I've always loved her, right through school, university and when we both got jobs.' As Josh is saying this, photos of Josh and me appear on screen. One when we are about eight and he is pushing my swing. I'm grinning, a gappy, toothless grin, and kicking my legs high. You can see my knickers. Josh looks intense and as though he's working hard to push me higher. In fact he was trying to push me off the swing so he could have a turn. Of course he was. He was a brother to me.

'I've always loved that photo,' says Mum. I scowl at her.

There's another one of us at university, getting our degree certificates. Josh is adjusting my gown. Then several others, where we are doing our own thing. Josh in his chambers, me at various parties or functions. The thing they have in common is that I'm always surrounded by men and holding a glass of champagne; Josh is always alone.

'Why haven't they shown any of you working?' asks Mum. 'Or any of Josh partying? He's such a cheerful young man and he seems a loner in these.'

'Exactly. That's what they want to imply.' I rake my hands

through my hair. I know exactly where this is going and I'm quite powerless to stop it. Issie pats me on the knee. We don't take our eyes off the screen.

'Cas seems quite a party girl,' pursues Katie.

'Well, yes, she is,' confirms Josh, and in case he's misinterpreted, he adds, 'But I like that in her.'

'When did you get engaged?'

'March, this year.'

'So you've waited for Cas for twenty-six years. You staying at home, whilst she's been having a high old time. I hope she's worth the wait.' Katie turns towards the camera and grimaces.

We don't get to hear what Josh replies. Even if he was honest enough to admit that he didn't exactly hang around in the wings for twenty-six years – more like bought shares in Durex – the audience don't get to find out because the camera cuts to some affidavits from my friends and colleagues. We see them say, 'Up for it,' 'Game on,' 'Wild,' 'Fun,' 'Skilled (laugh), if you know what I mean.' The audience has no idea what question was asked or how the interviewee was led into a certain response. They could have been talking about my attitude to work. They could have been talking about someone else. I know this because at TV6 we aren't always that consistent in our approach to interviewing for *Sex with an Ex* and we edit for maximum entertainment – rather than authenticity. In the past I've advocated this. Now I'm regretting it.

Katie gets Josh to talk about how he proposed to me. The audience lap up the cream rose, dimmed lights, huge diamonds. He omits to mention the fact that the weeping of the freshly ditched Jane was still echoing around the flat. Nor does he mention his New Year's resolution or the tax breaks.

Fair enough. I wouldn't either if I were him.

Josh talks about all the preparations, cost and care for our 'big, traditional wedding'. He doesn't say that my mum has done all the work. They cut to lots of footage of Josh talking to caterers, florists and the guys who erect the marquee. I can only assume this footage was filmed especially because, to my certain knowledge, Josh has not visited any of these people to actually plan for the wedding. My mother confirms this when she comments, 'But that's not the florist we are using.' She looks at me and corrects herself, 'Were using. That's not the florist we were using. Why do you think Josh is talking to them?'

She's far too innocent for me to be able to explain.

'Josh, it's clear to see that Jocasta is a bit of a flirt.'

The words cut. A neat incision.

'But why did you contact the studio? Is there a particular ex that you feel might threaten your relationship?' Katie Hunt tilts her head to one side and smiles sympathetically. I've seen her practise that in the mirror in the loos.

'There's this one guy, Darren Smith.'

The incision rips to a wider gash.

They play a film of the TV6 party. Even in this stupefied state I have to credit the editor. It's a fine piece of work. Because the cameras were concealed and I obviously haven't signed a release form allowing TV6 to film me, they have had to use a black stripe to obscure my eyes. But since they have just shown numerous stills of me, the strip doesn't conceal my identity. I just look sinister, a bit like a masked madame at a brothel. The film starts with a shot of me slipping my engagement ring into my pocket. This is repeated four times and then it shows me greeting (a masked) Darren. Cut to me beaming like a Cheshire cat. It shows Darren being attentive towards me, bringing me caviar and champagne. They speed that bit up and, because of my animated hand gestures and his vigilance, it looks as though I am bossing and directing him on an endless stream of jobs. Fetch this, bring that, go there and come here. Cut to Darren and me dancing together. We were actually dancing to an innocuous cover version of 'Let's Twist Again' but TV6 have dubbed in the husky, throbbing voice of Rod Stewart singing 'Do You Think I'm Sexy'. The camera angles are such that I look as though I'm gyrating my groin almost in Darren's face. Cut to me trying to get through the crowd of women hanging round Darren. Again this is speeded up, and by shaking the camera, the effect achieved is one of violence. It looks as though I'm shoving away the competition. There's a bit where we were chatting exuberantly, my hair cloaking our faces. It looks as though we were snogging, at it like hammer and tongs. We had openly left the party together. But by editing two different bits of footage, one of Darren going to the loo and another of me going out of the room for a moment to take a call on my mobile, it looks as though we deliberately left separately and then met furtively outside the building. If this were a film about anyone other than Darren and me, I'd be thrilled.

Darren.

I watch Darren and me walk along the river. I was right – we did start holding hands by the Mall. I see us get in a cab and arrive at a hotel. The masks hide the look of longing and apprehension in Darren's eyes and blank out the moment where the caution rinsed from mine.

It all makes sense now. That's why we were able to get a cab so easily – a plant. The cabby *knew* which hotel to take us to. The one with hidden cameras in the lobby, bar and corridors. That's why breakfast arrived even though we hadn't ordered it. TV6 needed an affidavit from the bellboy that we were in bed together. That's why the manager couldn't let us stay at the hotel for another night. Too right they needed to clean the room out – more like they needed to collect evidence.

I'm right. The film finishes with a number of shots of the debris of our love. A camera pans around the bedroom we left. Empty bottles of champagne, discarded sachets of bubble bath, crumpled sheets on the bed and used condom packets in the bin. The last two shots cause the audience to titter. There is no voiceover. No accusations are actually articulated because if they were I could sue the hides of TV6 but the implication is clear. The masked woman, identifiable as Jocasta Perry, has betrayed Josh, the smiley, affable chap on the stage. I feel betrayed. Exposed. Dirty.

Katie Hunt is exhilarated. Her obvious excitement is bordering on sexual arousal. She tries to contain it as she turns to Josh.

'So how does that film make you feel, Josh?'

There are no winners.

Poor Josh. Despite having watched every episode of *Sex with an Ex*, it is clear to me – his former best friend – that he had no perception of the humiliation, upset and pain he was about to bring upon himself by opening this Pandora's box. The same could be said of me but doubly so.

How had I ever thought this showing of bloodied sheets was entertainment? How could I have ever thought that it was OK to reduce love to petty gossip and to aggrandize betrayal to something glamorous rather than grubby?

Josh looks worn and defeated. He tries, but fails, to summon his charming smile. The audience sigh collectively. He looks as though he's going to cry. Oh my God, he is crying. It's excruciating.

'As I mentioned, Jocasta Perry was invited on to the show but refused to appear.'

'That's an outright lie. I'll get my lawyers on to that,' I snap, but I know the situation is beyond help or hope. TV6 have made a calculated gamble. Even if I sue for invasion of privacy, as this show has been much more intrusive than any other, they have a hit.

'We do, however, have a recorded interview with her.'

They show footage of me in a meeting, presenting on *Sex with an Ex*. I am not wearing a mask because I made this film for TV, to publicize the show. I gaze brazenly at the camera. I am in fact talking about the show when I comment, '*Sex with an Ex* is unbeatable. Risky, dirty, cheeky and above all fun.' But I know that the millions of viewers watching think I am talking about Darren.

'And let's leave the final word with Darren Smith,' beams Katie.

Close-up of Darren leaving the station after having seen me on to the tube. Even the black stripe over his eyes doesn't make him look comical – he looks more like a modern-day Lone Ranger. He leaps up the steps three at a time. He reaches the top of the steps and leaps into the air, punching it. Cut to me, winking and saying, 'Cheeky and above all fun', air punch, 'above all fun', air punch.

Issie and my mother stay silent as the credits roll. I switch off the TV.

'What did that last bit mean?' asks my mother.

'Do you, do you—' Issie's struggling. 'Do you think Darren was in on it?'

I pelt her with a silencing glance and she looks at her shoes. I finally find my voice.

'How could they do that to me? I hate the studio. I hate the media.'

'Er, you invented it. It's your baby,' points out Issie with uncalled-for reasonableness.

'This isn't a baby. Babies are cute. This is Frankenstein's

monster's more vicious big brother.' As I say this I know she's thinking this serves me right. I also know she's correct.

My eye flicks with tiredness, my head aches. I'm suddenly freezing. I go to my bedroom and unearth a jumper and some socks. Back in the sitting room my mother and Issie are sitting still, like statues, where I left them. I pull my jumper tighter around me. The chill seems to be coming from the inside.

'So do you think Darren set you up?' persists Issie.

'No.' I'm horrified that this thought has entered her head.

'You're certain.'

'I'm positive. Issie, I trust him.'

'It's just that he did seem to forgive you rather too easily. He might be a saint, but it seems more likely that he was part of the plot and wanted revenge.'

'You're wrong.' He couldn't have faked it. I know it was absolutely real. Everything from the party, to the walk along the river, to the hotel. He's my fiancé, for God's sake.

Hmmm.

But even considering that, I trust him. I keep hold of *my* pictures, him singing into the bathroom mirror, my hands towelling dry his soapy back after our bath, him shining his shoes with the little polishing kit they leave in hotel rooms. I don't allow the film to replace them. I know what I know.

The telephone starts to ring. Foolishly my mother answers it. It's a reporter from the *Mirror.* I take the handset from her and hang up. It immediately rings again. I disconnect the phone at the wall. Issie looks out of the window. She's right to expect to see the pack.

I start to think of the people who must have been involved in this set-up. Bale certainly must have given the go-ahead. But Bale has not betrayed me. Betrayal requires an atom of self-awareness. With Bale this kind of behaviour is closer to animal instinct. Unpleasant as I've always found him, I can certainly believe that he'd stitch me up in this way for ratings. He'd sell his mother to the white slave trade if he thought it would make good television. But he's not bright enough to have come up with the idea. That must have been Fi. I don't want to jump to conclusions, but Fi knew how I felt about Darren. She was unusually keen to help me arrange the party. I bet she suggested the party to Bale in the first place. Of course – why else would she have enough time to help me out? Bale makes sure all his staff are on overdrive all the time. She sent out the invitations and she never makes mistakes, mail merge or otherwise. How could Fi do that to me? I thought we were friends.

But were we?

Was I ever a real friend to her? When she joined the station she had tried to be agreeable but I made it clear our relationship was strictly business. I recognized the fact that she was fiercely intelligent and ambitious. I was threatened. So instead of developing her potential, working her into the team, recognizing her achievements, I tried to contain her talents. All I've taught her is ruthlessness, selfishness and egotism.

Still, she seems to have learnt those lessons pretty well.

And it's not just Fi. Debs and Di must have been working on the publicity for this. Jaki must have co-operated too, because the press have my telephone number and address – personal details that only Jaki has. Katie Hunt was having a great time exposing me as a bitch and I gave her her first big break! What could I possibly have done to offend her? Maybe she just thought I was fair game. Tom and Mark may have held a grudge because I slept with them and then dumped them. Gray because I didn't. Ricky's trickier. What have I done to hurt him? Failed to comment on how fetching he looked in his new Diesel shirt? I think of the time that he needed me to negotiate a schedule change with the homophobe executive. I'd agreed to go to lunch and then stayed with Darren. I didn't even remember to cancel the date. The executive never forgave Ricky and has made his life hell in a thousand small ways since. Obviously Ricky felt I'd let him down. And Jack the cameraman? Ed the editor? Mike on sound? How we've laughed about that – 'The mike Mike', we roar. Jen on special effects? We've shared KitKats! And then, when it came to the crunch, they all betrayed me. These are depressing thoughts but the worst of it is I know that I deserve it. It doesn't surprise me that I failed to inspire any loyalty anywhere with anyone. Because it has been my mantle: no trust, no honesty, no fucking possibility. I'm being treated badly because I treat people badly.

My mother and Issie stare at me cautiously, waiting to see the result of mixing the mortal cocktail of resentment and humiliation. They are expecting me to swear that I'll never, ever trust anyone again. Cautious before, impenetrable now. It wouldn't surprise them if I insisted on leaving the country, where my impenetrable aloofness would be further enhanced by the fact that I'd be struggling with a phrase book. They are waiting for the fury and the vows that I will never, ever confide, trust, respect or love again.

Instead I say, 'I'd better call Darren.'

19

'Josh.'

Silence.

'Josh, it's me, Cas.' I guess that this is more information than necessary, in the light of our history.

'Well, hello, little lady.' He sounds suspiciously joyous, which I know can't be the case.

'Josh, are you drunk?'

'Yes, and you'll still be beautiful in the morning.' He sounds wounded, regretful and disgraced.

'Oh Josh, I'm so sorry.' The inadequate words fall down the telephone line.

'Which bit are you sorry about, Cas? The twenty-six-year friendship? Agreeing to marry me? Committing infidelity in front of 12.4 million viewers, or the colour of the bridesmaids' dresses?'

I smile. I love him for being kind enough to joke with me, even though I am pretty sure I can hear his heart splintering at the other end of the phone.

12.4 million. A record for the programme and TV6. It's now unlikely that *Sex with an Ex* will be ousted into another time slot to accommodate blockbuster films. Fi's done her job. The irony is that I helped her to bring about my fall. If I hadn't been so determined to boost my own public image, by insisting on appearing in every tabloid, magazine and chat show, my marriage would never have been so interesting to the general masses. If I hadn't created resentment in the journalists by manipulating them, maybe, just maybe, they wouldn't be so keen to put the Russell & Bromley in now.

The press have jumped on the exposure story, inciting yet greater interest as each day passes. A number of the chat shows have run opinion pieces, asking their viewers to ring in and vote for who I should marry, Josh or Darren. The qualities also ran the story, turning it into a modern-day morality tale. And indeed all my ghosts have visited me: past, present and future. Josh is far too cute for anyone to want to consider his part in this, so the blame has been well and truly, and entirely, left at my door. The moral condemnation overlooks the fact that 12.4 million silently vindicated my infidelity by being entertained by it.

I understand.

The more vehement the condemnation of me is, the more entire their absolution. Clean hands. I don't blame them. I haven't exactly advocated collective responsibility in the past. Besides which, it *is* my fault – even I know that.

The florist who had been booked to provide flowers for the wedding is suing me. He claims that as *Sex with an Ex* filmed a substitute florist, he was denied the publicity which was rightly his. I don't think this will stand up in court, but a number of other suppliers have jumped on the bandwagon: the caterers, the cartoonist and the manager of the reception venue are demanding that they be paid in full. Even the vicar is looking for a public apology and, more secularly, compensation for the bellringers. But then I guess the fact that the number of weddings has declined by 35 per cent since the first episode of *Sex with an Ex* is reason enough for the Church to feel aggrieved.

Past guests of *Sex with an Ex* have emerged in droves. Reselling their stories with a new spin, i.e. how I incited the infidelities (which is not true – there are enough careless people in the world without me having to do that). Some guests say the channel gave them money to commit infidelity (untrue); others say that I offered sex for them to co-operate (lie). Nothing is so bad that it cannot be said of me.

Every one of my exes who could come forward, without jeopardizing his own relationship, has done so. Exactly how I give fellatio is now a matter of common knowledge. As is where I get my hair cut, how many fillings I have, how much I paid for my apartment, my bra size. I have been laid open, unmasked.

'I take it the wedding's off, is it, Cas?' Josh asks.

I think I hear hope in his voice. Which is worse than all the above. I know his heart rate and breathing have quickened. I know his mouth is parched and his stomach somersaulting.

'Cas, I'm sorry about the show. I should never have agreed to do it. I didn't know they were going to stitch you up that badly. I didn't approach the studio, they approached me. They didn't stick to the rehearsed questions. I didn't—'

'I know,' I sigh, cutting him off. He needn't explain. I'd assumed the best of him, blaming him for little more than naïvety. It is a pity that Josh didn't have enough confidence and trust in our relationship and therefore put us both through this. But he was right not to trust me, so the pity and shame are mine. 'It's not your fault, Josh. I'm sorry they used you—'

'Can't we just put it behind us?' Hopeful.

'No. We both know I can't marry you.' Firm. 'I am sorry they used you to get at me but I'm more sorry that I used you.' I take a deep breath. 'I love you, Josh, but I'm not in love with you. I agreed to marry you for the wrong reasons.' For the first time I understand what the expression 'cruel to be kind' really means; I'm not using it as an excuse to dump someone who's outgrown his use, become tedious or whom I've simply stopped fancying. Dare I add the next bit? 'And I don't think you are really *in love* with me.' I hear him take a sharp intake of breath. It sounds as though I've punctured his lung. I've certainly punctured his dreams.

'What the fuck do you know, Cas?' he snaps drunkenly.

'Not much,' I admit. I pause. There isn't a gentle way. 'But a bit more than when I agreed to marry you. I am so very sorry, Josh.'

'But it's so humiliating. The invites have gone out.' He's pleading with me, nearly begging, but instead of the cold delight that I used to derive from impassioned accounts of unrequited love, I hurt for him.

'Please, Josh, don't say any more.' If I wasn't so swollen with sadness I'd be amused that he hopes that anyone who's received an invitation will still consider it valid. All Britain knows I'm not going to be wafting down the aisle in a cloud of silk and lace this Saturday.

'You don't believe that thing about the One, so aren't I as good as the next one? Better than none?'

'Josh, you're wonderful. You'll make someone a fabulous husband,' I say truthfully.

'But not you.' There's no need for me to comment. 'And are you planning to keep the champagne on ice for your wedding to Darren?' he asks sarcastically. 'Your adulterous friend.' I try to be patient and remember he is within his constitutional right to be bitter and livid. I don't say that sleeping with Darren wasn't infidelity. Sleeping with Josh was.

'You know we can't ever see each other again?' he threatens.

This is complex. A fat tear splashes on to my telephone directory. Crying is now significantly more natural than breathing.

'If that's what you want,' I say, knowing this is not what I want but I have to respect his wishes now.

'You realize what I'm saying. There will be no one to fix your washing machine, or check the oil and water in your car. No one to send out for pizza in the middle of the afternoon because you and Issie are too engrossed in your movie to move your arses.' He's trying to sound angry, but I can still hear the tears in his voice.

'I'll miss you. I love you. I'm sorry,' I squeak and I put the phone down.

I know I can get in a plumber, take the car to the garage and order my own pizza. I can do it alone, but I'll miss him. I'll miss his stupid jokes and his stories about court. I'll miss his hugs and his cooking. I'll miss our shared history. I'll miss his friendship.

Darren.

His face cuts into my consciousness, explodes and sends tiny particles of emotion hurtling into my heart, knocking me sideways. It doesn't feel secure, it feels risky, but it feels safe too. I don't feel certain, but I am sure. It's right and it is fractious. I can't marry one man knowing I am in love with another.

The odd thing is, I've lost Darren.

Quite literally.

I have spent the last four days trying to track Darren down but he's vanished. His mobile is switched off. And when I went to his house his flatmate told me he hadn't seen him since the night before the TV6 party. I went to his laboratory and office to ask for him. No one had seen him for a few days. It was suggested that he might have been consigned to an away job. But if anyone knew where that might be, they weren't going to tell me – public enemy number one – no matter how much I cajoled, threatened or pleaded. Issie sees his disappearance as an admission of his involvement in the set-up; Mum's reserving judgement but as the days have slipped by, and there's been no contact, her face has become increasingly fraught.

I know he wasn't in with Bale and Fi. I don't know why he's disappeared but I know he didn't betray me.

So, after all my years of scepticism, mistrust, selfish hedonism, I find I have landed here, exactly where I was scrupulously avoiding.

In love.

But alone.

I guess that's evidence that there is a God, or at least my fifty-three cast-off lovers would think so.

I return to the office on Thursday. It's a difficult journey into work as journalists are constantly trailing me. One of them is more tenacious (or junior) than all the others and has been camped outside my door since Saturday. He's obviously unsuited to sleeping rough and now looks as bad as I feel. Seeing his chilled and crumpled state this morning, I take pity on him and pass a few pleasantries and offer him a cup of tea. He looks at me suspiciously but is too cold to turn down the tea. It may be July but it's a British July.

'You shouldn't believe everything you read, you know. I'm not Cruella De Vil.' He takes the tea. 'Are you planning on trailing me all day?' He nods. 'Well, I'm driving to work. I might as well give you a lift.' He doesn't know whether to accept my offer. Naturally he's trying to discern what my ulterior motive could be. There isn't one. I'm too worn out to formulate a come-back strategy. I'm not even sure that I want to.

I arrive at the office by 8.15 a.m., and although I haven't managed to go to the gym I enter with my kit bag over my shoulder to give the impression that not only is it business as normal, but I am healthy and sane. I'm wearing a charcoal-grey Armani suit – emotional armour – and dark glasses to hide the bags under my eyes, induced from lack of sleep and endless crying. But then I do work in media and as long as the glasses are designer no one thinks twice about my wearing them inside.

I walk through the glass, open-plan offices, cursing (not for the first time) the architect. Had he considered my public humiliation when he put together his design? I nod to a few faces and ignore the sniggering and whispering. I walk the marathon to my desk, sit down and put on my PC. I ring Jaki's extension number.

'Jaki, can you bring me a double espresso, please,' I ask, as I do every morning.

'You're back!' She doesn't trouble to hide her disbelief.

'I am. I had summer flu. But I'm back now.'

'Er, glad to hear you're better,' she stutters.

'Thank you, Jaki. Can you bring me my diary? Oh, and can you make room in it so that I can see Bale today?'

'Well, actually your diary is clear.'

I get it, but pretend not to.

'Fine, then I'll have time for some invoicing and it shouldn't be difficult for you to get me an appointment with Bale.' I hang up.

Bale agrees to see me at 11.00 a.m. In the meantime the entire staff studiously avoid me. My leper-like state is due to the widely held belief that luck is catching – both good and bad. When I was fast-tracking my way through promotions I'd been an extremely popular girl. Trixxie is the only exception. She does pop by my desk to say hi. But then I suspect that in her drug-induced state she has no idea what happened on last week's show.

I choose to wait until five past eleven before I walk into Bale's office. Fi is sitting there already.

'Bale, you've put on weight,' I smile. Pleasantries over, I close his office door. He reminds me of a walrus, his pink fleshiness indefinitely merging nose into lip, lip into chin, chin into neck into chest and suddenly we arrive at his feet. I try to think of his good points. I can't. He doesn't even close his mouth when he chews his food. I turn to Fi. She, on the other hand, looks magnificent. Triumphant, glowing. I think of Lady Macbeth. She's wearing an Alberta Ferretti suit, which, as I've never seen it before, I can only assume was bought from her ratings-achieved bonus.

'Nice suit, Fi,' I comment. 'I didn't realize that they took blood money at Harvey Nics. Thought it was just charge cards.'

'Oh, come off it, Cas. You know the game.' She looks sensational and I know for certain that my team will now be worshipping at the temple of Fiona. They can't see through her. Because they are dazzled. She's dazzling.

'Have a seat, Cas,' offers Bale. I note it's the low one. They'll tower inches above me if I sit in it.

'I prefer to stand.'

'Oh, not stopping?' asks Bale. They start to snigger.

'Did you catch the show on Saturday?' asks Fi. Which sends them into raptures.

'Have you seen the runs? Aren't you going to congratulate us on the ratings? You always said a show with Darren Smith would break all records,' pursues Bale.

'Ratings? Ratings? Is that all you think about?' I snap. Despite my vows to remain cool and calm throughout.

'Yes, Cas.' He thumps the desk and suddenly turns serious. 'Ratings are all *I* think about. And up until recently, when you fell in lurve, that's all *you* thought about.'

Slapped face. Even this repulsive cliché knew more about me than I did. I don't think there's any point in my trying to explain that the cost of ratings rocketing is hearts plummeting.

'You let us down, Cas. Running up north after that hippie gypsy. Coming back with loads of mumbo-jumbo ideas on emotionally profitable programmes. You're a disappointment.'

'Just because Darren isn't a materialistic, hedonistic, Fascist, that does not make him a hippie gypsy,' I yell back. I think about it for a moment and then add, 'And anyway what's wrong with hippie gypsies?'

Bale and Fi roar with laughter. Her boobs and his belly bounce up and down as their laughter ricochets around their bodies. I stay still.

'I expect this type of thing from you, Bale, but you, Fi – you've surprised me. How could you do this to me?' Fi stares back, insolent and unashamed. 'You knew that Josh and Darren would both be hurt and that I'd become public property.'

'Yeah, I heard that Dazza did a runner,' sneers Bale. 'Bad luck, Cas.'

'Still, look on the bright side,' comments Fi. 'There's been so much publicity about your abilities in the sack that, besides Darren, absolutely every man in the country wants to shag you.'

'And the bright side is?'

'Oh, come on, Cas. You've never been one to turn down a shag.'

'No,' I sigh and rub my forehead. 'Not in the past.' I'm sick of the small talk. 'Well, as jolly as it is passing pleasantries with the pair of you, I think it's time I got to the point. I'm resigning.'

'Accepted. I was going to fire you, for your recurring absences without doctor's certificates, but then we'd have to negotiate severance pay. It's so much cleaner this way. Although not as financially advantagous to you,' he taunts.

I don't care about the money. I turn to Fi.

'I've got to hand it to you, Fi. I thought you were going to have to fuck Bale to gain his favour. Instead all you had to do is fuck me. Good choice – I'm far prettier.'

I let the door slam behind me.

I walk out of the office, past my desk. I don't even bother to empty my cupboards. I walk to the lift, through the reception and keep walking out of the door.

And I surprise myself, because as the door swings behind me, I feel better than I've felt for a long time.

So I get my hair cut. All off.

'My God, your hair!' squeals my mother when I pop round to see her and Bob on Thursday night.

'Don't worry, it's not an act of self-loathing or penitence. I just wanted . . . I don't know . . . a change.'

My mother looks as though she's about to cry and so I'm grateful when Bob says, 'It's very fetching, Cas.' Bob's OK, quite a decent bloke, once you look past the brown cords.

'Thanks.' I force a smile across the fish fingers and beans. I see him gently nudge my mother.

'Well, I expect it's a good idea to herald a new beginning,' she stutters heroically. 'You might shake the press for a day or two.'

My head's much lighter – I estimate that my hair weighed pounds – but my heart is still heavy. After supper I turn down the offer to stay the night and hurry to catch the tube.

I spend the next day on the telephone. I re-call Darren's

mobile, flat, lab and office. No joy. I make a list of National Parks and call each one of them to see if he's working with any. He's not. I then start on London's parks and when I still don't unearth him I try twenty or thirty others up and down the country. There are plenty of sick trees but Darren's not ministering to any of them. I walk the streets hoping to spot him. It's futile. I then gather my courage and call the Smiths in Whitby.

His father answers the phone.

'Hello, Mr Smith. You probably don't remember me.' I had the impression that my stay at the Smith household passed Mr Smith by. I was merely an interlude between *Countdown* and the chat shows. 'It's Cas Perry. I'm a friend of Darren's. A sort of friend.' Somewhere between archenemy and fiancée.

'Hello, pet, of course I remember you. When you came on the telly, I said, "Wasn't she the one who was up here, chasing our Darren?" And Mother said I was right.'

I'm a bit stuck for what to say next. The fact that Mr Smith referred to my 'chasing' Darren is bad enough but my worst fear is confirmed: Darren's family saw the show.

'I've seen your picture in the paper, too.'

Marvellous.

'Well, I was just ringing – it's a bit awkward really. You see, I need to talk to Darren and I can't find him.'

'Aye.'

'Well, erm, I was wondering if you'd know where he is.'

'Aye.'

'And whether you'd tell me.' I cross my fingers. In fact, they've been crossed for days now, which makes it very difficult to hold a cup of hot coffee and almost impossible to tie my trainers.

'Well, that's something else. I'm not sure I can do that. I'll have to ask Mother. *Mother,*' he bellows.

I have a vision of Mrs Smith running along the corridor in a waft of baking smells and fury. I am terrified and want to put the phone down. But if I do I'll never find Darren. Mr Smith has put his hand over the handset but even so I can still distinguish distinctive wrathful mutterings: 'No better than she ought to be, the cheek of her, I'll give her what for.' I am paralyzed with fear and now can't put the phone down, even if I wanted to.

'Yes?' she barks. 'Who is this?'

'It's Cas Perry.' Meek.

'Who?' Insincere.

'Cas Perry, Darren's friend.' Tentative.

'Hardly!' Outraged.

'Mrs Smith, I can imagine how angry you are—'

'Oh, you can, can you?' She sniffs. 'I doubt it.'

'But I really do need to talk to Darren,' I persist.

Silence. I can hear the cogs of her mind whirl round.

'I won't help you.'

The phone goes dead and I'm left with the cold, continuous tone that tells me no one wants to speak to me.

I wonder if he is there? Perhaps he was in the yard kicking a ball around with Richard. Oblivious to the telephone wires that I am trying to crawl through to reach him. Or perhaps he did know I was on the phone and just didn't care.

Saturday is red hot. The sun is pouring in through my windows. Insensitively cheerful. I consider that this is the fine weather I hoped I'd wake up to on my wedding day; now the sun's mocking me. I pull down the blinds. I look around my flat and try to think of something to do to while away the next fifty-odd years. Throughout the last few days I have tidied, ordered, arranged and rearranged every aspect of my life. My cereal packets are arranged in descending size order, my knickers are arranged in colour and date purchased order, my cosmetic bottles are separated into sections – face, body and hands, and then subdivided by brand, and my CDs are alphabetically categorized. Everywhere I look is tidy, neat and trim. It's ironic that I know exactly where to locate the list of who I sent Christmas cards to in 1995, but I've no clue as to where to find my fiancé.

Besides the physical tidying up, I've had time to do a bit of mental cleaning out, too. I've written a list of the things that have gone wrong. Or more specifically, and much more humbling, the things I've done wrong. I approached my list methodically, subdividing my crimes into categories: 'Darren', 'Mum', 'friends', 'work', 'lovers', and an all-encompassing 'general'. The same themes recur in each section. I've selfishly pursued my own peace of mind, ruthlessly trampling on the feelings of others. Worse, I've justified my behaviour by sulkily holding a grudge against my parents for having the audacity to make their own decisions and live their own lives. I think of Fi's question, asked in some grotty pub after we'd both become careless with alcohol. 'Couldn't you have just, I don't know, muddled along like the rest of us?' Yes, in retrospect I suppose I could have. Should have. After all, I was given enough chances. Why didn't I see that my mother was teaching me about love, not restraint? She loved me so much that she put me before anyone else for years. Why did I have to resent that and see it as a pressure? I had amazing friends, and how did I repay them? By bossing one and using, then humiliating, the other. Issie's and my friendship is held together by a very slight thread right now. I know that the only way I can possibly hope to keep her as a friend is to learn to deal honestly and fairly. Josh, my dearest friend, is lost for ever. I can't see how either of us can ever recover from this. Too much hurt pride on his side. Too much shame on mine.

I used my power at work childishly, thoughtlessly. I was so heady on the success of ever-increasing ratings and advertising billings that I was blinkered to the destruction the programme was wreaking. I now force myself to consider every aspect: from the woman weeping in my reception on Christmas Eve to the silk farm that had to close down after their exports decreased so significantly. I wonder how many lives I altered the course of with *Sex with an Ex*? Was it fair to involve myself, and the general public, in people's loving and living? Would those people have muddled up the aisle if it hadn't been for my intervention? And if they had, would it necessarily have ended in disaster, as I'd always maintained? Perhaps it was unfair putting such emotional pressure on individuals just before their weddings. Perhaps it hadn't been a flat playing field. I realize now that *Sex with an Ex* was not much more than an elaborate way to try to prove that my father was the rule rather than the exception.

I had boasted about dealing in desolation, but I hadn't a clue what desolation was.

I feel sick. I stand up and walk into the kitchen, trying to put some distance between me and the ugly list.

I pour myself some Evian and hold the cold glass to my forehead. It soothes the aching momentarily, but I'm aware that my actions are similar to those of an air hostess asking 'Chicken or beef?' seconds before the plane crashes.

I pick up the pen. My ex-lovers. I'm resolute that the majority knew where they stood with me. Hearts and flowers were not part of our dialogues. These men were mostly the ones with wives or girlfriends. The ones who wanted a quick-no-questions-asked bonk, and I supplied it. But had the wives and girlfriends been in on the deal? Unlikely. Now, I wonder how many times I caused a heart to sink as those women found my telephone number scribbled on a scrap of paper.

And what if some of the men, especially the single ones, were surprised that I never called back, and a little hurt, perhaps insecure? Is it possible that Issie is right and men have feelings too? I think of Darren, I think of Josh. Of course it's possible that they have feelings.

My neat list has become a random mind map, with arrows and circles like Venn diagrams connecting one action to another. Looking at the amount of ink I've spilt this morning, it's not surprising that Darren has walked away from me. I don't deserve him.

I am so sorry. And this isn't simply because the press are trailing me, the show exposed me, the country and most specifically Darren hate me. I'm sorry because I got it wrong.

I don't deserve Darren, but he does deserve an explanation. I have to find him.

The phone rings and I fall on it.

'It'smeIssie,' says Issie quickly, establishing that it's her rather than Darren. She knows I really only want to hear from him. 'I didn't know whether to ring.'

'I'm glad you did.' I am. I am indescribably grateful that Issie was only able to sustain her state of acute pissed-off-with-me-ness for about two hours and has allowed her fury at me to fade somewhat. I guess that's the only good thing that came out of the show. Issie couldn't possibly turn her back on me in my hour of need; the fact that the rest of Britain loathes and despises me serves to increase Issie's commitment to our friendship.

'Has he called?'

'No.'

'You still think he's going to?

'Yes.'

'Why?'

I realize that I'm in serious trouble. If Issie, the last of the great romantics, has no faith in this ending in a tulle and organza number then I must have more chance of winning the lottery, on a roll-over week, than ever getting an opportunity to talk to Darren.

'I've told you, Issie, I trust him. He proposed to me. Darren wouldn't do that just for TV.'

'And I've told you, he might do it for revenge. After all, you did sleep with him for two weeks, all the time giving the impression that you were pretty committed, then you vamoosed. There's not a man on earth who would take kindly to that type of behaviour. His pride was kicked into touch. Don't you think that it's possible he's getting his own back?'

'I know he had nothing to do with the programme, Issie.' I'm trying not to become irate with her, but my personality transplant hasn't been so entire that I can stay patient in the face of a constant barrage of criticism of Darren. 'Look, Issie, why don't you ask Josh if he thinks Darren was involved in stitching me up? *He* must know.' I place a heavy emphasis on 'he'; if I can distract Issie with Josh's crimes for a while, maybe she'll get off Darren's case.

'Would you like me to do that for you?' she asks enthusiastically.

'Do it for you, Issie, so that you believe in Darren. I don't need anyone else's word.'

We sink into a huffy silence. I know I can outsulk Issie. I haven't even counted to three before she offers her olive branch.

'OK, supposing you are right and Darren wasn't knowingly involved in your unrestricted and unmitigated humiliation, why do you think he's done a disappearing act?'

'It's obvious, Issie. He thinks *I* set *him* up.'

'Oh.'

Issie is far too straightforward to pretend not to see why he'd make this assumption. She doesn't even blame him.

'I should have told him about the engagement!' I berate myself.

'So what are you going to do from here?'

'Good question. I need to talk to him but I've looked everywhere. Work, home, pubs. I've even walked the streets but it's futile. London's a big city; England's a big country.'

'Well, actually, it's quite small in geographical terms—'

'It's colossal when you are hunting someone who doesn't want to be found.'

'And of course he may not be in England, he may be abroad. He could be anywhere.'

I wonder if the position of Job's comforter is currently available in some other time dimension, because Issie has all the qualifications.

I sigh. She's right. I suddenly feel so small and the world feels so big.

'Issie, there's call waiting bleeping. Do you mind if I ring off?' We both know I'm hoping it will be Darren. We both know it won't be.

'Fine. I'll call you tonight,' says Issie.

'Hello,' says a tiny voice on the line. I try not to drown in the disappointment that it is a female voice as I struggle to place it.

'Linda?'

'Yes. Hello, Cas.' Linda sounds nervous and young. Even younger than her seventeen years.

'Linda, I'm so happy to hear from you.'

'Oh. Are you? I don't know if I should be talking to you.'

'Yes. Yes, you should,' I urge. 'Linda, I know things must look terrible from your point of view. I have done some very bad things, but you have to know I didn't set Darren up on that programme.' I'm speaking very quickly because I guess I have only a finite amount of time to convince her. She sounds on the edge of putting the phone down.

'I know,' says the tiny voice.

'You do?' I'm so relieved I can't say any more. To have someone believe in me is an overwhelming relief.

'I said to Mam that you loved our Darren. But Mam said I only believed that because I'm seventeen. No one else believes that you do.'

'But *you* are right, Linda. You *are* right. I do love Darren,' I repeat hysterically. It matters to me that she believes me.

'Mam said I mustn't call you.'

'I see.'

'It's just that Darren called last night and he mentioned that he might go to the Natural History Museum today and I thought you might—'

'Linda, Linda, I could kiss you,' I yell down the phone. Of course, his favourite building. That's where he goes to do his thinking. Suddenly my mind is splattered with a vision of Darren's childhood bedroom. Aladdin's cave meets Treasure Island meets Batman's cave. With the zillions of books, the cardboard models, the Meccano eco-system and the painted Milky Way. 'Thank you, Linda. Thank you so much. I promise you you've done the right thing. I love you, Linda!' I drop the telephone, grab my keys and fly out of the flat.

20

I run to the tube, my feet thudding on the pavement, my blood thundering to my heart, my heart pounding. I run all the way to Tower Hill station. I pass the happy crowds drinking pints in the street; they leer and jeer at me as I'm sweaty and not wearing a sports bra. I keep running. Although I usually run eight miles in the gym every day, I haven't been since 'the show'. Not that I've been afraid of the inevitable pointing fingers (they like notoriety better than celebrity at our gym – the receptionist nearly orgasms every time she spots Jeffrey Archer using the treadmill); it's just I've had no motivation. Every moment has been consumed with finding Darren. So now I'm panting heavily. Then again, the shortness of breath isn't just to do with the rapidly decreasing levels of fitness. It's also excitement. Hope. Possibility. A long shot. But a shot.

At the tube station I realize that I left the house in such a hurry that I didn't pick up my purse. When did I become so disorganized?

'Please can you let me have a ticket?' I smile sweetly; it really is my most dazzling.

'Where to?'

'To South Kensington.'

'£1.80.'

'I have no money.' The smile is frozen and stuck to my face.

The ticket officer snorts. 'We're not operating a charity.'

'Pleeeease. It's an emergency. I have to get to South Ken.' I have abandoned my tone of pleasant authority and I'm begging. He's impervious.

'Mind along. There are other customers. Ones with money.'

I stay still.

'Pleeeeease.' I think I might cry. Tears that I've managed to hold back for years are now constantly threatening and erupting. The officer doesn't even look at me.

'No money, no ticket. Bugger off.'

That's the proverbial straw. Huge, ugly overwhelming sobs storm out of me. I'm not sure where they come from – certainly not just my mouth, but my nose too and perhaps my ears.

'I've got to get there. He's there. He's there,' I sob, which is ridiculous on many counts. For a start, the Underground officer doesn't know who I am or 'he' is, and anyway, he cares less. Secondly, I don't *know* if I'll find Darren there. There's snot on my arm and days-old mascara on my cheeks. I'm blind with tears, bogies, regret, frustration, pain and loss. I slump to the floor. It's too much. I can't act any more. Years of acting as though I don't care, then I care, and now I've hurtled past caring, straight, slap bang into despair. It's too much. Life without Darren is not enough.

'I'll pay her fare.' I hear the lazy, warm drawl of an American accent. 'She sounds kinda desperate.' I daren't believe someone is being kind to me. The recent, constant volley of abuse has left me bereft of hope. I can only assume this guy has just arrived in England or that he doesn't read any newspapers. My Good Samaritan kneels down next to me and the crushed cans and cigarette stubs. This isn't easy for him, because he's obviously a man who enjoys a good breakfast, and lunch and dinner too by the look of it.

'Hey, ain't you that girl on the TV?' he whispers as he hands me the ticket.

'It wasn't how it looked,' I defend through my tears.

'Nothing ever is.' He staggers to his feet and offers me his hand. I let him pull me up.

'You're not a journalist, are you?' I ask nervously. He shakes his head and then melts back into the throng of people busy sightseeing.

I consider it. I look up and see a security camera. It is just possible that this is another set-up. That guy could be a plant.

Get a grip. Only Linda knows I'm coming here. She would never be part of a set-up.

But I could have been followed. I'm still breathing shallowly and quickly. The guy looked honest. Unlikely though it seems, I think he was just doing a good thing. I don't waste any more time thinking about it. I push my ticket through the machine and dash to the platform.

The sand and grey building creates a swell in my heart and I allow myself to hope, because, maybe, just maybe, he's in there, the Natural History Museum. I realize I have the money problem to face again. At the desk I lie and say I've had my bag stolen. The staff are far too polite to laugh outright at my claims.

'Have you reported the theft, miss?' asks the huge, sauf London bird.

'No,' I admit. 'I am planning to.'

'What, after you've visited the *Tyrannosaurus rex*?'

'Yes.'

'Naturally.'

I'm very short on patience, a life trait exasperated by recent events, but somehow I hold it together long enough to persuade the staff at the museum to let me ring Issie. She gives them a credit card number and they give me a ticket.

I burst through the turnstiles and then run directly to the galleries. I charge up and down the three flights of stairs, constantly looking to my left and right. I can't see him. I rush through the huge corridors, popping my head into all the exhibitions and restaurants as I pass by. I see innumerable creepy crawlies with their wings fettered; I see fossils, stuffed eagles and tigers. A taxidermist's dream. But no Darren. I check the exhibitions on crystals, mammals and dinosaurs. I see every animal, vegetable and mineral in every state of growth, maturity and decay, except for Darren. I do all this twice. After an hour and a half of frenetic and futile searching I find myself back in the main lobby. Other than attracting numerous odd looks and lots of unwanted attention, my wild goose chase hasn't achieved anything.

Of course it hasn't.

I sit under skeletons of dinosaurs, surrounded by Gothic arches and earnest foreign voices reading to each other from the guidebooks. It's pretty spooky. I've searched the entire building; he's not here. It was ridiculously far-fetched to hope he would be. Why didn't I ask Linda some more searching questions? Like what time had he planned to visit? Was it a definite plan? I'd been so delighted to get even a sniff of a lead that I hadn't followed it properly. I can't call Linda back. She'll get into trouble if her mother knows she's been in touch with me. I feel dumb and hopeless. The gargoyles obviously knew this all along because they look as though they are laughing at me.

I need to get some perspective.

I go to the cloakrooms. As usual there is a massive queue of women with bladders the size of peanuts. I stand listlessly, too exhausted to fidget impatiently or terrify anyone into peeing more rapidly. I catch sight of myself in a mirror and I'm shocked. I look like a down and out. My new crop requires minimum attention, a quick comb through, some gloss and then a ruffle to erase the effects of the combing. However, I haven't thought to carry out this simple operation, so my hair is tangled and snarled at the back of my head. Nor have I thought to change my clothes, apply any make-up or eat since the show. Normally slim, I know I look emaciated. Up until now, I've been with Wallis Simpson, but now I see – a woman can be too thin. I've smoked to abate hunger, to distract and comfort myself. The smell of stale fags lingers in my hair and clothes. My skin is grey and my eyes have sunk to the back of my head. I am a human ashtray. I splash cold water on my face and then decide to revisit the dinosaur collection; at least they look rougher than I do.

For three hours I slowly amble around the galleries and whilst I admit that fishes, amphibians and reptiles are interesting in their own way, they can't compete with Darren for mind share. Whilst I learn that dinosaurs lived between 230 million and 65 million years ago, I can't imagine it. I've been without Darren for a week and it seems like an eternity. I also learn that they lived on land and could not fly but walked on straight legs tucked beneath their bodies. I consider writing to the consistency editor in charge of film at the studio, because I'm sure I've seen blockbusters with flying dinosaurs, but I don't have the energy. I visit the human biology gallery and watch a film on reproduction and the growth of babies, which makes me feel squeamish. Not just because of the blood but because it's proof, if I needed it, that love and life and living that life are special and miraculous. I sigh and check my watch. Four thirty. I'm hungry. I decide to visit the Life Galleries one more time and then, reluctantly, I'll call it a day. Go home, have some pasta.

The Life Galleries are really spectacular. A series of exhibits demonstrating that each individual animal, plant and person is just one component in a complex system. There are some cool special-effects holograms of the atmosphere, hydrosphere and lithosphere. There's a reproduction of a bit of the rainforest, with sound effects of pouring rain and screeching birds. There's a bit about oceans and coastlines. The sound effects change to crashing waves and seagulls.

Whitby.

Him.

It could be my imagination but I think I can smell the sea.

Less romantically there is a stuffed rattlesnake and a decomposing rabbit.

I walk through howling gales and head towards the funky bell music, which puts me in mind of the stuff that's played in Camden market or in flotation tanks. I head along a dark corridor towards a series of mirrors that are arranged to reflect and refract light to create the impression that you are standing outside the earth and you are watching the hydrosphere. Water recycles endlessly, in all its many guises, water, steam, ice. I don't quite understand it. But the scale and silver holograms are awesome.

Darren.

Suddenly there are hundreds of him. I can see Darren. He's right next to me. He's left, next to me. I reach to touch him but my hand plummets through space. I *can* see him. He's in front of me, and he's behind me too. I look up, he's above me. Then he's gone.

My breath surges out of my body, creating a vacuum. I can't breathe. It gushes back in again, nearly knocking me over.

He was here. It was him. I try to work out where he must have been standing, and which were mere shadows and visions of him created by the mirrors. I can't calculate it. But he can only have gone one of two ways: back through the rainforest to the Waterhouse Way corridor or forward towards the Visions of Earth exhibitions.

Creepy crawlies or lost in space?

I pelt towards the Visions of Earth exhibitions. A series of six statues, representing different aspects of life on earth, are dominated by a dramatic sculpture of earth, which revolves between two giant walls. The walls depict the solar system and the night sky. I collide with a party of overseas schoolkids, universally noisy, happy and overexcited. They're all dressed in blue and merge into one homogenous mass of rucksacks, acne and ponytails.

He's in front of the party.

He's ascending the giant escalator that takes you up through the solar system.

I have no time to consider English tradition. I shove and barge and push my way through the queues of schoolchildren. They object noisily.

'There's a queue, you know, madam.'

They try and elbow me back, but their attempts are pathetic in the face of my love and panic-induced strength.

'Excuse me. You are going the wrong way.'

But I'm not. I'm finally going in the right direction. I fasten my eyes on Darren's head and don't drop the link. He isn't aware of me and I don't call out. The schoolchildren dividing us may prove to be too much of an obstacle if he decides to run. The escalator rises through sheets of beaten copper, which represents the core of the earth, and we are accompanied by Indie music, which represents the poor taste of the curator. I pass the stars Ursa Major, Draco and Ophiuchus at an achingly slow speed. I want to stamp my feet and although I've squeezed past a number of other gallery visitors, by intimidating them with my sense of urgency, I'm stumped now I've reached a woman with a double buggy. Short of climbing over her, I'm stuck.

At the top of the escalators I turn right and follow Darren through volcanic eruptions and earthquakes.

'Darren,' I scream. 'Darren!'

But my voice, usually powerful, doesn't cut through the natural disasters or the fourth-form chatter.

'*Darren.*'

He turns.

For a moment he doesn't recognize me because of the haircut and the unfashionable grunge look.

'Cas?' As the word edges from his brain to his vocal cords I see his face flicker in surprise, disbelief, pleasure and then settle in irritation.

'This is a coincidence.' Darren puts his rucksack on the floor and folds his arms across his chest. My brain computes that he's saying don't come near. My stomach is oblivious; it becomes gymnastic as I see the muscles in his arms flex.

'Not really. I've been looking for you.' I don't mention Linda's tip-off. I don't want to get her into trouble. 'I've been here for hours,' I stutter. He looks surprised. I push uphill. 'I tried everywhere I could think of in the last week.' I scratch my nose and pause. I'm looking for a credible place to start our conversation. He looks around too. I wonder what he's looking for.

'So where are the cameras?'

Ah, I see.

'There are no cameras – well, none that I know of,' I add nervously. He makes a sound, a mix between a snort of contempt and disbelief, which forces me to assert, 'I had nothing to do with the show.'

'Really?' It's just one word but I don't think a half-hour soliloquy could have communicated his disgust and sarcasm quite so clearly.

'I know it looks bad—'

'Bad,' he yells, attracting a number of curious stares from the wild children. 'Bad isn't how I'd describe it. I'd describe it as vile, corrupt, damning. You've made an arse of me, Cas, you've – ' He's shouting and stuttering. 'You've fucking hurt me. I can't believe you, *even you*, would sink so low. You slept with me for TV entertainment. You accepted my proposal for TV entertainment. What sort of animal are you? I can't believe it!' He's spraying angry spittle and his face is contorted with pain.

He's magnificent.

'Well, don't believe it, because it's not true. I didn't know that we were being filmed.' I try to grab hold of his arm. He violently jerks away from me as though I'm insanitary.

'You were engaged to Josh!' he fumes.

'Yes,' I confirm simply, dropping my arms to my side again.

'You were engaged and you didn't think to mention it?'

He's still shouting and we are now collecting a small crowd of onlookers. I don't think he's noticed. The teacher tries, but fails, to move the children along. She's right – this may be a PG-certificate viewing; bad language and violence threaten.

'Well, yes, I thought of it. But—'

'And you accepted my proposal?'

'Yes. But I didn't lie to you. I was going to tell you—' It sounds faulty, even to me.

'When? Before or after you married Josh?'

He's really furious. He is spitting, not blood, but pain and tension. His face is splintered into trillions of anxious particles and I can't look at him and see the whole face. I can only see a hurt mouth, an angry nostril or a ferocious eyebrow. Desperate eyes.

'I wasn't going to marry Josh. Not after I'd met you again. I didn't have anything to do with the show.' I'm trying to sound reasonable and in control. It's a tough act. 'I love you. Just you. I'm in love with you and I have been since we were in Whitby.'

It's a relief saying the big words.

'So why were you engaged to Josh?' Darren asks the floor this question. For the moment the anger has subsided and lapsed into a sadness. I like it even less. Deep breath. I know this is my last chance. And chance is probably far too generous a description. I choose each word carefully.

'I was scared I'd end up like my mother. Or at least how I thought my mother was. Falling in love was too risky. I knew that I'd be safe with Josh. He loved me more than I could ever love him, so he'd never be able to hurt me.'

'Didn't you think how unfair that was on him?'

'Not really,' I sigh. There's no option, other than to be honest. But the truth is so unflattering. I can't imagine my looking more unsightly.

'Jesus, Cas, do you know what you've just said?' Darren suddenly looks up and his gaze punches me. 'Josh is one of the few people I thought you truly loved. I had been heartened by your relationship with him because I thought it was indelible proof that you were capable of loving and the hard-bitch act was just that, an act. But you've just admitted you didn't even *think* about him. He was just another piece in your game.'

'It was what he wanted.'

'I doubt he wanted a wife who didn't love him.'

'It wasn't like that. I don't think I knew how to love then.' I try to wave the thought away.

'I heard you, Cas. I saw the programme. You said sex with me, and I quote, was "risky, dirty, cheeky and above all fun". I didn't hear you tell the world you loved me. Why not?' He doesn't let me answer but gives in to his anger again. 'Because you don't. You've made all this up because Josh has dumped you, and the studio has dumped you, and all Britain hates you. I'm nothing more to you than your only option.'

'You're wrong.'

'How many kick-backs am I supposed to take, Cas? What's an acceptable number? First I'm "too serious and homely". Then you fuck my brains out. Then you disappear. You ignored my calls, threatened to call the police. Then you're back and then you fuck my heart out and this time we get engaged and then that turns out to be for the titillation and edification of your audience.'

Put like this it sounds bad.

'You act like a psycho. How do I know that this latest declaration isn't just another publicity stunt? How can I trust you?'

'I just know you have it in you, Darren. Some people have and you are one of them.'

I concentrate on the slight cleft in his chin, and on the exact colour of his eyes. I note the way he moves his hands and the precise shape of his wristbone. I consume it all because there is a real possibility that I'll never see any of it again. If he walks away I'll live in a permanent eclipse. I look at the group of schoolchildren, who are all but splitting with laughter and jeering. 'Can we go somewhere more private to discuss this?' I hiss through clenched teeth.

'What's the bloody point, Cas? Our relationship is public property. Posh and Beckham have more privacy.'

I get the feeling I'm being tested, but I'm unsure of the nature of the exam. I certainly haven't prepared. I navigate through with as much sincerity as I can. I am conscious that behind me there is a reconstruction of an earthquake. Every fifteen seconds the world shudders and cracks up. I wonder if Darren also thinks this is ironic.

'I was very scared, Darren. Loving you so much left me petrified. Ecology is your thing, isn't it? Piecing things together for the whole picture? Come on, Darren, think about it. Think about where I was coming from. I'd never seen any good come out of loving. My father didn't love either my mother or me enough to stay. He left her, us, brokenhearted. My mother did her best but it wasn't just the money that was limited after he disappeared. She reined in her affection, or at least her displays of it. She was awash with caution and distrust. I wasn't taught to love. I was taught to be wary.'

'Wary, Cas, not wicked!'

I ignore his interruption. 'I know it's not an excuse, only an explanation. Before I hit puberty, I was certain sex and love were incompatible. And then the endless stream of lovers seemed to confirm my theory. There was man after man who was prepared to betray me or use me to betray someone else. I didn't want to be a victim. I wouldn't allow myself to love. I didn't even think I was capable of it.'

There's lead stuck in the pit of my stomach, but at least I have Darren's attention and that of every member of year four, *l'école de* Sprogsville. Where is this going? How can I tell him that loving him seemed like the worst thing that could have happened to me, but at the same time the best? That I miscalculated lots of things when I was young. Now I see that to have a figure like Barbie's I'd have to have an eighteen-inch waist, a forty-inch leg and a head the size of a beach ball. Spaghetti hoops are not the world's most exquisite culinary delight and Donny Osmond isn't sexy.

Being made happy by love is an option.

I notice that the neck of my T-shirt is wet. I touch my face and discover that I am sobbing. Fat, globular tears are falling at such a rate that I'm soaked.

'I'm sorry it took me so long to get here but I've learnt I am capable of loving. I did not set you up. I know how you feel about the programme. And for what it's worth, I see now that you were right. You have to believe me, Darren.' I wonder if there is any point in telling him that I've left TV6. I doubt it.

He'll probably believe the papers and think I was sacked. My face is aflame. My heart literally aches, a filthy agony. I try to read his thoughts. I know he'll be trying to understand, but will he be able to? And even if he does, will he care? He leans back against a glass display case. The fact that he needs propping up can't be good for me.

Can it?

He rubs his eyes with the balls of his fists.

'Believe me,' I plead.

He shakes his head. Very quietly, almost inaudibly, he whispers, 'I don't think I can. I'm sorry.' And he looks it. He looks devastated. Wounded. 'I wish I could.' He bends down and picks up his rucksack and starts to walk out of my life.

For a week I have vacillated between regret, fear and desperation. I've howled and cried privately. I've fought to appear collected and not too indulgent in public. I've been dogged and exposed. Discussed and dismissed at a micro and macro level. The experience has left me weak. The small amount of residual energy I had left was consumed whilst reasoning with Darren.

Wham.

Suddenly I'm whacked with an emotion that is struggling between passion and ire. Anger refuels my body and the resurgence explodes in torrents of undefined fury. Not the premenstrual monster that inhibits my body for three days every twenty-eight. Not the spitting anger that I used to feel when the ratings weren't robust or a production assistant had made some duff decision. Not the intense irritation I feel when Issie throws herself at some worthless oink. Or the scornful vexation that I've felt when Josh mistreated some bimbo. My anger is much more . . . painful than that. The storm of irritation and hurt begins to climb the Richter scale. Swelling up through my stomach, into my chest and heart, exploding – a veritable whirlwind – in my head.

'Is that it then, Darren?' I scream. 'That was your crack at being in love?'

He turns back to face me. 'Well, I think it was pretty crap actually!'

Being unreasonable is all I'm capable of again. I'm so bloody desperate. I don't know how to stop this inevitable, needless disaster.

'You've been loved and adored all your life. Swaddled. Protected. Encouraged to believe the best in people and here you are falling at the first serious hurdle. I thought you were better than that. You *are* better than that. Don't you dare walk away from me.' I stamp my right foot. 'Don't you dare stop trusting me.' Then my left. 'You said you loved me. Easy fucking words.' He's right in front of me. I spray some spittle into his face.

'OK, so I came to it a bit late in the day but I do believe in love and I do think that out of the billions of people in this world you're the one I should be with.' I jab my finger at him accusingly and I want to stamp again and flay my arms. There's so much anger inside me and it doesn't know how to get out.

'I've stopped being terrified by the "what ifs". And I know you're not my father. And I know that I shouldn't judge everyone by his iniquitous standards.' The hairs on the back of my neck stand viciously erect. Tears poke mercilessly at my eyes. 'And I'm sorry that I've hurt so many people in the past before I came to this understanding. I am so sorry. But trust me now. I did not do this for the bloody, fucking, crapping, pissing ratings.'

I think that even if I'd gone to a posh school, I'd have been struggling to come up with more appropriate vocabulary, under the circumstances. I give in and stamp my feet, harder and harder and harder and faster and faster and faster. The tears explode from my eyes and fall harder and harder and harder and faster and faster and faster. Eventually I am worn out.

Exhausted.

Defeated.

I stop stamping and try to find some equilibrium. My breathing is fast and desperate, my feet are throbbing with the violence of my stamping and my head is sore with shaking. I cannot look at Darren or the schoolkids. It is so intensely embarrassing. Over the last few days I've lost everything: both my fiancés – one my love, the other my best friend, my job, my privacy and now my reason. I've been cheated, deceived and humiliated. I've felt despair and loneliness and regret.

I take stock.

All that and I still believe in love.

Which means that just when I thought I'd lost track of the game, I've won.

I have Mum.

I have Issie.

I have learnt a lot.

I force myself to look up at Darren. My heart cartwheels. I rub the back of my hand across my face, cleaning up the excess of smudged mascara and tears. I pick up my museum map from the floor, where I'd thrown it.

'Do you know something, Darren? The irony is, I never stopped believing in you. I never thought you'd betrayed me. Not for a minute.'

We are both breathing deeply. Staring at one another. Our faces are a potent cocktail of anger and forgiveness, love and lust, trust and fear, potential and endings. Hope.

It's all been so intense, right from the beginning. Euphoric, desolate, euphoric again, desolate plus. What now?

Minutes go by. Neither of us says anything. Neither of us moves.

'Do you know the Camarasaurus weighs twenty-five tons?' asks Darren.

'Yes,' I say carefully, and then add, 'It's a plant eater, so I suggest the grapefruit diet.' It's a weak joke but Darren's face hints at a smile. He takes my arm and starts to lead me through the galleries. His fingers singe.

'So you've seen the dinosaur exhibition?'

'Yes.' I'm shaking.

'Have you seen the blue whale?'

'Yes.'

'So you've seen enough of the Natural History Museum for one day?' I feel as though I'm behind a number of veils but as he asks each question a veil drops and instead of feeling exposed, I feel more confident. I can see more clearly.

'Yes.'

'Do you think you'd like to go for a beer?'

This time I nod. I'm incapable of finding my voice. We leave the museum and go out into the London sun. We stop on the steps of the museum and squint at the brightness and crowds. Darren turns to me.

'Do you still believe in me, Cas?' he asks. His voice is patchy with emotion but it is still velvety and I recognize possibility and opportunity glimmering there.

'Yes.'

'Will you give me another chance?'

'Yes. I will. A huge, fat, full YES.'

I'm home.

Thank You

Jonny Geller, my agent, a unique blend of panache and sincerity. Louise Moore, more than just Editor of the Year to me. I feel extremely fortunate and honoured that you are both in my life.

My family, who have constantly and tirelessly spread the word. For the record, neither my sister nor her children are on commission, although I'm sure their friends think differently.

My friends, who have been enthusiastic and interested. You know who you are and how grateful I am.

Acknowledgements

People assume writing and producing a book is a one (wo)man show. It's anything but. I'd like to take this opportunity to thank all those involved in the success of *Playing Away* and those who currently have their fingers and toes crossed for the success of *Game Over*.

Especially Harrie Evans, John Bond, Tom Weldon, Nicky Stonehill, Peter Bowron and his entire sales team at Penguin. Everyone who ever sold a copy, everyone who ever bought one. I know none of this would have been possible without you.

Thank you to the people at Granada Media who gave up their time to talk to me, even though they are impossibly busy and work on a far tighter ship than TV6: John Creedon, Sally Blackburn, Martin Lowde, Ian Johnson, Bob Massie, Marina Webster and Keith Bryan.

Everyone remembers a good teacher; I'd like to formally thank a few of those who gave me challenges and chances and helped me become what I am (for better or worse!): Mrs Gunn (Durham Lane Primary School); Mr David Oliver, Mr John Beddow and Ms Margaret Maguire (Egglescliffe Comprehensive School); Professor Martin Stannard, Professor Sandy Cunningham and Professor Lois Potter (Leicester University).

Game Over and *Playing Away* are unlikely tributes to Colin Douglas, Mary Peacock, Dick Parks, Moyra Wilkinson and Emma Blythe, with love.

adele parks

about Adele Parks

about the book

whilst I was writing

the books

read more

about Adele Parks

author photo © Jimmy D

about Adele Parks

I was born in Cleveland, in the northeast of England and had a conventional 70s childhood, existing on a diet of convenience food and bad TV. My parents (still married after forty-odd years) devoted themselves to giving my sister and me as stable, loving and happy an environment as possible. I attended the local state primary school and then the local comprehensive. My fond memories aren't so much of a home town – more of a modern, well-kept housing estate, where everyone knows everyone and everything that there is to know.

Perversely, this stability nurtured in me wanderlust and a longing to do, be and see things that were different. I studied English Language and Literature at Leicester University. After I'd finished my degree I had the chance to fulfil my dream to see more of the world. I travelled to Italy and had a fabulous year teaching English: a time of hope and dreams and fun. Later, I also travelled to Botswana and lived there for two years – a place that provided a terrific sense of space, both physically and mentally. I'm still very envious whenever I hear of people who up-sticks and go trotting around the globe.

I've lived in London for most of my adult life. It's a city where dreams can come true – that said, it's easy to scratch the surface and find disappointment and disillusionment. Even whilst enjoying success, that is a disquieting thought.

I've wanted to write for as long as I can remember. As a child I read voraciously and wrote my own stories, mostly about witches, strange lands and magical adventures: flying carpets featured heavily, as I was a rather lazy child and this was the ultimate fantasy. By the time I was ten or eleven, I found that I often wrote about things in an effort to understand how I felt or thought about them. I referred to these scribbles as my jottings. When I was in the sixth form I read a book every second day.

It's possible that I would never have done more than fill notebooks with jottings, but when I was twenty-seven a number of friends and family died in quick succession. I felt desperate, scared and vulnerable, and became ill with severe back problems. I have heard other people say they've experienced similar runs of bad luck and ill-health. Usually some good comes out of these terrible situations, although it's hard to believe at the time. I turned to escapist jottings as a way of relief from the sadness that swamped me.

I started to write *Playing Away* – a novel in which the protagonist enjoys a seemingly perfect and utterly glamorous life, at least until she falls into an abyss of sexual obsession. I was disciplined and devoted three evenings a week and one full day of my weekend to writing. I was working in marketing at the time and so I fitted my writing in around the day job.

After I'd written a substantial chunk of *Playing Away*, I sent it to an agent I'd read about in a Sunday supplement. He liked it enormously and encouraged me to finish the script. Then he sent it out to a number of publishers. The interest around *Playing Away* was intense; it seemed that female infidelity hadn't been explored in literature since *Anna Karenina* – odd because male infidelity is ubiquitous and it can't possibly be that betrayal and misbehaviour is so one-sided! Following what is known in the trade as a bidding war, *Playing Away* was published by Penguin in March 2000 and became an instant bestseller. The rest, as they say, is history. I gave up my marketing job and became a full-time novelist.

I've now written six novels, I've published numerous articles and short stories in a variety of newspapers and magazines, and I've appeared on TV and radio. My books are sold all over the world. It's a dream come true.

I'm often asked whether I worry that I'll run out of ideas. I don't: I worry I'll run out of time before I've committed all my ideas to paper. People wonder where I get my ideas from. The answer is life – my own and other peoples'. I'm also asked what I like best about being a novelist. That's a hard one because I adore so many aspects of my profession. I believe I'm a supremely lucky individual in that I've had the opportunity to make a hobby into a viable living. I must be quite egotistical because I relish the opportunity to express my views, ideas and concerns, and I'm thrilled that copies of my books will be held in the British Library for ever. The flexible nature of my employment is a joy; as a working mum it's an invaluable aspect of what I do. But, if pushed, I think I'd say that the thing I like best about being a novelist is that I get the opportunity to entertain: maybe to provoke a moment of pondering or a wry smile. I thank each and every one of my readers who is good enough to give me a few hours of their lives. What greater gift is there?

Cas is actually quite difficult to like. What made you want to write about someone so manipulative?
It is very easy to write a character that is everyone's best friend and is entirely sugar and spice and all things nice. The 'conflict' in the novel would then have to be that she came up against an adversary who was completely bad. In the real world people are much more complex than that. Good people do bad things. Mean people are often motivated by explanations that are not immediately obvious. For example, Cas appears to be a super-bitch but she does care for her friends and family. Ultimately, she is simply vulnerable. It's a much greater test of my skill as an author if I can get the reader to like someone who doesn't deserve any admiration.

Did Cas deserve someone as delicious as Darren?
Probably not, initially. But Cas does undergo a transformation. Darren literally brings out the best in her. Besides, true love is about loving someone even when they don't deserve that love. Darren also learns things from Cas. In the end she has more faith in him than he does in her and her faith has never been nurtured the way his has. Hers is the greater leap. I love Cas's spirit just as much as Darren's morals.

Darren is so gorgeous. It's very easy to fall in love with him. Do you think there really are men like him out there?
We can live in hope.

Would you think of writing a sequel to *Game Over* to reveal what happens to Josh and Issie and whether Darren and Cas actually make it?
I doubt I'll write a sequel. Once I've finished a novel I like my characters to live in the imagination of my readers. However, I am a fan of happy endings so it is my belief that Issie does find true love. Perhaps, she'll meet a doctor. Josh will probably marry a model with a heart of gold and have a bunch of kids. Cas and Darren stay in love and grow old together but I'm not sure they'd actually get married.

about the book

Where does the inspiration for your characters come from?

Life sparks my imagination, but I never write biographies of individuals nor do I try to reproduce people I know; my friends are saved that indignity. My characters are an amalgamation of a number of people I've met, watched or heard about, plus a great big dose of 'but what if...?' The question 'but what if...?' is the one that kindles my imagination.

Did you have to do lots of research to write this novel?

Yes. I was lucky enough to have a number of friends and contacts who work at ITV. They kindly answered all my questions and introduced me to producers of real shows so that I had a clear idea of the mechanics of a TV channel. They even allowed me to work alongside of them for several weeks so that I had a thorough understanding of the vibe of TV production. In addition, I sat in the audience of a number of live and recorded shows so that I could get a handle on audiences' reactions. I also became a regular visitor to the Natural History Museum.

What do you think of reality TV shows? Do you watch and enjoy them?

I wrote this book before BIG BROTHER had hit our screens – funny to think of a time before BIG BROTHER ;-). Reality TV was just emerging and back then I watched them occasionally and something rather terrible in me enjoyed them, but I'm not particularly proud of that fact. I think reality TV is lazy TV. Producers no longer have to do much to produce a show. No time is given to clever scriptwriting, making beautiful costumes or training and hiring good actors. All that is required is a few ordinary people who are desperate for a bit of fame and don't mind being exploited.

Do you think *Sex with an Ex* could really be made into a TV programme?

Sadly yes. When I came up with this concept in 1999 my editor worried that the show was too far fetched. Since then we have seen an explosion of reality TV programmes hit our screens and the concept of *Sex with an Ex* is rather tame compared to those shows where people are prepared to marry on stage or live in a house for weeks with complete strangers, allowing the nation to watch them take a shower. I wonder if there are any limits left.

Is there a significant ex in your life?

Not now because I have been married and divorced and so I guess my ex-husband is the most significant ex I have, but I don't have any 'what if' fantasies about him as I know exactly what being with him was like. I guess it would be amusing to know what my exes were up to now and a rather vain part of me would be interested to know what they think of me.

You mentioned that you like happy endings; do you consider yourself a romantic?

Eternally.

Questions asked by Jan Murray

WHIST I WAS WRITING THIS BOOK I ALSO ...

1. Got pregnant
2. Gave up the day job
3. Celebrated the arrival of the new Millennium by watching fireworks on the River Thames
4. Lost my gold card holder status with the British Airways loyalty programme
5. Saw Shirley Bassey in concert for the first time
6. Made my first National TV appearance
7. Wrote articles for National newspapers and magazines, who dubbed me 'The Infidelity Expert' – a questionable honour
8. Bought a bike
9. Was part of a live TV audience, 19 times.
10. Saw PLAYING AWAY, my first novel, hit bookshop shelves at home and abroad

HUSBANDS

Bella secretly married her childhood sweetheart, Stevie, over a decade ago; they were at university, two big kids playing at being grown-ups. When it all unravelled and reality hit, Bella simply got up and left.

Years later, Bella meets Philip and, despite her vow never to marry again, she can't resist him. He is a catch. Funny, charming, interesting and kind. Only hitch is, she's still (technically, anyway) married to Stevie. And the moment to tell Philip never quite seems to arrive.

So Bella plans never to reveal her secret – after all, it's just a silly piece of paper, lodged at a registrar's office in Aberdeen, isn't it? She hasn't seen Stevie for years – probably never will again. Except when Bella's best friend Laura introduces her new man to the gang, it is none other than Stevie. Could things get any more complicated? Only if Bella and Stevie fall in love with each other again ...

LARGER THAN LIFE

Georgina fell in love with Hugh Williams the first moment she saw him.

She was eighteen. He was out of her league. So she reinvented herself and now, at thirty-two, she has him. The fact that he got married and had two kids in the meantime is not important.

At least, all this is what George has always believed. Until something happens, so momentous, so life-changing, that even her rock-solid faith in Hugh is challenged. Surely, she thinks, a baby will bring them close together?

Larger than Life is a funny, moving and truthful account of how a relationship copes when the unexpected happens. Something larger than just the two of you.

After all, what is bigger than the biggest love of your life?

STILL THINKING OF YOU

New love, old relationships and a question of fidelity from the bestselling author of *The Other Woman's Shoes*.

Tash and Rich are newly engaged and wild about each other. They can't wait to celebrate their wedding with their closest friends, all of whom have known each other since university, where they enjoyed a hedonistic whirl of parties, popularity, sex and success.

But is fun really as easy-come-easy-go in your thirties as it was in your twenties? How do relationships change once you leave college and have to cope with real life?

And what if the love of that life were to reappear now?

As old, long-buried passions are reawakened, the group realize that a lot can change in twelve years. And a lot can happen in seven days ...

PLAYING AWAY

'I'm married,' I said.
'I'm a tart,' John smiled.
Both the defence and the challenge.
I. Simply. Can't. Resist.

Connie has been happily married for a year. But she's just met John Harding. Imagine the sexiest man you can think of. He's a walking stag weekend. He's a funny, disrespectful, fast, confident, irreverent pub crawl. He is also completely unscrupulous. He's about to destroy Connie's peace of mind, her grand plan for living happily ever after with her gentle, loving husband Luke.

What will happen if her husband finds out? What will happen if he doesn't? Connie doesn't know the answers ... yet.

But she does know that she's playing against the rules, and she's playing with fire.

THE OTHER WOMAN'S SHOES

The Evergreen sisters are united – in their envy of each other's love life.

Martha and Michael have the perfect home, the perfect family and the perfect life. Until one day, he leaves her.

Eliza and Greg rent a one-bedroom flat where they make music and lots of love. Until one day, she leaves him.

Now the Evergreen sisters are united in separation. And suddenly, they're free to pursue the relationships they think they've always wanted.

Martha wants fun, and lots of it. Great sex and high excitement, courtesy of Jack-the-unpredictable-lad.

Eliza wants the ideal husband, and fast. Sensible conversation and dinner parties with a man who doesn't buy groceries at the local garage.

So when both women find exactly what they're looking for, everybody's happy ... aren't they? Or does chasing the perfect love only get more complicated when you're wearing another woman's shoes?

LARGER THAN LIFE

Are you good enough? Are you? Are you thin enough but not too thin? More Elle Macpherson than Kate Moss? Do you go to the gym? But do you starve yourself? I hope you don't starve yourself because it's so last century to starve yourself. Think of the Africans. Don't you? Don't you have a social conscience? Of course you recycle your bottles and your newspapers, but do you recycle your tins too? I know it's a nuisance and you often cut yourself washing them out and the recycling unit is miles away, but really you should make an effort. Where do you get your hair done? Really? Is it expensive? Because it should be expensive, you ought to take pride in yourself, but it shouldn't be too expensive, being flash isn't attractive. Are they new boots? Oh, you chose tan. You do know that olive is the new tan, the new brown, the new black. Black is a classic, of course, no matter what the magazines say. You do read the magazines, don't you? It is important to keep up. How's work going? Been promoted recently? Have you asked for a pay rise? Well, don't let them exploit you; it's important to know your own worth. But it doesn't do to be greedy. What time did you leave the office last night? Crazy, isn't it. The Brits work longer hours than anyone else in Europe, only the Americans do more. No wonder they're all in therapy. It's important to get time to yourself. I could never leave before seven o'clock, though, they depend on me. Your hands are very chapped. I know a good manicurist. Yes, it's the weather and the transport strikes, but what can you do about it? I know a fabulous girl who does a fabulous manicure and pedicure as well. It doesn't do to let yourself go. No time. Make time. Do you get out much? Did you see the Tracey Emin? They said she's become appallingly mainstream. Do you go to the theatre often? Did you catch that one, oh, what's it called? I forget, the latest one with the ex-soap star, she takes her clothes off. Oh, it doesn't matter what it's called, you ought to go, everyone is. Have you visited Tate Modern? Who did you go with? Who did you see? Who were you seen by? Did you ever do that Dome thingy? No, me neither, I rather regret that now. Are you studying? Well, everyone is doing a night class nowadays, aren't they? De rigueur. Modern Spanish history, IT, film appreciation, the semantics of women's literature, it's so useful to have something to talk about at dinner parties. Which book are you using at the moment? Are you still with Jamie Oliver, or have you tried anything from the latest Nigella Lawson yet? Melissa's doing very well. Yes twins, yes one of each, so that's the set. Clever girl. She's planning to be back in the gym a week on Monday. I don't know what I'd do if I had a baby. Which hospital? Which nurseries? Which schools? And you would have to go back to work; it doesn't do not to have anything to say to the hubby when he gets home from work, exhausted. The nurseries are all full, you know, from now until the year 2005, well at least the desirable ones are. There's always childminders. Yes, a nanny is probably the answer in terms of stimulation for the child, but you hear such stories, don't you? A really good girl is the very devil to find. It's so important to give them the very best start. Baby Beethoven, Lamaze, Montessori, organic nappies. Part-time might be the answer, but then you'd hardly earn enough to cover the childcare costs and buy your sandwich. Well, I must be going. It doesn't do to be late. By the way, you've spilt something down your shirt, is that silk? Is that olive oil? Oh dear, it won't come out. I do hope that stain hasn't been there since lunchtime. That wouldn't be good enough.

January

I

I don't go back to the office but instead drive to Hyde Park. I park and then walk. And walk. And walk. Stopping only to barf and retch unproductively en route. It's an icy cold January afternoon. There's hardly a soul around, unlike the summer when the park is heaving with revellers. The occasional tramp shuffles by, and I see the odd figure dashing home through the twilight, probably clerks who religiously leave their office at five. Not paid enough, or motivated at all, to stay a minute after clocking-out time. Oblivious to their surroundings, they don't glance left or right – the park is simply something that must be passed through on the way to centrally heated rooms and hot cups of tea. The odd mother rushes by with her toddler in a pushchair. The kids are invariably ugly, tired and dirty. The mothers are all that, and also harassed. I suppose that pushchairs, previously beneath my notice, will soon become significant to me.

Pushchairs and high chairs and baby baths and cots and nappies and it's impossible. It's alien. It's wrong.

Where is the unquashable exhilaration that, surely, should be the order of the day?

I'd settle for a faint flush of enthusiasm.

I walk on. I walk past the Serpentine, the desolate, deserted bandstand and around the Round Pond. I walk up and down. I circle. I walk so much that I'm actually warm even though it's freezing and late. My feet and legs ache. I'm starving. And I feel sick. How's that possible? On balance the hunger is more compelling than the nausea. I'm so desperate that, for the first time since I gave up watching *Black Beauty*, I buy a hot dog from a suspiciously filthy man pushing an off-white cart. The cart, man and hot dog would fail all health and hygiene regulations with spectacular success. I try not to think about it. He piles greasy onions into the bread bun and then smothers the hot dog with mustard and ketchup which squelch on to his fingers and down his arm. He wipes his dirty hands on his dusty trousers, runs his hand through his hair and, the final flourish, wipes the back of his hand over his mouth. I don't care. The hot dog looks delicious. I'm that hungry I would eat the man, dusty trousers and all, if necessary. Without even stopping to check if anyone can see me I gobble down the hot dog in approximately three bites. For about seven seconds I feel almost normal. My hunger is satiated and I don't feel sick, an exceptional state of affairs for the last month or so. On the eighth second my stomach lurches uncontrollably and I am hoying for Europe. The undigested hot dog, with onions, mustard, ketchup and trouser dust lies forlornly on the pavement. It's accompanied by two digestive biscuits, and I think that other thing is rye bread from my sandwiches at lunchtime.

'Ya fackin stupid bitch,' says the hot dog seller. 'What the fack did ya do that for? That ain't good for business, is it?'

I scrabble in my handbag and locate some tissues with which I wipe my mouth, sick-splattered trousers and boots, and then I walk away, too weary to fling back a clever retort, never mind reapply lipstick. I walk around the park again until I'm convinced that my boots are worn through. Finally, I throw myself on to the nearest park bench, not bothering about the bird excrement or chewing gum.

The park seems joyless. Littered with filthy vendors, rushing faceless people, dog muck and broken glass bottles.

I am growing a baby.

There is a baby inside my stomach. Or womb, or uterus. Or somewhere.

I try to think about that for a moment.

And can't.

It's so big. The thing, it . . . he or she is probably about the size of a single grain of couscous, but the *fact* that I'm pregnant is big. Too big.

Do I want to be pregnant? Do I want a baby (the natural conclusion)? I have no idea. My mind is completely blank. I rummage around a bit but there is only space, a yawning gap, a brilliant, dazzling, gleaming, glossy whiteness where a reaction or a response should be.

What will Hugh think? What will Hugh say?

Oh God.

I pull out my mobile and flick through the menu. Who to call? Hugh? God no. No. Not until I'm calmer, more certain. Of what? Certain of what to say, of how I feel. The idea of calling Drew, Karl, Brett or Julia, the people I work with, the people I've spent upwards of ten hours a day with, five days a week, for several years, makes me laugh, or at least it would if I didn't feel so much like crying. Whilst each of them is certainly sexually active, alert, even aggressive, I don't think any of them have ever connected the thing they do every Friday and Saturday night with making babies. In fact the primary concern has always been making sure sex didn't have anything to do with making babies. Sam? No point. Not unless I can somehow spin my pregnancy story so as to relate to finding her an eligible bachelor; she talks of nothing else. I dismiss a dozen or so other names, acquaintances that will trill that this is marvellous news. The thought terrifies me because I'm not certain that I'm ready to hear that.

Because I'm not certain it is.

There's Jessica, of course. She *is* my mother. Albeit the type of mother who insists I call her by her Christian name, as she hates to admit that she has a thirty-two-year-old daughter and she hyperventilates if I reveal our relationship in public. She is so much the epitome of a 'lady who lunches' that my father ought to have placed a copyright upon her when they married. She's all suntan and surgery, diets and drama. Her life's work is turning back the hands of time. To give credit where it's due, she's very successful in realizing this ambition. She looks about forty-five whereas she's nearly twenty years older than that. My parents live in Cannes in the summer and Cape Town in the winter. My father is a very silent man, more notable for the things he doesn't say than for the things he does. He is a retired diplomat, a career that suited him; he finds that the skills he developed in his professional life are still extremely useful as he negotiates his way towards his fortieth year of marriage. And Jessica, for her part, is the perfect wife for a diplomat. She knows things like how to address a bishop or a lord, which flowers last the longest in hot weather, and how to write an utterly charming thank-you note. She is at all times extremely practical and clear-sighted. To date, her maternal advice has ranged from which sunblocks are indispensable to the recommendation of personal trainers; I figure it's time to use my joker card.

'Darling, how lovely to hear from you. Oh God, it's not your birthday, is it? Have I forgotten your birthday?'

'No, Jessica.'

'No. Of course not. You were a summer baby. It's not mine, is it?'

Jessica hasn't celebrated a birthday since I was eight. Instead, she goes into a darkened room on the actual day and wears black for a week.

'No,' I assure.

'So why the call?' A sad but fair testament of our mother – daughter relationship.

I consider talking about the weather but realize it's pointless. 'I'm pregnant.'

There's a wail of horror. 'Oh darling. How could you do this to me? That will make me a – oh God, I'm going to have to sit down – a *grandmother.*' She hiss-whispers the last word, as though articulating a curse.

'I didn't do this to you,' I splutter, resisting the urge to scream, 'Bugger you, what about me? What about me!'

'I've been dreading this call since you were fourteen. Oh darling. You didn't plan this, did you?' She's incredulous. We are, in many ways, very similar.

'No.'

'Is it Hugh's?'

'Of course.' I try not to sound offended.

'Well, that's something, I suppose,' she mutters. 'It will, at least, be good-looking.' This is typical of my mother. Untouched by the traditional concerns, such as the facts that the child is unplanned, illegitimate and fathered by a married man, she focuses her attention on the aesthetics. I don't know why I was expecting her to be supportive or cheering. Since absolutely everyone's first question on seeing a baby is, 'How old is he/she?', my mother views children as little more than giant, depressing egg-timers. She's always made it clear that she finds it hard enough to understand how planned pregnancies are met with delight, so she thinks falling pregnant accidentally is one of the worst things that can happen to you. Obviously not as bad as finding out you are seriously ill or someone you love is dying. But certainly up there with losing your job or your lover, worse than being gazumped on a house sale or pranging the car.

'Do you want it?' she demands, unabashed. I don't have the chance to reply before she adds, 'Unlikely. I mean, who in their right mind actually wants a baby?' I try to forget the fact that this woman is my mother. 'They are highly inconvenient and not in the slightest bit rewarding until they are old enough to make one feel *ancient*.' She stretches the word ancient for an unfeasibly long time. 'And, goodness, the damage they do to your figure.' I have by now completely lost sight of the reason I chose to call my mother. 'It's irreparable. Darling, have you considered the stretch marks, the weight gain, the varicose veins?'

'It's good of you to remind me,' I snipe dryly.

'So, you don't want it?' Finally, I detect something like sympathy, or at least concern, in my mother's voice.

'I don't know,' I wail.

'Shush, darling. You mustn't cry. You'll get awful wrinkles, crying dries out the skin terribly.' She coos this instruction and it's soothing. It's vain and faintly ridiculous but soothing.

'I don't actively not want the baby. Or at least, I don't think so.'

'Goodness, so many negatives, does that make a positive?' Forever the grammarian.

'I don't know,' I mutter weakly. I deal with facts, data, information, and certainties. Agonizing over and trying to understand everything from my psyche to my G-spot has always seemed positively farcical, but now I'm considering, debating, procrastinating, *feeling* left, right and centre. All this not knowing is exhausting. I have always *known* things. I know the importance of identifying a single-minded, strategic focus. I know that standing orders are an efficient way to pay bills. I know the importance of owning at least one piece of jewellery from Tiffany. I know that the Burberry bandana has been done to death, I'm over it. I knew I wanted Hugh.

I knew he didn't want me, but I knew I could make him want me and I knew how to do it.

'Well?'

'I'm not ready for this, Jessica.'

She sighs. 'No one ever is. Even the couples who have spent years trying with IVF. They are not ready. They may want it more. But they're not ready either.'

Job. Lover. Home. Friends, all star quality. I have it all.

Including a sneaky suspicion that this is a little bit more than I bargained for. This wasn't part of my plan. 'Having kids seems like the end of life as I know it,' I mutter.

'It is exactly that.'

We both fall silent. I study the park bench. The graffiti reads *Andy Luvs Angie 4 Ever.* Will they? For ever? It seems such a long time. The time I have left is for ever. *George Feels Sick 4 Ever. George Changes Nappies 4 Ever.*

My mother interrupts my musings and asks quietly, 'So are we talking gin and hot baths?'

It's admirable that she does not shy away from the issue. I am, and always have been, pro-choice. Abortions are an option for teenagers, mothers of half a dozen children in increasing, overwhelming debt. They are an option for anyone who finds out that their baby is seriously ill. They are an option for rape victims. Abortion is not an option for me. I'm thirty-two, solvent and I love the father of my child. 'No. No gin or hot baths.'

'Oh good.' Jessica sighs with relief, although she hadn't betrayed her viewpoint until she'd heard my decision. This is her greatest strength – she never passes judgement. 'Well, darling, I hope you know that your father and I are always here for you.' She adds the caveat, 'Providing you never, ever use the Granny word. By the way, Georgina, when I said the damage to your body is irreparable, I wasn't being entirely honest. I can give you the name of a marvellous surgeon at Bart's. The very essence of discretion. Visit him within three months of the birth and everything will be as good as new, if not better.'

I know she's trying to be a comfort.

I hang up.

It's raining, and I wonder how long it has been doing so. It's the dark, relentless type of rain that offers no compensation or joy. Wind snakes its way into my coat and licks my back. Circles appear in puddles and disappear almost as quickly. It nearly always rains at commuter hour. I think of the sweaty tube carriages, damp and steamy with dripping people, bags and umbrellas. Irritated and exhausted shoppers tutting if someone opens the window, tutting if no one does. Tutting if someone stands on their toes, or they on someone else's. I imagine harassed office workers irritably fighting for an extra square inch of space, and drunks who sing and smell of streets and urine. In my mind I see the groups of Japanese girls who giggle quietly and relentlessly, neat and identical in their designer clothes. They are oblivious to the fact that all the other women in the compartment are glaring their resentment at the slim hips and advantageous exchange rate. I know all this life is happening right now, as it did yesterday, and as it will tomorrow. Everything going on as it went on before. No one aware that my life has changed, irredeemably.

I pull my coat an inch further around me and walk to the park gates.

Time to go home and tell Hugh the news.

2

I fell in love with Hugh Williams the first moment I saw him. Sam and I were first-year students at university and we couldn't believe Hugh was too. He appeared so much more mature. It turned out that he was twenty; he'd taken a couple of years out, to find himself, in India. Which he did in record time – he was there only about six weeks and spent the rest of his gap years stacking shelves in his local Sainsbury's. I always think this is why he's so good with people.

Just over thirteen years ago. Nearly half my lifetime. In all that time I've never loved another man. This all sounds *über*-romantic. People are generally bowled over by my story. Love at first sight and the idea of such constancy, etc., etc. Faces fall slightly when I mention that he was seeing someone else at the time, whom he subsequently married and had two children with. To be honest, I wasn't exactly thrilled either, but, hey girl, life's not a fairy tale.

A fairy-tale scenario goes something like this. Their eyes meet across a crowded room, she chastely looks away and then looks back again; he's still staring at her. He moves towards her holding two bottles of beer. They start talking, discover they have masses in common, he asks her for her phone number and tells her he'll call the next day. *He calls.* They meet several times over the next few weeks; each date is better than the last. He doesn't push for sex (she's marginally disappointed by this because she's gagging for it; why else leave home and go to university?). Eventually, after a respectable period of a number of weeks, after he's bought her flowers, poetry books and tastefully mounted Rothko prints, they fall into bed. Lovemaking is explosive, better than anything either of them has ever come across before – although, admittedly, their repertoire is rather limited (he is her first partner; she is his second or third, definitely not more than fourth). And, as they are smoking a post-coital cigarette, he tells her he loves her and that she's *the one*. At this point she is so besotted with him that she would happily agree to eat his pongy socks for the rest of her life, let alone wash them. They agree to finish their degrees, but set a date for their wedding to be soon after they've graduated. Then they live happily ever after.

My real-life scenario was almost identical, except for at the bit where they're smoking the post-coital. He didn't set a date, but instead flicked open his wallet and showed me a picture of his girlfriend. Girlfriend! And I know that makes him sound like a bit of a shyster but, really, he's not.

He is divine. A genuine god-like specimen. The most attractive man I've ever clapped eyes on, including anyone who's ever appeared on *Top of the Pops*, and all of the men in the Levi's adverts throughout the '80s. Which, I suppose, were the only men I'd had intimate relationships with pre-university. Well, you don't get much opportunity to meet boys, let alone men, at all-girls boarding schools. I left my school with high hopes of what uni would offer, and though I went to Sheffield, not Oxford, I was expecting the experience to be entirely *Brideshead Revisited* revisited. On sight Hugh fulfilled all my expectations and my fantasies and my dreams, and then some. Tall, blond, chiselled – classically handsome – with broad shoulders and a tight butt. He's the kind of bloke that when you see him in the distance you almost hope that, up close, he'll be a bit of a disappointment. Perhaps his eyes will be too close together, or he'll have blackheads nestling on his nose. Because, if he is as gorgeous as his distant silhouette promises, he'll be overwhelming.

Up close, he doesn't disappoint.

He was then, and is now, staggering. His eyes are huge, sparkling, green, dramatically offset by long lashes and perfectly arched eyebrows. He has high, jutting cheekbones and a square jaw. An eleven, on a scale of one to ten.

And they matched.

Becca's photo was testament to her above average beauty. Details? Think creamy, flawless skin, huge, laughing, blue eyes, long, blonde, curly tresses (the only time I've ever found an appropriate use for the word tresses is in relation to Becca), permanent, broad smile, revealing pearly-white teeth, big boobs, minute waist, hips, thighs, ankles, etc., etc. In short, irresistible.

Thank God it turned out that she didn't understand him.

And me? Well, even disqualifying British false modesty, facts have to be stated, and the fact is, or rather was, when Hugh and I met I was more of a five or five and a half – out of ten.

I also had long hair, but it didn't fall in long, blonde tresses – more brown, tangled rats' tails. I've got two crowns, you see. Not two heads, that really would be bad, but two crowns, and so my hair never parts properly, but sticks out at angles perpendicular to my head. My teeth could be described as straight(ish) and white(ish), but then again they could be described as crooked(ish) and grey(ish), and, let's face it, I didn't have a huge amount to smile about at the time. I didn't have a waist at all. I was the shape of a rather chunky toilet roll, which probably gives you an accurate enough picture of my thighs and ankles too.

It wasn't as though I could even take consolation in her being stupid or uninformed. No. Becca was one of those who sat for endless hours in the student union bar nursing warm beer and packets of cheese and onion crisps. Not that she ate the crisps. She always made a great show of buying and opening bags and bags of them and putting them on the tabletop and shouting, 'Dive in, dive in'. And whilst mere mortals like me, with excess fat and deficient self-control, did dive in, she held back and discussed 'issues'.

She had opinions on sanctions on Cuba, on whether Soviet troops ought to vacate Afghanistan, and on the environmental consequences of using CFC aerosol hairspray. She protested against apartheid in South Africa and wanted some answers about China's human rights record. She debated the intricate politics of Iran and Iraq, whereas I spent all my time trying to remember who was on which side. She'd even read *The Satanic Verses*, for God's sake. I had 'issues' too, but they were less lofty – mostly clothes, music and make-up. Regularly reading *Hello!* and knowing how much Marilyn Monroe's blouse was sold for at Sotheby's were as near as I got to current affairs (£7,150, if you're interested).

Becca was mesmerizing.

Everyone was captivated.

Even me.

I admit that if we had met under other circumstances, in another life, maybe we could have been friends. Maybe I would have liked her sense of humour, admired her compassion, conceded that she had impeccable skin and a pair of legs to die for. As it was, I simply loathed her.

I couldn't get over him. I couldn't let him go. I couldn't chalk him up to experience or carve a notch in my bedpost and move on. I really couldn't.

I sometimes wish I had been able to.

Our relationship makes the Grand Old Duke of York look spectacularly sedate and single-minded. *When they were up they were up, when they were down they were down*, just about has us in a nutshell. In the past thirteen years we've metamorphosed through all the possible boy/girl incarnations, including pen pal. The only consistency is that he's always been essential to my adult life. We've been 'just good friends', anguished lovers, not-so-good friends, the person with whom we had a drunken fumbling at the end of a party, anguished lovers again, and finally live-in lovers.

And – er – now parents to be.

Wow.

It was the beginning of December. Hugh had just been headhunted as MD for Rartle, Roguel and Spirity, renowned as one of the most creative agencies in London. A desperately coveted role throughout the advertising industry, the industry that we both work in. As a matter of fact, we'd both been approached and asked to apply for the position, but as soon as I heard that Hugh was seriously interested I stepped out of the running. Well, I didn't have a chance against him, and anyway it wouldn't have been good for our relationship. I firmly believe the best man won. To show my absolute support I went along to his welcoming party. It was a very tasteful affair starting with champagne and canapés in the boardroom, and then dinner at Nubo's. As is our way we drank a lot, partied until late and then made frantic, fervent love on the breakfast bar, the dining-room table and the rug in the sitting room. He asked, 'Is it the right time?' And whilst I was desperately trying to count the days on my fingers, well, let's just put it this way, by the time I'd done the maths he'd done the deed.

And as I lay awake in bed that night, gently doing my Pilates exercises whilst trying not to wake Hugh, I reasoned no one ever gets caught out the first time they take a risk.

No one.

3

I've read about telling your partner that you are pregnant, I've seen the films. I know how it's supposed to be. The champagne is supposed to be on ice (which immediately strikes me as unfair because I know that alcohol is already a long-lost friend to me). I'm meant to dress up in something that is at once feminine and intriguing. But this is out of the question, as I seem to have put on 5lb just in the drive from the doctor's to the park, and another five on the drive from the park home. I know I'll feel bloated and uncomfortable in all my favourite outfits. Besides which, I don't own anything in a floral print. He's meant to arrive home tired but handsome.

I say, 'Darling, you are going to be a father.'

Then I faint. Except in this case I might have to be more specific and say, 'Darling, you are going to be a father *again*.' He's then supposed to shrug off his tiredness long enough to gather me into his arms and whirl me around and around. It's essential at this point that he doesn't lose eye contact but gazes adoringly, whilst repeatedly telling me how clever I am.

I pour a great deal of concentration into visualizing this scenario but, try as I might, I simply cannot see Hugh and me in this state of domestic bliss. I guess ringing Becca for some tips is a little inappropriate. Besides, I know how Hugh felt when Becca became a mother.

Devastated.

He ran.

Directly into my arms.

Oh God.

It's fair to say becoming a mum didn't do Becca any favours. Quite the reverse. I'm rational enough to calculate that perhaps Hugh would have stayed with Becca if she hadn't fallen pregnant and become mind-numbingly boring. Plus fat. Yes, of course, it hurts knowing this. No one likes to think they won their man because his wife lost her sexual appetite and her ability to talk about anything other than baby poo and Winnie the Pooh. But kidding yourself is just that. It's wisest to understand, genuinely understand, where the other woman went wrong. In that way you can avoid making the same mistakes.

Or not, if you are haphazard with a calendar.

I mooch around the flat trying to submerge that last thought. *Think good stuff, think nice thoughts.* I instruct myself in the same way Jessica used to instruct me when, as a child, I woke up from a nightmare and couldn't fall asleep again in case the scary dream found its way back into my mind. OK. Good thoughts:

Hugh arriving on my doorstep eight months ago. I beam to myself remembering the exquisite mix of relief, breathtaking excitement and sheer, unadulterated joy. He's chosen me! After nearly two years of undignified sneaking about and before that eleven years of frustrating silence, Hugh and I were able to declare our love for each other, to each other *and* to the world at large. Good thought – it doesn't get better than that.

What was so utterly wonderful about that day was that Hugh didn't sneak up to my flat with a battered suitcase and heart, he arrived with a flourish, with pizzazz. The doorbell rang, which made me think it was a courier from work as Hugh had a key; Sam never arrives without calling first and who else would pop by? I opened the door, and lying on the mat was the most enormous bunch of starburst lilies; there must have been thirty stems. The bouquet was undoubtedly the most beautiful bouquet I had ever seen, or have seen since. It was a frenzied mass of colourful flowers and ribbons, with arty twigs jutting out at jaunty angles. It was a bouquet that declared celebration. At the very centre there was a yellow toothbrush. A toothbrush! Did this mean? Could this mean? I hardly dared hope. Giggling to myself I looked left to right but couldn't see any sign of a florist or Hugh. I picked up the enormous bouquet and, taking care not to brush the flowers – heavy with staining pollen – against the hall wall, I took it to the kitchen.

The card read, *I choose you.*

Yes. Yes. Yes. I punched the air, I screamed out loud. I literally jumped for joy; over and over again I jumped, pounding my feet on the floor until they hurt. He chose me. *Me. Chose* me. He did. My unrestrained delight was brooked (but only momentarily) when Hugh knocked on the kitchen window. He was laughing, it was clear he'd witnessed my entire response. Heart racing, I ran to the back door, pulled it open and flung myself into his arms. We kissed and kissed and kissed until he scraped my chin away, and my knickers.

That was eight months ago.

By the time Hugh arrives home I am trashed. Not woozy, not merry, not pleasantly inebriated, but trashed. Plastered. Wrecked. Far from becoming a long-lost friend, alcohol is my closest intimate. And whilst I know I absolutely should not be drinking now, let alone drinking enough to become legless, I simply can't stop myself. I might as well admit it: I am smoking my eighth cigarette of the day, too. I argue that if I hadn't found out about the pregnancy until tomorrow

I'd probably be at some wine bar right now, smoking and drinking myself into oblivion in happy ignorance.

I know it's a shoddy argument and I already feel guilty.

'Hello, gorgeous. Can I join you?' Hugh kisses me on the lips and nods towards the nearly empty bottle of Merlot. He throws his jacket over the back of a chair, it's a really simple action. But this simple, domestic action makes my heart zoom to my mouth and then ricochet to my knickers. He, at least, has fulfilled his part of the bargain; he does look handsome and tired. I really regret my lack of floral prints. I love him. Every tiny bit of him. From his dishevelled hair, which he has so obviously run his fingers through numerous times today, down to his immaculate, shiny shoes. He takes great care of his shoes. He has a shoe-tree for every pair he owns, and he never puts on or takes off a shoe without the aid of a shoehorn. This practice, although undeniably old-fashioned, endears him to me anew every time I witness it.

I love him so much it hurts. I love him so much I feel sick with it.

But then that could be the pregnancy.

'How was your day?' I ask.

He treats me to a half-grin, a half-shrug. We both know that the other's days are, as a matter of course, busy, stressful and political. We wouldn't have it any other way. He pours himself a glass of wine and tops up my glass. He joins me on the grey buckskin settee and we shuffle into our usual position – him upright, me slouched lengthways, with my feet resting on his legs. He absent-mindedly starts to rub my ankles.

'I like the nail varnish.' He nods towards my pedicured toes. 'So what's up?' he asks. Whilst I'm gratified that he knows me so well that he's immediately sensed that something is wrong, his question blows any hope I had that I'd kill time with polite small talk.

'I went to the doctor's today.'

The pressure of my foot massage increases marginally.

'You didn't tell me you were going to the doctor's. You're OK, aren't you?' And all that he wants to hear is a simple, 'Yes, I'm fine.' I'd like to oblige.

'Blooming,' I sigh, not able to keep the drunken weariness out of my voice. Bull by the horns: 'I'm pregnant.' The comforting circular motion on my feet draws to an abrupt halt.

'Pregnant?'

'Yes.'

'You're having a baby?'

'I don't know any other type of pregnant.' Unless you include the pregnant pause which follows. I watch him closely. But he's too much of a professional to rashly betray any emotion.

'How pregnant?'

'Nine weeks.' Which is something else that's been bothering me. I have no idea how the doctor came up with this date. It seems that it's nothing to do with when the deed was actually done. Apparently, it's a scientific calculation taking into account the date of the first day of my last period, whether or not there was a full moon that night or an 'r' in the month, and if Hugh was wearing blue socks.

'How?'

That's an original one. I bet the Treasury would like a pound for every time a man has asked a woman, 'How could this happen?' We'd probably clear our national debt.

'I guess we played Russian roulette just once too often.' I try to smile, but the muscles in my face are behaving treacherously and I'm sure I'm grimacing.

'You said it was your safe time.'

'I was wrong.' I know it seems odd to him. It does to me, too. I'm thirty-two, hardly at my fertile prime. I started successfully repressing my reproductive organs over thirteen years ago. Besides which, sperm counts are supposed to be down – there are always articles saying as much, and what about the stuff they put in London water and the effects of pesticides on our food? I watch Hugh compute the information, consider it, balance it, and then finally react to it.

'Well, that's big news.'

'Yes.'

'I never expected . . .'

'No.'

'And you want to keep it?'

'Yes.'

The caution that we are both exuding stains the air. It's a yellowish colour. I know what he's thinking. He's wondering whether we'll be any good at it. Parenting, I mean. Obviously he's at an advantage, he's already had a crack at it, but Becca had never allowed Hugh too much active involvement. I'm sure she limits his access so that she has the opportunity to bemoan his lack of commitment. He's nervous – what if the child is stupid, or ugly, or even beautiful and clever but depressed and a drug addict? And one child, more often than not, leads to another, doesn't it? Pregnancy, and ultimately a small person, will restrict our freedom (dinners out, holidays, entertaining, gym visits, etc.). Ditto sex life. Ditto our relationship generally. Ditto our careers. Well, probably just my career. Hugh's career will be unaffected by this, or possibly enhanced. Fertile men are still held in high esteem by their colleagues, visions of passing cigars around come to mind, as do conversations about golden bullets. A family man – however many families he has – is seen as stable and reputable. By contrast, a procreating woman is seen as unreliable, dizzy and a liability. He's thinking about sickness (mine), fatness (mine), lank hair (mine), spots, piles, skin flaps, skin colouration, loose vagina, uncontrollable gases escaping from the body (all mine). He's contemplating loss of sexual desire (both of ours!). He's considering the indignity of maternity clothes and the possibility of the eradication of adult conversation and foods. And, finally, there's the pain of labour (mine).

'Marvellous! It's marvellous news.'

Oh, the relief.

I thought that – well it seems stupid to even mention it now but I thought, no, not as strong as *thought*, but certainly *feared* that he'd . . . leave.

That's all I've thought about.

He flings his arms around me, hugs me very tightly for over a minute, then pulls away, takes my cigarette out of my hand and stubs it out.

'Well, that's the last one of those you're having. And of those.' He pours the remaining wine from my glass into his, goes to the kitchen and returns with a large glass of milk. I am so stupid! How could I have worried about Hugh's reaction? How unbalanced. How unnecessary. Of course Hugh's delighted. He's a wonderful man and he's bound to be delighted to hear he's having a child. What kind of man wouldn't be delighted?

What kind of woman?

4

After our one night of passion back in 1987, Hugh went back to Becca and I settled for becoming Hugh's best friend, or at least posing as such whilst disguising my more lascivious motives for wanting to spend every waking moment with him. Whenever he and Becca had a spat, he'd pop by my hall of residence and tell me all about it. Then we'd have a terrific time, eating garlic bread in cheap Italian restaurants, standing freezing and cheering on the sidelines as Sam played hockey, and drinking countless cups of coffee and eating countless slices of buttery toast in our bedrooms or the communal kitchens. The best times I had at university were definitely those times we spent together, and I treasure every single wonderful memory.

The more time I spent with Hugh, the more intensely, insanely, incurably I fell in love with him. It wasn't just his stomach-churning good looks, it was the fact that, by quite some way, he was the most vibrant, alive person I'd ever met. He had a sort of animal energy and a phenomenal curiosity in everything and everyone around him. His mind was a labyrinth and appeared insatiable. He was good at sport. He played the guitar and wrote his own songs. He could drink anyone who dared to challenge him under the table. He had a big dick. Becca obviously wasn't impervious to his charms either because she would always turn up a couple of days after their rows, all red-eyed and penitent, and I'd watch as with nauseating inevitability they kissed and made up.

Actually, *those* memories don't rank amongst my fondest.

Throughout my time at college Hugh was polite and friendly towards me. But then he was also polite and friendly towards Sam, and all of the hockey team, the first and second eights, all the reps on the student union, the librarians, the entire end-of-term ball committee and every female fresher – amongst others. He is just a polite and friendly sort of guy. Polite and friendly as in no flirting, no accidental touching of hands across the table or banging of knees underneath, no shrouded references to our night of hot sex. Hugh seemed to find me as gender specific as a teddy bear. And quite a lot less appealing.

I quickly came to realize that Becca was a better proposition than I was. Tragic but true. She was prettier, sportier, cleverer, more interesting and interested. She could leave half a Mars bar uneaten for months. But, I argued, *I* didn't owe Becca any loyalty. OK, so she saw him first and said *bagsie*, but that hardly seemed reason enough for me to throw in the towel. My undergraduate self reasoned that Hugh was still up for grabs until Becca had a ring on her finger. And the answer to wetting his whistle was that I'd have to become the better proposition.

Come on, I'm not the first, nor will I be the last, woman to try a homespun, crash-course, Pygmalion-like transmogrification with the aim of netting something delectable in the staminate department. Haven't you ever dyed your hair just to see if blondes do have a better ride? Haven't you ever pretended you've read a book that you'd only looked at the cover of – just to appear more interesting and informed? Do you honestly like football?

I began to read newspapers and I joined the debating society. I went out of my way to meet as wide and varied a group of people as possible. Naturally, this meant I squandered numerous evenings with bores and weirdos, but slowly I also began to build a base of knowledge on issues cultural, financial, historical, economic. I didn't waste any more of my vacations slouching around my parents' home, but instead visited a kibbutz in Israel, restoration projects in Naples, holiday camps for socially deprived children in the Bronx. And, whilst up until meeting Hugh I'd viewed studying as something to do when the bar closed and attending lectures simply as a means of checking out my mates' new clobber, I suddenly started to take my degree seriously. I worked hard. Very hard. I was able to quote Keynes, Einstein and Euclid at the drop of a hat; even now I can tell you anything you want to know about Benazir Bhutto, Manuel Noriega, the poll tax or De Klerk. Go on, test me.

I did all that walking-up-the-stairs-instead-of-taking-the-lift thing. I cut the fat off my ham when I made ham sandwiches, but I didn't melt away into a pre-pubescent nymph, so I cut out ham altogether, and other meats, too, pretty soon after. In fact, nothing ever passed my lips unless it was nutritionally valuable and had been interrogated in terms of fat and calorie content. I obliterated my couch-potato persona and reinvented myself as a fitness freak and, most particularly, as 'very outdoorsy'. The illusion I created has been so effective that I have subsequently found myself on skiing holidays in the winter and sailing holidays in the summer. The free time in between has been punctuated by hikes, treks, Saturday and Sunday afternoons standing on the touchlines of rugby and football pitches, crossing the London Marathon finish line – twice – jogging, swimming, serving, volleying, batting, running, biking, on one occasion kick-boxing, and the undisputed low point, pot-holing. Hell. Undoubtedly that's what hell is. A cold, damp hell, as opposed to the more traditional fiery hell. But hell. I suppose, sooner or later, I should tell Hugh that the only type of sweating, panting and grunting I want to do in front of him is, in fact, under him, and even going on top is more athletic than I'd ideally opt for.

I followed a strict regime of cleanse, tone and moisturize with exclusive La Prairie products, even though the products cost a term's rent. I had my hair cut every six weeks, and coloured every twelve. I used toothpaste that bleached my teeth. I paid to have six of them capped, and I wore a brace for several months and – this might sound extreme – I had a boob job. Why not make the best of yourself? If you have the money. Actually, I didn't have the money but I took out a loan.

Everything I read, I read to impress Hugh. Everywhere I visited I stored up stories to repeat to Hugh. Every purchase I made, I made with him in mind. I didn't stop to wonder whether any other man would do instead. I knew, simply knew, as clearly as I knew my own name, no other one would. All other men were grey. They seemed finite and unreliable.

For three long years I was always 'there' for Hugh. Helping with essay crises, his election campaign as president of the student union, being a shoulder to cry on when his parents divorced, running out to buy hangover cures after very heavy nights. Well, isn't this what best friends do for one another? In fact, it is because I did so much research for his milk-round interviews in advertising – studying every IPA paper and scrutinizing every issue of *Campaign*, the advertising industry's weekly bible, memorizing the business performance league tables and the names and faces of all the players – that I didn't have time to think about another career, one for myself, so we both interviewed. We were both accepted on a graduate trainee course with Saatchi and Saatchi, and I got a place with Q&A and JWT as well. Which was a bit freaky; I think the industry was discriminating positively in favour of women that year – why else would Hugh get only one place and I get three? I chose Q&A because they offered a four-month training course in New York and Hugh said I'd be mad to turn down that opportunity. I'm still with them almost eleven years on, although Hugh has worked at Saatchi and Saatchi, Leo Burnett, Lowe Lintas and now Rartle, Roguel and Spirity.

So I went to New York for no other reason than the fairly ignoble one that it would impress Hugh. And whilst I was there the worst thing that could happen did happen – as usually is the way. Becca and Hugh got engaged.

The news scalded my ears and tore at my heart. I ached. Every fibre of my body revolted as pain bounced from my kitten heels to the tips of my Paul Mitchell-conditioned hair. I felt as though my bloodstream were infected and polluted with grief, as my hopes, dreams and plans collapsed like a straw house, defeated by the breath of the huffing and puffing big, bad wolf. I bobbed like a bottle at sea, vacuous, without bearing. And the hardest part of all was admitting that I wasn't even surprised that Hugh chose Becca. I knew that despite my superficial reconstruction I wasn't good enough for him.Elevens marry elevens; they don't marry five and a halves masquerading as eights. That would be against the natural order of things. Darwin probably wrote a paragraph or so about this exact subject.

What can I say? It is not better to have loved and lost, as anyone who has ever lost will confirm. I felt raw and exposed. I missed him, or at least the chance of him, with a breathtaking, ferocious intensity. For a time I tried alcohol, drugs and pizzas – none of them soothed the agony. But after several weeks the wretchedness did dull to a quiet (although persistent) ache and I pulled myself together sufficiently to try a new line in survival.

I didn't go back to London in January as planned, or indeed for another five years after that. I couldn't. It represented all that I had lost. I persuaded Q&A to give me a full-time position in New York. I threw myself into my work, vowing to put Hugh out of my mind for good. I concentrated on gaining a reputation for dedication and professionalism. I also dated, constantly and unsatisfactorily, but often rather glamorously (my conquest list included several up-and-coming politicians, minor actors and one of the Kennedy cousins – distant). It was the ultimate frustration that so many other men believed in my reinvention whilst Hugh had not. Which just proved that Hugh was more discerning, more sagacious, more judicious. By rejecting me he showed himself the better man and became even more attractive to me. I dressed in designer labels, worked my ass off both in the gym and in the office, I holidayed on the West Coast, learnt to scuba-dive and to drive a Harley Davidson. Slowly I built up the reputation I longed for: I became a serious professional with great tits.

By the time I returned to London in late 1995, Becca and Hugh were married and living in Highgate, whilst Sam was only in the infancy of her search for the love of her life.

They all came to meet me off the plane at Heathrow. I had planned my emergence from behind the sliding doors for weeks, and to every last detail. I had neatly stacked my Prada luggage on a trolley (anything that wouldn't conveniently fit into these suitcases had been sent on ahead so as not to ruin the effect). I was wearing a black, halter-neck catsuit, which made my legs look longer than the reality, and exposed my now ferociously toned, muscular arms. My hair was immaculately styled and, despite the transatlantic flight, still hung in the sleek drop it was newly trained to; my Gucci sunglasses sat jauntily on top of my head. I wanted to look carefree. I wanted to prove, not least to myself, that I was over Hugh, that he'd been nothing more than a crush, escalated in my head by eight years of longing, which had *surely* been adolescent. As the doors swept back the gang let up a cheer and waved flowers and a ludicrous cuddly toy. I took one look at Hugh and knew that my self-imposed exile had been pointless. Far from diving, dating and dealing him out of my system, I loved him more.

My post-graduate self reasoned that Hugh was still up for grabs despite the ring on Becca's finger.

In 1996 Becca gave birth to Kate, and eighteen months later she gave birth to Tom. Six months after that I became Hugh's mistress. It's ugly, I know. I wish I could make it, the situation, or, more honestly, me in particular, sound more noble or at least less ignoble, but the fact is that in 1998 I became his mistress. And even if I tell you that she didn't appreciate him, that she's never worked since they married and has depended on him entirely for an income (whilst professing to disapprove of his career choice) . . . Even if I explain that she didn't like him going to the gym and she nagged him about the fact that he played rugby once a week and trained another evening . . . And she grumbled because she didn't think he did enough for the children and that she said he didn't pull his weight around the house . . . If I divulge that there is a serious probability that she had an affair with her tennis coach . . . Or if I elucidate by saying that she never read the books he read, she never laughed at his jokes, or noticed when he'd had his hair cut, or asked how his day had gone . . . It would be pointless; none of this would alter the fact that being a mistress is not a very heroic position, whichever way you look at it. I can't justify it. I can't make it seem right. I am still a mistress. *Still*, because technically he's still married to Becca, although he moved in with me eight months ago. Annoying, isn't it? One of life's little irritants. Colossal irritants, actually, because I am so tired of being apologetic. The truth is nice people (me) do not very nice things from time to time (sleep with other women's husbands, for example).

He should have been mine right from the beginning, he really should have.

But he wasn't, and when some things go wrong you can never, ever put them right.

5

There are lots of unwritten rules in the advertising profession; besides what to wear, eat and drive, you have to know how to conduct yourself from day to day. It is of paramount importance to be perky and productive at all times; no one wants to network with a dormouse. Getting from reception to desk in the mornings should be a social occasion. Smile at all times. Wide, toothy smiles.

'Watcha Georgie, you're looking gorgeous.'

Karl hasn't looked at me. He says the same thing every morning, to everybody. He's a very popular man. If he had looked at me, he might have noticed that the jacket of my Armani suit is swinging open, as opposed to fastened as is usual, and the top button of my trousers is also undone. Although I am now only nine weeks pregnant, I'm already struggling to find clothes that fit. It's not that I am fatter (I am, but it's not that); as unbelievable as it seems, my hips have widened. They've been aching for days, and now I can hardly fit any of my trousers over my hips, not even my emergency-fat-period trousers. Hips widening! I can only assume it is to make way for the baby's head, giving me a tiny insight into the torture which is ahead of me. And my ribcage has moved. No one tells you that; indeed it's probably better that they don't, otherwise I'm pretty certain the human race would die out.

'Why thank you, Karl,' I *smile*, barely glancing his way, and I add, 'And you. Have you been working out?' Karl is – get this – an Assemblage Account Director (meaning he manages a group of suits).

'Thought you'd be interested in this report, page nineteen hits the issues,' says Drew, the Emporium Strategist (basically a planner).

'Cheers,' I *smile*, taking the paper from him without breaking my stride towards my desk (that's another rule, never walk if you can stride, but never, ever run; it's cool to be busy but not frantic).

'Georgie, are you coming to the opening of Champagne Charlotte's tonight?' asks Brett, the Officiating Creative Director (the one with the crayons).

'Certainly, I'll be there,' I *smile*.

The boys and I are all ranked at the same level. Our current positions are mutually dependent upon one another's success, so we all frequently, loudly and, if necessary, insincerely expound on each other's talents and profess adoration. Our relationship smacks of 'friends close, enemies closer'. It's not that I don't like them; they are all smart, savvy, sexy and cocksure. They operate in a homogeneous mass; if they ever had individual personalities, they've long since been erased. They are the advertising world's equivalent of a boyband. I *do* like them. I just don't trust them. Experience has shown there's no advantage to being sentimental.

'Georgina, can you read this and give me your opinion on the IPC situation by close of play?' says Dean, the MD, everyone's boss, as he tosses an inch-thick report on to the already towering pile of papers I'm carrying.

'Sure thing.' I broaden my smile an incredible fraction further. I think my face might split. He's American, so I find myself sounding like a Wild West settler whenever I speak to him; it's entirely deliberate.

My title at Q&A is President of Neoteric Enterprise. Brand enhancement is our way of life; hence the overly grand and misleading job titles. Whilst my job is important to me and at times exhilarating (when I'm talking to a headhunter, for example), it does fall slightly short of the title imported from the US. If I didn't work for an American agency I'd probably have a more modest title, such as New Business Manager. But then we are talking about an office culture that calls cleaners Industrial Waste Executives, and the woman who doles out the slop in the canteen is a Protein and Vitamin Execution Executive (pronounced Vite-a-min).

My job essentially boils down to endlessly trawling through personal contacts, newspapers, annual reports, etc., in an effort to identify companies that don't currently advertise but might be persuaded to, or, rather more lucratively, those that currently advertise and spend heaps of money, but with another agency. I then put together a team and we plot, persuade, coax, cajole, entice and impel said companies to part with large amounts of cash in the hope that we can help them make yet larger amounts, which in turn we help them in spending. I seem to have quite a knack for this. I like to see it as a virtuous circle.

In truth, I often see it as a fairly undignified way to earn a living.

'Doughnut, Georgina?' offers Julia, my number two in the office, but also my mate after hours.

I shake my head and repeat the old adage, '*a moment on the lips, a month on the hips*'. I sing this through my smile, whilst mentally calculating the calories and fat units in a doughnut. Julia immediately throws the doughnut in the bin, which I wish I hadn't seen. I'll spend all day thinking of it, languishing there. Uneaten. My smile falters momentarily.

My usual practice is that I positively bounce into the office every morning, fired up for debating the brand properties of loo bleach or 'refreshing' versus 'thirst-quenching' as the unique selling position for the latest carbonated drink. But today I feel wiped out, low, feeble, exhausted. I am a used bin liner, as rubbish as that. My head hurts, I feel sick. Think pernicious hangover combined with worst period pains ever. Bingo. The important thing is no one must know this. I finally reach my office. I slump into my chair and lay my head on the desk. I usually conduct my entire day's business standing up; it's more intimidating for the audience and good exercise for the calves. Sod that, I'm exhausted. Without lifting my head I rummage inside the top drawer of my desk, where I keep a collection of remedies for all ills. Spare pair of tights in case of ladders, clear nail varnish in case of laddering spare pair (a little blob at the top and bottom of the ladder does the trick). Tippex to be used on ladder in spare pair of tights when I can't unscrew the lid of the clear nail-varnish bottle. Toothbrush, breath fresheners, comb, an assortment of Boots 17 cosmetics (anything more expensive would be nicked), nail file, tweezers, spare battery for my mobile, modem line, roughly £20 of change in six foreign currencies, a variety of pens, pencils, elastic bands, paper clips, string, business cards and, finally, aspirin. I reach for the packet of aspirin then read the instructions and discover I can't take any.

Because I'm pregnant.

I try thinking about butterflies and freshly squeezed orange juice but the visualization technique fails miserably. It's bollocks, actually. I feel even more nauseous and quite extraordinarily ravenous. The doughnut in the bin is the only thing that I can imagine will help. But only if I eat it now. *Now, now.* Not now as in how long it will take to nip out and buy another one. I *have* to eat *the* doughnut that is in the bin and I *have* to eat it *now.* I turn round and see that Julia is standing by the scanner, leaving her desk and, more particularly, the bin-languishing doughnut unguarded. Moving like James

Bond on blades, I speed back to her desk, retrieve the doughnut, hide it in between my files, dash towards the privacy of my own office, which thankfully has a door – a perk negotiated with my last promotion, along with a beechwood desk and a dry-cleaning allowance – and then I eat the doughnut. To put this into context, this is the first cake I've tasted since my twenty-first birthday. This 007-like operation takes me about four seconds. I feel well for a further four seconds and then I throw up into my bin – the white one, which is for paper. I suspect this is a little more than the office administrator was bargaining for in terms of recycling materials. I move the bin outside my office door, but I have the feeling that the stale smell of spew will linger all day.

The indignity is staggering.

I don't have time to spray perfume around the office before the phone starts to ring. I pick it up. Someone wants to know something about portfolio planning. My second line is ringing, a question about relative market shares, and then Julia is suddenly by my side, trying to get me to sign a pile of papers, which I do – with my free hand, whilst reading them with one eye. A coffee appears on my desk. I cradle the phone under my ear and then take a sip. I finish the call about commissioning market research into teenage girls' views on digital TV, put the phone down and it immediately rings again. My lead-like limbs are operating in their own time zone, refusing to keep pace with my mind, which, anyway, is lagging behind the required canter set by my job description. I knock back the plastic cup of coffee, hoping the caffeine will take effect a.s.a.p.

Yuk.

'Julia, have you switched coffee house?'

'No, it's the same old, same old,' Julia replies.

Julia wears her hair cropped short and spiky, a look which really only suits elf-like girls, which Julia is not, in fact, but she considers herself to be so. I am jealous of her misplaced confidence. It's odd, isn't it, that some girls who aren't naturally beautiful become intrinsically beautiful once they believe they are. And other girls, like Sam for instance, are gorgeous but can never really believe it. I'm somewhere in between. I know I'm beautiful when Hugh says I look 'good', then I'd happily sunbathe in a bikini next to Miss Universe. I disappear altogether when he doesn't notice my new outfit. Yes, I do realize that this is unhealthy. Every self-help book I've ever read has violently condemned over-reliance on other people's opinions and praise. I've given all my self-help books to the local Oxfam.

Julia changes her hair colour every week; this week it's plum. Her hairdresser's bill must run to thousands a year. She has huge, brown eyes (so laid-back they're insolent), which she frames with trendy, square, yellow Calvin Klein glasses. I'm not sure if she is genuinely short-sighted, or if the glasses are a fashion statement. She wears skimpy, clingy designer T-shirts with things like *roger me senseless* printed across her breasts. Diesel jeans and the latest, trendy, must-have sneakers from the States. She always looks cold and bored. But cool. At a guess I'd say she spends 90 per cent of her wages on clothes; the remaining 10 per cent is spent on newspapers and style magazines. Her father pays her rent and her 'friends' pay for her gigs and drinks; she doesn't eat. Julia has a low boredom threshold so the words 'same old, same old' are her anthem. She's been known to use them when referring to an outfit she purchased fifteen minutes earlier, or about a guy she's accepted her first drink from. I see a low boredom threshold as the sign of a lively mind, so whilst I don't mind her response, I do doubt it.

'Are you sure that you didn't get this from the vending machine?'

'I'm certain. I know how you feel about your double espresso from CaféCafé. Although your predictability in such matters does surprise me.'

Traditionally my life has lacked certainty, therefore sticking with a coffee brand is disproportionately important to me.

'Why, what's wrong with the coffee?'

'It tastes bitter and smells odd,' I complain.

Because I'm pregnant.

Of course, I shouldn't even be drinking coffee. I'm saved from explaining the fickle nature of my taste buds as my landline screeches at me at the exact same moment that my mobile pings to let me know I have a text message. I'm pretty certain that both desperate attempts at communication are from the same source.

'Hi, it's me. Have you got time to talk?'

I say no but Sam talks anyway.

I love her dearly; remembering her antics during Freshers' week still brings a smile to my face and a tear to my eye, and makes me wonder who her lawyer is. Yet her scatter-gun approach to her love life is irritating in the extreme. Oblivious to the fact that I may be very busy (which is normally the case), or that I am very pregnant and therefore feeling more filthy than a dog's arse (which is admittedly news), we, yet again, re-enact a conversation we have had several times a month for the last thirteen years. An endless, directionless flow of self-pity about her being very nearly thirty-five and 'half her life being over'. I point out that with extended life expectancy Sam can reasonably anticipate living into her nineties. She counters that a long life will be torturous as the best bit is already over, and then she starts comparing quality of life: roller-blades vis-à-vis Zimmer frames, blooming new bosoms and sagging tits, university and retirement homes. She has a point and she makes it well but my patience is stretched. Sam is not suffering from a deadly disease or redundancy, her flat hasn't fallen into negative equity, nor has she broken a nail. The source of her desolation is, in Julia's phrase, 'same old, same old'. Last night her date stood her up. Her life's over.

I hope my silence is condemnation enough. Sam knows I think she's pathetic. She thinks she's pathetic too – it's this refreshing honesty that makes me love her; everyone else our age pretends to like being single.

Sam's original life plan has gone way off course. According to it, by now, she should be a corporate wife, lovingly supporting a dynamic husband as he thunders his way up the corporate ladder. She should be mother of two adorable children, one boy, one girl – dark and blonde respectively. She should be living in a large detached house somewhere in the green belt, with a huge manicured garden and perhaps even a pool. She should be heavily involved in the PTA and organizing a weekly rota for the school run. Ideally, she'd be driving a Land-Rover.

Need I go on?

Sam's current position – lying under the duvet with nothing more than a box of Kleenex for company – is a situation which is horribly, depressingly familiar. Her life achievements to date (has made junior partner in a huge firm of management consultants; has swum with dolphins off the coast of South Africa; can fly a helicopter; has bungee-jumped from Victoria Falls; owns a racing-green MG) are forgotten. What grieves and shames Sam the most is that she could have lived without all that stuff if only she were surrounded by silver-plated photo frames displaying testaments to her success as a wife and mother. I can't think of any heartfelt words of consolation, so resort to the comfort of the cliché and mutter, 'Still. Never say die.' Sam complains that I've worked too long in advertising if I think an old saying like that is any help at all. This is hilarious coming from Sam, who speaks almost entirely in terms of 'fish in the sea', 'a change is as good as a rest', 'all that glitters', 'a stitch in time' and other such non-profundities. Anyway, what choice do I have? I can't tell her that she wears her desperation as conspicuously as most other people wear Vivienne Westwood – and, to men, it smells more intrusive than Poison perfume – although this undoubtedly is the case. Besides which, I simply can't see the mild embarrassment of being stood up as anywhere near as serious as the issues I'm currently facing – i.e., the embarrassment of the stench of regurgitated stolen doughnuts drifting condemningly through my office. I want to tell her that I'm pregnant, but don't know how. In the past it's been our habit to share our lives, entirely. We've always confessed to every love affair, emotion, victory, loss, piece of luck, joyless fuck and paranoia going.

But suddenly I'm stuck for words.

The thing is, I'm sure she'd tell me this is brilliant news and I'm sure it is. I know it is. Hugh says it is. I'm just waiting to feel that it is, or, more accurately, to feel that it is for longer than ninety consecutive seconds. I'm bound to get excited soon, aren't I? I'm bound to go gaga about little socks in babyGap. I wonder if they come with instructions on how to get them from the packet to the foot? It's just so new and unexpected and unplanned that I haven't had time to digest, process and react appropriately.

And I'm nothing if not appropriate.

I'm a slave to the magazines that tell you how to file your

nails, buff your skin, wash your hair for optimum shape/silkiness/shine. I know which shoes go with which length skirt. I know which denier stocking to wear for every occasion. I know how much to tip taxi drivers, bellboys and waiters in every European country, Canada and the States. I have an appropriate response to a discussion on any election – local, national or international. In fact, I have an appropriate response to just about any conversation: the arts ('fascinating'), food ('This is delicious, is that cinnamon I can taste?'), football ('I'd like to see it become a family sport again') and politics ('it's a serious matter'). For the record, I can discuss a number of other subjects in depth. I know an awful lot about Renaissance literature, Helmut Newton's early work and the history of Punch and Judy shows, amongst other topics. You'd be surprised how rarely an in-depth knowledge of anything is considered appropriate. My adult life has been a series of goals, which I've set, then achieved. I've always known the direction I was travelling in, even during those long years whilst I waited for Hugh – at least *I* had decided to wait for him. It was my choice, my decision. I have always been unquestionably, undoubtedly, assuredly, 100 per cent in control. The thing is, I don't make mistakes. I don't make blunders, miscalculations, slips. The only 'err' I've ever made is to err on the side of caution. I haven't so much as made an impulse purchase in a sale that I've later regretted.

And now this.

I decide against mentioning it over the phone and instead tersely advise Sam to get showered, get dressed and get into work before anyone notices her absence. I promise I'll ring her tomorrow and then I hang up quickly to avoid hearing her cry.

6

The morning passes in a smudge, not even a blur. A blur would at least suggest activity. I wonder if I appear to be exactly the same George to everyone else? Probably. Which is odd – in fact, I am entirely different.

At lunchtime I nip out to buy a maternity book, as it strikes me that whilst I have some vague notion that being pregnant means my periods stop and I'll get fat, this is all I know. I'm spectacularly uninformed on the subject.

The wet London streets are teeming with shoppers, hoping to take advantage of the dregs of the sales. I watch them scuttle from shop to bus trying and failing to avoid the rain. The shoppers are the only things moving. The rest of London is at a standstill, partly because of the pouring rain, and partly because the lorry drivers are protesting against something or other, they have a taste for it. I think that today they are objecting to the French exporting French cheese. A point of principle that evades me.

On the way to the bookshop a strange thing happens to me. I swear I have never, ever seen a pregnant woman in London. Not one in all the years I've lived here. But on the short walk from Golden Square to Piccadilly, which can be no more than a few hundred yards, I see three. *Three.* And two women with babies strapped to their front in those sling things, plus countless women with pushchairs (and therefore babies). I keep expecting Jeremy Beadle to jump out from behind a lamp-post and tell me that I've been framed, that this is all a joke, that the waddling women are really extras with cushions stuffed up their dresses for my benefit.

Although their misery looks real enough.

And they are miserable-looking. Tired, uncomfortable, fat. Not blooming, blossoming or benign as promised by prevailing myth.

Sigh.

It takes me about thirty minutes to locate the relevant section in the bookstore. It's on the third floor, which leads me to believe that a man, or a woman who has yet to discover her reproductive capacity, designed the store. I huff and puff my way up the stairs doing a good impersonation of Dawn French running the final mile of the London Marathon. Odd to think that not so long ago I prided myself on sprinting up stairs all over London, including that double set at Piccadilly tube station because the damn escalators are never working.

It's an eye-opener to discover that there is a whole industry devoted to the thus far invisible army of women that give birth. There is shelf after shelf after shelf of books about pregnancy. Straight books, funny books, medical books, books that look at the emotional, psychological, sociological, economic and political aspects of having a child. Books with diagrams, books with photos – black and white and *colour* (aahhh) – and books that rely entirely on text. There are books about conceiving, carrying and labour. There are books about the first days, weeks, months and years of childhood. The choice is overwhelming. I have no idea which book to buy. Despite the choice, all the books have two things in common. One, they all picture women with dodgy 1980s haircuts and sailor-collar dresses, and two, they are universally terrifying and depressing. In a near trance-like state I finally grab the two nearest to me. One is a week-by-week guide to pregnancy. I flick over some pages until I come to the section on the baby's development at week nine.

Week 9
Your baby's arms and legs are longer. Hands are flexed at the wrist and meet over the heart area. Your baby now moves its body and limbs.

I look at the diagram expecting to see something that could audition for a Huggies advert. In fact, there is a diagram of a small alien-like thingy. Its eyes look evil. The second book I choose is a lighthearted text detailing the things a best friend should tell you about pregnancy. Since I haven't actually managed to tell my best friends I am pregnant as yet I hope that this book will be a good enough surrogate.

There's another book, one that acts like mercury spilling into my nervous system. I can hardly bring myself to glance at the title on the spine. It's about dealing with miscarriage and stillbirth. So, for the first time since I was a Brownie, I say a prayer. A sort of prayer. I don't drop to my knees in the middle of the shop, but I sort of ask whoever is out there that if at all possible could (s)he see to it that the little grain of couscous grows to be a howling, mewling, spewing baby.

I want this so much that I think I've stopped breathing.

What does that mean? Could that be the first hint of an appropriate response? It feels right. In fact, it feels much more right than many of my other appropriate responses – for example, raving about *Pulp Fiction*; I'm aware I'm supposed to love the film, I just didn't but best we keep that to ourselves. It's definitely more appropriate than describing beds in galleries as informative and sophisticated, as opposed to wanky.

Exhausted from the effort of climbing three flights of

stairs, I decide to stop for a quick coffee. I reluctantly remember that I should no longer be drinking coffee, and so order a banana milkshake instead, another habit I kicked in the Brownies, but my churning stomach is threatening revolt yet again and is more or less demanding something creamy and calorific. I patiently queue in the bookshop café, nervously eyeing the only free table and wondering if it will be my stomach or my legs that will let me down first. I notice some guy walk into the café, put his bags on a chair at the free table and then join the queue behind me. Let's face it, we've all done it. The bagsie thing. So I'm not perturbed. I take my milkshake and sit on the other side of the table.

Have you ever read one of these books? Have you? I am carrying an alien! A puke-inducing, body-deforming, breast-engorging, amniotic-fluid-drinking (whatever that is) alien!

And the book I've chosen has an obsession with food, too. How tactless is that? Apparently the crown–rump length of the embryo is just over 2 cm; they liken it to an olive, and my uterus is a little bigger than a grapefruit. Yuk, yuk, yuk, yuk. Olives. Now there's a thought. I fancy an olive and some of those cherries they served in really naff drinks in the 1970s. I think I'll nip to Tesco Metro on the way back to the office.

The bagsie guy joins me, I smile, and for the sake of good form I add, 'Hope you don't mind me squatting, there was nowhere else to sit.'

I turn back to my pregnancy book, thus making it clear that I have no intention of talking to him and that my sitting at his table is entirely driven by necessity and not an attempt to leapfrog the lonely-hearts column.

The introduction reads: 'Whether this is your first pregnancy or whether you've already had a child and you are expecting for a second, third or fourth time –' get real '– this is a very exciting time for you. Having a baby developing inside you is an incredible experience.'

Incredible is a word I can agree with. As in unthinkable, unimaginable, suspect.

Turns out that pregnancy is not nine months but nearer ten, well at least forty weeks, a device to prolong the agony. Sorry, obviously I mean to prolong the excitement. And apparently, like the Queen, my foetus has two birthdays, fertilization age and gestational age. By page six, I'm dizzy with confusion brought upon by words such as mucus, cellular debris and endometrium.

'I do mind, actually,' says the bagsie man.

'Sorry?'

'I do mind you sitting here. I have some friends joining me.'

Somewhat taken aback I look up from my book. I doubt the friends bit – this chap looks like a lonely techie nerd, the only friends he'll have are virtual – but I can't very well call him an out-and-out liar.

'Besides I was here first,' he adds, quickly metamorphosing from a techie nerd to an awkward git.

He wasn't, strictly speaking, but I'm too sick and tired to argue; I simply reassure him, 'Don't worry I'll move when they come.' I ought to point out that this level of tolerance and compromise is unusual for me, and unprecedented in London.

'No. That's not good enough. I want you to move now,' says the miserable turd. He's glaring at me with fish-like eyes. Cold and wet.

'Well, I'm not going to, there's nowhere else to sit.' I wave my pregnancy book about a bit and try to stick out my stomach, hoping he'll pick up on my *condition* and feel shamed into leaving me alone. I feel appalling and don't think I could stand up to drink my creamy, gunky drink even if I wanted to. And actually part of me does want to, the part that doesn't like sitting with weirdos, but the other part, the stubborn, I-know-my-rights-you-miserable-twat part, is not prepared to budge.

This guy has glasses and a struggling goatee. He's wearing M&S jeans and a beige sweater. He weighs about nine stone. At a guess I'd say he went to university and studied geography. He reads the *Guardian* and tries to pretend he gets the jokes in *Private Eye*. His mother probably has her hair 'set' once a week at the local hairdresser's, and his father spends most of his day on the allotment. He hasn't got a girlfriend. He's not a threat. I'm prepared to ignore him, to overlook his obvious hostility, to drink my milkshake quickly and leave. But he has other plans.

'You're one of those fucking arseholes, aren't you?' he says.

He says that to me. *To me*.

Look, I live in a cosmopolitan city, I work in advertising, I am not unaccustomed to colourful language. We all know who he means when he says 'fucking arseholes'. He means the Sunday drivers who drive below the speed limit, he means the boy racers who cut you up at traffic lights, and he means traffic wardens who give you a ticket even though they are still writing it when you return to your car. And *he*, apparently, means *me*. I cannot reply. Literally cannot. I know if I speak I will shower the man with every expletive I know (many) in a way that would make a sailor run for cover.

Or I will cry.

Torrents.

It takes every ounce of self-control I possess to reject both these responses. Instead, I quickly finish my drink, gather up my books and leave. Hoping that he can't tell that I'm shaking.

Question: what kind of world is it that I am bringing a baby into? Answer: one where brutal words are said aloud, in a bookshop, by a middle-class, *Guardian*-reading man to a middle-class, milkshake-drinking woman.

7

We fall out of the lift, a rowdy crowd desperate for a drink, tobacco and irreverent chatter. I try not to resent the fact that only one of those three is still a viable option for me. We often have a drink after work – the theory is that this drink is to help us relax; the reality is that we often carry on discussing office politics and, rather than helping us to unwind, our drunken evenings only serve to wind each other up. Still, these nights out are irresistible. If we're drinking on expenses we visit trendy watering holes such as Mash, Attica and Titanic, but if there's no client spondulicks then we usually go to the Crown and Sceptre. This is the grotty local that sells warm, tasteless, overpriced beer; it has carpets splattered with cigarette burns, blood from brawls and vomit from those who can't understand the concept of 'one too many'. It has nothing to recommend it except that it's next door to our office. You can find us there most evenings. Tonight is different again. Brett has a friend who is opening a bar and he's blagged us invites, and although I'll be drinking fizzy water I'm still looking forward to it. Champagne Charlotte's has had the rare and dubious honour of being positively reviewed in *Time Out.* Everyone who is anyone will be there. The boyband is on a mission and I'm in remission. It's been a long day.

'My balls are aching, it's a necessity that I get laid tonight,' comments Karl.

'Darling, you are all charm,' I muse.

'Not getting enough, you effing shirt-lifter?' asks Drew

sensitively. It's the only way they know how to communicate.

Karl snarls some retort, but I miss it because at that moment I notice Hugh in reception. I'm thrilled – it's been a while since he's surprised me by meeting me after work like this. He's obviously being doubly thoughtful since I've told him that I'm pregnant. A fraction of a second later I notice Kate, Hugh's lovable little tyke – except she isn't in the slightest bit lovable – and Tom, who is still so tiny that he is a non-person without any personality at all, not even an offensive one.

My heart sinks. Obviously, I've forgotten some commitment or other. 'You guys go ahead, I'll catch you up.' I sigh.

As they walk towards the door Hugh exchanges a few pleasantries with the lads. They congratulate him on his job move and they all discuss football and bottled beer. They're nearly bosom buddies. In the background I'm beaming. I can't help it, he *is* proud-making. He fits so easily into any social situation, happily chatting and passing the time of day, and yet he's so much cleverer and more distinguished and remarkable than other men.

Although I think Karl is in exactly the same shirt, and Drew is wearing the same suit, but in a different shade.

'Babe.' Hugh turns to me and kisses me full on the lips, holding my face between his hands. I adore the openness, especially after the months of skulking. I cast a cheerful, victorious glance at the boyband, but it's wasted because they've already scooted out of the door, in pursuit of that first drink.

'Babes, you are looking hot,' murmurs Hugh.

'What do you want?'

He grins and I'm grinning too because seeing through his blatant flattery is another sign of our being a legitimate, established couple.

'Buggered up the childminding arrangements, haven't I?' Hugh shrugs and then bangs his hand against his head, managing to leave his hair helplessly ruffled. He plays the little boy lost to his advantage frequently, and whilst it's no longer quite as charming and endearing as it was thirteen years ago it is now quintessentially him and therefore irresistible. 'Becca's at some night course, I said we'd babysit. After all, the sooner she's retrained and back in the workplace the better it will be for us.'

This is undoubtedly true. Becca doesn't work, so Hugh still pays the mortgage on their place and lives rent-free at mine. Well, it would be ridiculous to ask him to contribute towards a mortgage that I can easily afford. We both earn serious salaries and we don't go short on luxuries, never mind necessities. Besides which, Hugh quite rightly points out that Kate and Tom shouldn't have their lifestyle compromised because of the choices that the adults around them made. They're used to having their mum at home. Having said all that, I sometimes wish that she was more financially independent, the emphasis being on independent.

'Fair enough,' I comment as I scoop up the wriggling Tom. Oh God, his nappy needs changing. 'What course is she doing?'

'Furniture restoration.'

I don't see this as a practical choice for a fully trained accountant trying to get back into the workforce. Surely, she should be updating one of her qualifications on tax fiddles. Furniture restoration! A bloody delaying tactic if I ever saw one. She's hardly likely to find employers queuing up to offer her a job bringing a Louis XIV chair back to life. A surge of irritation washes over me and I battle to suppress it. Deep breaths, deep breaths. Bloody Becca always seems to use the children to get what she wants. This reminds me of

Christmas, which was difficult. Naturally, Hugh and I had wanted to spend time together as it was our first official Christmas as a couple and, naturally, Hugh had wanted to spend time with his kids. Naturally, Becca had wanted the kids to be at home over Christmas and, naturally, she did not want to spend any time with me. The feeling was mutual. Besides these immediate warring factions, various grandparents, uncles and aunts had a claim on the kids' time too. If they continue to be so much in demand, they'll be on *Tatler*'s 'most wanted list' before they start prep school. From about August onwards all the various interested parties argued as to where and when they could spend an hour with the monsters. I really couldn't see the appeal of watching them carelessly rip open their carefully wrapped presents, eat the paper, squash the box and break the toy, but it seemed that I was the only person in the Western world that had no such urge.

Finally and unsatisfactorily Hugh spent Christmas morning with the children, at Becca's. I stayed in bed sipping champagne and deciding what underwear to put on for his return. I'd planned that we'd spend the rest of the day making love, only venturing out of bed to eat the amazing and exotic delicacies that I'd prepared. Delicious in a low-key way – ginger and lemon grass risotto served with mustard and black pepper crackers, homemade chocolate soufflé with violet and rose creams, a small *panettone*, and plenty of port. In truth there was absolutely nothing 'low key' about the twelve hours it took me to prepare the food, not to mention the time it took me to plan, source and purchase the ingredients. But, as I'd been waiting for this Christmas for years, nothing was too much trouble. I'd thought that the contrast between such a sensuous and indulgent Christmas and the raucous, chaotic household he'd just left would delight Hugh.

But when he finally arrived back from Becca's (three hours later than agreed) he explained that he'd already eaten as the children were expecting it of him.

Which was good of him, because it wouldn't be fair to disappoint Kate and Tom.

I do a quick calculation in my head and realize that by next Christmas I'll have my own mini-vandal. I believe it less than I believe in Father Christmas.

'Oh well, we can pick up pizzas on the way home.' Resigned, I move reluctantly towards the revolving glass doors. Tom nips my earlobe and Kate swiftly kicks my ankle. I can see we're in for a good night.

Hugh hangs back. 'Er, the thing is, my love, I can't stop. I'm meant to be meeting some clients for dinner. It's the whole intro thing, I can't very well let them down at the last minute like this.'

'Hugh.' My expression speaks volumes of irritation and I would complete the picture by putting my hands on my hips, but I'd drop Tom. I can't say too much in front of the ever-vigilant Kate. She's nearly five going on fifty and repeats everything I say back to Becca. She twists my words in a way that the editors of some of Britain's scummiest tabloids would be proud of. I'm not giving Becca the satisfaction of knowing she caused a fracas.

Hugh walks towards me and puts his arms around my shoulders and rests his forehead on mine. He tries to stare into my eyes but I won't look at him. Instead, I'm staring at the floor – not a very violent protest but my resources are low. There aren't any handy railings that I could chain myself to.

'If you knew how much I'd prefer to spend the evening in with you . . .'

'Really?' I immediately lock eye, forgetting my protest.

'Do you have to ask?' He's using a low, groany voice, the one that indicates that I'm sending him wild with desire. Despite the fact that Tom is pulling my hair clip out of my hair (effect created being chaotic rather than tousled) and I have vomit on my jacket, I am sending Hugh wild with desire. The thought instantly cheers me up. Poor Hugh having to work at night. Reinvigorated, I try to locate Kate. She's terrorizing the security guard; he's trying to shake her off but losing the battle. I try to prise her fingers off his legs but she has a vice-like grip, and the moment I loosen one finger she clamps another one down again.

'I knew you'd be cool with this. You are so good with the kids, you can tell you love them.' Hugh is not so much outright lying at this stage (although what he says is a lie), he's simply deluded. In fact I don't love them. They bore me at best. However, I've made a superb impression of being besotted with them since their births. I suppose I do feel a bit responsible for them. Even though I make their daddy happy (and nothing on this earth makes their mummy happy, so I've given up caring that I *may* have been responsible for some of her unhappiness), I do admit it would have been more textbook, from their point of view, if their parents had stayed together. That's why I'm generous with the mortgage payments and patient with the fact that Becca's lawyers are tardy with the decree nisi. That's why I encourage Hugh to spend as much time as possible with them, and I always drag myself along on their trips to Planet Hollywood or the Disney shop, even though there are other places I'd prefer to be on a Saturday afternoon, combing Bond Street or Harvey Nicks fourth floor, for example.

That's why I'm biting my tongue now, though Kate is biting my thigh. I drag her towards the door with one hand, whilst using the other to carry my files and laptop, and balancing Tom on one hip. I wonder if Kate's violent tendencies are because she's from a broken home or because she's intrinsically genuinely awful.

'It's not a problem,' I assure Hugh brightly and falsely, whilst mentally and reluctantly kissing bye-bye to my noisy night at Champagne Charlotte's. 'Come on, Kate, we'll walk your dad to the Tube and then go and buy a Häagen-Dazs.' She scowls – I might as well have offered to pull out her toenails or torch cute puppies. I reassure myself that the only person who is less enamoured with this childminding arrangement than me is Kate.

We set off towards the Tube station, dodging left and right to avoid large umbrellas belonging to harassed office workers who are dashing to the nearest pub or fighting over available cabs. I glance through the window of Champagne Charlotte's. It looks warm and inviting. It's already heaving with boisterous boys and girls. I look away quickly before Hugh notices my longing. Although he probably wouldn't notice anyway, because he's excitedly telling me about things that happened in the office today. He loves his new job. He's always been extremely driven, but I've never seen him quite so enthusiastic about work in years. He likes the people who work there, he likes the clients, he likes the creativity. He's never been happier and I'm really happy for him. We reach the Tube station. Hugh strides towards the ticket machine. It salves his social conscience to travel by Tube now and again rather than always by taxi. Bugger that, once he is safely on the Northern line I'm going to hail a cab. It's bad enough having to be responsible for Kate and Tom, there's no way I am going to attempt to be so on public transport.

Two of the ticket machines are out of order; two are not giving change; the fifth is surrounded by jubilant Italian teenagers who can't read English and, even if they could understand the instructions on the machine, would feel that it was unpatriotic to hurry. We stand in the miserably long queue, with people with miserably long faces. Kate lies on the floor and screams that she hates me. Hugh doesn't react to this antisocial behaviour ('don't pander to her, that's what she wants'), but grabs his ticket, kisses Tom and the space near my left ear and pushes his way through the ticket barrier.

Kate screams on. This she-devil is the half-sister of the being I'm carrying. That must count for something. I dig deep for some reserves of patience and understanding, whilst sighing silently and hoping to God Kate takes after her mother. I drag her along the dirty tiled floor whilst fruitlessly pleading with her to stand up. Besides the fact that I'm in serious danger of losing my balance and dropping Tom, I can't take any more tuts of disapproval. I want to shout at passers-by that she's not mine, that I'm just shagging her father, but I don't think it will help. God, I'm tired, I'd love to go home right now and hide away under the duvet. Still, there's no chance of that for the next several hours. Scrub that, the next several years. I rally and think of my grandmother's motto, 'make do and mend'. Of course, she was referring to a ripped shirt or frayed basket; I'm battling with shredded patience and tattered nerves.

Surprisingly, we all do make it to the Häagen-Dazs store in one piece. I hand Kate and Tom cones stuffed with tutti-frutti and strawberry ice cream. I know that Becca wouldn't approve of me feeding them ice cream, which secretly motivates me. Kate's cone sways precariously for a split second and then the tutti-frutti hits the deck, leaving evidence of its fall on Kate's school coat and my trousers. She lets up an enormous wail; the horrifying pitch is such that it prompts at least three other customers to consider calling the police and the social services. I quickly buy her a replacement, which she accepts ungracefully, shooting me looks that clearly indicate she holds me responsible for the catastrophe. I have a distinct feeling that it's going to be a long evening.

8

It's Kate who first notices Sam camping on my doorstep. I live in Clapham, and there are often down-and-outs rolling around my neat residential street – it's one of the many colourful juxtapositions that make up London life. However, the vagrants are rarely dressed in Karen Millen and hoofed in L. K. Bennett. Sam and her sadness stand out like Scary Spice on a Saga holiday. Her red-rimmed eyes tell me everything I need to know at a glance. She explains that she couldn't face either checking out ancient names in her palm pilot or going home to her empty flat, which offers little more in the way of company than a bottle of wine and a box of microwave chips. She adds that there's only me who understands 'because we are so alike'. I'm extremely shocked and offended by this comment. It truly terrifies me. Does the outside world see me as such a dismal throwback? Sam thinks the suffragettes were a 1970s pop band. She's a pushover where guys are concerned. It's embarrassing. I may have bemoaned a lack of Hugh in my life in the past, but the difference is I've only ever bemoaned the lack of *Hugh* in my life; Sam has bemoaned Alan, Bart, Clive, Doug, right through to Zachary, all with equal vehemence. It's a big difference. Her inconsistency is maddening, and threatens any real sympathy I might be persuaded to muster.

There again, she found my consistency absolutely bewildering, yet she was always the other end of a handkerchief.

(G&)tea and sympathy are the order of the day.

I try to view her presence as a blessing; at least she always knows how to entertain Kate and Tom. And it's a good thing Hugh had to go out; he wouldn't have seen Sam's presence as anything other than an irritant. Listening to Sam's stories of her countless near misses is some way away from his idea of fun. He claims that her stories depress me and that she causes me to be irritable. This simply isn't true. In fact, the reverse is the case. It's not very nice to admit, but Sam's stories of her hapless love life make me mentally jump with joy that I have Hugh and that I'm in such a great relationship – I mean, there but for the grace of God. Anyway, whenever Sam comes round for a debrief of her unromantic liaisons, Hugh grabs his car keys and mumbles something about 'taking it for a wash' and leaves me alone to the job of supergluing together Sam's shattered heart and self-esteem. I wonder if I could pull the same stunt and leave Kate or Tom in charge of Sam; looking at the state Sam's in, there is only a minuscule chance of the more conventional alternative being a viable option.

Kate falls through the door and runs directly to the sofa. She picks up the remote and tunes in to Cartoon Network. I know that the only way Hugh can ever persuade her to stay in with me is with the bribe of Cable TV. Still, I'm not complaining; one down, two to go. I change Tom's nappy (there really isn't anything more disgusting in the entire world and I simply don't believe mothers who say that you get used to it) and I pop him to bed in the spare room. Finally, I deal with Sam. I pour her an enormous G&T and whilst the kettle is boiling I eat three slices of toast.

'Kate, give me a hug,' demands Sam. I'm amazed to see Kate actually skip across the room into Sam's open arms.

'Can I have one too?' I ask. I can only assume this request is hormone-driven. Kate tuts and sidles reluctantly towards me. Too well drilled to actively refuse, too much of a four-year-old to pretend to enjoy complying. I wish I'd never asked. Her second journey across my coir matting floor leaves another set of muddy wellington-boot prints, and as she hugs me she blows an enormous gum bubble that pops in my hair.

I'd say it was deliberate sabotage but I have no absolute proof.

'I'm sure I've heard your daddy say that bubble gum is not allowed,' says Sam, through her smudged mascara and sniffles. 'Take your wellies off and go and wash your hands before you touch anything.' It amazes me that even a distracted, heartbroken Sam is more capable of babysitting than I am, especially since I'm trying hard. However, the instructions, although well-intentioned, come too late. I can already see sticky fingerprints on the B&O stereo, the aluminium coffee table, the TV, the remote. I'll have to go to the hairdresser's to get the effects of the burst bubble cut out of my hair and, for some reason, logical only to a four-year-old brain, Kate has chosen to take off her muddy wellington boots whilst sat on my white goatskin rug. I sigh but say nothing.

I pour Sam another large G&T (lordy, she got through that one quickly enough) and I try to silence Kate's demands for peanut-butter sandwiches, Coke and Twiglets. I can supply the Coke and Twiglets, as I bought them especially for her, but I don't have any peanut butter. When she visited last week her undisputed favourite sandwich filler was Nutella. Last week I hadn't any Nutella, this week I've stocked up heavily on it, but Kate simply stares at me as though I've suggested poisoning her.

'Yuk. Never touch it,' she yells categorically. 'It's so calorific.'

I'm tempted to tell her that peanut butter is more calorific, but realize that this is not a dignified argument to have with a four-year-old. I offer her avocado and mozzarella, a banana or French plum jam. It appears that neither my fridge nor my life are particularly child-friendly. She finally accepts the banana, pulling a face, which clearly communicates her belief that I am trying to poison her. I wait, expecting her to demand that Sam act as food taster, rather like Queen Elizabeth I. Finally she settles back in front of the TV.

I decide to concentrate on cheering up Sam, at least I'm practised in that skill, but I realize that I am doing a fairly poor job when I can't even remember the name of the guy she's been seeing. Nor do I help myself with my defence – that it isn't my fault; I've only met him once and they've only been an item for five minutes. Sam struggles to hide her irritation and points out that they've been seeing each other for three months. To be pedantic, they've been seeing each other two months, two weeks – she always rounds up. Coincidentally it's the same length of time I've been pregnant. I tell her that she doesn't need a man to define her. She tells me that she *knows* she doesn't *need* a man, and if she had a pound for every time someone has said that she'd stop applying for a slot on *Who Wants to Be a Millionaire?* She just '*wants* one'.

Sam is thirty-five. Her life story is roughly as follows. From the age of nought to fifteen she spent looking beautiful and imagining being Cinderella, or similar (it is my personal belief that this is the reason behind Sam's shoe fetish – in her mind pretty shoes are intrinsically linked to the happily ever after). Aged sixteen to twenty-four she latched on to a specific boy or man for a period of two to three years in the hope he'd propose. This strategy was so extreme and followed so strictly it even led to her delaying her university entrance for three years as she was 'so close' to a proposal from some guy or other. The proposal didn't come, so she changed track and went to university to meet more men. Turned out to be more of the same men because, despite an impressive array of candidates and considerable effort on Sam's behalf, a diamond ring never materialized. When she graduated, aged twenty-four, she heard her body clock ticking so loudly that she thought the wake-up call was coming from Big Ben. In response she shortened the probation period she'd allow for prospective husbands to demonstrate their commitment. Her boyfriends were given anything from a month to six months, maximum. If at that point there was no indication of serious intent (at the very least the suggestion of a weekend break in the Lake District) she dumped ruthlessly. Problem is, Sam attracts commitment-phobes like Winnie the Pooh's pantry attracts wasps. As time passes and Sam panics, she swaps one hopeless case for another with increasing, and alarming, rapidity. The result is that despite being gorgeous, funny, kind and generous, she's still alone.

She's lonely.

Becca is doing a night class in furniture restoration.

And I'm pregnant.

We all have our crosses to bear.

It's a melancholy evening, which bizarrely recommends itself to me. Between us we consume (besides the G&Ts and toast) four pots of tea, an entire packet of chocolate-covered Hobnobs and a fish-and-chips supper (two and a half weeks' calories in less than two and a half hours). Sam also smokes twenty Marlboro Lights and drinks a bottle of Chardonnay.

'You're not drinking?' Sam refills her own glass. She is so absorbed in her own problems that she barely pauses for my response.

'No.'

'Not smoking?' She offers me the pack for a brief second and then lights up and inhales deeply.

'No,' I mutter.

'Another detox programme?'

'Sort of.'

'But you are eating chocolate?' she insists.

'Yes.'

'Odd detox programme. Whose is it?' But she doesn't wait for a reply. It's quite depressing that an absolute reversal of thirteen years of ruthlessly strict habits draws no more attention than this from my best friend, which makes me wonder if we are on different planets. At the very least we are operating in different time zones.

Melancholy tips into maudlin, slips into depression and finally nose-dives into full-scale despair by about 9 p.m. and after the second bottle of Chardonnay. I am actually relieved when Becca arrives to pick up Kate and Tom, as she interrupts Sam's monologue about how she feels incomplete and if that's so wrong, saying a man completes her, then come the revolution put her against the wall and shoot her. I am tempted to shoot her there and then when she crashes into my telephone table, knocking over a vase of flowers, breaking it and spilling water on to a pile of papers that Hugh has left in the hallway.

'I'm not saying all girls are incomplete without guys.' She still calls women 'girls', even though nearly everyone she knows is in their thirties; some would think this endearing. 'But I am saying people, human beings, are incomplete without other human beings; and having one special human being to love me above all others is my nirvana. I'm always the bridesmaid, never the bride.' And so she spews forth her words of wisdom as I encourage her to put on her coat and pashmina and fold her into a waiting taxi. 'I know it's not a fashionable point of view, but it is *my* point of view. I want someone to buy a house with, celebrate birthdays with, have kids with and' – she hesitates – 'recently I've begun to feel fed up that "someone" is always a "different one" or, worse, "anyone".' She grabs my hair and stares at me with an intensity that can only be achieved if you have consumed more than half a dozen units on an empty stomach (you can't count Hobnobs as food) and a dozen more after some fish and chips. 'You understand, you felt just this way about Hugh.'

Yes I did, do.

9

Hugh finally comes home some time after one in the morning. He wakes me up as he gets into bed but I don't let on. If I admit to being awake I'll have to ask where he's been until this time of night. And I don't want to have to do that. He probably persuaded his clients to go to his club after the dinner, which will have undoubtedly been a success (Hugh's charming most of the time, and when he makes the effort he's irresistible). They'll have been bowled over by the fact that he has a private membership at Monte's, especially as Jamie Oliver was actually cooking tonight. It's worth staying late because the lovely Jamie often pops out front after he's hung up his oven gloves. Hugh knows how to show his clients a good time.

Probably.

What am I thinking? Of course he's been with his clients. Bloody hell, I'm becoming really paranoid. If I asked him now he'd tell me all about it.

I think I will ask. Just to prove to myself how stupid I'm being.

On second thoughts, best not, I don't want Hugh to think I'm mistrustful. Besides which, he's unlikely to say, 'Actually, I've been having wild sex with Scandinavian nymphomaniac twins.' Instead I lie very still, trying to ignore the fact that I feel nauseous again. Hugh falls asleep immediately. The smell of alcohol seeps from his pores and his snores reverberate around the room; weirdly I find this comforting. I've never minded his snoring. This is what I wanted. It's intimate. It's us. The street light is leaking through the roller blinds, illuminating the room in parts, and casting shadows in other parts. I can just about make out the silver frames on the Klimt prints, but not the detail of the pictures. Not that I actually need to see them, I know them off by heart. *The Kiss* and the one with the pregnant redhead. Hugh bought me them for my twenty-first birthday. They're just posters bought from Athena but I was thrilled; at the time every other student room was decorated with black and white photos of women wearing big hats and too much make-up or men with bare chests holding naked babies. I had the Klimt posters framed in silver, which the guy in the shop advised against, he was pushing us towards the more traditional gold frame. But Hugh pointed out that gold was such an obvious choice, everyone framed Klimt in gold. So I held out for what I wanted.

Looking at them now I think they might have been better with gold frames.

Still, no point losing sleep over a decision I made donkey's years ago.

I can see the chair at the end of the bed. It's wooden, with a white seat. Hugh has carefully folded his trousers and left them on the chair back. The trousers and a small pile of loose coins next to his side of the bed are the only obvious signs of his inhabitance. Naturally, his other clothes are hanging in the wardrobe and his CDs dominate the rack, his razors are in the bathroom and he has some travel books on my bookshelves – he's not a great reader of novels – but it doesn't seem to add up to very much. Suddenly it doesn't seem very permanent.

God, girl, get a grip.

Talk about middle-of-the-night heebie-jeebies. Of course Hugh's permanent. He was delighted when I told him about the baby. *A baby.* Our baby. That's more permanent than anything we've ever done before. More permanent than touring Mexico, or trekking in China, more permanent than choosing Christmas presents together or visiting aged aunts, more permanent than anything, full stop. And permanency with Hugh is all I've ever wanted. I need the loo. I really, really need to wee. My bladder is groaning. It feels exactly like a balloon stretched to its limit and full of water. And I feel sick. I thought it was supposed to be *morning* sickness. The strain I've got is obviously insomniac and has no regard for time of day. Right now, in terms of permanency, I'd have settled for Hugh putting his name on the deeds of the apartment.

Joke.

I've already been to the loo twice tonight and it's freezing on those bathroom tiles. I lie still for a few more minutes and will the inflated balloon to go away, but it doesn't. In fact, all I can think of is Victoria Falls. I get up, brave the icy tiles and then decide to read a brief Julia has drafted. It's all about odour control in shoes. It's a good paper, and I only have to mark one or two amendments in red ink, like a teacher correcting an essay. One of Brett's team already has the creative solution anyway, so it doesn't much matter what Julia's brief says. He wants to use Moby's song 'Why Does My Heart Feel so Bad?' and change the words to 'Why Do My Soles Smell so Bad?' I'm torn. It's a really beautiful, gravelly, soulful song. If Moby (or more likely, his agent) gives us permission, we'll probably make a great ad that will render odour eaters cool and undoubtedly send the record back up the charts; but I can't help thinking that it will be a shame if Moby's agent does accept the offer. I mean, which lyricist can seriously want their song associated with pongy feet? Just as I am contemplating getting back into bed and fighting Hugh for my half of the duvet, the phone rings. I dash to it, heart pounding; I hate middle-of-the-night calls. They invariably spell trouble.

'George, George. It's me. It's happened!'

'What has, Sam? Are you OK?'

'Never better. George, *it's* happened. Gilbert's proposed!'

'Who?'

'Gilbert.'

Is she still drunk? Isn't he the one we've been questioning the parentage of all evening?

'Gilbert, as in the one who stood you up the night before last?'

'Well, yes, but he explained all that.'

'He was working late, right?'

'No, his tyre blew.'

'And he couldn't get to a phone?' I ask sceptically.

Sam ignores my question. 'George, he's proposed!'

'Right. Yeah. God, how embarrassing, you hardly know him. How did you get out of that?'

Silence.

I suppose I should want to eat my words, but I've only said what everybody must be thinking.

'I didn't want to get out of it,' says Sam, trying desperately to keep the offence out of her voice. 'I accepted.'

'Oh.'

'He's lovely.'

'Good.'

'Seriously lovely.'

'Oh, seriously good, then.'

'Aren't you going to congratulate me?'

I stare at the carpet that is still wet with the water from the broken vase. It seems an indecently short amount of time since I was spooning a sobbing Sam into the waiting cab. Admittedly, I'm not good with sudden change. I'm known to be a creature of habit but this strikes me as the opposite extreme.

'It just seems a little sudden. It would be a mistake to accept the first proposal that comes along, you know, Sam. Just because you want to get married.'

'Oh, and do you suggest I wait for a second one? At the current rate that will be when I'm seventy,' she snaps. 'I love G and he loves me.'

'Who's G?' I ask, momentarily confused.

'Gilbert. I've decided to call Gilbert "G".'

'To make him sound more twenty-first century?'

'No, because I want a pet name for him,' she defends.

'How about G-spot? I mean, he must have hidden talents that you're not telling me about.'

'That's very nasty, Georgina.' Besides which it's stupid, because she's told me everything about G. Me and everyone else for that matter.

'So you love him?'

'Yes. He's reliable and honest.' Except when he stands her up and tells lies about it.

'Those are the reasons you employ a plumber or buy a car,' I point out.

She ignores me. Of course she loves him. Nearly every woman would agree that to be a single woman in London after the age of thirty is not pleasant and when you're tipping thirty-five it is distinctly uncomfortable. Sam thinks it's absolute social failure.

I weigh it up. Should I continue my honesty policy? Which is obviously as popular as a naked Keith Chegwin. Or do I tell her what she wants to hear? I hear myself mutter an apology and I do my best to sound sincere. That is the problem with saying what you think, it's rarely popular.

Better to stick to the appropriate responses. Sod honesty.

'Well, congratulations, Bird. I'm really happy for you.' I struggle for something nice to say about him and finally come up with, 'Good bridge player.' I'm referring to a tiresome evening Hugh and I spent with Gilbert and Sam last month. We had dinner at her place and, naturally, got very drunk during the evening. I suggested we play cards. A light and easy game of 'Aces High' was what I had in mind, but Gilbert was tediously competitive and insisted that we played bridge instead.

'That was a fun evening, wasn't it?'

'Hilarious,' I lie.

'To think I'll be married by the end of the year. I've always wanted to be a winter bride.' This at least is true. In as much as she's always wanted to be a spring, summer, autumn or winter bride.

'Have you told Julia?' I'm interested to hear what Julia has to say about the hasty engagement. I introduced Julia and Sam to one another a year or so back. As they are both single they took to going out together, ostensibly to be independent and go clubbing, patently to find men. However, whilst Sam was hunting for someone to glide down the aisle with, Julia was looking for something altogether less churchy. Her idea of permanency is two dances in a row. Julia, the queen of treat-them-mean-keep-them-keen, does however have a far greater success rate when it comes to follow-up calls. They both regularly treat me to (radically different) accounts of their exploits. Sam is dangerously romantic, poetical and idealistic; the three things that are most notable about Julia are that she is spiky, funny and a bigger bitch than Bette Davis. Therefore she is an excellent gossip; I can't wait to hear what she has to say about this engagement.

'No. I haven't called Julia yet. I thought you should be the first to know.'

I'm itching to swap notes.

I sit down on the floor and settle with my back against the radiator; I sweep the skirting boards with my little finger in an attempt to eradicate all dust.

'OK, so tell me everything,' I instruct, summoning every molecule of enthusiasm in my body.

And she does. She tells me how when she got home from my flat he was waiting for her, armed with bribes (a bouquet of red roses, a magnum of champagne – not that she needed anything more to drink – and a reservation at the Ivy).

'They let you in?'

'Yes.'

'But . . .' But she could hardly stand. I can hardly say so.

She reads my mind. 'They've seen worse.'

I suppose they have. The Ivy is famous for its lush celebs; the alcoholics count is second only to the Groucho club. Besides which, it will have been late. Ten o'clock maybe. Those who go to the Ivy to see and be seen go for eight-thirty.

She tells me that when they got to the Ivy, they didn't eat anything from the menu because he had already prearranged a bespoke selection. He'd chosen all his favourite foods that he wanted to introduce her to. Wasn't that sweet? They started with oysters, which actually Sam hates but she ate them anyway, she's swallowed worse things. Then they had foie gras and water biscuits. It's a good job that Sam had already eaten a fish-and-chips supper, that way she could pretend to have the appetite of a bird, an impression every woman feels compelled to give. And the waiters made such a fuss of them. Gilbert is a regular, and Sam thinks they'll both be dining there frequently in the future. They had such a fun time, neither of them stopped laughing and there wasn't a single pause in the conversation. The food just kept coming, as did the champagne. And it is so elegant. Proper linen tablecloths and decent-sized tables. I let her repeat every word, gesture, inflexion, several times, and largely I manage to stay awake.

'Well, I'm very happy for you, Sam,' I say, trying to bring the conversation to a close. Bored to death, I wiggle my toes; my legs and bum are so numb I fear that rigor mortis has set in. I check my watch – Sam has been on the phone for an hour and a half.

'How are you?' she asks dutifully, obviously feeling a teensy bit guilty that she's neglected this social nicety for ninety minutes.

'Fine.' Instinctively I know that this isn't the 'I'm pregnant!' moment either.

The tedium of Sam detailing the entire contents of the Pronuptia catalogue overwhelms me. I congratulate her again, then I hang up. I'm not sure she notices.

10

I've been in the office precisely ninety seconds. Julia and I don't bother with niceties, but cut to the chase.

'What do you think?' I demand.

'Astounding.'

'At first I didn't have a clue who she was talking about.'

'How could you fail to recognize the hallmark of "G", the International Man of Mystery?' sniggers Julia. (It's natural that we should be a tiny bit bitchy.) 'I bet that pissed her off.'

'Well, I recovered by pointing out that she had called me at 3 a.m.,' I defend myself.

'I'm glad that you're known for your enthusiasm and that I'm known for my lack of it, because otherwise I'd be the one receiving the excited calls at ungodly hours.'

Am I? I consider 'being known for my enthusiasm' for a moment. Is it a good thing? Enthusiasm strikes me as a bit amateurish. Not very cool. Why can't I be known for my sound advice? Or my level-headedness?

'She just called me. I made a huge effort to summon up the proper amount of delight. Should I be delighted?' asks Julia. 'What's he like? It's all happened so fast that I haven't even met him.'

The thing is, we both love Sam.

'Gushing is not my thing,' I lie, trying on a level-headed persona which is alien to me. 'But, yeah, I think we can be happy for her. He seems nice enough. I've only met him once but, unusually for a man of Sam's, he seems genuinely interested in her, her friends, family, job, et al.' I'm saying this partly because it's true but mostly because I want it to be true. 'And he's certainly willing to commit.'

'Definitely a point in his favour as far as Sam is concerned.'

'A necessity.'

'Don't you think the speed is a bit suspect? Could he be a psychopath?'

'Well, he's getting on a bit. Mid-forties, he doesn't have time to hang around.'

'She said that the proposal was everything she ever wanted and more.'

I find that hard to believe. 'Good.'

'She said he looks like a film star – does he?'

I consider. 'Well, not any particular film star that I could name. Not a Ben Affleck or Jude Law, not really a Tom Cruise either, but thinking about it' (generously) 'he does have a generic film-star quality. Perhaps Cary Grant – before we knew he was gay – crossed with Errol Flynn.'

'He wears green tights?' chortles Julia again.

'Stop being mean. He's other-worldly, decent and charming.'

'Dull, then?'

'As ditchwater,' I confirm. 'Still, she's happy that he's so other-worldly, because most men that she's been with have been so "of this world" that their main hobby was downloading porn from the Internet.'

'And she did say that the ring was the one she'd have picked out herself if she'd been given the choice.'

'Oh, my God, the ring, I forgot to ask. It must be the square solitaire from Tiffany.'

'No. I thought that, but it's an emerald cluster.'

'Oh.'

'Still.'

'Still.'

'She seems happy.'

'That's the main thing.'

'Hmmm.'

Having said very little it's obvious that we are in total agreement.

I ring Jessica to tell her about Sam's engagement.

'How lovely for her. I hadn't realized she was seeing anyone seriously. You girls are so secretive.'

'No, we're not.'

'What did she say about your pregnancy?'

'Er, I haven't mentioned it yet.'

My mother chooses to think better of me than I deserve. 'Didn't want to steal her thunder?'

'Something like that,' I mutter.

'Well, what's he like, this Gilbert?'

'He's a 47-year-old, nice enough guy who is a cautiously efficient MD of a small, reasonably successful firm that writes mildly interesting computer programmes,' I say bluntly. I resist adding that he reminds me of everyone's father.

'You don't sound very enthusiastic.'

'I hadn't realized until today that my enthusiasm was so conspicuous,' I grumble.

'And now you have noticed, you're trying to eradicate it?' I can hear exasperation leak into Jessica's voice.

'Sort of.'

'Why? Being enthusiastic isn't a bad thing. Just because you are it, it doesn't necessarily mean it is a bad thing to be. Why do you insist on always trying to be something you're not?' Jessica scolds. I wonder if she's being ironic when she turns the conversation and mentions that she's considering liposuction on her thighs.

February

11

Hugh ruins my Saturday morning almost the instant I open my eyes by asking, 'Are you coming to the gym?' I wish, and not for the first time, that I'd wake up to an offer that we go to the King's Road together or, better yet, out for lunch. Ever since I met Hugh, or more accurately ever since he showed me the photo of the elegant, elongated Becca, the gym has been my torture chamber. It represents all that is evil in the world, i.e. the fact that my genetic make-up veers towards rotund, and the fact that naturally skinny is simply a cruel myth perpetuated by people who starve themselves. I find little comfort that for almost fourteen years I have been one of those perpetuating the myth. My natural state of slothfulness is further exaggerated as during the night someone has poured cement down my throat and now my legs are tonne weights. My back and boobs ache, gold-medal style.

Hugh repeats the question about the gym but, before I can answer him, I have to make a dash to the bathroom to throw up last night's supper. A ritual that has become as intrinsic to my morning routine as applying Estée Lauder moisturizer, or fishing around in the cereal boxes to find plastic models of dinosaurs.

It's almost impossible to think that this is the same bathroom that used to be a zone of erotic pleasure. Hugh and I used to have frantic, fantastic sex in the shower and long, loving bubble baths. The numerous candles and sensuous massage oils are being neglected. I can hardly bear Hugh being in the same flat as me when I puke, so the chances of him getting into the bathroom are microscopic; he's having to grow a goatee.

I am seriously considering suing the publishers and authors of all the maternity books I've read for printing incorrect information. Information that raised my hopes and allowed me to believe that pregnancy was in some way a bearable, if not a desirable, state to be in. The books warn me that a 'small amount of nausea is normal'. Ha! Nausea. It strikes me that nausea is a pitiful word, woefully inadequate, far too refined to describe the reality of the state I'm in. 'Ill' is also a euphemism, because ill suggests that there will be a recovery. 'Queasy' is insultingly mellow, considering there is a huge and constant ball of bile and vomit swelling in my gut. A ball of spew that is insidiously leaking into my nervous and capillary systems, infecting every part of my body. Nothing helps. Not dry biscuits, nor ginger, nor sucking lemons. I consider explaining this to Hugh, but decide there's no point – he gets squeamish if he sees me putting bikini-line wax in the trolley at Tesco's. Instead, I stick to the facts.

'No, I'm not coming to the gym. My personal trainer was a bit shirty when I threw up on the stationary bike last week.'

'You threw up on a stationary bike? How embarrassing.'

'It was. And I threw up in an umbrella stand in Harvey Nicks. The accuracy of my aim cost me £180. Nothing's sacred.'

'Poor you.'

Yes, poor me. I climb back under the duvet and wait, hoping that he'll offer to stay with me and while away the rainy Saturday. He could help me find something to satiate my hunger and at the same time calm my churning stomach.

So far I've come up with pickled onions and tinned pears (simultaneously).

'Well, come for a sauna or a session on the sun bed,' suggests Hugh cheerfully, oblivious to my telepathic plea for company and sloth.

'I can't use the sauna or sun lamps any more,' I reply, not trying too hard to keep the self-pity out of my voice. Pregnancy, I've found, isn't simply about washing vegetables and giving up raw meat.

'Well, it is much more fashionable to use fake tan,' Hugh says.

It's not. It's much more vogue to say you use fake tan but still use sun beds; they give a more even cover. I don't say so. Nor do I comment that some of the maternity books I've been reading suggest it's better to avoid fake tan as well for the duration of the pregnancy. The books are American; I can't take them too seriously. Hugh doesn't offer to stay with me, but simply comments, 'Perhaps it's a good thing that you're throwing up so much if your workouts are going to be restricted.' I can't be bothered to point out that even if I do more tactical chunders than a supermodel, between now and the delivery, I'll still be obese.

'Well, if you're not coming to the gym, can you pick up my suit from the dry-cleaner's?' asks Hugh, as he starts to pack his sports bag. He sweeps the bathroom shelves, collecting up deodorant, shampoo, shower gel, shaving cream.

'Yes,' I mutter, although I had planned to hide in bed all day. I ought to buy him a double set of all his toiletries; then he could keep one lot in his gym bag and one lot in the bathroom – it would make things much easier for him.

'And buy a birthday card for my mother.'

'I already have, you just have to sign it.'

'Oh, great. Well done.' He starts to search his drawers for

something. As he becomes more frantic he scatters socks and T-shirts on to the floor like confetti.

'What are you looking for?'

'Sports socks.'

'Second drawer down on the left.'

'Oh, right, thanks. And my blue Nike shirt?'

'In the dryer.'

'Great.' He rushes downstairs, leaving a Hansel and Gretel trail of clothes behind him. He comes back into the room with his squash racket but no Nike shirt.

'Your shirt,' I remind him.

'Absolutely. Right.' He grins and runs back downstairs. 'What would I do without you?'

'You'll never have to find out,' I shout after him. Which is true, and a much nicer thing to say than, 'Just leave, just go and play squash!' which is on the tip of my tongue.

The door bangs behind him.

Bye, then.

Even under the duvet I can see that there's regurgitated Weetabix on my shirt. Without surrendering my horizontal position I wiggle out of the shirt and throw it in the general direction of the dirty-laundry basket. Then I sleep.

The telephone ringing wakes me up. I feel around for the handset.

'Hello.' I try and project an alert and jolly tone into my voice, so that whoever is calling can't tell I was asleep.

'Were you asleep?' demands Hugh.

'Er.' Truth or tiny, little, white lie?

'It's midday,' he adds, his tone betraying exasperation and disgust.

Lie then. 'No, I was just by the telephone, dusting.'

'Oh. Isn't that what we have a cleaner for?'

Maybe I should have said painting my toenails; dusting gives off all the wrong vibes. It's too domestic. Also, it implies I don't manage the cleaner properly.

Luckily Hugh has much bigger things on his mind. 'I've had a brilliant idea.'

'What?'

'Let's throw a dinner party to tell all our friends about the baby.'

'That *is* a good idea.' Sweetie. He's so pleased about this baby!

'Knew you'd think so. How about tomorrow?'

'Bit short notice, isn't it?' We often throw lunch or dinner parties, and in my experience they cannot be pulled together at the last minute. At least, not if you serve a minimum of three different nibbles with the four different cocktails, a starter, a main course and a pudding, mints, coffees and cognac. Handmade pastry, hand-whisked soufflé, hand-ground coffee. And we always want to do all this.

'You like a challenge,' he urges.

I don't like to look incapable so I stall. 'Not the cooking.' I manage to hit a note which implies 'Ha, cooking, that will be a breeze'. 'Short notice for the guests. Everyone will be doing something.'

'Don't worry. I sounded out a couple of the chaps at work yesterday. They said they could make it for seven-thirty.'

Right.

'Did you ask Sam or Julia?'

'Babes, I thought you'd want to tell your closest girly friends the big news in a more personal way, not at a dinner party. You should call them.'

True. I should. It's odd to think that when I got my job at Q&A Sam knew within hours of my signing the contract. When I first kissed Hugh, illegally, I called her within minutes to give her the details. In the past neither of us would have considered it odd if I phoned her to ask her opinion on whether I should buy 'the red one or the blue one' (dresses, that she'd never even seen). I'm eleven and a half weeks pregnant; according to the scary books, this being I'm carrying is close to 0.18 oz (5 g), and is the size of a small plum. (The food obsession continues.) It has eyelids and clearly defined fingers and toes and yet Sam doesn't even know of its existence. Sam who knows how many lipsticks I own and the precise shades of all thirty-seven handbags in my wardrobe.

Perhaps that's why the handbags still seem more real.

I call Sam and Julia and get them to agree to meet me at the Bluebird Café, on the King's Road. I think that the service is dire and the food is overpriced, but it is terminally trendy and I'm a sucker for the glamour. Besides, the supermarket there stocks the most gorgeous delicacies. I'll be able to pick up some 'cheating' groceries for the dinner party.

12

It's a dark, February Saturday afternoon. Shop windows, sporting vast displays of red nylon underwear and faded boxes of Milk Tray, are the only interruption to the greyness of the streets, the weather, the people. The hope is that these Valentine's window displays will rekindle the flagging passion of the British public. Not so much a long shot, more an Olympic challenge. Thank God Hugh has more style. He's not a curry and a couple of pints type of guy; the lingerie he buys me is always silk, wrapped in enough tissue paper to cover the Empire State Building. I imagine that he'll whisk me to the George V, in Paris, for a weekend.

Not that he's mentioned anything, and Valentine's Day is now less than two weeks away. Still, I love surprises.

Julia arrives first.

'God, you're looking rough, another hangover?'

I wish. She immediately points out that my trousers are held together by a complex engineering feat involving safety pins and a belt belonging to Hugh. I try to convince her it's high fashion.

Sam arrives in a halo of happiness. Her first words are, 'I can't stay too late, G is expecting me.' This isn't necessarily true, but it allows Sam to introduce Gilbert into the conversation within seven syllables. Then with suitable aplomb she orders champagne. It may only be mid-afternoon but she hasn't drunk anything else since she got engaged. I order a mineral water.

'So, why the council of war?' asks Sam, as she takes a sip

of the champers. I can only imagine how good it must taste. Dry, crisp, off-limits.

'Problem at work?' asks Julia, as though I'm single-minded.

'I've some news.'

'Oh, my God, *you are getting married*,' yells Sam, jumping up and spilling her drink. She flings her arms around my neck and starts to sing the wedding march. I stay utterly still. 'That's absolutely *the* most fantastic news I could have hoped to hear,' she giggles.

'You're pregnant,' says Julia, identifying the look of bemused vulnerability and desperation that I'm sporting as something other than pre-wedding jitters.

'Yes,' I confirm, 'I'm pregnant.' I am sure there are more elegant ways of breaking this news. But, 'I'm blessed' or 'the stork is going to be making a delivery' must have seemed ridiculous even in the nineteenth century. 'I'm up the duff' or 'creek without paddle' may be more accurate but are more emotive than I want to be at this stage in the conversation.

Sam stops dancing around me. For a moment she is lost for words. She rallies and says, 'That's the second best piece of news I could hope to hear.' Then, because she's not entirely ensconced in cloud-cuckoo land, she adds, 'Isn't it?'

I try to pull my face into an appropriate celebratory expression and I try to nod, but I think the gesture ends up looking like a shrug.

I should be ecstatic, shouldn't I? Because Hugh is, isn't he? We are going to be a family, how perfect is that? Although I hadn't really envisaged the culmination of all my dreams as me spending days cleaning puke off the bathroom tiles. Whilst I'm sure ecstasy is waiting in the wings, my immediate response is considerably less gung-ho.

Sam and Julia stare at me expectantly.

Maybe I'll just tell them that some of it unnerves me. Some of it has left me a little out of sorts.

Surely they'll laugh and tell me that lots of their friends/cousins/sisters/neighbours felt exactly like this. That they too were held hostage by their emotions and were victimized by their bodies in the same way. We always have consoling counter-examples to hand to comfort one another, whatever the situation:

'So he said he wanted more space and can only see you one night a week, don't worry. A friend of mine had a boyfriend who wanted more space so he trained as an astronaut.'

'Not giving you a house key is not an inability to commit. My cousin was dating this guy for three months and he wouldn't give her his telephone number. Now that's an inability to commit.'

'I've been feeling quite ill,' I mutter, the crowning glory of understatement. 'I still don't quite believe it.' My luck, or lack of it, that is. However, neither of them rush to make me feel part of the human race. Instead Sam giggles disproportionately and asks, haven't I ever heard of the old adage, 'If you can't be good, be careful.' I nearly argue that, 'It's easy to be wise after the event', but then I catch myself. She's really going to have to stop resorting to these pathetic old sayings, not least because they're infectious.

They ask the same questions as my mother and Hugh did.

'How long have you been trying?' (Sam). Oh, *pleeease.*

'How far gone?' (Julia). Too far.

Sam adds a new one. 'Well, accidents will happen. So when will you be getting married?'

'No plans as yet,' I comment breezily and make a pretence of trying to catch the eye of the waiter.

'But you will be getting married,' insists Sam.

'We're not really the type of couple to be tied down by all that conventional stuff,' I bluff.

'So he hasn't mentioned it, then?' asks Julia.

'No,' I admit.

'But Hugh's pleased.' It's half statement, half question, from Sam.

'Oh, yes,' I assure them. I consider telling them about the dinner party he's throwing to celebrate the news, then I remember that neither of them are invited and so I keep quiet.

'That's what all the flower business was about,' adds Julia.

'Yes.'

The day after I told him, Hugh sent the most enormous bouquet of pink roses to my desk at Q&A. An hour later I received irises. An hour after that pink lilies, and then cornflowers. He alternated pink and blue flowers every hour for the entire day.

Sam almost wets herself when I tell her this and I know she's making a mental note to instruct Gilbert that he must do the same when the time comes. This makes me feel dreadful, because my reaction to Hugh's generosity wasn't as enthusiastic. The gesture was ridiculously generous; I couldn't carry them all home and had to give most of them to the secretaries. But besides being ridiculously generous it was in fact just plain ridiculous. Karl guessed that I must be pregnant and cranked the rumour machine into operation, within twenty minutes of the second bouquet. Brett suggested starting a whip-round to buy me a carrycot. I'm surprised Julia missed the furore; she must have been doing some serious drugs the night before and sleeping it off in the boardroom, as is her way. It was all slightly embarrassing, because I hadn't had a chance to discuss my pregnancy with Dean, my boss. He sent me an e-mail demanding to know whether he had to 'write me off to the great pool of gaga women on maternity leave'. This is probably against some

European employment law, and when I pointed out as much to him he succinctly replied, 'Bollocks to the garlic-eaters.' In the advertising industry a sympathetic employer is one who puts a Tampax machine in the loos.

Besides which, I know that Hugh did exactly the same for Becca when she fell pregnant with both Kate and Tom. I remember her telling me.

'And you are pleased, aren't you?' asks Julia again.

There is a slight, almost indiscernible tension in the air. I should be. I know I should be. I want to be. But can 'want' and 'should' combined counter the distinct feeling that I'm not?

'Because your car only has two seats,' Julia prompts.

'Joseph doesn't do maternity wear,' adds Sam.

'It will be the end of your exotic holidays.'

'And sex on the stairs.'

'And sex, full stop. So, are you?' prods Julia.

And I barely hesitate before I answer, 'Absolutely. Thrilled. Absolutely thrilled.'

The girls beam at me, reassuring me that I've just hit upon the appropriate answer. And it's probably a good thing that the voice that said I'm 'thrilled. Absolutely thrilled' sounded more committed and cheerful than I really am.

13

We spend the rest of the afternoon talking about Sam's wedding, a safe topic for me, the only topic for Sam, and a foray into a foreign country for Julia. Sam is sky-high. Bugger drugs, this is her answer: an emerald and a cluster of diamonds on the third finger of her left hand. She holds her ring up to the window for about the zillionth time today and then turns back to us with a smile as wide as the Eurotunnel.

'Can you believe that I've been engaged for two weeks and two days, a whole three weeks next Thursday.'

'Really.' Seems a lot longer.

'Where has the time gone? Not so much flown past as rocketed.'

I wipe the steamy window of the café and lose myself in the world outside, leaving the burden of conversation to Julia. I don't expect Sam will require too much active participation.

I'm glad I chose the Bluebird because the King's Road always cheers me up. The shops are divine, as are the people who frequent them. Admittedly, they aren't often very polite or smiley, but they look amazing. I'd wager that there's not a man who earns less than £60K, nor a woman who is bigger than a size 10, on the King's Road today.

Except me, of course.

Suddenly the thought isn't as cheering as it usually is.

What is Sam saying now?

'The last couple of weeks have been awash with champagne and goodwill. It's true everyone loves a lover. You only have to drop the slightest hint to your hairdresser that you are newly engaged and suddenly it's all free honey and primrose conditioner, coffees and magazines.'

I can always buy my own.

'It's the same in shops – assistants positively crowd around my ring, sizing it up and admiring it.'

Wondering how much he thinks she's worth. It's probably just my hormones that won't allow me to be as happy for Sam as she'd like.

As I'd like.

I wish I knew Gilbert a bit better. Perhaps I can persuade her to have a long engagement.

'Would you like to try on my ring? It's lucky, you know; if you twist it around your wedding finger three times you can make a wish,' Sam offers.

I notice Julia is looking as sick as I feel. Macabrely, I find this a comfort. I do wish Sam'd stop all this 'Wanna be in my gang, my gang' stuff. If I wanted to be married, I would be married, but I wanted Hugh and Hugh's already married. My head suddenly fills with cotton wool. Why would I want to be married? Marriage comes with in-laws, and, in this case, stepchildren. Isn't marriage synonymous with endless sock-washing and family teas? I've never imagined myself married.

But then I've never imagined myself not married, either.

And I already wash his socks.

'I'm almost worn out with celebrating. I wish you'd seen my parents' reaction.'

'Pleased, were they?'

'Delighted. Daddy never says much at all, but I could tell by the way he opened his malt whisky and offered G a cigar that he approved of my choice.'

'I bet they have loads in common,' says Julia. I snigger

and try not to catch her eye as I catch her oblique reference to Gilbert's age. Sam, wrapped in dreams like tissue paper, doesn't catch it either.

'I *was* rather annoyed with Eddie when he commented that Mummy and Daddy had probably spent the money they'd put aside for my wedding as they must have "given up hope of anyone actually proposing".' Whilst Sam is doing her best not to appear troubled by her brother's insensitivity I can see indignation burns in her eyes. Quite right. It may be an open secret between her family and friends that she's always been extremely keen to marry and have a family, but it does seem in rather bad taste to mention it in front of Gilbert.

'What did Gilbert say?' asks Julia.

'Oh, G was the perfect gentleman, assuring Eddie that he imagined that "Samantha must've been fighting off suitors for years", and anyway he'd be more than happy to pay for the day of my dreams.'

'Samantha?' I ask.

'He calls me Samantha, he prefers it, he thinks it's more sophisticated than Sam.'

He's trying to make her sound older, she's trying to make him sound younger – is there hope that they'll collide somewhere in the middle? I feel like a bit part in *Back to the Future*.

'Good for him. I bet that shut baby bruv up,' comments Julia. 'Who are you having for bridesmaids?' She is obviously angling for an invite. Bloody cheek, she can get in line. Julia's only known Sam a year or so, I've known her a lifetime.

'Well.' Sam is suddenly and unusually reticent. She obviously finds this question excruciatingly difficult to answer. Her reticence ensures my absolute undivided attention much more easily than her earlier recital of the order of service had. 'Well, there's Connie who I used to work with, my friend Daisy, because I was bridesmaid for her, and I was gong to ask both of you,' she says, looking at Julia but without looking at me. 'But . . .' The but is loud and clear.

'In light of my news.'

'Exactly.'

'Now, I'm pregnant, it's out of the question.' I bite out the words, furious with myself for making it easier for her to slight me. I try to smile and try to look unconcerned. It's not that I desperately want to be a bridesmaid. Just because I'm her oldest and bestest friend. I mean, who wants to dress up in fuchsia and frills?

Me.

Me.

I do.

That's how irrational I am. It's not my fault, it's my hormones.

I smile a brittle smile that is all teeth and that definitely hasn't made it to my eyes. OK, so there would be a serious possibility that I would look like an Easter egg staggering up the aisle, but I'm her best-friend Easter egg. Sam might want four identical size-10 bridesmaids, but it's not very real, is it? Couldn't she get married after I've given birth? Or not care that I'd look like an Easter egg? She shouldn't see it as me ruining her photos, she should think of it as enhancement – she'd look like Kate Moss in comparison.

Julia tactfully picks up one of the many bridal books that Sam has taken to carrying around with her, *How to Create Your Perfect Wedding Day*, and asks whether it's any good. I know that she couldn't care less, but Sam answers the inquiry as though it was genuine.

'It's very helpful. It tells you all about the order of service and wedding lists and civil services. It's terribly modern, suggesting seating arrangements if the bride or groom's parents have divorced and remarried, up to three times each. And there's a section that you might find useful, George – it outlines the proper etiquette as to whether the groom should mention the unborn child in his speech. It seems to depend upon whether the bump is desperately obvious. It also has suggestions as to where stepchildren should sit. All very interesting stuff.' Yeah, right. 'And there's a handy wedding planner at the back of the book. It's tear-out, so you can carry the planner around in your handbag. It's extremely useful, timetabling when to send out invites, book cars and order almond favours. There are neat little boxes where you can tick off each task as you complete it, which I've always found very satisfying.'

I bet Julia wishes she'd never asked.

My mobile rings, saving me from having to slice out Sam's tongue. It's Hugh. When he hears that we are at the Bluebird Café, he says he'll swing by and pick me up. I'm delighted and don't try very hard to keep the smugness out of my voice when I tell the others his plans. Sam might have the ring but where's Gilbert, hey? At least Hugh actually wants to spend time with me. The wind is somewhat stolen from my sails when Sam announces that Gilbert is busy taking *her* mother to *her* great-aunt's, and she didn't even have to go along. Whichever way I look at this (soppy, wet creep or amazing, gentle man), I have to admit it's the action of a devoted lover.

I leap ahead again on the silent 'I have the better deal' poll when Hugh arrives. He looks sweaty and relaxed from his game of squash and unquestionably knicker-dropping gorgeous. I know for a fact that when Sam looks at Gilbert her first thought is not that she must dash to Agent Provocateur and stock up on scanty panties. The sexiest thing that

Sam has ever said about G is that 'there's many a fine tune to be played on an old fiddle'. This is the only reference that Sam has ever made to their sex life. Which is odd, when you think that in the past Sam has always told us about her conquests in such gratifying and gratuitous detail that after her debriefs I always felt like going to confession, and I'm not even Catholic.

I turn my lips to Hugh's (which always look bee-stung tender). He kisses me on the forehead and asks if I've told everyone our news. Establishing that I have, he orders a bottle of Bolly, shunning the house champers that Sam and Julia have been drinking all afternoon. Then he engages Sam in a conversation about bridal magazines. I feel ridiculously smug, even if I can't enjoy the Bolly.

'Aren't they all the same?'

'Not at all. There's *Brides*, *Brides and Setting up Home*, *Bride and Groom*, *Bridal Beauty*, *Beautiful Bride*, *Just Brides*, *For Brides*, *Wedding Day*, and *Beautiful Weddings*. You've only flicked through them; if you read them properly, you'd realize that each and every one has its own individual style.'

If he read them properly I'd have him committed.

'Doesn't it make you want to take the plunge?' asks Sam. She playfully pokes Hugh in the ribs, and at this point I'd cheerfully kill her.

'What, tie the knot?' he asks.

'Yes.'

'Are you oblivious to the connotations? Tie the noose, more like. If you looked up knot in a thesaurus, you'd find "snarl", "tangle", "web", "difficulty", "conundrum".' Hugh laughs. 'Once was enough for me.'

I've always thought it's best to know where you stand.

Julia diverts the conversation, but I don't think her intentions are entirely altruistic towards me, more mischievous towards Sam, whom Julia finds too easy a target to resist ridiculing. 'It must be a relief for you to actually be able to purchase one of these, sorry, several of these, magazines, Sam.'

Sam, bless her, doesn't take offence, but takes the comment at face value and nods enthusiastically. The truth is that for years Sam has visited newsagents and surreptitiously flicked through the glossy pages, fantasizing about flowing white dresses, debating tiara or flowers, agonizing over the cut of the bridesmaids' dresses. She'd almost wear the pages thin with handling. I know this because she once told me that she felt bad about leaving the mags in less than pristine condition for real brides-to-be to buy; but then she comforted herself with the thought that *they were real brides*. Whereas she used to have to wear a ring (that she'd bought for herself in Turkey) on her wedding finger to convince the shop assistant there was serious intent to purchase.

We stay in the Bluebird until Hugh, Sam and Julia are guaranteed hangovers tomorrow, which worries me a bit because I haven't started to prepare for tomorrow's dinner party. I have garlic to peel, chillies to chop and deseed, prawns to marinate . . . Still, at least I won't feel as isolated when my body is convulsed with nausea in the morning. I pay the bill, hail cabs for Sam and for Julia, and then help Hugh back to his car.

Hugh wraps his arms around me, trying to find the place where my waist used to be. I make a small manoeuvre to avoid his grasp; I'm too podgy to touch. As he's obviously in no fit state to drive, I take the keys. I'm beginning to feel queasy again; which seems unfair, because I haven't eaten anything rich and I've only drunk water all day.

'Kate and Tom are coming over tomorrow,' he says.

Whoopee do.

'Really? Had any ideas as to what we should do with them?' I ask, as I lower him into the car. We always do something. I usually arrange tickets for the London Eye, or a visit to an aquarium or the London Zoo, etc. Hugh's kids never sit in and simply watch *Little House on the Prairie*, like I had to when I was a kid. What I really fancy is an ice pop or a Yorkshire pudding.

'No,' comments Hugh, 'any suggestions?'

'I'll put my mind to it.' Between skewering and chilling and chopping and sautéing. I sigh. Tinned peaches with salt and vinegar crisps might help. I don't mean for the dinner party, I mean now.

'Did you buy Kate any Nutella?' asks Hugh.

Ah, Nutella, that's the answer. I screech the Boxster to a halt outside a Cullens, flick on the hazard lights and dash in to buy a jar of Nutella. I'm parked on a double red line but, after all, this is an emergency – I can't wait to get home to eat the jar in the fridge. Hugh initially assumes I'm being particularly solicitous of Kate and his face oozes pride and pleasure, but as soon as I'm back in the car I open the jar and scoop a large dollop on to my finger and cram it into my mouth. Hugh says nothing, but his look of approval dissolves and he stares with open disgust as I continue shovelling.

'Kate prefers peanut butter,' I mutter by way of a defence.

14

'So, what's on the menu?'

'Coriander-marinated prawns, chilli and lemon olives and herb-chicken skewers as nibbles. Linguine with sardines to start, monkfish baked with crème fraiche and panzanella for main, and a chocolate soufflé to finish.'

'Hope no one is allergic to fish. Have you bought flowers?'

'Yes, but I haven't had chance to put them in vases yet; they're still in a bucket of water in the utility room.'

'Oh, George, isn't it a bit warm in there for flowers? They'll open prematurely.'

'Yeah, sorry,' I mumble as I quickly rub moisturizer into my neck. How old do I look? Twenty-eight? Fifty-five? I can't decide. I looked about twenty-eight this morning, but after a day with Kate and Tom I could probably apply for a bus pass and no questions would be asked. I snatch a pair of tights from my top drawer and start to examine them for runs.

'What are you wearing?' asks Hugh.

'Er, maybe my grey hipsters from Joseph.' If I can still get into them.

I rattle through my extensive wardrobe in a hapless attempt to locate a pair of trousers or a skirt that will negotiate my spreading hips and protruding stomach. I gather up four or five outfits and take them into the bathroom. I want to try them on where Hugh can't be a witness. I have a horrible feeling that none of my clothes, selected to emphasize my normally board-flat stomach, will now zip up. Oh

God. Stop the sushi bar, I want to get off. Hugh is unaware that I'm trying to carve out some privacy and follows me into the bathroom. He sits on the loo and chatters. This intimacy is lovely, obviously. But I would much prefer it if I could simply *emerge*, dressed, made-up and accessorized. I don't want him witnessing my undignified wrestle with fashion; besides he'd be much better employed in the kitchen. I haven't made the champagne framboise or the manhattans yet, let alone stoned the dates or chilled the mascarpone for pudding.

Eventually I find a Cerruti skirt, which I am able to bribe and tease my corpulent flesh into. It looks OK with the Carolina Herrera shirt, providing I don't tuck the shirt in but leave it hanging over the groaning zip. I look in the mirror and try to decide whether I'm presentable enough.

'How do I look?' I ask, as I nervously run my hands over the skirt in a pointless attempt to flatten it.

Hugh stands behind me and looks in the mirror at my reflection. He doesn't answer, but starts to kiss my neck and his hands weave their way to my breasts as though on autopilot. In a matter of weeks I've grown from a very attractive 32C cup to a 36DD. Personally, I think my big bosoms are farcical, it's a look that should be confined to postcards sold on Blackpool pier. Luckily, Hugh is more enamoured but, less luckily, he shows his appreciation by constantly lurching at his new toys. The thing is, my swollen breasts are so painful that I swear if he tries to touch them again I will not be responsible.

Knifing him is too humane. Why should I be the one left alone to cope with the baby? Kneeing him in the groin or hitting him with the nearest blunt instrument are options. I've often wondered why there's always a copy of the Gideon Bible in the bedside drawer in hotels; now it's clear.

Just kidding.

I check my watch. The guests are due in forty minutes. The wine is still under the stairs and not in the fridge. Hugh kisses my neck and then he turns me towards him and starts to unbutton my shirt. If we make love, the seared and marinated tuna, the herb-chicken skewers, the coriander-marinated prawns and the chilli and lemon olives will not be ready in time for the guests' arrival. Hugh's kisses become increasingly intense. Well, we do have some Bombay mix in the cupboard. I could put that in little bowls. That always looks nice.

Forty minutes later the doorbell rings; Hugh is in the shower and yells to me to answer it. There hasn't been time for me to get showered so I greet the guests feeling distinctly shabby. I suppose that it is some consolation that the just-shagged look is undoubtedly better than the just-vomited one I've been wearing so openly of late.

Hugh had said this supper was an opportunity to announce the pregnancy to our friends, so I'm a bit taken aback when I open the door to six smiling faces, none of which I recognize. I comfort myself that everyone seems pleasant enough and I try to think that strangers are just friends not yet made. The strangers who are friends not yet made beam at me and shout out all at once, 'Seth', 'Piers', 'Hedley', 'Jasmine', 'Eve', 'Viv'. It's not easy to know who owns which name. I beam back and offer to take their coats. The embarrassment increases substantially when the first chap through the door makes the mistake of assuming I'm Hugh's wife. Hugh canters down the stairs in time to explain, 'This isn't Becca, this is George.' Which seems to clear the matter up.

'Oh, I am sorry,' says Seth/Piers/Hedley, colouring, but

the others help him out of the excruciating moment by laughing raucously at his mistake. Which is nice of them.

Hugh leads his guests through to the sitting room and I try not to dwell on how Seth/Piers/Hedley could mistake me for Becca. Indeed, how they even know about Becca's existence. Why would Hugh have a need to talk about Becca to his new work colleagues? Becca is history. I pass around the Bombay mix and then go to the kitchen to pour drinks and check on the food in the oven. Hugh follows me through.

'Have you come to help? You could mix the dressing for the salad,' I suggest.

'Oh, I'd best not.' He smiles and pulls a face that clearly communicates Christ-no-don't-let-me-near-I'd-mean-well-but-undoubtedly-cock-it-up-so-sorry-old-thing.' Honestly, I think Hugh Grant copied it off my Hugh. 'Best leave the cooking to the expert,' he adds, then he smiles and pats my bottom. Before I get chance to bask in the glory of the compliment he adds, 'Bombay mix, though, darling – what's going on?'

'Well, you distracted me.' I smile and try to catch his eye so we can share the joke, but it's hard because he's concentrating on opening a bottle of wine. He shakes his head in genuine bewilderment, then comments, 'You need to blend in your foundation along your jawline.' And, whilst it probably isn't relevant, I can't help but remember that, besides the indiscretion with the tennis coach, Becca made the fatal mistake of 'letting herself go'. Too many coffee mornings and finishing up the kids' plates.

I feel as though I've just been shown the yellow card.

Despite the inauspicious start, the dinner party turns out to be a relative success. I say relative in so much as the monkfish is delicious and the soufflé is perfect. And I suppose it is a good thing that I can't drink – I'm certainly more efficient when it comes to pouring other people's drinks; in the past Hugh has often mentioned that when I've had one too many I forget to pour the guests drinks and just keep refilling my glass. Which is unforgivable.

But perhaps understandable if our guests are always so mind-numbingly boring.

How can Seth, Hedley and Piers possibly think that talking exclusively about advertising is interesting? I know we are all 'in the business', as advertising people like to say (as though there were only one business to be in), but surely their interests extend beyond this single topic. More perplexing still, how could Jasmine, Viv and Eve think that not talking at all, but simply smiling and simpering, is a valid contribution? I cooked for them, didn't I? The least they could do is bring a bottle of wine and an entertaining anecdote. Despite having to keep one eye on the oven timer I try a number of different topics, all to no avail. It's pretty clear, within the first twenty minutes, that a conversation about UN law is going to be a stretch, but they stare equally vacantly as I recall a particularly amusing sketch in the last episode of *South Park*. I then try something more hallowed in the hall of comedy fame and start to recite Monty Python scripts – not a flicker. They don't have opinions on West End plays, whether Posh is too thin, or even the current *Corrie* story line. All of my usual conversation starters are met with polite but firm rebuffs.

I'm not sure what I'm doing wrong.

Hugh obviously knows how to communicate with them. Eve laughs at every word he utters, including, 'Refill?' and Jasmine practically has an orgasm when he passes the cheese board and asks, 'Can I tempt you?'

Still, accepting the fairly dire company I cannot help but wait with bated breath for Hugh's announcement. I've waited throughout starter, main and pud, but he's made no hint. I pour the coffee and pass the brandy, and I'm almost giving up hope that Hugh has remembered what this dinner party is supposed to be about when, suddenly, he goes to the kitchen and comes back with a magnum of champagne. I rush to find the glasses.

'I'd like to make a small announcement.' He grins, naturally basking in the fact that he has everyone's attention. He fills the glasses and passes them around. Hugh raises his glass and the light from the candles dances giddily with the bubbles in the champagne. Everyone waits – the chaps are genuinely interested, as they are probably assuming that Hugh is about to announce that RR&S have won a new account, the girls are affecting polite interest whilst desperate to feel the champers hit their throats, as champagne always represents an explosion of possibilities.

'Please raise your glasses to toast the beautiful Georgie, who is about to become the mother of my third child.'

There is a fractional pause before Seth/Piers/Hedley find their manners. 'To Georgie, congratulations,' they affirm. I think that as they've had a fair bit to drink it took a moment for the news to sink in, and perhaps it would have been better if Hugh hadn't mentioned that this is his third child, although obviously the first one with me. But then again I can't expect him to ignore Kate and Tom's presence. Viv giggles but does manage 'fabulous news'. Eve and Jasmine barely mutter 'congrats' before quaffing the champers and holding out their glasses for a refill.

'Are you having it privately? At one of the "too posh to push" hospitals?' asks Hedley.

'I haven't thought about it,' I confess, and I turn to Hugh

to gauge his opinion. He doesn't comment as he's busy pouring drinks.

'Names, had any thoughts?' asks Eve.

'I like Lizzie,' I offer tentatively.

Eve turns to Hugh. 'What do you think of Lizzie?' she demands.

'Don't know her, what does she look like?' asks Hugh.

And everyone laughs loudly, as though his joke was absolutely the funniest thing anyone's ever said.

15

'Darling, how are you?'

'Fat, sick and tired.'

My mother ignores my answer because it's not what she wants to hear, and I'm left wondering if I spoke at all.

'Guess where I am.' Before I can take a breath to reply, she continues, 'Heathrow. Quick stop before I go to New York. I *have* to shop.'

She says that she 'has to shop' with the same seriousness that other people reserve for 'I have to pass these final exams' or 'I have to battle this debilitating disease'.

'Cape Town does a marvellous sunset, but it's rather dire when it comes to retail therapy. Let's meet up.'

What will I wear? It was a depressing day when I could no longer button my jeans all the way to the top, but it was nothing on today. Today I couldn't tug them past my knees. Every bit of me has metamorphosed. I knew pregnancy was about getting a big stomach; if only it stopped there. It's about big stomachs, big legs, big arms, big bum, big cheeks, big ankles, big bosoms.

And small self-esteem.

I've religiously read the pregnancy book and followed, with some trepidation, its obsession with comparing the foetus to food. It grew in size from a small lime to a peach, and is now the size of a grapefruit. It's puzzling, therefore, that I am the size of a baby elephant.

I look down; my present garb could hardly be described as high fashion. I have resorted to wearing Hugh's clothes because they are the only things in the flat that fit. However, he won't let me wear anything half decent (not since I was sick on his Nicole Farhi flannel trousers), and so I am forced into wearing the stuff that has lurked at the back of his wardrobe since his student days. This morning I was underwhelmed with the choice between a sweatshirt embroidered with his college crest or a Meatloaf T-shirt. To be twinned with tie-dye trousers (purchased in India during his years out) or a green suit with a double-breasted jacket (apparently it was his first interview suit and he kept it for sentimental reasons). I opted for the sweatshirt and hippy trousers and then called in sick – it was easier than washing my lank and unmanageable hair or trying to conceal my sallow skin under layers of foundation. The bags under my eyes are bigger than Posh carries home from Bond Street.

I can't let Jessica see me like this. She has standards.

'I have an invite to an art exhibition at a gallery in Walton Street. Some ghastly new artist. Hermia something or other, I forget. Unlikely to be her real name anyway. Probably be dismal but I have to go, it's Clarissa's daughter's gallery.'

Clarissa and my mother have known each other longer than either of them care to remember. Clarissa's daughter Freya and I are roughly the same age and therefore we have endured a lifetime of being compared and contrasted by our highly competitive mothers. Jessica had always been perfectly happy to enter into this comparative game, providing I won. I passed my piano and violin grades before Freya, I thrashed her at gymkhanas, exceeded her marks at school and, whilst advertising wouldn't have been my mother's first choice of career, she takes comfort in the fact that I earn shed-loads of cash. Things were fine until the mid 1990s, when Freya netted herself a count or duke, or something or other. Jessica never really forgave me. Freya then went on to have three bouncing babies in quick succession. Not that Jessica was in a great hurry to be a grandmother; she wasn't. But she hated, on principle, my coming second to Freya. To add to my mother's irritation, Freya never put on more than 18 lb for any one of her pregnancies – I've already put on twelve, even though I'm just fourteen weeks pregnant. Nor was she sick or spotty; she positively glowed and no doubt made shampoo from the placenta. I can't imagine ever being able to retrieve my position.

'Are you having lots of beautiful thoughts to help your baby's karma?' asks Jessica.

'Mostly murderous.'

'Darling, I thought you said you wanted this.'

'I do want it. I just didn't want it to be so hard.'

'Well, you can't have everything.'

Apparently not. Even accepting that the pregnancy has left me – what were my words? – 'Thrilled, absolutely thrilled', I can't help but think there's a design fault somewhere along the line. Why can't I just go and pick up a baby in John Lewis? The fact that giving birth is supposed to be the most exquisite, enriching, natural and substantive thing a woman can do has passed me by. Zoom, straight by. I don't feel mother-earthy; looking at me no one in their right mind would 'give it up' for the fertility gods, or high-five for Aphrodite. And whilst I concede that it is a miracle that you can hear the baby's heartbeat at this point, I'm less thrilled about the fact that the small intestine had developed and is now capable of producing the contractions that push food through the bowels, reducing me to little more than a public convenience.

'Are you listening to whale music? Freya listened to whale voices throughout her pregnancies and then had water births. Personally, I find that rather gimmicky but from all accounts the children are angels. They all slept through for eight hours by the third night.'

'Really.'

'Gospel. So I recommend whales.'

Well, this little bugger should be all right then, as it's being born to a whale.

'And plenty of exercise, darling. You are still visiting the gym, aren't you? At least three times a week.'

Yes, I'm exercising – I've nearly worn through the carpet en route from the settee to the fridge and the loo. I avoid answering the question directly by agreeing to meet at the gallery at six-thirty. This gives me roughly five and a quarter hours to transform myself from grungy hippo to something that she may recognize.

My first stop in the search for my former self is the bathroom. I know that it is paramount to wash and style your hair before you visit the salon. If you go in looking dire the stylist assumes you have low standards and then proceeds to disappoint them. If you go in looking good you have a chance of leaving looking spectacular. In fact, I have a hair-salon league, and it has been known for me to visit a division-two stylist in the morning, just as prep for an afternoon appointment with a premier-league stylist. The same is true of clothes- and shoe-shopping. I've learnt that it's vital that you wear your current best outfit to shop for new clothes, and always polish your shoes and check your hosiery is in order if you are shoe-shopping (time permitting have a manicure and pedicure as well). My problem today is that in my present state I look too awful even to visit my beautician, so I resign myself to home treatments. This demands a battle with my lethargy, but will save me the humiliation of being seen by my beautician.

I shower using my Aveda body polish and moisturizing gel. I try to lose myself in the fragrance and strive not to notice that the power shower feels like pins and needles being jabbed into my tender boobs. When I do have thoughts like, 'Whose ankles are these?' (mine are slim, toned, worked out and for – the ones on the ends of my legs are podgy, puffy and distended), I attempt to push them from my head. I endeavour not to get too depressed when I finger the place where my hip bone used to make an appearance; the bone is now safely shielded behind inches of flesh. I comfort myself that, whilst at the moment I simply look fat, in a couple of months I'll look pregnant and that will be a genuine improvement.

Which just goes to show how bad things are.

After I have cleansed, toned, moisturized, loofahed, exfoliated, brushed and pummelled every inch of flesh I have (side benefit: this is a really good upper-arm workout) and shampooed, conditioned, brushed, blow-dried, serumed and rebrushed every hair (including my eyelashes and muff – you really can never be too well-prepared), I am beginning to feel vaguely human. I carefully apply my make-up (to a stranger's face – even my eyes have changed colour; the emerald green is now more of a Thames-river-sludge colour; surely that's my paranoia).

I consider what to wear. I root through my lingerie drawer, ignoring the flimsy little bras with cups that would no longer support my nipple, never mind a complete breast, and locate a clean boulder-holder. I'm tempted not to bother with knickers at all, on the grounds that, at the moment, they are about as comfortable as sitting on a cheese grater; I'll have to buy the next size up as soon as I have an opportunity. I wish I had a tent to wear but I don't, so I root through my summer clothes, which tend to be less tailored than my winter wardrobe. I try on a number of cashmere cardigans and cotton T-shirts, but the cardigans won't fasten and whilst some of the T-shirts do stretch across my Pammy Anderson tits, the hem rises at the front, so I look farcical. In the end I opt for a button-up shirt of Hugh's, which is outsize enough to make me look still not quite elephantine. And I settle for a pair of linen trousers. Unsuited to the climate maybe, but they are a step up the sartorial ladder from the tie-dye number or the green interview suit. I grab the car keys and my credit card and set off.

My second stop, in search of my former self, is Bond Street. I automatically dismiss the smart boutiques that sell sexy, skimpy numbers (which are normally the staple of my wardrobe) and I walk right past the large designer stores that don't stock anything bigger than a size 10. Effing fashion fascism. The retail environment may be more relaxing if you don't have to encounter heaving women in the changing rooms, women that are universally depressed about their cellulite thighs and post-pubescent figures, but it's not very real, is it?

I head for a small maternity-wear shop, the stock of which has been described to me as 'adorable, perfect, divine', so I'm quite hopeful that I'll be able to buy something glam and appropriate. I'm feeling surprisingly upbeat. It's been a couple of months since I've indulged in any retail therapy and my credit card is feeling as under-exercised as my inner thighs.

After five seconds in the shop I realize that the description of the clothes as 'adorable, perfect, divine' omitted the all-important caveat, '*for maternity clothes*'. The disappointment is breathtaking. There are row after row of machine-wash trousers with elasticated waists. Of course machine wash is essential, as I discovered by week ten of my pregnancy, when I deposited no fewer than thirty-six outfits at the dry cleaner's. The bill on collection could have bought me a week's holiday in the Caribbean. Of course the trousers have to be elasticated, but does elasticated have to mean ugly? Apparently, yes. There's nothing sheer, fun, flirty or exciting. There's not a single tailored garment. There's nothing high fashion (or even mid fashion). There's nothing catwalk or statement. In summary, there's nothing to get my libidinous glands secreting.

The shop appears crowded. In fact, there are only four other women in the store, but three are pregnant and therefore space is at a premium; it feels similar to Harrods on the first day of the sale, except without the optimism. We don't look at each other, but can't peel our eyes away from one another's bumps. The biggest dollop of resentment rests on the neat bump owned by the woman who is telling the assistant that she really *is* seven months pregnant, and, yes, everybody says that she looks tiny. It's the yoga! The shop assistant also looks genuinely cheerful, but then she's a size 8 and hasn't spent the last few months staring at limescale on the inside of the toilet rim. I take a deep breath and push towards her. I explain that I need something special for a reception plus, with a sigh, I concede that I need some work suits and shirts, casual clothes and nightwear. Why do I feel like I'm losing the school trophy?

The assistant bundles me into a changing room (small) together with a pile of clothes (large and occasionally large enough). The biggest shock is the pouch of material hidden in the front panels of the trousers; surely my stomach will never fill those excess yards. I try the trousers on and discover that they are too snug already and I need the next size up. The colours are drab, mostly beige, which I presume is selected for its camouflage properties; I suppose I should be grateful that there are no polka dots in sight. The 'special' outfit the assistant suggests is a black Empire-line, on-the-knee dress. Despite the fact that it has sequins around the neckline, it appears promising. And, whilst these clothes are obviously not a patch on anything Alberta Ferretti, Givenchy Couture or Marc Jacobs would produce, in the end I buy all the things she gives me to try on – just because they fasten right to the top. Relieved, I wait for my credit card to clear. It astounds me that whilst the fabrics, tailoring, designs and names don't match my usual purchases the prices are about the same. The assistant smiles as she hands me the bags; obviously she has no conscience about fleecing the deformed.

My third stop is the hairdresser's. My stylist is very sympathetic. 'Darling, lank, greasy hair is to be expected. Be thankful you don't have a moustache.' The floor stubbornly refuses to open and swallow me up, so there is nothing I can do except accept a herbal tea and sit through the catalogue of horror stories about pregnancy that the shampoo girl, my colour technician and stylist all insist on relaying.

At six-thirty on the dot, my mother's cab pulls up outside the gallery. I watch her hand over the correct money for the fare and tip, pull a comb through her hair and snap open a compact case so that she can check her reflection. I quickly turn to the gallery window, to check (as taught at the breast) that my teeth aren't smeared with lipstick. My reflection isn't bad, *considering I'm pregnant.* It's been a lot of effort, but the outfit and blow-dry works, I think. I look . . . pleasant. Jessica will be pleased.

Jessica hops out of the cab and almost walks straight past me. I stop her by leaning in for an air kiss.

'Georgina?' she demands, lifting her sunglasses on to the top of her head (an unnecessary accessory as it's February and the chance of seeing the sun in the UK within the next five months is slim). 'Georgina,' she repeats, not quite believing her own eyes.

I smile hesitantly.

'We'll have to do something with your hair.'

16

It's the kind of party that I adore, or used to. It's obvious to me from the moment I walk through the door that I'm not going to enjoy myself. The gallery is huge and white, with a polished wooden floor. There are two or, tops, three pieces of art hanging on the wall. They are very modern, mostly solid blocks of colour. If they have a meaning it passes me by. Heaving crowds of shadowy people try to compensate for the empty walls and empty pictures.

'What did you say the name of the artist is?' I ask Jessica.

Jessica shrugs. 'Some Italian woman – I forget.'

'Well, she is certainly very well connected.' I nod around at the guests. 'All of London's Great and Good are here.'

'Or at least those who like to consider themselves to be so,' adds Jessica haughtily. She prides herself on never being impressed.

'Isn't that Jemima Khan?' I ask, genuinely thrilled.

'Yes – don't stare. Note, Georgina, she has two sons and has retained her figure.'

I sigh, and point out someone who looks a lot like Elton John; no one can accuse him of keeping his figure. To describe the guest list in the vaguest terms, there are a number of politicians, TV celebs, journalists, and a liberal scattering of lords and ladies, marquesses and marchionesses, barons and baronesses. To be specific, there is every wealthy, powerful, jowly man in London and every beautiful, scare-crow-thin, peroxide woman. My black sequined number suddenly seems woefully inadequate. Between us, my mother and I know, at least by sight, nearly every guest, and we are intimately acquainted with a respectable number. So why am I standing alone with only the peanut bowl for company?

I survey the champagne-swilling and vol-au-vent-eating room (the vol-au-vents are filled with goat's cheese or Parma ham, so I can't indulge), and wonder who I should speak to.

'This one represents the legitimacy of death.' A platinum-blonde, skeletal woman is staring at a red square and a black rectangle. Her companion, equally skinny but with titian hair, nods and comments, 'A superb depiction, the very epitome of the lawfulness of dissolution.'

Actually, it's still a red square and a black rectangle. I ponder their words, trying to make sense of them and then I decide I can't; they don't make sense. The words, like the pictures, mean nothing. The skeletal women may or may not know that their words mean nothing; they may or may not care that their words mean nothing. I suspect their real reason for being at the gallery today is to be seen, and if they can also manage to spout a bit of nonsense, which is mistaken for a profundity, all the better.

I could talk to Patsy Kensit's agent; he's always good for a natter. I suppose I should congratulate the artist and tell Freya how beautiful her gallery is. I decide against this when Jessica announces Freya's expecting her fourth child.

'Really. Is she due much after me?' I ask.

'Six weeks before you,' says Jessica, not even bothering to hide her flames of fury (ignited by her competitive streak, and well and truly fanned because it's a competition she's already lost). 'You can't tell, can you?' she adds.

I glance in Freya's direction. No, you can't tell. Her stomach is flatter than a two-day-old bottle of Veuve Clicquot. Why does my mother want to torture me in this manner? Why does she hate me? Why did she give birth to me? Why did Clarissa give birth to Freya? Why did Freya have to get pregnant at the same time as me? Why am I fat? Oh, back there again. I note that, as with Freya's other three pregnancies, her skin is amazing and her hair is growing madly, I've never seen it so long. She looks terrific.

'I chatted to her on the phone earlier today,' comments Jessica. 'She was so calm about this party and the exhibition. She's definitely more serene than I have ever known her to be.'

We can assume a comatose state, then, because Freya is normally so cool that she can chill a bottle of Chardonnay with a single glance. But why? Why isn't she hostage to the roller-coaster ride that leaves me feeling delighted, bitter, blissed, blistering, all in as many minutes? I can't resist twisting the knife. 'Was she sick a lot in the first few months?'

'If she was she didn't mention it,' Jessica admits.

'Listless? Unable to concentrate?'

'No.'

'Sweaty feet?'

'Georgina! As if anyone ever talks about such things.' Actually pregnant women do, and about excess hair growth, and skin flaps and loose vaginas, amongst many things. I've forgotten what passes as an acceptable level of familiarity.

'Haemorrhoids?' I ask, hopefully.

'What are haemorrhoids?'

'Piles.' I blush. The English term is much more disgusting than the US one.

'Oh, goodness, Georgina, is there any call for you to be so bestial? Don't tell me you have piles.'

'Not me, no. But some women do get them,' I lie hastily.

'Oh, there was one thing.'

'Yes?' I hope for a grim morsel of consolation.

'She says her nails are growing at an extraordinary rate and she's spending a fortune on extra manicures.'

Big shame.

It's obvious that Freya is having the pregnancy that was intended for me.

I can't help but think that pregnancy is some sort of device to expose me. To show me up for what I am (a five and a half out of ten), not what I've become (the quintessential twenty-first-century woman).

Desperately, I try to find someone else to talk to who will serve as a diversion. Is that thingy? Oh, what's her name? She won the Barclays Businesswoman of the Year Award last year. I went to her wedding, so I should be able to remember her name, it's err . . . thingy . . . It can't be her, can it? Has she lost weight? She can't have, she had none to lose. I smile at her. It's the smile I've perfected to ensure that if she does cut me dead then I can catch the eye of a passing waiter and take a glass of champagne, thus not losing face. She throws back a half smile, betraying that she can't quite place me, then quickly (but not quickly enough) breaks into a genuine grin.

'George, darling, how lovely to see you.' Air kiss, air kiss.

'You know Jessica.' It's as near as I can get to an introduction, as I still can't remember her name. Bloody pregnancy spongie-brain.

'Of course.'

They smile and shake hands.

'I almost failed to recognize you.' The words are out of Ms Barclays Businesswoman of the Year's mouth before she can calculate their damage. The thing is, she's quite a decent woman and wouldn't deliberately hurt me. She blushes. 'You're blooming.' We both know this is a lie, especially when she adds, 'A spring baby, how adorable. I think you are so brave coming out. When I was reaching the end of my pregnancy I wouldn't be seen dead.'

The baby isn't due until the end of August. I don't say as much but instead mutter something unconvincing about water retention.

'But you are well, generally?'

'Oh yes, absolutely fine. We're thrilled.'

She nods, smiles, looks over my shoulder and then makes her excuses and goes on to find someone more useful to talk to.

'Slept with one of the judges to get that award,' comments my mother loyally but untruthfully.

It's not accurate to say that everyone fails to recognize me; some do, and these ghouls take great delight in swarming in for a closer look – my size can be established from a distance, but the poor condition of my skin can only be vouched for on near inspection.

'Darling.' Air kiss, air kiss. 'You look so well.'

Everyone knows that 'well' is a deliberately facile code to crack. It means anything on the scale from plump, fleshy, corpulent, chubby, obese, right through to lard-arse.

'I didn't even have an inkling that you were married, let alone pregnant,' smiles Mindy, a vague acquaintance of mine whom I have bumped into at several parties over the years.

'And, Mindy darling, how is your husband? Remind me, is this number three or number four?' asks Jessica, the very picture of innocence. She draws Mindy to one side and whispers, 'Tell me, do you recycle your gowns?'

'George, sweetie. I see you are pregnant. How very year 2000. It's not like you to be so appallingly behind the times,' smiles Dulcie. It's true. At least if I'd had a baby in 2000 I'd have been in good company. Last year everyone was at it – Madonna, Cherie Blair, Catherine Zeta Jones, even Zoë Ball managed to make the deadline. Having a baby in 2001 obviously isn't a fashion statement; it's simply a contraceptive gaffe and no amount of insisting on my part that we are thrilled will convince otherwise.

'Dulcie, darling, have you seen the "art", that's with an "f". Absolutely appalling, entirely emperor's new clothes, don't you think?'

Dulcie looks furious. 'Actually, you may not be aware, but Hermia Vicci is my partner.'

My mother flashes one of her most charming and flirtatious smiles. 'Oh, I do apologize.' The Machiavellian smile almost convinces me that she's sorry. Almost. 'What do I know? I'm sure she'll be an enormous hit.' We move on.

My mother is reassuringly rude throughout the evening, she sends back the champagne, insisting it is Asti spumante, orders Krug for herself and cranberry juice for me. On my behalf she bats back the slights, the snubs and implied insults like the true pro she is. She also insists that we circulate constantly and fires instructions at me such as 'chin up', and 'don't let that smile falter, not for a nano-second.'

I repeat, no fewer than fourteen times, that I'm 'thrilled, absolutely thrilled'. It's an exhausting evening but I'm grateful.

We find the time between vol-au-vents and catty comments to catch up on the family news. I establish that my father is accompanying Jessica on this shopping trip to New York and is currently preparing himself and his credit cards for the inevitable battering by spending a restful evening at his gentlemen's club. My brother is pursuing the unlikely profession of DJ; Jessica comforts herself with the fact that it is no more unlikely than all the other professions he's tried since being sent down from Durham ten years ago. He's been a film extra, a musician, a car mechanic and a gardener, to her certain knowledge. A 'courier' in South America, and an 'escort' in Las Vegas, to mine.

'And that thing with the cameras, how did that go?' I have no idea what Jessica means. She elaborates, 'What's it called? The scan.'

'Oh, it's tomorrow.'

'Do you want me to come along?'

'I thought you were flying out tomorrow.'

'I am, but I can change it if need be.'

I'm touched. 'No, don't worry. I'm sure Hugh will be coming along.'

'I hope it's all good news. Not twins.' My mother grins mischievously.

At eight-thirty Jessica concedes that I've done enough. She puts me in a taxi and comments, 'Now that wasn't too bad, was it?'

It was bloody awful but, because we both know it, neither of us is prepared to admit it. I wind the cab window down and ask, 'Did I ever like those people?'

'I doubt it,' she smiles.

I catch her hand and squeeze it. 'Thanks, Jessica.'

She returns the squeeze. 'That's what mothers are for, George.'

17

Week 12
It is important to involve your partner in the miracle that is happening in your body. He can be a big support to you. This can be a time of communication and growth in your relationship. But you may have to work a little to make your partner feel that he is part of what is happening to you.

More jobs, I sniff resentfully.

Hugh can't join me for the scan; he's too busy. I try to understand, he is very important. And, anyway, who needs all that hand-holding nonsense?

Every other pregnant woman in the room, apparently.

I hate doctors' waiting rooms. They are so embarrassing. The lack of reading matter forces you to notice the other patients. (I don't count dog-eared copies of *Hello!* magazine as reading matter; was there ever anything charming about puff-ball skirts?) A number of the patients are in an even more distressing state than me. Their arms are hanging off, or they are sneezing so much that they've obviously got bubonic plague. I try not to sit too close to anyone else in case I leave the surgery with something awful. Really, couldn't they have made an effort? I have. I've put on a pair of trousers that fasten and I've wiped the puke off my shoes. After all, the poor man has trained long and hard to get where he is now, and he doesn't want to have to look in more dirty or badly presented crevices than absolutely necessary. Couldn't they have brushed their hair, taken off their slippers, closed their mouths? What does it take to apply a little bit of lipstick? Also, I find those posters of rotting vages completely offensive.

I had my tonsils taken out privately. In Harley Street everything is a little more discreet. The walls are white, and the only things hanging are tasteful reproductions of Monet's waterlilies. All the patients were immaculately presented and wore the uniform of the rich: white shirts tucked into dark jeans, lots of gold jewellery, flat navy shoes, and sunglasses resting on top of recently highlighted hair (this was just the men).

It's a straightforward procedure, the scan. Once you're past the full bladder/empty bladder dilemma. The books say a full bladder is necessary for best pictorial results. As usual, the books are woefully out of date. The doctors now use cameras that prefer not to have a filter of urine between lens and alien, but I only discover this after having kept my legs crossed for three hours in the waiting room. Then I endure the indignity of emptying my bladder in an aluminium loo whilst the midwife waits for me next door; she has nothing more to do than listen to my wee splash against the pan. Oh joy. Then she puts a freezing cream on my stomach and rubs a microphone-like device over the Mount Everest bulge.

It's amazing.

The alien thingy, it's *amazing*. I'm surprised that, at the right angle, the alien thingy looks recognizably human. I can definitely make out its head bent over its chest, and I can see its arms and legs.

It can swim.

And mine is particularly athletic.

18

Increasingly, work is hell. I work in a glass office that looks out on to long rows of desks, piled high with PCs, identical except for the screen savers. The thirty-odd account handlers sit, stand and shout at each other from these desks for eight hours a day and more. This used to be my idea of heaven. I can see who and what is coming and going on, up and down. However, now that the thing coming up is my breakfast, the open-plan structure is a disaster.

Brett, Karl and Drew charge into my office and catch me stuffing a cream-cheese bagel into my mouth.

'You shouldn't be eating that,' comments Brett. I'm not sure if he means because it's unpasteurized cheese or because I'm the size of a house.

Ostensibly, we're meeting to discuss the agenda for our strategy meeting for our pitch meeting, for a toilet-tissue account. It's a high-profile pitch as this business is worth a media spend of an astounding six million: the agency would take approximately 10 per cent of that in revenue.

However, the boys have little interest in 'Puppy Salience', 'Puppy Love' or 'Puppy Metaphor', the attributes the existing incumbent agency exploits so magnificently. They're irked that I won't play Fantasy Football but insist on sticking to the point instead.

'The client says he considers the current ads to be strategically sound,' I offer.

'He means boring,' Karl dismisses.

True, he probably does; traditionally this is a business

where one thing is said and something altogether different is meant, but the ritual of at least appearing to believe what is said must be observed.

'And well branded,' I add.

'He means very boring,' dismisses Brett. As Creative Director he sees branding as a heinous crime – 'Intrusive branding is diametrically opposed to creativity.' The others make noises of agreement.

'It's imperative that we remember that creating, fashioning, forming a brand, a mark of ownership, a seal, a *name*, can be a near-religious experience. A veritable adventure,' comments Drew, as he nods sagely.

Everyone in the room nods too, except me. I feel as though I'm back in Freya's art gallery. I'm not sure he's said anything at all but, if he has, he's just said the opposite to Brett, so why is Brett nodding? There's a board at one end of the room on which Karl has written the words *Prominence*, *Commotion*, *Style*, *Elegance*, *Divertissement*, *Well-being*, *Negotiate*, *Personal*, *Amour*, *Culture* and *Accessibility*. We all stare at the wash-down whiteboard and nod some more. The words are not relevant to our discussion. It's an old trick – whenever we meet we write some hocus-pocus on the board. In this way we are free to discuss the fact that Dave in production is shagging Cindy, the receptionist, or whether a Stella Artois is a cleaner drink than a Budweiser Budvar, whilst giving the impression that we are brainstorming the brand's properties. I wonder why Dean has never noticed that it's always the same words, irrespective of whether we are supposed to be branding an insurance company or a loo roll.

'Look, this pitch doesn't have to be so hard,' grumbles Karl. 'We'll end up doing what we always do. Show a few of the ads we've made for other clients, make some short, pithy generalizations, show some dull charts demonstrating that we've done the number-crunching, add a line or two 'in summary', and then present the creative solution, which is all anyone is ever interested in anyway.'

I sigh a lament at his cavalier attitude, and a little bit of me also sighs because he's probably right.

'Don't you miss the days when we just sent George in, and she so set their rocks on fire that it didn't matter what she said?' teases Brett.

I treat him to a weary look.

After about fifteen minutes, it's decided that the best plan is to have a *pre*-meeting to discuss the long list of possible agenda items and narrow them down and *then* have a meeting to discuss the agenda for our strategy meeting for our pitch meeting, for the toilet-tissue account. It's agreed that the best time for this meeting is tomorrow lunchtime, and the best venue is Mezzo restaurant. The current meeting is adjourned and the boys go back to their offices feeling that they've done a good day's work.

I'm less confident.

I often think that I chose the wrong career. Well, rather, I ended up in the wrong career. 'Chose' is far too active a verb to describe how I ended up in advertising. I suppose I should be grateful that Hugh wasn't interested in joining NASA or the armed forces. Although there would have been an undeniable cachet telling people at parties that I was an astro-physicist and Hugh certainly would have looked cute in uniform. Advertising is meant to be a laugh, everyone in the industry knows that. The only people that ever take advertising seriously are the moral brigade, who regularly object to ads for underwear. Everyone else sees the job for what it is; a great way to avoid growing up but at the same time making more money than you would make if, say, you'd stayed on at university to do a PhD.

Not me.

I haven't got the *je ne sais quoi.* I'm simply not chilled. I try to be (which is certainly my first mistake). I really *wish* I could perfect that fly-by-the-seat-of-my-pants-write-the-strategy-in-the-lift-on-the-way-up-to-the-clients'-office-put-the-whizz-in-spin-doctor-bullshitter approach. But I can't. I really do think it's immoral to fill in your own questionnaires as a basis to recommending a creative direction to the client, call it research and charge them thirty grand for the pleasure. I can't agree that the only work that is ever 'on strategy' is the work created by those who can advance my career. Nor is my best friend Alberto, the office administrator, just because he has the keys to the stationery cupboard and the corporate drinks fridge (to be honest, he's a git).

I work really hard to keep my head above water. I am the only person I know in the industry who has actually read Levitt, Kotler, Ansoff and Porter. I know the difference between sales volume, net sales volume, sterling sales at RSP, gross contribution, net contribution and break-even point. Moreover, I do care about our clients' profit margins. I've worked on creative award-winning businesses. I've worked with the world's best photographers, directors and film editors. I've helped create brand equity on a number of household names. I don't simply use acronyms such as ECR, FMCG, FMPG and KVI as a way of confusing the person I'm presenting to; I use them because these words are basic currency. I understand the importance of agency culture, a fat expense account and a big Christmas party. I'm firm but fair with all my staff and I never resort to political shafting. Yet, despite all this, I live every day thinking someone is going to find me out.

Find out that I'm not effortlessly chic, but that I spend half my salary on face creams and half my life in the beautician's. That my personal trainer terrifies me, that my personal shopper exploits me, that I don't even like avocado, never mind caviar, and, worse still, I don't even know the proper pronunciation of Renaud Pellegrino. I mean, is it 'green-o' or 'grin-o'?

It's a terrifying way to live.

The people I work with are entirely Jekyll and Hyde. Affable and amusing company at dinner parties, unscrupulous, greedy and insecure during office hours. A noxious cocktail. It strikes me that some of the most dangerous people in London work in advertising. It's populated by those who were born at the end of the baby boom and then suffered over a decade of Thatcher rule – how can they be anything but self-centred and overly ambitious? Therefore my falling pregnant, and suddenly doing convincing impressions of a dizzy Sigourney Weaver from *Alien*, is seen by most as a huge opportunity to supplant me.

Returning from my lunch hour (spent in the bathroom), I find the office deserted.

'Where is everyone?' I ask Julia. I notice that there is a huge box of Jelly Belly Beans on her desk. Without waiting for an invitation I start to hoover them up, red ones first.

'Help yourself,' smiles Julia. Immediately guilty, I try to resist by clasping my hands behind my back. I last about four seconds before I start to eat the lime ones. The thing is, all I want to do is eat. Eat and eat and eat and eat. Anything. Everything. I just want to stuff food into my mouth and chew it very quickly so I can stuff something new into my mouth. I eat as though I want to compensate, in the next fifteen minutes, for nearly fourteen years of starving.

Thinking about it, this is absolutely the case.

'Didn't you get the memo? Some speaker is over from the US office. A three-line whip that everyone attends.'

Funny, no one mentioned an imperative meeting when we were discussing diaries this morning, not Brett, nor Karl, nor Drew. Or maybe not so funny.

'No, I didn't get the memo.' I resist adding that, as my number two, it is Julia's responsibility to see that I do get memos and that important meetings are put in my diary. It's so tricky managing a colleague/friend relationship. She's unconcerned, more involved in applying another coat of nail varnish. Julia is not ambitious. She's 'in advertising' simply because she spent so long in bars in Soho that a number of people assumed she already had a job in some agency or other and eventually she was 'headhunted' from a job she didn't have into this one, a job she barely does. She's extremely bright, but has a trust fund and is too wealthy to care about actually doing the job well.

'You should have gone, there's free sandwiches and champagne,' she comments.

Besides the free lunch I should have gone. It turns out that the 'speaker' from the US office is none other than the new Global Chief Executive, Philip Marx. He recently inherited the role after a rather savage and sleazy power struggle. The entire corporation was split into two rival camps of supporters. Anyone with any commercial and survival instinct knows that it's career suicide not to be seen to be endorsing, and celebrating with, Marx. The war cry of the office is 'the best man won'. Not because Marx is the best man for the job, but because he won. *Fuck.*

'Why aren't you there?' I demand. Her absence combined with mine will be interpreted as departmental mutiny.

'I offered to man the phones.' At that point a phone rings. Julia ignores it, as she is busy blow-drying her nails.

'Any messages, then?' I ask but I'm not hopeful.

'Er, yeah, there was one.' She roots around tentatively on her desk; it's a mass of cosmetics, but there are one or two pieces of paper interspersed with the mess. 'Here.'

She waves a Post-it note triumphantly. However, on reading the message it's about as clear as the Enigma code.

'Who's Gar?' I ask. Apparently he wants me to call him.

'AAR,' she clarifies.

The Advertising Agency Register. The AAR contact me when Q&A have made it on to a pitch list. This is good news, I suppose, although frankly I'm so stretched with my current workload that getting on to another pitch list is a mixed blessing. To be accurate, it's not that my workload has increased at all, it's just that I can't tackle my in-tray when my head is down the loo.

I sit at my desk and hope that no one has noticed my non-attendance. Fifteen minutes later everyone starts to file out of the boardroom and back to their seats.

'Oh, Georgina, you *are* here,' says Karl. 'We thought you'd gone shopping.'

Bastard.

'When have you ever known me to go shopping at lunch-time?' I smile.

Karl raises his eyebrows. A gesture that succinctly implies, to anyone taking an interest, that women simply can't help themselves and, important business meeting or not, we will be out abusing the plastic. I adore shopping but I've never, ever shopped on company time.

'I was expecting an important phone call, I couldn't leave my desk,' I lie.

'Really,' smiles Karl. 'Shame. Interesting meeting. You were missed. Marx even sent someone to look for you.'

Bugger. I mutter something about being in the loo at the time and decide not to tell Karl that he has a cress seed stuck between his teeth.

Things go from bad to worse when that afternoon, unable to fight the overwhelming fatigue of pregnancy, I twice fall asleep at my desk, only being brought back to consciousness by banging my head on my computer screen. Dean notices my fiery ambition has been dampened to smouldering embers when during a team meeting I lose my train of thought three times. On the fourth occasion he leaves the room without even excusing himself. By doing so he makes it clear I'm wasting his time.

I call Hugh because I need to be soothed by his sympathetic tones.

'Can you talk?' I ask, as I know how irritating it is to be called at work when you are right in the middle of something tricky.

'Not a good time, Babes, is it important?'

To me, yes. 'Nothing that can't wait until this evening,' I mutter and carefully place the phone back in the cradle. I pick the phone up again, just to check, but the line is dead and the dead tone isn't in the slightest bit sympathetic.

At six the computers are slowly switched off as thoughts turn towards cool lagers. Most people are bushed with the exertion of trying to impress Philip Marx. I'm bushed with the exertion of trying to stay awake.

'Drew, fancy a beer?' asks Karl.

'Ever known me to say no?'

'Brett?'

'Damn right, I do.'

'Where are we going?' I ask. The silence can be heard in Asia.

'Look, Georgie, no offence, Babes, but we're planning on

a bit of a lads' night. No skirt,' explains Karl. 'I'm sure you understand.'

'Sure,' I smile, 'I understand.' And I do. It's crystal clear. 'I have plans, anyway. I'd have had to rearrange.'

'Of course you do. See you tomorrow. Enjoy. Take care.'

He throws out a couple more facile, insincere comforters and they leave. Karl knows I haven't got plans tonight as plainly as he knows that I always attend the boys' nights out in the local pub, where all the real wheeling and dealing is conducted. He doesn't give a damn if I enjoy my evening or if I take care. These platitudes are spun to the losers and no-mates simply as a conversational salve. Finding myself abruptly excluded from the high-powered meetings in the boardroom is serious; exclusion from high-jinks meetings in the pub is the signing of my death warrant. If I don't receive the latest hints and tips, as I have always done in the past, my job (as much dependent upon rumour as on share-of-voice reports) will become increasingly difficult. Just fifteen weeks pregnant and already I'm history.

I should fight back. I should rally, reassemble, charge and counter-attack. And I would. I certainly would. I've done it before. Only now I can't think how. My mind is a fog.

The best thing is for me to have an early night and to get in at the crack of dawn tomorrow morning to strategize. I mustn't get this out of proportion; after all it's not as though I've received my P45 in the internal mail.

Julia is reapplying her lipstick. It's unlike her to stay a minute after five-thirty. She must be going somewhere special.

'Going somewhere funky?' I ask, half-wondering if she'll invite me along. We haven't been out together for a couple of weeks, in fact since the afternoon at the Bluebird. Whilst I do feel a bit guilty for neglecting our social life (it's always me that arranges the nights out), right now clubbing is so low down on my agenda it doesn't even make it to AOB.

'Nowhere special. Just out with Karl and the boys for a drink.' She snaps her bag and her smile closed.

I see.

19

I can't consider waiting at a bus or Tube stop so I decide to jump in a cab. I know this is a big mistake when I have to endure a solid twenty-minutes monologue on foreign and domestic policy according to Mr Cabby. None of it is original or enlightened; most of it is offensive. Although when I think about it carefully, he's not saying anything I haven't heard before and it's never bothered me in the past. But, suddenly, I object to the barely disguised bigotry; it's not made any more acceptable just because it appears in most of our national newspapers. The cab driver puts me in mind of the difficult man in the bookshop. He makes me think that however much Milton sterilizing fluid I use this world will never be clean enough to bring my baby into. I'm not in a good mood. It's not my idea of fun to crawl through town at about three miles per hour, breathing in toxic fumes. It amazes me that even at this speed he can manage to brake so suddenly that I am flung from the backseat and only just prevent bashing my head on the glass partition by rolling into the brace position. Whilst there I fall asleep; when I wake up the meter reads nearly forty quid, even though ordinarily the journey home costs me seven. I know the cab driver has been driving around in circles, taking advantage of my chronic fatigue. I tell him so but he argues that the traffic was bad. I know he knows I don't believe him but I'm too strung out to argue. The only form of protest I have available to me is to refuse to leave a tip.

I tip him.

And then stumble out of the cab and into my flat, dazed with the humiliation of being so weak as to accept his bullshit.

I don't bother to hang up my coat but fling it over the back of a chair. I pull myself up the stairs and into the bedroom. I start to take off my suit and shirt. My breasts ache and then bounce about as I release them from my boulder-holder bra. There's a limited range in maternity underwear – big knickers, big bras and not a suspender belt to be had, not for lust nor riches; all of it is less aesthetically pleasing than the Hunchback of Notre-Dame's vest. My boobs finally settle down long enough for me to examine the red welts where my engorged flesh, swollen to unrecognizable proportions, has chafed against the generous elastic straps.

Oh God, I forgot to call AAR. I must do that first thing tomorrow. Sod it. There's nothing for it. I can't fight it. I struggle out of the rest of my clothes, rummage around Hugh's drawers for a roomy T-shirt and, although it's not yet seven, I slip between the cool cotton sheets.

To sleep.

I wake up to see Hugh rip off his tie; too impatient to unfasten the buttons on his shirt, he removes it by seizing it at the back of the neck and hauling it over his head in one swift efficient movement. It's almost as though he doesn't like having his face covered by the shirt in case he misses anything. The muscles in his back and shoulders flex tantalizingly. My heart leaps to my throat and I have to swallow it back down again. He pulls off his trousers and boxers, throws his socks into a corner of the room and slips between the covers.

'This is a nice surprise. What are you doing home so early?' he asks.

I'm a no-mark, a has-been, a loser. I say that only in my head because if I say it out loud it might ring too true. His hands are already running up my thighs; he encounters the T-shirt and halts. 'Oh.'

Oh indeed.

I'm a girl with serious aspirations to glamour. In all the time we've been together, Hugh has never seen me in anything other than designer underwear. If I bother with nightwear at all, it is always silk. This is not because I keep my best underwear for the nights when I think we'll have sex; I simply don't have anything other than sexy stuff. My wearing an outsize cotton T-shirt in bed is the equivalent to other women leaving a note that reads, 'Your dinner is in the dog'. Finding me in bed early of an evening, Hugh had obviously thought I was requesting a steamy session.

Wrong.

Very wrong. My libido has absconded. It is possibly nestling under my many acres of stomach. How can I feel sexy when my body is a pincushion and a professional producer of urine?

I grab his wandering hand and force him into conversation. 'How was your day?'

'Fine; yours?' He doesn't care. He wriggles so that he can start to caress my hair with his left hand. I consider clutching his hand in my vice-like grip, but then I notice that the caresses feel nice. If only he'd leave it at that, then I could relax. But I know that the hair-caressing stunt is just to lull me into a false sense of security, then he'll move in on my tits.

'Terrible.' I start to tell him about missing Philip Marx's introduction meeting and then the scene with my boss during the team meeting. Ours is a small industry so Hugh knows Dean and therefore tries to reassure me.

'Dean is known for conducting his meetings like that,

leaving before they are over, taking calls in the middle, it's a way of reminding everyone how important he is.'

'No, it was more sinister than that, he was marking my card.'

'You're over-reacting, it's your hormones. Your body is going through a lot of remarkable changes right now. That's why you are being so extreme, tearful, overly sensitive and moody.' Suddenly he's turned into Dr Hilary Jones, but even more patronizing.

I glare at him but don't reply. Instead I reach for my week-by-week guide. I almost find it funny when I read that in week fifteen 'growth continues to be rapid, but the skin is very thin'. I can't help but be concerned that the skin may have to toughen up, with Hugh as a father. Both mine and the baby's. Apparently its entire body is covered in a fine hair called lanugo. Yet more similarities. I nudge the duvet surreptitiously and try to quickly appraise my body without drawing Hugh's attention. Besides the great mass that is my stomach, the other obvious sign of my pregnancy is that my bikini line has hit my knees. This entire process is designed to humiliate.

Hugh starts to massage my neck. It's pointless, I'm so tense it feels like he's nipping me. I tell him about barfing on my keyboard. His eyes glaze over and I don't blame him, I'm boring myself. In an effort to rediscover the woman I consider myself to be I put down the book and give way to his caresses. I'm pretty sure a really substantial orgasm will make me feel at one with the world again.

Sex is unworkable.

Hopeless.

However hard I try I cannot summon up the tiniest residue of desire. Even when I try to stay absolutely still my stomach thinks it's competing in a gymkhana. I feel entirely separate and alone. Hugh's hand runs up and down my thigh but it feels as though he is peeling off my skin. He tries to kiss my stomach, which causes me to shudder; I don't want him to touch the squelchy bits. Bastard lying maternity books say I 'might be suffering some slight discomfort in the breasts, a tingling sensation' – in reality they feel as though they're being tackled by the entire national rugby team, so they are entirely off-limits. He interprets my brushing him away and dismissing foreplay as an indication that I want a quickie. I suppose I do, in as much as I certainly don't want to prolong this.

I'm ashamed of my loss of desire and so hide it by faking orgasm. This is the first time in my life that I've ever faked and it's with the man I love more than myself. Where's the sense in that? I'm not even very good at faking it. I find myself impersonating people on TV pretending to orgasm and not imitating my own.

'God, yes, yes, yes. Oh that's it. Don't stop. Oh wow. Oh angel.'

Hugh sees through me and this hurts both of us equally. He rolls away from me, picks up a packet of cigarettes and then puts them down again. He does this in an extremely pointed manner. He wants me to note his huge sacrifice. But I don't feel grateful that he's restricting his smoking because I know he can still drink whisky.

'Is this still about Valentine's Day, Georgina?'

He means the fact that he forgot Valentine's Day and had to resort to buying me a bunch of carnations from the local garage, the type of bouquet that makes a dusty box of Milk Tray look positively thoughtful.

'I just don't feel in the mood, that's all. I'm not well,' I mumble. 'It's ironic that I feel permanently premenstrual when in fact that's something I simply am not.' I try to smile.

'Well, that's something to be pleased about, isn't it?' he says encouragingly. 'No more periods for months. You've always grumbled about your periods. You said that they were the worst plague inflicted on womankind.'

I'm now having a rethink but I don't say as much.

'I'm sorry about Valentine's Day. And I'm sorry I've been working such long hours. I'm very involved in . . .' I tune out. Again, it's unprecedented but I'm not sure I care what's going on in Hugh's office. I only start to listen again when I hear the words, 'You need a holiday.'

Love.

Incredible, wonderful love.

Yes, yes, I do. Somewhere glamorous, somewhere peaceful, somewhere hot. The Caribbean? The Maldives?

'We should go away with the kids.' Hugh turns to me, enthusiasm oozing out of every pore. 'Why didn't I think of it earlier? We can tell them about the baby.'

Pig.

Misogynistic, chauvinistic pig.

No, no, I won't. However, because I'm pregnant my brain appears to be operating in reverse and I can't formulate an excuse quickly enough. Holiday and kids in the same sentence is an oxymoron.

Hugh interprets my silence as an assent. 'Not abroad but somewhere in the country. We could take long bracing walks.'

Holiday and long bracing walks is another contradiction. Holiday equals white, private beaches and long days lying in the sun. However Hugh is too approving of his own idea to notice my doubts. I can only hope that Becca vetoes the suggestion.

March

20

Becca thinks it's a brilliant idea for Hugh and me to take the kids away. She even suggests that we team up with Hugh's brother Henry and his family. I'd have never credited her with so much spite.

Henry is a pleasant enough guy, but his wife, Penny, and I don't see eye to eye. She's Becca's friend and, as such, is never going to be mine. Their three children, whose names escape me, are devil's spawn. Suddenly I'm noticing how many badly behaved children I know. I wonder if there is any other variety. Ideally I'd like one that comes with a volume-control button and self-clean surfaces.

To avoid the weekend away being an unmitigated disaster I suggest that Sam and Gilbert join us. Hugh has enough sense to realize that, in this case, dilution is desirable and readily agrees. Moreover, when Sam rings up and asks if Gilbert's brother James can join the party too, we fall over ourselves and agree.

'Will there be enough room?' she asks.

'Yes. The cottage we've hired is more of a country house. It has four bedrooms and a caravan. That's a bedroom for Henry and Penny, you and Gilbert, Hugh and me, and the kids can bunk in together. James can have the caravan. Do you think he'll mind?'

'Can't say for certain, I've never met him, but I don't expect so. He lives in Africa. He's some sort of safari guide. He's probably used to sleeping in odd places. He's taking a season off and coming to England. G's delighted. He obviously adores him.'

'Older or younger?'

'Younger, quite a bit. And, from what I can gather, very unstable.'

Oh, I hope so. I could do with the excitement. 'What makes you think that?'

'Well, what sort of a job is a safari guide for a thirty-six-year-old? Why can't he get a boring job like everyone else? I'm sure he's only coming home to watch his old mother into the grave.'

'Sam. How unlike you to be bitchy. Isn't it great that you can get to know him before the wedding? You must be excited about meeting Gilbert's nearest and dearest?' The subtext is, of course, that in the normal course of events this nicety would have been observed before the engagement ring was slipped on to her finger.

Sam is silent for a minute. 'Suppose. Sorry.' She isn't. 'It's just that G has been behaving so strangely since he heard that James is coming home.'

'Really.' I'm very interested. I wonder if it will turn out that Gilbert is more interesting than assumed thus far.

'Like a cat on a hot tin roof. He is so keen to make a good impression on James, it's ridiculous.'

'I thought it was supposed to be the younger brother that hero-worshipped the older one.'

'Exactly. Get this, last night G tried on three different outfits in order to choose which is the most suitable to wear to meet his brother at the airport.'

'Odd, but not a hanging offence,' I point out reasonably.

'He wouldn't agree to this weekend away unless his precious brother came along too. Apparently he "doesn't see enough of James as it is".'

So, nothing sinister in Gilbert's past then. The mystery is solved. Sam is having a bout of the green-eyed monster. She's used to having G's attention, full and devoted. It seems her pique against James is nothing more than a reluctance to share the stage.

'Be nice, Sam,' I warn her.

'OK. I suppose there's "nowt as queer as folk".' She falls back on a cliché. 'Er, by the way, should have asked, how are you feeling?'

Hugh and I have agreed to make a supreme effort to leave work at a relatively reasonable time this Friday. We plan to collect Kate and Tom and then head down the M4 (with about half of London's population) for a 'relaxing' weekend in the country. The relaxing bit starts after the four-and-a-half-hour traffic jam.

However, I'm the only one who sticks to the bargain. I get home early, pack for both of us, make supper, eat my half, put his half in the fridge, shower and change clothes. It's seven o'clock and he hasn't called. I eat his supper and try to comfort myself with the thought that we will have missed the worst of the rush hour. I open the post and am irritated to see that Sam has sent me a package of magazines, a tactless mix of bridal and maternity. There's a note attached: *Wouldn't a double wedding be a scream?! Hint, hint!!*

As subtle as a brick through a glass window. Cow, she would never have suggested a double wedding if I'd still been a size 10; the dates she's picked for her ceremony mean that I'd be waddling down the aisle in a mound of organza, praying that the contractions didn't start.

It's surprised me that so many people have assumed Hugh and I will now announce a wedding date. Unsolicited, friends, family and colleagues launch into the debate as to whether we should have a shotgun marriage immediately, or whether it would be better to wait until after the baby is born so that I'll have my figure back. Last week my mother called to express an opinion, or more accurately, to give directions.

'Darling, I'm assuming that you'll want the family christening robe.'

'Haven't given it any thought.'

'It's in storage somewhere. I'll locate it and forward it to you.' Without pausing for breath she added, 'It would be tidiest if you could marry before the baby is born. How much weight have you put on?'

'Sixteen pounds,' I muttered sulkily.

'In as many weeks!' she yelled. 'Well, in that case, a wedding is out of the question until after the baby is born. You have to live with the photos for a long time.'

I repeated the conversation to Hugh, hoping for a dose of sympathy about my weight gain. 'I know that she thinks I'm a self-indulgent, gluttonous slut. I can't expect her to understand – in her day they were allowed to smoke. Oh, the relief of putting something in your mouth that isn't calorific.'

'How about my penis?' asked Hugh, completely missing the point.

Both points, actually.

Because whilst everyone from my mother to the local greengrocer has expressed a view on when Hugh and I should get married, the one contribution which has been notably lacking is Hugh's. It's not that I want to get married. I think marriage is an outdated, restrictive, misogynistic, one-way deal.

But it would be nice to be asked.

Although fairly impractical since Hugh is, technically, still married.

But it would be nice to be asked.

I pick up *Beautiful Brides*. There's a bewildering mass of photos of models with supercilious grins (which I find inexplicable – how can anyone feel supercilious dressed as an extra for a low-budget costume drama?). Those that don't look like a smug Mr Whippy have obviously been instructed to appear beguiling or demure. Neither look appeals to me. There isn't a man in sight. If these magazines are to be believed, grooms are incidental to the whole marriage process. It's horrible, it's terrifying. It's the nastiest thing I've ever seen.

I pick up *Mothering* and instantly change my mind. This magazine redefines horrible and terrifying; in comparison *Beautiful Brides* is a walk in the park. There's picture after picture of fat women, followed by picture after picture of bloody, bawling, tiny William Hague lookalikes. There are pictures of hospital wards, which are grim and drab, with the women in the hospital beds looking exhausted and defeated; they're real, they aren't models, and so there's not a hint of serenity or superciliousness. I keep turning the pages, looking for cute gurgling bundles and blissed-out mums in white silk nightgowns – there are none. There are articles on pain relief (none of it appears to be foolproof), treating engorged nipples (ditto) and incontinence (ditto). There are a couple of articles on how to dress well during pregnancy, but the editor's tone isn't hopeful. The article admits disappointment even before it begins, because, frankly, how can anyone look good when she's carrying an extra three stones? Once again, there isn't a man in sight. The impression I'm left with is that it's perfectly normal for the male partner to make an efficient appearance at the conception, but he doesn't actively participate again until the child graduates or scores its first century playing for England. I shiver involuntarily.

The telephone rings and I dash to it. But it's not Hugh, it's some poor sod from BT trying to sell their latest marketing package – friends, family, vague acquaintances and dodgy chatlines, or something like that. I can't be bothered to listen to him so I pretend to be my Polish cleaner instead. I catch sight of myself in the mirror that hangs above the phone. My cleaner is better presented.

The doorbell rings, I fly to the door – Hugh!

'Becca.'

'Hello, Georgina.' Before she says anything else Kate and Tom charge past me into the flat. Becca starts to unload more baggage than Geri Halliwell travels with. 'Hugh called me.'

He didn't call me.

'To explain that he's stuck in a meeting. We agreed that it was best that I drop the kids off here. That way you can make an early start tomorrow.' She doesn't pause but tells me these facts in a clinical, straightforward way. Becca and I have an unwritten agreement to be calm and polite with one another on all occasions but especially in front of the children – that is Kate, Tom and Hugh. If I were generous I would assume that she behaves in this reasonable way because she is a proud woman who loves her kids. The less generous side of my nature is more inclined to believe that her reasonableness is to do with the fact that she's financially dependent upon Hugh and me. I behave in this reasonable way because I won; winning creates capacity for refinement. We both recognize the need to be civil, but our motivations are so diverse that, naturally, the arrangement is an uneasy one.

'Becca, you've lost weight.' I silently congratulate myself on this choice of double-edged compliment.

'No, I don't think so. Perhaps you've gained,' she smiles, but only with her mouth – her eyes remain flint.

I find the comment quite droll, not least because of its unlikely source, but then I consider that it's true and don't find it in the slightest bit amusing.

'I understand that congratulations are in order,' she adds.

So he's told her. Or maybe not; I'm kidding myself if I think this is the type of pregnancy you can hide. I summon up the sort of smile that my mother used to wear on her official duties, wide, exaggerated, all teeth, and I beam back. 'They certainly are.'

'Well, congratulations, then.' Becca moves her head too quickly and I can't be quite sure how to interpret the look in her eyes. She seems genuinely pleased. But she can't be. Which woman would be pleased that her husband and the mistress he absconded with are having a child? Except perhaps if Becca knows something I don't. Like how unsuited I am to the task. Or Hugh is. Or we both are. Just at that moment Kate tips out the contents of my handbag on to the floor. Perhaps Becca simply knows how hard the task is.

'I don't think I've ever seen you without make-up,' Becca comments. I don't tell her that I'm wearing the full quota but my face must betray me because, slightly more sympathetically, she adds, 'Have you been very sick?'

'As a dog.' I don't even consider lying to save face. It's that bad. 'I was seventeen weeks yesterday. I'd placed a lot of faith in the idea that the sickness fades in the second trimester. But it doesn't seem to be easing. I'd heard that this is when I'll feel glorious and blooming and –' I'm about to add that, most importantly, my sex drive will come back, but I remember who I'm talking to so I simply say, 'But . . .' and leave it hanging there.

'Don't hold your breath. I was sick for nearly six months.'

Bitch.

'Seventeen weeks, so the baby must be about 100 g by

now, that's 3.5 oz.' Becca drops her eyes to my bulging stomach. She's obviously trying to account for the other 15 lb 13 oz weight gain.

It's typical that Becca would know stuff like this even though she's not pregnant right now. I try and demonstrate that I'm not altogether ignorant by parroting a fact I read just thirty minutes ago. 'The crown–rump length of the baby is 11–12 cm.'

'Really, it's amazing, isn't it.' Becca holds her hands up in the air and estimates 11 cm.

I hope she's no good at measuring because 11 cm look big to me. Very big. Eleven centimetres is about the length of a banana, but how wide? That's the pertinent question. How the hell does this thing get out?

I take the final bag from Becca and put it in the pile with the other 430. Why does she always pack as though the children were going on a year-long explorative trip to all six continents? We are only going to Wales for a couple of days. It's a hallmark of Becca's to make child-rearing appear as complex as possible; I'm sure she does it to intimidate me. She then begins to recite the list of instructions for the weekend. Yes, I'll remember to give Kate her penicillin. Yes, I do know that Tom is allergic to nuts and yes, I know he has an inhaler to treat his asthma. Wimps. I hope all these defects are on her side of the family.

'One more thing – Hugh asked if you've remembered to pack his walking boots?'

If I knife Becca, would a woman judge be more or less sympathetic than a male one? I wonder.

'Yes, I have.' I glower.

'Goodo.' Suddenly Becca checks her watch and then hastily kisses the children goodbye, explaining she has to dash or else she'll be late for her date.

Date?

I know I shouldn't be surprised – Becca used to be a beauty and recently she's lost a bit of weight and started to smile again in a way that does bring to mind her past loveliness. But I am surprised. I've never considered the possibility of life after Hugh. There certainly wasn't life before him. Not for me, at least.

Date.

So this explains why Becca is so unexpectedly (and treacherously) compliant with regard to access. Historically, Hugh has always had to visit the children at her home (*their* old home, stuffed with poignant memories – a transparent tactic) or somewhere neutral, but rarely here in my apartment. Obviously, Becca tries to exclude me as much as possible. Now it appears she's happy to offload the kids on to me, the Wicked Witch of the West, at the drop of a hat. Although I doubt it's that she's planning on dropping tonight.

I close the door behind her and turn back to the children. Kate is crayoning on the dining-room table. Literally. There is no paper involved in this creative endeavour. And Tom is kicking repeatedly the leg of a barstool, for no apparent reason other than that he can.

Enjoy your date, Becca.

21

It's not accurate to say that you can cut the atmosphere with a knife – you'd need a hacksaw.

Hugh finally rolled in last night at 11.15 p.m. I, in the meantime, had just got Kate and Tom to bed, after playing a seemingly endless game of jungles. The game was free play, there were no rules, boundaries or limits, but after playing for about twenty minutes I began to realize that there was an aim. It was for them to keep me tied up and on all fours for as long as humanly possible. Apparently I was a captured hippopotamus (a distressingly accurate analogy). I'd been ensnared by traffickers for an illegal zoo. I had to endure two and a half hours cramped under the dining-room table, which I would have objected to but it seemed the safest place in the flat; they used the rest of the rooms to terrorize each other. They ran, jumped, wailed, fought, bit, kicked, screamed, nipped, cried and crashed their way towards oblivion, and eventually wore themselves into that state Jessica used to refer to as 'past tired'. I then gave them a glass of milk each, a reasonably successful operation as only Tom broke his glass, and finally ushered them into bed. Then there was the lights-on-or-off fiasco – which involved my trying out more illumination combinations than there are on Blackpool front: main light off, hall light on door open, or main light on but dimmed, or main light off bedside lamp and hall light on, or all lights on, or all lights off but the radio on. We settled for bedside lamp on but with a cloth over it so it wasn't too bright. Then at last they fell asleep.

Silence.

I've never appreciated stillness quite so much in my entire life. By this time it was 10.45 p.m. The effects of spilt milk, chocolate handprints and crawling on all fours for hours had obliterated any efforts I had made with my hair and clothes. I considered that at least the constant activity required to amuse and occupy Kate and Tom had stopped me thinking about my nausea. It must be this that cajoles a woman into having a big family; it appears that this particular strain of exhaustion is the only effective antidote to sickness.

Suddenly it struck me that at least the children were company of sorts; now they were in bed the silence taunted me. This was possibly the most depressing thought I'd had in the last couple of months and, believe me, my thoughts have been fairly bleak.

Truth is, I'm lonely. Recently I've spent so many evenings at home alone that I'm beginning to think that I have something special going with the talking clock. In the eight months before the two blue lines, Hugh and I had probably less than a dozen nights in (if you include going to the gym as a night out). We were to be found at parties and receptions, in bars, restaurants, cinemas and pubs. In the last two months I've been out twice. Where the hell's Hugh? Whatever he's working on can't be this important, can it? I resent the bloating pregnancy. In the circles I mix in the only parts of the body that are meant to bulge are botoxed lips or silicon boobs. No wonder Hugh doesn't want to spend any time with me. That said, it was his bulging trousers that put me here.

When Hugh finally got home he tried to tell me he'd been working late, whilst the distinct smell of a good time – booze and fags and fun bars – wafted over from his suit and smile, betraying him.

'You bastard,' I yelled, not waiting to hear his full explanation. And that was about the nicest thing I said to him for the following hour and a half. The energy, which had been eluding me recently, came flooding back with venomous, Incredible Hulk-like proportions. I screamed, ranted, hollered and raved, not allowing his entreaties – that yes, he had been to a restaurant but it really was work – to interrupt me.

'So why didn't you call me?'

'We were short on time.'

'You had time to call Becca.'

'Well, I knew she had to make arrangements for the kids. I knew she was going out.'

'Oh, so you considered Becca's plans but not mine? You kept your promises to her but not to me.'

Hugh's face was flooded with confusion, as well it might be; no one had ever accused him of that before. Hugh rarely makes me mad and on the odd occasion he does I never show it. Being angry is hardly attractive, is it? Screeching and crying achieve nothing but premature ageing. If we do argue, the subject matter is never more serious than what we should watch on TV. We'd never had an actual fight. I shout infrequently, and I'm never jealous. Or, at least, if I am, I take care not to display it. This, our first proper row, was spectacular. Without allowing reason or rationale to direct my soliloquy I yelled about random things that had been niggling me. And, when I'd run out of those, I alighted on new things that don't really irritate me at all, but at least fuelled the row, giving me the opportunity to vent further my ill-defined fury. Throughout my roaring Hugh remained irritatingly calm and tried to persuade me to lower my voice so I didn't wake the children.

'Oh, so suddenly you remember you have children?' I yelled, managing to sound accusatory, bitter and self-righteous in just one sentence – quite a feat. I didn't allow him to answer but demanded, 'And what about the broken tile in the bathroom?'

'What *are* you talking about?'

'Didn't you notice the broken tile in the bathroom, near the sink?' I marched off in the direction of the bathroom and pointed at the broken tile triumphantly. 'It needs replacing,' I insisted. All at once it seemed like an atrocity. 'Didn't you notice?' I demanded again.

'Well, no,' he muttered, amazed at this sudden turn in the conversation.

'*No*?'

'Yes,' he tried tentatively, but I could see from his face that he didn't think that this answer was going to be any more palatable to me. He was right.

'Well, if you noticed, then why didn't you do something about it?'

'I didn't notice,' he yelled, finally breaking in the face of my persistent hysteria.

Perversely, I found his loss of calm rather soothing. 'Ah.' I smiled with morbid satisfaction. 'And do you know why you didn't notice?' He looked around the room, obviously hoping to find the correct answer scribbled on a wall or graffitied on the shower curtain. 'I'll tell you why not. Because it's too domestic, that's why not. It's nothing to do with you. The domestic arrangements of this home are nothing to do with you. You aren't interested.'

'You're not interested either, that's why we have a cleaner,' he pleaded.

Whilst this was a fair point I was determined not to fold that easily. 'And you're not interested in Kate or Tom or me either, because if you were you'd have come home at 6.30 p.m. as per our agreement.' I hadn't realized I thought this, at least not until I'd said it. All I could think was, Thank God I'm not married to this selfish, thoughtless git. I'd sooner swim with crocodiles than shackle myself to this wanker.

But I am shackled to him. The baby that's growing inside me is more binding than a bloody wedding band, and although it only weighs 100 g it's more constraining than a ball and chain.

And he's not a wanker. He's Hugh and I love him and I've always loved him and I will always love him. There isn't any alternative. It was my own self-pity that finally broke me. The emotional hurricane that had whipped me into such frenzy passed, leaving me with the devastation wreaked by the words I'd used. I am not the sort of woman who behaves in an insane, illogical, preposterous way and then blames it pathetically (and disloyally) on her 'time of month'. I've never 'absent-mindedly' shoplifted, I've never cut out the crotch of my ex-lover's designer suits. I am in control of my body, my emotions, my future, and I'm responsible for my past. I would have told him all of this, but I was crying and couldn't get the words out between the sobs. Lying prone on the settee, two things crossed my mind: one, Hugh is no more used to seeing me cry than seeing me rant. Normally I really am the very epitome of rational behaviour. I've often sobbed about him, but I usually employ a policy of stiff upper lip in front of him. Even when I watched him return to Becca, over and over again. Even when I watched him get married. Even when I drove Becca to the hospital to have Kate (there was no one else to do the honours). Yet, now, when I'm having his baby, I start to sob. Where's the logic in that?

The second thing that crossed my mind was that I was wearing pop socks.

I'm the size of a whale and my trousers are riding up to expose pop socks. This bout of histrionics would almost certainly have been more effective if I still weighed eight stone four and was wearing stockings.

With relief Hugh realized that the storm was over and gathered me in his arms, whilst making soothing, cooing sounds. I instantly forgot that it was him I was angry with in the first place and clung tightly, wrapping myself around him like a limpet.

So, naturally, the atmosphere this morning requires a hacksaw to penetrate through the confusion, regrets and fear. We are both being overly polite. Trying just a bit too hard to show that last night, our first-ever row, is forgotten, and by doing so we betray the fact that neither of us is thinking of anything but.

First ever.

Hugh and I often take weekend breaks. Usually abroad – Barcelona, Prague, Paris or Rome – but sometimes in the UK too. Just before Christmas we spent a weekend at Babington House, enjoying the hotel spa, the countryside and the fact that we were miles away from Christmas shoppers. I can't help but compare that car journey to this. Then, as now, we sat in a seemingly endless traffic jam, but then it was distinctly fun. Our CDs were playing on the Boxster stereo and we sang along at the tops of our voices. I kept popping squares of bitter, dark Lindt chocolate into his mouth (although not into mine) and each time he sucked on my fingers. The traffic was moving so slowly that it was possible for him to lean over and kiss me or grab my thigh every now and then. And we chattered, non-stop, about our week at work, treatments we'd indulge in at the spa, our plans for Christmas, anything really. That was three months ago. It might as well have been three years ago or three million years ago.

I wonder if Hugh is remembering that journey too. I can't decide if I hope he is or I hope he isn't.

Hugh is bewildered. He often has to stay at work for impromptu dinners with clients; normally I don't mind and I do know that he is working on a big pitch for something or other. I can't remember which brand; it's definitely not Mothercare or Avent. I, more than anyone, should understand the pressure of big pitches; they demand copious amounts of time and energy. He is under a lot of pressure proving to Rartle, Roguel and Spirity that he's worth the six-figure salary his new job commands. He needs a couple of big new business wins under his belt. OK, so he had time to make only one call, he knew that Becca would relay his position to me, and he expected me to understand because, as I say, it's a regular occurrence. I've always understood in the past. Because that's what mistresses do, don't they? They understand. It's the wife who traditionally has a comprehension problem. And mistresses don't do shouting; again that's the wife's domain. Still, I suppose I should find some comfort in the fact that I slipped into the role with a certain confidence, despite the lack of a ring on my left hand.

I'm confused too. Why should a regular occurrence, which has never bothered me in the past, suddenly annoy me with such a ferocious intensity? On the other hand, why can't he see how insensitive his behaviour was? I'm also annoyed at myself for having presented my grievances in such a hysterical manner; my genuine injuries were washed away with the murky gripes that came to mind when I was playing the wrought-up shrew. The broken tile, for example – definitely more minor battle than war. I sigh, exhausted with trying to decide who was in the right and who was in the wrong.

I force myself to concentrate on the weekend in front of us. After all, it's supposed to be a holiday. I politely offer Hugh a boiled sweet and he politely accepts it. He comments on the weather, I mention that it's cold inside the car, he tries to adjust the heating, fiddling with unfamiliar dials. We've hired a saloon to accommodate the children; I know Hugh would have preferred a four-by-four. I'm afraid I didn't ring the car-hire place in time, this was all that was available. I ask him if he wants to listen to a CD or the radio, he insists it's my choice. The kids somehow sense that this isn't a good moment to misbehave and therefore do fairly good impressions of a couple of angels; there's so much caution swilling around in the car I think I might drown.

About half an hour into the journey, Hugh yells, 'Oh shit.'

'Shit,' shouts Tom.

'"Sit, sit still," Daddy said "sit still",' counter Hugh and I in unison. We take a second to grin at one another, relieved that the formality has been blown away with Tom's expletive.

'What's up?' I ask.

'I've forgotten a file I need for work. I brought it home last night but I've left it on the breakfast bar. It's really important that I read it this weekend. I have to take a conference call on Sunday night and need to be up to speed. We'll have to go back for it. Sorry.'

I don't mind in the least; in fact, I even remember (just) when I had the energy and inclination to work at the weekends. At the moment, it's all I can do to drag myself into the office to work conventional hours. I know I'm coasting; my hope is that I'm the only one who knows.

When we arrive back in London I jump out of the car and run up to the flat to save the time of Hugh finding a parking space.

'Got it.' I smile, waving the file at Hugh. He takes it off me before I've even fastened my seat belt.

'You were a long time,' he comments.

Was I? It is so cute that Hugh guards my every moment so jealously.

'Becca rang to see if we'd set off,' I say as I roll my eyes. Hugh smiles and leans forward to kiss me. Everything is going to be OK. For the second time that morning we head off towards Wales.

22

We arrive at the cottage at about midday. It's not the Maldives, nor the Bahamas. There are no white beaches, no designer boutiques and no five-star restaurants. However, since I look more like a beached whale than a beach babe, since I can't fit into any designer labels, and since most restaurants have menus littered with dishes solely composed of soft cheese, raw meat, and soft-boiled eggs – all of which are off-limits – Wales is perhaps a more reasonable holiday destination.

Except, of course, we have brought the children with us. Becca's children. And there's Penny. Becca's friend.

I wonder if the facts that the cottage is thatched and has a working chimney, and that there are window boxes at every window, dribbling snowdrops and daffodils, will be enough to make the weekend a success. Pull yourself together, girl. I'm surprised at myself. Normally I'm so good at looking on the bright side. I'm here with Hugh, aren't I? And that's always been enough for me in the past; just being with Hugh guarantees I have a good time, no matter where we are.

Although it's mid-March, it is Wales, so spring has not yet sprung. Snow is still lying in thick rolls on the hills and there is a light dusting of frost in the cottage garden. The sky is electric blue and a frail but brave sun is seeping through the clouds that slice up the view. It is very different from the soggy and grey sight of Clapham High Street. I have to admit it's spectacular. I breathe in, deeply. Trying to budge the nausea.

I can see Henry around the side of the cottage – he is chopping wood, which I think rather quaint and endearing. Hugh and Henry look alike, or, rather, Henry looks exactly as Hugh would have looked if I hadn't rescued him. Henry is four years older and looks about ten years older. They have the same square jaws and strong Roman noses and they have the same laughing green eyes and sandy blond hair, but Henry is carrying an extra stone and a half and his laughing green eyes are invariably clouded with worries about promotions, parking tickets and pets with lice, issues that I shield Hugh from. In my opinion, Henry's overwhelming domestic concerns would be somewhat alleviated if only Penny would allow him to shag her senseless now and again; she'd look better for it, too. Her complexion would benefit.

Henry's eyes do light up when he sees us arrive. He is one of the few people who manages not to betray any signs of whether he approves or disapproves of Hugh and me. He simply chugs along with it, endeavouring to be civil and courteous to me and, no doubt, to Becca too when he sees her. Everyone else we know feels duty-bound to pass an opinion. Most mount a moral high horse (standards notably lacking in their own lives); this is extremely annoying. One or two try to be open-minded and encouraging, which is more annoying still. Henry's diplomatic silence makes him very relaxing company.

It turns out that there's another surprise guest, a friend of Penny's, Libby. I don't hold out much hope for her entertainment value, not if she's a friend of Penny's.

'She's really, really nice,' assures Henry.

This doesn't recommend her. It turns me off. 'Nice' means she'll be boring. 'Nice' means I'll feel inadequate. Still, Sam will be delighted she can pair Libby off with James; since Sam got engaged her number-one pastime is matchmaking.

Henry is thinking the exact opposite. 'We'll have to do something about the sleeping arrangements,' he points out. 'Penny suggested that Libby could take the caravan, and the single chap – what's the name of Gilbert's brother?'

'James.'

'Yes, James, he'll have to make do with the futon.'

'Very sensible,' I say, nodding. I know Penny will have given the sleeping arrangements a lot of thought. I wonder if she'll insist that James wears a dressing gown at all times. Risqué, as far as Penny is concerned, is hanging underwear on the washing line.

I politely inquire as to where Penny is, although in truth I'm not interested, and as to whether the others have arrived. I'm told that Sam, Gilbert and James all arrived last night and they are currently out walking. Libby is due any minute.

'Penny's in the kitchen,' says Henry. 'Let's go and say hello.'

Because it's impossible to refuse, I agree.

The kitchen is a hive of activity. The smallest child is squashed into a sticky high chair. I think it's a girl, but it's difficult to tell because it has so much organic and freshly pulped baby food on its face that it's rather hard to distinguish its features. I notice the racks of organic vegetables in the corner of the kitchen. Oh, another formidable criterion against which I will soon be measuring myself. I know I won't have the courage to use baby food in jars. The child smells. Not of nappies (thank God), but of regurgitated food, child sweat and tears. Henry ruffles its hair. I notice Hugh smile warily from a distance – I think he's waiting for Henry to rinse his hands.

We let Kate and Tom loose on the other two children (definitely boys, I can tell by their clothes) who are sitting on the floor, playing with large Lego pieces and small cars. I nearly tread on them as I cross the kitchen to air-kiss Penny. Penny endures my physical proximity because she's too polite not to, but I can tell she wishes that I'd disappear. She hugs Hugh because no one can help but like him. And whilst I love him, I am his greatest fan, it does cross my mind how unfair it is that I am seen as scarlet, positively radioactive, whilst he, the one who took the wedding vows, is seen as a victim. I never asked Hugh to leave Becca for me. Which I think is to my credit, since it was the thing I wanted most in the world. I never once suggested that we needed a resolution to our affair. I simply accepted whatever I was offered. I made sure that we had good times when we were together and I left Becca to destroy her own marriage. Which she did, very successfully.

Penny isn't wearing any make-up but she is sporting a healthy ruddy glow, and only the faintest film of sweat from the heat of the kitchen. She's been baking bread and fairy cakes. Hugh steals a cake and Penny playfully slaps his wrist. I ask if anyone wants a Bloody Mary, and even though I plan to have a Virgin Mary, Penny throws me a look that is intended to turn me to stone. I deflect it with a huge smile, which wins over Hugh and Henry, at least. I also steal a fairy cake. Penny shoots me another withering look and moves the baking tray out of reach. I hope I've sabotaged the catering plan.

'Have we missed breakfast?' I smile my inquiry. It's obvious that we've missed breakfast. For a start, it's after midday and whilst I don't know much about children I do know they demand their sugar-coated E additives at about seven in the morning. Besides which, the great pile of gleaming, newly washed pans shows that a large cooked breakfast has just been cleared away.

'Penny could knock you up some scrambled eggs. I think

we have some salmon,' offers Henry helpfully. He moves towards the fridge.

'The salmon is for a quiche for Sunday tea,' protests Penny. Henry tuts as though she's being a killjoy. I know that it's more likely that she's simply concerned that if we eat out of turn there won't be enough food for the rest of the weekend. Which is sensible of her and therefore the tone *is* killjoy.

'Oh, don't worry, I'll nibble on an apple until lunch is ready,' I smile, nicely making myself out as compliant and her as difficult.

I'm immediately ashamed of myself. Penny brings out the worst in me. I sigh, suddenly exhausted. Since Hugh and I got together I seem to have entered into hundreds of these small battles with first wives. All at once they tire me. I wish that Penny liked me more or at least loathed me less. I wonder if that will ever happen and what I can do to make it happen. I wish that the resentment and mistrust could be wafted away by the yummy, sweet smells of her baking. I look up hopefully at Penny. Of course she can't read my mind and doesn't see the olive branch. She sees a big sign that reads THREAT hanging over my head.

'Let me show you around, George,' offers Henry. 'Hugh, you two are in the front bedroom, kids next door, if you want to settle in.' Hugh takes the bags up to our bedroom and lights a fire in there, whilst Henry shows me around the beautiful cottage.

It is textbook. There's plenty of room to house the tasteful rustic furniture and big Persian rugs. Every window boasts a stunning vista of rolling hills and possibilities. There are two big, noisy black Labradors playing in the garden, a fat, squelchy cat in front of the fire, piles of dusty old books and even a piano. Twee and clichéd, exactly what I want for a weekend break in the country. Hugh catches us up in the sitting room.

'The kids will love this big garden.' I beam at Hugh to see if he's caught my enthusiasm, but he's not concentrating on what I'm saying; he's looking for somewhere to plug in his ISDN line.

'Libby's here,' shouts Penny from the kitchen. Curiosity gets the better of me and I lean out of the window to watch the new guest get out of her car.

Libby is quite a surprise. I was expecting a Penny clone, plump and mumsy, but Libby is anything but. She's about five foot eight, slim, with long mid-blonde hair, which is only just visible as she is wearing a large hat with flaps tied under her chin. She looks young, probably still in her twenties. She's wearing a knee-length sheepskin coat and a long multicoloured scarf – I'd put money on it that she knitted the scarf herself or found it in a trendy little vintage-clothes store in Brighton. The effect is extraordinarily chic. Libby's look announces to the world that she is a unique combination of artisan meets trendsetter; yet, whilst she looks as though she's just stepped out of the pages of a style magazine, the whole outfit probably only cost a few quid. Just as I'm beginning to be quite hopeful that Libby's presence will tip the balance of the weekend away from conversations about jam-making and towards something a little more exhilarating, I notice another kid. A sticky girl, aged about seven, climbs out of the back of the car; the scales have just plummeted back down on the jam-making side. The young girl is tall, slim and blonde. She's wearing hipster jeans from GAP kids and, despite the fact that you can see your breath, she's wearing a cropped top, emblazoned with pictures of Westlife. However, her sophisticated look is ruined because she is also sporting a milkshake moustache and she is sucking her thumb. Naturally, because she is a child, she's sulking about some disaster or other – I think it has something to do with the number of sweets she was allowed on the journey. She must be Libby's kid sister.

Penny does the introductions. 'This is Hugh, Henry's brother. This is Libby and her daughter, Millie.'

'Daughter?' I ask, not bothering to hide my amazement.

'Yes, daughter,' says Penny, as though she were talking to an idiot.

'Millie's your daughter?' I ask Libby, just to be sure.

'Yes.' She smiles pleasantly.

Libby is oblivious to the fact that she has just *ruined* my theory. Since I've become pregnant I've separated all women into two distinct categories. Non-mothers are easy to recognize. No baby sick dripping down their shoulders or clinging to their calves; they wear a jaunty, celebratory, carefree look, as distinguishable as the morning-after glow; in fact, interchangeable with that look, because this lot are the only ones getting the type of sex that makes you smile the morning after. Mothers, on the other hand, look harassed, defeated and traumatized. Their faces are set with grim determination as they battle with the will of a minor and the indignity of doing so. Weary with self-sacrifice, they walk a thin line between arbitrator, disciplinarian and comforter. They walk it in snagged tights and ugly clothes. They smell of sick and wee.

Except Libby smells of a Calvin Klein perfume. I'm stunned.

'I'm sorry, I didn't catch your name?' says Libby. That's because Penny didn't give it.

'Georgina, but call me George.' I smile.

'Hugh's partner,' chips in Henry for clarity, rather ruining

Penny's chances of labelling me as the local whore. Henry pats Millie on the head, obviously mistaking her for a pet dog: she rolls her eyes and snorts her derision, but doesn't get the chance to say anything rude as Penny ushers us through to the dining room.

Throughout lunch (a generous and elaborate Ploughman's, with apple pie and cream for pudding) the conversation, rather tediously, revolves around what I should avoid eating. Whilst I can't complain that being pregnant means everyone ignores me, I'm still not happy. I've read the books. I know what I should avoid.

'Raw eggs,' says Penny.

'Peanuts,' adds Henry.

'Pâté,' adds Hugh.

'Goat's and sheep's milk,' adds Penny.

'Caffeine,' adds Henry.

'Saccharin,' adds Hugh.

Pregnancy comes with lots of problems; varicose veins, swollen ankles and unwanted advice are but a few. I glare at them around the table and defiantly dip my finger into the melting Brie. I don't actually want to eat it as I'm aware of the dangers of listeria, but the bloody food-fascists have riled me into defiance. I don't like receiving unsolicited advice at the best of times; I've never bought into the theory that it's well intentioned, I consider it impertinent. Throughout my relationship with Hugh 'well-meaning' friends have offered advice, which nine times out of ten could be boiled down to 'forget it, he'll never leave his wife' – now, it's a good job I ignored that advice, isn't it? If you *ask* for direction you must roll with it, take it or leave it, but roll with it. If it's uninvited I feel almost duty-bound to be uncivil. Without doubt the most irritating counsel comes from women who haven't had children and men whose wives have.

'What are you doing?' demands Henry, when he sees the dollop of Brie resting on my finger, hovering between my plate and palate.

'You haven't even had a baby, Henry. What makes you think you're qualified?' I snipe.

'Yes, I have. I've had three.'

'No, *you* haven't,' I insist. I would have elaborated but, luckily for him, long before the steaming apple pie is placed on the table I have to dash to the loo to accommodate the pickle's second appearance of the day.

By the time I emerge from the bathroom, lunch has been cleared away and everyone is settled in the living room. There's nowhere for me to sit, and the after-lunch cigarettes (and in Henry's case cigar) make me feel queasy again. I'd rather hoped that we would go for a walk and get a bit of fresh air. But when I say this, mutters go up about arctic climes. I point out that Sam and Gilbert are out walking, but I know my reasoning is falling on deaf ears. From the number of beer cans and wine bottles on the coffee table it's obviously been agreed that the only march we are making this afternoon is the one towards alcoholic oblivion. Even Penny has a glass of wine.

I feel like a leper.

Even here, the arse end of nowhere, I don't fit in. I look out of the window.

It *is* a very pretty arse end. Maybe I should just go for a walk on my own, do my own thing.

But then that would appear churlish.

The children seem to recognize that I'm the only sober adult and pester me constantly.

'Why does water freeze?'

'I'm hungry.'

'Where is my comfy cloth? Have you seen it, Georgina?'

I ignore most requests and demands and eventually the children turn their appeals to Penny and Libby. I wonder if kids have a radar system that identifies mums as being the people who are the most likely to replenish the cup of Ribena or wipe bottoms, noses and faces. If so, it's a pretty primitive system, it doesn't seem to identify fathers; neither Hugh nor Henry are much help. Hugh's effort to explain how water freezes is far too complex; it bores and confuses the children. Whilst Henry does *offer* to make some sandwiches, his attempts are ham-fisted. Rather than shout out a constant stream of instructions – 'the butter's out', 'there's some chicken or jam', 'the knives are in the top drawer on the right-hand side' – Penny, in the end, gets up to make the snacks. The snacks don't appease them and the children quickly start to snipe at one another. The adults are all a bit tipsy and so they start to snipe at one another as well. There's nothing on TV except an old black and white musical. Penny and Libby want to watch it, but Henry is the king of the remote and irritates everyone by constantly flicking between channels.

'We can't even look forward to *Brookside*,' comments Libby.

'Why not?'

'Get this! Wales doesn't receive Channel 4.'

I notice Millie emptying the entire contents of my make-up bag on to the tiled kitchen floor. I watch helplessly as a twenty-quid mascara rolls into the black hole that is the space under the fridge and as she liberally applies my foundation to Kate's face, hands and T-shirt.

The initial holiday mood is fading fast. I fear that I'll suffocate in the dull domesticity that abounds.

Luckily, Sam, Gilbert and Gilbert's brother, James arrive on the scene. I haven't seen Sam for nearly a month, we still talk on the telephone, but as I'm not a florist or a dressmaker it's nearly impossible to actually get to see her. Even before they've taken off their hiking boots, I notice that Sam has never looked more radiant. I'm not sure if it is the day's hiking or the stop off at the pub that has put the glow in her cheeks but she looks fabulous. I hug her, greet Gilbert and then turn my attention to James.

I'm immediately pleased that he's joined our party; James is instantly identifiable as a good laugh. He's obviously a bit of a flirt and immediately sets to charming Libby. Sam will be thrilled.

I'm not.

I can't help but notice that neither his face nor his trousers flickered with appreciation on greeting me. Not that I fancy James. I don't, not in the least. I'm with Hugh and there's never been anyone else for me.

But.

But when did I become invisible? Historically men have not been impervious. Even with the most decent man – who is absolutely besotted with one of my friends, who would never think of trying it on, who has no real interest at all – his eyes would always sparkle in appreciation for a fraction of a millisecond. And the majority of men make it clear they'd like to peel my knickers off with their teeth.

Something's changed.

Who am I kidding? Everything's changed.

I take consolation in the fact that James's eyes and smile do betray that he is bright, easy-going and entertaining. His insistence that we 'get off our arses and get outside to play a game of rounders' confirms it.

'In this weather?' protests Penny.

'"You can keep your hat on",' sings Gilbert, giving a reasonable impersonation of Tom Jones.

I actually agree with Penny that it's far too cold for a ball game, but I'd rather pull out my fingernails than say so. I don't want to appear as miserable as she is, so I rush to the door.

The rounders game turns out to have been a brainwave. It involves everyone, kids and adults alike (except for Penny who excuses herself by insisting that she has potatoes to peel), and it blows away the cobwebs of an afternoon sat in front of the box, drinking and eating too much. We split into teams naturally. Libby, Hugh, Henry and I play against Sam, James and Gilbert (my presence is obviously seen as a handicap; once again I'm eleven years old and the last to be picked for the netball team). The gaggle of kids who are old enough to run stay involved by randomly fielding the ball for both sides. They are too young to be genuinely useful but at least they hamper each team equally.

Hugh and Henry immediately revert to their teen selves. Even though they are on the same team they jostle competitively with one another, often risking dropping a ball altogether rather than allowing the other the glory of a clean catch. Gilbert and James's approach is entirely different. They work with each other. Gilbert allows James to field a catch. James raucously cheers Gilbert throughout the game and Gilbert does move surprisingly quickly, for an older man.

We play until it is dark, and then we put on all the lights in the house and play a bit more. Eventually we have to give up because the electric light is proving inadequate and, anyway, none of us can stand Penny's constant harping about the waste of electricity. Sam checks her watch – it is 8 p.m. exactly. Her team are a single point ahead, so she throws her arms around James's neck and declares that the match is over and that they are the winners. If it's true that, 'it's not the winning but the taking part that counts', why does she look so smug? Gilbert takes up the cheer and they are so noisy that it is impossible for our team to argue that we are each owed another bat. Instead we concede defeat gracefully, well, quite gracefully – Hugh keeps insisting that my performance was sub-standard due to my pregnancy, and whilst he's probably right I'm not sure it needs saying.

23

Libby and Sam bath the kids, and James proves to be as good a sport off the rounders pitch as on by offering to read a bedtime story. By the time he re-emerges Penny is just putting an enormous fish pie on the table.

'I put six kids to bed, is that right?'

Everyone falls silent and does the maths. Kate, Tom, Millie plus Penny and Henry's three, yup, six in total. Bloody hell, so many. They're everywhere, and yet we still had fun, despite Millie cheating on the scores and Kate biting Josh. A lot of fun.

How odd.

Another oddity is that staying sober turns out to be OK, quite interesting in fact; it gives me the opportunity to people-watch. Everyone else is drinking copious amounts and as a consequence becoming increasingly odious, flirtatious, argumentative or charming. By the time the pregnancy is over I'll have several months of embarrassing stories about my nearest and dearest. I could blackmail them for large sums of money and give up my day job.

Sam has obviously forgiven James for being held in high esteem by Gilbert and is making a huge effort to put him at ease amongst so many strangers. Not that he seems to require any particular care or attention. He's one of those blokes who quickly makes himself at home and he obviously expects to be popular, which he is, so fair play to him. He entertains Sam, Hugh and me with stories about safaris in Africa. The stories excite Hugh so much that he starts to make plans for us to visit Namibia or Botswana.

Sam points out that I can't take malaria tablets at the moment and that by the time I can take them again we'll have a baby. 'Africa is hardly the place to take babies.'

Her comment is accurate, but I can't see Hugh at Butlins. Henry and Libby are chatting merrily about music. Most people have Henry down as a Mr All-work-and-no-play, and it's true his clubbing and gigging days are behind him but, rather sweetly, he still buys NME and therefore does have a reasonable knowledge of what's pop and what's not. They are exchanging views on who was the main influence on the Aloof. Turns out that both of them prefer the radio edit of Groove Armada's 'At the River' (as opposed to what, I don't know, the non-radio edit?). I wish Henry wouldn't monopolize Libby; the more I watch her the more I want to get to know her. All day her conversation has interested me. A unique mix of high(ish) brow topics and a healthy interest in the tawdry goings-on of the rich and famous as reported in *OK* and *Hello!* She seems good fun; I want to know more. Is she married? Who is Millie's father? Where did she buy those jeans?

I notice that Gilbert is spending most of his evening talking to Penny, which is noble of him but can't be much of a laugh.

'Supper was marvellous, Penny,' comments Gilbert.

'Oh, it was nothing, very easy, anyone could have done it.'

'Ahh, but you did,' he smiles.

'Really, it was nothing. In fact, I think it could have done with a hint of basil and perhaps a touch more salt.'

'It was delicious.'

'No, not at all. My friend Becca gave me the recipe.' Penny glances in my direction. I affect to be fascinated by the candle wax melting down the sides of the wine bottles. I consider assuring her that I know how perfect Becca is. I've known since 1987, which is why my life has been one long struggle. But I stay silent and remind myself that Hugh is mine now.

'Now, when *she* bakes fish pie it really is something to write home about. I thought mine was a bit bland.'

Gilbert sighs and gives up on the compliment. I don't blame him. For God's sake, why can't Penny simply say thank you and leave it at that?

Penny's next conversation non-starter is, 'I know other people's dreams are the most boring things on earth, but I had the strangest dream last night.' She's right, for once, other people's dreams are the dullest things on earth, but she starts to relay hers anyway. The story, something about a train and a fish, is lacking in humour, exoticism and eroticism; it doesn't even have an ending. Gilbert nods and smiles throughout, not betraying for a moment that he's so bored that his blood has ceased circulating to his brain. I can't decide if I admire his politeness or find him wet.

At a quarter to ten Gilbert suggests a game of cards. I've fallen prey to his tedious competitiveness as far as bridge is concerned before, so I decline the offer, as does Libby. Sam, Gilbert, Hugh and James make up a four, Henry looks on and Penny starts to wash up, despite everyone's entreaties to leave it until the morning (she really does know how to break up a party). So, finally, I get to chat to Libby.

'Is it too smoky for you in here?' she asks thoughtfully.

'To be honest, I am beginning to feel a bit queasy,' I admit.

'Come on, let's go and have a walk outside.'

I don't mind giving up the open fire, even though it's an outrageously cold night. I grab my coat, scarf and gloves and follow Libby up the garden path. The air bites at my skin and makes me doubt that spring will ever arrive.

'It's a shocker of a year weather-wise, isn't it?' I comment.

'Yeah, but you don't want a hot summer anyway, it will only make you feel more uncomfortable.'

I could kiss her. It's not that I've suddenly developed lesbian tendencies, it's just that that comment is the first I've heard from anyone that suggests they know how difficult pregnancy can be. I was beginning to think that there's only ever been me, in the entire history of mankind (or, to be technically accurate, womankind) who has struggled with this pregnancy thing. Everyone else seems to imply that it's as easy as a lady of the night, as natural as the waves coming in. Libby hasn't said much about the pregnancy but, notably, she hasn't said that I must be 'excited' or 'delighted'. She hasn't offered any advice on what to eat, nor has she asked me how much weight I've put on. I'm very, very grateful.

'You work in advertising, right?'

'Yeah, I'm a New Business Director at an agency called Q&A.' I briefly tell her what I do. In my experience, people don't much care or understand what other people do for a living – it's just one of those questions we feel under some obligation to ask – but surprisingly Libby seems genuinely interested.

'And Hugh?'

'He's at another agency, R, R&S.'

'What's with this initial thing? Why can't advertising agencies have proper names? I thought that was the point of advertising agencies, to make distinct brands.'

I smile. 'Good point. It's designed to confuse.'

'Hugh was talking about pitching for new business too. But he's not a New Business Director, is he?'

'No. He's the MD.' And I can't help myself, I shimmer

with pride. 'But the MD is always intrinsically involved in new business. I report into a guy called Dean, who's my MD.'

'Is he a good boss?'

I think about it, perhaps for the first time, and find that my not very inspirational answer is, 'Mostly good enough.'

'Do you like your job?'

'Ditto. Mostly good enough,' I admit. Oddly enough, I haven't ever really given it that much thought. It's what I do. I'm reasonably good at it, or at least I am when I concentrate. 'What about you?'

'I work in an STD clinic, in the city. I deal with the bankers that are more than wankers,' she grins.

'I bet you have some stories to tell.'

'I do,' says Libby, laughing to herself. I think that she's about to enlighten me, but we fall silent when Libby notices a fox. We watch it cross the path sleekly and glide into nothingness in the hedgerow.

'So, do you like your job?' I ask.

'Funnily enough, working as a receptionist in an STD clinic wasn't my ambition,' admits Libby with a wry smile.

'What was?'

'I wanted to be a doctor; the surprise arrival of Millie put paid to that idea. I was in my third year at medical school.'

'Where's Millie's dad?'

'Missing since action.'

'Oh. That's hard.'

'It was when I was alone in my bedsit, counting stretch marks, whilst my mates were out on the razz, chasing tequilas, but it got easier and now I see that Millie is definitely the best thing that ever happened to me.'

Libby must be doing some weird drugs. I mumble that indeed it must be a relief now that Millie is out of nappies and can put her own bread in the toaster. Libby laughs, although I wasn't making a joke. I am so lucky. I am. At least Hugh isn't about to do a Houdini.

'What was Millie's father like?'

I know I'm behaving like a student again. Not just because I'm doing a credible line in asking, 'Where do you come from?', 'What grade A levels did you get?' and 'What position on the UCCA form was this university?' There's something else very studenty about this conversation; it's direct and honest and seems drunken. I'm not asking Libby polite questions that I know would be socially acceptable (as is usually my way); I'm not asking pointless questions such as 'what type of tree is that?', which would be safe and give the impression that I give a damn about stuff. I'm asking her the things I want to know. It's a relief, it's unusual. Libby doesn't seem fazed by my directness but answers me in the same straightforward way that the question was intended.

'What was Millie's father like?' She repeats the question to herself and then shrugs, 'I can't *really* remember.'

I don't think she means that she can't remember who Millie's father is; her tone suggests that time has eroded the memory of how he was.

'Quite funny and not entirely useless in bed. Millie has his smile,' she adds.

I try to think of Millie's smile. Today, she has done a fair amount of scowling, snarling and sulking – have I seen her smile? Yes, I think I do remember her bestowing it at teatime. Suddenly her smile burns my retina. It's wide and sincere. A charming smile, although I presume her father had more teeth.

'How did you meet Penny?' The more I know about Libby the less likely their friendship seems.

'At prenatal groups. Josh is the same age as Millie.'

'And you've stayed friends all this time?'

I obviously don't do a very good job of keeping the incredulity out of my voice, because Libby answers. 'She can be a bit straight, but her heart is in the right place. She's been very good to me over the years. There are times when I'd never have managed without her. Girl friends really come into their own when you're pregnant, don't they?'

I don't reply because, to be frank, mine haven't. None of my friends have experience in this department. Ask them what you like about lymphatic drainage, calorie content, the effects of grape seed as an antioxidant and the advice is limitless. They can list over 100 uses for Vaseline (thickening lashes, conditioning nails, a cheap lip gloss . . .) but I doubt soothing baby's bottom would be one of them. They don't do babies. Sam always asks, 'So, how are you?' but before I can answer she comments, 'Gilbert and I can't wait to start a family,' and then she talks about Gilbert or, more accurately, the wedding. I don't spend as much time at work and I never see Julia after work now; even if I did I don't think she'd be interested in my pregnancy. In fact, I know she wouldn't. I'm beginning to realize that work was all we ever had in common. The champagne-swilling, vol-au-vent-eating women who I used to meet at parties and receptions were never more than acquaintances. On hearing about the pregnancy, many of them have telephoned – once. Which is the correct thing to do. I've assured them all that I'm thrilled and excited, the correct thing to say, and I haven't mentioned my mood swings, hot flushes or frightening discharges, as these are distinctly incorrect things to discuss. I don't wallow, but return to the question of Libby's career.

'Maybe you could go back to uni and finish your training, now Millie's a bit older and at school.'

'Yeah, I keep saying I will. The people at the clinic are

really good about Millie's childcare arrangements, so I bet they would be flexible about study time, if that's what I really wanted. It's just that I've never quite got round to putting pen to paper to apply. If I ever have five minutes spare I eat chocolate or drink a glass of wine.'

'Perhaps it's for the best.'

'Why do you say that?'

'What year did you say you were in when you fell pregnant?'

'My third.'

'Well, consider your basic grasp of biology – surely they'd done the birds-and-the-bees bit by then?'

Libby laughs out loud, as I'd hoped she would. It's a strong confident laugh that rings through the woods. She links my arm in hers and we walk back to the cottage, discussing whether Jude Law's arrogance is off-putting or gob-smackingly sexy.

24

At eleven-thirty I decide to turn in. I'm far too tired and sober to stay up to argue the pros and cons of Leo Sayer's voice versus Barry Manilow's.

'Where's Hugh?' I ask Sam.

'Dunno,' she slurs back. To be fair, she is juggling her wine glass, a fag and a hand of cards, so I can't reasonably expect her to keep an eye on the whereabouts of my boyfriend as well.

'We whipped their hides,' adds James, giggling drunkenly, then he turns back to Sam to make another toast to their victory. I almost pity them the hangover that is certainly scheduled for tomorrow. I wander through to the kitchen, where Gilbert is helping Penny dry the pots.

'Have you seen Hugh?' I ask.

'Yes. He and Henry are fetching firewood from the shed,' replies Gilbert.

'They took the whisky bottle,' says Penny, not bothering to hide her irritation. It's code, of course, for, 'They've gone for the night', but why is she being so testy about it? It's not a criminal offence.

I throw on my coat and gloves and scarf once again and brave the 'arctic climes'. It's such a clear, cold night; it really wouldn't surprise me if it snowed again. I hear Henry and Hugh before I see them.

'Congratulations,' says Henry, and he bangs his whisky tumbler up against Hugh's.

'Thank you,' Hugh over-articulates, immediately betraying that he's more than a bit merry.

I turn a corner and spot them by the barn, although they can't see me as they have their backs to me. They are sat on a huge, neat pile of chopped logs, looking out into the black night rather than at each other. The sight is quite touching, brother sat with brother, shoulder to shoulder, so I pause to take it in.

'How are you er . . . managing with the . . . erm . . . pregnancy?' asks Henry. The question makes me smile to myself. Hugh and Henry are equally ill at ease with discussing anything remotely emotional or female. The mix of both pernicious subjects is crippling. They are archetypal products of a single-sex boarding-school education. They are charming, independent, witty emotional cripples. However, I'm sure that if Hugh is going to talk to anyone about how he feels about the baby it will be Henry, so I stand mute and still.

'Clipped your wings a bit, no doubt.'

Now I really can't move, it's simply not possible. I'm rooted, waiting for Hugh's response. I'm not sure what it will be. It strikes me that I don't know how he's 'er . . . managing with the . . . erm . . . pregnancy'.

'In a way, but they can be rather fun, though, can't they? Children?' says Hugh.

Isn't that lovely? I start to breathe again, but I don't move, maybe I'll hear more lovely stuff.

'If only George was a bit more fun.'

Or maybe not.

'She's not taking it too well, then?' asks Henry, and I can hear concern in his voice.

'You'd think she was the first woman on earth ever to get pregnant, the way she's going on.'

Going on! I've hardly said one hundredth of what I feel. Going on!

'Don't you think she wants it?'

'She says she does, but she's behaving very strangely.'

'Eating coal?'

'Spitting fire.' They both laugh, 'A total dragon.'

I can hear whisky glugging from the bottle into the tumblers, another drink, and then silence as they savour the woody taste. A total dragon! It's just not true. One row. We've had one row! I consider coughing and letting them know I've arrived on the scene because I am aware that people who eavesdrop never hear good things about themselves. I stay silent.

The giggling subsides and in a more serious tone Henry comments, 'Well, it must have been a shock to her. You didn't plan it, did you?'

'Good God, no.'

'And she's quite a career woman. That won't be easy to give up.'

'No. I suppose not.'

So I'm giving up my career? Or at least Hugh seems to think so. We haven't talked about it. I thought I'd be carrying on after the baby is born. We need the money and, besides that, I may not be saving lives but it is *my* career. I know that only half an hour ago, on this very spot, I described my job to Libby in the lacklustre terms, 'mostly good enough' but it is *my* mostly good enough career.

'And you two have had a high old time living the fast life – holidays, parties, restaurants, bars – you can't do all that after the baby is born.'

'*I* can,' insists Hugh, and, scarily, I believe him.

'Shame that they all become victims of their hormones in the end.' Henry shakes his head with genuine regret. I'm not sure what it is he's regretting; the fact that women have the vote, perhaps? 'I always had George down as fairly rational, quite considered. In many ways, I've always thought she was more of a man than I am,' chuckles Henry. 'Certainly has a better car and stereo.'

'Not very good at maths, though, look at her blunder over her safe dates.' Hugh starts to laugh at his own joke but I don't think it's very funny.

'She was unnecessarily sharp over the Brie this lunchtime,' admits Henry. 'She does seem a bit tetchy.' His disloyalty inspires a rage in me that makes me think hanging is too humane a punishment for such treachery.

Which possibly proves his point. Possibly.

'Yes, she is,' agrees Hugh.

'And she always used to be so –'

'Compliant, accommodating,' Hugh fills in the gap.

'Yes,' nods Henry.

'Such comfortable company,' adds Hugh.

'Yes.'

'But now she's always angry, tearful, neurotic.'

'Yes. Well, I'm sure it's her hormones. They all get neurotic. I'm certain she's no more neurotic than any other pregnant woman is. Hormones are to blame. Things will settle down after she's had the baby,' comforts Henry, with the sensitivity of a genocidal Neanderthal.

'I hope you're right, Henry. I do hope you're right.'

I'm gutted. This is terrible. Absolutely irreparable. Hugh thinks of me as compliant, accommodating and comfortable. I thought he thought I was sexy, stylish and sassy. Not at this precise moment, admittedly. But generally.

My head starts to spin as I desperately try to compute what I've just heard. For once, I'm certain that the dizzy rush is nothing to do with plummeting sugar levels and the pregnancy. Compliant, accommodating and comfortable! Hugh thinks I'm docile, submissive and subservient! Which is just one step away from imbecilic. It's so insulting. My breathing is shallow and fast. I can see it on the chilly night air, which is a small comfort. Seeing my breath cloud the icy night at least proves that I exist. That I'm here. Hearing your lover say such things can obliterate your very sense of self. The physical assurance of my presence helps me to remain calm. I watch my breathing become slower and more regular. Deep breaths. Deep breaths. Maybe this is good news. Maybe I'm being too hasty and judgemental. Hugh probably means compliant as in kind and gentle. Gracious. And comfortable is a compliment. At ease. I put him at ease. Hugh thinks I'm gentle, gracious and tender. And as Hugh is with me because I'm gentle, gracious and tender, then it doesn't matter if I'm not sexy, stylish and sassy. Which I'm not at the moment. Oh joy, oh joy, he's not simply interested in my looks, he's interested in the core me.

Providing, of course, that the core me is compliant.

Meaning gracious. It's just semantics.

He did say that he was looking forward to having a child with me. That it will be fun. Which is a very positive thing to hear. I smile to myself. I'm thrilled, ecstatic, amazed. Hugh is interested in how I *am*, not how I look. Which is fantastic. What's he saying now?

'And she looks bloody terrible. She's piling on weight and she used to have the most amazing tits but now they are fast beginning to resemble cows' udders, decorated with veins and stretch marks that look like the Tube map.'

'Big, though,' Henry tries to be positive.

'Yes, great big boobies,' says Hugh with audible disgust.

It's my own fault. No one ever hears good things about themselves when they listen to other people's conversations.

It's my fault.

It has to be.

Hugh finally comes to bed after 2 a.m. He starts to play with my breasts; obviously after a bottle of whisky it's not always easy to tell the difference between 'amazing tits' and 'cows' udders'.

I chase the bitterness out of my head and heart and I try to remind myself that I shouldn't have listened in to the conversation. It was a private conversation. And he wasn't sober. Nowhere near. We can't really be held accountable for the things we say when under the influence. We all say things we don't mean. He did say that he was thrilled to be having a baby with me and that he couldn't imagine anything being more fun. I can't help but think of Libby, who hasn't anything other than her bedsocks to keep her warm (unless she got lucky with James), so I cling to Hugh as though my life depended on it.

As indeed it always has.

We make love and, whilst it's not planet-scattering, it does have the advantage of being well rehearsed; it's warm and comfortable. I must make a bit more of an effort to be more 'up' when I'm around Hugh. I always used to ensure that he only ever saw me at my happy best. And although it is much harder now that I see him every day, rather than on two week nights and every second Sunday, I simply must try harder. I have been unnecessarily snivelly recently.

I fold my body into Hugh's and murmur that the fresh air must suit me. 'I haven't been sick for hours.'

'It must suit Sam too; she hasn't mentioned her wedding for hours, either,' he quips.

We giggle. I start to tell Hugh about Libby, but quickly discover that I am wasting my time. He's asleep. His breath gently pours on to the back of my neck, his left arm cradles my pillow, his right arm is thrown across my body, my back is toasted by his chest, and our legs are so entangled that it's nearly impossible to work out who is giving whom cramp. It's only when we are wrapped around one another like this that I feel really warm and truly safe. It is at moments like this that I remember where and why I've been travelling all these years. This is it, I have arrived.

Haven't I?

25

I wake the entire house with my retching. The only consolation is that I'm not the only one feeling rough; those who are feeling vaguely human are in the minority. Surprisingly, Hugh is one of them. I can only assume his hangover is yet to kick in, because when I got up at seven – to empty my insides into the plumbing system – he got up too and went for a run. Penny obviously isn't hung over as she only ever drinks moderate amounts. However, pretty much everyone else is reaching for the Alka-Seltzer. I realize that I can't be a very nice person as I find being ill with company infinitely more palatable than being ill alone.

I wonder if that's something I should work on.

'I'm too old for such late nights,' comments Henry.

Not for a second do any of us believe that his hangdog expression, pounding head and overactive sweat glands are the result of lack of sleep.

'I could make a cooked breakfast,' offers Sam. There is a roar of unanimous approval.

'Good girl.'

'Fine idea.'

'Well done, you.'

I catch Penny's eye. She's wearing rubber gloves as she's washing the kitchen floor and has just finished cleaning the bathrooms. Although she planned the menus, did all the shopping for the weekend's catering and has made every meal so far, she has not received as much praise as Sam gets for offering to stick a couple of rashers of bacon under the grill. I wonder if she's noticed. Libby obviously has, because when Sam leaves the kitchen to go and find her fag packet Libby comments, 'I wouldn't waste your time cleaning loos if you want to get noticed.' She drops three teaspoons of instant coffee into a mug. She does this in slow motion; it's obvious that she feels wrecked too. 'Men don't see dirt, they don't notice when it's messy, so why would they care if you tidy up?' She shuffles to the fridge and pulls out a pint of milk. She sniffs it carefully, but of course it is fresh because Penny wouldn't have sour milk in any fridge that she's in charge of. 'They notice drink. Pour them a glass of wine or fetch a can and a cheer goes up.' And whilst she doesn't have to be explicit, it's obvious that Libby's next observation is that men notice the food that soaks up hangovers. Therefore, despite the fact that breakfast is the simplest meal to prepare, it's always the meal that earns the most lavish praise.

I think it's pretty good of Libby to share this advice with Penny, but Penny doesn't thank her, she doesn't say anything at all. She waits until Sam reappears from the sitting room and simply says, 'Would you make breakfast, Sam?' (Although I do notice that the smile is a little stiff.) 'Then I can take the children to church. I looked up the mass times yesterday. There's one at eleven.'

'Do they go to church every week?' I ask.

'Most.'

Religion. What will we do? Will I instruct my baby that there is a God (other than the modern-day ones, such as Amex and Robbie Williams) or will I admit that, as far as I'm concerned, the jury is still out? There's so much more to parenting than buying the latest Nike trainers and, not for the first time, I wonder if I'm qualified. Hugh and I have yet to discuss the God issue. We must, and soon. Maybe I'll broach the subject on the car ride home. And I'll find a way to bring up the fact that I am planning on going back to work after the baby is born. It strikes me that besides sex we haven't done much together to actually prepare for this baby's birth. We haven't even agreed a name and I can't pin him down on whether he's planning on attending the birth or not.

'I'll come with you,' I offer. It's so out of character that Penny initially thinks she's misheard me. It's true that I don't regularly attend church – in fact, I limit my visits to weddings and funerals. 'You'll never manage all the kids on your own,' I justify. I don't suppose Penny wants me to go to church with her but on the other hand she can't refuse my offer. It wouldn't be very godly; it wouldn't be very Penny.

I bully Kate and Tom into wearing something vaguely smart, or at least clean, and, as Libby has shuffled back to bed to take advantage of the, I assume, rare chance of a lie-in, I ask Millie if she wants to come too.

'Why should I?' she demands. Fair question.

'We're stopping off at the newsagent's on the way home to buy newspapers and sweets,' I reply. It's a tough call. Millie will have to leave her Barbie and Steps videos or trust someone else to choose her favourite sweets.

'OK, then, I'll come,' she sighs, making it clear that her agreement is reluctant.

Millie won't put on anything suitable for church. To be fair, it soon becomes obvious that she doesn't actually own clothes that would be considered suitable. God is just going to have to accept her fluorescent-green mini skirt, silver halter-neck top and ruby-red sling-back sandals, worn (with undeniable flair and a dollop of unconventionality) with multicoloured, stripy tights. To prove she knows she's going somewhere a bit special, Millie also chooses to wear about twenty friendship bangles; it looks as though the weight of them is going to make her tumble sideways. Penny is obviously horrified and if I'd realized that Millie's appearance was going to upset her so much I would have allowed Millie to put on her fake tattoos; as it is, we have to hurry.

By some miracle, we manage to get all children to the church on time and, by another, they all look set to behave impeccably throughout the service.

My motivation for coming to the service is ill-defined. I know for definite that I didn't want to sit amongst the smells of a fried breakfast, yet another trigger which my oh-so-sensitive stomach reacts to. And a tiny bit of me thinks that, however self-righteous and irritating Penny is, it isn't fair to expect her to manage all the children on her own all the time. Who would have thought that rubber gloves could unleash such sympathy?

And then again there is something more than that.

It may be curiosity. It's certainly a novelty spending a Sunday morning in church rather than simply spending in the supermarket or on the King's Road. It's not that I want to pray or anything. It's not that I have anything particular that I need help with. My life is just fine. Hugh and I are having a baby and he speaks of me in glowing terms to his brother. Everything is fine. And, anyway, even if it wasn't fine, mumbling silently in my head, to a silent something in my head, is unlikely to be much practical help. Having said that, I find myself mumbling anyway. Something about 'please, silent something in my head, let it be fine'. Because it can't harm, can it?

There is no flash of lightning, no parting of the seas, no obvious sign of divine intervention. But, sat amongst the shiny wooden benches and smiley old women, singing hymns that I sang as a child, and watching the early spring sun filter through the stained-glass windows on to the worn marble floor, I feel peaceful. Supported. I lose myself to the sound of the choir and simply enjoy the confident, understated harmony of combined voices.

It's a relief.

The feeling of calm doesn't last as long as the sermon.

Penny has to take her youngest two outside the church – one is screaming louder than the tenor is singing, the other has peed his pants. A fact revealed to us during silent prayer, when Tom yelled at the top of his voice, 'Naughty Marcus has done splashy wee-wee all over the floor.' Penny's oldest child, Josh, has listened to more propaganda than your average Russian during the Cold War, and sees me as the devil incarnate. Given a choice of companions he'd rather spend time with Cruella DeVil. He eyes me warily and I know that I have only a matter of minutes before he starts to bawl. Kate and Tom are fighting because, apparently, Tom's coin for the collection box is shinier than Kate's. Millie is bored and keeps kicking the pew in front of her. Each time she does so she apologizes in a loud voice and explains to the angry occupants that she comes from a one-parent family and has never been in a church before, not even to be baptized. The entire congregation sigh communally for her poor lost soul and glare at me. The ones who still possess the majority of their faculties look at my ringless left hand and my swelling stomach. They mutter something about cushy number on the welfare state, tut their disgust and turn back to their hymn books.

I no longer feel supported.

I just want a fag.

And a stiff gin.

When the service is over I quickly usher the kids outside, trying to avoid the vicar's handshake and Marcus's pee. I'm delighted to see that Sam and Libby are waiting with Penny.

'We thought we'd come and meet you and we can all walk back together,' smiles Libby.

'Or pop to the pub,' suggests Sam. She catches Penny's eye and adds defensively, 'For a lemonade, there's a garden.'

'I don't think so,' comments killjoy Penny.

'Well, I do,' I assert. I'm in need of a drink, even if the only stiff thing about it is the straw.

Penny insists on taking Kate and Tom home with her. She exercises her right as auntie and I, common-law stepmother, have no rights at all. Oh, I don't care, let her take them. It can't be healthy that I've started to actively seek Kate and Tom's company. I am pleased that Libby opts to join Sam and me. It's understandable. As Londoners we are all deprived of fresh air and we think it's a luxury to sit on a bench near a tree, even if it is still chilly and we have to keep our coats on.

'Shame Penny didn't want to join us,' ventures Sam. Whilst I'm not losing sleep over her absence, I don't say as much. It's unnecessary to be mean to a woman whose idea of a good time is donning rubber gloves and cleaning loos. 'Penny is awash with old-fashioned housewifery skills that are dying out. I feel I could learn a lot from her. She does her own decorating, hangs wallpaper and everything. She showed me some photos of the children's rooms; she's painted adorable stencil designs all around the walls and ceiling.'

'Really?' I try to stifle my yawn behind a polite smile, but fail.

'She can ice cakes, arrange flowers. She knows stuff like the importance of turning a mattress.' Sam sighs her adoration. 'You'd find her interesting, too, if only you'd give her a chance. Remember, they say it takes all sorts to make a world.'

This is the second time in twenty-four hours that I've been given this advice and still I doubt it. Indeed, I'm piqued beyond reason that Sam would even think so.

'What makes you think that just because I'm pregnant I want to turn into the type of woman who knows how to remove stains?' I demand. Libby and Sam look at me pityingly. My example was a bad choice; likelihood is I will want and need to know how to remove stains from shirts, dressing gowns, carpets, coats and car seats; all sorts of stains, sick, milk, milky sick, Ribena, squashed banana and worse. It's a dismal train of thought, so I change the subject and ask, 'Where are the chaps? Didn't they want to join us?'

'James has gone back to bed,' says Libby.

'Wise,' I approve.

'Gilbert never drinks at lunchtime,' says Sam.

'Old fart,' I comment, but dilute the harsh words with my sweetest smile; my gesture is unnecessary as Sam doesn't seem to be listening to me. 'And how are your heads?' I probe.

'I have to stop drinking so much,' says Libby, laying her head on the wooden table and moaning. 'It wasn't just last night; I had a very heavy session on Friday as well.'

I *really* like Libby, more and more. This is more like it. Forget stencilling and turning mattresses. There's no need to assume that mums throw in the towel as far as having fun goes. It's obvious that Libby's life is no picnic, but I'm thrilled to note that she isn't letting her spirit, youth and beauty go to waste.

'Did you have a good time?' I ask.

'Millie, why don't you go and play on the swings?' suggests Libby.

'Don't want to.' Millie can obviously sniff a good debrief from quite a distance and is not prepared to lose out. Libby glares at her daughter and, after a short but undignified battle involving bribes of a bottle of Coke and a packet of crisps, Millie slinks off towards the swings, which puts her out of earshot – although her mother warns us that she's quite good at lip-reading. Libby chooses to answer my question anyway.

'Kind of. Some of the gang from work invited me out for a few drinks, and as Millie was having tea at one of her friends' and I'd arranged for her to be picked up from there by her babysitter . . .' Self-justification elegantly mixed with guilt is possibly Libby's natural state.

'So you were young, free and single, as it were,' I say, trying to hurry her along.

She nods. 'Well, a quick one turned into a slow several. The works: beers, wine, tequilas, a nightclub and . . . sordid S.E.X. with a friend of one of the junior consultants.' She whispers the last bit.

'Oh no.'

'Oh yes,' she assures, half cheerfully, half ruefully. We pause to open a packet of crisps for Millie; personally, I doubt whether this will be a robust enough distraction.

'And was it any good?' I ask dutifully. No one ever makes a confession of this kind except in the hope that they'll be asked for details.

'Not sure,' whispers Libby. 'When I woke up the next morning there were two things on my mind. One, who is this P.E.R.S.O.N. L.Y.I.N.G. next to me? Two, how can I remove H.I.M. without attracting the attention of you know who.' She spells it out quickly although Millie is at least fifty yards away; Libby obviously thinks she's currently in training for MI5.

I smile sympathetically.

'Actually, there were numerous other questions springing

to mind, vying for attention. What time is it? What day is it? If it's a weekday what shall I put in Millie's sandwiches? Is her school shirt ironed? How did I get home? How did my K.N.I.C.K.E.R.S. get stuck on top of the headboard? Who blew out the candles? Is that a red wine stain on the carpet? If so, will Fabriclean remove it? I decided that my rudimentary decision to concentrate on the original two questions was wisest.'

Sam and I laugh and Sam asks, 'Did you get rid of him without inciting the wrath of the scary . . .' She makes a movement that's a cross between a wink and a nod as she motions towards Millie.

I notice Millie tut. Obviously our attempts to preserve her childhood innocence are as ineffective as they are ludicrous.

'Yes and no. Getting rid of him was a doddle. He seemed rather too keen to make an exit, especially after he spotted the Pokémon stickers on the fridge door and the Mickey Mouse toothpaste in the bathroom. However, we didn't manage to accomplish his flit without being spied on by the ever-vigilant . . .' Libby points at Millie.

Millie breaks her sulky silence as she re-approaches our bench and comments, 'My mother is a disgrace' in her best Mary Whitehouse accent, behaving as though she were Libby's mother, rather than her daughter.

'Show no fear,' I whisper. Libby tries to smile but I can tell she's concerned. I don't know what to say to her to make her feel better. But I can't just sit back and watch her drown in guilt and responsibility. 'OK, so you slept with a handsome stranger. How bad can that be?'

'Not bad at all if I were simply single, rather than a single mum,' mutters Libby. It seems that Millie is an albatross and a lifebuoy all at once.

'We've all done it,' says Sam, patting Libby's hand comfortingly. 'Well, except for George,' she adds, which makes me distinctly uncomfortable.

'Haven't you ever had a one-night stand, George?'

'No, well not unless you count my first night with Hugh.' I briefly fill her in with the background of my and Hugh's relationship. It takes a remarkable amount of self-control to stick to the broad brush strokes rather than give her the minutiae, but then I am restricted by time – we have to be back at the cottage for lunch in a couple of hours.

When I've finished, Libby asks, 'Can I ask you a personal question?'

'Go on,' I agree cautiously. It must be bad if Libby feels she has to ask to be personal; we've assumed a girly level of intimacy and honesty thus far.

'How many men have you slept with besides Hugh?'

I'm sure if we'd met in our early twenties this question would have been included in the first five questions on meeting one another. Name, age, occupation, which Tube line do you use to get into work and how many notches on the bedpost? The order of questions four and five is interchangeable. But meeting a little later in life normally demands more reticence; I'd hoped to avoid it altogether. 'Besides Hugh?' I clarify.

'Yes.'

'How many?' I stall.

'Yes.'

'Err.' I take a moment; my answer is frighteningly unfashionable. If Sam wasn't here I'd lie, but Sam knows the truth. 'Em, well, none,' I finally confess.

'None!' Libby is so shocked that she nearly drops her drink. 'No one other than Hugh?'

'No,' I confirm.

'But you work in advertising?'

'A few near misses. Quite a few. But no actual, you know.'

'Hiding the sausage.'

'Exactly.'

She stops to do the maths. She's so obviously aghast that I'm distressed for her. 'That means you were celibate for roughly ten years, most of your adult life,' she says, incredulous.

'Yes.'

'But you give the impression that you are so worldly.'

I shrug, what can I say? He was worth waiting for. I hunt for a fresh packet of crisps amongst the debris. At least the rustling breaks the silence.

'Why?'

'Why what?'

'Why just Hugh?'

'I love him. I've only ever loved him.' It seems straightforward to me, but I guess mine could be regarded as a fairly complex moral code. I slept with Hugh although he was married to Becca, but I've never slept with anyone else because I've never loved anyone else.

'God, Hugh must be amazing to have kept you so . . .' she searches for the word, 'focused.' Libby can't take her eyes off me. In her mind I'm obviously akin to something that's just landed from another planet. I sometimes wish I were Madonna.

'Don't look at me like that.'

'How am I looking at you?'

'As though I've wasted my life.'

'How should I be looking?'

I can't think of an answer.

At great personal expense, Sam creates a diversion. Or maybe she just wants to talk about herself again.

'I'm giving up alcohol too. I feel as rough as budgie crap.'

Millie giggles and seems to forget her mother's one-night stand and my lack of them as, this time, she skips off toward the swings, appearing every inch the adorable, compliant seven-year-old. I can only assume she thinks she's achieved her mischief quota in church this morning.

'I didn't get to sleep until after 5 a.m. this morning,' says Sam.

'Show-off. Nooky in the early hours of the morning. I'm beginning to understand why you're engaged to Gilbert,' I say, coarsely winking and elbowing Sam in the ribs. It's funny, since I've become pregnant I don't seem to be able to do anything elegantly, not even discuss the lurid details of my friends' sex lives. Actually, thinking about it maybe that's not so odd.

'I wasn't with Gilbert. He went to bed just after you.'

'So what were you up to?' asks Libby, guffawing. If Libby knew Sam better she'd know *for a fact* that Sam won't ever be 'up to' anything again. Sam is engaged now, which was her lifelong ambition and therefore that's that.

'I was up till late with James. We went for a walk, actually.'

What?

'Just you and James?' I want to be sure of my data.

'Yes,' Sam is talking to something at the bottom of her glass, and she suddenly seems to be extremely interested in the grain on the wooden bench.

'Gilbert's brother James?' I ask.

'There aren't two Jameses staying at the cottage,' she points out, mildly aggravated.

'A walk? At night? Alone?' I persist.

'Yes. Yes. And yes.' The irritation is mounting.

'Why?'

'I don't know,' she admits. Suddenly deflated, the irritation disappearing in a puff of smoke. She tries to replace it with mock bravado. 'He's a great guy. We get on well. He's going to be my brother-in-law. I'm just trying to get to know him. We've spent the week together, he's a great guy.' She completes her ever-decreasing circle of reasoning.

And why shouldn't she? What's wrong with taking a walk with the guy who's going to be your brother-in-law?

Nothing.

Something.

Yes, something is definitely wrong. A vision of Sam falling through the door of the cottage yesterday afternoon, laughing raucously, her entire demeanour radiant and luminous. I'd thought it was the fresh air. Another vision, this time Sam flinging her arms around James when they won the rounders match – why didn't she give Gilbert the victory hug? And last night she hardly said two words to Gilbert, she spent her entire evening in deep and often exclusive conversation with James. I'd thought she was simply being welcoming and polite, but now I'm not so sure. My misgivings are further fuelled when Sam takes the unprecedented step of saying, 'Look, if you don't mind, I don't want to talk about it. Best we forget all about it.'

'Absolutely,' says Libby.

I just nod. This is Sam! Sam who has been known to accost strangers in the street and force them to listen to the bloody details of her love life because she's running out of willing listeners.

We fall into awkward silence again. I feel I owe Sam for helping me avoid Libby's tricky questioning so I accept the conversational onus and try to provide some entertainment.

'Hugh and I had a huge row on Friday night,' I confess.

'A row?' Sam doesn't try too hard to hide her surprise.

'Yes,' I sigh.

'You and Hugh?'

'Yes. I was furious with him.'

'Furious?'

'Yes.'

'With Hugh?'

'Yes!' I'm beginning to wish I hadn't said anything.

Sam lets out a long, low whistle. She's so taken aback that she doesn't even ask what the row was about.

Luckily, Libby is on hand to fulfil this social nicety. 'What about?'

'He was late. Five hours. I was stuck at home with his kids.'

'Look on it as practice,' comments Libby, then she drains her drink.

Funnily enough I don't see this as a comfort. 'He's started to call my tits boobies,' I blurt. The girls stare at me non-comprehendingly. 'I hate it. There are so many awful connotations. It makes me think of *Carry On* films and booby traps, booby prizes.' The girls both stare at me, obviously still not grasping the problem. I try to be crystal: 'Tits are sexy, breasts are sensuous, boobies are indubitably ludicrous.'

Their faces are vacant.

I give up. 'Fancy another lemonade?'

26

We arrive back at the cottage at about five minutes to two. Penny is just about to serve up an enormous roast lamb. A small twinge of guilt nips me. Unassisted, Penny has managed to entertain five kids and cook what promises to be a delicious roast for fourteen. I consider skulking off to the sitting room to kill the last five minutes before lunch as a way of avoiding her cold gaze, then I think better of it. I think of the countless brunches, lunches, dinners and suppers I've prepared in the past that have passed by uncommented on. Plates cleared, glasses drained, napkins discarded without so much as a 'Well done, George, very nice'.

I lift the lid off a pot and peer in. 'Looks very tasty,' I comment, and then more warmly I mutter, 'I'm sorry we left you on your own, Penny.' Half of me hopes that she won't hear me.

'Oh, it's OK, I'm used to it,' she breezes.

Instantly irritated, I fume that this woman is devoid of social graces.

Almost as quickly I acknowledge that she's within her rights not to let me off the hook that easily. 'I'll wash up afterwards,' I offer, then I quickly leave the kitchen before I change my mind.

Lunch is fabulous and everyone enjoys it, except for poor Sam who isn't eating; presumably she's dieting for the wedding. Apparently a must, irrespective of your size or shape.

'You're not dieting for a wedding, are you?' asks Gilbert

as he spoons a generous portion of roast potatoes on to my plate.

'No.' Sadly not.

'Nice to be pregnant and temporarily released from the tyranny of calorie-counting, isn't it?' smiles Penny, smoothing over any potential discomfort Gilbert's comment could have caused. All at once I'm glad I offered to do the washing-up.

'I suppose you're right. I've never looked at it like that.' I smile back and nod as she piles the works on to my plate. Lamb, mashed potatoes, three different vegetables, Yorkshire puddings, mint sauce and gravy. I even chew on the crackling, something I haven't done in donkey's years. Hugh stares at me with barely disguised disgust but doesn't say anything openly, so I pretend not to notice his disapproval.

It's not so hard.

Crackling tastes fantastic. Chewy and crunchy at once. The mash is made with real butter, not a low-fat spread. It melts in a creamy delicious mush on my tongue. How did I ever give it up? And because I can't drink alcohol I have lime and lemonade with the children. The full-sugar version. It tastes syrupy and luscious, rather than acidic and caustic like diet lemonade.

'This is really gorgeous, Penny. I can't remember when I last had a full Sunday roast lunch.'

'I don't know why you starve yourself.'

'To stay thin.'

'Well, it's not natural, we're supposed to eat. Do you know that your baby is sucking and swallowing by fourteen weeks?' says Penny.

'Really?' I probably have read that. But I hadn't taken it in. When I read the pregnancy books I tend to concentrate on weight gain; mine and its. Or abnormal foetal development, infections, the many ways in which this pregnancy limits my lifestyle. The bad stuff. I pause for a moment and consider the miracles Penny is talking about.

'And, incredibly, your baby's permanent teeth are already forming as tiny buds behind the milk-teeth buds in its jaw by nineteen weeks.'

'That's fascinating. Imagine how minute they must be.'

'They can already distinguish between sweet and savoury.' Penny is on a roll; this is obviously her specialist topic.

'Better not have any of the bread-and-butter pudding then,' advises Hugh, intercepting the plate that Penny is handing me. I look at it with longing. 'You don't want to be teaching the baby bad habits this early on. A little restraint wouldn't go amiss.' He laughs to himself but no one joins in. Nor do they comment when I quietly take the plate from him and firmly start to fork the sticky pudding into my mouth.

After lunch everyone settles down in front of the TV except Hugh, who finds a quiet room to read his file. It strikes me that we could all have been thus engaged in London and it seems a waste of Wales. I mean, there are hills and things, aren't there? We should be walking up them, or at least looking at them. Once again I'm sorely tempted to strike out on my own and go for a walk.

But I don't.

Instead, I offer to give Hugh a hand with his work, but he points out that he's pitching for an account that demands a certain level of confidentiality. He hints darkly that Q&A might also be pitching for this business and therefore we can't discuss our strategies with one another. He must be on about the Sun 'n' Sauce Hols account; both Q&A and Rartle, Roguel and Spirity are on the pitch list. As are WCRS, Ogilvy and Mather, Y&R, Saatchi & Saatchi – in fact most of the advertising agencies in London. MKJL already run the account, and it's my belief that they are doing a terrific job. Sun 'n' Sauce Hols have just hired a new Marketing Manager. He's called a pitch simply to flex his muscles; I very much doubt he has any real intention of moving the business, he just wants a few free lunches. He must be a very hungry man if the number of agencies he's invited to pitch is anything to go by. I think Hugh may be sulking because of the incident over the pudding – I can't believe he is genuinely interested in winning this pitch; it's not worth more than a few hundred thousand in a media spend. Perhaps he sees it as a potential creative-award winner. Arguably, any half-decent agency could create fun and attention-grabbing ads for such a cheeky brand. That said, our strap line at Q&A is a clumsy and unimaginative play on the words *Get off on Sun and Fun*. I think we've lost the pitch before it's even begun and so I'm not biting my nails. Oh well, if Hugh doesn't want my help it looks like I have no excuse for not keeping my promise to do the washing-up.

The pans are so numerous and so large that I estimate that the task may take me a week. I'm just musing on the fact that every idyllic little cottage with window boxes should come with an efficient little electric dishwasher when Libby follows me into the kitchen. She picks up a tea towel and quietly starts to dry the plates I've washed.

'So, are you attending all your prenatal check-ups?' Libby is drying the dinner plates with slug-like speed. She stares at the little red rosebuds that adorn the crockery with such interest that you'd be forgiven for believing that they held the answer to the eternal questions, such as 'Why are we here?', 'Which is the one true religion?' and 'Who will win the Derby?'

'Yes. I go to my check-ups,' I confirm.

'That's a good sign, well done,' beams Libby. I look round for the child with learning difficulties to whom she is so obviously addressing her praise. 'Some women in your position go into total denial. They don't attend their check-ups, they continue to smoke and drink. They exercise fanatically and generally try to live their lives exactly as they did pre-pregnancy.'

'My position?'

'Our position. Unplanned. Unmarried.'

I'm not in Libby's position – she was also unsupported – but it doesn't seem polite to say so.

'Going to the doctor's is a nightmare, though,' I confess, plunging my hands into the suds again.

'Why so?'

I look at Libby. There's something about her slightly harassed, shiny face that makes me realize that I'd actually relish a girly chat. Which is odd, because the only thing in anyone's face in the past that has inspired such a sentiment was something on the face, i.e., 'Is that the new Chanel lipstick you are wearing? Does it last?' Libby's smile gives me permission to be a bit more frank with her than I am with, say, Julia or even Sam. Maybe it's because her face is unadorned (other than with a faint alcohol-induced flush), and her hair is carelessly tied back in a stubby ponytail. Last time I looked, Julia's hair was ebony with red streaks (signature Toni&Guy) and she was wearing a Stella McCartney T-shirt and Joseph jeans. Sam's look is quite different but, if anything, even more expensive. It's all Hermès, Escada and Chanel. I'm not sure why both looks prohibit a swapping of confidences about the safety or otherwise of douching, itchy flesh and bladder infections, but they do. I wonder when Libby last blew more than

£25 on anything for herself (Dyson vacuum cleaners don't count). Knowing that it's much more likely that she has to spend her Saturday mornings in the Early Learning Centre and then McDonald's, rather than in Jigsaw and a neat little French bistro, is somehow comforting.

'It's odd. I've never worried about demanding answers from doctors, nurses or other medical bods in the past. They're just people.'

'Absolutely,' agrees Libby. 'I've slept with an anaesthetist.' The ultimate leveller. 'It was a complete disaster, his technique was appalling, although as an anaesthetist he was probably very skilled,' she muses.

I giggle, allowing trust to flow into our relationship. I offer a confession to meet her own. 'And at university I drank a number of medics under the table. I do know them for what they are. I've always considered it my God-given right – no, duty – to cross-examine them on exactly what they are prodding and why,' I pronounce.

'Absolutely,' agrees Libby again. And then she prompts, 'But . . .'

The bubbles dance prettily around the greasy plates, oblivious to my difficulty. 'But suddenly doctors and midwives have become deus-like. I'm convinced that no one other than the Virgin Mary could have ever looked her midwife in the eye. When talking to a midwife, my line of inquiry is something like this, "Excuse me. I wonder if you can help. I don't mean to be too much trouble. I am *very* sorry for asking, but could you possibly explain why you are treating my private parts with a battering ram . . . Oh, it's procedure. Fabulous. Thank you. So sorry to be a bother. Thank you."'

Libby is laughing.

I'm not.

I seem to have lost all my assurance, all my confidence,

and it took me so long to collect it. For years I have tried to be better informed, wittier, sharper, more intelligent, more sagacious, more lucid and perceptive. None of the above adjectives have ever applied to the pregnant women or new mums I've come across. Nearly fourteen years of effort. It's demoralizing to think that fifteen minutes of duvet action have reversed all that.

'I remember the prenatal examinations being intimidating,' Libby admits. 'It's natural that you feel a bit apprehensive, you are sailing uncharted waters.'

'There is so much to learn, and, however many books I read, or however many strangers stop me in the street to offer unsolicited advice, I don't seem to be any the wiser.' I raise my eyebrows and Libby laughs again.

'But everything's OK, isn't it?' she asks, suddenly serious. She asks the question without lifting her eyes, allowing me some privacy as I procrastinate about how honest I want to be. Whilst I've never actually been in a confessional box I think this is what it must be like. Frightening, difficult and yet enticing. It would be a huge relief to be honest. To admit that I'm nervous, that I feel overwhelmed and under-qualified. It might help to explain that I find it disconcerting that my body, which has always been just that, *my* body, for the exclusive use of G&Ts and Helmut Lang dresses, is now public property. It is peculiar that my vagina has had more tourists than the Dome.

It's not just my body; my life is not my own.

It would be a huge relief not to have to use 'the voice' to tell her 'everything is fine' and that 'I'm doing beautifully'. I'd like to say fuck 'the voice'.

'Absolutely fine,' I smile. 'I'm doing beautifully. Well, you know how marvellous it is to be expecting.'

Libby stares at me for the longest time but says nothing.

The moment passes, and I'm left with the distinct feeling that the only person I've let down is myself.

Libby hangs her tea towel to dry out on the back of a chair. 'Millie and I are heading back to London soon. We want to miss the worst of the Sunday afternoon traffic. Here's my number – I thought we might get together for a coffee or something.'

'I'd like that,' I beam. And whilst it's true that I haven't exactly been inundated with invites recently I realize that her offer for coffee is the only social engagement I've actually wanted to accept in two months.

'Well, give me a call,' she smiles. 'Soon.'

27

Hugh, Kate, Tom and I leave the cottage at about 5 p.m. after Hugh's important conference call and about two hours after the optimum time for departure; we catch the traffic and the children's Sunday evening blues. Still, on a more positive note, the long journey home does give me plenty of time to talk with Hugh. Until this weekend I hadn't realized how much we haven't talked about. I'd never thought of ours as a house of taboos.

I start with the question of childcare. 'Do you think we should have a nanny or send the baby to a nursery when I go back to work?' I ask. I've considered this question for twenty minutes before I put it to him. I've decided it's best to rule out any ambiguity as to *whether* or not I will be going back to work.

'Oh, you are going back to work, are you?' His question isn't challenging the assumption; he merely sounds mildly surprised.

'Yes. Had you expected me to stay at home?' Of course I know he had, but I can hardly admit as much without revealing that I listened in on his conversation with Henry.

'Hadn't given it much thought.' He smiles. 'I suppose that because Becca didn't go back, nor Penny, come to think of it, I'd assumed you wouldn't want to, either. But, by all means, if you want to work, do so.' He grins at his own benevolence.

'So nanny or nursery then?'

'Your call.'

'Do you think the baby should be christened?'

'Up to you.'

'If we do have it baptized we should go to church too, on a regular basis; there doesn't seem much point otherwise.'

'Oh, I'm not sure about that, George. Sundays are very busy as it is. There's golf, rugby and the papers.'

'Right.' I pause and look out the window. Everyone is in such a hurry to get home. All three lanes of the motorway are cluttered. I peer into each car that passes and watch the occupants. There are lots of couples. Some happy and relaxed; some obviously rowing; some weary, hardly talking to one another at all but already thinking about the towering in-trays and endless e-mails that will greet them in the morning. I pay particular attention to the cars full of families. It surprises me that there is no noticeable disparity between the cars full of families and those with couples only. The families are also a mix of happy and relaxed, or weary and rowing. The only discernible difference is that the family cars tend to have boxes of tissues on the back shelf and hand prints on the windows, not such a monumental distinction. The light fades and it becomes more difficult to people-watch, as the car headlights are dazzling. I turn back to Hugh.

'Have you read that literature I gave you on epidurals?'

'Most of it.'

'And you're happy for me to go ahead if necessary?'

'Well, it's up to you. Becca didn't have anything other than gas and air.'

'I know.' I bloody know.

'I feel sick,' shouts Kate from the back of the car.

'Stop looking at your book then,' I instruct. 'Here, suck this.' I pass her some boiled sweets. She doesn't thank me. 'What do you say?' I ask.

'Thank you.' She mutters this with all the sincerity of a *Big Brother* contestant expressing regret that they have to pick a nominee for eviction.

'Have you given any thought to names?' I ask Hugh.

'Have you?'

'I like Jake for a boy, or Isabel for a girl.'

'Not Jake,' yells Kate. 'There's a Jake in my class at school and he's horrible.'

'Isabelly,' lisps Tom, 'really smelly.'

Hugh laughs and says, 'Not Jake or Isabel then; you'll have to think of something else. Now how about some music?' He turns on the radio and the children let out a squeal of approval as they hear the charts countdown.

Conversation finished.

I lie back and close my eyes. I know it will only be a matter of minutes before the motion of the car and the hum of the various indistinguishable songs will lull me to sleep.

I'll be asleep before the end of this track.

Or the next one.

I'll soon be in the Land of Nod.

I sit bolt upright, I'm not even drowsy.

After weeks of battling with killer lethargy, why, when I'm given this perfect opportunity to nap, can't I sleep?

I wish I'd been more frank with Libby. She appears entirely trustworthy – I should have been more forthcoming. I mean, that stuff about the midwife, whilst true, is only part of the problem. As indeed is the stuff about getting fat and missing fun and flirtation. So what's really bothering me? Why do I feel so desperate, so defeated, so despondent?

I glance across at Hugh. He's singing. He's got a great voice. And beautiful eyes. A wicked grin. His eleven out of ten-ness shines brightly. I look down at my swelling hands and can't help but think that once a five and a half, always a five and a half. I've spent half my life at gyms and beauticians' trying to drag myself up to an eight. Don't make the mistake of thinking I'm vain. I'm not vain. The botox, the designer clothes, the bleached teeth, the diets, the gym, the implants, are not about vanity. The vain ones are the ones who go out without any make-up. I'd never have the confidence to inflict my nude face on the world at large. I admit I *am* finding the symptoms of pregnancy a strain; I sometimes can't imagine ever feeling human again, but that's not the problem. I don't resent the fatness, the spots, the lank, greasy hair per se. I fear them.

Hugh bought into the size-10, hard-body me who drank at the right watering holes, wore the correct Christian Blanken garb. He chose the skinny-ribbed, dainty babe. I was sharp, too.

As in funny.

That was what attracted Hugh, and I secured him by making his life as comfortable as possible. Feminists gasp, suffragettes spin, and my friends throw their arms up in the air and use words like 'mug' and 'doormat'. But, the thing is, I know we are meant for each other. I am a better person because I met him. Without him I'd have an average degree and a dull job, I'd shop at Etam, and I'd probably get my hair cut at the local hairdresser's. I might not even know who Christian Blanken is. Wouldn't that be awful? So, yes, I fawn and flatter and fall into line. All relationships are compromises.

Things have been a bit wobbly recently. No one said a perfect life is easy to maintain. You need to put a lot of effort in. It is possible that by not going to the gym I've ruined everything – I'm not talking jinxes; it's more scientific than that. If you don't go to the gym, you get fat, you become unattractive – and your boyfriend leaves you. If you don't read the newspapers, concentrate at work, you become dull company – and your boyfriend leaves you. If you don't go out with your friends and keep up with the latest trends and gossip, you become boring – and your boyfriend leaves you. Being pregnant is just another ball I have to juggle. It's not an excuse. What would I do if he left me? I could not survive. I wouldn't even want to. Vicious and virtuous circles are entirely the product of the manufacturer. I just need to get back on track. I should have a manicure or read *The Economist.*

I can hold this together despite Mother Nature being a class-A bitch.

I'm sure I can.

April

28

'Let's cast our minds back to this time last year when you came to us, to share your marketing objectives. Three simple objectives. Firstly, to take a 2 per cent share of the fruit-flavoured carbonated-drinks market by the end of year one – bearing in mind that this market is extremely fragmented and crowded, with no one brand taking even as much as a 9 per cent share. Two, to minimize the cannibalization of our clients' extremely prestigious fruit-flavoured portfolio.' Karl pauses at this point to flash a winning smile at the young Brand Manager. She smiles back, succumbing to the blatant flirting. 'And three –' Karl pauses again. Yes, and three?

I wait expectantly. Karl looks around the room in desperation and then I remember it's at this point I'm supposed to interrupt him and say, 'Karl, I really don't think we need to teach Ms Carter how to suck eggs; she knows her own brand objectives better than we do.'

Actually, we didn't achieve the third objective, which was to come in on budget. A fact that we obviously don't want to dwell on. I manage to jump in just in time. Karl shoots me a look that would sour sherbet; I nearly dropped him in it. Drew is shaking his head, too. Whoops. I don't know why they are looking so stressed. Ms Carter clearly has the hots for Karl and, if push comes to shove, I'm sure Karl will oblige to keep her sweet, all in the name of duty, you understand. Besides which, Karl has delivered his little intro perfectly. He commands the room and hijacks everyone's attention. This act *is* impressive the first couple of times you see it, but recently I've longed for him to drop the show; he uses it in his business and private lives alike and it bores me. I imagine that if he ever does decide to propose to his long-suffering girlfriend of nine years he'll use a PowerPoint presentation.

Point One: why I'm proposing, subdivided into three categories – a, Karl is an irresistible proposition; b, the demographic-trend data detailing average age of those tying the knot; c, financial considerations.

Point Two: why Jenny should accept . . .

I deliver the next part of the presentation and, luckily, Ms Carter doesn't notice the fact that we overspent on her budget by about 17 per cent.

I'm torn.

I'd wanted to come clean and explain to the client why we had overspent. The fact is, the repeat fees for the actress who starred in the advert broke the bank. The client was informed of the cost at the time and agreed to it, 'providing we tried to cut back elsewhere'. We did try, but not too hard. When we were preparing for this annual review, I suggested that we simply remind the client that she did sign this cost off. Karl disagreed and was annoyed that I should want to be so 'naively transparent'. Drew doesn't dirty his hands with anything as grubby as money, preferring instead to stay resident of his personal ivory tower, and Brett didn't support me much either because he'd been the one who had insisted on that particular actress. I hadn't the energy to argue the point of principle. To be honest, it surprised me how little I cared – it's only a fizzy drink. So we resorted to the one, two, but not three, set-up. I have to admit Karl was right – we got away with it.

I'm barely concentrating on my part of the presentation,

but that's OK, because neither is Ms Carter – she's too busy playing eye tennis with Karl, the consummate flirt. I suppose Karl *is* attractive, in an obvious sort of way and, arguably, what other way is there? He's just flashed her a smile that regularly causes meltdown in the West End. He has Ms Carter's undivided.

I stagger out of the room and am planning to slope off early this evening to the chemist's to pick up some vitamins, but my plan is brought to an abrupt halt when Dean catches me sneaking out of the door. He calls me into his office. His tone is neutral, but I feel like I've been caught smoking behind the bike sheds and have been ordered to the headmaster's for a big bad bollocking. I wonder what the summons is about. I rack my brains for things I've forgotten or failed to do, or have simply done in a fairly inadequate way; I stop counting when I run out of fingers and toes. Therefore it's a pleasant surprise when Dean turns to me with a smile.

'Great news that we're on this pitch, George. High five.'

I take the letter he's waving and read it. It's from the AAR and says that a well-known luxury-car brand has decided to allow us to pitch for their advertising business. I would tell you the name of the car brand, but then I'd have to kill you.

'Make Project Zoom your priority,' Dean insists.

'Project Zoom.' I chortle at the unimaginative code name.

'My code name. Cool, don't you think?'

'Oh great.' I conceal my snigger and cynicism under a pretence of enthusiasm.

For some reason that I am yet to fathom there is always a dark veil of secrecy around pitches. The bigger the account the more tightly that veil is drawn. And this is big business. We're talking a multinational account with a media spend of £80 million, which is worth £8 million in revenue for the agency. My target this year is to grow the agency income by £3 million. Wow. Even in my half-baked-pregnant-mind-for-mush state I can see the importance of this pitch.

'I've already met the Marketing Director. Nice Chap,' says Dean. 'He mentioned you. Apparently you met at the Marketing Forum last September and then again at the IPA ball. Frank Robson. Does the name ring any bells?'

'Yes, I remember.' A shrewd enough guy. I was pleasant to him and did talk at length about the advertising strategy he is currently pursuing. I made him laugh with my summary on product life cycle. One, development: an expensive time that generates small revenues and little profit (we rarely muddy our hands at this stage). Two, a period of growth with rapidly rising sales and profits (count us in). Three, maturity, and then four, decline. I told him to call me when his brand hit Stage Two, but not a minute before. He laughed a lot and said he appreciated my honesty. It just goes to show it's worth being nice to everyone; you never know when your hens might come home to roost and it seems that this time the hen may be laying the golden egg. I feel almost excited. I almost feel like the old me.

'Well, apparently, he remembers you. You made a big impression, George.' Dean sniggers, he can't help himself, he just has to repeat, 'A *big* impression, although I dare say you'd make a much bigger one now.'

I glare at him and he tries to rein in his buoyancy. 'Well done. Attagirl. Just when I was beginning to think you'd lost your edge, you pull the rabbit out of the hat.' He chuckles to himself and starts to root through his desk drawer for a cigar. 'I needn't spend so much time wondering about your severance package now, ha, ha.' He smiles, but part of me knows part of him isn't joking.

Lost my edge! Lost my edge! I want to say something

cutting, but then I consider that the criticism is fair enough. A fact confirmed to me when I notice that at the bottom of the letter from the AAR there is a paragraph noting that they've been trying to discuss this pitch with me for over a month and I've failed to return their calls. Presumably Dean has overlooked this passage in his euphoria at Q&A actually having made it on to the pitch list. I hastily gather up the letter and say, 'I'm all over it like a rash already, Dean. It's all under control.'

'The client's insisting on absolute secrecy with regard to who's made it on to the pitch list. Even within the agency we should only discuss this with those who will be directly involved.'

'Well, that code name will be a tough nut to crack,' I comment. Luckily, Dean takes himself far too seriously to suspect that anyone else would do otherwise.

'We don't want to come across as a leaky ship. I want Chinese walls, not bloody Chinese whispers. See to it, George.'

'Will do.'

'Thought of a team yet?' he demands.

No. 'Yes. Obviously, with such an important piece of business we need some heavy management guys. Karl, Drew and Brett should all be very much involved.'

'Absolutely.'

'Karl and I will discuss the finer points of who we should draft in to make up the best account-management team; we'll get back to you with details.'

'Go get 'em, George.'

Lost my fucking edge.

I'll show him. It will be the best pitch in advertising history. I'll wow them with the strategy; I'll schmooze the client to within an inch of his life; I'll pull together the sharpest, keenest, brightest the agency has to offer; I'll use the most innovative media yet – we'll advertise on waterfalls if we have to. I'll be galvanized, I'll be energized, I'll be motivated.

I better go and buy those vitamins.

29

Chemists' are awful places. The smell – a noxious mix of suffering and sanitation mingling to create the most unwelcoming aroma possible – is worse than fishmongers' or even pet shops. In addition the queues are always endless and, like doctors' waiting rooms, there is a serious possibility that standing in line will turn out to be lethal. I try to avoid the other customers' eyes and illnesses by studying the produce on sale – incontinence underwear, support tights and powders for athlete's foot. How can a chemist's be a pleasant retail environment if the nicest thing on sale is TCP throat pastels? I shuffle to the front of the queue and hand over the prescription.

OK. The pitch is just another ball to juggle. I can do it. The vitamins will help with the pregnancy and I'll cook for Hugh tonight. Something special. Although I think he mentioned that he'd be late tonight. Never mind, I can use the time to read the brief for Project Zoom. I can do this.

'You can buy these over the counter,' the assistant yawns. What does she mean? That's what I'm trying to do. 'They're all the same.'

'Whatever.' I shrug non-committally.

'Well, which ones?' she demands. The rest of the people in the queue begin to groan impatiently and glare angrily because I don't know the system.

'I'll just have whatever it says,' I comment, nonplussed.

'Over the counter or from this prescription?' she pursues.

What's the difference? Do I care?

'Over the counter is cheaper if you pay for your prescriptions. Do you pay for your prescriptions?' she stalks her point.

'Yes.' I'm shocked that she'd ask me. The rest of the customers seem shocked that I pay and tut their disapproval.

The pharmacist scrutinizes the prescription and then glares at my bulge. 'Oh no, you don't. Not now that you are pregnant,' she sneers.

Why does her tone suggest that she thinks she's caught me trying to defraud several governments so as to provide illegal funds to terrorists? My only mistake is that I tried to pay for a prescription that she wants to give me for free.

'Sit.'

Her Barbara Woodhouse tone is extremely effective. I grab a seat and wonder when life became so complicated. I know the answer. I can date it back to the two blue lines on the baton. The lines that broke the camel's back. My surge of confidence at hearing we are on the pitch list begins to wane. What if I can't pull it off? What if being pregnant really has mushed my mind? After all, I can't seem to manage efficiently the simple task of buying vitamins. Has Dean really been thinking about my severance package? Damn, I've spent so much time worrying about how ugly and lonely this pregnancy has rendered me that I haven't been paying attention to the big stuff. If twenty-second jingles can be considered the big stuff, that is. I'll simply have to try harder. Try harder to be more efficient and effective at work. Try harder to be more pleasant company around Hugh. And try harder to be better presented.

I have a dull headache starting just above my right eye; it's irritation that I'm sat in a chemist's and yet there's no chance of any medical intervention. I look around to find something to distract me. There's not much choice – leaflets and posters about treating acne or demonstrating the correct application of an ankle bandage. The leaflet on acne makes me itch so I opt for the one on ankle-bandage application.

Although I've offered no encouragement, the woman sat next to me, who has a double buggy and a bump, decides to strike up conversation.

'When are you due?'

'August,' I reply and return to the fascinating topic of ankle bandages. I'm not in the mood for chit-chat.

'Really? I thought you were further gone,' comments the bump woman.

I'm halfway through my pregnancy and, although this morning I marked the milestone on my calendar and I felt OK about it all, suddenly I simply feel like a fat failure again. If only I could stop eating – I reach for a packet of breath-fresheners (the only 'food' on sale in the chemist's), and start to munch them.

'I'm due in June,' she tells me, although I didn't ask. 'You must be having a girl as your bump has spread everywhere, even your arms,' she chuckles. I shift uncomfortably in my chair. I have no idea if I am having a boy or a girl. I haven't given it much thought beyond the fact I'd like a healthy one, preferably with Hugh's eyes. I try not to become riled by the fact that this complete stranger has noticed that I have enough fat stored under my arms to feed a starving family of five for an entire drought season. I try and see it as something that could come in useful if, say, I find myself in Africa.

'No, it's a boy,' chips in another woman. She's licensed to comment by the fact that sticky twins are clinging to her legs. 'Stand up,' she barks. Silently and stupidly I comply. 'Look, she's carrying a lot of weight on her bottom – "A lazy boy is all behind", they say.'

Do they now.

'No,' disagrees the first woman, with conviction, 'a boy bump is neat and all upfront. Nobody could describe that bump as neat.'

I sink back into my chair and a prayer that they will argue it out together without requiring any more input from me. I close my eyes and hot tears sting my lids.

This is worse than potholing. This is hell.

Bored by the guess-the-sex conversation (after all neither of them can emerge triumphant in the immediate short term), the first woman turns back to me. 'Are you using the microwave?'

I wonder if this is a trick question, but before I can work out the punchline I hear myself answer truthfully, 'Yes.'

'But what about the radiation and the foetus!?' she screams, and the odd thing is the other customers look at me as though *I'm* mad. I furiously blink back the tears; the dull headache is starting to pound. Bang, bang, bang.

'And I can see that you have your hair highlighted,' she adds accusingly.

My hand automatically reaches up for my head. I hate admitting to this at the best of times. 'Yes. I was feeling rather dowdy,' I mutter in explanation. The truth is that I look so crap at the moment that there is a serious possibility that my child will find the placenta more aesthetically pleasing than its mother. Having my hair highlighted was an attempt to stop the rot.

'But what about the chemicals?'

'Chemicals?'

'Do you want to poison your baby? They can be born with such horrible deformities if you've highlighted your hair and injected all those horrible chemicals into your system. You might as well inject heroin into your eyeballs.'

Thank you for that. Bang, bang.

'Do you swim?'

I nod, assuming this at least will earn me Brownie points and somehow distinguish me from Hannibal Lector. All the maternity books advise gentle exercise and, whilst I have been forced to abandon my hour-and-a-half, high-intensity aerobic workouts (big shame that my personal trainer never forgave me for vomiting on the stationary bikes), surely the effort I make dragging myself to the baths every week or so will be regarded as a good thing.

Wrong.

There is a collective sharp intake of breath by all the women in the chemist's (all of whom, I suddenly notice, have buggies and babies and rolls of post-natal fat).

'You shouldn't be swimming, think of the damage the chlorine can do. Would you consider drinking bleach?'

Yes, if I have to listen to any more of this nonsense.

The hammering inside my head is escalating and I really have to concentrate to hear what the bump woman is saying. I seriously doubt that it's worth the effort. She goes on to give me her qualifications for offering this advice. 'It's my third. All Caesareans. Look.' And before I have a chance to object she whips her jumper up and trousers down and flashes her scars at me. What to say?

Nothing.

Pregnancy seems to be a rite of passage to a club, and all the other members (mums and mums-to-be) think that we've bonded naturally, just because we're in this club together. And whilst I concede that listening to Penny's illuminating little facts about pregnancy wasn't altogether irritating – in fact it was interesting – her information was accompanied by a roast lunch by way of an incentive. I no more want to share my gynaecological details with a complete stranger than I want to go to war, which, I might add, seems to be a very close analogy for childbirth if these women are to be believed. This isn't the first time a complete stranger has taken it upon herself to share her battle scars. Last week in Café Rouge I met a woman in the queue for the loo who insisted on showing me her stretch marks, and there was another woman at the checkout in Marks and Spencer's who was determined to share more information than necessary about her problems with incontinence. Marks and Spencer's, not Netto!

It's repulsive.

On the other hand, who else am I going to play with? Sam only wants to talk about veil lengths; she and all my other childless friends and acquaintances are running ahead in their open-toed, kitten-heeled shoes, dashing into wine bars and designer-boutique changing rooms – I can't keep up. I'm not even sure if I want to. Whereas the bump woman would like nothing better than to discuss pelvic-floor exercises.

One of the grubby kids sneezes, and the bump woman slowly bends down to dig out a tissue from her bag and then dig out the snot from the child's nose. He doesn't appreciate her devotion and starts up an almighty wail. My brain splinters with pain.

I feel my life is over.

I have two choices right now: I could cry and scream and rant and rave, I could stamp my feet and kick and scratch (a little like the snot-nosed kid is doing). Or I could call Libby.

I reach into my bag and pull out my mobile. After all, with so much commotion I'm not sure my tantrum would even be heard in the chemist's.

30

I briefly tell Libby about my day, then I start to sob down the phone that I'm sick of trying and can't try any harder and yet I don't seem to be good enough as I am. It reminds me of a conversation I had with Jessica when I was seven and stranded at Brownie camp. Confused about how to make a washing-up-bowl stand from twigs and unsure of the genuine demand for such a product, I rang her in tears and begged her to pick me up. For the record, she didn't. She believed grubbing about with creepy-crawlies and having to ration loo roll was character-building.

Luckily Libby has experience with seven-year-olds.

'I'm not sure how I'll manage. I'm fire-fighting on too many fronts. I'm sick of trying. Trying to be what Hugh wants in a partner. Trying to be what Kate and Tom want – or at least will tolerate. Trying to be a patient and good friend, which I'm failing miserably at – I recently told Sam that I didn't give a toss if marrying in August was reputed to be more fortuitous than marrying in, say, May, as per some dodgy old wives' tale. Trying to be thin is a battle I've lost. I'm also defeated in my battle to try to be attractive, witty or coherent. How am I ever going to handle this enormous pitch when I have this enormous body?'

Somehow, despite my sobbing, Libby manages to get the gist of what I'm saying. She immediately says she'll put the kettle on and that I'm to come straight round to hers. I don't need any further persuasion, but I'm delighted when she tells me that Millie is at her grandparents' for the evening.

Libby lives in Earls Court, in the top-floor flat of a Victorian terraced house, above various transient yet consistently pleasant Australian travellers. Her flat is tiny, but whilst there's not much space there is lots of life. She greets me with a hug, which isn't very London but is very her, and I feel better for it. I follow her through to the skinny kitchen at the back of the flat, trying not to trip on the numerous piles of stuff that litter every surface. There are magazines, Millie's shoes, comics, crayons and toys, yet-to-be-unpacked shopping, piles of washing (needs to be washed, needs to be ironed, needs to be put away). The flat is cluttered with half-completed creative endeavours (knitting, tapestry, tile mosaics – Libby's; paper-tissue butterflies, splatter-paint pictures and cardboard models of HGVs–Millie's). There are dozens of Millie's works of art pinned to the fridge, the freezer and any available cupboard door. There are coloured fairy lights hung on every wall, as though Libby and Millie celebrate Christmas all year round. Then there are the books, the most impressive collection of books I've ever seen outside a library. The books are integral to their home. They crowd the shelves, tables, windowsills, the TV top and the sideboard. They are scattered randomly on the floor and are stacked neatly in piles in the loo, under the settee, on the stairs. Added to this there are the surprise stores – books in the kitchen cupboards, the cutlery drawer and on the shelf where she keeps tinned spaghetti and cornflakes. There are thousands of books, quite literally.

I'm feeling a bit shy after my histrionics, so I try to make general conversation to lighten the mood. 'Have you read them all?' I ask.

'Yes,' says Libby, 'why else would I have them?' I don't tell her that my shelves are mostly stacked with lifestyle magazines. The books I do have are made up of: 50 per cent

I have read, 25 per cent that I keep meaning to read, and 25 per cent that I feel I should read. Libby has worthy books discussing theology, politics, history. There are poetry books, literary books, books about music, travel, law and biology. There are dozens of novels, every Whitbread and Booker contender since the year dot, and her shelves also boast the odd sexy, trashy novel, which, I think, shows a certain amount of quirky independence.

I follow Libby through to the kitchen whilst she gathers up the necessities for a comfortable evening debrief. I watch her efficiently pull together teapot, mugs, biscuits, milk and sugar, and put them on a tray. Her crockery doesn't match, but is a hotchpotch of brightly coloured hand-painted affairs. They look great, comfortable, inviting, which makes me wonder why I spend time combing the shops for the exact replacement cup or matching milk jug when a piece of my Conran crockery gets chipped. Would the world draw to a halt if my crockery didn't match?

The window is open a couple of inches allowing, if not fresh air, then certainly the noise of the street to seep into the flat. I can hear an irate driver rowing with a traffic warden and, in the distance, a pneumatic drill. They are digging up the Cromwell Road again. It's spring, the season of fertility and promise, but only according to the calendar. April is having an identity crisis; it thinks it is January. Everything is still extremely bleak. The rainfall has been record-breaking, the freezing temperature ball-breaking.

Libby leads me through to the sitting room, where she has set up an ironing board, surrounded by yet more piles of clothes. She doesn't seem bothered or embarrassed by the mess. Nor does she appear to be fazed by my outburst; she says nothing about my hysterical phone call. I, on the other hand, am horrified. It's hardly accepted behaviour in front of someone you've met only once. I head towards the tatty, squashy settee, which is positioned close to the fireplace, and I fall into it. The clock ticks and the iron makes a swishing sound as it lets off steam. I'm here for the same purpose; despite this, I'm mute. Libby's question wasn't a difficult one. Did I enjoy Wales? It should be easy enough to answer and yet I'm struggling. The shame is overwhelming. I know I've said too much to pretend I was simply joking when I called from the chemist's. I said I couldn't cope. Me who's always coped, no, excelled. I wonder if I can blame my hormones?

'So did you enjoy Wales?' Libby asks again.

'Mostly.'

'Did you and Hugh manage to relax?'

I've already noticed that Libby never opens her mouth without carefully considering the effect of every word she intends to utter. She looks out of the window as she asks me this question but she doesn't take her eyes off me whilst I reply – an interrogation technique that creates the impression that she is omnipresent and omnipotent. She's somewhere between a god and a librarian; it's not just the books. She reminds me of the type of librarian who knows when little boys are looking up pictures of breasts in medical books or swear words in dictionaries. Finally she fiddles with the temperature dial on the iron, giving me the opportunity to consider how truthful I want my answer to be.

My shame starts to recede as my desperation to talk honestly takes over. 'It seemed to be a temporary solution to my constant fatigue, if not to our bickering.'

'What are you bickering about?'

'Anything. Nothing.'

It's odd, that first row in almost fourteen years, which happened just before we went to Wales, has turned out to be a watershed; now we seem to do little else. However positive and productive I intend my conversations with Hugh to be, we always end up squarely in the middle of a fight. We fight about anything and everything – his lateness, my tiredness, his selfishness, my lack of sex drive, Becca's alimony, whose responsibility it is to sort out child-care, who put the empty milk carton in the fridge. Yet, whilst the arguments are always about something different, they are all the same – pointless, directionless, bitter and remorseful. If the first trimester were to be summed up in one word, it would be 'puke'; for the second, it would be 'hostility'.

'We are having one or two difficulties,' I confess to Libby. 'My hormones are . . . unreliable.'

'Ah.'

'The maternity books are full of laughable understatements. Apparently, I may expect to feel "occasionally teary or cross".'

'In fact you've been rendered less reasonable than Attila the Hun,' suggests Libby.

'Exactly.' And I laugh despite myself.

It's as if, when I conceived, a small particle of anger, no greater than the size of a grain of sand, got trapped in my body and it is gathering velocity and volume with each passing day; only the foetus is growing more heartily and ferociously. Now, five months into the pregnancy, the grit of sand is about the size of a cannon ball and twice as explosive. Suddenly, I'm so bloody angry. I'm furious with everyone and everything. I'm blisteringly furious with Hugh for something new every day. But, besides that, I'm cross with my female friends who've lost interest and contact since I became pregnant. I'm enraged with my male friends, who were previously a source of harmless flirtatious fun, for ignoring or abusing me now. Both the stupid women in the chemist's and their unruly, imbecilic children incense me. Christ, if I were one of my friends I'd have crossed my name off my own Christmas-card list by now.

'How's Hugh's dealing with it?'

'I mentioned to Hugh that our recent rows could be a result of my hormone imbalance and he commented, "Thank fuck you've finally realized as much, you really should do something about it."' I feel a bit disloyal repeating Hugh's words out of context. A bit.

'He's entirely a new man,' mutters Libby.

'Jessica, somewhat more helpfully, swears that vitamins will restore some calm.'

'She's right, you should mention it to your midwife.'

'I did and, quite surprisingly, instead of simply confusing and terrifying me with talk of crown–rump length, efface-ment, chorion, alpha foeto-protein, Mittelschmerz and the like, she agreed with Jessica and has given me a prescription.'

'Progress,' says Libby cheerfully.

'Suppose,' I mutter grimly. 'But I was collecting the pre-scription when I called you, and I wasn't particularly calm then.'

'You have to eat them, not keep them in your bag. It is normal, you know, to feel . . .'

Whilst Libby is searching for the right words I beat her to it. '*Fucked off*.'

'Yes,' she admits.

'I'm just no good at it.' And for the first time since I arrived I lock eye with Libby. She doesn't flinch, but meets my confession head on. She stays silent but her gaze oozes empathy and understanding. The tiny brown flecks in her otherwise blue eyes tell me it's OK to be honest. Even if honest is abominable, vulnerable or unfashionable.

I carry on. 'I'm tired and emotional. I'm spotty, my hair is falling out, and I'm fat.'

Libby demonstrates her integrity by not rushing to assure me that my face hasn't changed at all, or that, from the back, I don't even look pregnant.

This is undoubtedly a good thing.

Although I wouldn't have minded just a tiny smidgen of insincerity, simply to cheer me up.

'It isn't a competition,' she says. I cast her a withering look. Her naivety is unprecedented.

'It is. Everything is.'

'But you are looking forward to the birth, aren't you?'

'Huffing and puffing?' I ask incredulously.

'No. I mean actually having a child, being a mother.'

I could bluff. I could summon up 'the voice' and repeat for the millionth time that I'm 'thrilled, absolutely thrilled', but that wouldn't be the whole story. I stare at the crumpled tissue I'm gripping in my hand. It's heavy with my snot and tears, an unromantic testament and a timely reminder of my recent hysterics.

'I'm terrified,' I reveal. I stir the Earl Grey and watch the leaves dance with the water in the cup.

'Of?'

Deep breath. Plunge. 'All of it. The ugly pregnancy, the ugly labour and being a mother. I'm not "thrilled, absolutely thrilled" as much as "terrified, absolutely terrified".'

'Ah.'

'Pregnancy is too big for me. It's too much of a challenge. I don't like the small bladder, the large stomach, the vomiting, the breathlessness, or the isolation. And motherhood? More small bladders, fussy stomachs, more vomiting, breathless tantrums and isolation. I'm just not sure I'm up to it.' She stays absolutely still and her inertia pushes me to add, 'It scares me, being needed that much. I'm scared of the dependency.'

Libby comments sensibly and gently, 'They don't stay in nappies for ever.'

But even the sensibleness of her tone doesn't stop me pointing out, 'I don't even know which nappies. Presumably you've seen the bewildering array available on supermarket shelves. Towelling, disposable, waterproof, recycled, maxi, mini, freedom, newborn, front-loaded, back-loaded, super-absorbent, elasticated legs, and all of the above come in about twenty different sizes.'

I'm on a roll. All the anxiety, fear, self-doubt that I've been bottling up for weeks, no, years, comes tumbling out.

'There is no end in sight. When it finally does stop peeing and shitting, in that disgustingly dependent way, when it finally sleeps through for an entire night and perhaps even manages to say something cute, I still have to negotiate it through nursery and primary school, with all their associated horrors. Head lice, bullying, OFSTED and end-of-term reports.' I fling myself back against the settee, nearly upsetting my teacup. Libby cautiously puts down the iron, but she doesn't interrupt.

'And which nursery school?' I demand. 'Or should I have a nanny or a childminder? And am I damaging this child if I go back to work? If I am, tough, because I simply could not stay in with it all day every day.' I glare at Libby as though she personally has insisted that I should. 'Which school?' I yell, and if she were to suggest one right there and then I would take her up on it because, really, I don't have a clue. A few 'helpful friends' and acquaintances have already telephoned me to say that it's too late to put my name down at any of the best prep schools, as the places are all taken for the next million years. I've only just managed to restrain myself from screaming down the telephone line, 'But it's still a foetus!'

I'm exhausted.

Tired of trying to pretend everything is fine. Tired of having to pretend that it's even better than fine. 'Fine' would be failure that I have to eclipse. I pause, reflect and then divulge, 'I feel as though I've been exposed as the fraud I am.'

'What do you mean?'

'I'm not an eight, let alone a ten. I'm a five and a half.'

Libby doesn't understand, so I explain that whilst I appear to be the epitome of self-confidence – *appear* is the operative word – I'm not a natural at anything much.

'It isn't enough to have a good job, a lover, a lovely home, great friends and a gym membership; suddenly there's a new measure. I have to give birth without putting on weight and whilst repeating yoga chants, and then I have to nurture another Einstein without giving up the day job,' I yell my frustration.

'I think you are too hard on yourself. Who set these unreasonable standards?'

Who, indeed? Did I? Did Hugh? Did Becca, way back in 1987? Was it Hollywood?

'Perhaps it would be wisest if you didn't worry about the school at the moment,' says Libby, dragging me back to the problem in hand, or at least to the problem I'm prepared to admit to. 'One step at a time.'

One step at a time, what nonsense! I've always prided myself on my ability to multi-task. Although, recently, I've done nothing but drop balls. Libby unplugs the iron and starts to wind the cord around the handle. Then she moves a pile of freshly ironed clothes so that she can sit next to me. She squeezes my arm.

'The thing is, as I'm going to be a mother I want to be a good one,' I plead.

'You will be,' Libby assures.

I wish I could be as certain. I wonder if I can admit to Libby why my relationship with women like Penny is so complex. As much as it pains me to say so, I do admire Penny. In many ways she is exactly the type of mother I want to be. In other ways she horrifies me. Her eternal self-sacrifice is at once resplendent and repugnant. I do want to be the sort of mum that feeds her child homemade, organic, nutritionally balanced food. I want to take my child to ballet, tennis and French lessons (although not necessarily before it is three years old), yet this means that my life won't be my own. I'll simply be the chauffeur; constantly scheduling car runs to Tumble Tots and Water Babies. How will I ever have time to fit it all in? Will I ever moisturize my knees and elbows again? Then there are the teenage years when my child will hate me anyway, however much time and effort I have devoted to it. If it's a boy it will become smelly, moronic and uncommunicative, and if it's a girl it will undoubtedly be hysterical, anorexic and shrewish. Final insult to injury is that it will make me a grandmother.

As though she's reading my mind Libby says, 'Motherhood is not all anxiety, uncertainty and defeat, you know. Far from it.'

'What is it like, then?'

She pauses. Someone less serious would be able to answer this question very easily. They'd say 'fantastic' or 'awful' or 'hard' or 'relentless'. But whatever answer they'd give would be over-simplified, one word, or perhaps one line. Or they might give me a cliché, because mums often describe motherhood by resorting to clichés. They say, 'It's changed my life', or 'It's like falling in love.' Libby doesn't do either of these things. She picks up a KitKat, takes a bite and then stares into space; or she could be looking at the huge pile of laundry that still needs to be ploughed through. She takes a deep breath.

'It is the most overwhelming experience I've ever had. It consumes my every waking moment, and, actually, a fair amount of my sleeping moments too. I have so much to say about being a mum that I am always tempted to stay silent. It's an amalgamation of a zillion squabbling emotions: joy, rapture, satisfaction, fear, guilt, wonder, relief, worry. Especially worry. I sometimes think that I might be made physically ill with worry. Am I too strict? Not strict enough? Am I teaching her wrong from right, and who am I to make the distinction? Will it matter anyway because possibly something unimaginably ugly will happen to her –'

'Libby!'

'I know it's awful just letting the thought flit into your head, never mind articulating it aloud, but it does come into every parent's head. The fear of cracked skulls, broken bones, broken hearts, and so much worse. And sometimes I want to collapse with the weight of my fears and responsibilities. I want to crawl under the duvet and let someone else take over. Of course there isn't anyone else, so I can't, and besides which I only have to look at her and I'm' – Libby searches for a particular word – 'renewed. She's my reason to live, but more than that she's everybody's reason to live, even for those people who have no idea of her existence. She is the future.'

I stare at Libby, wondering if she's joined some mad cult, but she looks just the same. Slightly frazzled and pretty. Does she think Millie is going to be the first female President of the USA? I mean, she's a bright enough kid and I don't want to burst the bubble, but there's the small question of the passport.

I realize that perhaps I'm on the wrong track when she adds, 'Aren't they? Children? The babies we bear, not just mine or yours but all of them, they are the sum of everything and everyone that has gone before and here they are, our future. There's renewed hope and possibility in every one of them. I suppose, thinking about it, I do occasionally miss a spontaneous trip to the pub but I don't hanker after it. And if I make myself remember, then, yes, the labour was painful, the sleepless nights were irritating, but with all that I still wouldn't change a thing. Fact is, giving birth may seem crappy and disturbing now, but I can guarantee that you'll think it is the best news in the world fifteen seconds after the afterbirth slithers out. It's not orderly. It's messy and complex but it is beautiful and amazing, too.' She rolls the KitKat wrapper into a ball and tosses it in the direction of the waste-paper bin; it misses. 'That said, sometimes I could scream because she's asked me just once too often why she can't have another ice cream or Barbie doll and I think I might kill her, and, for a second, I hate, I'm so tired.'

'You hate her?'

'Not her, I just hate. But mostly she's about joy. An indescribable, unrepeatable splash of colourful, wonderful joy.'

As I walk home from Libby's her words swim around my head. She made it sound so simple. A baby being 'the best news in the world'. A baby being the 'reason to live . . . everybody's reason to live . . . the future'.

So simple and convincing.

Even though it's drizzling I've decided to walk a few Tube stops; I could do with the fresh air (or at least London's apology for fresh air), it might clear my head. I don't bother with my umbrella but let the rain fall on to me. I'm aware it's full of pollutants, but it still feels symbolic and cleansing.

I'm all mixed up. Partly because I don't understand what Libby is on about. Partly because I do. A 'splash of colourful, wonderful joy'. Colour? Which colour? Thinking about it, there's not much colour in my life. Traditionally, I've always worn black; after all, I was a student in the late 1980s and my career is in advertising, so what other colour is there? I did flirt with the whole brown/purple/grey-is-the-new-black thing – that happened towards the end of the last decade – but Hugh brought me back down to earth and reminded me that black is the one true classic. My flat used to be decorated in a dozen subtle tones of mauve but I painted it in a dozen subtle tones of brown when Hugh moved in. I couldn't expect a man to live with such girliness. To be honest, neither the sludgy mauves nor the sludgy browns could be fairly described as colours.

A huge canary-yellow street cleaner trundles past, spraying and splashing puddles left and right. Pedestrians grumble and swear as their coats are drenched, but I start to laugh. Even though I got sprayed too. I know that in the past I'd have been screaming and cursing. My blood pressure would have been soaring. I'd have already been calculating how and when I could change into another pristine outfit before anyone saw me in such a state. In fact, I keep spare clothes at work just for this type of crisis. But today I simply laugh and brush off the worst of the spray from my coat because it's not the end of the world, is it? So I'm a bit grubbier and damper than I was a few minutes ago and I don't look quite so perfect. I've lived to tell the tale.

I think I'll paint the nursery canary yellow.

Then a double-decker bus flies by too, drenching me for a second time.

Yellow and red.

31

Since Libby's description of children as our future (I'm sure I'm paraphrasing to the detriment of her beautiful speech in favour of a fairly obvious, tacky song – but you know what I'm on about), I've started to allow thoughts of what this might be like. Beyond pregnancy, to when I am a mum. A mummy. A mother. Someone's mother. My baby's mother.

And I'm so excited I can hardly think.

Yes, I'm fat, but, now that I'm so fat that I'm beyond help, I've decided to surrender and that feels good. So good. Now when I wake up on a Saturday morning and it is past midday I do not feel guilty about the depths of sluggardly behaviour I have sunk to. Because sleeping is good for the baby. It makes a nice change to lie in bed and do absolutely nothing. I no longer believe that Saturdays have to be spent reading the papers to keep informed. Or visiting farm-produce market shops to buy cheese, the fishmonger's to buy bream or cod, the Italian deli to buy sun-dried tomato and rosemary bread because Hugh hates the 'processed muck that all the supermarkets churn out'.

I no longer feel guilty when I fail to run six miles or swim thirty lengths. Total surrender to my body shape feels like an honourable discharge. I embrace the freedom of eating what I like, because eating is good for the baby. Each mouthful of previously forbidden food feels like I'm sticking my fingers up to the blokes on the building sites who torment you if they do whistle, insult you if they don't. Have you tasted chips with salt and vinegar, eaten from a bag? I mean, really tasted? Not just gobbled them down, guiltily, hardly allowing their fat, squishy gorgeousness to hit your taste buds. But slowly chewed them, luxuriated in the burning crispiness of the outside and then creamy corpulence of the inside. You should do.

I've grown so large that I'm invisible. I've vanished off the fashion-despotism radar screen and I feel liberated. It no longer matters if I'm wearing the very latest shade of black, in the very latest length. As a child I always thought being the invisible man would be rather fun, and it is. It allows you to arrive late and leave early from the office, it allows you to sit out of strenuous exercise (including sex) if you so choose, and it allows you to dawdle around supermarkets.

I still have piles, which are excruciating and a humiliation, and I've got odd patches of funny-coloured skin on my stomach but, as I'm invisible, only I know this.

Instead of resenting the pregnancy and regarding it as a reversal of everything I've spent almost the last fourteen years trying to achieve, I've started to consider the possibility that I was trying to achieve the wrong things. I'm beginning to accept and, on occasion, actively enjoy the pregnancy, because after all there's no other way to a baby, is there? And I so want this baby.

BANG.

I have turned gaga. I have become obsessed. It's happened to me. I show people the baby scan, I tell them when it kicks me, I talk about my plans to breastfeed – it's official, I am captivated. I go back to my maternity books and read them all over again. How could I ever have thought of my baby as an alien? Admittedly, its head is still a little bit out of proportion, but this is definitely a baby. I hold the book to my stomach and try to imagine that little being inside me. A tiny thing with fingers and toes, and ears, eyes, a mouth and a nose. It is gorgeous. How could I have missed the fact that it sucks its thumb from fifteen weeks onwards? How adorable. Even the fact that the baby weighs approximately 200 g, 'a figure that will increase more than fifteen times between now and delivery' – this doesn't faze me. I've been asking what is there to life if there are no bars, no restaurants, no shops, no massages; well, it's obvious, there's life itself. The baby has replaced my work, my gym, and my friends' infatuations. Everything. It *is* true the absolute sweetest things on this earth are the little socks that babyGAP sells. The most beautiful, wondrous things on this earth are babies' hands (all babies are now lovely, although mine will obviously be the loveliest).

However, my enthusiasm for the coming baby and the fat me is possibly not shared by Hugh. I tried to ignite him in the same way as Libby had me. I encouraged him to talk about any fears or doubts he might have about the upcoming birth, but he sniggered and asked if I'd recently attended an American workshop about 'sharing emotions'. So I told him about the splash of colourful, wonderful joy – only I can't be quite as good an orator as Libby, because Hugh simply stared at me.

'Don't you see what she's getting at?' I persisted.

'Babes, I've told you I'm delighted about the baby,' smiled Hugh. I bite my tongue and resist begging him to tell me again. 'Have you seen my golf socks?'

'Third drawer down on the left.'

I know he *said* he was pleased and he did send flowers to the office, and I want to believe him, but I can't help but notice that since then he's rarely mentioned the pregnancy. Well, other than to ask me where he will store his LP collection if we are going to convert the spare room into a nursery. I pointed out that we don't even have a record player any more and suggested he sold them. We could do with the extra cash.

And I can't help but feel disappointed that Hugh didn't keep his promise to sit down with Kate and Tom in Wales and tell them our news. I'd imagined us all sitting in front of an open fire. Hugh cuddling a newly scrubbed, straight after bathtime, angelic-looking Kate and Tom (I know it's a stretch but it was a fantasy). I'd rehearsed with him how he should explain, very gently and carefully, that a new brother or sister wasn't anything for them to worry about because each baby comes with its own extra bag of love. That the love he had for them wouldn't have to be shared or spread more thinly (we'd gloss over the fact that time, however, would be at a premium). As it was, Kate caught me with my head down the loo on Sunday morning.

'Are you poorly?' she asked with what could have been mistaken for glee, if a minor hadn't delivered the question.

'No, she's pregnant,' sighed the world-weary Millie. Kate stared non-comprehendingly, so Millie took her off to give her a lesson in basic biology using Barbie and Ken as props. I would have been concerned, but how much damage can a couple of eunuch dolls do? Anyway, I couldn't leave my sentry position, and where the hell was Hugh?

Hugh doesn't find the scans fascinating, nor the books frustrating, nor the biology miraculous. Admittedly, none of it is new to Hugh and it's all new to me . . . still. His attitude was best summed up in Wales when Henry asked him if he wanted a boy or girl.

'All the same to me.'

I was thrilled and waited for the statutory line, 'as long as it's healthy'.

He surprised me. 'After all, I've already got one of each flavour.'

Oh . . .

It's odd, but this is the first genuine difference of opinion I think we've ever had. We're normally so in sync. I can't think of anything more absorbing than talking about the baby, thinking about the baby, planning for the baby. I'm not saying that Hugh doesn't want it – I'd say he's neutral.

Quite a big difference of opinion; perhaps it would have been better if we'd started with a disagreement about which colour to paint the downstairs loo.

God, I really should be thinking about this pitch.

The phone rings, giving me the perfect excuse not to think about it right now.

'Hello, darling.'

'Hello, Jessica.'

'What does the book say?'

Luckily, Jessica has filled Hugh's shoes in terms of being appropriately enthusiastic and excited about the coming birth, although I remain careful not to make an outright reference to the fact that the birth will make her a grandmother. She rings once a week and I read the appropriate chapter from the maternity book.

Week 21

The skin covering your baby begins growing in two layers. These layers are the epidermis, which is on the surface, and the dermis, which is the deeper layer . . . The epidermis is arranged in four layers. One of these layers contains epidermal ridges. These are responsible for patterns on surfaces of fingertips, palms and soles of the feet. They are genetically determined.

We both fall silent in amazement.

'How can something so tiny be so intricate and perfect?' asks my mother. 'To think, right from the moment of conception, it's all mapped out, what sex it will be, what colour eyes it will have, even its tiny fingerprints are already forming.' I normally interrupt my mother with an effervescent flow; my silence startles her. 'Are you still there, Georgina? Are you all right?'

'Yes. I'm fine.'

'What did Hugh think of the colour that you painted the nursery?'

'He said it was fine.'

And I believe him, I do. Because it has to be, hasn't it? It has to be fine. I know Hugh said I'm angry, tearful, neurotic, and before that he thought I was compliant, accommodating and comfortable, which are not the attributes I imagined our relationship would be based on. And, recently, I've begun to think that he isn't quite as considerate as I imagined. He isn't quite as interested or forgiving. But still, everything is fine. Because things really do have to be fine now. This child I'm carrying is half his. Half him. The soles of my baby's feet have been genetically destined by this man. So he can't be a disappointment. He simply can't.

32

I buy Kate and Tom Easter eggs from Thorntons. Big ones. The biggest in the shop, and I have their names iced on them. They'd possibly prefer Barbie and Bob the Builder eggs respectively, and Becca very probably will be furious that I've bought them eggs at all. I think she has a no-chocolate, no-sweets, no-fun policy, which she intends to follow until the children are at least twenty-one. However, that is not my motivation for choosing these eggs. I chose them because, when I was a child, my uncle bought me a Thorntons egg, and he had my name iced on it and I still think it was the best Easter egg I ever received. The best in the world.

On Easter Monday I am sat at home, flicking between channels. Rather disappointingly, *Jesus Christ Superstar* is not being repeated, I have to make do with *Jesus of Nazareth* with Robert Powell. And whilst his performance is excellent, only outdone by his amazing eyes, I'm not sure that I feel quite right about finding Jesus sexy. I switch over, but the alternatives don't interest me either. There's a western, a documentary on the Rolling Stones, or rugby.

Hugh is playing golf, which is an Easter Monday tradition. I feel that my Easter has lacked the structure that marks the holiday, or indeed distinguishes it from any other bank holiday. Surely someone (other than myself) should have bought me an Easter egg (I bought six, actually, and have them stashed in secret hidey-holes throughout the flat). And shouldn't there have been fish on Friday and hot cross buns? Shouldn't there have been a roast lamb on Sunday? Last year Becca took the kids to her parents' and Hugh and I took advantage of her absence. We played house and entertained. We had a fish supper for six on the Friday (I wore a black boob tube and bootleg trousers – Joseph). We went out for lunch with four other couples on the Saturday (I wore a black Sportmax trouser suit) and we held a roast-dinner party, for ten, on the Sunday. I wore a Prada shift dress, in grey – well, it was Easter Sunday. We drank champagne, vodka shots and highballs, and whilst each meal was upward of three courses, followed by coffee and petit fours, I picked at salads throughout.

Still, that was a tradition of sorts.

This year, when we are a real couple, we've marked the resurrection of Christ by arguing about whether we should visit a gallery (my choice) or go for a walk in the country (Hugh's preference). Hugh is astounded that I won't fall in line with his plan. I am too. As all I've ever wanted was Hugh, I've only ever wanted the things he wanted. Everything I have ever thought of for the last thirteen years I have thought about through a Hugh filter. Would Hugh prefer pink or red nail varnish on my toes? Would Hugh like to see this film or that film? Has he ever eaten at such and such restaurant? His answers would shape mine, blur into mine, become mine. But I don't want to go for a walk. I haven't got maternity rambling gear; besides, I really want to see the new exhibition at the National Portrait Gallery.

'No one is going to that exhibition,' Hugh argued.

'I know it hasn't had much publicity, but I really want to see it.'

'No one's going, Babes.'

Including us, apparently.

In the end we do nothing.

Next year things will be very different, because next year we will be a family and, at the very least, our baby will be dressed as an Easter bunny, with floppy ears and a pompon tail. I'll wear various flirty, little dresses with tiny flowers, in turquoise, lilac and pink. I'll accessorize them with colourful cardigans, hemmed with sequins and frills. Hugh will wash the car. The sun will shine. We'll have a proper Easter.

The phone rings, interrupting my daydream. I winch myself out of the settee and think, not for the first time, how much I'd like a domestic crane to help me get about the flat.

'Hello.' For a moment I can't place the voice. 'Hello, it's Becca.'

'Hugh's not here,' I answer automatically. 'I'll tell him you called.'

I'm about to hang up when I catch Becca's garbled, 'Actually, I rang for you.' She coughs, clearly as surprised to find herself ringing me as I am.

I force myself to remember the conversational social niceties that get one by in awkward situations such as these. 'Hello Becca. Are you having a nice Easter?' Like I care.

'Fine, fine. Very nice. And you?'

'Fine.'

'Really?' The question surprises me. It's genuine.

'I've stopped being sick,' I report. Becca had been right; the books were wrong, I stopped being sick nearer the six-month mark than the third. I can't bring myself to admit as much.

'That's good.'

'I'm a bit spaced, not very good at remembering things for more than two minutes in a row, but I'm fine.'

'This is a nice stage of pregnancy before you get too –'

'Fat.'

‘I was going to say, uncomfortable.’

We both laugh, it amounts to the same. What am I doing having this conversation with Becca? I pause, waiting for her to enlighten me as to why she called. I wonder if the kids want new bikes.

‘I rang to thank you for the Easter eggs.’

‘Oh. Err, that’s OK. Hugh chose them,’ I lie. My motivation for lying is complex. I want Becca to think Hugh is more thoughtful with regard to Kate and Tom than he is, and I also want her to think I am less so. I’m not sure why I want her to believe it’s this way round; perhaps because it should be.

‘Oh, I don’t believe that for a second,’ she dismisses, and I haven’t the energy to lie again. There’s no point – she was married to him. ‘I also rang to see if you’ve signed up for NCT.’

‘Err, not yet,’ I confess.

‘Well, you must. They fill up extremely quickly and it’s invaluable.’

I haven’t a clue what she’s talking about. NCT? Is it a union? However, I can’t bring myself to confess this to Becca because a sixth sense tells me that if I do I’ll show how inadequately prepared I am to be a mother because NCT is certainly something to do with being a mother.

‘Give them a call tomorrow, I’d say it’s imperative.’ I sigh, relieved at the re-emergence of the bossy Becca, it’s the one I feel much more at home with. Then she adds, ‘I always wanted a Thorntons egg when I was a child.’

And the human Becca is one that terrifies me.

May

33

Why, oh why, can't we have meetings in offices, like everyone else? Offices with tables and chairs, instead of in trendy boardrooms that are disguised as private bars (lots of thick cigarette smoke and big squashy leather settees). I'm sat on one of said settees; in fact, I'm drowning in it. How will I heave myself out? Why did I wear a skirt today? What are they saying?

'And that's a task for you Georgina, OK?' asks Dean. 'It's a real responsibility.'

I nod. I'm not sure what I've just agreed to, I hope Julia is taking notes. Whatever it is, since it's been described as 'a real responsibility', I know it's something no one else can be bothered to tackle.

'So let's meet again, say next Tuesday? We could have a working session to bang the final proposition into shape. What time's a good time?' asks Karl.

Everyone instantly reaches for their palm pilots; I struggle to my feet and then just about manage to bend to pick up my handbag, when I hear them agree to Tuesday at 4 p.m. I drop back on to the settee and sigh. No doubt the plan is for the meeting to run into the evening. This achieves two objectives. One, by working late the team can convince themselves and everyone else that they are very busy and, two, by working late they can avoid confronting the fact that they have no life outside the office.

'Err, actually, I have a problem with Tuesday,' I say.

'Turn a problem into an opportunity, Georgina. I'm

interested in solutions. Am I crystal?' Dean flashes a smile; it's designed to terrify.

'It's just that Tuesday isn't very good for me,' I persist. The room stops, and everyone stares at me with a level of horror which really ought to be preserved until I announce my waters have broken. The usual form is to cancel any previous commitments. 'I'm going to my parental water-conditioning class at 8 p.m. Can you guarantee that I'll be out of here by seven-thirty?'

'No, Georgina, I can't guarantee that. You'll have to reschedule. We're working to a deadline here.'

We are, but it's not imminent. It's May now; by the end of June we have to have a clear strategic positioning. In July we have the actual pitch, where we'll present our proposed brand strategy and an idea for an advert (the creative concept, daaaarling). At the rate we are currently working we're in danger of hitting burn-out before the end of this month.

Dean stands up, indicating that as far as he's concerned the issue is not up for debate. He's obviously very irritated with me, but I can't bring myself to care.

'Thing is, Dean, the baby is working to a deadline too. I'm six months pregnant. I've religiously worked ten-hour days ever since you employed me in 1990, and I've regularly supplemented those hours with weekend work too. All overtime unpaid. I need some time to prepare for the baby. I only get one shot at this and I'm not going to jeopardize its health. Let's agree to meet at 2 p.m. and then we can finish by seven. OK.'

'I've a lunch on Tuesday, I won't be through by 2 p.m.,' comments Karl. I stare at him. I'm pretty sure I've done Medusa proud when he mumbles, 'Well, I'll see if I can rearrange.'

'Yes, do that.' I relaunch myself from the settee, relinquishing only a small amount of dignity. We've just spent five hours debating how we would staff the account if we win it. This information will be boiled down to only one page of an inch-thick presentation document. We'll be lucky if the client is still awake at the point when this chart is presented. If only there was an award for time-wasting meetings we'd win the golden pencil. We've spent this long on this issue because it's Karl's issue to resolve, and he wants to make it appear trickier than it is.

In an effort to finally wrap up the meeting and summarize the discussions I comment, 'The way I see it, Project Zoom requires a pretty straightforward management proposition. A two-pronged attack. A very simple division between the detail of retail and–'

'I love the way you loyally stay with the small stuff,' interrupts Karl, with a barely disguised snigger. 'Such attention to detail is always commendable.'

Arse.

In advertising, attention to detail is essential but often dismissed as myopic. I wish I had money on the fact that his next comment will be, 'But where's the bigger picture? Where's the vision?'

'Have you given any thought to the bigger picture, George?' He smiles around the room but doesn't look at me.

'It's a *two*-pronged attack,' I continue, not allowing him to push me off track. 'A very simple division between the detail of retail and the larger brand-equity proposition. I'll jot something down and deliver it to you by this Thursday, Dean. That will give you a chance to consider it before our Tuesday meeting. This should save us some time on the day.'

Whilst my job consists of galvanizing the troops and

ensuring that the strands of the pitch – the creative proposition, the finance, the staffing, the breakfast on the day – all come together in an impressive and coherent way, I often help write the deck, too. Karl's torn between being offended that I'm stepping into his territory and being relieved that he'll have less to do. For all his chat throughout the meeting, I know he hasn't given Project Zoom much thought; earlier on today I caught him drawing tits on a whiteboard – he said it was a diffusion curve.

'What do you say, Karl?' asks Dean.

'Yeah, it could work.' All capital ideas are received with a degree of cynicism, as are crap ideas. No one knows the difference.

'Obviously, Karl and I have worked on this at length and very closely,' I lie. It's true that in the past I would have worked alongside Karl, keeping all the guys to the strict timetable agreed months previously, liaising with the media agency, talking to the international clients to find out as much as I can about cultural differences, and generally making sure that we do our utmost to win the business. Or, at the very least, not get caught with our pants down. But nowadays Karl and I rarely discuss anything much; that's not what Dean wants to hear, he wants a cooperative team, and if I pretend we are such Karl will feel grateful. His gratitude is useful. I'd rather keep him sweet; I've seen how he deals with people who cross him.

'That's the spirit,' says Dean. 'There's no "I" in team.'

'But there is "M.E.",' laughs Karl.

'Good one, Karl,' chuckles Dean.

I wonder if he really is stupid enough to think Karl is joking.

34

It turns out that NCT is not a union (oh, how Libby laughed when I asked her that one), but a sort of national educational club/charity for parents-to-be, new parents and children. They run prenatal classes, which is what Becca was referring to. It's a good way to make friends with other mums-to-be. And, whilst only a matter of weeks ago I'd have argued that I didn't want to be friends with other hormonally unbalanced beached whales, now I can think of nothing I'd like more. I have a need and desire to learn as much as I possibly can about labour and the aftermath.

Hugh is not coming to the prenatal classes or the confidence-in-water course that I've signed up to (I'm contemplating a water birth – just because it worked for Freya, doesn't mean I have to rule it out). Libby has just called to offer to come with me to the classes, but I don't want to look like a lesbian.

'You won't,' she argues.

'I will.' I'm almost crying; I'm certainly whining.

'You won't,' she asserts. Once again demonstrating her expertise at handling petulant children. 'I bet when you get there that there'll be loads of women with their friends or their mums accompanying them.'

'You think so?'

'Yes.'

'Who did you go with to your prenatal classes?'

'No one.'

'Oh.'

'It felt very lonely,' she adds quietly. 'Personally, I'd have been happier to have been mistaken as a turkey-baster type.'

Suddenly terrified, I'm not even embarrassed by my 180-degree U-turn. 'I'll pick you up at seven-forty.'

'Us. Millie will have to come too. I can't get a babysitter this late in the day.'

Ah, Millie. Well, every silver lining has a cloud. Of course, Millie and Libby. Libby and Millie. Libby can't do anything without considering Millie. *Anything at all.* She can't have a night out or visit Tesco's. 'Yes, see you both at seven-forty.'

I put the phone down and it immediately rings again. This doesn't surprise me; my social life is now more or less restricted to telephone conversations. In my hall it doesn't matter if I sit naked except for a pair of socks. It doesn't matter if I have to hang up several times to dash the short distance to the loo, and at least I know the loo will be clean. No one can see how much ice cream I'm spooning into my mouth, or the fact that I'm combining it with Weetabix.

It's Jessica.

'How are you?'

Her imperious tones almost shock the truth out of me (fat and beginning to like it), but, just in time, I realize that my mother would regard this as a sure sign of deep depression, so instead I lie. 'Fine, weight gain has stabilized.' (Lie.) 'Skin clear.' (Lie.) 'And I'm just on my way out to the gym.' (Not a lie, but perhaps a misrepresentation.) Jessica seems suitably appeased; she's imagining a neater, more groomed me and I'm probably wearing low-slung white linen trousers and revealing a tanned, shapely bump. In fact, I'm in an outsize T-shirt from M&S, and I'm wearing XXL joggers that I once bought in the States for a fancy-dress party. Hugh and I went as a pair of Charlies (as in Chaplin) – we wore a leg each and we were (literally) inseparable. I'm now happily filling them on my own. I count it as a blessing that video telephones are still a figment of the imagination of the guys on *Tomorrow's World* and haven't yet gone into general circulation. I dread the day when technology will reveal the less picturesque truth. I know I should be snacking on dried fruit or wholemeal bread and I would, if only it tasted more like chocolate.

'How's the heartburn?' she asks.

The maternity book warned that 'overeating and eating before going to bed at night are two major causes of heartburn. Eating five or six small, nutritious meals a day instead of three large ones may make you feel better.' I took that as licence to eat five or six large meals a day and really I feel much better.

'Fine. I start the third trimester in two days; I'll be twenty-seven weeks.' The countdown is obsessive.

'Ah, the home stretch,' laughs Jessica, excitedly. 'Oh, read it to me,' she urges.

Although I'm in a hurry and it's breaking the rules (we don't normally allow ourselves to look ahead in the book, I suppose it's superstition), I decide to read it to her anyway. '"In early development the eyes are on the side of the head. They move towards the middle of the face between weeks 7 and 10 of pregnancy. Eyelids cover the eyes until about week 27, when they open."' We both gasp in amazement. 'I wonder what it can see?'

Jessica gives some instruction about what to eat to maximize iron absorption and then she hangs up.

I rush around the flat trying to locate my maternity bathing costume and a big towel, which, after some unseemly dashing, I find and push into a waterproof bag. Actually, when I say dash, I mean move around the flat in a clumsy lumber, which is as near to a dash as possible if you are carrying an extra three stone.

I start to hunt for twenty-pence pieces and pound coins for the meter and locker. At the point when I am precariously balanced on a dining-room chair, reaching up to a small shelf above the door in the kitchen, the phone rings again. I know that behind the pile of old *Economist* magazines there is a tin in which I used to save twenty-pence pieces when they first came out; there's probably a fortune in there. I feel around blindly and have only just located the tin when Sam's (woeful) tones float up towards me. Bugger.

'Hi, it's me. If you're there, pick up.'

It's probably just yet another crisis about the wedding, something along the lines of she can't source table linen to match the shade of Gilbert's cravat. Big tragedy. There's a pause during which I try to decide whether it's worth my while making the effort to get down off the chair. Will I accomplish this feat in time to pick up the phone before the answering machine cuts out?

'I know you're there.'

It's depressing that she assumes I have no social life. We haven't seen much of each other and I'm not sure why. We've played telephone tennis for weeks, leaving messages on one another's machines, but never actually getting to talk. When we do fix up a lunch or supper Sam cancels at the last minute. She's very wrapped up in the wedding plans and I'm very wrapped up in the pregnancy. For the first time ever, our lives are moving at a different pace and in different, although not opposing, directions. This shouldn't be enough of a reason to dissolve a thirteen-year friendship, should it? I lower myself down off the chair and rush into the hall to pick up the phone; the moment I get there the line goes dead. I decide against calling her straight back. I'll ring later tonight when I have more time to talk.

I climb back on the chair and seize the tin, the contents of which are unhelpful, mostly buttons, paperclips and about £2-worth of Lira. I look in all the usual change-gathering receptacles in the flat – soap dish in the downstairs loo, the fruit bowl on the hall table, a coffee mug on the breakfast bar, my desk drawer. Not a penny. In desperation, I start to hunt behind the cushions on the settee and under the bed. God, look at this, my box of old diaries!

In the past I've always been a strict and dutiful diary writer. Ever since I went to university, I've religiously made an entry every day, sharing my thoughts, experiences, hopes, dreams and fears with myself – at least this way I could guarantee a receptive and sympathetic audience. I haven't looked at my diaries for weeks. I stopped making entries shortly after I found out I was pregnant. The early days were so miserable, entry after entry describing vomit; the reading was too boring and, frankly, if your own diary is boring, then you are the last person who should remind yourself that this is the case. I may now start keeping a diary again to detail the amazing changes in my head and my body, which, I now concede, are fascinating.

I pick up a heavy brown leather diary for 1999 and hold it close to my nose to drink in the familiar creamy, warm smell. The pages are well worn on this one. I can't resist, I lower myself to my knees and then my bottom, every movement is as tricky as a three-point turn, and I sit on the floor with my back against the bed and start to read.

Oh yes, we went ballooning! God, that was terrifying! And here's a whole section on our holiday in the Maldives. That was an amazing holiday. What times we had! I can almost feel the sand between my toes, and everywhere else for that matter! Sex on the beach, sex on loungers, sex in the pool and, almost disappointingly, sex in the hotel. I'm suddenly thrust back into a world of skinny limbs and scanty underwear. I smile fondly to myself. I turn back the pages of the diary. My birthday. Sam arranged a big dinner at Titanic. Everyone came, Julia and Karl, Drew, Brett. Not Hugh. So many people; yet I remember the birthday as being excruciatingly lonely. I rush on. Christmas. The Christmas Hugh ate two dinners and didn't tell me until he was sick on Boxing Day! He was still living with Becca and he nipped to my flat for an hour or so on Christmas Day in the evening, under the pretence of walking the dog. That was good of him. Wasn't it?

Was it?

Suddenly the euphoria starts to dissolve. The hair on the back of my neck twitches then stands up and my tongue feels sticky and dry. If I didn't know better, I'd identify this feeling as guilt or, more accurately, shame. What was Becca doing on that Christmas night when Hugh was walking the dog? Was she pleased with him for getting the dog out from under her feet, or did she resent having to struggle to bath and put two over-excited children to bed on her own? How come I've never thought about that before?

I shiver.

I can't help thinking about the fact that Becca wanted a Thorntons egg when she was a girl and although it seems unrelated to my present state of uneasiness, it isn't. If she wanted an egg, what else did she want out of life? Almost certainly not to be a single parent. Because who wants that?

It's *Becca*, for God's sake.

What am I doing feeling sorry for *Becca*?

She can look after herself. It's all history now. And we are where we are. And she did have a fling with her tennis coach.

Or at least she probably did; she always denies it but Hugh is almost certain. And she's dating again now, isn't she? She's happy. I turn to another page, desperately trying to recapture the delicious feeling of euphoria that I felt when I first opened the diaries. I know which bit always cheers me up. I pick up the cream suede diary for 1998 and turn to March 5. It's a bit about a party. *The* party actually. The party when Hugh and I stepped over the boundary from 'just good friends' to '*very* good friends'.

It was a party to celebrate my promotion at Q&A to President of Neoteric Enterprise; I'd invited Sam and Hugh and Becca. Becca, predictably, turned the invite down, said she couldn't get a babysitter. She pretty much handed Hugh to me on a plate. Q&A had hired a limo to drive me home, anticipating that I'd drink so much I'd be incapable of getting a cab, let alone remembering my own address. I suggested Hugh share the limo home. We didn't exactly live near each other (he was north London, I was south), so by accepting the offer he was making his intentions clear. I'll never really understand where that first kiss came from. One moment we were talking about the fact that 54 per cent of carbonated drinks are consumed by under-24-year-olds, and the next he was kissing me. All those years wishing and wanting and waiting and sounding like a 1960s track, then suddenly it was happening and it seemed the most natural thing on the earth. As innocent as bending to tie his shoelace. Well, actually, not so innocent, as we ended up having sex in the back of the limo.

'We could barely contain our wanting. I felt so sexy that the action of crossing my legs in the back of the limo nearly sent me into orbit.'

I reread the phrase. Four times.

We could barely contain our wanting.

It doesn't make me feel euphoric.

It's my handwriting and it's my diary. I assume, then, that this was my life. But I'm not certain. I don't recognize it. I flick through April, May, June. By the summer, we couldn't keep our hands off each other; every opportunity and, hey presto, knickers down. I return to the 1999 diary. We had sex in five countries before I broke my New Year's resolution not to drink more than three units in one night; now that is what I call going some. God, and what detail I went into! If I ever get fed up at Q&A I might seriously consider a career in writing hard-core Mills and Boons. I read another passage and then another. They are all the same. They either detail us having sex, or reasons why we couldn't meet and have sex. I pick up the year 2000 diary and start to make a list of the places we made love. Besides beds – in numerous hotels, mine, the spare one in Sam's flat – there was also my office, his office, my boss's office, my bathroom (shower, bath, floor), kitchen (breakfast bar, washing-machine – on top, not inside, ha, ha), sitting room (settee, chair), dining room (table, floor), and stairway. Aside from the fact that I bought this flat before the property boom, it certainly appears that I've had my money's worth from every single room. I continue with the list. In the year 2000 we made love in greenhouses, sheds, swimming pools, laundry rooms and pantries, in parks, cottages, cars, cinemas, beach huts and on beaches. On planes, trains, ships, yachts, in rowing boats and once, most uncomfortably, in a punt.

The adventurous nature of our rendezvous naturally came to a close in the middle of 2000, when Hugh moved into my flat. The urgency fell out of the relationship, although the frequency was still impressive. This year has scored pretty poorly on both counts. I snap shut my diaries and place them back in the shoebox and push the shoebox back under the bed.

I'm depressed. Not just because I can't remember when we last made love but because I can't remember when I last wanted to.

Yes, I can, it was Easter. I wanted sex with Robert Powell.

The phone rings again; this time I do get there in time. It's Hugh, who has called to tell me he's working late. I suppose that it's progress that he's called at all. He sounds really pleased that I'm going to the gym, which cheers me up somewhat. For reasons I can't explain, even to myself, I keep him on the line longer than necessary. For reasons I've never been able to explain, it does the trick – as it always has – his voice cheers and soothes me.

'Are you happy?' I ask. It's a risky, unadvisable question, but his answer heartens me.

'No, I'm Sneezy,' he jokes back.

Of course it doesn't matter if we don't have acrobatic sex any more; I certainly don't miss the carpet burns. Nor does it matter that Hugh once ate two Christmas dinners. I thought it was funny at the time. We pass five minutes more in pleasantries and then he hangs up. I place the phone back in its cradle and try very hard to hang on to the uneasy calm that the conversation has reinstated.

I check the time. I'm really going to have to get my arse in gear if I want to make it to the water-confidence class on time.

Now, what was I doing before the phone call? I know, looking for money for the meter and locker. Ah ha, Hugh's jacket pockets. I often find loose change in the pockets of his jackets when I'm taking them to the dry-cleaner's. I lumber back upstairs and start to rummage through the numerous garments. We really need a sort-out. We've both got far too many clothes, and we won't have as much space when the baby comes. Nor can I imagine I'll need my extensive, exclusively black, dry-clean only wardrobe. I rummage through his jacket pockets. Spare office key – he can never find that when he's looking for it. Chewing gum. Condoms; God, they must have been in there for ages. Blockbuster membership card. Receipts for taxis and restaurants and clothes. I can't believe he thinks he'll get that through expenses! That's odd, we've never been to the Lucky 7 restaurant. I wonder when he went there? I must ask him what he thought of it. I've read rave reviews in all the lifestyle mags. Eventually I find two pound coins in his sports jacket. I pocket them and rush out to meet Libby.

I know what you're thinking. Condoms and a receipt for a restaurant. A bill that comes to about £80, a bill that means a meal for two. You think Hugh's having an affair.

Me too.

It's not just the baby that's opening its eyes.

35

Libby, Millie and I settle down to hot chocolates and king-size Mars bars. The beauty of going places with a seven-year-old is that I don't have to apologize for this gluttony. Despite showering, we all still smell of chlorine and disinfectant. Only Millie has bothered to blow-dry her hair; I do this as infrequently as I possibly can nowadays because it requires exhausting arm-raising. Nor have I reapplied my make-up. Why bother? It's nearly nine o'clock – we'll have to take it off again in a couple of hours. Still, I feel beautiful.

Radiant.

For the last forty-five minutes I've just floated and bobbed about in a pool with about a dozen other mums-to-be (at least four of whom were actually bigger than me!) and I feel fantastic.

'I thought I'd die laughing when the instructor told us to jump but keep our legs together, and you shouted back, "It's a bit late for that",' says Libby.

We both giggle uncontrollably and cackle unattractively until snot comes out of our noses and tears out of our eyes.

You had to be there.

Millie, who I now try to regard as 'a splash of colourful, wonderful joy', looks at us with contempt and suggests that we've lost the plot. Then she asks, 'Are you going to get married? Because then I could be your bridesmaid.' Since she discovered that Kate is being one of Sam's bridesmaids it has become Millie's greatest ambition in life to be one too. I know how she feels.

'It's tricky,' I comment, and stall by blotting a tissue on all the damp bits of my face.

'Why?'

Her directness no longer takes me aback. I've now realized that this is how children operate. They have a sixth sense that identifies which question you'd least like to be asked, and then they ask it.

'He's still married.'

'Is he planning on getting divorced?'

'Oh yes, we've lived together for nearly two years now.' I barely blush as I use Sam's technique of rounding up; in fact we've been living together barely over a year. 'It's only a matter of time.'

'How much time? What's the delay?' Normally Libby would step in at this point and tell Millie not to be impertinent. The fact that she doesn't suggests to me that she also wants to hear the answer.

I really don't know.

I fall back on 'It's tricky' once again.

'Is Becca making things difficult?' This time it's Libby who asks the question.

'I can't honestly say she is. Her lawyer has been a bit tardy, but . . .' I don't know what else to say. I try and remember what Hugh says to me when he is explaining the delay. I can remember the words he uses. Something about minimizing the disruption for the kids, trying to coincide it with a school year. But we've had a new school year and, anyway, Tom hasn't even started school yet. Hugh goes on about financial implications and I know he wanted to wait until his grandmother passed away, but she's been pushing up daisies for eight months now. When he explains it to me it always sounds so perfectly reasonable, but repeating it back, even to myself, the delay is inexplicable. I patch together a party line from the things he's said to me in the past. Surely, if I can make Millie understand then I'll have a chance of getting it too.

'There are a lot of people to consider, that's the thing about marriage and divorce, it's not just about two people or even two people plus two kids.'

'But you must have known that before you started the affair,' points out Libby, with irritating reasonableness.

'Yes, I did, but no, I didn't,' I sigh. 'His mother is distraught – she loves Becca.'

'Even after she had the affair with her tennis coach?'

I admit that I *might* have misled Libby a little bit here. Upgrading a probability into a certainty.

'Oh God, Hugh hasn't told his mother about that; it would break her heart and he is far too considerate.' That's probably why Hugh is careful to minimize my visits to his mother too, just out of respect for her sensibilities. 'I see quite a lot of his father,' I justify. 'His attitude is slightly more accepting.' As I'm talking I slurp my hot chocolate. I think the conversation would have rested there; perhaps we'd have started to talk about the virtues of a crib versus a Moses basket – only I add, 'Of course, there's the little matter of him having an affair.'

'Another one?'

Despite Libby being one of the coolest and most liberated people I know, this does get the net curtains twitching.

'Another one,' I sigh.

It was something about saying aloud that Hugh was considerate that prompted this confession. It is after all a great big fat lie. I used to think he was. But I don't believe it any more.

I tell Libby about the restaurant receipt, the condoms, and that he has been doing unreasonably long hours in the office recently. I ask her where else could he possibly be channelling his sex drive; it's certainly not coming my way. She knows about the endless rows. I've already decided that these are not things that I'll be telling Sam or Jessica. How can I? They've listened to me worshipping Hugh for a lifetime.

'What do you think?' I ask Libby. 'Do you think he's having an affair?'

'Sounds as though you do.'

'Well, it's pretty conclusive evidence, isn't it?'

She moves her shoulders – it's a cross between a nod and a shrug; I'd say sixty–forty in favour of a nod.

'So, what are you going to do?'

'I don't know.'

And I don't. I could confront him, ask questions, demand answers. Scream, shout, rant, rave, cut up his clothes, scratch his car. Theoretically I could leave him, although, if I'm honest with myself, this is unlikely. I mean, not only have I spent all my adult life trying to be with this man but now I'm having his baby; it hardly seems to be the optimum moment to pack up the old kitbag. I could ignore him. I could ignore the evidence. I could wait. After the baby I'll be sexy and thin and interested and interesting. I could order another hot chocolate. I decide to do that.

It's easiest.

36

I get home at ten. Hugh is still stood in the hall, flicking through mail; it's obvious that he hasn't been home long.

'Another late night?' I ask and only just resist adding ominously, 'At the office.'

'Yes, but worth it, I think. We're making some progress.' I don't ask what on. Hugh notices my wet hair and gym bag. He throws out a broad smile; it's not the smile of appreciation he bestowed in the old days, it's more one of relief. It's a smile, though. 'You've been to the gym.'

'Water-confidence classes with Libby,' I remind him, even though we discussed it less than three hours ago. 'In case we go in for a water birth.'

He puts down the mostly brown envelopes and asks, 'Have you eaten?'

'Not a thing.' Well, besides the Mars Bar and the prawn-and-avocado triple-pack sandwich that I bought on the way home from the baths.

'Let's go out for dinner; you can tell me all about your evening with Lizzie.'

'Libby,' I correct, but he doesn't hear me – he's already on his way out of the door.

I am hungry. I'm always hungry, but what I'd like most in the world is to curl up on the settee and watch TV; yet I realize that saying so would be tantamount to a declaration of war. For weeks I've moaned that Hugh never takes me out any more. A dinner invite is not to be sniffed at. I'm being ungrateful. It is neglectful women who cause their partners to have affairs.

That or the male inability to control their knobs.

Hugh lets me choose the venue and I pick a noisy, trendy restaurant, which used to be a regular haunt of ours pre-pregnancy. The second we arrive I know my choice is a mistake. I'd have been wiser to pick a quieter, more intimate restaurant. London's glitterati hold little allure for me right now. I wish Hugh had given me time to put some make-up on, or at least change out of my tracksuit and into my Mamasoon shift dress; it's my 'posh frock' by virtue of being my only frock. I open the door and hit a wall of cigarette smoke. I silently calculate the probability of projectile-vomiting over a waiter.

We are shown to our table. It's positioned at the back of the restaurant; the waiter pulls out a chair for me, the one facing the wall. This is the direct opposite of the etiquette that the female guest is usually shown to the seat that faces out on to the action. Am I being overly sensitive or am I being hidden? A quick glance around confirms that I probably am being hidden. The restaurant is packed to bursting with women whose breasts still stick out further than their stomachs. I hate them. It's wall to wall with toned arms and slim hips. Now that it's May, the first tentative signs of summer are finally visible in London. Not just lighter evenings and leaves on the trees, but skirts and dresses which are shorter and tighter and the occasional sighting of a colour other than black. I know that this summer I am going to resemble a sumo wrestler; half an hour ago this didn't matter but, suddenly, it does matter again. The happiness that I felt at the swimming pool starts to dissolve. Libby (and even Millie, to an extent) put me at my ease; sitting opposite Hugh I suddenly feel as though I'm sat on a couple of mating hedgehogs.

He doesn't make me happy.

I'm not happy when I'm with him. That is not particularly fine, whichever way you look at it.

No, it's not true.

It can't be.

I won't let it be.

I'm unhappy because I'm surrounded by toned abs. I was happy with Libby because I was surrounded by other bumps. This is not about Hugh.

I peek over the menu and take a look at Hugh. Quite a big part of me is expecting a 666 to be tattooed on to his forehead, or perhaps when he meets mine his eyes will be bloodshot, because surely there has to be some outward manifestation of his ugliness, his evil betrayal.

His eyes are still green and sparkling merrily.

He looks confident, happy, relaxed. He does not look like a guilty man. Maybe I've been too quick to condemn. A restaurant receipt is hardly a confession signed in sperm. Look how overwrought Othello became about a handkerchief, and no good came of that. Hugh's demeanour radiates innocence.

Although he's well practised at deceit.

A skill that I used to be grateful for.

Fool.

My brain is about to spontaneously combust. I don't know what to think. The sickness in my stomach has migrated to my head. I home in on Hugh's cuff links; they are shiny white gold, engraved with his initials. I bought them for him to celebrate his new position at R,R&S. The shiny gold cuff links, his clean, square fingernails, the sharp creases in the cuffs of his shirt, all conspire to convince me that he is the same man I said goodbye to this morning. The tiny specks of stubble that are peeking out of his chiselled jaw also want me to believe in him. His long eyelashes that gently brush his brows, putting me in mind of a horse swishing its tail, can't be wrong.

I push the hazy, scary thoughts from my mind and try to amuse myself by looking around the restaurant again.

Besides the superwaifs, there's a liberal scattering of other advertising bods and the odd dot-com nearly there millionaire, average age twenty-two. I feel ancient. Hugh looks tired but relaxed. He still fits. I'm not sure what terrifies me the most – the fact that I don't fit in, or the fact that he does.

Hugh smiles and says, 'So tell me about this swimming class that you and Lizzie went to.'

I do, but I know he's not listening. He keeps glancing around the room, checking out who he should be shaking hands with, who he should be waving to, who should be waving to him. I take a deep breath and resist commenting on how little of the menu's selection is appropriate; most of the dishes are soused in rich, soft cream-cheese sauces or alcohol; raw fish and rare meat make up the remainder. I choose a tuna salad. Hugh drains his Martini, orders two courses and a bottle of wine. I tell him about the baby kicking like crazy when the music is pumped up at the pool and about it being still throughout the Mozart. He raises his eyebrow, which is his devilishly handsome way of expressing interest. It looks genuine enough, but then I've seen him practise it in the bathroom mirror. I know he uses it in presentations to clients. Still, I blunder on. I tell him about the legs-together joke and he does laugh.

It still feels fabulous to make him laugh.

Even though the man sitting opposite me is still married to Becca and is perhaps having an affair with yet another woman, I still adore him. I do love him. As much now in the teeth of confrontation as I do in the grip of orgasm. I can't stop myself. It still feels fabulous to hear him laugh.

'You could come if you wanted. Most of the other women there take their partners along.' Unwilling often, but all the same present and correct.

'You can't suddenly uninvite Lizzie, Babes,' says Hugh and he manages to sound honestly regretful.

'Libby.'

OK. The best thing is not to think about the condoms in the jacket pocket. Or the restaurant receipt. Or the late nights at the office. Hugh is mine. I've waited a long time for him and I'm not allowing an insignificant little dalliance, which is very probably a figment of my imagination anyway, to get in the way of the important stuff. And the important stuff is that Hugh lives with me now. He chose me. And I'm carrying his child.

We should get married.

Hugh married Becca, I silently lament. Never one to sit imagining the great white meringue, it surprises me that suddenly, violently, this is all I want. I want to be a wife. I need to be a wife. I want a ring on my finger. I want the guarantees. Oh, I know it's not a guarantee, but I want what she had. Even if I take it off her. Even if someone else has already taken it off me. In the car on the way home from the baths I tried to think of things from Hugh's point of view. He has been very stressed recently, very busy indeed. And I haven't really been paying any attention to that, none at all. The problem is that, however fascinating Hugh's career used to be, I can now only see it in terms of what it will provide for our child. I want him to be successful but not because I care whether he feels the buzz of being a successful man, I just need him to continue to earn a good salary. Perhaps that *is* unfair of me. In addition I know that, as far as Hugh's concerned, by becoming twice my usual size I've become half the woman I was. I don't talk to him, or about him, or about anything that interests him the way I used to. I don't watch him play rugby or cricket. I don't drink with him. I don't smoke with him. I don't have sex with him.

I do argue with him.

Perhaps he is getting a bum deal.

'I had a really great time at the pool,' I smile. 'At least it's big enough. Or at least it is as long as half the water jumps out when I jump in.'

I pull a funny face, which hopefully conveys I'm laughing at myself, not feeling sorry for myself.

'Did you learn anything?'

'Yes. There were about a dozen women there, nine of whom had not planned to be parents; I learnt not to trust the rhythm method.'

Hugh laughs again. Suddenly he takes my hand. This voluntary touch is the first one I can recall for quite some time; it sends shivers up my back and into my crown – I think that even the ends of my hair are on fire.

'I can't wait until the baby is born,' Hugh says.

Tears of delight spring to my eyes. God, how I've misjudged him. How quickly I moved to condemn. Hugh is by some way the kindest, most terrific man I have ever known. The most sympathetic, understanding, gentle male on the entire planet.

'Can't you?' My grin stretches from earring to earring.

'No. I can't wait to get the old you back again.'

'The old me?'

'You know the –' He lets go of my hand so that he can draw a picture of an egg-timer in the air with both hands. 'Although I think you're going to have your work cut out for you, the way you've been piling on the pounds. You really are going to have to stop bingeing on Mars bars. It's not healthy.'

Piling! Bingeing!

Bastard.

In the car I decided that the important thing was to stop the rot, right now. I'd planned to entertain him with amusing anecdotes about the water-confidence class and the funny things that happened at work today. I'd rehearsed these stories, carefully eradicating any trace of pain or humiliation so that we'd simply be left with pleasantries and humour. I had planned to pretend that today's work meetings had excited and lifted me the way they had always done in the past, but suddenly I can't be bothered. I can't be bothered to make my day sound better than it was. Nor can I be bothered to tell him about my actual day. I don't think I'll be bothered to fight for my former figure, either. I'm not sure I'm prepared to put the effort in again. All that skipping and running and lifting and jumping and starving. It suddenly seems pointless; besides I'll have a baby and won't have time. God, I wish I was at home, under the duvet.

Alone.

The waiter arrives with Hugh's starter. I should have ordered one as well; it would at least have given me something to do with my tongue – it's apparent I've lost the skill of biting it, because whilst I don't plan to say it I suddenly hear, 'Jessica loves me even when I'm fat. So does Libby.'

'I love you even when you're fat.'

'So you think I'm fat.' Hugh sighs and doesn't comment but it's an articulate sigh.

We both fall silent. He chews and looks around the restaurant. I stare at my hands and rack my brains for something to say. What was the plan? Entertain him with amusing anecdotes or stab him to death with a fish knife? I can't remember.

Hugh seems to be equally stumped for a line in witty repertoire.

'Sam called for you this evening.'

'Did she? Any message?'

'No.'

'I expect it was some crisis about her wedding.'

'Expect so.'

I had promised myself that I'd call her back tonight. I wish I'd done so, rather than come out on this pathetic excuse for a date with Hugh. We fall silent again. I pick up a knife and start to carelessly draw it along the edge of the table. I hope I'm making him feel nervous.

I'm not. Hugh rebukes me with a stare and I feel as though I am Tom or Kate. I put the knife down and fold my hands in my lap. This isn't what I had in mind when I agreed to supper out. Why aren't we laughing and chatting and making each other randy? I rack my brains for *anything* to say. Something elegant or witty or pleasing. Something entertaining that will make Hugh smile or even laugh out loud, that raucous, charming laugh that still bewitches me. I'm confounded.

'Or maybe Sam rang up to offer some advice on sterilizing bottles. Since I became pregnant none of my friends are capable of having a conversation with me without mentioning the pregnancy.' I realize this wouldn't win awards for conversational brilliance, but it's all I can manage.

'Maybe that's you,' comments Hugh, as he shovels another fork full of meat that's practically still mooing into his mouth.

'Me?'

'Maybe.'

'Are you saying I'm boring?'

'No.'

'Well, what are you saying?' Even I can hear the hysteria mounting in my voice. I no longer care whether I'm elegant or witty or amusing. And if Hugh were to laugh his supercilious, arrogant, overconfident laugh right now, I'd shove it where the sun don't shine.

'You talk about the pregnancy a lot and the er . . .'

'Baby,' I prompt.

'Yeah. That's all. That's all I'm saying.'

'So what's wrong with that?'

'Nothing. I didn't say anything was wrong with you talking about it a lot. I just said that maybe it's you that introduces the subject into conversations, not your friends.'

'You *are* saying I'm boring.'

'No.'

He means yes.

Hugh is saved from elaborating because the waiter comes to take his plate away. I'm about to object and point out that Hugh has hardly touched his carpaccio but Hugh waves it away and says he's finished.

The thing is, it's quite possibly true. Since my road-to-Damascus conversion I probably have turned into one of those awful women who talk about nothing other than pregnancy and the associated horrors. But Sam talks about weddings. Doesn't she? Oh God, I can already see my friends gathering at dinner parties in years to come, their eyes glassy with boredom, as I retell the funny little stories that all begin, 'Jamie/Mirabelle/Giles/Hatty [I haven't decided on a name yet] said the funniest thing today . . .'

If I'm not vigilant, I could end up being one of those ghastly women who insist on showing photos of the baby, packs and packs of them, whilst running a video of its first Christmas, even though the baby is sat right there. How awful! I promise myself that I can and will talk about something else. From this moment on I will not mention my aching back or swollen ankles. The word pregnancy will not pass my lips. How hard can it be? It's not as though I talk about it all the time. I do have other topics of conversation.

'So how was your day?' I ask Hugh with a bright, wide smile.

'Very interesting as it happens . . .' I don't catch exactly what's interesting because I'm considering the pros and cons of breastfeeding. Halfway through my salad and his roast wood pigeon I notice that Hugh has noticed I'm not listening. He stares coldly. In an effort to dispel his (correct) belief that I'm thinking about the pregnancy, I say the first thing that comes into my mind.

'Have you heard anything more from the solicitors about the decree nisi?' I see immediately that it would have been wiser to confess to my thoughts on whether I ought to pack bedsocks in my hospital bag; they say your feet turn to ice during labour.

'No.'

'They're a bit slow, aren't they? You could have passed an act of Parliament in a more efficient time frame.'

'Are you suggesting it's my fault?'

'No. But I do think you ought to know what the delay is. Is Becca stalling?'

'Why the sudden interest?' Hugh's tone is that of someone trying (desperately) not to lose his temper but (obviously) about to do so. I can hardly say, 'Because Libby and I were just discussing it and, on public inspection, your excuses to date fell at the first hurdle', nor can I comment, 'Because I have reason to believe you're having an affair. Another one.'

Instead, I try to appear breezily efficient and cool. 'Oh well, it's not important.'

'Whether I'm divorced or not is unimportant to you?' It's obvious that, rather than breezily efficient and cool, I've managed to appear brutally indifferent and cold. This conversation is running down the same tract as the 'love me when I'm fat' conversation. It's a lose/lose situation. Hugh mops his lips with his napkin and flings it on to his plate.

'I didn't say that,' I spit.

'Yes, you did,' he hisses.

'Why are you being argumentative?' I seethe, throwing my knife and fork down on to the barely touched salad.

'I'm not being argumentative.' We fall silent again. Hugh lights a cigarette; I think he's being provocative. I stare my silent objection. The waiter clears our plates and he uses a small silver dustpan to clear away the crumbs and spills on the tablecloth but he can't budge the atmosphere.

Another successful evening, then.

37

'You did *what*?'

'It's not like I'm confessing to joining the Foreign Legion.'

'I'd possibly be less surprised.'

'Julia, it's not so heinous.'

'Well, how did you hear about it?'

'Sam gave me the number.'

'Yeah, it sounds just up Sam's street.'

'I simply needed a change,' I justify.

'Whatever,' comments Julia as she drifts back to her desk, clearly mystified.

The nature of my crime is that I visited a Color Me Beautiful technician. You know, one of those women who advise you on what colours you should be wearing and what make-up tones suit you. It was fascinating. Well it was, after we got past the 'Is your hair brown or blonde?' question. (Answer: blonde at the moment except for an inch or two at the roots. Not that I actually believe all that rubbish the bump-woman in the chemist spouted, but you never can be too careful, can you? I'd never forgive myself if there was any truth in the things she said and it's not worth the risk just for a few months' vanity.) Once we'd established that I'd become a 'natural' blonde again after the birth, Cecilia (my Color Me Beautiful technician) was able to advise me as to what I should be wearing. She held little duster-size pieces of material to my neck, and pulled my hair back with a series of colourful scrunchies in an effort to discover which 'season' I am. It was a surprisingly good laugh. For the first time in months I felt feminine and fun. When I said as much to Cecilia she asked, 'So why haven't you been feeling feminine?'

'Ha, isn't it obvious?' I pointed towards my huge stomach.

'But you're more feminine now than ever!' she gasped.

Apparently, I suit baby blue, indigo and the lightest tones of purple. I should wear mint in the summer (which I'm finding a bit hard to swallow) and when I have serious meetings where I want to influence I ought to wear jade. Which is what I'm wearing today. I haven't gone for the full-on jade suit – in fact I'm still in a long white dress (it hides a multitude of sins), but I am wearing a jade scarf around my bump, à la Nicole Appleton, and carrying a funky little green handbag. I thought I looked rather swish; Julia clearly believes that this is another aberration driven by my hormones.

She pops her head back into my office. I wait for her to continue her tirade on black being the only appropriate colour for an agency, and certainly for a client meeting, but she surprises me. 'Here, if you are serious about this we might as well go the whole hog.' She holds out a bottle of emerald-green nail varnish, 'Give me a shout when you want your toes done. I assume you'll need some help as you can't reach them any more,' she grins.

I used to spend hours, literally hours, drifting around beauty counters. My idea of Elysian Fields definitely was spending unending Saturday afternoons with my fingers in pots of buttery creams, or testing shimmery powders on the back of my hand. If Anna Sui had a new body paint out then I'd have tried it even before it was reviewed in *Vogue*. If Urban Decay brought out a new test tube of lilac glisteny stuff and a dinky puff to go with, no questions asked, I'd whip out my plastic. I can fall in love with well-presented and packaged beauty products sat in delightful tempting rows as easily as other women fall in love with Brad Pitt. Boots is, unquestionably, the grown-up girl's candy store. Yet, whilst I really enjoyed playing 'girl's world' with Cecilia and Julia (for the record I did 'influence' the meeting today, in so much as I persuaded the boys that a sushi bar was not a great venue for lunch), I realize that make-up is not the reason I was born to be female.

That thing Cecilia said about me being more feminine now than ever – I think she's right. I lie awake at night and rest my hand on my stomach. On *my baby*, and it doesn't feel ugly. It isn't just a protruding mass of fatness. It feels entirely womanly and breathtakingly beautiful. And I know, absolutely know, that this is the most important thing I can ever do. At the risk of sounding too American, it's a privilege that a baby is growing in my body.

I think I might dissolve with excitement.

June

38

Suddenly in June as I hit month seven I become Herculean. I brim with energy and anticipation. And whilst I have shaken off my lethargy, I know I am still being held to ransom by my hormones. Instead of avidly consuming *Campaign* and *Marketing*, or even shopping, I decide that the most useful way to channel my energy is to wash skirting boards, paint walls and polish floors. Then I start to plant window boxes, grow herbs, and hoover behind the settee. Libby is delighted. She insists I'm 'nesting'.

I dismiss this as the idiocy that it surely is. 'I am not nesting,' I yell. 'I simply want everything to be clean and comfortable and . . . ready.'

'You're right. How could I have muddled that up with nesting?' she asks with a grin.

'I'm simply doing it to avoid being seen in public,' I defend, taking care to cross my fingers.

It's eight o'clock in the evening, I am bent double over a steaming bucket of water, plunging my rubber-gloved hands into the mass of soap suds when, suddenly, I catch my reflection in the long bathroom mirror. Except it can't be me. Can it? Because the woman scrubbing floors, well, for a start she's scrubbing floors, secondly she's wearing paint-splattered non-designer jeans, which aren't fastened but held up with a scarf. Her hair has dark roots showing through, it needs a wash and so is pulled back into a severe knot. She's rotund. More alarming yet, she is half-smiling to herself as though she is gaining some satisfaction out of scrubbing floors and being inventive enough to use the small scouring pad to really get at the dirt in the grout between the tiles. Surely that isn't my reflection. That woman looks familiar, but she doesn't look like me . . . she looks more like . . . Penny or Becca. I peel off my rubber gloves and cast them aside. They slap against the bucket and the scourer.

In panic I call Sam to ask her if I'm turning into Becca. I can ask this, safe in the knowledge that Sam would rather lie to me than hurt my feelings and therefore will deny it vociferously, making us both feel good.

Surprisingly, she's in.

'At last, we speak,' I say. Our answering-machine-message trail has continued recently and besides grabbing a quick coffee last month I haven't seen her since we went to Wales. The coffee meeting was unsatisfactory. Sam was glowing and giggly one moment and then took a call from her seamstress. There was some problem about veil length that totally broke the mood. Sam became distracted and jittery. I don't think she's eating enough.

'I'm desperate to see you,' she says.

'I don't suppose you're free now, are you?'

'Yes, brilliant, I'll come over.'

I pause and look around the flat; it's in an amazing state of disarray. Before I started scrubbing the floor I had been tidying my wardrobes. I'd just got to the point of emptying the entire contents – jackets, suits, tops, trousers, handbags, shoes, hat boxes and false boobs (which look a bit like chicken giblets) – on to every available surface, when I noticed that the bathroom floor needed scrubbing. I've had the Klimt posters reframed. They look better in gold frames after all, but I haven't had a chance to hang them in the bedroom so they are propped against the skirting board in the living room. I went to Tesco's yesterday and did a big shop, only half of which has been unpacked. I can see about three piles of ironing and any remaining floor space is decorated with open maternity books and magazines. My flat looks like Libby's home. It's light years away from the serene, *feng shuied* abode that I used to keep.

'No, let's go out. I'm a bit stir-crazy myself.'

Sam is more successful than she'd have you believe. You have to be very tough and very good to be a management consultant, and she's an exemplary management consultant. She's accustomed to fancy restaurants as she dines with clients most lunchtimes and evenings. I've arrived at the restaurant before her, and from my seat I watch her as she efficiently drops off her jacket, expertly touches up her lipstick and orders vodka before she sits down. As the crisp white napkin is settling on her lap I ask, 'So what news?' This question comes at enormous personal expense, as I put my own concerns on hold (Am I turning into Becca? And names – does she like Jack or Toby if it's a boy? Ellen, if it's a girl?).

I allow Sam to dive in first. 'Oh, nothing special. I just thought it would be nice to meet up, just the two of us,' she mutters. I'm not convinced for a nano-second. Sam's vodka and orange arrives with surprising speed and she drinks it equally smartly, then she orders another. I can spot them at a hundred-mile radius; Sam is a woman on a mission.

'I'll have a still mineral water with a twist of lime,' I instruct the waiter loudly. Recently, I've revelled in my virtue and no longer hanker after a glass of champagne. 'So, how are the wedding plans?' Over the last five months I've started every conversation I've had with Sam like this. Indeed, I occasionally used it as conversational filler with her even before she'd met Gilbert.

Normally her response is both enthusiastic and verbose; today she is surprisingly reticent. 'Fine.'

'That's it? Fine?'

'Yes. What else do you want me to say?'

'Well, isn't there some minor catastrophe? Like being unable to match the ribbons on the bridesmaids' dresses with the exact shade of the roses in the church floral displays? Or maybe something really serious is happening, like you've timed the car route from your flat to the church three times, and now have to decide how to find an average journey length. Should it be the mean, the mode or the medium?'

'Oh, it's all one big laugh to you, isn't it?' snaps Sam.

This is absolutely unprecedented. I have never, ever, in all the years I've known Sam, heard her snap at anyone. She is the absolute epitome of kindness, appeasement and tact. She would rather walk a tightrope without a safety net than appear confrontational. I've often wondered how this gentleness and occasionally giddy attitude accomplished anything at work. But it does.

'I'm a big laugh, a big joke,' she hisses, downing her second vodka and immediately ordering a bottle of Chablis.

I cautiously sip my mineral water and, on putting it down, I reach across the table and squeeze Sam's hand. 'You are not a joke, Babes. I never laugh at you.' And whilst this isn't absolutely 100 per cent truthful, it is the reassurance Sam needs. 'Have I done something wrong?' I ask.

'No, this is nothing to do with you.'

Relieved, I encourage Sam to look at the menu. However, I notice that whilst I mentally devour every dish and get an enormous amount of entertainment just imagining what everything will taste like, Sam can't seem to concentrate on the delicacies that ought to tempt her. For all the interest she takes in red peppers stuffed with codfish mousse, or the creamed gazpacho with cured ham, we might as well have been at McDonald's and ordered two cheeseburgers with fries. I order an oriental salad with delights such as crispy duck and an orange and cashew nut dressing, then baked turbot with calamari. I ask the waiter to replenish the bread basket and comment to Sam that I think I'll have room for pudding. She's in a bad way – she doesn't show even a flicker of surprise at the amount I'm ordering. I'm in a bad way. I think that even after eating this lot I could still happily devour a cheeseburger and fries. Sam looks desperate and can't seem to make a choice. I presume she's still on a calorie-, fat- and taste-control diet for the wedding, so I point out a couple of the least artery-hardening options; after all, this used to be one of the most essential dinner-party skills I possessed. She nods, mutely accepting my suggestions; obviously she couldn't care less what she eats.

I wonder what can be throwing her equilibrium so completely.

'I've kissed James.'

Ah.

'With tongues, and I enjoyed it,' she confesses in a rush. I don't know if she's expecting to be struck by lightning or handed a cigar.

'James, as in . . .'

'My future brother-in-law, yes,' she adds impatiently.

With depressing regularity in the past, Sam and a number of my other friends have come to me with confessions of this kind. Normally, I defuse the situation by yelling out something flip like, 'Scores out of ten?' because that's what girl friends are born for. Today I'm wary of saying anything before I've had a chance to weigh up exactly what this means.

'Just the once?' I try to establish the extent of the indiscretion.

Sam nods ferociously, but then after a couple of wholehearted declarations of, 'Yes, of course, just the once', the nod dissolves into a shake.

'Twice?'

Shake of the head.

'On an on-going basis?'

Nodding again.

Ah.

'Sober?'

More nodding.

'Just kissed him?'

Shaking head again. I feel like a Victorian dentist trying to extract teeth with a cumbersome and painful pair of four-foot-long tweezers.

'We're having an' – she pauses and checks who is sitting at the tables nearby – 'an affair, for want of a better word,' and then more bravely and firmly she repeats, 'We're having an affair.'

I check my reflection in the mirror on the wall; I'm searching for something priestly in my face that prompts or demands confessions such as these. I try and fail to appear unfazed. An affair, Sam! Sam, an affair! What's the world coming to? I grab another roll covered in pumpkin seeds and start to butter it vigorously.

'Since when?'

'Since Wales.'

Now that I count my life in weeks I'm quickly able to calculate. 'This has been going on for fourteen weeks, over three months?'

'Yes.'

'But you've been so happy in the past few months.'

'Yes.'

'I thought it was Gilbert making you happy, and the wedding preparations.'

'No.'

Sam is in agony. It's obvious. I quickly try to assess the situation. James is fun, extremely charming, intelligent, and he has a quite overwhelming physical presence. He is definitely a horn, even I noticed as much in my near-eunuch state.

'Is it just sex?' And I almost want her answer to be in the affirmative. It will be easier for her in the long run.

But she shakes her head. 'I think I'm in love with him. I didn't want it to happen, but the moment I met him I knew it was going to. He's all the things I like about Gilbert except that he's younger and spunkier and more' – she searches for the word in the bottom of her wine glass – 'more alive. At first I thought it was just sex. It is true to say that there is an unprecedented sexual attraction between us. The air was crackling on the drive down to Wales, I was certain that Gilbert would pick up, but he didn't.'

Poor trusting Gilbert.

Silly sod Gilbert.

'After the rounders game and the fish pie—'

'A well-known aphrodisiac.'

'It seemed inevitable. We went walking in the woods—'

'In the dead of night?' She nods reluctantly. 'Oh, Sam you went for a PISS!' I'm not referring to the bodily function here, but to a Potential Illicit Snog Situation. Sam nods unwillingly. After all, you don't just happen to find yourself in a situation like that, you have to put yourself there. Sometimes you go for a PISS with no intention of letting things get out of hand, and sometimes you desperately want them to.

'And there was this moment. You know, The Moment. When you know you are going to kiss each other and you know you shouldn't, but you know you are going to anyway.

You look at the floor and then at his eyes and then back at the floor again.'

'Sam, no one does that except in films.'

'I do. I did. He's not like a film, George, everyone else was but he's not.'

And despite my gruffness I do know. I remember that moment exactly. She's talking about the sort of moment when Hugh and I first kissed in the limo. I, too, had put myself in a Potential Illicit Snog Situation; in fact I'd been putting myself in one for years, and eventually Hugh noticed he was there too. I drag myself back to Sam.

'And did you have sex with him then and there in the woods?'

'No, of course not.' Sam's shocked at my presumption, which is unfair. After all, she's the one that's shagging her brother-in-law to be. It's not so odd that I should inquire whether there was a bit of action in the woods à la Titania and Bottom.

'We've been seeing each other and trying not to sleep with each other ever since.'

Oh, that old one.

'Until last week.'

'When I presume . . .'

'You presume correctly. You told me to be nice,' she justifies.

'Do you sleep with every man you are nice to? Don't answer that.'

Our food arrives. Sam leaves hers untouched and, whilst I know I am running the risk of looking insensitive, I am thirty-one weeks pregnant, nearly full-term, so I dive in.

'Go on.' I encourage her to finish her story, not least because it gives me the opportunity to eat my food uninterrupted.

Sam doesn't need much prompting. 'He's it. He's the One. My teapot's lid.'

How romantic. Despite the seriousness of the situation, it takes every ounce of my will-power to suppress my giggles.

'He makes me feel I can be entirely myself. He makes me feel that I can be *more* than I am. He is potential. He's realization. I'm in love with him.' She smiles so broadly I think her face will split. Her huge brown eyes radiate unreserved delight. 'He is the first man that I have ever been with where I feel I can confidently be me. You know what I mean.'

Of course I do.

I think I do.

I should do. I stay silent and allow her to fall into a stream of gibberish.

'I don't have to adapt myself, edit, mould or change myself in any way. I don't have to fake an interest in his hobbies or quash any passions of my own. We can talk about anything, our childhood, work, ambitions, travel and friends. And he *listens* to me. It's not just me doing all the polite inquiring and sympathetic nodding of the head. He doesn't seem to need me as an emotional crutch or as a hostess or for money, like all the other men I've dated have done, but he does seem to really want me.'

I think it's time I injected a bit of caution, a smattering of reality. 'Sam, you have said similar stuff before.'

'I know,' she admits. 'I've said it before because I've wanted it to be true. But this really is different. He really is different.'

I've heard this before, too.

'What should I do?'

I sigh. 'What do you want me to say, Sam? Do you want me to tell you to call it all off, draw a halt? Or full steam ahead?' In my experience these confessions are never shared in the hope that the story teller will get some genuine advice, but more so they can tell you what they are going to do and square it with their own conscience. Sam looks at me with fear and despair, and love and hope, but she doesn't answer my question. 'How does James feel?'

'The same,' she replies confidently.

'You're sure?'

'Certain.'

'No fifty-fifty, do you want to ask the audience? Call a friend?' She glares at me. I know I'm being flip but actually I'm relieved. This is difficult but not a disaster. So she loves her fiancé's brother; that's not the most convenient scenario, I admit. But if he loves her too then it's not an irretrievable situation. She hasn't been seeing Gilbert that long, less than a year. Yes, there will be a lot of heartbreak and embarrassment in the short term, but providing they both have the courage of their convictions then they will pull through. I say as much to Sam.

'You're suggesting we tell Gilbert and weather the storm?' She's incredulous.

'Yes, I am. You're lucky you've discovered how you feel about one another before the wedding.'

'I can't do that.'

This surprises me enough to make me put my fork down, possibly the first time in months that I have voluntarily done so rather than had it wrestled from my hand.

'Why can't you?'

'Because I'm marrying Gilbert.'

'But you love James.'

'Yes.'

'And he loves you.'

She nods.

'So?'

Sam becomes impatient. 'Aren't you listening? I'm *marrying* Gilbert. *Marrying* him. James hasn't mentioned marriage.'

I'm astounded.

Sam sees as much and tries to explain.

'Some people, no, to be accurate, most people think my obsession with getting married is sad and pathetic.' Yes. 'Outdated and restrictive.' Yes. 'But it's not.' Oh yes, it is. The pantomime is in my head. 'Those people misunderstand me. They assume I need a man to define me. It's not true. I know who I am. What I like. What I want from life. So how can I be sad?' I assume it's a rhetorical question, so I don't jump in with my response that marrying one man whilst loving his brother seems pretty sad to me. 'The career thing has never done it for me. I admit there is a certain excitement to foreign travel, managing a team of twelve people, and I'm definitely not knocking the terrific salary, but . . .'

The 'but' hovers in the air like an annoying mosquito. The 'but' represents all that fails to keep her warm at night.

'But my greatest ambition, what I really want, always wanted, all I've *ever* wanted is to be married.'

This is hardly breaking news.

'But surely *who* you marry is of vital importance?' I probe.

'Not really. Not any more.'

I think this is the most honest thing I have ever heard anyone say. It's also the most pitiful.

'Oh Sam,' I murmur, for want of anything more articulate to say.

'Look, Gilbert is a firm offer.'

'You're not selling a house!' I almost scream. I notice that a number of other diners have now abandoned their conversations, preferring instead to listen to ours. I can hardly blame them; this is better than Jerry Springer.

'Better the devil you know,' shrugs Sam. I know she's trying to sound brave. I know she's not feeling it.

'But you know both James and Gilbert.' It's not the first time one of her clichés has appeared woefully inadequate.

'Oh well, then, a bird in the hand is worth two in the bush.' I scowl, frustrated. 'I can't risk it,' Sam explains. 'I'm not going to repeat my past mistakes.'

It is true that Sam has been known to misread the signs of the guys she's been dating, assuming they were further along the commitment chain than they obviously were. She's often entertained me with tales of misadventure and misconstruing. For example, when she was eighteen she was extremely disappointed when her boyfriend at the time failed to propose at her birthday party and, instead of giving her a ring with a precious stone, he presented her with a Culture Club video and the *Rocky Horror* soundtrack LP. Far more useful in my opinion, but not in Sam's. When she turned twenty-one she was sure all the signs were there that Terry was going to propose. She managed to ignore the fact that he'd repeatedly told her that he wanted to travel after he graduated, she thought he was teasing. He wasn't. And then there was Matt, whom she dated when she was twenty-three. He kept telling her she'd make a lovely wife. Not his, apparently. Nick (she was twenty-five) did say he wanted to demonstrate his commitment, but again this declaration failed to produce a diamond ring – just a bag of dirty laundry every Sunday evening. And then there was Steve, and then Rod and then . . .

'Nothing,' Sam screeches, as though she's been following my thoughts. 'Not a single proposal in over seventeen years. And I used to ask, "Why not? Why not? Why not?"' I notice that the Chablis bottle is empty. So does Sam. She beckons to a waiter and orders another. Her starter is still untouched.

'I'm not ugly,' she shouts defiantly.

'You're lovely,' I confirm. I want to say more, but she's in full flow and it's fuelled by alcohol; there's nothing I can do except listen and hope that none of the diners are her clients, or are related to her mother.

'I work out. I try to be pleasant and liberal and informed. I may be past my initial bloom, but, the point is, even when I was bursting with youth no one made an offer. I'm not dull or smelly and I don't have any unsocial diseases. I'm fairly good at Trivial Pursuit; I nearly always win the pie pieces. I read the *FT* every day, for God's sake. But for years there was nothing doing. I used to watch them on the Tube – married women – and they're not all that special.'

I focus on the red patch of skin on her neck, which I know as well as I know my own hand. When Sam is riled or embarrassed or excited her neck blushes. Apparently, when she orgasms she looks exactly like a vine-ripened tomato.

'Yes, of course some of them look lovely but some are real hounds, and some are obviously above average intelligence but others seem to be just one up from pond life. So I'd ask myself, why not me? It's not that I was overly fussy, not a fact that I'm unduly proud of. And then, finally, there was Gilbert.'

She pauses not so much for breath but to replenish her glass. I start forking up bits of her starter and shovelling them into my mouth. Well, she's barely glanced at it and I don't want to offend the chef.

'George, before Gilbert proposed I was at the stage where I didn't mind if a man was short, earned less than me or used his knife and fork incorrectly. Gilbert saved me.'

I notice that Sam has stopped calling Gilbert 'G'. He's become Gilbert once more. Indication that she is seeing him for what he is.

Sam is blinking ferociously, because the only thing that is more embarrassing than a woman ranting in a restaurant is a woman sobbing in a restaurant. We are both glad when the waiter interrupts us to clear our plates and deposit our main course. He takes Sam's plate away, although I am still cramming her food into my mouth.

'The proposal was *so* perfect.' She's trying to convince herself.

'You were drunk,' I remind her.

She brushes my objections away. 'He'd booked a table at the Ivy. The Ivy! Usually you have to be featured in *Hello!* at least twice before you can hope to secure a table at the Ivy.'

Personally, I'm not all that gung-ho on proposals at a table in public. I find the other diners intrusive, but whatever lights your fire. I've always known that Sam is scarily starry-eyed and idealistic.

'The ring is beautiful.'

But not the one she wanted.

'He thanked me for agreeing to marry him.'

This almost touches me.

'Getting married is all I ever wanted and I've wanted it so desperately, for such a long time. I don't know how to want anything else.' She pauses. 'James isn't talking marriage.'

'Are you sure?'

'Yes, I asked him.' She has no shame. 'It's so unfair. If we were in a film he'd propose. He'd offer me a marriage proposal to replace the one he's asking me to sacrifice. No one in a film says, "Don't marry him, shag me", do they?'

'What did James say when you talked about marriage?'

She waves her hand, drunkenly, 'Oh, some nonsense about not ruling it out. Blah, blah. One day both of us may be ready to make that kind of commitment to each other. Etc.,

etc. Too big a decision to make in the heat of the moment. So on and so forth.'

'Sounds pretty sensible to me.'

'Sounds like a get-out clause to me.'

Even I am now beginning to lose my appetite. How has this happened under my nose with my failing to notice? Sam's right. It has always been a joke that she's desperate to marry but suddenly it seems dark and deadly serious. She is prepared to marry one man whilst loving another rather than go through life ringless. It's as if Germaine Greer never existed. I feel irredeemably depressed. What's left for us in the twenty-first century? We have no religion, we don't believe in everlasting love, and the only comfort available is a handful of confetti and a three-tier fruitcake. I've never even met anyone who likes fruitcake. There has to be more to it than that. Doesn't there?

Sam, oblivious to my profound pondering, comments, 'Men they are like buses, aren't they? You wait for ever and then two come along at once. Perhaps it's a case of the grass is always greener,' she tries to comfort herself.

If I think back through our relationship, it has not been one punctuated by thoughtful pauses. The opposite is true, as we've always preferred chatter and irrelevant observation to silence. Our evenings together were a foggy mass of excited gossip, scandal, palaver and prattle. More babbling brook than still waters. So I know lots of stuff about Sam. I know when and where she had her first kiss, and who she lost her virginity to. I know that her favourite meal is jacket potato with curried baked beans and mayonnaise, although it's never been fashionable. I know the sound she makes when she orgasms. I know she 'sort of' believes in God, although she only goes to church for weddings, christenings, funerals and midnight mass on Christmas Eve. I know she always believes the best of people, she invariably looks on the bright side and she doesn't even find Anthea Turner irritating. I know how many times she's been in love, and how many times she's been in lust. I know which hairspray she uses, where she buys her hosiery, what she wants to call her children. In short, I know the contents of her fridge, her bathroom cabinet and her heart. And she knows lots of stuff about me – she knows I lost my virginity to Hugh. That my taste in food, art, music and film were all formed with, through or for Hugh. Well, Hugh is pretty much all there is to me.

I also know one or two things about Sam that she's never told me; things that she's possibly oblivious to. Things like, she's the most generous, magnanimous, sweet-natured woman in the city of London. She's beautiful, talented, inimitable, and the reason she's not married isn't because no one's offered to date, but because she's too good to settle for the flotsam and jetsam that has washed up on her beach. And even the flotsam and jetsam have known this.

How has this happened? What should I do or say? I can't let her make this mistake. I've always followed a policy of non-interference; I'm there for my friends if they ask for help but I don't thrust it upon them. It's too messy. Too complex. Last time I tried to be honest with Sam was when I told her not to rush into an engagement. She's hardly going to thank me if I underline my point with a 'told you so'.

So she's marrying the wrong bloke. How bad can it be, spending the rest of your life paying for a mistake?

Bad. Bloody, fucking bad. I *have* to be honest. I've been amused and indulgent for too long. I can't stand by and let her destroy her life.

'Sam, for goodness sake! You can't go on living your life by following a handful of outdated old wives' tales and clichés. It might make things appear simpler, but you're kidding yourself,' I burst.

'But it is better to be safe than sorry,' she whines.

'This nonsense might be useful until secondary school but grown-up life's too complex for you to retreat into *The Oxford Dictionary of English Idioms* every time you have a dilemma.' Sam is silent. 'You have to get yourself your own set of values and opinions,' I insist. 'You have to think about this very carefully. You have to think what is best for you. And being married to one man whilst loving another won't make you happy. You're not being fair to yourself, or to James or Gilbert for that matter. You have to think about Gilbert too.'

'The way you thought about Becca?' Sam looks up and stares into my eyes.

'What's that got to do with anything?' I ask, genuinely bemused. We're talking about Sam, not me.

'Don't you see, George? Don't you know why I came to you?'

'Because I'm your friend.'

'Because we're exactly alike.'

Whoa, hold your horses, matey. No, we are not. Sam may be the most generous, magnanimous, sweet-natured woman in the city of London. She is beautiful, talented, inimitable, but she's also an appalling throwback as far as the cause of female independence is concerned. She thinks that being married is the only way to be happy. She believes this so strongly that she's prepared to marry the brother of the man she loves just to ensure a dual-pension policy. I'm quite different. I'm with Hugh although the wedding band is noticeably lacking.

'No, we are not. I'm with the man I love.'

'Be imaginative,' she spits nastily. 'For Hugh, read

marriage. You pursued Hugh with the same grim determination that I pursued an engagement ring. The only difference is I'm more honest with myself. You didn't allow the fact that he was married to someone else to distract you, nor the subsequent births of his daughter and son. You've hardly got the steadiest grip on reality, have you? Physician, heal thyself.'

'You've got it all wrong.'

'Have I? Well, as long as you're sure.' I've never seen her so angry and bitter before. Where's Sam gone? Gentle Sam, lovely Sam. 'George, you punched, kicked and clawed your way to where you are now. You suffered countless humiliations. For years he ignored you. He forgets your birthday, he doesn't pay any bills, and this is what you reinvented yourself for.'

La, la, la, la. I'm not listening. Mentally, although not physically, I've put my fingers in my ears. La, la, la, la. It is a technique I used to use when watching horror movies as a teenager. I'd pretend to be brave, but I'd sing to myself so the scary reality didn't sink into my consciousness. I want this conversation back on track. I want to talk about Sam, Gilbert and James.

'You're marrying for the dress, the day, the fantasy,' I accuse.

'And why are you with Hugh?'

'We are alike.' But are we? I used to think we were, but now I'm not so sure. I push on as much to convince myself as Sam. 'We have the same tastes in music and books and art.'

'You don't even have tastes of your own! You imitate his tastes.'

'I wanted him from the moment I saw him and I've never wanted anyone else.'

'Yeah, well, sometimes we have the best sex with the worst people. It's God's April fool.'

I try and be patient; after all, I've seen her knock back a fair amount to drink tonight, all on an empty stomach. She probably doesn't mean most of this. 'You're twisting this, Sam. I'm not the one with the problem. You are. You're deluded.'

'At least Gilbert is a nice guy to be deluded about.'

'Meaning?' Actually, I'm not sure I want her to tell me.

'Hugh is a prat, George.'

'He is not a prat,' I counter automatically, although mentally I know the insult has already seeped into my mind and heart, and I'll haul it up for closer inspection when I'm next alone.

'He is a selfish, childish, petulant, inconsiderate prat,' says Sam, who never says anything bad about anyone.

'I thought you liked him,' I stutter in disbelief. 'You've been his friend as long as I have.'

'He's a funny enough guy to spend Rag Week with. He's pleasant company at a dinner party. But that's it. You're wasting your life.' She stubs out her cigarette.

I'm beginning to think I should stay at home. I certainly should avoid restaurants. Bad karma.

Our dinner ends fairly swiftly after this outburst. Sam and I struggle through the main course, she hardly eats a thing, I hoover up everything edible in the vicinity, and then we promptly pay the bill. There's little left to be said.

39

To use a Sam phrase, 'you could have knocked me over with a feather'. To be more original about it, I am shattered, shocked, stabbed and (this is the hardest to admit) somewhat contrite. Sam has chucked me. My status as her best friend is no more. I haven't been seeing that much of Sam recently, but the fact that I'm unlikely to see her again sends shivers of horror bouncing up and down my spine. Another void. I used to be very good at filling gaps. I'd visit the gym, buy clothes, have a facial. In fact, these methods for filling the terrible nothingness that haunted my existence were so effective they became my life. But the pregnancy has slowed me down. I can't shop or skip, which gives me more time to think. Forces me to think.

Sam's right, of course, I didn't think about Becca. Not really. If I thought of Becca at all, I thought of her as the antithesis of me. Initially, when I had spreading hips, rats' tails hair and a limited general knowledge, she had slim hips, flowing tresses and was a serious contender for the *Krypton Factor.* I rarely thought of her except in terms of what I was not. Or, rather more accurately, what I had not got.

Hugh.

As I worked off the spare inches and devoted more and more time to the *Times* crossword, she appeared to be sliding down the slippery slope of smug marriedness, landing in a sludgy mess of mushed veg, mushed mind and mushed skin tone. It's only now that my hands are back in the rubber gloves and the steaming bucket of hot water that

I consider Becca may be, *must* be, more than that which I am not.

After years and years of seeing Becca as the devil incarnate, recently, since supper with Sam, I lie awake at night thinking, 'Maybe she isn't'. In fact, she's beginning to look more and more like a victim in all of this. And if she's the victim, then I'm the aggressor. Which is not how I like to see myself.

It didn't work. La, la, la, la didn't work. The cruel home truths have stained my consciousness and, however hard I try, it's impossible to ignore what Sam said. *Punched, kicked and clawed my way to where I am now . . . suffered countless humiliations . . . he ignored me . . . this is what I reinvented myself for . . . Hugh is a prat, George . . . a selfish, childish, petulant, inconsiderate prat. I am wasting my life.*

The funniest thing is she doesn't even know about the suspected affair and she thinks this. Of course, I'm using funny in a post-modern, ironic sense. There's nothing funny about this situation.

It isn't news.

She thought she was telling me something I didn't know, but she was wrong. I've known it for a while. I can't exactly date it. I didn't wake up one morning and think, '*Fuck*, what a waste of fourteen years', it was a more insidious, cumulative process. It possibly started when he announced our pregnancy to our 'six closest friends', and I'd never met any of them before, or, for that matter, since. I was very tired and sick and I'm not sure they were worth the effort. His endless jokes about my expanding waistline have also worn me down. Hugh has never understood that putting on weight is a necessity when producing a baby. The endless long and lonely nights haven't done much to persuade me that he's a great guy. I've added them up. I've been pregnant for 224 days, we've known I've been pregnant for 161 days, Hugh and

I have spent thirty-five evenings together in that time. I know I'm anal, I'm bored. I'm desperate; it makes you anal. The condoms and the receipt didn't do much to improve my confidence in him, either. I can't name the exact moment when I realized that my issues about being pregnant were not about the discomfort of haemorrhoids, the restricted social life, the swelling stomach. I didn't fear losing my status as a goddess per se, I feared that losing that status meant I would lose Hugh. I'd like to think that he's not the type of man to walk out just because I'm the size of a house. I'd like to think that. But Sam's right, isn't she? Don't even answer that, I know the answer. I've known for quite some time that Hugh is a prat.

But he's my prat, and love is a really hard habit to kick. So, before you ask, I'm not going to leave him.

I'm staying with him because of my baby, because it deserves a father. And because of Becca's babies, because I stole their father. It's the only way I can make amends. It's possible that my actions haven't been 100 per cent honourable to date. The fact that I've been blinkered by love explains it, but doesn't excuse it. I want to do the right thing. If I were to leave Hugh now I'd have ripped their lives apart for nothing and that's not fair. It doesn't seem much, but at least if our relationship works and Kate and Tom grow up believing that their father left their mother for the love of his live – as I'd always believed – then maybe they'll find it in their hearts to forgive us both. Maybe we'll all muddle along as a fairly unconventional family. And if that's too much to hope for, at the very least I can guarantee that they'll get Christmas and birthday presents. It's not much, but it's all I can offer in the way of making it up.

So I must not think about the possibility that Hugh is having an affair. It doesn't have to mean anything significant. It doesn't mean anything at all, unless I say it does. I have to get our relationship back on track because the stakes we are playing to are terrifyingly high. Two children and a foetus. Nor can I think about the fact that Sam might be marrying one man whilst loving another. I can't even think about the pregnancy. The thing is, the chances are, if I managed to miss the fact that my best friend is ensconced in an affair just weeks before her wedding, then there's a serious possibility that this isn't the only sail that is blowing me up shit creek. I know that recently I've been far too installed in babyville. I know that I haven't paid enough attention to Hugh or to my job. I can only fix one thing at a time, and I've decided it ought to be my job.

Because it is *my* job and Hugh is just Hugh. He's not my Hugh. Or at least not exclusively mine, which might as well mean not mine, mightn't it? I'm staying with him, but I've woken up to the fact that he's not my sun, my moon, my stars. I hope one day he will be again, when I stop being angry. In the short term it's probably wisest to concentrate on something else.

I *have* to win the Project Zoom pitch. I have to be entirely and unreservedly focused. I have to be pithy, witty, droll, keen, jocular and waggish. My knowledge base as far as cars are concerned is traditionally female: the colour (interior and exterior), the presence of power-assisted steering and a CD player are important. As is not breaking down. If a car conversation gets deeper than that I find it very difficult to avoid my eyes glazing over. So my first stop is the newsagent's, where I buy ten car magazines and set about learning everything there is to know about luxury-car brands. At least that way I'd be able to appear credible at a factory visit or when I meet the dealers.

I utilize my sleepless nights studying engine sizes, understanding suspension – front, rear and standard issue – I now know what a chassis is. I can hold a plausible conversation about the wheel base and engine transmission of most luxury cars. I know about tyre tread, width and grip. I know that a car with rear-wheel drive and a low centre of gravity holds the road like a sports car. I am able to say things like, 'Well, the straight-line speed and performance are beyond dispute on the Jaguar V6, but it sounds trouncey at high revs compared with a BMW's honeyed straight six', and I know what I mean. I know that an aluminium- rather than steel-built car is better for the environment, although 'real drivers' bemoan the bastardization of the driving experience. They like to feel the car grip the road under them.

And whilst this might not be everyone's solution to a lack of best friend and to a philandering lover, it's the best I can come up with at short notice.

July

40

I call Libby to show off my new knowledge. She's not exactly impressed, even when I tell her that a Volkswagen Golf 2.0 GTI is 3 mm shorter than a Ford Focus 2.0 Zetec, and these cars aren't even Project Zoom competitors. Her lack of enthusiasm could be something to do with the fact that it is after midnight.

'Did I disturb you?' I ask guiltily.

'Not really. I was ironing Millie's school uniform. Then I'm going to go to bed.'

'It would be easier to park,' I insist.

'What would?'

'The Volkswagen.'

'Three millimetres, no one would notice the difference,' she scoffs, betraying that whilst she might not be that interested in what I have to say she was at least listening to me, which is good of her. 'Especially me as I'm not very good at judging lengths.'

'That's because every man you've ever slept with has told you he has an eight-inch penis.'

We both laugh.

'Anyway,' I persist, 'the Volkswagen Golf 2.0 GTI is 36 mm wider than a Ford Focus 2.0 Zetec, so it's back to the eternal short-and-fat versus long-and-thin debate.'

'Well, my vote is with short and fat every time.'

We giggle again and then I comment, 'God, cars *are* sexy. Really sexy. Suddenly I get it. I understand the penis-substitute thing.'

'Oh-oh, your hormones are raging again,' Libby comments.

'What makes you think that?'

'Every one of your conversations reverts back to sex, whatever you're talking about.'

'But haven't you noticed that the vocabulary used when talking about cars is desperately provocative? All the car mags go on about is size, performance, grip, how the cars "respond" when "handled".'

Libby is laughing again. 'I think it's going to be Hugh's lucky night.'

Not Hugh's.

'Sex is definitely the right territory for Project Zoom. Or at least passion is. It's an Italian brand. I think I'm on to something.'

Libby laughs and points out that even if I was trying to sell thermal bedsocks to the old and infirm, I'd probably give it a sexy spin right now. We laugh and then hang up. She goes back to ironing Millie's uniform. I go back to lying on my bed, staring at the ceiling.

Libby is right – I do feel more randy than a fifteen-year-old schoolboy at the *Playboy* mansion, but my 33-week bulging stomach definitely doesn't do it for Hugh; he doesn't think my popped tummy button is in the slightest bit dinky. I think it looks great. Nor does he think the dark stretch marks that have oozed across my belly are exotic. The other day he came into the bedroom, and maybe he would have made overtures; after all I was lying naked and spreadeagled on the bed. However, he sensed that I was thus reclining due to the overwhelming, somewhat startling and sudden appearance of summer, not because I was feeling unbearably randy. Cooking a baby is hot work. Besides, he caught me scratching my boobs and I thought he was going to hoy.

Anyway, even if he were willing, I'm not sure I am. I'm staying, I'm just not playing – as yet. Not when there are so many unresolved issues swirling around. The receipt, the condoms, the late nights 'working' are all still burnished on my mind. I do try to submerge the issues with thoughts of Project Zoom and, largely, I'm successful. It's only late at night when I lie awake staring at the ceiling, like this, and I find myself counting cobwebs rather than reading about throttles and clutch control, that uninvited thoughts and images charge into my mind. Like gatecrashers at a party, they are difficult to evict without a row.

As a mistress I've long since been accustomed to the thought of Hugh kissing someone else's body. Laughing at someone else's jokes, making breakfast, even making babies with someone else. I'd quickly become accustomed to the fact that anything I did with Hugh – picnics in National Trust gardens, watching fireworks in the park, making fireworks in the bedroom, selecting prams from the Mamas & Papas catalogue – the chances were Becca had already done that, been there, written the book, starred in the movie. I'd got used to being the understudy, waiting to step into the limelight. There had always been someone before me. I'd just never imagined that there would be anyone *after* me.

This woman. The other 'other woman', what is she like? Is she brilliant and ballsy, or ephemeral and feminine? Is she blonde or dark or a redhead? Is she skinny? What size are her feet? What perfume does she wear? What are her favourite flowers? Does she like it when he kisses that tiny groove where her back stops and her bottom starts, the place where sweat sits after energetic lovemaking? Does he suck her toes? And if he does, does it make her come? Has he ever put his tongue up her nostril just for a laugh? Do her wardrobes smell of his clothes? Of wool and sweat and stale aftershave mingling, fusing to create a bomb that is guaranteed to blow me away.

Most nights I deal with the heebie-jeebies.

Tonight I want my mum. I grab the phone and press memory three. Hugh's mobile is memory one; I rarely use that nowadays. Sam is memory two; I never use that. A change in my telephone patterns shouldn't amount to much, but it does; I feel my life is unravelling like an old jumper.

'Out of all of Henry VIII's wives which one would you have *least* wanted to be?'

'Darling, what a philosophical question for you to put to me at –' I sense her scrabbling around for her alarm clock, even though we are miles away from one another. 'Two in the morning.' (That's taking the time difference into consideration.) 'I'm so pleased your very expensive education was entirely wasted.'

I cut through her ill-humoured sarcasm. 'Which one?'

'The last one,' she says finally.

'But she outlived him,' I protest.

'Maybe so, but she had to treat his gouty feet for years, which is definitely my idea of hell on earth.'

'Well, I think Anne Boleyn was the most put upon,' I pronounce. And before my mother even has the chance to ask why, I tell her. 'She didn't even have the dignity of being the first and she was followed by the one he loved the most.'

'Oh, and here's me thinking you were going to say something conventional, like she was executed.'

I stay silent for a moment, considering that I have possibly just shown my hand.

In a tone that my mother often uses, the one that suggests she knows more than I give her credit for, she adds, 'Still, the Princess Elizabeth must have been great revenge.'

'She was frigid and red-haired,' I whine petulantly.

'The red hair was her father's and saved her from losing the head it sat on. And her decision to remain celibate was incredibly wise. I wonder if she inherited her intelligence from her mother? Is everything all right, George?' asks Jessica. She almost tricks me into being truthful; she sounds so entirely out of character, so very mum-like.

'Fine,' I assert resolutely.

'It's just that it is the middle of the night.'

'No, really, I'm fine.' It is going to be OK. This dalliance of Hugh's will burn out. I'll win Project Zoom. The baby will be born fit and well and we'll be OK. Kate and Tom will continue to get their Christmas and birthday pressies on time.

'Well, since you've woken me in the middle of the night you might as well read out the book.'

'Good idea.' I scrabble about on the floor next to my bed, the book is never far away. "Week 33". It's official, it's a watermelon. How's it ever going to come out?'

'What else does it say?'

'"Wearing rings and watches can cause circulation problems. Sometimes a ring becomes so tight on a pregnant woman's finger that it has to be cut off by a jeweller." Well, that's one indignity Hugh has saved me,' I joke. '"You might not want to wear your rings if swelling occurs. Some pregnant women purchase inexpensive rings in larger sizes to wear during pregnancy."' I trail off as I think of Sam with her fake engagement ring, looking through bridal magazines. It shouldn't matter to me but it does. I hear a cab pull up outside. I don't want to risk another row with Hugh. 'It really is very late. I'll let you get back to your beauty sleep. I'll call you in the morning,' I say.

'You are OK, aren't you?'

'Never better. Got to go, Mum.'

I pull the covers around my ears. I close my eyes and pretend that I've been asleep for hours. I hope Jessica doesn't jump to the wrong conclusion because I called her Mum. Or worse, the right one.

41

I look out of my office window on to Golden Square; it is littered with groups of picnickers and pigeons. Every inch of grass and cement is taken up. The sun has decided to put in a rare appearance and, in response, Londoners have flooded out of their offices in their droves. There's an abundance of trendy, Soho types who work for one of the many nearby advertising agencies or media houses or, more enigmatically, are 'in film'. They lie in silent, smoking huddles; their only concern is achieving an even tan as quickly as possible. There's every shop assistant, waiter and hairdresser in the West End who has been able to swing a lunch hour. There are a number of beautiful girls, long-limbed and languid, reading magazines about how to be yet more beautiful. There are tourists, relieved to be discarding their waterproofs at last. There are couriers pausing to smoke a fag, their bikes propped against them, enjoying the fleeting sensation of freedom that pretending to be Mediterranean creates. There are some oldies with grey hair and walking sticks, and they are thinking that whilst many things were different in their day perhaps some things were just the same. The oldies, like me, find their gazes repeatedly drawn to the lazy couples, lying on the grass, benches and each other – kissing, caressing – not caring who sees their explicit intimacy because, after all, it's London, it's summertime and they love each other.

There are no pregnant women.

So I'm glad to be tucked up in my cool air-conditioned

office; it's a relief and we are making some headway on the pitch. I'm channelling my Herculean energy injection into becoming the George of old. I have called Frank Robson, the Zoom Marketing Director, and by befriending him I have become Q&A's Trojan horse.

'Frank, it's Georgina Richardson here . . . Yes, delighted . . . Thrilled . . . It's an honour . . . Our approach is different, Frank, we're not here to tell you about your advertising, we're going to set up an integrated partnership . . . Absolutely . . . Look, ideas aren't the problem; every agency could come to you with a good idea, we're looking at the competitive advantage . . . We're looking at your bottom line . . . We want to talk to you about every aspect of your communication strategy, dealership, staff, trade marketing, event marketing, direct marketing, product placement, sponsorship, PR . . . No, BMW already own that territory . . . You don't want to touch it. No, that's Audi's positioning, wouldn't go near it with a barge pole. The last thing you want, Frank, is another "me too" branding. Or, worse yet, a "me too late" . . . I'm looking forward to seeing you as well, Frank.'

He bought it.

He respects me, he trusts me, he likes me and, because he hasn't seen me for several months, there's a fairly good chance that he fancies me. I think I'll limit our relationship to the telephone until the actual pitch date and then, and only then, he can discover the truth. The fact that he's been flirting with the Michelin man. By then it won't matter because we'll blow him away with the high standard of our work.

In all the years of trying to impress Hugh, Dean, Karl et al, I have never worked so hard on a pitch. This is the big one. Besides the massive amount of revenue that winning

Project Zoom would create for the agency, there is another much more personal issue at stake. In advertising you're only as good as your last ad or, in my department, you are only as good as your last pitch win. Since my last pitch win was for odour eaters, with a net income of a few hundred thousand pounds – hardly enough to cover the cost of the team's salary and the market research – things could be better. I want to prove to Dean that I haven't 'lost my edge' but, more than that, I want to prove it to myself.

Recently, I've been wondering if Hugh and I had both applied for the position as MD at Rartle, Roguel and Spirity, who would have got it?

Could I?

How good am I?

How good would I be on my own if, say, if I had to be?

Julia interrupts my thoughts by slamming an inch-thick document on to my desk; every fibre of her body is screaming resentment. She obviously feels my insistence that she deliver the research on unit shift and share of voice for every saloon, coupé, convertible and roadster that Lexus, Jaguar, Mercedes, Volvo, Audi, Saab and BMW have produced to be somewhat unnecessary. Especially as I insisted that she provide the information by today, and she's had to sacrifice her lunch hour in the sun to do so. However, my experience has always proven that Julia's 'research' is rarely that; there will be more holes in it than there are in fishnet tights at a tarts and vicars' party. I do feel guilty that by missing today's sun Julia may have missed the British summer altogether, so I promise to read the research and give her feedback a.s.a.p. I'm hoping she'll see that her contribution is valuable and that the deadline I set her was an actual deadline, rather than a deadline drawn in sand.

'Whatever,' sighs Julia, betraying her lack of passion about tracking car sales since 1980. I make a mental note to mention this lack of enthusiasm at her next appraisal, but I doubt that I will. When it comes to the crunch, I'll probably tell her she's doing marvellously and is a great asset; I'll then give her a pay rise even though she already earns about double what she's worth.

'Is everyone ready for the pitch practice?' I ask.

'Suppose.' She barely hides her indifference.

I bite back my irritation. For the past couple of weeks I've been working around the clock. I've attended research groups as far north as Edinburgh and as far south as Hove. I've talked to Zoom marketing managers in France, Italy, Germany, Sweden and Japan. I've visited countless dealers' stores. I've masterminded a workshop with the client so that we can try to understand the brand as much as possible. I've commissioned creative briefs, vox pop interviews, and helped pull together a mood tape that represents the brand as it stands, and another to demonstrate where we'd like to take it. We've seen and understood the client's market plans, or at least one strain of them. The strain that rewrites all that's gone before and creates unrealistic expectations of what can be achieved in the future. We've studied the brand plan, the marketing strategy and the budget. Karl, Drew and I have met on a daily basis to debate the brand positioning and Brett drops in on our meetings with unprecedented regularity, demanding to see a creative brief. Everyone in the agency knows how important this pitch is to us.

I stride into the meeting room that we have commandeered for the pitch; we call it the 'war room'. This is blatantly an act of self-aggrandizement, but I work mostly with men so it's necessary for their egos; as are sweat rings under their armpits, the bigger the better, and to think I used to worry that my bump was disgusting. There are pieces of paper haphazardly Blu-Tacked to the walls of the war room; these are the fruits of our recent efforts. They are titled: *Future Product Line-up. Brand Personality. Brand Personality Index-linked Against the Competitors. Driver Profile. Competitive Encroachment.* There are charts showing the competitive ad spend of every car brand in this category, broken down by media type and year spend, share of voice, share of mind. There are examples of competitive ads, Websites and communication propositions. Our job is to develop a communication strategy that is at once relevant but different. It's a struggle. All car adverts are the same – they show cars speeding around the Swiss Alps. The same-colour car, the same stretch of road, the same Swiss Alp.

I catch Karl reading the *Sun*; he tells me he's doing research into the minds of real people.

'It's a luxury-car brand,' I argue. 'You haven't got time to waste.'

He closes the paper and rubs his temples. 'God, George, what hormone is it that's giving you all this energy suddenly? I'm knackered. We haven't stopped for breath in weeks.'

'Two weeks until we present the strategy, Karl; we both know this isn't the time to slow down.'

'Suppose not,' he agrees reluctantly.

Secretly I know he's thrilled that the old George has made a reappearance, and secretly I am too. OK, so I may not have toned calves (or indeed toned anything), I may not be able to wear tailored, sexy suits (although everything I wear is clingy, this is an accident of nature), but at least I'm able to write an impressive pitch document. It's a thrill to be appreciated for my mind. It's a first.

The rest of the team join us: Drew, Brett, Julia, a pair of creatives, an Account Director and an Account Manager.

'According to the research, which brand has the benchmark status in this category, Jaguar or BMW?' I demand.

'BMW,' replies the Account Manager.

'OK, well, let's interrogate BMW then,' I bark. I mean, let's understand as much as we possibly can about BMW's communication and advertising strategy, but it would be social death to be as straightforward as to say that – jargon to advertising is of equivalent importance as sun-blushed tomatoes are to the Bluebird Café.

'Have we considered this sufficiently from the consumer's point of view?' asks Drew. 'Have we done enough research into current perceptions of the brand?'

'Yes. We've segmented the results of the group research and the vox pop research by age, class, sex, sexual orientation, income, religion, marital status, usage level and personality factors,' assures the Account Director. The idea is that a clear understanding of the customers will mean that we can advertise to them more effectively. In reality, research is used as a post-rationalization to push through the creative endeavour, which Brett and Dean prefer.

'OK, well, let's run through the deck then,' I instruct. 'We'll start with agency credentials, show them lots of ads that look pretty, then we'll go on to the agency philosophy . . .'

'Excellent concept, Brett, the boys have done good,' smiles Dean; his attempt at an English idiom is proof that he's really pleased with the creative team's work.

I smile, relieved, not least because the concept is actually mine. I don't want the praise, I just wanted something that Brett, as Creative Director, signed off, and Dean, as MD, was delighted with. Not as simple a process as it sounds. For weeks, Drew, Karl and I have been arguing the positioning for the Project Zoom brand. As usual, we spent 90 per cent of our time outdoing one another in the up-your-own-bum stakes.

'Our job is to communicate the brand's desire to admit to its humanity.' (Drew.)

'It's a car,' I reminded him, playing with the ring-pull on my can of fizzy orange.

'We must gradually move the brand tonality from clinically severe and strategic to something more congenial and charismatic. More sunrise than seascape.' (Brett.)

'It's a car,' I repeated, as I munched on the soft bourbon biscuits. They are my least favourite biscuits in the whole world, but I'd eaten the chocolate fingers and the custard creams, needs must.

Then we spent roughly 7 per cent of our time arguing like children.

'There has to be a picture of the car.' (Karl.)

'No, there doesn't.' (Me.)

'But all car advertising has a picture of a car.' (Karl.)

'Exactly.' (Me.)

'Well, then, *we* have to have a picture of a car.'

'We don't.'

'Do.'

'Don't.'

'Do.'

'Don't. Don't. Don't.' I only just resisted stamping my feet.

The remaining 3 per cent of our time was spent feeding the creative team ideas that we then wanted them to present back to us. The trick is that they have to think the ideas are their ideas in the first place; any creative worth his DKNY trainers will seriously oppose anything that management might actually like. Karl, Drew and I then had to pretend we believed our idea was their idea and whilst we 'quite liked it' we 'had reservations' as it was 'too outlandish'. The creatives then told us we were 'dull tossers' and wouldn't know a good idea if 'it bit our lardy fucking arses'. Finally, faux-reluctantly, we agreed to use 'the idea' for the pitch.

Downing Street looks decidedly un-spin in comparison.

The idea is this:

The cars look beautiful, but then you expect that; if you are spending anything upward of twenty grand on a car, it's a given it's going to look good. Karl has argued for various adverts that, boiled down in a melting pot, are little more than beautiful shots of the cars. I've argued that Zoom is the master brand in terms of engineering genius, technical innovation and excellence, and this is what we have to communicate. At the risk of appearing a bit wanky, it is possible to refer to their cars as having intelligent wheels, an engine with a brain, a sequential gearbox that contributes to a unique driving experience, and functional lightweight steering. These cars are in fact the ultimate boy-toy, a Swiss Army knife on wheels, the dog's bollocks. And that's the creative solution.

There are no pictures of cars; there are no winding Alpine roads. There's a black screen. Then, first of all, there's a simple line drawing of a Swiss Army knife. The Swiss Army knife morphs into line drawings of other boy-toys such as a WAP phone and then an iPAQ. These pictures morph again into ground-breaking inventions such as the Enigma code machine, the Apollo II capsule – inventions that have, arguably, altered the course of history. The penultimate drawing is of a dog's bollocks. The final shot is of the car's badge. It's brave, it's risky, and we're all unsure as to whether the client will let a picture of dog's bollocks get into production. However, the concept will raise a laugh in the pitch presentation and it does the necessary in terms of shock, cut-through and communication. We've tested the ad concept in six European countries and it went down a storm with the target audience of males aged twenty-five to thirty-five. Guy Ritchie has agreed to direct the ad, and Ewan McGregor has agreed to do the voice-over, providing we remain 'edgy' (i.e., keep the bollocks).

I think it might work.

We've backed up this sixty-second ad with a number of shorter adverts that draw attention to specific technical innovations. In addition we have a strong, efficient and differentiating media plan.

I think it might just work.

By the time the rehearsal is over it's after nine o'clock in the evening.

The team has had enough. I give them my credit card and tell them to put it behind the bar at the Crown and Sceptre and then go on and get slaughtered; I'll pick up the tab tomorrow. They're grateful; they don't need to be asked twice.

'Are you joining us?' asks Drew. And, whilst it's nice to be invited, it's been a while, I say no because I want to go home and have another read through the deck. As I turn the lights out in the war room I can smell something in the air. Not just summertime, not just the fat, creamy lilies that are scattered in vases throughout the agency, with a liberality that suggests we are expecting to host a wedding for *OK* magazine. There is a faint whiff of possibility, of power, of success. The perfumes I used to drench myself in, which have eluded me of late. And I love that smell.

42

Despite the fact that the Tube is heaving and I have to stand for the entire journey home (the age of chivalry is not only dead, it's entombed), and despite the fact that I am wedged between a cheesy armpit and a girl who is weeping into her mobile phone, I still manage to walk through my door feeling positive.

I waddle to the bathroom and start to run a cool bath. I might even paint my toenails because open-toed shoes are eternally sexy, irrespective of hip width and stomach girth. Although looking at my swollen feet I may be kidding myself.

I wish Hugh would rinse his stubby hairs away and not leave them cleaving to the porcelain; how difficult is it to swill a bit of water around a sink? I notice that he's left his empty can of shaving cream on the loo seat, too. This is his way of asking me to buy him another can. Doesn't he know that there is a Boots on every high street? Anyway, where is Hugh tonight? He must have said. I remember that he was asking for his dress shirt this morning; he must be at some awards do or client dinner. When he asked where his dress shirt was, I wanted to yell, 'On the floor, in the smoky heap that you left it last time you went to a black-tie function.' But, of course, it wasn't. Because I also want to be perfectly efficient and the drive to be perfectly efficient is the one that made me pick up the shirt, wash it (with all the other white washing on a very high temperature), press it and return it to his wardrobe. Just call me the laundry fairy.

Don't think about it. Don't think about it. Don't get

wound up, not after such a successful day, I instruct myself.

I slowly and carefully ease myself into the bath, enjoying the sensation of the cool water enveloping my body and the feeling of buoyancy, which temporarily releases me from my feeling of off-the-scale massiveness. I stroke the baby and start to talk to it.

'Mummy's been a ball-breaker today,' I brag, and then I apologize in case 'it' is a 'he' and 'he' is feeling intimidated. Slowly the Radox works its way into my skin and psyche and I begin to drift, mentally as well as physically. I begin to daydream about my perfect life. My perfect life is this. It's a hot summer afternoon and I'm sat in a garden under an umbrella; I'm watching my baby crawl and gurgle on a picnic rug on the grass nearby. Various friends are with me, and we're all drinking Pimm's, and there's a smell of barbecued sausages drifting towards us (although, because this is a fantasy, there's no smoke choking the guests, and I have remembered to bring my washing in off the line). There's a medley of children running around the garden; I can identify Millie, Kate and Tom, but there are others too and, again because this is a fantasy, none of them are squabbling. Libby's there, and Sam with James (go on, then, I'll throw in a wedding ring for Sam). I've won Project Zoom and therefore Dean has awarded me a generous maternity-leave package, so I know that this time of languid summer afternoons, whilst not endless, is at least extended.

Suddenly, I sit bolt upright in the bath, sending waves of water crashing over the edge on to the tiles.

I can't see Hugh.

The water floods past the bath mat and really has made an awful mess.

I suppose he must be doing the barbecue. Mustn't he?

After my bath I wash the bathroom floor, and as I'm on

my knees I wash the kitchen floor too. Then I tidy the drawer where I keep the cookbooks and the money-off coupons. I should probably have done this before I got in the bath, but my ability to think sequentially is impaired at the moment; it's another pregnancy symptom, and not one any woman should ever confess to any man.

At 9.15 p.m. I pour myself a large glass of iced water and add a slice of lemon. I'm trying to trick my mind, my body and soul into believing that I'm enjoying a hefty G&T. It's boiling hot and the sun is streaming through the blinds, which I've pulled down because I'm naked but for a pair of Mothercare maternity knickers – although, arguably, these knickers are more modest than some of the skirts I used to wear pre-pregnancy. My thighs stick together, and when I prise them apart they make a thwack sound, not unlike a plunger relieving a sink of years of hair and dead skin.

'Who could resist me?' I ask ironically. I giggle to myself, because this doesn't horrify me as it would undoubtedly have done in the past. In fact, it makes me laugh so much that I let my thighs melt and mash together over and over again, just for the pleasure of pulling them apart and hearing the thwack sound.

The doorbell rings.

Bugger, I could ignore it. I look down at my naked state, and state is definitely the appropriate word – boobs hitting my knees, sweat running over my bump in rivers. There's no one on this earth I'd let see me dressed like this. Or, rather, undressed like this.

Except.

Sam!

Thrilled, I dash to the door and am about to fling it open to reveal my naked, corpulent self, but at the last second I'm infected with a hint of caution. I spy through the letterbox.

'James?' I yell.

'Sorry to arrive unannounced. I know it's rude of me, but–' The 'but' is so desperate that I barely remember to fling a jacket on to protect my modesty and protect his sensibilities. I open the door.

'Come in.'

This time his face does flicker on greeting me, but I can't kid myself – it's not appreciation, it's bewilderment.

'Er, if I've come at a bad moment . . .' he starts to apologize, as he scans my semi-nude, nearly immodest state.

'Oh, don't worry, we're not swinging from the chandeliers. I'm on my own actually. It's fantastic to see you.' I realize this sounds a bit like a come-on and I'm mortified. I've obviously spent too many evenings on my own; I'm pretty hopeless at deciding what's acceptable chit-chat. I decide not to worry too much; I suspect James has more on his mind than my semi-nakedness. 'Come in, fix yourself a drink, I'll go and find some clothes,' I urge, pulling him over the threshold before he can run away and before the neighbours start talking.

Five minutes later, I come down the stairs again and this time I'm decently clad. James is sat in the kitchen at the breakfast bar. I'm pleased to see he has poured himself a beer – it shows he's relaxed – and I'm delighted that he's poured me a glass of milk – it shows he's thoughtful.

'You must think it's odd my coming round here like this.'

'Not really.' I head towards the more comfortable chairs in the living room and James follows me through.

'You've got to talk her out of marrying my brother,' he splutters before he's even sat down. 'You're her best friend; surely you don't think she should marry him, she loves me.' James turns a bit pink as he realizes that what he's said could sound irresponsibly arrogant.

'I've tried.'

'Have you?' He looks up at me with surprise and scary intensity. James has very deep-brown eyes and, although my personal favourite has always been green eyes, I have to admit that his are exceptionally beautiful. They are aflame. The fire is unmistakable, unambiguous, unequivocal.

His eyes are lit up by love.

I haven't seen that for a while.

'So you don't think she should marry him?' he asks.

'Well, not if you love each other, no.' I'm being cautious. Because, after all, I don't want to say anything that will compromise Sam's position. She is my best friend, albeit a best friend who can't stand being in the same room as me.

'It's such a mistake.' James runs his hands through his hair and hangs his head. His pain and frustration are almost tangible. He really is delicious – what can Sam be thinking of by looking a gift horse like this in the mouth? 'I don't get this obsession with being married.' He suddenly looks up at me and is obviously hoping I can explain it to him. I can't, he's the wrong sex. How can I explain that Sam has come to the end of her tether? She can't bear to be the spare female at even one more cosy dinner party hosted by smug couples. She's been a bridesmaid about six times. She's woken up in her share of strange and familiar beds only to be asked to drop the latch on her way out. In short, she's seen love come and go more often than is decent and she can't risk it again.

'Well, from her point of view, you're a bit of a gamble, a wild card,' I stutter. I'm trying not to offend him, because he looks genuine enough sat on my sofa with his tan and his pecs and his burning eyes; on the other hand, he is shagging his brother's fiancée, which isn't exactly the epitome of trustworthy behaviour.

As though he were reading my mind, James says, 'There's no reason for you to trust me, I'm behaving treacherously towards Gilbert. I'm aware of that.'

'Yes.'

'But you have to believe me that I've never done anything like this before.'

'That doesn't necessarily make it OK,' I comment, and after all I should know. James looks as though I've just punched him.

'I love her.' He stares at me for about two weeks. I've met dozens of Sam's boyfriends in the past. I have even heard one or two say exactly the same thing. I can't look convinced, because James feels compelled to add, 'I love the way she scrunches her nose up when she laughs. I love her because she is the most altruistic, forgiving, sweet-natured woman I've ever met. I love her because she is beautiful, capable and peerless. I love her because she buys at least three copies of the *Big Issue* every week even though she has a direct debit for Shelter. I love the way she can drink me under the table. I love it that she's competitive. I even love her flat feet and the fact she scratches her head when she's thinking.'

I don't think I've ever heard any man say such things about any woman to a third party, not even grooms about their brides in their speeches at the many weddings I've attended. James loves Sam for the same reasons I do; well, except I could take or leave her flat feet and scratching.

'What about Africa? Aren't you supposed to be going back soon?' I can't see Sam living anywhere without there being a Chanel or Dior or Estée Lauder concession within spitting distance. He can't seriously think she'd go with him.

'I'll get a job here. I'll work in a travel agency. I'll find something. I'd do anything.'

Considering that it's been difficult to persuade Sam's

boyfriends to move over in bed or give her a share of the duvet in the past, I admit this is serious.

James stands up and moves towards the door. He's leaving because we both know I'm not the one he needs to convince.

'Sorry, to – er – have barged in like this. I just needed to say it.'

'Don't be sorry.' I sweep his embarrassment away as best I can. 'Have you thought of telling Gilbert about your affair?' I ask.

'I can't do that to either of them.'

'No, I suppose not.' I open the front door and James starts to walk up the path. 'Have you thought of proposing?' I yell.

'Not whilst she's engaged to my brother.' He shrugs.

'No, suppose not,' I repeat and then add, 'Er, good luck.'

I realize that my parting shot is inadequate and imperfect in the face of his pain and passion.

Oh God, being an adult is so difficult.

Hugh comes in at one-thirty in the morning. I'm at the dining-room table, ostensibly reflecting on the enthusiastic, almost unearthly preoccupation the engineers and designers at Zoom have with building the ultimate driving machine; in reality I'm worrying about Sam and James and Gilbert. Hugh has been through the door for about thirty seconds and he still hasn't mentioned the shiny kitchen floor. I don't think I can forgive him.

'Where have you been?'

He doesn't answer immediately, but empties his pockets of his mobile, loose change and keys. To think I used to find this little ritual endearing, when obviously it's as irritating as someone scraping their fingernails down a blackboard.

'I told you, we went to the Unilever clients' summer ball.'

'We?'

'Yes, me and the team.' He seems confused.

'Why didn't you ask me to go with you? I suppose it's because I'm too fat to be seen with. Where was this ball? So who's on this team?' I know, I make those involved in the Spanish Inquisition look inadequate.

Hugh doesn't look at me, but tells the breakfast bar that no one took their partners. That the ball was at Grosvenor House. That he had mentioned it this morning, and that the team members are Mark, Tom, and Toni.

'With an "i" or a "y"?'

'What?'

'Toni. With an "i" or a "y"? Male or female Toni?'

Hugh almost grins. 'Well, I suppose, strictly speaking, she's female, but not easily identifiable as such. She's a real bulldog. Good brain, though,' he adds as an afterthought.

'Really,' I snipe. It's not Hugh's style to comment on female intelligence. He rarely walks along the street turning to check out the pert grey matter. He's never commented, 'Fantastic pair of medulla oblongata.' I'm not convinced for a second. I've heard it all before. Well, at least if not first-hand then certainly second, through films and girl friends. No one ever admits to a colleague being attractive. The bulldog is undoubtedly far from being a bruiser. I can see her now – a leggy, skinny, redhead. A number of Hugh's sexual fantasies involve redheads.

'I'm telling you the truth,' he insists.

'As though you'd know what it is,' I mutter.

'What's that supposed to mean, George?'

I don't bother answering. I walk to the kitchen, open the fridge and hunt around for the milk.

'How many copies of the *Big Issue* do I buy a week?' I ask Hugh.

Hugh stares at me as though I've just confessed to a three-in-the-bed but doesn't answer.

'What do you love about me, Hugh?'

He loosens his tie. 'Your ability to hold a sequential conversation,' he mutters sarcastically.

I pour myself a glass of milk and head off to bed with my week-by-week pregnancy guidebook.

43

It's hard to say how things are going. The Managing Director, Marketing Director, the Marketing Controller, two Marketing Managers and the Brand Manager all appear rapt. But it crosses my mind that they could have learnt that encouraging-nodding-of-the-head technique on a course in Tunbridge Wells.

Karl is being predictably slick and efficient.

'The health of the brand is excellent. Sales are at record levels, the product continues to improve and goodwill amongst consumers has never been higher. Why, then, I hear you ask, would we suggest that now is an appropriate time for a change in the communications strategy?'

Actually, none of the clients has asked any such thing, and I have a horrible feeling that one of the Marketing Managers has just started writing a shopping list on the agency-supplied notepad, with the agency-supplied pencil. Undaunted, Karl carries on, his rhino-like skin is an invaluable asset at times like this; a more sensitive man would crumble.

'Given the success of the brand, you may be inclined to simply repeat what you've already been doing. More of the same. But that's not a good idea. Why not? I'll tell you why not.' Karl pauses dramatically. 'The environment in which we are operating is constantly changing, and we need to change with it. After all, once you're at the top there's only one way to go.' He starts to crank up the emotional pressure. If you can't impress them then depress them was not the agreed strategy. I fling him a warning look. He ignores it.

'Success is invariably followed by plummeting decline and the decline can always be traced back to the unwillingness of an old dog to learn new tricks. Think of the Roman and Soviet empires, think Thatcher. Or, more prosaically, think Spam and Red Mountain . . .' Karl continues to try to intimidate the client as he briefly touches on some media-buying issues. 'There is increased competition in advertising in the car category on TV, in in-flight, in the press and on posters . . . So-called "innovative" media ideas offer no respite as they are copied immediately . . . And we all know that TV does not deliver as it used to.'

The clients are just reaching for the Prozac when I cut Karl short by pointing out that the best brands, with the appropriate communication, can always cut through the clutter.

The clients smile at me gracefully. Karl winks at me, and I realize that we have just played good cop/bad cop to perfection – without even rehearsing it. I feel a flicker of excitement dart up my calves and then explode in my stomach. We're a good team. I'd almost forgotten how good we could be.

Drew is suitably academic and incomprehensible. He asks, 'Are there truly any real brands?' No one knows how to answer this, although he has been asking it at every pitch for as long as I've known him. I don't mind; it's the planner's job to be obscure. One of the uppity Marketing Managers starts to attack the segmentation chart that Drew is presenting. Drew bats back by pointing out that this is the same chart that Mars always use, and, if it's good enough for Mars, well then . . . Drew then adds, 'Why keep a dog and bark yourself; after all, it's better if you stick to the knitting.' No one has a clue what he's on about, least of all himself, or the uppity Marketing Manager. No one wants to admit to being ignorant, so his point is conceded.

Drew then shows over forty slides on the market-research results, sprinkling his presentation with details on continuous surveys, retail-audit presentations, consumer panels and tracking studies. He uses so many acronyms I'm beginning to think *I'm* in the wrong meeting, so I have no idea what the clients must be thinking. AGB, TGI, EPOS, DAR, ECG, NRS. I, for one, fear he's gone OTT. Even if he has a point, we're so bored that we can't be bothered to let him make it; the pitch process is fast turning into a kind of slow-water torture.

When Frank looks confused enough, I start to chip in with my thinly disguised sales pitch. It's a unique mix of: flattery – 'We're all aware of the exacting standards you set'; glossing – 'So what did the brand research tell us? We did credibly well against all the key dimensions of performance, engineering quality, technology and design'; and telling him how it is – 'But I'm afraid the brand performed poorly against the aspirational characteristics, dynamic, sporty, contemporary and prestigious.'

I can see the clients sinking into their seats; it's my job to lift them.

'But don't worry, we do have the solution.'

Drum roll, and then Brett presents the creative concepts, which are all anyone is ever interested in anyway. Brett shocks us all. He's very keen and largely articulate. When questioned by Frank about why we went with this direction, he doesn't say, 'because black is my favourite colour', he shows an astonishing amount of acumen. 'What we are trying to do is exploit the dissonance between the brand's residual association with yuppies and the 1980s, and current cultural values of anti-badge advertising. This is all about not taking yourself too seriously, about being big enough to take a pop at yourself . . .'

It's clear, they love them. The MD slaps Frank on the back, Frank beams and winks at me. The Marketing Managers are already getting excited about the prospect of meeting Guy Ritchie. Now all I have to do is draw the meeting to an accurate and memorable conclusion.

I start with a bit of reassuring good sense about knowing what their company is good at, about never underestimating the workload, nor the importance of selling the idea to the sales force – at which point Frank surprises me by stealing back the show.

'Do you mean that?'

'What?'

'The bit about the importance of selling the idea to the sales force?'

I can hardly say no. 'Yes.'

'Good. Let's do it. We've seen six agencies and I'd say it's down to two. You and one other.' He doesn't pause to say congratulations. 'You can both present to our sales force, and we'll see what they think.'

This is great news.

'You can do it this afternoon.'

This is bad news.

It's an unusual situation. Frank's on-the-spot decision to take advantage of a sales conference that just happens to be taking place today (I smell a rat) is unlikely to be a genuine impulse. I don't seriously believe that the decision of who will handle the advertising business will rest with the sales force. I think the MD and Frank's marketing department are just trying to keep the unions happy. My experience is that really good advertising never comes from committee approval. However, the client is god and if they want their potential agency to sweat blood and tears in front of a 200-strong audience we'll do it.

And then some.

Although, as Dean, Drew, Karl, Brett and I pack up our charts and tapes (in the knowledge that we have less than fifty minutes to get to Euston station, buy our tickets and board the train for Milton Keynes), it's hard to view the 'opportunity' to pitch our creative concepts to the entire sales force as quite the victory it surely is. This morning we were running on adrenalin (well, at least I was; I can't vouch for Brett, his adrenalin quite possibly comes from something a little stronger than black coffee and Pro Plus). The adrenalin rush lasted throughout the morning's presentation, and whilst we are all trying hard to cling on to the can-do attitude we're all feeling a bit nervy and jaded.

Thank God it's a bright sunny July day and all of London is celebrating this fact. The parks are full, the cafés are heaving, and the streets are bubbling over. The world is awash with optimism. People are actually smiling at one another in the street as though they were living in a different century. Black clothes seem to have been banished overnight as effervescent beauties and uglies dress in flirty, colourful summer dresses that are unashamedly feminine. Blokes grin their appreciation, trying but failing to pluck up the courage to strike up a conversation. There's nowhere quite like London, on a hot summer's day, to convey possibility. The smells of sweet sweat (barely disguised by designer perfumes), sun oil, lager and garlic all collide into one another to create an infusion of expectation. Even the facts that my previously toned upper arms are rubbing the edge of my maternity bra, and that the sweat is running down the chafed flesh, don't upset me.

'I think we can really do this, guys. I think we might just win it.'

Karl looks doubtful, Brett looks sulky (he had a big lunch planned) and Drew is simply looking out of the cab window.

'Really. I have a good feeling,' I enthuse.

Only Dean picks up my ebullience, and that's only because he's American. 'You're all ready to wow them, Georgina?'

'Sure thing, Dean,' I grin.

'Attagirl, go get 'em.' He thumps my back and I regret my lack of pompons. Dean definitely sees me as the team cheerleader.

The pitch is perfect.

Karl is pleasantly polished and effective. Drew cuts his presentation in half, which still means it's twice as long as necessary, but it is an improvement. And, most importantly, Brett's presentation of the creative concept sends a ripple of excitement through the audience.

It's in the bag. It's in the bloody bag! I'm sure of it. All I have to do is make a careful and notable summary. No flannel, no frills, no problem.

I stand in front of the mike, which immediately squeaks irresponsibly. Rather than yell 'testing, one, two, three', which is so unoriginal, I cough and realize that the sound hasn't been picked up. I glare my irritation towards the back of the hall. A scruffy individual, in jeans and square glasses, begins to panic and run around, as though there is a rocket up his boxers. If only. I turn to Dean and smile prettily, trying to convey that everything is under control. An outright lie. The mike makes another high-pitched squeaky sound; this one apparently indicates that the blip in the sound system has now been rectified. I'm meant to understand this because the geek in the jeans and glasses has stopped sweating buckets and is holding his thumbs up in the air.

I approach the mike for the second time, rehearsing my opening under my breath. 'It's an unusual position you find yourselves in. You are a victim of your own success. The sheer volume of sales . . .'

Then it happens.

It starts in my shoes, or at least I think it must because it certainly builds from somewhere, and my shoes are as far away from my mouth as any other part of my anatomy. It builds in my stomach and pauses there for a fraction of time. Long enough for me to recognize it for what it is, but not long enough for me to stifle its progress. My stomach growls and rumbles. Then it rises up my oesophagus; there's a moment where I can't breathe. Then the sulphurous, clamorous, ruinous BURP explodes.

I'm so pleased that the mike is working efficiently and that it picks *that* up.

Not.

A number of the more juvenile members of the audience (about three-quarters) start to titter, and, before I can quickly look around for someone to blame the bodily explosion on, the worst thing happens. I fart. A rip-roaring, resounding, wall-reverberating, ripe FART.

I'm finished.

The room erupts into riotous laughter. The members of the audience, on average, earn £30K apiece and yet their mental age is equivalent to their shoe size. I notice the odd woman in the audience trying to keep a straight and loyal face but then their solidarity breaks as they hear repeated imitation farts, which the majority are indulging in.

What can I do? I can hardly ask for everyone's understanding that the uncontrollable gases are the result of my being thirty-four weeks pregnant. Sales forces rarely do understanding. I catch Dean's eye and immediately wish I hadn't. He looks like he's just had intercourse with a cactus. His face is puce, his eyes are rolling, I think that is genuine steam emitting from his body. Surely he can't think I did that on purpose. Surely he knows I'd rather eat my own eyeballs than fart in public. Of course I've farted, and for that matter burped, in public before. Once at Christmas 1997, and another time near the turn of the millennium. But on both occasions I was at noisy parties and able to walk swiftly away before anyone attributed them to me. I'd rather curl up with agonizing stomach cramps than fart in front of Hugh, I'd rather excuse myself from bed at 3 a.m. saying I need to walk the dog than let loose, and we don't even have a dog. And now I've farted in front of 200 potential clients, my most important colleagues, and my boss.

I see no reason to carry on living.

I stumble through the presentation, but I'm not sure anyone is listening. I battle against the tasteless gas jokes, which are heckled intermittently, and after twenty minutes I ask, 'Are there any questions from the floor?' About one hundred hands shoot up.

'Can I offer you a Settler?' Snigger.

'Can you run through the budget? I do hope your claims to cost efficiencies aren't all *gas and air*.' Titter.

'I liked your adverts – at least they're not a *rip off* of anything else I've seen.' Chortle.

So I did have their attention.

44

The alarm clock interrupts my nightmare. I'm grateful. I was dreaming that I was presenting to a huge audience of a company's sales force, and it was a really important pitch for business, worth millions of pounds in advertising revenue. It was essential to Dean that Q&A win this high-profile, multimedia, international account, and I ruined the presentation by uncontrollably letting rip. As I mooch into consciousness I'm struck with a hideous thought – this was not a dream. This really happened. I sigh and pull the covers back over my head. I can smell Hugh's early morning body and it's some comfort; at least it is until he says, 'So are you going to face up to' – he hesitates and then sniggers – 'your gaffe and go into work today?'

However big the man, farts and burps are irresistible joke fodder, it's genetic.

I peek out from under the covers and scowl at him. I wish I'd never told him about the incident. It would be nice to get some sympathy, but I realize my chances are anorexic.

'Come on, George, you can't hide away for the rest of your life.'

'I'm not planning to hide away for the rest of my life – just until after the pregnancy,' I mutter.

Hugh shows no mercy but flings the duvet completely off the bed. I dash to the shower, not least because I don't want him to see my corpulent flesh. As I close the bathroom door he asks, 'Who were you presenting to, anyway?'

I hesitate. In the past I've sometimes broken agency

confidentiality and discussed with Hugh an account that Q&A were pitching for. He's often a help when bandying ideas about, but this time I have observed Dean's instructions for absolute secrecy and I haven't discussed the fact that Q&A are on this luxury-car pitch. *The* pitch that the *entire* industry is talking about. Well, at least I haven't discussed it with Hugh, although Libby does know what's going on. It's not that I don't trust Hugh to keep tight-lipped, it's just that . . . I don't trust Hugh.

I turn the shower on full blast and pretend I didn't hear his question.

The pitch is over. I've obviously blown any chance we had of winning, and, for a moment there, I thought we did have a chance. I dread to think what the consequences might be. I can't imagine Dean suddenly developing a sense of humour. He's probably already started to reconsider my severance package. His threat wasn't so decent as to be veiled.

Worse still, the pitch is over and so I no longer have an excuse to avoid thinking about the possibility that Hugh is having an affair. The possibility that he's betraying me. Because no matter how many times I tell myself that it's best to ignore the signs, I can't. Because no matter how many times I tell myself that an affair isn't significant, it is.

I'm tired. Really tired. Tired because recently I've put enormous effort into trying to win the pitch. The long hours and deep concentration were arduous. And I'm tired because I'm pregnant. My body, proficient at lifting weights and running marathons, has never endured anything quite so physically gruelling and demanding as this. But mostly, I think I'm tired of Hugh.

I know, big news.

When I emerge from the shower, Hugh has already left

for the gym; he still works out before going into the office and then showers at the gym. On the bed there's a breakfast tray. Tea and toast and croissants, with honey on the side (my favourite accompaniment) – not in a jar but carefully decanted into a little bowl, which looks so much better. There's also orange juice, and when I taste it I note it's freshly squeezed. There's a small vase of sweet peas that must have been cut from our garden; they are still dripping with morning dew. The tray looks beautiful. It looks just like something you'd find in the pages of a lifestyle magazine. I sit on the bed and stare at the tray. A large tear rolls down my cheek and splashes on to the toast. I'm not sure if I'm crying with relief, regret or rapture.

45

'You are a fucking genius,' laughs Brett.

Have I walked into the wrong office?

'Yeah, well done, George. Fair play, who'd have thought it?' Karl shakes his head with mystified delight.

I don't react. It could be a wind up. Trust no one is closer to scripture than mantra in advertising.

'Congratulations, Georgina. Congratulations, every one of you. Well done for all your hard work. Take the rest of the day off,' booms Dean.

A cheer engulfs the war room and within seconds ripples through the agency. It sounds genuine enough.

We've won.

'We've won?' I know I'm being slow – the champagne corks are already popping and it's unlikely that I've got the wrong end of the stick, but I want to be sure.

'Yes, we fucking won,' laughs Karl. He sits back in his chair, putting his hands behind his head as he rests his feet on his desk. He's trying to look like a man who knew all along that Project Zoom was in the bag. Not like a man who berated me for the entire journey home from Milton Keynes for 'throwing away the pitch'.

'And it's all thanks to you,' smiles Dean, pumping my hand.

'No, not really. Karl, Drew, Brett, the whole team . . .' I splutter modestly. I've never known the New Business Director get such direct verbal praise for winning a pitch. A bonus yes, but not so much of the glory.

'You're being modest,' smiles Dean.

I am.

I wrote most of the pitch and the creative idea was mine (cleverly planted to appear to have been generated in the creative department so as not to offend anyone, but in fact mine).

'No, really, it was a team effort.'

'Oh yes, the pitch document was.' With a dismissive air Dean waves his cigar-holding hand and brushes away months of work.

'But then . . .' I don't grasp it.

'The gas thing, that was *yours*,' Dean chuckles. I stare, uncomprehending. He tries to enlighten me. 'Apparently, Frank couldn't make his mind up between the two agencies on the shortlist, but that – er – gas thing you did swung the vote. The dealers loved it. They thought it made our agency appear less poncy than the other contender. They liked our down-to-earth attitude. So we were awarded the £80 million account, and Q&A are now £8 million better off. Let me buy you lunch.'

So we won.

But not because I spent hours arguing over the appropriateness of the word 'intelligent' rather than 'efficient' to describe an engine. Not because I trawled through endless videotapes of groups of men talking about their passion for revs. Not because our team was the most committed, thorough and creative. Not because I worked so hard that sometimes my head burnt and my eyes turned fizzy. Not because I ate, drank and slept cars for weeks. But because I had wind.

'Good job you're pregnant, Georgina,' adds Dean as he slaps my back. 'The old George was far too sexy for gas. Far too polished to pull a stunt like that.'

'Yes, it's a blessing.' I try to smile.

It *is* a good thing we won the pitch. A brilliant thing. I look around the agency and everybody is laughing and smiling and joking. No doubt they've already mentally spent their bonuses dozens of times over. They radiate confidence and self-belief; nothing lifts an agency like a pitch win and a multinational, multimillion-pound win is the jackpot. Part of me really wants to join in the celebration, but part of me holds back. The office revellers appear to be at a 100-mile distance from me. It's as though I'm looking at them through a lens; a lens smeared with Vaseline, like photographers use when they are taking one of those tacky wedding shots. Take the Vaseline gimmick away and what are you left with? Inappropriately dressed people, with glued-on smiles. I did want to win this pitch, so, so much, but surely there ought to be more dignity involved in winning. Surely the actual work I do, the way I spend my day, all my days, my life, ought to mean more. I try to explain my feelings to Karl.

'Don't you think it's an odd tie-break?'

'Who can drop the biggest clanger? Who the hell cares? We won, didn't we?'

'I suppose.'

He's right, I'm being churlish. We won, that's the main thing. Who'd have thought it? I was worried that my pregnancy would destroy my career; in fact, it's galvanized it. I was so sure that I no longer fitted in this world now I no longer fit into my jeans, but perhaps I do. Perhaps there is another way of doing things. I would have preferred to be appreciated for my ability to effectively position a brand rather than my ability to make trumpeting sounds, but the point is I won the pitch. I begin to smile and allow myself to feel if not proud, then at least pleased.

'We screwed the arses off Rartle, Roguel and Spirity,' laughs Karl.

'Who?' The agency name is so familiar, but it's the last one I expected to hear in this context. 'Rartle, Roguel and Spirity were in the pitch?' I ask. My stomach lurches, but, for once, this isn't to do with the pregnancy sickness. The lurch stubs out the flicker of pleasure at winning the pitch. Suddenly everything slams into focus and I can see the whole picture far too clearly.

'Duhhh. Yes. Keep up. They were on the shortlist. Apparently, it was down to them or us. Don't you read *Campaign*?' Karl rolls up a copy of *Campaign*, and playfully hits me over the head with it. 'They leaked their involvement last week,' he explains. 'Quite a good publicity stunt if you are sure you're going to win, which they obviously thought they were. Bloody suicide if the client is snatched from under your nose.' Karl sniggers. He leaves the magazine with me and wanders away to refill his champagne glass.

Rartle, Roguel and Spirity.

Hugh.

So this is what Hugh has been working on all this time. This might even explain the late nights. Although not the condoms. Oh my God, he'll be devastated. He must have spent months, literally months, on this pitch. Why didn't I know this? It's so obvious. How can I have been so wrapped up in the pregnancy as not to have known this? Poor, poor Hugh.

I read the article, which clearly states Rartle, Roguel and Spirity's involvement in the pitch. It gets worse. There's a picture of Hugh and a quote from him. Stupidly, arrogantly, he's quoted as saying he'd lay his job on the line that no one could come up with a more thorough response to a client brief than the one R,R&S had come up with. Surely he wouldn't have said that if he hadn't had insider information that he'd already won the pitch, even before it had taken place. Sadly, such things do happen in our business. But he hasn't won. We've won it and we've won it because I farted.

This is a disaster.

I bolt into my office and close the door behind me. I call Hugh, but his secretary says that he's in a meeting and she can't put me through. He might be, or he might just hate me. I beg her to get him to call as soon as he's free. She grunts; I'm not sure if it's in agreement.

I call Jessica and briefly fill her in on the events of the last twenty-four hours.

'But, darling, that's marvellous news,' she trills.

'No, it's not, Hugh is going to be broken-hearted.' I try to convey how prestigious it would have been for Hugh, as the new MD of Rartle, Roguel and Spirity, to have brought in the Zoom business.

'But, surely, as President of Neoteric Enterprise at Q&A, it's an extremely prestigious win for you. And isn't your salary dependent upon how much new business you win?'

'Well, yes,' I agree.

'Hugh's isn't.'

'Well, no.'

'And didn't your boss make it clear that he thought you weren't up to the job now that you're pregnant?'

'He hinted as much.'

'So then. From what I can see it was down to either Hugh or you being made unhappy. You're my daughter, Georgina; this is clearly the better result.'

'But I won it for a stupid reason.' I sigh. I'm literally banging my head on my desk; metaphorically it's against a number of brick walls.

'No, you didn't, Georgina. Get a grip.' Jessica's clipped tones jolt me into taking notice. 'Do you honestly think £80 million of business is awarded on a whim? It seems to me that the win being attributed to the incident' – (neither of us can bring ourselves to be more graphic than this with regard to my bodily functions, God knows how we'll get through labour) – 'is just one of those urban myths that you advertising types are so fond of.' I stop banging my head; she may have a point. 'I imagine you won the pitch because of good old-fashioned hard work. You tried hard. You were successful. Just be proud of yourself.'

'But I feel terrible for Hugh.' How can I explain to Jessica that I'm more used to wanting what Hugh wants and what is good for Hugh than I am at even identifying what I want? 'He will assume that I *knew* I was pitching against him.'

'Why didn't you know? Ought you to have known?' she asks.

It's a tricky one. I don't like to admit that I didn't know that R,R&S were pitching partly because I've been neglecting the industry press and partly because I've been neglecting Hugh. My silence is very telling.

Jessica adds, 'Hugh's big enough and pretty enough to look after himself, George; it's about time you realized that.'

'I thought you liked him,' I wail.

'I thought you loved him,' she comments.

46

Hugh, somewhat predictably, doesn't come home from work until very late. I'm lying in bed but I'm far from asleep and that's not just to do with the growing baby pushing against my bladder.

Today should have been a perfect day. Dean insisted on taking the Project Zoom team out for lunch. Most of the team are still there, twelve hours later, scoffing and quaffing. However it was all I could do to force down a couple of mouthfuls of prawn and glass-noodle salad with sesame and ginger, and my modest portion had nothing to do with the fact that I had to pick out the prawns. For once I was glad to have a legitimate excuse to avoid champagne. I didn't want to taste that dry crackle at the back of my throat. I didn't want to feel that intrinsic headiness of bubbles zapping my brain cells that definitely signals celebration. Because I didn't feel much like celebrating.

'Cheer up, George. It's not a bloody wake, you know,' laughed Karl as he ordered a double brandy and cut himself some blue cheese from the board.

I realize that it is absolutely impossible to explain to Karl or Drew or Brett why I'm sad. They can't understand that I'd rather Hugh had won Project Zoom. None of them are in a serious relationship, even Brett, and he's married. They never have 'issues' or 'problems' or things they 'need to discuss'. If a woman that they are sleeping with ever suggests that she needs to talk she is swiftly shown the door. They all had emotional lobotomies before they left prep school. It's a pity we can't have a chat because they could give me a great insight into Hugh's state of mind.

I didn't enjoy the lunch.

I wonder how many more lunches Hugh's going to ruin for me.

I can tell from listening to the sounds he makes as he closes the door and takes off his jacket that he's drunk. I hear him throw his jacket on the back of the chair and I hear it miss and fall into a crumpled mess on the floor. He stumbles upstairs, crashing from one side of the stairway to the other; I hear a picture fall off the wall. It's a good thing we haven't yet got a baby for him to wake. He swings into the bedroom and then pauses for a moment; it's obvious that he's attempting to appear sober.

I pretend to be convinced because he needs me to be so. 'Hi.' I smile, falsely bright. I don't ask where he's been. Or who with.

'Hello, Georgina,' he articulates carefully. He sits on the end of the bed and starts to take off his shoes. He doesn't put them carefully in his wardrobe but casually throws them across the room. His shoes are unimportant now and my grandmother always said you could tell a lot by a man's shoes.

'I was just going to make a cup of tea, do you want one?' I offer with sham geniality. I know, by the way his eyes are dangerously dancing around, that he needs to sober up.

'No.' He starts to take off his clothes and then wanders into the bathroom. I get out of bed and follow him.

'Hugh, I think we should talk.' This is perhaps unconsidered of me; as a bloke he's never going to welcome this opener. His extreme anger, bruised pride and stupendous alcohol intake aren't likely to increase his inclination for a heart-to-heart. But we do have to talk, sooner or later. There's a lot to be said.

'What about?' He stares at his own reflection and doesn't look at me.

'I'm sorry about the pitch.' It's as good as any place to start.

'Liar.'

'I am.'

'Oh well, if you're sorry that's that then, isn't it? Apology accepted.' His tone is scathing and cruel. I'd like to blame it on the drink.

'I didn't know you were pitching for the business,' I explain. He still won't look at me so I'm also talking to his reflection.

'Liar, liar, pants on fire,' he sings, and then he dances a small jig around the bathroom. I take a deep breath and try to see this as great practice for when the baby is born. His juvenile behaviour is exposed as astonishingly inappropriate when he stumbles and bangs into my bump. I move away from him and wrap a protective arm around the baby; he doesn't notice.

'I didn't know,' I insist.

'Did.'

'Didn't.'

'Did.'

This isn't getting us anywhere.

'Even if I had known, what could I have done? Would you have expected me to pull out of the pitch?' I try to hold his gaze and to reason with him but he looks away. Surely this has hit a nerve. He can't possibly have expected me to throw the pitch. He can't have needed me to do that.

Hugh doesn't answer for the longest time. Finally he replies, 'Yes. You should have pulled out.'

'Yes?' I'm astounded.

I can hear the tap in the shower dripping and the cistern

of the loo is filling up, but I can't hear the words Hugh is saying. His mouth is moving but I must have got it wrong.

'Yes. You pulled out of the race for the MD position at R,R&S, didn't you? One more small sacrifice wouldn't have made any difference to you. You're about to have a baby, for Christ's sake, what do you care about Q&A's end-of-year billings? Your loyalties lie with me.'

He's finally turned towards me, but I wish he hadn't. His face is just centimetres away from mine; as he shouts he sprays spittle on my cheek. I've never seen him so furious. Tiny little lines of bitterness are engraved on his forehead, small shafts of resentment run along his cheeks up to his eyes and down to his mouth. I'm sure they weren't there this morning. He looks ugly. This man, who has always appeared the epitome of beauty and fineness, is ludicrous.

I try to remain logical. 'Yes, my loyalties lie with you. And yours with me. Winning this business is not about billings, Hugh, or the business-performance league tables. I'll have to go back to work after my maternity leave. We need the money. Leaving on the high of a big account win is invaluable for me. It will make such a difference to my reputation, and Dean has promised me a bonus. Think how handy that will be, what with a new baby and the money we pay Becca and the kids.' I'm trying to remind him that we are a team.

The truth is we need my job with its big salary and expense account. The offer of a company car and private health-care scheme are useful too. At this precise moment I'm even feeling affectionate towards the annoying little card that I swipe in the vending machine to get a cup of watery tea.

'I'm wounded, George. I've nothing more to say to you,' says Hugh. He has definitely missed his vocation and his era. He makes Oscar Wilde look underplayed.

'There *are* other things to talk about,' I insist. I'm getting heartily sick of him deciding the parameters. I try to provoke a response. 'I'm not sure if I even care about the bloody car account,' I mutter, not really under my breath, because I do know how to flick his switches.

'What?' Suddenly I have his attention. Surprise. Surprise. 'You don't care about the pitch?'

'Well, not on the scale of things, no. It's just business. It's got nothing to do with you and me. And our particular business has very little to do with anything really important.'

'Really important?'

'Gear sticks versus the war-crimes tribunal and Slobodan Milosevic. Wheel girth takes on illegal immigrants suffocating in lorries. Two-tone metallic finish versus child soldiers.'

No response. I go for something a little closer to home. 'Leather interior over and against Tom's birthday tomorrow. You forgot to sign his birthday card even though I bought it over a week ago and left it on the dining-room table all this time. I had to forge your signature.'

It's as though I haven't spoken.

'You're not sure you care about the car account? So you wrecked my life for something you're not really sure about. How could you, George?'

And he's brimming, absolutely flowing, with indignation and self-righteousness. It's almost laughable. In fact, it is laughable. I can't help myself – I start to chortle. These inappropriate responses may or may not be a result of the pregnancy, but they are liberating; I do hope they last. I no longer care if R,R&S lost the pitch, I no longer feel guilty that Q&A won the pitch. In fact, I think I'm rather pleased. I don't want what Hugh wants because I no longer believe that what Hugh wants is right. His halo has slipped from his head to around his neck; a little bit of me hopes it strangles him.

'Oh Hugh, I didn't wreck your life.' I giggle at his melodrama. 'They haven't even sacked you. I hurt your pride. No, that's not even true. You set yourself up for a fall by doing the interview for *Campaign*, by being the big man, saying your balls were on the line and that R,R&S had an unsurpassable pitch. I didn't do this to you.'

'Why didn't you tell me you were working on the pitch?' he screams, frustrated by my amused stance.

'I never realized you considered me such a threat.'

Hugh snorts. I can't make out any particular words but I'm pretty sure that whatever he's saying involves plenty of blasphemy and lots of expletives.

I start to think about the films we've seen together, the meals we've eaten together, the miles we've run together, the holidays we've lazed through together. I'm thinking about the hours I've spent on StairMaster equipment, under hairdryers, in boutique changing rooms, cooking in the kitchen, body-brushing in the bathroom, loving in the bedroom, and I wonder why they don't count for more. And I wonder why it doesn't bother me that they count for so little. How did we end up here, so angry with each other and ourselves? Incapable of a civil exchange about the weather, never mind meaningful communication about our life together. Why can't he calm me like he used to? Why can't he excite me? Why can't he reach me?

Why can't I reach him?

'Why didn't you tell me you'd been to the Lucky 7 restaurant?'

I'm trying to keep my voice free of accusation, but Hugh knows me too well. I watch him in the bathroom mirror as he freezes, thinks for a second, and shouts (unnecessarily loudly, as I'm in the room), 'Didn't I?' In that second his face sweeps through a rush of emotions. Initially angry, he suddenly becomes contrite, and then his contrition dissolves as a wave of irritation washes over his face and, almost instantly, disappears. If I hadn't been watching him so intently I might have missed it. But then, I'm always watching him so intently.

He puts down his toothbrush which he's been bandying around to help him express just how indignant he is; he's oblivious to the little flecks of Colgate he's sprayed everywhere – after all, he won't be the one cleaning the bathroom tiles. He picks up a bar of soap and climbs into the shower. He turns the tap on and zillions of little particles of water whiz out of the faucet; even so I don't think he'll wash himself clean.

'Didn't I mention I'd been?'

'No, you didn't. Which is odd, don't you think? Because normally you're so keen to impress when you've been to a cutting-edge restaurant.' I'm still sniggering to myself because, really, how stupid is it to show off about which restaurant you've been to? It's not as though he goes to these fancy restaurants to actually enjoy the food. The wine list – yes; the prices – yes; who else was there – yes; but not what he ate. Still, I digress.

I open the shower door. The hope is that his nakedness will make him feel vulnerable, evening up the score – my inches of flesh make me feel very vulnerable. Not the fatness, that doesn't bother me any more. The fact that this is a baby. I've made a little person with this man. This silly, spoilt, angry man is the father of my child. How can I retrieve this situation? What result do I want?

'George, you're getting water on the floor.'

'Are you seeing someone else?' Because this matters to us more than an £80 million pitch or £8 million of revenue ever could.

'No,' he says simply.

And in the past I know I'd have accepted his word, I'd have argued with myself that there could be any number of reasons that he'd eaten at Lucky 7. It could have been work. He hasn't tried to deny that he was there, has he? I'd have told myself that I was being silly and that it was wrong and unfair of me to jump to conclusions. I'd have told myself not to rock the boat, to be grateful that this man, the pinnacle of everything I ever wanted, has chosen to be with me. I'd have glossed over the fact that, in terms of adultery, this man has form.

As it is I can't.

'I'm sick of these rows, George. I've had these rows before. Now if I can just have my shower in peace and then get to bed. Is that so much to ask?' Hugh tries to push me away from the shower door and close it. I jam my foot in the door. I won't be ignored.

'When? Tell me. With Becca? Tell me. Say it. When have you had these rows before?'

'OK, yes, I've had these rows with Becca,' Hugh concedes, not getting my point.

'And she was right, wasn't she? You *were* screwing someone else. You were screwing me. So who are you screwing now?'

47

'I'm desperately in need of some light relief.'

'I'll send Millie round.'

'I didn't mean light as in weighs less than four stone, I meant as in humorous.'

'So did I,' says Libby, indignantly.

Thinking about it, it is true that Libby laughs more than nearly anyone else I know. Could that be because she has a child? Well, you certainly do need a sense of humour to be with Millie twenty-four seven.

'Are you going to leave him?' she asks. Not one for beating about the bush. I've just spent thirty minutes on the phone bringing Libby up to date.

'Fourteen years. Nearly half my life. Twice Millie's,' I justify.

'Suppose,' she comments, instantly understanding my investment. I don't think I can explain about the fact that I feel truly guilty about splitting Becca and Hugh up. I can't find the words to clarify that it would be OK if we were for real, for love, for ever.

'And I'm carrying his child.'

'True.'

'I don't *want* to be a single mother.'

'Is there any other kind?'

I laugh grimly. The thing is, I still believe in the happy ending. Bloody hell, no one wanted a happy ending more than I did (well, except Sam possibly). 'I think there is another kind,' I answer truthfully. 'I have seen concerned and conscientious fathers at the water-conditioning class. I've spotted nervous and sweating dads-to-be waiting hopefully for the scan results. There have been sightings in Tesco's and in the park on Saturday mornings. I watch them all the time.'

We're both silent. It would be easier to pretend this type of man didn't exist than admit that we've made bad choices. But I know they do.

'I don't think I'm up to being a single mother. I'm not as brave as you. Not as strong. You do a brilliant job but I don't think I'd be up to it.'

I have these fantasies, you see. It's Christmas Day and Hugh is carving the turkey, the flat is full of tinsel and good cheer. The baby is sat in front of a log fire opening its presents, Jessica and my father are there, even Henry and Penny and their kids have joined us.

Not that we have an open fire.

And, anyway, they are very dangerous with small children around.

OK, another fantasy, a bit lower on the risk list of accidents in the home. Hugh and I are lying in bed on a Sunday morning and the baby is lying propped up on pillows between us, gurgling, giggling. That's not too much to ask, is it?

Although, in reality, Hugh would probably expect to continue his morning visits to the gym, even after the baby is born. I'll probably spend Sunday mornings juggling the baby and the roasting dish, because Hugh has said that he'd like to reintroduce Sunday roasts once we have the baby. Even though the baby won't be tucking into a joint and three veg for quite some time yet.

I sigh. If I'm honest with myself I know that the fantasy will always be light years away from the reality. He will never help me choose clothes in babyGAP; even now I pick out

Kate and Tom's pressies. I usually do that in my lunch hour. I'm the one who washes floors, I cook, I shop, I iron and take our suits to the dry-cleaner's and pick them up again. I buy loo rolls and change the water filter. Hugh only need mention that he fancies the new REM album (his tastes are mainstream, but he is thirty-four; he's unlikely to express an interest in that-new-indie-revival-band-that-played-in-the-pub-in-Camden ever again). He expresses the interest and the next thing the CD appears in our stereo, as if by magic.

No, actually, as if I'd bought it and put it there.

Yet he looked horrified when I hinted that I might like a small token of his esteem as a thank you for having the baby. He said, 'Don't you buy the presents now?'

I order furniture. It's me who arranges to be at home whenever there is a delivery of any kind. I arrange the payment of all bills – Barclaycard, Amex, gas, electricity, TV licence, council tax, mortgage. I am the one acting as a human incubator.

Hugh goes to work.

Abruptly, it seems extremely unbalanced.

I admit I used to do all these things for myself when I lived on my own, of course I did. But then the mess was my mess. My cereal bowl, my empty yogurt carton, my clothes in the washing basket and my wet towels on the bathroom floor.

What am I saying? That I'd be better off alone? No. Of course not. I can't be saying that. I'm just saying it seems unfair.

Libby must have been thinking along the same lines because she says, 'I don't know why you think you couldn't manage on your own. You have a highly paid job, you bring in massive revenues for your agency. You own your own flat, your own car. You're the one who runs marathons for fun. You lived in New York, New York, for five years; you did all that on your own.' (She says New York, New York, with a twang; a bad impersonation of a US accent is essential when saying those four words, however serious the discussion. I'm so pleased Libby has remembered this.)

'That was the old me,' I insist.

'You'll be the old you again, after the baby is born.'

The odd thing is I don't know if I want to be. For a start, I don't think I have the energy to read another article that promises I'll banish cellulite for life, or that I'll lose 15 lb in a month or that I'll learn twenty-five sure-fire ways to increase my sexual energy. Sometimes I feel my head is bursting, it's holding so much stuff – how to be brighter, better, wiser, thinner, more fashionable. I try so hard. Too hard. I try at every aspect of life. I try to be the perfect woman for Hugh, the perfect friend, the perfect employee. I even try to be the perfect stranger, for goodness sake. I sometimes think I'm going mad. The other day I found myself wishing I were a video recorder. Right now, I could do with a rewind, fast-forward and erase button. Although, notably, there's still not much call for play or stop.

Secondly, even assuming I had the energy (and time – unlikely) I don't think I want to be the old me, because I'm not that keen on her any more. I'm not even sure if *I* ever really existed beyond being what I thought Hugh wanted. I don't blame him for this. I blame myself. And I'm even sick of that, blaming myself. I want to fix things and move on. But what would be a 'fix' in this situation? I do know that I don't want to put my considerable energy and whatever talent I might have into regaining skinny thighs because there *has* to be more to life than being a perfect size 10. I know there is; I put my hand on my stretched stomach and gently rub my bump. Besides which, trying all the time is exhausting and demoralizing because, however hard I try, I'm never quite good enough. There's always something I've forgotten to do, even if it's only applying a second coat of lipstick.

I want to articulate some of this to Libby.

'I need to fix some things.'

'Such as?'

I sigh. 'It was Sam's hen weekend last weekend; she didn't even invite me.'

'Was it one of those outdoor-pursuits things? She probably thought it was too active at this stage in your pregnancy.' Libby is already trying to find excuses.

'No, it was nothing to do with the pregnancy.'

'Have you had a disagreement?'

'Sort of.' I'm pretty certain that my wedding invite is invalid. Which strikes me as odd, I've been on the guest list for fourteen years and now I'm NFI. 'It's complicated. I'm sorry I can't tell you the details, it would be breaking her confidence.' I know Libby is itching to ask me to spill the juicy gossip and I am tempted, but I resist.

'Call her, uncomplicate it,' suggests Libby, offering a solution as though she were a man.

I ache to call Sam. I miss her with such ferocity that I feel an emptiness that's as real as hunger. We haven't spoken since the evening at the restaurant when she confessed to her affair with James. I'd love for her to see the size of my bump now, it's unreal. I just keep growing and growing and when it seems impossible that I can stretch any more without popping, then I grow some more. I'm sure she'd love to feel the baby kick. I'd like to tell her about the pitch win. But, most of all, I'd like to explain that I do understand; now I know exactly what she meant when she said getting married was all she ever wanted and she'd wanted it for such a long time she didn't know how to want anything else. I know why she compared her obsession with getting married to mine with getting Hugh. I now understand how brave I was asking her to be when I suggested she dump the fantasy. I'm not sure I can, either.

'And there's Becca,' I add.

'Becca?' Libby is understandably surprised.

'I feel guilty, seriously guilty about breaking up Hugh's marriage. I'm beginning to think I owed Becca a bit more . . .' I hesitate. I know the word but don't think I can bring myself to say it. 'A bit more solidarity.'

'Oh, call her and say as much, I'm sure she'll understand,' says Libby glibly.

'I think I might.'

'I wasn't being serious!' She's horrified. 'People don't just call each other and say, "Look, I've been giving this some thought, maybe I shouldn't have run off with your husband." People just don't do that.'

'I might.'

Because, for the first time in my life, not doing the done thing seems to be exactly what I ought to be doing.

August

48

Sam or Becca? Becca or Sam? Both are foul calls to have to make. Both involve eating a gag-inducing amount of humble pie. Libby says that I'm just trying to avoid the really big issue of Hugh's philandering. It's possible.

Two more weeks go by and I've done nothing. Well, I've been to work; at least there I'm still basking in the glory of the pitch win. I've edged closer and closer to my expected date of delivery. I've passed Hugh in the hallway. I've even slept in the same bed with him but I haven't called Sam or Becca and I haven't pushed Hugh on the pertinent question of who he's screwing now.

'Are we going to Sam's wedding, then?' asks Hugh.

It's the first sentence we've exchanged in over two weeks so I feel a bit of a spoilsport when I have to answer in the negative. 'I don't think so.'

'Christ, George, she's your best friend. I can't believe you're missing the wedding because you're too fat to fasten your strappy sandals.'

I glare at him. 'That is not the reason I'm not going to the wedding. For your information, as it's so obviously passed you by, Sam and I have had a falling-out.'

'Really?' It's touching that he does pause to look at me before he asks, 'Because she wouldn't let you be bridesmaid?' Believing that I'd cut off my best friend over something so trivial is less touching.

'No, Hugh, because we had a major disagreement about love, life and the reason we are here.'

'Girls! You really overcomplicate things. Why do you talk about such stuff?'

'Because neither of us follow football,' I mutter, and then I turn back to my book on breastfeeding.

Hugh leaves the room.

Even for a pregnancy outfit my wedding outfit is gorgeous, by virtue of it being a wedding outfit. I'd planned to wear a long red dress that pretty much covers everything from shoulders to ankles. The only thing it does expose is my vast cleavage, as the dress has a great plunging neckline. I know that my heaving bosoms are my best attribute at the moment (although, admittedly, the competition from the rest of my body is at an all-time low). I'm working on a theory of drawing the eye up over or down over, actually anywhere away from my expansiveness, and so have bought scarlet, shockingly high sandals and a very wide-brimmed hat. Both of which are swathed in sequins, feathers, glitter and all manner of girliness. Weeks ago, Hugh suggested I wear my black shift from Mamasoon, presumably so I'd blend in and minimize myself as much as humanly possible. I did buy black shoes and a black hat but later rejected them; I don't want to disappear. I want to be loud and proud, I want to celebrate my fertility and femininity.

And, anyway, I can no longer fasten the black number.

Not that it matters either way, as things have turned out. The hat and the sandals are still in their boxes. I haven't called Sam. Sam hasn't called me. I won't be throwing any confetti today.

It's five to eleven. Right now Sam is climbing into a cream Rolls-Royce and heading to the church. I'm lying on my bed in my bedroom. The windows are open and bright sunshine is bathing the room. I can hear next door's kids squabbling over a tennis racket; I can hear a lawnmower and I can smell the freshly cut grass. It is a beautiful August day, a perfect day for a wedding. I can't help but grin to myself because I know, absolutely know, could put money on it, that Sam will have woken up this morning and said, 'Happy is the bride whom the sun shines on.' I know exactly what's happening.

The bridesmaids are wearing gold. The readings are a mix of the secular and the divine. Obviously the congregation are obliged to sit through I Corinthians 13 – 'Love is patient and kind . . .' – because no wedding is complete without it, but Sam has also chosen a John Donne poem, one of the raunchy ones. She'll walk down the aisle to Handel's 'Arrival of the Queen of Sheba' and leave to Mendelssohn's 'Wedding March'. She chose all this before she completed her university finals. It's not easy finding a comfortable position at thirty-seven weeks but this thought doesn't help.

Hugh comes back into the bedroom. I spend most of my time here now, often asleep, sometimes just lying on my bed thinking. I'm working on a theory of Why stand when you can sit? Why sit when you can lie? It's not as easy as it sounds. The thinking that is, not the lying. I realize that there is a genuine possibility that I've never thought before. I've fantasized, imagined, idealized. The pitch is over and I've started to think. I've been the Dutch boy with my finger in the damaged dam wall. I've been trying to hold back a tidal wave of thoughts and now, carefully, slowly, I've dared to remove my finger. I want the flood. Hugh spends most of his time downstairs in the living room. He's taken to playing his CDs at a very high volume. I use his track selection to follow his mood. In many ways it's a more reliable form of communication than actually talking to him ever was. He's worked his way from Gloria Gaynor's 'I Will Survive', to Culture Club's 'Do You Really Want to Hurt Me?', which I never did like. And this morning he listened to Tom Jones singing 'I (Who Have Nothing)'. This, if I needed it, is absolute proof that he's not gay, and that he doesn't understand the female psyche. In situations like this you should end with Gloria.

I close my eyes. I don't want another row. I'm just not up to it.

'I thought you might like some lemonade. It's homemade.' He puts the glass down on the bedside table.

I open my eyes (not least to check that this is for real and I'm not dreaming; towards the end of my pregnancy my dreams have become extremely vivid). I heave myself up to take a sip. 'It's lovely, thank you.' I only just resist asking, 'What's brought this on?'

'Do you want a pillow for under your feet? I read that it helps with the water retention.'

Call the FBI – the body-snatchers have got him! Hugh goes into the wardrobe and rummages around for the spare pillows, and then he helps me to stuff them in between my knees, under my bump and under my feet. I know I look like a stranded hippo but I don't care. After years and years of trying to be skinny, lithe and energetic for him, it's a relief to be so peaceful just being me. He can take me or leave me – what am I talking about? He already has.

Hugh sits on the edge of the bed. 'I can't believe we're not at Sam's wedding.'

'No, nor can I.'

'After all these years.' He pauses and gazes out of the window. I half wonder what he's thinking but I'm no longer curious enough to ask. Yet, somewhat out of character, he volunteers his thoughts. 'We all go back such a long way, don't we?'

'Yes.'

'She's wanted this for a long time, hasn't she?'

'Yes.'

'Do you remember how Sam always dressed up as a bride for all the fancy-dress parties at uni? Every Halloween party she went as Frankenstein's bride. The Tudor party, she went as all six of Henry VIII's wives. The bondage party, she went as wedlock. She always wore white gowns at the end of term ball.'

'At the Christmas party she went as a fairy on the top of the tree,' I defend.

'She looked like a bride.'

'True, she did,' I concede. It's no good; her behaviour was transparent and as such difficult to defend.

'Can you name Sam's three favourite films?'

'*Four Weddings and a Funeral*, *My Best Friend's Wedding* and *Muriel's Wedding*.' I giggle, everyone can name Sam's three favourite movies. '*Seven Brides for Seven Brothers* comes a close fourth.'

'I love playing charades with her,' smiles Hugh. Whilst it's a bit disloyal poking gentle fun, even Sam would admit that we are entitled. Hugh and I have watched all these videos on so many rainy Sunday afternoons that our tapes have worn thin. Hugh jumps up and grabs the chair from the end of the bed. He drags it towards the wardrobes and stands on it. He starts to rummage around in the cupboard space above the wardrobe. Hat boxes, shoeboxes, sacks of old clothes and bundles of old letters and cards cascade to the floor.

'What are you looking for?'

'These,' he pronounces cheerfully as he carefully pulls out my photo albums from the top of the cupboard. He picks out the large black leather albums housing the photos from my university days. I'm meticulous in the categorization of my memories – black leather equals university. Blue leather for the photos from New York; there are five of those albums, one for every year. Then I have brown albums until 1998, when the albums become red. I would never have guessed that Hugh knew my code. It's odd that he can still surprise me.

Pleasantly.

I turn the pages of the album; the tissue paper between the card pages wafts gently, promising unlimited treasures.

'That was Freshers' Week,' I say, pointing to a shot of Hugh stood by the table where they were recruiting rowers.

'Look at your hair on that one. It's almost brown, I'd forgotten.'

'There's Sam as Frankenstein's bride.' I laugh.

'God, I hope she looks better today.'

'There you are with the rugby team,' I comment. A young Hugh smiles his boyish smile from under his blond fringe.

'You look lovely on that one.' Hugh is pointing to a picture of me in my third year. My transformation was in process. My hair is blonde and I'm slim, but it's early days because I'm smiling and I look careless. I'm stood next to Sam, who looks just like Sam. Happy, hopeful and wearing a white ball dress. It's probably just my hormones, but I'm crying again.

Hugh lays his hand on my leg and says, 'I'm sorry.' Then he squeezes my leg and leaves the room.

I'm overwhelmed. Hugh is not prone to bouts of sentimentality. I'm moved that he cares that he's missing Sam's wedding, that he cares that I am. Isn't it the strangest thing? After countless displays of Hugh's insensitivity and neglect, as unreasonable as it sounds, it is in this moment of tenderness that I finally realize.

I don't love Hugh any more.

I wish I could. I wish I believed that the lemonade and the pillows and the breakfast in bed the other week were motivated by genuine repentance, but I fear they are the result of an inflamed conscience. I wish I could forgive him for ignoring his growing child, for his countless examples of irritability and selfishness. I wish I could forgive myself for falling in love with an idol and ending up living with a man. I really wish I could love the man. I stroke my stomach and apologize to the baby for getting everything wrong. And whilst I'm still not sure how to go about getting it right, I promise, I swear to the baby that I will.

I must have fallen asleep again, because the sound of the phone ringing wakes me up. In my half-conscious state I feel around for the handset.

'George?'

'Sam!' She's rung me with a debrief! She's rung me to ask me to go along to the reception. I'm already reaching for my red frock. Oh, I love her, I love her. I just want us to be friends again. I want to un-say all the stuff I said. It wasn't worth saying, not if it meant I would lose her. Even if I was just being honest. I forgive her all the things she said. She was just telling it like it is.

'Sam, I'm so glad you called. I've missed you so much. How was the wedding? I'm very sorry I wasn't there. I *am* glad you called,' I start to repeat myself as I rush on. Excitement is mixed with self-consciousness, mixed with absolute glee. 'How was it? Are you beautiful?'

'I am officially show-stopping,' she laughs. Her laugh is high-pitched and hysterical. I wonder if she's been swallowing helium from the balloons. I pull myself to a sitting position and start to inch out of the massive, shapeless T-shirt that I live in. I wonder if I'll have time to wash my hair.

'Congratulations, Mrs Crompton,' I trill.

'Actually, it's congratulations, Ms Martin.'

'You're keeping your name?' I'm stunned; it's a very un-Sam thing to do.

'Well, imagine the scenario, I'm in all my finery and, oh George, I did look good.'

I'm struggling to undress with one hand, hold the phone with the other and try to listen to every particular at the same time. In the end I give up dressing and pause to drink up the details. Pregnancy has left me unable to multi-task, which will be a bloody disaster after the baby is born if I'm handicapped thus.

'Did you go for a tiara in the end, or flowers?'

'Tiara.'

'Hair up or down?'

'Up.'

'Oh God, I bet you were gorgeous. I wish I'd been there.' Sam is silent. 'Go on, I want to hear everything, from start to finish.' I'm now propped up against the headboard, the phone is cradled under my ear. My fingers are itching to unwrap the sandals and hat, to release them from their boxes and expose their finery. If I hurry, I might still make it in time for the first dance and maybe even the speeches.

'Well, the thing is, I'm sat in the Rolls on the way to the church . . .'

'Yes.'

'And my father is telling me some funny story about his and Mummy's wedding day, but I can't *hear* him. I'm staring right at him, and I can see his mouth opening and closing, and he's sat right next to me, but I couldn't hear him.' She pauses for breath, I'm trying to catch mine too. 'I could hear you,' she says.

Oh God.

'I could hear you telling me to get my own set of values and opinions. *You* telling me to think very carefully. *You* saying that marrying Gilbert isn't fair to him or to James or to me. I couldn't get that stuff you said out of my head.'

The hat box slips off the bed and falls to the floor.

'You—' My heart slows, almost stops.

'Yes. I thought I could ignore you, but I couldn't. I realized, you're right.'

Oh no. Oh no. I mean, oh yes. Yes, I am right, but oh no.

'It's not about the dress, or the flowers, or the canapés, or the swans—'

'You had swans?' Even at this undoubted code-red moment I think swans are worth commenting on.

'Yes,' says Sam with some dignity and then she continues, 'it's about the man. And as nice as Gilbert is, he's not *the* man. James is.'

I can't believe what I'm hearing. 'You stopped the wedding?'

'Yes.' Sam is trying to sound brave but I know her well enough to appreciate that she's seconds away from boohooing for an Olympic medal. 'So you see that's why it's congratulations, Ms Martin.'

Sam dissolves into tears and I tell her I'll order a cab.

49

I'm sat at my desk, making a 'to do' list for Julia, who is going to cover for me whilst I'm on maternity leave. My heart's not really in it, particularly as I know that Julia will lose this list within the first thirty minutes of being in sole charge. I am not going on maternity leave until I actually go into labour. Obviously, this isn't an ideal case scenario; all the maternity books suggest that you take at least a fortnight, if not four weeks, off work before the birth. However, Dean isn't keen to give me more than three months' leave in total, and I want to spend as much time as I possibly can with the baby. I'm still negotiating for six months, but Dean keeps insisting that Q&A need me; suddenly, he seems to think I'm single-handedly keeping his agency afloat. This is no nearer the truth than when he thought I was losing my touch, but he, like many advertising-agency types, likes to operate in extremes. I can understand why, it makes life so much simpler. The hues and tones I've been dealing with of late are terrifically complex.

I am now just one week away from my EDD. Just seven days, or 168 hours, or 10,080 minutes, or 604,800 seconds, depending on how you look at it. And whilst I know that many, many babies are late and that first babies are notorious for being so, I still have my fingers crossed in the hope that mine will be on time. I know that every day after the EDD will seem like another month, because every day that's passed in the last few weeks has seemed an aeon. For a while, after Sam called off her wedding, time flew past as I was genuinely immersed in her problems, all of which seemed more immediate than anything I had to worry about. Suddenly, I was in charge of the disposal of 200 chicken drumsticks and returning several toasters. Her constant bemoaning her fate was definitely a welcome distraction; not that it was easy to see her in such a bad way. She hasn't yet plucked up the courage to face James, Gilbert, or her mother. She spent the first ten days after the non-wedding hidden in her flat with the blinds down, the answering machine on and the doors locked. I intravenously dripped pizza and gin into her system, and listened whilst she beat herself up for being 'so cruel', 'so blinkered' and, finally, after several pizzas (*ai funghi* and Fiorentina), 'so fat'. After she'd crawled in and out of her hair shirt I persuaded her to take a holiday (after all, she was due a honeymoon, she was waxed in all the appropriate places, and her bikini was packed). So at the moment she's soaking up the rays in the south of France, although she did promise that she'd catch the first plane home the moment my contractions start.

I can't wait.

Obviously, I have to, there's no alternative, but I'm beginning to really understand the term 'expecting'. I've never longed for something so much in my life; I've never anticipated, yearned, craved or dreamed for anything with such ferocity; not even Hugh. Yet I am exhausted, and I could probably do with some time resting; if the baby is late I should put my feet up. If I'm honest with myself it may be my last opportunity.

Ever.

There has been so much to organize before the birth. Over three months ago I drew up a list of jobs that I wanted to complete before the baby was born. There were forty-nine necessary jobs on the list. Fifty would have been neater.

The list was deceptive. A job such as 'sort childcare' took no more space on the piece of paper than 'pack hospital bag', but in fact it took an unfeasibly long time. I've visited eleven nurseries, the homes of six childminders, and interviewed twelve nannies, six of whom could actually speak English. I'm still undecided. I have my name down on two nursery waiting lists and, assuming I do negotiate six months' leave, there's an Australian nanny who is planning to come to England after Christmas; I liked the sound of her over the phone but would still have to meet her. Other things on the list included: clear out cupboard under the stairs, clear out kitchen cupboards, paint nursery wall, put up shelf in nursery, put up curtain rail in nursery, make up cot, fix video recorder, fix camera, update address list, buy announcement cards, plug hospital telephone number into my mobile phone, buy all baby equipment (as per list B), pick up pram, etc., etc., and so on and so forth. Although there seemed to be an enormous amount to accomplish, the list did give me a greater sense of control. But, then, it crossed my mind as I packed labour massage oil into my hospital bag, that I'm fooling myself. The fact that I've packed bedsocks and sanitary towels doesn't mean I'm any more prepared to be a mother. I'm still going off into the unknown with little or no relevant experience. The difference is this no longer terrifies me – it excites me.

I subdivided the job list into three categories: those jobs I reasonably thought I could tackle, those that necessitated outside labour, and those I thought Hugh could be responsible for. The split was roughly thirty-five, eleven, and three.

Three jobs are still outstanding.

Four, if you include 'Make peace with Becca'.

My only outstanding job.

Interestingly, it's this one that will probably prepare me

best for being a mother. I want my child to be born into as much love as possible, and whilst it's messier and more perplexing than the traditional two-point-two-with-a-dog-family, this is the family the stork has pre-destined for my little bundle of joy. I don't want any jealousy or cruelty or bitterness between Kate and Tom and my baby. I mean, I know I've always found Kate and Tom ghastly, but I'm hoping that this is a stage – mine. If possible I'd like them to know each other, grow with each other and even love each other. This won't happen without Becca's support. But Becca doesn't owe me any loyalty. So, although it's a long shot, it is my only shot – I have to ring her up. I want to assure her that after the baby is born, Kate and Tom will still be as much a part of their father's life as they've ever been. I want to apologize for the fact that he's not as much a part of their life as he should have been. I'm not sure if things could ever have turned out differently. I still believe I couldn't help loving Hugh as much as I did. So, whilst I can't undo what's done, I can try to salvage some of the relationships and stop there being any more human debris.

I pick up the phone and start to key in Becca's number.

Christ, Libby's right, people don't make this sort of call.

It's madness.

I hang up before I've pressed the final digit. I take a deep breath. For the last fourteen years every action, every deed, every impulse I have ever made has been driven by my passion for Hugh. I know for certain that Hugh would not approve of my making this call. He's always been very strict that I don't discuss the past with Becca, he said it was too painful for her, which I understand. Besides, he maintains that we have nothing to apologize for. He's often saying that true love operates on a higher plane than the concerns of the everyday. Which presumably includes his children, a thought that appears almost obscene now. In his more romantic moments of old, he used to say we simply couldn't help ourselves, that we were destined for one another. Besides which she was having an affair, a fact he never tires of repeating.

Even so I have to make this call. Not just for the baby. For me. It seems right to me.

I punch the numbers in.

'Hello, Becca.'

'George, are you in labour?' She sounds startled, as well she might – there's not much call for us to phone each other to natter.

My hand is shaking and I reach for the glass of water that's on my desk. This is definitely the hardest thing I've ever done. But then I haven't been in labour yet. 'No.'

'Oh.' She's stumped but too polite to ask, 'So why the call?' 'Well, to be fair, I owe you one,' she laughs.

'Sorry?' She *owes* me?

'An emergency dash to the maternity ward,' she explains.

'Oh, of course.' I now understand that she's referring to our mad dash when she went into labour with Kate. Hugh was away at a conference and I'd promised to look in on Becca as she was past her due date. I was there when her contractions started; I dashed through the traffic giving the finger to those who hindered our speedy progress across London. It was way before the affair began, of course. So much has changed since. Some things are the same, though. I mean, what was Hugh thinking of, booking a conference after his wife's due date? I work in the business, I know that it's unlikely that the cure for cancer or even for the common cold would be discovered at one of our conferences. I know 'conference' is a generous euphemism for piss-up.

'I think you broke every traffic law. Speeding, U-turns,

stopping on red routes,' laughs Becca. It had indeed been a cinematic dash.

'I was scared,' I defend.

'*You* were scared! I was petrified.' We both fall silent. 'You were very good about my waters breaking in your car.'

'No problem,' I say, as I'd said then. In fact the stench was so gross and so pungent I'd had to sell my beloved Spider at a ridiculous discount – in fact, I'd have paid someone to take it away.

'After having seen that labour I'm surprised you ever went in for a baby,' adds Becca.

'I'm not going to be as stoical as you with regard to drugs. My policy is, yes please, as many as you can, as fast as you can.' Becca laughs, as women who have only used gas and air throughout labour do laugh. It's an odd mix of envy and pity; there's always a smidgen of superciliousness – they are probably entitled to the superciliousness. Probably. The current 'right thing' with regard to labour is to want a natural birth because 'we've had natural births for centuries'. My thinking is that for centuries we've thrown Christians to lions and drowned women with PMT, calling them witches, and we don't any more – it's seen as progress. I've been held ransom to the arbitrary 'right thing' for decades and now I moonie at it. Give me drugs.

I stayed with Becca for most of her labour until her mother arrived. Hugh arrived just in time to catch the froth from the champagne bottle. He missed the placenta slopping into a bucket. I'd thought at the time that this was further proof of how unsuited they were to one another. I'd even taken a certain amount of pleasure from the fact that Hugh obviously didn't feel compelled to be with his wife at that unrepeatable moment, the birth of their child. Why didn't I see it as a measure of the type of man he is? Why did I insist on believing it was a measure of their relationship? A cold film of shame drenches my entire body and simultaneously hardens my resolve. I *owe* her the apology. What sort of woman watches another woman in labour and gets pleasure from the fact her husband missed the event?

Not a very honourable sort. Not the type of woman I want my baby to be brought into the world by. I used to think that when certain things went wrong they could never be put right – what a defeatist attitude.

That said, I've no idea where to begin. The silence yawns between us.

Becca resorts to the weather. 'The heat is stifling. How are you managing? Are you wearing hippie-chick floaty dresses?'

'No. The look I'm going for is more elephant man. I stay in as much as I can and if I could wear a paper bag, then I would, but they don't make them in gross size,' I admit, laughing. Becca laughs too. I wonder which one of us is most surprised by my honesty.

'Nearly there,' she encourages.

'My weight and blood pressure are soaring with the temperature.'

'And your spirits?'

'Soaring too.'

'Well, that's the main thing.'

I see an opening. 'Would you like me to call when I go into labour? I would . . . you know . . . if you wanted me to,' I offer hesitantly. I mean, what is the etiquette?

'Well, you needn't call me when you go into labour, but call as soon as you know anything, sex, weight, mother and baby doing fine. That sort of thing.'

'Yes. I will. Because Kate and Tom will be interested,' I clarify.

'Yes. Kate and Tom will be,' she agrees.

'A half-brother or sister,' I add cautiously.

'Indeed.' She doesn't sound overjoyed, but then nor does she sound at all distressed.

'I'm sorry,' I rush.

I didn't mean it to come out like that. I'm hardly being particularly clear about what I'm sorry about. I'm certainly not sorry I'm having a baby, a half-brother or sister for Kate and Tom. But I am sorry for so many other things. However, it quickly becomes clear that this is one of those unsurpassably embarrassing and painful moments in life, when you think you have just said something absolutely momentous, and the other person thinks you're making small talk about the shocking price of organic vegetables.

'I've been meaning to ask you, Georgina, it's probably a bit late now, but I have a baby bath, a Moses basket and a high chair' – she pauses – 'well, I'm sure you've bought everything new.'

'No, no, we haven't.' That's a lie, actually we have. Or rather I have, but I want to accept Becca's offer in the spirit it was intended.

'Well, you're welcome to borrow them,' Becca says generously. And then she adds, 'As long as you're careful.' I'm pleased to recognize the bossy perfectionist; she's less disarming. 'You never know, I might have need for them again, one day.'

'What?' I know I should have made an effort to hide my astonishment.

Becca laughs. 'I'm only your age, George, I haven't thrown in the towel.'

'No, of course not,' I rush to cover my gaffe. Becca having more children is something I've never considered. Why does she insist on proving that there is life after Hugh?

'I made a mistake once, but I can't let that dictate my

whole life, can I? Sorry, I probably shouldn't refer to Hugh as a mistake when speaking to you, but so much water has passed under the bridge that I think we can talk about it like adults, don't you?'

'Absolutely.' We can talk about it, I wanted to talk about it, but this isn't the conversation I was expecting. She doesn't sound like a woman waiting for me to apologize. Apologize for wanting Hugh so much, for tempting him away, for not giving them a fair chance.

'They say one man's meat is another's poison, don't they? Or, in this case, one woman's poison is another woman's meat.'

I let the cliché pass. I remember the trouble I got into last time I pulled someone up on their over-reliance on these clichés. I'm beginning to reappraise my view of the wisdom available from Garfield desk diaries; perhaps it's an important social currency.

'I always knew you'd be there to pick up the pieces. That was a great comfort to me when I threw him out. I'd long suspected that you were in love with him. I knew that he'd fallen in love again and as cruel as it sounds that's quite a relief for the conscience.'

'I'm sorry? Are you referring to your affair with your tennis coach?' Suddenly I'm piqued. I'm confused. What is she saying? This isn't what happened. She didn't throw him out. She had an affair. She became sloppy and unreasonable and then Hugh left her *for me.*

Becca laughs somewhat indulgently. 'Poor Hugh. I never had an affair. He never would believe me; he had to think that I threw him out for someone else because he just couldn't believe I simply didn't want him.' Suddenly Becca remembers who she is talking to. 'Goodness, this is hardly a cheerful conversation for you, is it? I'm not saying you got my leftovers or anything. You two seem much better suited; you always had so much more in common. I never could get excited about advertising concepts or pot-holing but you like all that, don't you?' She stops digging. 'Perhaps I could give the baby stuff to Hugh next time he picks up the children?'

It is possible that she's lying, that she's trying to wind me up, but I don't think so. Oddly, I trust Becca more than I trust Hugh. Hugh never left Becca for me. He didn't *choose* me. She never even knew he was having an affair. In light of this it seems unlikely then that she begged him to stay, not even 'for the sake of the children'. It seems unlikely that she's spent the last fifteen months sat by the phone waiting for me to call and apologize. I don't owe her or Kate or Tom anything.

Well, that's a relief.

And it's the most shocking, galling, abominable deceit Hugh has ever thrown at me.

Julia pops her head around the door. 'Dean wants to see you, George.'

Oh bugger, I'm not in the mood to argue about maternity leave.

50

The flat is thick with silence. Accusations hang in the air like fine cobwebs – when you walk into them they cling, impossible to brush off.

I hear Hugh's key turn in the lock. Slowly the door opens and I hear his footsteps, normally strong, one, two, three, and he's in the sitting room; today they are hesitant. I hear him take off his jacket and the gentle clink of coat-hangers banging together as he hangs it up (unprecedented – normally his jacket stays on the back of a chair until the next use). It's obvious that he is delaying the inevitable.

I am sat on the settee, curled up into the smallest ball I can possibly make my 39-weeks pregnant body shrink into. If I could, I'd disappear altogether. To say it's been a bad day is a woeful understatement. First the call with Becca, and then Dean.

Obviously Hugh has heard about the security escort that frogmarched me out of Q&A. Every advertising agency in the city will have heard by now. Always a hotbed of gossip, such a momentous occasion could not have passed by uncommented upon. I doubt very much that electricity was needed to power the thousands of PCs in the West End this afternoon; the buzz from this scandal will have been power enough.

I've been fired. For stealing a creative concept from Rartle, Roguel and Spirity. The Project Zoom creative concept, to be accurate. From Hugh, to be explicit.

'Hello.' Hugh's voice, although expected and well known

is a shock, precisely because it is so familiar to me. How could he have done it? I ask myself for the millionth time that day. How could he have thought so badly of me and betrayed me so completely? Talk about Judas's kiss.

'Why did you do it?' I ask.

'You shouldn't have looked in my file.'

'You think I looked in your file?'

'Well, didn't you?'

I don't bother to dignify the outrageous slur with anything more than a very articulate 'you bastard'. I am so splintered with fury that it takes quite a few seconds before I'm composed enough to add, 'You faithless, untrusting bastard.'

'Are you saying you didn't read my files?'

'Of course I didn't. I can't believe you think I would have.'

'I kept telling them it was unlikely.'

'Unlikely?' I yell. 'Unlikely? You signed my death warrant. Why didn't you say it was impossible?'

'But it was possible, George. I did bring a paper file home. Besides that there were electronic details of the concept on my PC. You have access to that.'

It takes every ounce of reasonableness I possess to resist physically evicting him from my flat there and then. I think I could do it; what with my Incredible Hulk-like proportions and rages, I'm sure I could. Instead, I take a metaphorical and literal deep breath.

'So let's get this straight. Frank Robson showed your CEO Q&A's winning creative concepts – a highly unprofessional move since they are still only in pre-production, I might add.'

'My CEO and Frank are quite friendly. I think that's why my CEO was so sure we'd won the pitch.'

Ah, now I understand why Hugh did the ill-advised interview with *Campaign*. How stupid of him. He, more than anyone, ought to know that personal relationships count for very little in this business.

'Then your CEO showed the concepts to you and you said that they were *your* idea.' I want to get my facts right.

'Yes. I recognized then instantly.' Hugh pours himself a whisky and sits down on the sofa opposite me. He doesn't even appear concerned.

'But they weren't your idea,' I splutter.

Hugh opens his briefcase and lays on the coffee table some illustrations of a penknife, a telephone, and a laptop. I have to admit the concept is oddly similar to the one we used on the Project Zoom creative pitch. I'm pleased to note, even in my wrought-up state, that they are not as good. We used a Swiss Army knife, not a penknife. We used a WAP mobile, not a land-line telephone, an iPAQ, not a laptop. Hugh's concepts have no edge. There's no Guy Ritchie, no Ewan McGregor, no suggestion that this car is the dog's bollocks.

'These were in the file that I took to Wales, a file you handled,' comments Hugh snippily. 'I had to report that you had access to that file.'

'I've never seen these concepts before in my life,' I insist.

'Well, you would say that, wouldn't you?'

'Yes, because it's true!' I yell.

'I didn't say to the board that you'd cheated for certain.'

'Oh, that was good of you.'

'I just said that you were very ambitious and I suggested Frank ask Q&A who came up with the winning concept.'

Of course the ensuing investigation quickly threw up the fact that I had planted the idea in the creative department. Not so long ago Brett had been only too happy for his team to accept the glory of winning the pitch; however he dropped all ownership as though it were a particularly angry python the moment the idea became immersed in controversy. I don't blame him. He was simply telling the truth; I did plant the idea in the creative department. However, I was aggrieved when he went so far as to suggest it was *peculiar* that I should 'hide my light under a bushel', and that the circuitous route of bringing my idea to the table was *suspect.* He implied that my planting a creative idea in his department was the most bewildering and treacherous act of industrial espionage ever. No one is prepared to admit that this is how it always works in advertising if the account management or the new business department have a creative idea. If we admitted as much, the bottom would fall out of the industry. The client has taken a dim view of the 'skulduggery' and is threatening to take the account away from Q&A. Dean fired me in an attempt to appease the client. A complex chain of events, but, if I trace it back, Hugh's lack of faith in me is the catalyst.

But it was *my* idea. I did not copy it. 'It has to be a coincidence. Things like this do happen. We live together, we talk together, we have similar tastes, we've been thinking along the same lines. That must be it.' It must be. Suddenly, I see a glimmer of hope. 'You have to vouch for me, Hugh. You have to say I wouldn't look in your file. You have to tell them, your CEO, Frank, Dean, everyone, you have to tell them that you believe we both could have come up with this idea independently.'

The glimmer of hope is a mirage.

'No can do, Babes,' says Hugh, lying back to stare at the ceiling with his hands behind his head. There isn't an iota in his tone to suggest he's regretful. 'They wouldn't believe me. They'd think I was trying to protect you.'

Not if they know him.

We sit in silence, the unmistakable sound of a relationship

cracking. Pain, shock and disbelief have left indelible stains.

'There's no need for any histrionics, George; I can forgive you.'

I'll never be able to forgive myself. I say nothing, and reasonably enough Hugh takes this to be agreement.

'Do you fancy a whisky, then? No, of course not. Sorry. Well, I'll have another if it's all the same to you,' he adds.

And it is.

That's just it.

It's the same to me. Being with Hugh has lost its colour and sparkle, and it's all the same to me. Hugh sits back down with his tumbler of whisky and reaches for the remote; he starts to flick through the channels. Obviously he considers the conversation closed. I gaze at the TV but can't make out the words. Even the noise of the traffic, drifting up from the high street, normally so intrusive and vibrant a hullabaloo, seems muffled and distant. I turn to study Hugh. In many ways he looks just the same as when I first met him fourteen years ago. He is divine. His height is imposing. His eyes are still huge, sparkling, green, still dramatically offset by long lashes and perfectly arched eyebrows. He's still blond; I can't imagine a grey hair ever having the nerve to find its way on to Hugh's glorious crown. His features remain chiselled; if anything, age has worked for him, he hasn't piled on the pounds, he's become leaner, sharper. His jutting cheekbones and square jaw are indisputably, classically handsome.

But do you know what? Up close, he's a crashing off-the-scale disappointment.

I stand up and walk to the bathroom. Pulling a handful of tissue paper from the roll, I blow my nose. It's a loud, guttural sound; it's hardly attractive. I hardly care. I stare into the bathroom mirror. I don't look anything like I looked when I met Hugh – I was plump and cheerful then. Nor do I look anything like I did this time last year – I was lean and nervous then. An obese, ringless, pregnant woman stares back at me from the mirror. For a moment I feel so dreadfully sorry for her. In the last nine months she's lost her sex drive, her ambition, her job, her body shape. She's just realized that she never had an identity, she doesn't want her lover, and nor does she want to live in a world where you might as well be dead than be bigger than a size 10. Fleetingly she looks pitiful. She looks tired. She is a great swelling, not much more than a mass of hormones, punctuated by blood-red eyes and acne. She even has a downy upper lip. The obvious thing to do now is to get pissed, but it's not an option for her. Nor is having a cigarette, or even a water biscuit with a spot of Brie. She can't descend into pizza-box frenzy as she has nutritional values for her baby to think of. She realizes she doesn't have another line in disaster management.

'Did you pitch the penknife concepts?' I yell through to Hugh.

'No, we dumped them. We went with some beautiful shots of the car racing around—'

'The Swiss Alps.'

'Yes,' he shouts back.

'Bad call,' I mutter.

And I smile at the pregnant hormonal woman and she smiles back. She also thinks it's funny. She's in on the joke. Hers is a wide, life-seizing grin that almost splits her face.

And do you know what? On a scale of one to ten, she's an eleven.

I'm an eleven.

It strikes me that Hugh isn't very good at his job. He should have recognized that car on winding road on Swiss

Alp has been done to death. For the first time, I really believe that Q&A won the pitch because we had the better concept, not because I had wind. I'll get another job, if I want one, because I am good at my job. I'll get another job with a huge salary and an expense account and a company car and private health care. I'll even get another annoying little card for the vending machine.

Hugh, by contrast, isn't very good at his job. Or, indeed, any of his jobs, MD, father, husband or lover.

I walk back into the sitting room.

'Hugh?'

'Yes, Babes?'

'Get out, Hugh.'

'What?'

'Get out.'

He nearly chokes on his whisky; spluttering, he asks, 'You're throwing me out because of a pitch?'

He can't believe what I've just said. I can't believe it's taken me so long.

I'm not throwing him out because of a pitch. I'm throwing him out because he's selfish and faithless. I'm throwing him out because he lied to me about how he and Becca broke up, because he's probably having another affair, because he forgot Tom's birthday, because he didn't come to the water-confidence classes, because he's never massaged my aching back, not once in nine months. I'm throwing him out because fourteen years is long enough to pay for an error of judgement.

Epilogue

Sam was right about being in love. It's not about worshipping from afar. It's not about adapting yourself, editing yourself, moulding yourself or changing yourself.

He makes me feel I can be entirely myself. He makes me feel that I can be *more* than I am. He is potential. He is realization. I'm in love with him.

He needs his nappy changing.

I scoop him up and take him upstairs. I do the necessary, which isn't pleasant but it isn't as awful as I'd imagined it would be. It's made bearable by the fact that he coos and gurgles and smiles at me throughout. Flashing his sparkly eyes, which are beautiful, although they are not green like Hugh's, but blue, like Jessica's. I kiss his stomach, letting my lips dissolve into his luscious skin, which is as soft and creamy as melting butter. I drink in his smell, more delicious than freshly baked bread or recently brewed coffee and sweeter, purer, clearer than a spring morning or new Egyptian-cotton sheets.

My son, Samuel (obviously named after Sam) arrived exactly on the expected date of delivery. Only days after I had finally reconciled myself to trading my Chanel LBD for a backless, paper hospital gown. Whilst the labour hurt more than even I'd feared, I can't really remember precisely what the pain was like. On the other hand, I won't ever forget that giving birth is the most exquisite, enriching, material and substantive thing I have ever done.

I could have picked my darling splash of colour's christening to give some insight into our life together. He was christened on Christmas Eve. It was bitterly cold and wet. There was no sign of romantic snow; however, there were candles, and carols, and choirboys and choirgirls. Hugh came with his new bint and his best intentions. At this distance I can see his best intentions for what they are, largely inadequate. But with this amount of space and time between us I can forgive him his mistakes and I can forgive myself mine. After all, we produced an adorable baby boy between us, which means something. It means everything.

Libby is Samuel's godmother. She's going to fit this duty in around restraining Millie from rushing into her teens, and retraining as a doctor. Sam and James came too; they are currently blissfully unmarried, although James did accept my offer to become Samuel's godfather, which suggested (to Sam at least) that he plans to stay the duration. I think he does. Becca and the kids were there. Becca brought a date, Miles; he's not a tennis player. Jessica and my dad travelled in from Cape Town. The big surprise is that one and all now know Jessica as 'Grandma'. Although some things never change, her hat was bigger than mine, her waist smaller. Still, I didn't feel inadequate, I felt proud of her and content with myself.

After the baptism all the guests came back to my flat and we drank masses of champagne and took scores of photos of Samuel. This day does give an insight into our lives because it was a day full of fun and promise and love and laughter, but then it was his christening and as such was biased towards being a successful day.

It's perhaps fairest to describe any old ordinary day. Today, for instance. It's an icy cold January afternoon. After I've changed Samuel's nappy, I pack his (huge) day bag, put him in the car and drive across town to Hyde Park. We park and then walk. And walk. And walk. Stopping only to shelter from the rain showers or buy a cup of hot chocolate for me. We walk past the Serpentine, which looks austere but grand. We walk past the deserted bandstand and I think it looks rather charming and other-worldly; it makes me want to rush home and read some Jane Austen. This is an extremely unrealistic expectation; nowadays I rarely have the time to read the bus timetable, let alone the opportunity to pick up a book. Any spare time I do stumble across I use to sleep.

We walk around the Round Pond and I chatter constantly to Samuel, pointing out ducks and pigeons to him, although he's really too young to be aware. I promise him that I'll bring him back to Hyde Park in the summer when it's heaving with happy revellers. He smiles and gurgles but then he's not particularly discerning, he smiles and gurgles at almost anything I say; he'd probably have had the same response if I'd offered to take him to Oxford Street in rush hour. I walk up and down. I circle. I walk so much that I'm actually warm even though it's freezing and late.

I pause near a park bench, check for bird excrement and chewing gum, then sit down to watch the city relinquish the day to the onslaught of twilight. Even though Samuel hasn't been fed in the last two hours and I haven't thrown him up into the air recently, I notice that he's dribbling sick. I scrabble about in my handbag and locate some tissues with which I wipe his mouth, sick-splattered coat and blanket. There's hardly a soul around, except for the occasional tramp and office clerk. I smile and nod but don't get a response. This shouldn't surprise me but it does. My life is so changed I often have to remind myself that others haven't gone through this transformation. That woman in the Burberry raincoat, for instance, she can't see me. I have a pram; I'm beneath her notice. But then she probably doesn't know what chips taste like either. The occasional mother rushes by with her toddler in a pushchair. The kids are invariably ugly, tired and dirty. At least they are to me. Their mothers probably think they ought to be models in Huggies commercials. All the mothers nod and smile at me. Some even stop and ask me how old my baby is. Sometimes I meet a mum in a park and I think we could become really good friends, if I had the time to go for a coffee and a chat. I don't often have the time, but it's nice to know it's a possibility. I'm sure that in the spring, when Samuel is sleeping through and is in a better routine, my social life will pick up again. It will be different, more playdough than pantyhose, certainly more gooey than Gucci, but I'm really looking forward to long hours rolling on picnic rugs and eating strawberries with cream. I'm also looking forward to starting my new job. In the spring I'm going back to work four days a week at a market-research company in Battersea.

Samuel starts to scream. It's a really loud, unforgiving, piercing scream, which tells me in no uncertain terms that I've missed the slot when he expects me to whip out my boob and supply supper. I sometimes do miss this slot but now, at least, I recognize the scream that communicates as much. I pick him up and try but fail to pacify him with cuddles. I consider, should I rush him back to the car and suffer his ear-splitting cries until we get there, or should I feed him here? Samuel is five months old but I still make mistakes, I know I always will. Progress is that I now realize that the mistakes I make are unlikely to be irrevocably harmful. I'm not perfect, I am good enough. I start to fiddle with my coat buttons, wondering if it is possible to get across to my breast without forfeiting all my modesty. For the record, my boobs have changed shape. But I'm pleased and relieved to note that they still defy gravity.

Although they no longer defy belief.

As Samuel starts to feed his wails subside. I look up and catch the eye of another new mum rushing by with her pram. She smiles proudly, first at her baby and then at me. I smile back. The smile we've exchanged is the secret smile of the initiated. It's a smile that conveys a unique mix of total exhaustion with unquashable exhilaration; it combines bewilderment and wonderment. It's a smile that acknowledges that our days are seemingly endless battles against soiled nappies, sticky hands and spew, yet, as each day passes by we feel cleaner, more dignified, more elevated than ever before.

I am good enough.

Acknowledgements

This book is dedicated to mams, mummies, mums and mothers everywhere. Especially the mums of the following indescribable, unrepeatable splashes of colourful, wonderful joy: Claudia, Felicity and William Dent, Harry and Alice James, Olivia and Charlie Buckley, Imogen Harwood-Matthews, Megan, Ella and Conor Woods, Thomas, Henry and Dominic Woods, Calum and Elizabeth Butler, Madeline May Allen, Amelia Boyle, Charlotte, James and George Gillies, Zuli and Leo Stannard, Eamon Burke, Jemima, Imogen and Oliver Middleton, Tearin, Darcy, Cody and Dylan Gray, Isabel Gibbons, Billie, Emily and Eddie Rudolf, Patrick and Rhys Davis, Miles and Helena Weatherseed, Laura Wheatley, Mia and Ezra Honeghan-Bates, Ruby Bond, Joe and Ben Geller, Polly and Lola Hodges, Joshua and Corbin Harkness, Eliza and Imogen Lander, Virginia, Patrick and Edward Hickey, William and James Taylor, Jamie and Oliver Hewitt, Lily-Beth Peacock, Amelie Peacock, Ethan Danielle-Brewe, Carly and Lia Downes, Molly Issac, Hector and Celeste Crosbie, Conner and Jasmine de Trafford, Megan MacDonald, Sally Moore and Amy Wilson.

I always seem to be a year behind on my thank-yous and there are so many people to thank. First and foremost, the biggest thank-you goes to my parents, especially as I now have some idea how hard your job has been (arguably, still is!) Thank you, Louise Moore and Jonny Geller, for being professionals, for being pals. Thank you, Harrie Evans, for caring enough about the book to argue with me, for caring enough about me to listen to me, and for graciously accepting that various bits of yourself and your conversations pop up in my books. Thanks to all at Penguin: John Bond, Abigail Hanna, Peter Bowron, Ami Smithson, Jessica Ward, Nicola Milner, Elisabeth Merriman, and the entire sales team. Thank you, Carol Jackson, for your enthusiasm home and abroad. Camilla Harrisson, for your insight into new business deals. Bob McBrain, for being a long-suffering mate and letting me use your office. Nicole Ingram, for your big smile that broke through writer's block. Alex King, for friendship and for editing genius at the last moment. Elaine Donoghue, for believing in my dream before I did. Marian Keyes, for sending the most wonderful letter. Thank you.

The author found the following books extremely useful throughout her own pregnancy:

What to Expect When You're Expecting, by Arlene Eisenberg, Heidi E. Murkoff and Sandee E. Hathaway, BSN (Simon & Schuster)

Your Pregnancy Week by Week, by Glade B. Curtis MD, FACOG (Element)

The Contented Little Baby Book, by Gina Ford (Vermilion)

adele parks

about Adele Parks

about the book

whilst I was writing

the books

read more

about Adele Parks

about Adele Parks

I was born in Cleveland, northeast of England and had a conventional 70s childhood, existing on a diet of convenience food and bad TV. My parents (still married after 40-odd years) devoted themselves to giving my sister and me as stable, loving and happy an environment as possible. I attended the local state primary school and then the local comprehensive. My fond memories aren't so much of a home town – more of a modern, well-kept housing estate, where everyone knows everyone and everything that there is to know.

Perversely, this stability nurtured in me wanderlust and a longing to do, be and see things that were different. I studied English Language and Literature at Leicester University. After I'd finished my degree I had the chance to fulfil my dream to see more of the world. I travelled to Italy and had a fabulous year teaching English: a time of hope and dreams and fun. Later, I also travelled to Botswana and lived there for two years – a place that provided a terrific sense of space, both physically and mentally. I'm still very envious whenever I hear of people who up-sticks and go trotting around the globe.

I've lived in London for most of my adult life. It's a city where dreams can come true – that said, it's easy to scratch the surface and find disappointment and disillusionment. Even whilst enjoying success, that is a disquieting thought.

I've wanted to write for as long as I can remember. As a child I read voraciously and wrote my own stories, mostly wrote about witches, strange lands and magical adventures: flying carpets featured heavily, as I was a rather lazy child and this was the ultimate fantasy. By the time I was ten or eleven, I found that I often wrote about things, in an effort to understand how I felt or thought about them. I referred to these scribbles as my jottings. When I was in the sixth form I read a book every second day.

It's possible that I would never have done more than fill notebooks with jottings but when I was twenty-seven a number of friends and family died in quick succession. I felt desperate, scared and vulnerable, and became ill with severe back problems. I have heard other people say they've experienced similar runs of bad luck and ill-health. Usually some good comes out of these terrible situations, although it's hard to believe at the time. I turned to escapist jottings as a way of relief from the sadness that swamped me.

I started to write *Playing Away* – a novel in which the protagonist enjoys a seemingly perfect and utterly glamorous life, at least until she falls into an abyss of sexual obsession. I was disciplined and devoted three evenings a week and one full day of my weekend to writing. I was working in marketing at the time and so I fitted my writing in around the day job.

After I'd written a substantial chunk of *Playing Away*, I sent it to an agent I'd read about in a Sunday supplement. He liked it enormously and encouraged me to finish the script. Then he sent it out to a number of publishers. The interest around *Playing Away* was intense; it seemed that female infidelity hadn't been explored in literature since *Anna Karenina* – odd because male infidelity is ubiquitous and it can't possibly be that betrayal and misbehaviour is so one sided! Following what is known in the trade as a bidding war, *Playing Away* was published by Penguin in March 2000 and became an instant bestseller. The rest, as they say, is history. I gave up my marketing job and became a full-time novelist.

I've now written six novels, I've published numerous articles and short stories in a variety of newspapers and magazines and I've appeared on TV and radio. My books are sold all over the world. It's a dream come true.

I'm often asked whether I worry that I'll run out of ideas. I don't: I worry I'll run out of time before I've committed all my ideas to paper. People wonder where I get my ideas from. The answer is life – my own and other peoples'. I'm also asked what I like best about being a novelist. That's a hard one because I adore so many aspects of my profession. I believe I'm a supremely lucky individual that I've had the opportunity to make a hobby into a viable living. I must be quite egotistical because I relish the opportunity to express my views, ideas and concerns, and I'm thrilled that copies of my books will be held in the British Library for ever. The flexible nature of my employment is a joy; as a working mum it's an invaluable aspect of what I do. But, if pushed, I think I'd say that the thing I like best about being a novelist is that I get the opportunity to entertain: maybe to provoke a moment of pondering or a wry smile. I thank each and every one of my readers who are good enough to give me a few hours of their lives. What greater gift is there?

Is this book autobiographical?

When I first handed in the manuscript of *Larger than Life* to my publisher, she read it and then immediately telephoned me as she was very concerned. She wanted to know if everything was 'OK at home?' I remember being grateful for her concern but laughing and assuring her that *Larger than Life* was, 'just a story'.

'Are you sure?' She persisted, 'It's just I can't imagine how any one could have written so convincingly about a break up of a relationship without having been through it.'

I laughed and assured her my husband and I were 'extremely happy'. We split up less than two months later. I was stunned at the time. It wasn't that I had been lying to my editor/friend; the truth is stranger than that. I, like George, had been deluding myself. I believed everything was OK in my relationship because I wanted to believe it. I remember writing the scene where George finally has enough of Hugh and she kicks him out and I remember thinking, 'would anybody ever be so brave as to choose single parenting?' It was odd then, to find myself saying the same words to my husband only weeks later.

I ought, in defence of my ex-husband, who is still a good friend of mine, to point out that our circumstances were very different and that Hugh was not modelled on him.

Can you be more specific? What were the differences between your life with your ex and George's with Hugh?

George and Hugh are both fairly extreme characters, my ex and I are more moderate! My ex-husband and I met when we were in our early twenties; at the time we were very much in love (with each other – I hasten to add!). My ex and I didn't work in the same business, as Hugh and George do and he is good at his job, unlike Hugh. Neither of us had ever been married before, nor had we any other children. These are all big differences between our relationship and George and Hugh's.

We were married for four years when we planned to conceive our first child. My pregnancy was straight forward, although like George I suffered overwhelming nausea and, on occasion, feelings of isolation and displacement. So, whilst the parameters of the story were very different from my real life, the emotions I felt mirrored George's almost exactly. Like her, I eventually came to realize that I was a stronger woman than I'd initially assumed myself to be and, like her, I realized that I was being dismissed and silenced within my relationship.

I think I, like George, tried too hard to be the perfect woman (I'll let you into a secret, there's no such thing!). Having a child was not the reason for our relationship breaking down but having a child did highlight that we had different values, dreams and priorities.

George was obsessive about reading about her pregnancy. Did you find books about pregnancy helpful? Do you have any recommendations?

My experience was very similar to George's in this respect. At first I found the books superficial, inaccurate, euphemistic or depressing. Later, I found them fascinating and couldn't get enough of them. But that's just to do with my personality. I like being well read on subjects; for example, if I am visiting a foreign country I will read a guide book and I might even carry a phrase book. Being pregnant was like visiting a foreign galaxy, never mind a foreign country! Reading helped me to be a little bit prepared. After my son was born I did use a book to help me guide him into a sleeping routine. I try not to be evangelical about the right way to deal with pregnancy and parenting because I think there is such a thing as advice and information overload. Do what suits you. If you are the sort of person who normally reads around a subject, do so. If you think ignorance is bliss, it might be. Above all, keep a perspective.

There was a point in your life when you were a working single mum. How did you manage to strike a balance between looking after your child and your career?

I was in an extremely privileged position in that as a writer I was able to work from home and therefore I have a career that I love, as well as being able to be mum, with little or no guilt. I don't have to clock in or out of a job; I don't have a boss or even a commute, so I enjoy greater flexibility than most working people.

As I say, this is a privilege. I know mums that work out of the home, mums that work in the home and mums that are not paid for the work they do. Nearly all of

them are wracked with guilt as to whether they are neglecting their children, their careers or both. There is no easy answer but it is worth pointing out that all these women work. A bit of solidarity please ladies!
Some mums work out of the home and make alternative childcare arrangements for their children. They might do this out of financial necessity or they might do this because they like their work. These women are cool. They have nothing to feel guilty about; it is their right to work. Some mums give up their careers to care for their children on a full time basis. These women are cool. They are not silly or boring, nor are they quitters – certainly not that! The work they do is tremendously important even if (no, scrub that) especially as it is unpaid. Some mums try to manage a part time career and still mind their children. These women are cool. They are not overstretching, neglecting or screwing up. Please be nice to each other. Whatever choice your neighbour is making, try to support her. It's pretty tough out there.

I take it from what you've said there that your experience has been that women don't support each other throughout pregnancy and motherhood?
No, not at all. Since becoming a mum I have become much closer to a number of my girl friends and made many, many more new friends through the child support groups. Women are fabulously supportive, funny, relaxing, honest, witty, exciting company. There is definitely a 'silent club' that you join as soon as you become a mum, and I'm proud and happy to be a member. However, ever so occasionally, I've witnessed women letting each other down by condemning one another's choices. It's clear to me that the psychology behind this is justifying their own choices. It's unnecessary.

You made your heroine 'the other woman' and initially she appears rather vain and cold. Why did you choose to do that? Why didn't you make your heroine more traditionally nice, and therefore easier to like?
Because I like a challenge and because I like to think my books tackle life's realities. Life is not 'yes or no', it's a scramble of 'maybes, what-ifs and good intentions.' George is an obsessive. Her personality disorder clearly comes from a lack of inner confidence. Unfortunately one sexual experience, when she was

very young and naive, has formed her outlook for her entire adult life. She is wrong to have an affair with a married man but she is so convinced that she is in love and 'meant for' Hugh that she justifies her unfair actions. Equally, she is wrong to starve herself and place so much emphasis on outward appearances; again she justifies this by saying her passion is motive enough.

Some people actively dislike George initially; I just feel sorry for her – but then I've a very forgiving nature. By the end of the book readers are always cheering for her, which is important to me. It was essential that George came to understand the unreasonableness of her actions and that she repents and puts right as much as she can, so that she can go on to live a more worthwhile life. I guess that makes me a moralist or at least a believer in happy endings.

Your other books, *Playing Away* and *Game Over*, are about infidelity and clearly in *Larger than Life* infidelity is still an important theme to you – why?

Because being unfaithful is so damaging and painful to everyone involved, and whilst everybody knows this, infidelity still thrives. This fact bemuses and fascinates me. And I'm not just talking about sexual infidelity. Sexual infidelity is clearly the most cut and dried permutation of infidelity but I'm also talking about broken promises, lies and the lack of trust between any two people.

The world would be so much simpler if we were all more faithful in our actions and words. Yet the reality is so far from that. It's a pity, but a reality, that nice people sometimes do not very nice things. I find that unsettling. In *Larger than Life*, Sam and James have an affair. They are both lovely characters and yet one is cheating on her fiancé, the other on his brother – why? Passion's a strange one! I think I'll keep writing about it forever, as I'll never understand it.

Are you saying you write to help you understand things?

Yes I suppose I do. I write to explore and explain the mysteries, misunderstandings and mistakes in my own life as much as anything else. I've always found writing very therapeutic. It was always an automatic reaction to any type of excitement or trauma for me. I was never disciplined enough to keep a diary but ever since I was a child if ever I wanted to understand something, or express my self clearly, I wrote it down. I've been fascinated, and somewhat overwhelmed, by the power of my subconscious. It is now clear to me that when I wrote *Larger Than Life* I was preparing myself for admitting that my relationship wasn't a happy one, although I'd always insisted it was.

Do you think about your reader when you are writing?

It sounds rude to say 'not much', but in fact I don't. I dare not. I think as soon as a writer starts to wonder, 'what would they like to read about?' then he/she will tie themselves into knots. If I do imagine my readers I always imagine them as sympathetic friends who are cheering me on, which may not always be accurate, but it is a comfort! I absolutely love hearing from my readers. I'm still utterly thrilled and astonished when someone tells me that they've read one of my books and that they enjoyed it or that it even made them laugh or cry. I think this is an honour.

What next? More babies or more books?

My son is perfect. I can't improve on him so I'd better stick to producing more books.

Questions asked by Jan Murray

whilst i was writing

WHIST I WAS WRITING THIS BOOK I ALSO ...

1. Became a Mummy!
2. Deleted 60,000 words of this novel and started again
3. Became addicted to Boots, loyalty card
4. Became a godmother to Harry James
5. Joined the National Childbirth Trust (NCT)
6. Had leaky breasts on National TV – it's wall to wall glamour being a novelist!
7. Visited Kew Gardens almost daily
8. Painted my son's nursery with a nautical theme
9. Stopped having any form of social life
10. Separated from my husband

HUSBANDS

Bella secretly married her childhood sweetheart, Stevie, over a decade ago; they were at university, two big kids playing at being grownups. When it all unravelled and reality hit, Bella simply got up and left.

Years later, Bella meets Philip and, despite her vow never to marry again, she can't resist him. He is a catch. Funny, charming, interesting and kind. Only hitch is, she's still (technically, anyway) married to Stevie. And the moment to tell Philip never quite seems to arrive.

So Bella plans never to reveal her secret – after all, it's just a silly piece of paper, lodged at a registrar's office in Aberdeen, isn't it? She hasn't seen Stevie for years – probably never will again. Except when Bella's best friend Laura introduces her new man to the gang, it is none other than Stevie. Could things get any more complicated? Only if Bella and Stevie fall in love with each other again ...

THE OTHER WOMAN'S SHOES

The Evergreen sisters are united – in their envy of each other's love life.

Martha and Michael have the perfect home, the perfect family and the perfect life. Until one day, he leaves her.

Eliza and Greg rent a one-bedroom flat where they make music and lots of love. Until one day, she leaves him.

Now the Evergreen sisters are united in separation. And suddenly, they're free to pursue the relationships they think they've always wanted.

Martha wants fun, and lots of it. Great sex and high excitement, courtesy of Jack-the-unpredictable-lad.

Eliza wants the ideal husband, and fast. Sensible conversation and dinner parties with a man who doesn't buy groceries at the local garage.

So when both women find exactly what they're looking for, everybody's happy ... aren't they? Or does chasing the perfect love only get more complicated when you're wearing another woman's shoes?

STILL THINKING OF YOU

New love, old relationships and a question of fidelity from the bestselling author of *The Other Woman's Shoes*.

Tash and Rich are newly engaged and wild about each other. They can't wait to celebrate their wedding with their closest friends, all of whom have known each other since university, where they enjoyed a hedonistic whirl of parties, popularity, sex and success.

But is fun really as easy-come-easy-go in your thirties as it was in your twenties? How do relationships change once you leave college and have to cope with real life?

And what if the love of that life were to reappear now?

As old, long-buried passions are reawakened, the group realize that a lot can change in twelve years. And a lot can happen in seven days ...

PLAYING AWAY

'I'm married,' I said.
'I'm a tart,' John smiled.
Both the defence and the challenge.
I. Simply. Can't. Resist.

Connie has been happily married for a year. But she's just met John Harding. Imagine the sexiest man you can think of. He's a walking stag weekend. He's a funny, disrespectful, fast, confident, irreverent pub crawl. He is also completely unscrupulous. He's about to destroy Connie's peace of mind, her grand plan for living happily ever after with her gentle, loving husband Luke.

What will happen if her husband finds out? What will happen if he doesn't? Connie doesn't know the answers ... yet.

But she does know that she's playing against the rules, and she's playing with fire.

GAME OVER

'I've turned my heart to steel. In fact even my closest friends ask if I have one at all', I try to grin.

'You have a heart to break, Cas, just like everyone else.'

'I do not,' I assert defiantly.

Cas Perry doesn't want a relationship. When her father walked out on her and her mother she decided relationships, love, marriage, the whole shebang, simply weren't worth the heartache.

But is Cas, immoral most of the time and amoral when it comes to business, going too far with her new TV programme, *Sex with an Ex*? Unfeeling and unscrupulous, she ruthlessly manipulates everyone she comes into contact with.

Until she meets Darren. A babe. Trouble is, he's a highly principled babe. He believes in love, marriage, fidelity and constancy, so can he believe in Cas? Is it possible the world is a better place than she imagined? And if it is – after a lifetime of playing games – is this discovery too late?

Game Over is a book about the lethal game we play in the name of love.